L.R. Montgomery

ATTAWONDARONK

J. R. Montgomery

iUniverse, Inc.
Bloomington

Attawondaronk

Copyright © 2011 J. R. Montgomery

All rights reserved. No part of this book may be used or reproduced by any means, graphic, electronic, or mechanical, including photocopying, recording, taping or by any information storage retrieval system without the written permission of the publisher except in the case of brief quotations embodied in critical articles and reviews.

Certain characters in this work are historical figures, and certain events portrayed did take place. However, this is a work of fiction. All of the other characters, names, and events as well as all places, incidents, organizations, and dialogue in this novel are either the products of the author's imagination or are used fictitiously.

iUniverse books may be ordered through booksellers or by contacting:

iUniverse
1663 Liberty Drive
Bloomington, IN 47403
www.iuniverse.com
1-800-Authors (1-800-288-4677)

Because of the dynamic nature of the Internet, any Web addresses or links contained in this book may have changed since publication and may no longer be valid. The views expressed in this work are solely those of the author and do not necessarily reflect the views of the publisher, and the publisher hereby disclaims any responsibility for them.

Any people depicted in stock imagery provided by Thinkstock are models, and such images are being used for illustrative purposes only.

Certain stock imagery © Thinkstock.

ISBN: 978-1-4620-4916-5 (sc)
ISBN: 978-1-4620-4915-8 (hc)
ISBN: 978-1-4620-4914-1 (e)

Library of Congress Control Number: 2011915093

Printed in the United States of America

iUniverse rev. date: 10/28/2011

Cover Art by Cathy Groulx

Interior Art by Kierstin Montgomery

Author's Note

The people in this story were known to their neighbors—friends and enemies alike—by many different names. The name most commonly used today is Attawondaron, but other names refer to these people as well, such as Petun, for the potent strain of tobacco they grew, and Neutrals, for their ability to remain neutral from the ongoing raids and retaliations between the Hurons and the Iroquois Confederation of upstate New York.

Attawondaronk takes place in Southern Ontario, approximately three generations prior to the first contacts with Europeans. Only a few whites ever actually met this fascinating culture, but from these brief contacts, a limited firsthand account of town names and locations—as well as the names of a handful of chiefs and subchiefs—were recorded.

The towns in this story are real; the characters are the product of an imagination trying to explain three Indian graves found in a walnut grove by a young child.

ACKNOWLEDGMENTS

In writing *Attawondaronk* I utilized a great many resources to verify the knowledge I have gleaned over years of reading and research of First Nation peoples. In addition to periodicals, reference books, and publications too numerous to mention, I would like to thank the Ontario Archeological Society. Its extensive work interpreting and recording the prehistoric and protohistoric eras of Southern Ontario from the simple everyday items left behind has revealed a culture that would otherwise have been long forgotten.

Thanks also to those at the University of Western Ontario who offered help and advice along the way, especially Linda, who read the first copy of the manuscript with an eye to possible historical errors, and of course to Cathy and Kierstin for their artistic help in completing this undertaking.

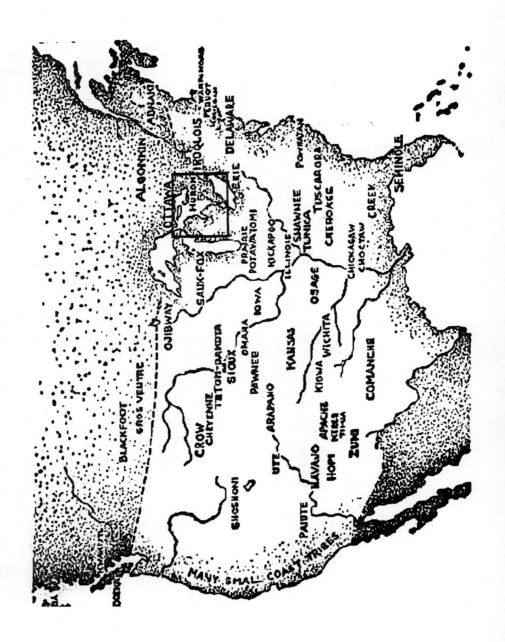

For every warrior who has sacrificed his—or her—life in defense of another

Main Characters and Towns

Ounontisaston: chief town of the Attawondaronks

Sannisen: war chief of the Attawondaronks; Land clan

Shanoka: born Ojibwa; raised Sennikae; mate to Sannisen

Ontarra: oldest son of Sannisen and Shanoka; Land clan

Taiwa: daughter of Sannisen and Shanoka; Land clan

Teota: youngest son of Sannisen and Shanoka; Land clan

Toutsou: Ontarra's closest friend; Land clan

Ounsasta: nation's oldest warrior; mentor to Sannisen; now honored by appointment to the prestigious position of "Keeper of the Wampum." Ounsasta is Bird clan. (It is a rarity for a Bird clan member to be allowed into the warrior society.)

Soutoten: hunt chief; Sannisen's friend since childhood; Land clan

Sounia: daughter of Soutoten; Land clan

Tsohahissen: chief of chiefs; father to Sannisen and Hiatsou (different mothers); confidants call him "Tsoha"; Land clan

Yadwena: young wife of Tsohahissen; Land clan

Hiatsou: chief shaman. Attawondaronk lineage descends through the mother (matriarchal). Although Tsohahissen is father to both Sannisen and Hiatsou, they have different mothers (hence, Sannisen is Land clan, but Hiatsou is Bird clan).

Poutassa: maniacal son of Hiatsou; Bird clan

Winona: grandmother of all Bird clans; Bird clan

Yadak: arrogant grandson of Winona; Bird clan

Kratcha: erratic old woman living as a recluse on the lower branch of the Tranchi near Teotonguiaton; Land clan

Outsiders

Dekari: unscrupulous Erieehronon trader acting as guide to the Tunicans

Manak: Tunican war leader masquerading as a trader in order to travel unmolested through other nations

Mox: dull Tunican warrior, pretending to be a trader

Matoupa: Tunican trader

Joneadih: chief town of the Sennikae

Togo: false face of the Sennikae; stepfather to Shanoka

Tadodaroh: Onondaga warrior who, by happenstance, has learned unusual fighting skills

Shonennkari: Onondaga warrior; Tadodaroh's brother

Introduction

Todd hunched down and stalked toward the bend in the river. Crouching on the bank, he nocked an arrow and poked it through the cattails to study his prey. Sucking a breath, he threw himself upright, pulling the drawstring to his cheek in a practiced motion. His hand quivered an instant, and the stubby walnut branch launched in a wobbling arc, descending into the midst of a school of striped sucker fish, scattering them to the four directions.

Todd's mouth twisted in frustration as he rubbed the raw abrasions the butcher's cord bowstring had left on his forearm. Wading down into the knee-deep water, he retrieved his precious homemade arrow before it could drift away. He'd never managed to hit one of the fish, but the joy of the hunt was always a thrill.

Sloshing back to the bank, Todd dumped water from green rubber boots, tightening the baler twine that passed for a belt as he scanned the grove for his next quarry. He loved this part of the farm—pristine and secluded—never used for anything but pasture. Two steep ridges wrapped around a shady grove, one meandering north–south, the other east–west, rising to the same height as the walnut trees that filled the river flat. The two ridges joined in an elbow, forming a shallow ravine that sloped down into the grove. A creek snaked its way through the trees, twining and curling to form small ponds in each loop, flowing along the base of the south ridge until it merged with the main river.

Buildings and roads were not even visible from down here. An abandoned rail line in the distance was the only sign that man had even been here. Best of all, there were no adults to encroach on Todd's secret world. He could hide back here all day, catching frogs, hunting with his bow, and occasionally tormenting the big snapping turtle whose lair he'd come upon last spring.

In the crook where the two ridges joined, a deep wash had formed. Over eons the scree and rubble coming down had created a saddle several feet high that looked like a finger pointing out into the grove. Todd had spent many hours dragging rocks from a pile of dumped fieldstones up onto the saddle, arranging a lopsided circle that in Todd's mind supported real walls.

He trudged up onto the knoll and sat within the security of his fortress, surveying his domain. In a stand of ironwood on the slope behind, a hollow trunk concealed his cache of treasures. The labored chugging of his father's Massey drifted down from the field above. It could barely haul the two-furrow plow through the rocky soil that was better suited for gravel than crops. Todd scowled at the modern-day intrusion and decided to add more stones to his fort.

Trotting down to the pile, he rolled out some suitable stones and for the first time, he uncovered a bottom layer. He was surprised to see that the ground-level stones were different from the rest—rounded, smooth, and black. They'd settled down into the topsoil, years of detritus practically covering them over. They'd been there a long time. Todd found a sturdy limb and pried a few from the dark soil, rolling one over curiously in his hands. *These are old. The first settlers must have cleared these.* He levered out some more, brushing tingling fingers over the smooth surfaces before rolling each one aside. He lost all track of time, until the slanting shadows of evening caught his attention. He'd pried out an entire corner of what appeared to be a rectangle of embedded rocks, but more fieldstones would need to be moved to get at the rest.

It was late. He sat on his haunches, exhausted, wiping grimy hands over his tattered jeans. He had to go—Mother would be worried. Something caught his eye. He knelt and dug some more, wiggling a stone from its earthen socket. Black as coal … perfectly round … the top and bottom like mushroom caps. Todd scurried to the creek, washed the mud away, and set it on his palm to admire the perfect shape. He noticed some marks on the top and traced a finger along them. A triangle was etched into the surface.

Todd sprinted across the fields for home. His family was already seated for supper. His jam-faced little brother smirked as Todd's mother took a look at his grimy condition and started to scold. He hastily set his find on the table, and the tongue-lashing fizzled out. His father reached over and picked it up, nestling it on a callused palm. "Interesting. It seems to be man-made. Someone spent a lot of time smoothing the surface." He rolled it over. "And it's been painted black. Where did you find this?"

"In that pile of fieldstones out in the walnut grove." Todd hooked his thumbs into the baler twine around his waist.

"It looks as if it's for some kind of game," his father surmised. "Curling or lawn bowling, maybe. The Scot settlers, I'll bet. I'll take it to the museum in town tomorrow—they'll know what it is." Todd's dad set the stone beside his plate and returned to his pork chop.

A sudden apprehension swept into Todd's mind. "No!" he blurted out. "I want to keep it!" His father stopped mid-chew and pressed his palms on the plastic tablecloth, annoyance rearranging the wrinkles at the corners of his eyes. Todd lowered his chin. "Sorry, Father, I don't know why I shouted, but I want to keep it—it belongs here." His father sighed, running a hand over his stubbled gray hair and lifting the stone again.

Todd's mom came to his rescue. "Let him have it, Bob. I doubt it has any value."

Bob exhaled, fixing Todd with soft blue eyes. "All right." He handed back the saucer-shaped stone. "But don't lose it. Someday you will want to know what that is."

"Thank you, Father!" Todd scooped up the stone and bolted for the safety of his room.

"What about your supper?" his mother's exasperated voice called after him.

"I'll eat later!"

Todd cleared a space on the dresser for his new prized possession. Wondering what the stone's purpose could be, he fell into an exhausted sleep and didn't open his eyes until the first hints of dawn were creeping through the window. His dirty clothes had mysteriously disappeared in the night. Todd studied the rock as he rummaged in a drawer for another shirt and something that would pass as pants. Something wasn't right. He ran fingers through his hair, wincing as they caught in a knot. The triangle on the stone was pointed in a different direction than he remembered. Todd dug beneath his bed, with fossils, a raccoon skull, and deer antler flying, until he came out with a stubby stick of yellow chalk. Drawing a line on the dresser, he positioned the stone on top.

Todd spent that entire day in the walnut grove, rolling fieldstones off the dark layer of rocks embedded beneath. By dusk he'd exposed a rectangular patch of blackened rocks, three paces by five. He settled down, resting with his back to a walnut trunk, wondering what those old rocks might be hiding, as his heavy eyelids slowly drifted shut. Something touched his face, and Todd jerked his head backward. It felt as if a feather had just been drawn across his cheek. He sensed an eerie presence and swept his gaze across the grove. Slowly, his eyes climbed to the crest of the south ridge.

A woman in a white dress stood there, long tendrils of ebony hair fluttering across her face in the breeze. She smiled as swaying branches blocked his view. He crabbed sideways—but she was gone.

When he got home that evening, he crept silently up to his room and checked on the stone—the same as he'd left it. Too exhausted to care, he collapsed on the bed. When his mother brought supper up, he was already sleeping. Auburn curls tickled his eyelids as she kissed a freckled cheek, set the tray on the floor, and silently closed the door.

Todd slept late the next morning. Yawning, he walked over to the dresser, and his jaw dropped. The stone was turned a full half-circle. Holding his breath, he poked it, and then slowly turned the point of the triangle back to the yellow line.

He didn't go to the grove that day. The remote isolation that he loved so much suddenly seemed ... sinister. Todd hung around on the porch until late in the day, mulling over his thoughts as he absently watched his father working the back fields.

"Are you all right?" His mother startled him. She was on her way out with his father's supper in a wicker basket.

"I'm okay; just tired." Todd followed her flowered dress with his eyes as she strolled out to the idling Massey. He wanted to go out and dig up that dark patch of rocks in the grove, but something was holding him back. Not fear, really, just a vague feeling that it wouldn't be right. His father shouted, beckoning to Todd with sweeps of his arm. Todd absently trudged up the lane, summers of running on bare feet making them immune to the sharp gravel.

"Look at this." A thin smile curled his father's dusty lips. "The plow turned it up." He tossed a gray hand-sized object, and Todd caught it. "A stone ax head," his dad said with a grin. "I'll bet that could tell you some stories."

Todd rolled it over in his hands. It really was an ax head. An image flashed in Todd's mind, and his eyes shifted to the walnut grove a stone's throw away. "Can I keep it, Father?" Todd's voice quavered with the excitement of a sudden revelation.

Bob snorted a chuckle, his rugged fingers tousling Todd's scraggly brown locks. "We kind of figured that our little pack rat might find a place for it in his midden."

Todd examined the weapon as he walked back to the house, wondering to whom it might have belonged and how that person possibly could have lost such an obviously valuable item. He ran a thumb over the blunt edge, marveling at its smoothness. "Like the rocks in the grove," he whispered. *I think the Indians hid something down there.*

Todd devoured the cheese sandwich his mother had left him in a few bites, realizing he was famished. Despite sitting idle all day, he was mentally exhausted. He climbed the stairs and set the ax head next to the saucer-shaped stone on the dresser and settled back against his pillow. Todd's eyelids drifted shut, something nagging at the back of his mind. His mother checked on him at dusk, smiled and tugged his clothes off.

Night waxed. Todd sat up with a start as early dawn was painting the eastern sky. He'd been dreaming of the grove but couldn't bring back the images. He closed his eyes and drifted back down, into that halfway place between this world and dreams. A raven-haired woman in a white dress fashioned from animal skins brushed his cheek with the tip of a feather and smiled. Todd jarred awake, knowing exactly what he had to do. Shivering, he tiptoed over to the dresser. The stone had turned—the triangle now pointed north. He pulled his clothes on and wrapped the ax head in a towel.

Todd softly closed the screen door and slipped out of the house before anyone else was awake. He slogged up the riverbank to where the river held the deepest hole he knew of and lobbed the ax head out into the middle.

That afternoon he went back to the walnut grove, fit all the old rocks into their original settings, and rolled the fieldstones back on top. The grove felt friendly again.

Todd grew to manhood and took a job in the city. He never discussed that strange summer of his youth. He knew that no one else would understand. Over the years he kept the saucer-stone in a special spot, often turning its position at night so he could find it aligned with the poles again the next morning. If he lifted it at first light and cradled it between his palms, he sensed a warmth and a feeling of … harmony.

After county officials visited Todd's father—they intended to expropriate land from the back of the farm for a new road—Todd returned once again to the pleasant little walnut grove. He sat up on the saddle, contemplating the rock pile and drifting back in time. The thought of earthmovers violating the landscape that he loved so much made his heart ache. He walked along the line of surveyor stakes, his suede shoes and pressed cotton pants picking up burrs and pitchfork seeds. As he pictured the path of destruction, a plan slowly formed in his mind.

He applied for a land severance, proposing to build a house directly in the path of the intended road. The Land Division Committee swiftly rejected the application. He fought it all the way up to the Ontario Municipal Board, which postponed the devastation until a ruling was passed. The county struck a deal to prevent any further delay. The road was moved south by eighty feet to accommodate the building lot.

The following spring, Todd watched as bulldozers leveled a section of the north–south ridge. They buried the rock pile beneath thirty feet of fill and plowed a hideous swath through the walnut grove. It was gut-wrenching, but he'd done all that he could.

That night Todd dreamed he was a young boy again, stalking the creek with a spindly stick for an arrow. The dusky lady in white beckoned from up on the saddle. Dark, luminous eyes and a radiant smile drew him to her. She knelt with a hug. "Tell them what happened," she said softly and kissed his forehead. Todd lurched upright, blankets flying in a heap. He stared into darkness to where the saucer-stone sat on a shelf. Slowly, he eased back into his pillow, palming moisture from the corners of his eyes.

A compulsion grew to unlock the mystery of the beautiful lady of the grove. Todd's search unraveled the lives of a people who once shared this land with their deities. An obscure, once Powerful nation that controlled a huge territory that today is known as Southern Ontario. The only hard evidence that these people ever really existed was brought to light by archeologists, from a scattering of excavated towns and mass graves. Much of the people's wealth and Power was derived from a potent strain of tobacco known as *petun*, coveted by others for its spiritual and healing Powers.

A handful of Jesuit priests briefly ventured into the people's realm in a futile attempt to Christianize them; the whites were summarily demonized and banished. The sketchy records left by these men of the cross are the only firsthand accounts of an unusual culture—a society that for some reason perpetuated archaic beliefs from a bygone era.

Gradually, a picture of their world etched itself into Todd's subconscious. Years later, he would ponder whether he'd imagined their lives or if a more intimate knowledge had somehow been bestowed upon him. He saw towns, fields, faces; he heard their laughter and felt their fears.

In his mind's eye, Todd saw a Powerful shaman society tightening its grip on the people, wielding fear and superstition to secure their control. Shunning all outside influence as a threat to their authority, they shackled minds to the past with little regard for the welfare of the nation or where this type of thinking might lead. The intrigues of these men divided communities, disrupting the binding loyalties essential to survival in a hostile and unforgiving wilderness.

Todd saw a family that was Powerful in ways they themselves never fully understood, a family that attempted to put an end to the destructive stranglehold of the shamans. And in an all-too-vivid nightmare, he saw the terrible consequences of such selfless courage.

The alienation of this family resulted in a vendetta spanning three generations. When the final reckoning came, an entire nation melted into the misty veil of time. When Europeans arrived again, the land was empty and desolate.

The Fire Nation called them Petun; the Sennikae called them … Attawondaronk.

Prologue

Three elm-bark canoes sliced downriver in near silence. Only the swirl of Powerful strokes broke the stillness. The men wore tanned tunics and leggings fashioned from the skins of deer and bear. Ebony hair was greased flat with bear fat and pulled into tight braids behind the ears; headbands ensured that stray strands wouldn't hinder their vision.

They had set out at early dawn, heading south, downriver. All had traveled the route before and knew it well. From northeast to southwest this pristine waterway cut through the heartland of their territory, eventually spilling out into Lake Between the Sunset Rivers, the western boundary of their nation. The canoes rounded a bend, and the river widened to nine canoe-lengths across. Upstream, banks were low. Here, the river had cut a deep scar into Mother Earth, with precipitous banks rising to the height of treetops crowding the shore.

The canoes slid gracefully to midstream without slowing. Quiet, cautious, the movements came as naturally to these men as breathing, instilled by years of survival in a tangled and unforgiving wilderness. Travel packs were nestled between the two men in each canoe, serving as ballast, and a platform for the arrows and bows lay ready for any emergency.

In the lead, Sannisen scanned the brilliant colors of the autumn forest, calculating the path an arrow would take from the high banks to his position on the river—*an easy shot.* His head bobbed with his thoughts. The possibility of an attack on him and his companions in the middle of their own territory was remote, he considered, but not impossible. As war chief, he contemplated how easily this channel could be defended against intruders.

They arrived at a smaller river flowing out from a narrow side valley. It rolled and churned in eddies and currents, mingling with the waters of the main course. Sannisen pointed, slicing the elm-bark nose of his craft around to force his way up the smaller stream. The canoes slipped into single file to negotiate the narrow waters, slowing perceptibly in the tumbling current. Progress was hindered further by trees fallen from the banks, almost blocking their passage in places. The main river was lost from sight in bends and turns as the smaller watercourse drew them steadily westward.

Sannisen had scouted this area in the spring. He studied his companions' faces as the canoes rounded a sharp turn and a huge bluff loomed up from the forest. The river continued on to the right of the bluff. A small stream tumbled down out of a ravine along the left face. The bluff jutted out into a blunt point, towering over the confluence where the two waters merged.

Sannisen thudded his canoe in to shore where the streams joined in the shadow of the bluff. The other two canoes thumped in beside him. He studied expressions intently, trying to read the thoughts of his companions who were seeing this place for the first time. These were important men—and his friends.

Soutoten hopped out and dragged the bow of his canoe up onto shore, grimacing as the side rail dragged along the scarred lump of two fingers that had been ripped out at the base knuckles of his right hand. Soutoten was hunt chief, an honor he had held since his twenty-eighth summer, two cycles past. He and Sannisen had grown to men together.

Thadayo slid over the rail, removing his weight to lend a hand. They wrestled the canoes up onto dry ground and then sat on their heels, catching their breath as they scanned the surroundings. Soutoten noted pathways running down the bluff to watering holes along the river; he nodded silently. Many animals were here to feed and clothe his people.

Thadayo wasn't a chief. His status derived from his ability to negotiate and settle disputes with other tribes and various factions among their own people. Thadayo was soft-spoken and reasonable, even when tempers flared—a talent that provided him the same privileges and status as a chief. His support was sought in all major decisions. Always seeking harmony and balance, Thadayo dug into his hide waistpouch and sprinkled some petun on the ground to appease the spirits of this virgin place.

Ahratota and Dahtka hauled their canoe up, squatting down to settle their ragged breathing. Ahratota was building chief. Now in his twenty-sixth summer, he was youngest of the subchiefs because the rigors of his work required an undamaged body. As only eighteen summers, Dahtka had just completed his vision quest, the final step in becoming a man. He would take Ahratota's place, when time or injury made it necessary.

Ounsasta shared Sannisen's canoe. Fifteen years Sannisen's senior, Ounsasta was an elderly man, although in his prime he'd been a fierce warrior. A hero of their people, he'd fought seven different tribes, taking many heads. His trophy feather pointed straight back from the part on top of his head to show that his warrior achievements were now behind him. His feather had more cuts and notches than any in the land, except for Sannisen's, which carried one more notch. Ounsasta had lost his right eye in the incessant raiding against the people who called themselves the Fire Nation. To Ounsasta they were simply "Agwa," his people's greatest enemy.

Ounsasta looked and dressed like the dangerous man that he was. A war club the length of his forearm dangled from his waistband. Carved of rockwood, the shank curved slightly, culminating in an intricately detailed lynx head holding a wooden ball between open jaws. It was highly efficient at splitting skulls in a single blow. Ounsasta was now "Keeper of the Wampum" and "Guardian of the Sacred Calumet," positions of great honor that entrusted him with his nation's greatest treasures. His words carried weight at council, but it also meant that he would not die in battle as he had always wished.

Sannisen's chest always tightened when that distant look clouded Ounsasta's face. Sannisen laid a palm on Ounsasta's shoulder to bring him back. "We will camp atop the point tonight." Ounsasta's eye refocused; he nodded.

They carried weapons and travel packs up a deer trail that meandered back and forth as it ascended the face. The tangled brush near rivers was nearly impenetrable unless they followed the animal trails. On top they quickly built lean-tos around a shallow fire pit. The sun was settling into its tunnel in the west as they sparked a flame. A lively fire took hold, licking at the deadfall and branches they piled on. With no time to hunt, they had to settle for boiled cornmeal. Pounded venison added body and flavor. Hunger made the simple fare taste delicious.

Sannisen allowed an inward smile as he dipped his travel spoon into the bark pot and listened to the conversations. There had been enough daylight only for a scanty survey, but excitement already tinged their words. Tomorrow they could reconnoiter the entire area, with judgment honed by cycles of personal experience. Each man would study this place with his own particular skills.

They slept the sleep of exhaustion. Animals scurried through the brush, scuttling quietly around the circle of firelight. Wolves viciously attacked a feeble deer at the river, but it was a common sound, and the men were oblivious to it. Just beyond the fringe of the firelight, a pair of yellow slitted eyes studied the men for a long while as they slept. Saliva dripped from a fang. They seemed an easy kill, but they smelled bad, and the flickering flames were strange and frightening. The eyes retreated into the night.

First hints of dawn colored the eastern sky as Ounsasta stoked the fire. Twigs and pine needles from the ground still were stuck in the gray streaks of his hair. The men wolfed down a quick meal of smoked fish. Eager to see as much as possible, each hurried off in the direction that interested him. Ounsasta remained to guard the camp. At dusk they straggled back in. Ounsasta had two rabbits spitted, and cattail roots sizzled on the coals. Soutoten lumbered in with a fawn over his shoulder. The men feasted and began a lively discussion. Sannisen gnawed on a rabbit thigh, careful not to get grease on the trophy feather dangling over his right cheek. Smiling, he listened to the fervor in their voices.

"The area is full of mature elms for lodges and canoes," Ahratota said, tossing a bone in the fire and dragging greasy fingers over his well-stained leggings. "The river flat is full of young saplings suitable for framing." He rubbed the irritating scar that ran down his right cheek from his eye to his chin, planted there by a birch sapling that had resisted becoming a roof arch. Twisting a shoulder from the roasting fawn, he pointed with the dripping meat toward the north. "A short distance that way is a grove of cedar for palisade posts." He clamped down with his teeth and tore an unexpectedly large chunk from the shank, grimacing as steaming meat sagged onto his chin. They all grinned at his sudden predicament.

Dahtka sat with his back to a tree, rubbing rabbit fat into the heavy forearm bands that protected him from the cuts and abrasions of his work. He couldn't wait any longer for Ahratota to finish chewing. "There are plenty of maple trees if the elms should run out, and there's firewood on the ground to last a hand of cycles." Ahratota tried to say something but his mouth was still plugged, so he nodded his agreement.

Soutoten stabbed the deer's liver with a bone awl he'd fashioned for lifting meat off coals. He clamped the organ between his teeth, pulling his lips back and hanging his head to let it cool. When his fingers could stand the heat, he gripped and slashed with his skinning knife. The razor-sharp chert severed a juicy morsel that disappeared with a slurp, revealing a prominent nose with a bead of blood forming where the knife had left a nick. "Game is everywhere," he mumbled through his food, chewing a moment before continuing. "As your bellies can tell you, there are deer everywhere. I saw sign of moose, elk, and bear. Plenty of small game too. The river is teeming with fish. The Tranchi is wide here. It will attract ducks and geese. All the men will be happy with this place."

Sannisen was pleased; he shifted his gaze to Thadayo. "Thadayo, what did you find?"

Thadayo crossed his legs, rubbing his hands up and down frilled leggings as he considered his response. "I walked far to the north on the uplands. The soil is perfect for the sister crops. Not the best for petun, though; it likes a sandier soil. It will grow after we burn the brush to feed the earth, but it won't be of a ceremonial quality."

The men fell silent as they considered this. "What about the river flats?" Sannisen asked.

Thadayo shook his head. "No good for petun, but the soil is dark and rich. It will provide bumper crops of sunflower, squash, and beans. Spring flooding will revitalize the soil each cycle. Crops will grow indefinitely down there."

Sannisen stroked the veins of his trophy feather, thoughtful for a moment. He nestled some deadfall on the coals and watched the flames take hold. "What first drew my attention to this place was this bluff we are sitting on. Its shape is like an arrowhead—steep sides, the entry river flowing along its eastern base, and the creek along the bottom of the west face. It is the most defensible natural position I have seen in all of our lands." He paused to give his next words effect. "We are far enough back from the Tranchi to be hidden from prying eyes, yet we can still reach the river in less than a hand of time."

Ounsasta stood and began to pace. He tugged at the bone earspool in his left ear that was carved in the shape of an acorn cap. He had never shared its significance with anyone, and no one had ever dared to ask. Ounsasta had been Sannisen's mentor since Sannisen was a young boy, and he'd come to think of him more as a nephew than as his war chief. Pride swelled in Ounsasta's chest when he saw the respect others held for Sannisen. "I walked the crest of the bluff today. The entire river flat is an easy arrow shot. I paced the distance across the point. If we build the palisades along both crests, we can still fit eleven longhouses inside. With our walls along the precipice, this place is unassailable from three directions." Ounsasta pulled his club, raising it over his head for emphasis. "I could hold this place with a handful of men against ten times our number!"

Sannisen always enjoyed Ounsasta's blunt speeches. "I agree." He flashed an easy grin. "The size of the entry river would force intruders to approach in single file. They would be under our fire long before they could organize an attack up the bluff; it would be madness to even try."

"Yes," Soutoten added, pausing as his palm covered the two bear canines that hung from a sinew thong at the hollow of his neck—teeth that once belonged to a bear with the misfortune of having removed two of Soutoten's fingers. "Our fishermen will be out on the Tranchi day and night. They would give us ample warning of anyone who approached uninvited." He lowered his hand, resting it on the hilt of the big skinning knife in his waistband. "The Tranchi has high banks here. We could ambush intruders out on the main river."

"Your hunting skills have made you sly and observant, old friend," Sannisen shifted his eyes from face to face. "So we would be secure from attack, except from the north, and that is the least likely approach. Our adversaries would have to take a circular route overland; the outlying lodges would see them. I've been thinking"—Sannisen steepled his fingers as he envisioned the plan—"that we could plant only beans and squash in the upper fields, as far as an arrow-flight in every direction. Our enemies would be offered no cover, and we would have a clear field of fire. The tapering shape of the bluff top would force them into a dense mass as they drew close. Even with all of our nation's four thousand warriors, I would not want to attack this place." Sannisen looked to Thadayo. "What will the women say?"

"Well … they'll want to see it, of course." He stared at the ground, arranging his thoughts. "And they will certainly find something to complain about—they always do." The men chuckled, mumbling back and forth about Thadayo's understanding of women. "But," he said, his voice brightening, "once they've voiced their opinions, they will decide they like this place. After a cycle here, they will probably convince themselves that they discovered it."

Ahratota rested his chin on gnarled fingers and studied Dahtka's sun-bronzed face to be sure that he agreed. ""If we start now, we can have all the poles and timber ready by first snow and begin building in the spring."

"The bark could be slashed and left on the trees," Dahtka added.

Thadayo stared into the thick forest to the north as he pictured the future. "We can build a deer drive out there and bring the women to help us burn the fields for next cycle's crops, and let them get accustomed to this place."

Sannisen shifted his eyes from face to face. "We are in agreement then. Here we will build a fortress for Tsohahissen, our chief of chiefs. In this place will stand the new town of Ounontisaston."

1

Ontarra sensed a movement in the lodge. Sliding the sleep robe down from his face, he forced an eye open. The hearth glowed but offered no light. A silhouette approached, hovered over him a moment, and then drifted away again. The fresh scent of his mother's hair relaxed him; he spat a long black tendril of unruly hair from his lips, tugged the fur back up, and nuzzled it to his face. The lilting melody of her morning psalms lulled him back to his dreams.

Shanoka crossed her ankles and folded herself down at the hearth. She set her prayer stone reverently on a floor skin. A breath of spring air fluttered in past the door skin. The embers ebbed and flowed with a life of their own as she added more wood. Tongues of flame licked upward instantly, casting lively shadows on the walls and sleep platforms.

Shanoka had performed this rite each day since her sixth summer. She was Midewiwin of the Ojibwa, born to a long lineage of healers and seers. Since marrying Sannisen she had tried to forget that life and transform herself into the dutiful wife of an Attawondaronk chief. She loved Sannisen and the children who slept around her in the lodge, but she had never been able to fully reconcile herself with their strange beliefs.

Shanoka shook off her thoughts and nestled the prayer stone on her right palm. Rotating it until the line on top ran north–south, she cupped her left hand on top, enfolding it in a light grasp. She felt Earth's forces align with the stone. Shanoka drew a deep breath as the familiar tingle flowed through her fingertips. Humming the ancient mantra, she called on the forces of nature to retain the balances that kept the world's order and held chaos at bay. Fond memories of childhood and her mother crept into her mind. She finished the ritual and set the stone aside, her soul at peace.

Predawn light turned her thoughts to the morning meal. Shanoka brushed her ebony locks back over her shoulders and returned the prayer stone to its place beneath her sleep platform. She glanced quickly at Teota, Taiwa, and Ontarra to be sure she hadn't disturbed them and then reached for her bark pot.

Ontarra woke to the sound of a child's laughter and the tantalizing smell of corn cakes. He rolled to his side and saw Teota, his chubby brown arms wrapped around his mother's neck while she tried to ladle corn mush onto a cooking rock. A depression in the hearth ring balanced a bark pot. Sannisen often chided her for not using ceramic pots like the other women, but cooking was a ritual she'd learned in childhood, and habits were hard to break. Shanoka lifted cooking stones from the coals and dropped them into the fish stew left over from last night's meal. The food and wood smoke blended into a comforting aroma.

"Mother, let me help! I want to help!" Teota chattered.

"You are small yet to work at the fire." Shanoka's voice was soft and held infinite patience. She held him back with a hand while using wooden tongs to pluck the cooled heating stones from the stew, replacing them with hot ones from the fire. They sputtered and popped as they plopped in; one broke with a loud crack.

Ontarra yawned, squirming over onto his back. Despite the fire, the lodge was chilly. He snuggled the robe to his chin, thinking about sleeping longer, when his robes were suddenly ripped away, leaving him naked and exposed. Impish laughter erupted as Teota ran for safety behind his mother's buckskin dress. He peeked around, still giggling. "Ontarra, get up and play with me. No one is outside yet."

Ontarra bounded to the fire, hunching over to capture some heat. "Mosquito, instead of a practice bow, I think I'll make you a hoe to work the fields with the women." Ontarra tried his best to look angry. It worked well with hair that had been slept in and one eye stuck shut with sleep crust.

Teota mistook his brother's mockery for real anger and was crestfallen. "I'm sorry, Ontarra." Teota's lower lip pouted outward. "I just wanted you to get up."

Ontarra relinquished a smirk. "All right, let me dress and eat." Ontarra pranced over to his sleep platform, digging his tunic and leggings out of the furs. With teeth starting to chatter, he hopped from foot to foot as he tugged the buckskins over the shiver-bumps rising on his legs. "What is that awful smell over here?" He shook his head and then moved back to the fire and gently pried his eye open. He tested the air and noticed his body odor was getting rather ripe, but the river was still awfully cold. Ontarra stretched and glanced around the lodge, thankful they didn't live in one of the longhouses with ten hands of people and squalling infants to wake up to.

Lodges of secondary chiefs and other dignitaries were built in the same style as the longhouses. Saplings were stripped and their trunks planted in a rectangle. The tops were then bent inward and fastened with hide strips, forming an arch. A framework of saplings was attached horizontally, and then the walls were covered with sheets of elm bark stripped from the surrounding forest, forming a single room four paces wide and eight paces long. Sleeping platforms lined the walls at knee level, doubling as seats and providing storage underneath.

Everything above shoulder height was blackened by hearth smoke. Shocks of corn, clothing, meat, and petun hung from the rafters for curing and preservation. It was snug and warm, even in winter, unless the east wind blew for more than a day. When that happened, no one in the town could stay warm. Ontarra accepted the hot tea his mother handed him and sipped gingerly from the wooden bowl. It was the pine-nut tea that refreshed the senses. She'd learned to make it as a child.

One of the town's dogs poked his head past the doorskin and whimpered. "Go away, you lazy creature," Ontarra grumbled. "Go to the refuse heap if you want to eat." The head retreated. Ontarra contemplated the shifting embers. "Mother, is it true that dogs were once people, but they grew too lazy to feed themselves?"

"No, the Sennikae say something like that about bears," she said as her slender brown fingers reached into the hearth and gingerly flipped a corn bread, "but I believe it is because a skinned bear looks so human. I'm sure that dogs came from wolves. They look exactly alike. They just decided that living with us is easier than hunting."

"When will you tell us more about Togo, Mother?" Taiwa's voice bubbled up from beneath her sleep robes.

Shanoka arranged her thoughts before answering. "Your father and I agreed long ago that it was best for everyone if some of my past remains secret. Considering what has been happening, though"—Shanoka stirred the coals with a wooden poker—"I think the time may have arrived to reveal a few things." Shanoka sucked in the corner of her lip and chewed on it, deciding it was still best to evade the subject for the moment. "Get out of bed!" She tossed a flat of cornbread at the hump in Taiwa's bedding.

"Mother! You shouldn't rush me from my dreams. It could be dangerous." Taiwa sat up, caught the bread just before it hit the earthen floor, and stuffed it in her mouth.

"You and your dreams," Ontarra chuckled. "Was Pierce Head chasing you, or was it the okis dragging you into the river this time?"

"Don't joke about dreams; they're important." Taiwa slid her dainty brown feet to the floor and scooted over to the fire. "I just wish I could fathom their meanings better." She scooped stew onto another cornbread with a wooden ladle, lifted it, and took a whiff. It was Taiwa's fourteenth summer. She was becoming a pretty young maiden, but it seemed she didn't want it to happen. "I think the spirits of the animals are angry. We don't thank them properly for feeding us, and we kill them when we don't need the food."

Shanoka dipped a barely discernible nod, surprised at how often Taiwa's dreams mirrored her own feelings. The Attawondaronks felt they must kill all animals they encountered to prevent them from warning each other to avoid the dangerous humans in their midst. Shanoka knew that the deities of the Ojibwa would be offended by this, and it made her uneasy. "Don't speak beyond our lodge about your dreams, Taiwa. They will not be well received by some."

Shanoka's dreams were always a meaningless jumble of unconnected events, but her mother had been a Powerful dreamer and seer. It appeared Taiwa had her grandmother's gift. Unfortunately, she lived in a place where she might never be allowed to use such a skill. Taiwa scooped more cornbread from the cooking stone, juggling it from hand to hand as it cooled. Teota snuggled up beside her and pressed his glossy black bangs to her cheek with a hug.

"Mother, I saw Yadwena yesterday when we were preparing the fire and hides for maple syrup. She was crying again. I think that she pines for a baby." Taiwa tore a chunk from the bread and threw it to the dog nose poking past the doorskin again. She dipped the remainder into the pot, scooping out as much of the stew as the bread could hold.

Shanoka's lips thinned, but the humor lines at the corners of her eyes wrinkled. "Taiwa, eat like a human."

"Ontarra does it all the time when you're not looking. Besides, I'm too hungry to be proper." Taiwa jammed the sloppy bread in her mouth, licking at the juices that dripped through her fingers. "It must be hard for Yadwena, being married to Tsohahissen. He's so much older. She's young, and he can no longer make babies. You should use your mide bag to help her."

"Careful, Taiwa, Hiatsou flies into a rage if my mide bag is even mentioned, and we don't need any more trouble in the town right now."

"Everyone knows you're a better healer than Hiatsou. Since you saved Tsohahissen from the coughs, everyone asks for you. Your mide bag holds the Power to change things—you said so yourself. You should help Yadwena."

"Even when I lived with Togo, I couldn't use my mide bag in public. It frightens some people, so we'll discuss it no more."

Taiwa knew better than to press. She switched subjects. "Tell us how Father saved you and Togo. I've always wondered."

"It's me," a bright voice called from outside. "May I enter?" Sounia poked her head through the doorskin, her long black hair still holding a damp sheen from her morning bathe at Snake Creek.

Taiwa jumped up, pulling Sounia past the hide that covered the entrance and greeting her with a hug. Taiwa yanked her head back. "Ooh! You're still wet!"

Shanoka grinned, motioning for Sounia to be seated. "Have you eaten yet?"

"I have," Sounia said, nodding, "but I'll have some of your tea—if there's any left." Sounia settled down across from Ontarra, flashing a demure smile as their eyes met. Shanoka rocked a ceramic pot down into the coals to warm the tea, a subtle grin curling the corner of her mouth as she caught the hidden greeting.

Ontarra smiled back, unable to pull his gaze from her. "You look fresh this morning." He loved the way those bottomless eyes reflected any light that touched them. "Perhaps you could give Taiwa some lessons in acceptable appearance and manners."

Taiwa placed her fists on her hips with mock disgust. "Ontarra, your breath is bad, your clothes are filthy, and now is about the time you usually start rubbing your belly and belching; so why don't you go do whatever it is that a warrior—one who is not quite a warrior—does all day."

Before Ontarra could fashion a reply, the doorskin lifted and two more faces appeared. Tonita and Brata were midwives; Shanoka often helped them. Between the two, they knew just about everything that happened in the town, and if they didn't know, they improvised. Brata's face had more lines etched into it than any face should possibly hold. Brata had been old when Ontarra learned to walk.

"It is good to see you both. I hope all is well at your hearths." Shanoka used the traditional greeting, but Brata was never one to abide by formalities.

"Don't ask about my hearth, Shanoka. My useless mate left early and let it burn out. These old bones were frozen when I woke. I swear that he's the reason for my aching joints and thinning hair. If I could hunt, I'd cast him out!"

Tonita laughed. "Has anything good ever happened to you?"

Brata considered this as she lowered herself to the warmth of the hearth. "Yes ... when I was young I found a beautiful bone hair comb by the river. I treasured it that whole summer. At Green Corn, another girl saw it in my hair and swore that I had stolen it from her." Brata was quiet a moment, ancient memories and the scowl returning. "Hmph! I guess that didn't turn out either."

Ontarra wanted to talk with Sounia, but this many women in one lodge was uncomfortable, and old ones were always so crotchety. Climbing to his feet, he shot another smile to Sounia and nodded to his mother. Before he made the door, Teota snagged a leg and hung on. "Can I still come with you today?"

"Yes, Mosquito, I haven't forgotten. Toutsou and Yadak are coming too."

"I'm going fishing, Mother!" Teota had waited forever for this. His enthusiasm brought grins to faces as he rushed around the lodge, frantically gathering items he wanted to take, discarding them, and starting again. His smile faded, and he looked up at Ontarra with sad, puppy-dog eyes. "What about my practice bow, Ontarra?"

"I'll still make it," he assured his brother, pushing back Teota's thick bangs and ruffling his hair. "Now, everything we'll need today is in the carry pouch under my sleep platform. Just grab that and then go to the Woodpecker clan lodge and wake Yadak."

"Why don't you wait and go together?" Shanoka asked.

"I want to talk to Toutsou alone for a moment." Ontarra didn't want to tell her that he never felt welcome in the Bird clan lodges. "We'll meet you outside the north entry, Teota."

Ontarra turned on a heel and ducked out into the morning bustle of Ounontisaston. The inner palisades were finally complete, their layout and shape dictated by the bluff they skirted. Nine completed longhouses sat within the safety of the walls. Two sat askew from all the others, conforming to irregularities in the terrain. Everyone was up now, moving about their morning chores. Near the west wall, Ahratota and Dahtka, dressed in heavy protective skins, supervised construction of the tenth longhouse in the impressive row. With outcamps counted, the town was now home to thirteen hundred souls.

Ontarra headed down the path that fronted the longhouses. Naked children darted from doorways and down secondary paths, playing tag. Older boys rolled hoops and fired practice arrows through them. The town's dogs loved hoops, running off with them to create their own game of try-and-get-your-hoop-back. Women gathered at community mortars, chattering like jays as they pounded corn and nuts into meal. Smoke from a hundred cooking fires twined and curled skyward in the still morning air.

Butterflied fish from nets in the river were already being hung on racks near the south entry. Drying huts scattered through the town were being filled with river muck to germinate petun seed. Ontarra marveled at all the activity. Only two cycles past, he'd first stood on this bluff with his father. It had been a tangle of brush then, impossible to walk through. Now, a vibrant community had been hacked into the wilderness. Everything was abundant here. The chief town of the nation attracted the most talented people. Everyone wanted to live at Ounontisaston. As the town filled, bribes to gain acceptance became commonplace.

The Bird clans took advantage of a need for fishermen, most of whom were Bird clan men, quickly moving them in from the other towns. After the fishermen were accepted, they brought the rest of their families, which quickly swelled the Bird clan presence before the practice was ended. Ounontisaston could grow no further now, hemmed in as it was by the bluff top. Any expansion would make the palisades indefensible. Council decreed that no newcomers could be accepted.

Shriveled old men sat around the doorways of longhouses, smoking their pipes. The first warm days after a long winter brought everyone out. Elders smiled, nodding to Ontarra as he passed. He dipped his chin and smiled, acknowledging each greeting. Sannisen might be chief of chiefs someday, and his son was well known. His pleasant easygoing manner made him well liked.

At the front entry to the Doe clan longhouse, Ontarra waited, listening a moment before entering. Walking into a family squabble unannounced could be hazardous, but he heard only the normal hubbub of a building teeming with people. Announcing himself, he stepped inside, pausing at the entry while his eyes adjusted. Smoke hung like fog just above his head. He knew the smoke wouldn't bother him after a hand of time, but he never got used to the initial discomfort. If a person was lucky enough to live fifty summers, his eyesight usually failed him. His mother said it was because of the smoke. Ontarra believed her.

Ten hearth fires ran down the center of the building. Light flickered and danced, casting eerie shadows on food, clothes, and tools dangling from rafters. The smell of food, smoke, sweat, and urine assaulted his nostrils as Ontarra threaded his way around half-dressed children, dogs, and eating utensils. People drifted in and out of the doors at each end constantly. Ontarra's presence was barely noticed. From somewhere ahead in the bowels of the longhouse, a shout was directed at him.

"Ho! Ontarra! Over here!" Toutsou waved from the far end. Ontarra navigated around the hearth fires, stepping over babies, and barely avoiding a collision with two boys running in circles. He managed to make it to the far end without a serious mishap. Toutsou greeted him with a friendly thump on the shoulder.

"Whew!" Toutsou stepped back, scrunching up his long, thin face. "You smell like you've been cleaning fish. Have you started doing women's work, or are you just afraid of water?"

Ontarra rolled his eyes, a grin spreading. He enjoyed Toutsou's constant insults and could usually snap one back. "I can go to the river and wash away the stench today, but you could wash to the end of time and that awful face will still be there."

"Now that I think about it, too much cleaning isn't natural or healthy," Toutsou said with a smirk. Everything about Toutsou was long and lanky. Ontarra was always surprised how many of the young maidens in the town watched and flirted with Toutsou and how Toutsou never seemed to notice.

Toutsou's plump, good-natured mother plodded around, gathering up sleeping furs to hang out on the palisade for airing. "Have you eaten yet, Ontarra?"

"Yes, thank you, Wasika. Mother won't let me leave without eating first."

"Is all well at your lodge today? I heard Hiatsou complaining to the shamans about your mother again last night."

Ontarra sighed, dropping his gaze to Toutsou's scruffy dog as it nuzzled his leg. He gave the obligatory ear rub as he thought about the uncle who had plagued his family for as long as he could remember. Hiatsou was chief shaman of the entire nation. He wanted to be the next chief of chiefs and saw Sannisen as his only rival. He was sly, conniving, and mean-spirited. Ontarra hated him. "All is well, Wasika. I wouldn't worry about Hiatsou's complaining. That's all he ever does."

Wasika agreed with an amused smile and headed outside with her armload of furs.

"Toutsou," Ontarra said, "I want to get a blank to make a practice bow for Teota while we're out fishing. Will you keep an eye on him for me when I leave?"

Toutsou nodded. "Sure. And I know where there's a hickory full of suitable limbs."

"Hickory is too stiff for Teota. I want to use maple. I saw some good trees when we burned the new fields. They're just to the north of the spawning hole upstream."

"That's a long way," Toutsou objected. "Why don't we head down to the Tranchi?"

"The fishermen have nets in all the prime spots. We're better off going up the Entry River and get the fish that escaped the nets. There will be rabbits and squirrels," Ontarra added for incentive.

A smile spread on Toutsou's face. "I'll bring my throw-stick, my skinning knife, and my bow."

Ontarra shook his head with an amused grin. Toutsou always wanted to hunt. "Forget the bow, Toutsou. The large animals have been scared off by the fires and smoke, but bring your fish spears."

"Well … all right." Toutsou returned the bow to an antler hook but slid the knife and throw-stick into his waistband. He dug in the storage area below his sleep platform and pulled out two three-pronged spears. The precisely carved points were fashioned from deer antler into a curve that fit neatly around a fish's body. Inward barbs held the fish, while a third point in the center severed the spinal column, ending the creature's struggles instantly.

"Whewf!" Ontarra studied the bone point in the center. "How did you ever come up with this?"

"When we were boys at old Ounon, I used to catch fish with a deer rack. Then I added a handle, but I kept losing the big ones, so I put a point in the center. I'm thinking of adding a line so I can throw it and retrieve it."

Ontarra bobbed his head as he pictured it. "Why not make an arrow with barbs and add a line?" Toutsou held Ontarra with his eyes, a smile slowly rearranging the lines of his angular face.

They ducked outside, shielding their eyes from glaring sunlight as they headed for the north entry. Toutsou called for his dog. A yellow form came snuffling around the end of a lodge. The shaggy mutt always traveled with his nose to the ground, tail standing straight up. He seemed confused as he tried to follow the maze of scent trails covering the worn pathways. Ontarra watched the dog's antics and decided his mother was right—dogs did look just like wolves. Bored with the jumbled smells, the dog lifted his snout and snorted a whiff of Ontarra's crotch.

"Quit that!" Ontarra slapped an ear. The dog jumped sideways, offended. "That's a bad habit he has."

"You should take that as a compliment," Toutsou said with a grin. "He likes you." Abruptly, Toutsou jerked to a stop, and Ontarra pulled up short. "Look at that."

Ontarra followed Toutsou's gaze to the plaza. Poutassa was there, dressed in gaudy red leggings. His skinny upper body was bare, and his ribs were blackened with charcoal. The headdress of a full shaman was perched arrogantly on his head. Hiatsou's apprentices performed the morning rituals while Poutassa shouted orders, belittling their efforts with each outburst.

A few people were gathered, obviously wondering why a real shaman wasn't present, especially since all the nation's shamans were all visiting Ounontisaston at Hiatsou's request. "Still obnoxious as ever," Toutsou muttered, pushing past some onlookers for a better view.

Ontarra watched as Poutassa humiliated one of the apprentices for painting his face the wrong color. Ontarra remembered how Poutassa had bullied him as a child, and his animosity beginning to boil. As if he could feel eyes burning into his skin, Poutassa turned to stare defiantly at his cousin. "What are you two gawking at?"

"Just wondering that ourselves," Ontarra shot back. "Why doesn't Hiatsou perform his own duties instead of endangering our town with your useless prattle?"

Poutassa's serpent-like eyes glared out from sockets uncomfortably deep and dark. He shuffled his weight from foot to foot, aware that people were watching. "My father has important spiritual business to attend to, and this is no concern of yours."

"Let's go." Toutsou's voice was suddenly anxious, but Ontarra wasn't ready to let up.

"Why are you masquerading as a full shaman, Poutassa? You aren't fooling anyone."

"It is an insult to the sun for anyone less than a full shaman to address it," Poutassa spat back. "This headdress gives weight to my words."

"I pass wind that has more weight than your words!" Ontarra shouted for everyone to hear.

Toutsou's eyes widened. He tugged nervously on Ontarra's arm. "Let's go." Ontarra reluctantly turned away, allowing Toutsou to drag him toward the north entry. "By the okis, Ontarra! You can't talk to a shaman like that! Don't you remember what he did to Kanda when we were children?"

Ontarra thought back. Poutassa had intimidated everyone. He was only one cycle older than Ontarra, but he'd been bigger than the other children their age, and when he couldn't get his way by physical threats, he tried to frighten people by cursing them. It didn't work on Kanda. Kanda dealt Poutassa a severe beating while the other children taunted and jeered.

"Kanda caught a fever sickness and died—that's all," Ontarra said, trying to sound certain.

"Sure, right after Poutassa made a doll from a piece of Kanda's clothing and burned it in front of us." Toutsou shivered as he recalled the uncanny ritual.

At the north entry, loads of saplings and bark were being carried in for the new longhouse. They had to wait until the switchbacks cleared. The guard up on the parapet had apparently heard the exchange between Ontarra and Poutassa. He dipped an amused nod of consent, allowing them to pass through. The entry was constructed of three parallel rows of saplings. They forced anyone entering or leaving to turn back and forth twice. Anyone uninvited would have arrows and rocks rained down upon them from above while they were caught in the switchbacks.

Outside along the north palisade, the town's craftsmen were enjoying the weather. All manner of essential goods were being fashioned. Projectile points, bows, arrows, clay pipes, field tools, war clubs, bone hooks, and fishnets were the male crafts. The women had laid claim to the bluff top along the south palisade, with its magnificent view of the river valley. They could watch the activities in the canoe area and see the field workers. In colder weather, the sun warmed the south exposure. In summer, the trees on the bluff shaded the area. Men and women always worked poorly together. Since the women occupied the crest on the east and west faces, the men were relegated to the north side. No one bothered to argue.

Yadak and Teota were watching arrow points being hafted onto shafts. Yadak was a grandson of Winona, grandmother of all the Bird clans. Ontarra had liked him when they were young, but it became apparent that Yadak had no ambition, and his penchant for bullying was contemptible. He had developed a permanent scowl that made him appear as if someone had just taken something important from him.

Yadak avoided Ontarra's eyes again, and Ontarra pretended not to notice. "I brought night worms." Yadak probed into a pouch on his waistband, drawing out a writhing piece of brown flesh. It slithered and coiled around his fingers.

"Can I see one?" Teota held out a hand and was rewarded with a fat crawler that required all of his attention and dexterity to keep from squirming free.

Ontarra shaded his eyes and stared out across the fields to the distant treeline at the ridge above the creek. "We're going there," he said, pointing, "where that smoke is rising. They're burning more fields today." He glanced at Toutsou and realized he wasn't listening; instead, he was staring at the billowing clouds forming in the sky.

"My mother says they are puffs of smoke from the calumets of the manitos," Toutsou muttered softly. "They are content and will give us a fine day."

Ontarra shot a dubious look at the clouds, shook his head, and set off across the fields, leaving Toutsou to catch up when he finished with his daydream. In two cycles, the uplands had been transformed from wilderness to a massive garden. Burning the brush pleased the soil and ensured good crops. Only the charred trunks of the largest trees survived the conflagration; their blackened skeletons were scattered through the fields like sentinels guarding the crops.

Women were busy hoeing mounds for planting. Everyone worked together, preparing one clan's fields each day so that no one would seem favored. They worked around the blackened trunks, but when the corn, beans, and squash came to life, the rows would be straight and orderly. It was a way of honoring the three sister goddesses that brought life to these crops. The women watched the fields mature with pride. It was cause for shame if a clan's rows were not straight or their plants appeared stunted. As summer progressed, women would tie corn leaves to the charred trunks to scare off marauding flocks of birds.

"The Wendat traders say our petun is prized everywhere," Toutsou chattered breathlessly, his long, muscular legs making it easy to catch up again. "They told me that the Caribou people can go for days without eating, just smoking our petun. And they never get hungry."

"Our uplands grow reasonable petun, but wait until you see the petun they grow at Tontiaton." Ontarra referred to their sister town built a half-day's journey to the south. "Petun likes the sandy soil there. It grows taller, and the leaves are—"

"Let's walk along the ridge above the river," Toutsou interrupted, his mind already wandering to other things. "We'll see game down in the ravine, and

I can show you how to use a throw-stick." He trotted off, forcing a revised route on everyone. Teota was mesmerized by the uncanny strength of his night worm and had to run after the others when he missed the course change.

Yadak trudged up alongside. "Ontarra, have you been with Tonayata lately?"

Ontarra let out a frustrated sigh. "Yadak, Sounia and I are promised. I have no interest in Tonayata. Why won't you believe that?" Yadak scowled, and Ontarra could see that he wasn't convinced. "She asked me to go with her to the creek a couple of times," Ontarra said, "but I found her to be … well, let's just say she is not for me."

Yadak's tone turned spiteful. "You are Land clan! You shouldn't have been sniffing after a Bird clan maiden!"

Ontarra stopped and faced Yadak. "Since when can the Land and Bird clans not mix?"

"Hiatsou says that the moieties should remain pure," Yadak snarled scornfully.

"Hiatsou speaks for his own benefit!" Ontarra shot back. "He tries to manipulate everyone. He—" Yadak turned away, but Ontarra gripped Yadak's shoulder, and they locked eyes. "Listen to me, Yadak. Tonayata is mean and spiteful. I want nothing to do with her. You'd be far better off with someone else."

Yadak twisted away. "I will not listen to you besmirch her like that. I know she's been seeing someone, and I'll find out who it is!" Yadak stomped off.

Ontarra shook his head and waited for Teota to catch up. They continued on in silence. He wondered if he'd said too much. *I spoke the truth. I could do nothing more.* They walked the crest in single file. Toutsou stalked the treeline, stopping occasionally to scan the hillside below. He stopped suddenly, looked over at Ontarra, pointed, and then headed down to Yadak.

Ontarra and Teota ducked and swerved through grasping branches as they followed Toutsou and Yadak down a deer trail. Teota was short enough to walk upright, but brush whipped and slapped at the taller boys. At the bottom, they stopped to inspect their scratches and scrapes. Teota anxiously eyed the river below, wondering what all the grumbling was about.

The Entry River blossomed out into a large hole here; the marshy edges were a morass of lily pads and tawny cattails. Toutsou prowled down the shoreline, keen eyes searching for spawning fish. Yadak crossed over at the rapids, preferring to keep his own company. Ontarra exhaled wearily and shook his head. Teota tugged Ontarra to the water's edge. "Show me what to do," he said, bubbling with excitement.

Ontarra untied his waistpouch and removed a length of dowel with a gut line carefully spooled around it. The deer intestine had been weighted and hung from a tree branch until it stretched to the length of a longhouse—it was no thicker than a leaf stem. A bone hook was firmly knotted and sealed with pine gum. "Give me the worm. Slide it on like this." When he impaled the worm, Teota grimaced. "Throw it out as far as you can," Ontarra said, tossing it to the center of the pond, "and then pull it back with short hops, winding up the slack as you go." He handed the dowel to Teota. Teota wound it up and lobbed the hook out into the weeds. After several futile attempts, he finally managed to hit the pond and retrieve the bait.

Toutsou let out a whoop. Everyone looked to where he was standing waist-deep in the lily pads. He had the butt end of his spear jammed into a hole hidden beneath the surface. He leaned back, digging his feet into the stony bottom as he hauled the spear back out of the watery lair. A dark blob appeared, thrashing just beneath the surface. Toutsou let go of the spear and lunged. Struggling a moment, he got a grip, and heaved a big snapping turtle up onto the shore. The witless creature had clamped onto the spear shaft with such single-minded tenacity that he still wouldn't let it go. Toutsou scrambled up onto the bank and, with a single slash, removed the head.

"Turtle soup at the Doe clan hearth tonight!" Toutsou held up the spear with the turtle's head still firmly attached.

"Nice catch!" Ontarra yelled. He turned to his brother. "Teota, I need to go and look for something. I won't be long."

"Okay," Teota answered absently, tossing his hook into the lily pads again.

Ontarra glanced over at Yadak on the opposite shore. "Yadak is in a foul mood. If you need help, call Toutsou." Teota nodded and tossed again. Ontarra watched the line sail out into the cattails. He smirked and shook his head and then headed for the uplands to find a blank for Teota's bow.

Teota fished without success until the sun was high. He was ready to give it up when he felt a heavy tug on the line. He yanked and felt the fish. "I've got one, Toutsou! I've got one! Help me!"

"No, you must land it yourself!" Toutsou hollered. "Keep the line tight! Try to slowly pull him in to the shore!" Teota wrapped the line around his fingers, turned and ran, dragging the fish a stone's cast up into the grass and weeds on the bank before Toutsou could get in another word. Teota dropped the line, ran back and dove on top of the flopping fish to prevent any escape attempts.

"It's a big mooneye, Toutsou! I caught one!" Teota couldn't contain himself. "What do I do now?"

Toutsou had to laugh at Teota's total lack of finesse. "If you have a knife, you'd best gut it out!"

Teota ran to the pouch and dug inside. He found Ontarra's knife and went scurrying back to the bouncing fish. It lay still for a moment, one glassy eye staring up at him. "I'm sorry, fish, but I need you to feed my family." Teota pressed the chert point to the belly and looked deeply into the fish's eye as it began to haze. He tapped the knife against his leg. He couldn't bring himself to separate the mooneye from his spirit.

"Give me the knife." The blunt voice startled Teota. Yadak bent down, peeling the knife from Teota's fingers. With plunging strokes, he opened the belly and clawed out the entrails. He left the head on so the fish could be carried by its gill-plates. "Run home now, and show off your prize." Yadak turned on a heel and sloshed back across the rapids.

Yadak's black mood couldn't spoil Teota's excitement. He gathered up Ontarra's fishing gear and hastily jammed everything into the pouch. "I'm heading back!" he called to Toutsou.

Toutsou thought about it a moment and then nodded. "All right. But go straight to town. We'll wait here for Ontarra."

Teota dragged the pouch in one hand and the big fish in the other. Halfway up the slope, he noticed another trail angling off. Resting on his knees, he decided the angled path would be an easier climb, but the fish grew heavier as the trail meandered aimlessly up and down the face of the ravine. Teota found himself stopping more frequently. He seemed to be making no progress toward the top. He considered trying to force his way up through the brush, but the tangle of branches was just too thick. He sat on the path, laying the fish aside to rub his aching arms. He heard something—voices.

Teota hunched down and stalked along the path as he imagined that the hunters would do. The voices were just ahead. Crouching behind a big oak,

Attawondaronk

he peered around the side—and yanked his head back with a startled gasp. He drew a few ragged breaths, and took another peek.

The shamans of the Attawondaronk Nation were gathered in a clearing below. Hiatsou had his back to Teota, but Teota recognized him by his bulk and greasy gray hair. Hiatsou lifted a screaming turkey up by its neck, silencing it with a bone-cracking shake. Another shaman approached with a knife and opened the bird from gullet to gut. The body cavity emptied onto the ground. Hiatsou dabbed his fingers in the bird's blood and stroked it onto his cheeks and arms. Without warning, Hiatsou made a terrible wailing sound, and Teota's heart jumped into his throat. The shamans gathered round, as if searching for something in the gory pile.

Teota reeled around, slumping against the tree. Only shamans were allowed to see a Ring of Fire ceremony. He had to get away before he was noticed. He crawled until he was what seemed a safe distance toward the top of the slope, and then he pushed to his feet. A furry shape stepped into his path. The thing grabbed him.

Teota screamed, struggling to break free. A blood-curdling growl froze him. He looked up, and what he saw sent a wave of horror through every fiber of his being. It was not of this world. The legs of a man; the body of a bear. Paws with wicked claws were wrapped around Teota's arm. Where a face should be, there was a blunt muzzle, sharp teeth, and huge cavernous eyes. Teota twisted and with the supernatural strength of terror, he wrenched himself free. He charged up the hill until he found himself tangled in a thicket of wild rose thorns. The thing came after him. Claws raked at his leg. Teota dropped and rolled to his back, kicking at the furry snout, wailing at the top of his lungs as he scrambled backward up the slope. He gained some distance, rolled onto his belly and wormed his way through the bushes and briers until he reached the top. He got his feet under him and ran shrieking across the fields.

"Taiwa! Taiwa, slow down!" Sounia trotted to keep up as Taiwa beelined for the south entry.

Taiwa turned and propped her hands on her hips, a misshapen braid with a goose-down feather at its tip sliding over her shoulder. "I want to get some distance before Mother thinks up something for me to do." She waited for

Sounia to catch up before continuing at a more leisurely pace. They skirted around the petun drying huts that lined the inner palisade. New shoots sprouted from the river muck already. In a few days, the women growers would sow three plants into every seventh mound of the upper fields. The women would guard the petun all summer, keeping vermin and meddlesome men away until it was ready for harvest. Petun was far too precious to risk losing even one plant.

Sounia's clothes were always clean and neat. She preferred a buckskin dress that fell to the knees, rather than the more traditional skirt and tunic. Moose-hide moccasins protected her feet. Long, lustrous black hair was woven into a single braid behind her left ear and then draped over her shoulder—a style that Taiwa was quick to claim as her own.

Sounia's clothing was the envy of all the maidens. Her father, Soutoten, was hunt chief and provided her with many hides of large animals, like bear and moose. The Wendat traders had just made a gift of three elk hides that would make beautiful winter clothing, but now that her mother was at the Village of the Dead, it had fallen to Sounia to provide a comfortable lodge, so she had decided to make sleeping robes instead.

Taiwa's old moccasins were grimy and tattered; her skirt was streaked with greasy finger swipes. She wore no top at all, preferring the warmth of the sun on her back and budding breasts.

"Aren't you cold?" Sounia asked.

"No, I love these first warm days. Don't worry; it's sheltered and warm where we're going."

Sounia arched a brow. "And just where is that? You told your mother we were going to pick cattail shoots."

"You'll see."

The husky guard above the south entry dipped his chin as they passed below. The girls strolled out through the switchbacks. The gate was wide enough for people coming and going, but if a load of fish or meat was coming through, people exiting were obliged to back up and let the bearer pass.

The girls paused outside the palisade, taking in the vista below. Crop fields spread out across the valley on each side of the Entry River. Blackened tree trunks dotted the landscape. Where Snake Creek and the Entry River merged below, the canoe area was a hive of activity. As soon as the ice was off the rivers, the fishermen and hunters came and went constantly. Fishermen studied the habits of fish and knew exactly where to find them as the seasons changed. They had six moon cycles in which to net, spear, or hook enough fish to provide for Ounontisaston all winter.

Hunters were bringing in the blackhead geese. The big birds were on the long journey to their summer homes. Noisy flocks landed on the Tranchi, squabbling with decoys fashioned from reeds that floated along the river to lure them in. When a sufficient number had landed, men burst from blinds, scaring the geese downstream. As the mottled gray bodies slowly lifted from the water, a net fashioned from bark fiber and vines was yanked across in front of them. They pounded into the mesh, where they were quickly clubbed or had their necks wrung.

The rivers were so busy in the kind seasons, it wasn't even necessary to guard them. Any intruder was seen and challenged long before reaching the Entry River.

Taiwa walked along the west brow of the bluff, studying the activities below. "Look at all the people washing clothes at the creek."

Sounia squinted through the tree branches. A festival atmosphere wound up and down the meandering watercourse. "Everyone is glad that winter is over." Sounia turned and wandered along the palisade to admire the work of the craftswomen. "Look at this, Taiwa." She stopped at a knot of women who chattered as they worked, glanced out occasionally at the valley, and chattered some more. "Avoya, what is it you're making?"

The old woman looked past Sounia with murky eyes. "Is that you, Sounia?" A smile touched her lips. "It's a cradleboard for Ahratota's wife. Her baby should arrive any day." Avoya ran her fingers across the brims of the baskets that surrounded her. She fumbled around in one, found a quill, and held it up to her eye. The quills had been softened in water and then dyed with bloodroot, wild plum bark, blueberries, or walnut husks. If she held a quill a fingerspan from her left eye, Avoya could just make out its color. Satisfied with her choice, Avoya drew the quill between her teeth, flattening it into a ribbon. She then wove it into the series of parallel thongs on the cradleboard, using only her sense of touch to create the beautiful design of a Thunderbird.

Avoya lifted her rheumy eyes to the sound of Taiwa's breathing. "Say nothing to your mother, child. If Brata hears, the whole town will know."

But Taiwa wasn't listening. Her attention was stolen by a girl of four summers who was making her first clay pot. The misshapen lump of clay was molded tightly around her fist. The girl studied her mother's pot beside her, gave up trying to get hers off her fist, and started poking chevrons around the brim with her thumbnail instead. The woman grinned up at Taiwa, eyes twinkling with silent amusement.

The girls continued on along the palisade. Fresh hides were stretched on the wall for their initial scraping with grooved deer antlers. The animals' brains would be churned into a paste and then rubbed into the skins to soften and preserve them. Several more scrapings would be required before they could be smoked, giving them their unique color.

All along the palisade, craftswomen were busily working on moccasins, pouches, pots, hoes, canoe paddles, and hair combs, all to be bartered for other necessities of life. These women were highly respected and generally wealthy.

Taiwa grew bored and headed for one of the paths that threaded down the bluff. She stopped at a smoking rack that was loaded with fish to stare at the woman who tended the coals. Blackened with soot, the woman rolled smoldering cross-sections of log out of the pit. Next she scraped and gouged the charcoal away with a stone adze and sharpened antlers, hollowing out wooden bowls in the process.

Sounia caught up. "Let's go over to the canoe area."

Taiwa glanced down at the organized chaos, estimating there were at least ten hands of canoes scattered amongst the trees and along the riverbank. "No. It's too busy. I want to get over the creek and go out across the fields."

They padded down the hill to the creek. Infants propped up in cradleboards dozed while their mothers scrubbed clothes and bedding. Washing was usually done by maidens Sounia's age, but today the older women needed an excuse to enjoy the sunshine. They smiled, dipping greetings as the girls passed. A clutch of maidens farther upstream splashed in the water, pretending not to notice the unattached youths who always gathered to show off when the girls were around.

The boys were stripped naked. Pushing, shoving, and chasing each other around, they watched the girls from the corners of their eyes. If a girl smiled or spoke, it provided an opportunity to talk. It was a socially accepted mating ritual. Couples would soon be wandering off, arm in arm, to some secluded spot for a secret liaison. Some would eventually agree to share a hearth; many more would not. The maidens were encouraged by their mothers to ask for gifts to increase their dowries.

"The games they play are ridiculous," Taiwa scrunched up her face as if she'd just discovered dog shit on her moccasin. "The boys act like bucks in rut, and the girls pretend not to notice." She tilted her head to Sounia. "Do you ever come here and flirt?"

"A few times last cycle, but I haven't since."

Taiwa shot a sidelong glance and grinned. "You don't come because of Ontarra. Am I right? You've agreed to share a hearth. I always knew you would." Taiwa suddenly pictured Ontarra's empty sleep platform, and her grin faded. She kicked a stone, sending it skittering into the creek.

They reached a bend where the stream squeezed in close to the bluff. The girls found themselves alone for the first time all morning. Taiwa pulled off her moccasins and stepped onto a moss-covered rock. "This is where I cross." She immediately lost her balance and slid in. "*Ahh!* It's cold!" Taiwa arched up on her toes to get more skin out of the water.

Sounia ignored the rocks and stepped in gingerly. "You m-might want … to … to consider w-washing … while … while we're here," she stammered through chattering teeth. "Boys admire a girl who is clean."

"Boys are a nuisance!" Taiwa placed her feet carefully, leaning into the icy current to keep them planted. "I can't even walk around naked anymore. They all stare at me!" Taiwa concentrated on her balance as the tumbling current tried to push her downstream. She frowned. "What is it you like about Ontarra?"

Sounia pondered a moment before answering. "I don't know how to explain it. When he looks at me … I get this feeling in the pit of my stomach."

"A feeling in your stomach?" Taiwa flashed an impish grin. "Mother makes a willow-bark tea that might help you with that."

"You're exasperating, Taiwa." Sounia winced as the frigid water crept up her legs. "Are you going to bathe or not?"

"Later." Taiwa tugged at roots poking from the bank to pull herself up. "Ooh, the ground feels good, and—" She froze momentarily and then called out, "Tonayata! What are you doing here?"

Sounia followed Taiwa's eyes, but a patch of blossoming willow brush blocked her vision.

"I'm trying to have some privacy while I wash!" an irritated voice snarled back.

Taiwa offered a hand to help Sounia up. "We're heading out across the fields," Taiwa apologized. "You may have your privacy."

Sounia could see Tonayata now, standing knee-deep in the stream and hidden by the bushes. She was holding a dress up in front of her with uncharacteristic modesty. Tonayata scowled at Sounia. "Why did you follow me here? Go away!"

"You shouldn't be so nasty all the time!" Taiwa snapped back. "Perhaps Ontarra would have liked you more."

Tonayata's eyes blazed as she looked from Sounia to Taiwa. "There are no men in this town for me. And it is obvious that Ontarra has no sense in women!"

"Why do you hide yourself, Tonayata?" Taiwa chided. "I can see enough to know that your body is growing as fat as your ego."

Sounia tugged at Taiwa's arm. "Forget her. You have something to show me, remember?"

Taiwa spun on her heel, walking off without looking back. Sounia had to take long strides to catch up. They didn't see Tonayata lower her dress, revealing a row of angry scars on her thigh and buttock. Tonayata sagged onto the bank, burying her face in her hands to muffle her sobs.

"Taiwa, you forgot your moccasins," Sounia said.

"I'm not going back there! I'll get them later."

"Your feet are going to look like elm bark," Sounia scolded.

Taiwa stomped on. "They will be useful boy-deterrents then, won't they?"

Wedged between the bluff, the Entry River, and the Tranchi, the floodplain had been transformed from a tangle of brush and undergrowth, into a bountiful cropland. Women were busy hoeing the lush black soil into mounds for sunflowers. They had discovered that flowers grew to fantastic heights down here, with massive heads full of fat seeds. Sunflowers could be planted before other crops; they were hardy enough to withstand cold snaps or even a late frost. Frost sometimes damaged crops on the uplands and left the lowland crops unscathed. The women believed that the good water spirits spread warmth across the valley to protect the crops. They threw petun in the rivers to ensure the spirits' continued benevolence.

The women paid little attention to the girls as they passed amongst them; concentrated as they were on working their hoes. All the hoes had wooden handles, but the blades were made from a variety of items. A limb that curved at the proper angle could be easily shaped into a hoe but usually only lasted one season. When the blade wore down, an antler or hipbone could be hafted to the handle. The best hoes used slate blades, brought in from the gray cliff near Teotonguiaton.

Soil was cultivated into loose piles that would hold eight or ten seeds. Every third grow-mound in corn or sunflower fields was larger. In this mound, pumpkin, squash, and beans were sown. As the taller plants grew, the vines twined up their stalks for support. Squash provided ground cover, choking out weeds. Beans added nutrients to the soil. The sister crops nurtured themselves.

Taiwa found a piece of driftwood that made a perfect walking stick. She slid her hand up and down the grain, and her fingers tingled on the glossy surface. She walked in silence, lost to her thoughts. Sounia never interrupted when Taiwa wore that distant look. "When you marry Ontarra," Taiwa said, "will he leave the Lynx clan and become Wolf clan, like you?" Taiwa sounded as if this had just occurred to her.

"Of course." Sounia raised a brow, surprised that Taiwa would mention something so obvious.

Taiwa stopped and grabbed Sounia's wrist. "I love Ontarra. I don't want him to leave."

"Ontarra isn't going anywhere. We will live here at Ounontisaston. You'll see us every day. When you marry and have children, Ontarra will teach your boys to hunt, and fish, and fight. It is the circle of life."

Taiwa sighed and started walking again. She'd never really thought about Ontarra leaving before. It seemed so sudden—she had a feeling of loss, like something that had always been, had changed when she wasn't looking.

Sounia eyed the sad expression. "Don't worry," she said, her tone reassuring. "Ontarra will always be your brother, and I will be your sister."

Taiwa brightened. "My sister ... who is also my best friend. Many of the girls don't even like their sisters. You're right; it will be a good thing." She pointed her walking stick. "Come on, we're going over there."

"Your thoughts change direction faster than a hummingbird," Sounia said with a smirk. "Why are we going up there? I thought we were going to pull cattail shoots."

"Maybe later. Follow me." Taiwa pulled Sounia's hand. "There's a trail." Taiwa dipped and weaved through the brush as they struggled up the ravine. The hillside was still in its wild, impenetrable state, and it would have been an impossible climb, except for the tiny passage left by animals as they moved down to the river flat to drink and pilfer crops from the fields. They reached a ledge where large boulders had tumbled down in the distant past. Taiwa eased herself down to one and pointed out through the branches. "Look."

Sounia turned. The fields and rivers spread out below, the palisades of the town standing vigil over the entire area. "It's beautiful. I've never seen the town from up high like this. We should show the craftswomen. Perhaps they could render it onto a hide."

"No!" Taiwa grabbed Sounia's wrist. "This is my secret place. No one else can know. Promise me, Sounia."

Sounia twisted around, annoyed at the childish outburst. "You and your games, Taiwa," Sounia sighed. "All right; it will be our secret."

"Good. Then I can show you the rest." Taiwa sidled onto the rock pile and shoved a flat stone aside. She reached into the crevice and retrieved a small bundle. Unfolding the skin, she produced a chunk of dried fish. "Watch." Taiwa climbed up the boulders, laying the fish on the highest one. She clambered back down and began a chant, interspersed with clucking noises that she made with her tongue. She stared up at the fish and then started again.

Brush rustled above them. "Something's up there!" Sounia jumped to pull Taiwa back. Taiwa twisted free, gesturing to keep quiet. There was a flash of tawny fur. A creature pounced on the fish. Sounia gasped, recoiling backward. "Taiwa, get away." Sounia's voice quavered and her frightened eyes darted around for an escape route.

The lynx hunched down—it seemed ready to launch an attack. Instead, it picked up the fish and bounced down the boulders to sit beside Taiwa. "Don't worry, Sounia," she said calmly. "He's my friend." Taiwa raked her fingers along the cat's back. He arched into her fingers and made a low, rumbling noise. The cat dropped the fish and held it under a fat paw. He tore off strips, canting his head to study Sounia as he chewed. "I have something for you,"

Taiwa cooed to the lynx. She pulled an armband from her waist pouch and tied it around the lynx's neck.

Sounia studied the geometric beadwork. "Taiwa, what are you doing? That's your mother's armband!"

"She never wears it. There." Taiwa sat back. "Isn't he handsome?"

Sounia was shocked. Other than dogs, she'd never heard of an animal that accepted humans—and dogs only hung around because they were once people. Her mind reeled. Sounia backed slowly toward the path. Could an animal spirit have entered Taiwa's body? Was Taiwa a witch? "Taiwa ... you're frightening me. How did ... why have you ... what's going on here?"

"It's all right, Sounia," Taiwa assured her. "Calm yourself. He's just a kit. I found him after the snows melted. He was in that hole up there." Taiwa indicated a large cleft in the boulders. "I heard him crying. When I peeked in, I found his mother had died. She was old, and he was her last child." Taiwa scratched the cat's ears; he rocked his head to help. "I've been feeding him ever since. I believe he thinks I'm his mother."

"Taiwa, this is wrong." Sounia fought her urge to run. She had to bring Taiwa to her senses. "You can't befriend an animal. It's evil. He'll bring harm. He might attack women in the fields or come and eat our babies in the night."

Taiwa looked as if her family had been insulted. "No, he won't! He's come here to protect me—and Ontarra."

"Protect Ontarra? What does Ontarra have to do with this?" Sounia heard her voice rising. "Ontarra would be livid if he knew that you befriended a creature of the night. It will tell the other animals how to avoid the hunters. We'll starve!" Sounia felt a sudden chill and scanned the woods to see if any other animals were watching. "Taiwa, we must get away from here and never come back!"

"Sounia, come over here. Touch him," Taiwa coaxed softly. "He likes to be touched." She scratched behind his ears. The cat stretched up and then flopped over on his side, offering his belly for a rub.

Sounia watched, bewildered. She felt some of her fear melting away and found herself wondering what he felt like. Stepping closer, she stretched out a hand. The cat rolled onto his belly, studying her warily, but he made no attempt to move. Sounia touched the top of his head. He made a rumbling noise, and she snatched her hand back. "He growled at me!" Fear flickered in her eyes.

"He makes that sound when he's happy. Try again." Taiwa tipped her head.

Sounia ran trembling fingers down the cat's back. He pressed into them. Sounia giggled. "He feels ... nice." She whirled her fingers through his fur with more confidence. He stretched, making a soft gurgling sound, and then started licking his paws, as if this was all part of a normal day. Sounia laughed, her fear diminishing with each stroke. "What do you mean, he has come to protect you and Ontarra?"

Taiwa's smile turned pensive. "I had a dream. Slammer talked to me. I can't really remember it all ... only that he's here to protect us."

"Slammer? You've named him?" Naming an animal was more bizarre than petting one.

"If you ever see him catch a rabbit, you'll understand the name." Taiwa grinned. "It's amazing to watch. Sounia, you promised to keep this a secret."

Sounia chewed on her lip. If people knew, Taiwa could be banished—or worse. Slammer seemed harmless enough. He was certainly friendly. As Sounia agonized, Slammer rolled onto his back and offered her his belly. Sounia had to laugh. "All right," she relented. "It will remain our secret. No one would believe this if I did tell them."

Near a mighty river that flowed to a saltwater sea, the town of Quizquiz guarded a land that had never seen snow. A spectral presence enshrouded the town like a mist from the river.

In the eerie predawn shadows of the temple mounds, warriors prodded a weeping girl ahead of them. Katia's mind whirled—the effects of the dark drink. The men pushed her up the log steps that ascended White Woman's mound. She pleaded, but her words were cut short by a heave of her stomach. A warrior peeled the infant from her arms. The others hauled Katia on up. Rough-hewn logs tore at her ankles and toes. Wooden shards pierced her skin.

An impressive wattle-and-daub dwelling adorned the crest of the mound. The warriors hadn't the courage to enter. Katia was tossed inside, sprawling to the floor beside the crossed square of a sacred fire. Thick tobacco smoke hung in the air, burning her nostrils. Her stomach clenched again. She swallowed hard to hold back the bile—and her terror. Katia had never been here before, nor ever wished to be. Her eyes adjusted to the flickering gloom. She saw the shadowy outline of White Woman staring down through the veil of smoke. A frail old priest, Nakabo, shuffled over to the door. Katia's boy-child was handed through.

"Fanacia, please ..." Katia choked, and her voice failed her.

"Tell this presumptuous creature not to address me directly! I am White Woman! Sister of the sun in the sky! I converse with deities, not with lowly stinkards!" Her venomous words seemed ethereal, drifting through the muddled pathways of Katia's mind.

A smothering dread tightened Katia's chest. The priest's skeletal hand forced Katia's head down until she could see nothing but the hard-packed floor. "I'm sorry, mistress," she sobbed. "I'm frightened. I forgot myself." She saw the priest's shadow hobble around the fire to Fanacia's side, but she didn't dare to lift her eyes.

Nakabo's face weighed heavy with pity for this poor girl. His soul grieved at her plight—and his inability to help her. To be a commoner of uncommon vigor and beauty had been her misfortune. He watched Katia tremble and sway from fear and from the stupefying effects of the dark drink. He resolved to try again, speaking softly to the fire with words intended for Fanacia. "Mistress, you have performed this ritual many times now. The spirits take no heed because it is not a proper rite."

Fanacia made no reply, her silence more intimidating than words. Nakabo lifted a tentative glance. Madness burned in her eyes. She shrugged off her feathered cloak and tossed it to the floor. A necklace of fresh-water pearls hung down between sagging breasts. Bags of flesh hung from her arms. Silver and turquoise bands strained to pinch it all in. Thirty cycles of opulence and sloth sagged over the waistband of a short cloth skirt that bulged at its seams. Ocher and other pigments made every wrinkle and fold seem bottomless. Nakabo had little trouble averting his eyes.

"Don't presume to advise me of what the deities desire, old man. I am of the sacred lineage. Proceed!"

Katia sobbed. Her baby mewed softly in Nakabo's arms. Nakabo wished that he could take the child's place. He had lived far too long, he realized.

This world made no sense anymore. The copper ear spools and fine clothing he wore displayed the trappings of rank and privilege, but it all meant nothing.

Nakabo motioned to the warriors at the door. They moved quickly, efficiently. A cloth bag was slipped over Katia's head, and the garrote was wound tight. Nakabo couldn't watch. He stared out the door at the hazy orange globe of the sun spirit peeking over the eastern horizon. *How many times have we seen each other? I've lost track. You have forsaken us. Why must you return each morning and prolong our torment?*

The warriors hustled out, dragging Katia by her ankles. Nakabo turned back to the sacred fire. White Woman was smeared in the child's blood. She drained more into a bowl, mixing it with powdered tobacco and roots. Satisfied the proportions were right, she drank and then raised the bowl to the sun. "I have done your bidding, my brother. The child's blood is mixed with mine." She poured the remaining liquid onto the coals. "This I offer to you." Fanacia closed her eyes, basking in the Power coursing through her veins. "Have the bodies removed to my burial mound, old man."

Nakabo heard Fanacia's voice from a distant place, but it no longer held meaning to him. He shuffled out the door and teetered down the steps of the mound. He paused at the bottom, bracing himself against the earthen structure. He barely noticed the bite of chilled morning air. Wrapping his arms around himself, he wandered the pathways through the town until he recognized his lodge.

Nakabo stumbled in, slumped onto a stool, and buried his face in his hands. A silent wail rose from deep in his core. He dragged a huge wicker basket to his side and flipped the lid to the floor. Startled snakes twined and coiled at the intrusion. A water moccasin spat venom, splattering it across Nakabo's chest. He heard Fanacia raving in the distance. Nakabo closed his eyes; moisture squeezed out at the corners. His gnarled hand floated out and hovered over the knotted ball of reptiles. The hand trembled and then slowly sank toward oblivion.

At the river, the northern boundary of Quizquiz, three huge trade canoes were being prepared for a journey. Two traders and four warriors disguised as traders supervised the bearers who loaded the dugouts. The men's heads were shaved, leaving only a fringe above the ears. A braided topknot adorned the back of each head. On Manak's right shoulder, the tattoo of a cross within a circle marked him as a noble-class warrior of the fiercest tradition. More tattoos of dots lined his jaw and circled his biceps.

Manak watched the stinkards heading out to the fields. All the laughter and banter he remembered from his youth was long gone. He studied the haunted faces of people preoccupied with their own mortality. This was a bad time to leave, but disobeying White Woman would bring a horrible death, even for the greatest warrior of the Yoron.

Spring flooding was ended. He had no excuses left. The silt-laden water seemed slower than normal. "Even the river has lost its spirit," Manak whispered to himself.

A frightful wail rose up from the town. Manak spun, and hundreds of eyes were riveted on the mortifying spectacle of Fanacia casting a bloodied child down the side of her mound. Her cry rent the morning air. "Nakabo! You old fool! I ordered you to take this wretch to my burial mound!"

"Aiyee," one of the bearers muttered. "She's been touched by the dark spirits."

Eyes still fixed on White Woman, Manak stepped back and wrapped his left arm around the bearer's neck. With sudden finality, an obsidian blade plunged deep under the stinkard's rib cage. For a fleeting instant, their eyes met. Manak peered into the man's soul. The blade twisted, and the soul fluttered away. Before the body could hit the ground, Manak spun into a crouch with the knife prepared for its next victim. The unexpected attack jarred everyone. Bearers fell over themselves in a rush to get some distance between themselves and that blade. Recovering from the surprise, warriors averted their eyes in proper deference to Manak's rank and prerogative.

Manak straightened and sheathed his knife. "Take him to White Woman," he exhaled. "A heretic for her retinue." He turned to the warriors, a resigned scowl on his face as he gestured to the canoes. "We are ordered up the Father Water to the City of the Ancients."

2

SANNISEN NORMALLY ENJOYED THIS SECTION of the Tranchi. It was familiar and close to home. He scanned above the treetops for the smoke of cooking fires at Ounontisaston. Even when trees shed their leaves, the town was not visible from any point along the river. It was always the smoke that betrayed a town's presence. Sannisen made mental notes of where the first twining columns of gray could be seen—information that might prove useful someday.

Events at Khioetoa preoccupied his thoughts. At the forks where the Tranchi split into a north and south branch, Soutoten, in the lead canoe, swung hard left, keeping to the main channel. Sannisen overshot the turn. When he caught up, the other canoes were slowing to a halt at the island just below the Entry River. Fishermen were anchoring nets in the right channel. They waved, shouting questions about the trip.

"We will call a council tonight!" Soutoten called back. "All the clans will hear our news together!" He let his canoe slip back with the current and then led the procession up the shallower left channel.

In a hand of time, the canoes turned into the Entry River. Sannisen's men began a lively banter, happy to be home, and let their guard down. A thin smile brushed Sannisen's lips. His original description of the stream had become its official name.

He felt some of his tension drain away as the forest opened up into crop fields. At Sannisen's urging, Tsohahissen had ordered no fields to be cleared below the last feeder creek on the Entry River, a precaution that ensured the forest would always shield any view of the palisades from the Tranchi. More than any other, Sannisen was responsible for the security this place provided.

He couldn't help admiring the majestic fortress when it came into view. Ahratota had agreed with Sannisen's suggestions for many improvements to the palisades before they were built. A ditch the height of a man was dug around the entire town. It skirted the edge of the bluff on three sides. Earth from the trench was piled to the inside, creating a moat. A second ditch was dug three paces inside the first. The palisade poles were planted in the mounds. Anyone who managed to scale the first palisade would drop into a shooting gallery, where rocks and arrows would rain down. A row of poles leaned into the inner walls, intersecting at an angle. They created an overhanging barrier on the outside, making the palisades impossible to scale without ladders. A gallery was built around the inside, on top of the intersecting poles. Hewn-log ladders allowed access to the ramparts, and Sannisen's warriors kept a constant vigil.

Ahratota later added his own innovation. He lined the inside of the palisades to the height of a man's shoulders with elm bark. Men could fire arrows through cracks between the poles in nearly complete security. The design created such a formidable barrier that it was now being copied at Tontiaton.

The Tonti River ran north from Lake Iannaoa on the nation's southern boundary, pointing like an arrow at the Tranchi and Ounontisaston. Sannisen saw immediately that the short overland route from the Tonti to the Tranchi would have to be guarded against hostile incursions, so a sister town was being built. Tontiaton would also provide revenues in tolls charged to traders from the lake who wanted to get to the Tranchi and the easy east–west route it provided. Tontiaton would be completed by autumn, and Festival of the Dead ceremonies would be held to inter bones that hung in lodges throughout the nation.

The canoes nosed into the landing area. Sannisen hopped out and heaved the bow on shore. Straightening up, he stretched to get the knots out of his cramped legs. Some men were mending nets. He beckoned to them. The canoes were loaded with deer and bear meat. They had to be handled carefully to prevent damaging the delicate elm-bark hulls.

While they were being skidded onto dry land, Sannisen studied the intricate web of pathways winding up the bluff, illuminated in fading sunlight. He admired its beauty for only a moment and then turned to Soutoten. "Do you have enough help for the meat and hides? I need to see Tsohahissen and arrange for a council."

Soutoten glanced at the throng of fishermen gathering around. "Fishermen like red meat." He jerked his head and flashed a grin. "I'm sure I can arrange something."

A man reeking of river meat stepped forward. "A hunter should carry his own kill," he jibed, taking a long look at the contents of the canoes, "but I'll lend a hand for some of that bear meat."

Sannisen chuckled and trudged off through the bustling canoe area. He threaded his way through piles of entrails, and racks loaded with drying fish, and canoes haphazardly scattered about. Nets were draped over the hanging meat to deter scavengers. Older men would remain all night, lying about the day's catch and bemoaning the reduced size and quantity of fish since their childhood. Their presence would keep animals at bay, except for the audacious raccoons that feared nothing.

Sannisen's concerns for the outpost town of Khioetoa intruded as he labored up the bluff. He negotiated the pathways by memory as he considered all of his options. Shanoka taught him long ago to be firm and concise at council, so that less reasonable voices would never prevail. He was a master at presenting his ideas forcefully, and his opinion was highly regarded. When he reached the south entry, his decision was made.

"Ho, Sannisen. It is good to see you."

"Ho, Adonwa." Sannisen nodded to his man above the entry. "Do I have permission to enter?" Sannisen was always careful to abide by his own rules, though they irritated him at times.

"You may enter, Sannisen," Adonwa said, bowing with mock formality, "but only if you find me other duties. I've been up here for three days."

Sannisen plodded through. It took a moment for Adonwa's words to settle in. He stopped and looked back, smirking at the deliberate insolence. "I'm sorry, Adonwa. It will have to wait until tomorrow."

With long strides, Sannisen walked to Tsohahissen's lodge. When he rounded the corner, a young warrior guarding the door jumped to his feet and nervously barred the entrance. "Sannisen ... I ... didn't know you were back."

"Relax. I realize that you can't stand all day. I need to see Tsohahissen."

"He's resting. He asked that he not be disturbed until Yadwena returns. I'm sure he'll want to see *you*, though."

Sannisen rubbed at his chin. "No. Let him rest. But tell him I'm back, and I wish to call a council tonight."

The warrior acknowledged the order with a dip of his head. "Sannisen ..."

Sannisen felt a ripple of concern at the young man's tone and turned to see his eyes. "What's wrong?"

"You better go straight to your lodge. Some women brought Teota in from the upper fields a short time ago. He seemed to be injured; they were carrying him."

Sannisen spun and walked swiftly along the backs of the longhouses, where he would encounter fewer people. Those he did meet saw that he was in no mood for small talk. He reached his lodge and brushed the doorskin aside. The women who had brought Teota home were still inside. Teota was curled in a ball on his sleep platform.

One of the women stood. "We are just leaving," she said. The rest all rose as one.

"Thank you for bringing him," Shanoka murmured, unable to take her eyes from the lump under the sleep robes.

Sannisen nodded to each of the women as she went by; then he stepped to Shanoka's side. Teota's moaning worried him. "What happened?"

Shanoka palmed moisture from the corner of her eye and leaned her head on the frills at Sannisen's shoulder. "The women saw him running through the fields like a demon was after him. He was crazed with fright. He won't even talk—just makes that whimpering sound."

Sannisen slid the fur down, his heart jumping when he saw the vacant stare. "Shanoka ... his spirit has left him."

Shanoka fought back a sob. "Yes ... I've seen it before. A person can be so frightened that his spirit starts the journey along Atiskein Andahatey, leaving the physical body to shrivel away. Look at this." Shanoka peeled the furs up from Teota's grimy legs. "He has cuts and scrapes to up above his knees, like he was crawling."

Teota whimpered as Shanoka gently unfolded one leg, revealing four deep lacerations on the calf.

Sannisen settled back on his heels. "It's a claw wound. Something attacked him."

Shanoka tugged the covers back over Teota and brushed a tear from her cheek. "Sannisen, remember why I had to leave the Sennikae?"

He scowled. "That's ridiculous. That could never happen here. He ran into a mother cat or a bear with her cub." Sannisen canted a look. "What was he doing out there?"

"Ontarra took him fishing, and Ontarra hasn't returned. I'm worried. He wouldn't leave Teota by himself."

"I've already called a council. I'll have to ask Soutoten to send some men out." Sannisen crossed his ankles and folded down at the hearth to check the pot. He dug inside, found a chunk of golden squash, and popped it in his mouth. Footsteps padded along the outside wall of the lodge, and Ontarra ducked inside.

Shanoka jumped up and hugged him. "I'm so relieved to see you."

"The women in the fields told me. How is he?"

"Tell us what happened." Sannisen forced himself not to sound angry before he heard Ontarra's explanation.

"We were fishing upstream on the Entry River. I left him with Toutsou and Yadak while I searched for a bow blank. Toutsou told me that he caught a big mooneye. He was so excited that he headed back to show it off."

"You never saw what attacked him?" Shanoka raised the furs and started wiping the cuts on Teota's legs with a damp rabbit skin.

"Something attacked him?" Ontarra knelt to check the wounds. Shanoka straightened the leg. Ontarra shook his head,. "We never saw or heard anything unusual."

"Sannisen," a voice called from outside, "council has assembled at Tsohahissen's lodge."

"Very well." Sannisen stood and stepped to the door. "I have to go."

"Taiwa and Sounia went down below this morning, and they aren't back yet," Shanoka began.

"I'll tell Soutoten." Sannisen disappeared out the door.

At Tsohahissen's lodge, the young warrior dipped his head, grunted permission for Sannisen to enter council, and moved to one side. "Everyone is here," he said. Sannisen leaned in. Council members sat in a half circle facing the door. No one sat with his back to the entry. Walking behind a seated man was a dangerous breach of conduct, resulting in certain confrontation and a forcible expulsion of the miscreant. Sannisen beckoned to Soutoten. The hunt chief joined him outside. When they came back in, Sannisen took his seat, and Soutoten excused himself.

Land clans—Lynx, Bear, Wolf, and Turtle—were represented by Soutoten, Sannisen, and Tsohahissen. Only two members of the council were Bird clan. Ounsasta was Owl, and Hiatsou, Killdeer. Thadayo was Snipe but considered impartial. He spoke for any missing clans at council and presented all of the women's issues.

"Has your woman been advising you again on the matters of men?" Hiatsou mocked with an infuriating smile.

The room fell instantly quiet. Only the crackling of the fire disturbed the silence. Sannisen glared at Hiatsou, feeling his anger rise, but something Shanoka once said came back to him: *Hiatsou is like a squirrel ... full of useless chatter ... always throwing his tail up over his head to make himself appear larger than he really is.*

Sannisen burst into laughter. "Yes, Hiat', and I think she should take your seat. When the council sticks are passed, we could hear words of substance for a change." The lodge roared with laughter. This was not Sannisen's usual style. He was a man of physical action and withering words. His use of a childhood nickname had been especially effective. Hiatsou was speechless, which was a welcome change. His pudgy lips opened and closed as he tried to come up with a reply. Soutoten returned, taking his seat beside Sannisen and wondering what he'd just missed.

Tsohahissen struggled to control his expression. He adjusted the flat-topped muskrat fur he always wore to cover the angry scar left by an Agwa war club when Sannisen was just a sprout. He held a hand up for silence. "Hiatsou, I think you should claim your seat." Unable to wrap his mind around a rebuttal, Hiatsou scowled and lowered his ample backside to the ground.

Still chuckling, Ounsasta's scarred fingers unlaced an elaborately decorated beaver-skin bag and started the meeting by passing council petun to his left. The plugs were cured by pressing leaf into holes bored in hickory logs. No one spoke while each savored the first pipeful. The aromatic smoke needed time to go to the head and enlighten a man's thoughts. It relaxed the mind and promoted wisdom.

Tsohahissen pulled five council sticks from his rabbit-fur robe, handing the longest to Sannisen to indicated that he should speak first. The others were passed left. Hiatsou shook his head in disgust when he saw he had pulled the shortest.

Tsohahissen took a long draw, blowing white-gray smoke up at the rafters. "Speak to us of your trip, Sannisen."

Sannisen crossed his ankles and rested his elbows on his knees. "We traveled down the Tranchi to Khioetoa. It was not our intention to hunt, but Soutoten's men are fast when game appears. The canoes are loaded with deer and bear." Everyone nodded approval to Soutoten who accepted the praise without expression. "On the second night we stayed with Nadawa at Sucker Fish Camp. We left the meat with his people. They cut and dried it in return for half. His wife and daughters scraped the hides. Nadawa and Soutoten offer this." Sannisen handed a folded black-bear hide to Tsohahissen.

Tsohahissen ran his hand through the thick, lustrous fur, a faint smile wrinkling the corners of his eyes but not making its way to his mouth. "I thank you for this fine gift, Soutoten." He laid the fur to one side, dipping his chin to Sannisen to continue.

"When we reached the canoe area at Khioetoa, Shadaki was waiting. We smoked and feasted in his lodge that night, discussing what the Wendat traders had told us. He sent for some men who had just returned from the land of the Tionnontates with elk hides. When they passed the large island in the Lake Between the Sunset Rivers, several warriors appeared and fired on them." Sannisen glanced around. "They were Fire Nation warriors."

Tsohahissen's brow furrowed. "Are you certain of this?"

"Yes," Sannisen replied flatly. "The traders had this." Sannisen produced an arrow, broken halfway up, the fletching still attached.

The chiefs murmured as they passed the arrow shaft around. "Agwa," Ounsasta cursed, blowing a gob into the fire. It sizzled and hissed while everyone considered the ramifications of enemies in their land. Tsohahissen examined the fletching again, as if there had to be a mistake.

"Why are they there, Sannisen?"

"We aren't sure, and we don't know how many. Shadaki sent a party out to locate their camp. I want to take two hands of canoes and four hands of my best warriors back. If the Agwa are few in numbers, we will attack them. If they are too many, we'll evacuate Khioetoa and bring everyone back here. Ounontisaston favors us greatly in a large fight." Sannisen watched the expressions closely, noting the silent nods as the chiefs considered his words.

"May I speak?" Ounsasta asked. Tsohahissen nodded. Sannisen handed his council stick over. Ounsasta held it between a thumb and forefinger, tugging on his earspool as he chose his words. "Sannisen, if they are a large war party and you evacuate Khioetoa, we will lose it to them. We should take many warriors and hold the town."

"I have considered that," Sannisen said, rubbing his chin as he studied the coals, "but we cannot leave Ounontisaston undefended. If Khioetoa is their object, it will probably be attacked before we return anyway. If they are a small group, our efforts would be wasted and we endanger Ounon'. Khioetoa can be rebuilt; the people are not so easily replaced. This way, we have the least risk to our people and the best chance of winning a major fight."

Hiatsou was still fuming, lost in the devious pathways of his mind. He possessed information of which no one else was aware. These unexpected events could prove fortuitous. He climbed to his feet, shook a turtle-shell rattle over his head, and started a loud and annoying chant.

"Hiatsou, sit down! Sannisen is speaking!" A rare flash of anger colored Tsohahissen's voice.

Hiatsou pointed his rattle accusingly at Sannisen. "The plan of our war chief is a cowardly approach! I will take our shamans to Khioetoa and call upon the manitos to hurl storms upon the Agwa. We will appeal to the okis and pummel them with waves. The shamans can crush them without a fight!"

Tsohahissen's age had robbed him of patience. "Hiatsou, be seated or leave the council fire!"

Hiatsou glared defiantly at the faces. "Since our people allowed warriors to become their chiefs, we have had war. When shamans were the chiefs, the deities protected us. We lived in peace. Let the shamans save Khioetoa—you will see that I am right."

"If the Fire People intend to attack us with their warriors," Sannisen replied in a controlled monotone, "I will oblige them with my warriors."

"You arrogant fool!" Hiatsou snarled. "You think—"

Tsohahissen clapped his hands for silence. "Enough! Hiatsou, you have disrupted this council for the last time. Leave! Or I will have you removed!"

"You cannot speak to me in that manner!" Hiatsou glanced around the fire for support, but no one would look at him. His face flushed. "You would eject me from council? Fools! You offend the spirits of our ancestors!" He stormed toward the doorskin but then turned back. "You will regret this!"

Ounsasta stood and handed the council stick back to Sannisen. "You're right, Sannisen. We cannot afford to have all our warriors away at once."

"Thank you, Ounsasta." Sannisen looked to Tsohahissen. "I will leave in two days."

Tsohahissen nodded and then reached out to touch Sannisen's arm. "How is Teota?"

Sannisen pursed his lips. "He was attacked by an animal. His spirit has fled. Shanoka says that all we can do now is to wait."

Tsohahissen sighed and stared into the shimmering embers. "She is the best healer I have ever known. I'm sure she will bring him back."

Sannisen ducked out into the cool evening air, lifting his gaze to the star-spackled sky.

Ounsasta appeared at his side. "I would like to go downriver with you."

Sannisen had expected this. He grasped Ounsasta's thick forearm. "You know that I need you here. The town must be guarded—duties assigned. The warriors respect you and will do as you ask."

Ounsasta lifted his eyes to the heavens. "As you wish." He walked off slowly.

Sannisen strode the deserted path along the front of the longhouses. The rhythms of the town flowed with the sun and the moon, and life had moved indoors. Only fishermen, spearing fish on the Tranchi by torchlight, and the sentries were still outside. Firelight spilled from doorways, casting long, grotesque shadows across the ground, playing tricks with the mind. Since childhood, Sannisen could see the spirits of dead ancestors in those shadows. They roamed the town at night in search of food and petun. He wondered how many more spirits would wander the town if he had to fight the Fire People.

He reached the lodge, and his thoughts turned to Teota. Sannisen squinted at the palisades and saw his men on the ramparts, silhouetted against the night sky. Satisfied that the town was well guarded, he ducked inside. Ontarra and Taiwa were already asleep. He could see their faces reflected in the orange light of pulsing embers. Shanoka sat on her heels at Teota's platform, gently bathing his face and neck with a dampened swath.

"How is he?" Sannisen knelt, placing a hand on Teota's forehead.

"He's been calling to his spirit," Shanoka said softly, pulling the fur up to cover Teota's clammy skin. "He cried out a few times. I think he said something about the shamans, but I'm not sure. He's sleeping now."

"The shamans," Sannisen snorted in disgust. "How long have they been here?"

"They arrived just after you left for Khioetoa. They've been meeting a lot lately. I don't like it. I think they're up to something."

Sannisen rubbed his jaw. "You may be right. Hiatsou tried to convince the chiefs to let the shamans protect us from the Agwa. Tsoha' dismissed him."

Shanoka reached over and folded her hand around Sannisen's. He caressed it, shifting his gaze to the sculpted face and luminous eyes that he loved so much. "What are the Agwa up to?" she asked.

"We aren't sure. I have to return to Khioetoa to find out. I don't like the thought of leaving with all the shamans here, though."

Shanoka tugged her hand away to stoke the fire, stirring the coals as she organized her thoughts. "Sannisen … we've hidden my past to keep peace with the shamans long enough. They've already split the people into clan factions. The Bird clan women have started spreading rumors about me. I'm sure Hiatsou is behind it. He wants to be the next Tsohahissen, and it's up to us to stop him."

Sannisen lowered himself to the hearth, propping his elbows on his knees. "More than half the people in Ounon are Bird clan. They would back the shamans."

Shanoka settled at his side. "I'm not so sure. Many of the Bird clan women sneak to our lodge when they're sick now. They see Hiatsou for the charlatan that he is—always strutting around in gaudy costumes, muttering his silly chants. They're sick of him always asking for petun and furs before he does anything for them."

"Perhaps." Sannisen let out a weary sigh. "But we need to be sure that we have the support of at least one of the Bird clans, or we will tear the town apart."

"If Hiatsou is banned from council, he's bound to try something. I'm a threat to the petun and furs that he extorts from everyone, and you are a threat to his becoming chief of chiefs. I think it's time for people to know about my past, before he finds a way to use it against us."

Sannisen was silent a moment. "We will tell a few people, and let the story spread on its own." He stood and pulled his frilled tunic over his head. "I must try and get some sleep." He bent, checking Teota a last time before easing down to the sleep platform. Shanoka cuddled in behind him, listening as his breathing quickly fell into an exhausted rhythm. She rose again, quietly padding over to get her prayer stone.

She was twenty-nine summers this cycle and found herself thinking more often of her childhood home. Somehow, she knew she would never see it again. Amikwe sat on the northern shore of the Sweetwater Sea. She smiled, recalling the happy times with her mother when they had traveled to the sacred places on the Island of the Manitos. Shedota had begun teaching her the ways of the Midewiwin as soon as Shanoka could walk. Shanoka heard her mother's voice from the past.

Dreams are important, Shanoka. Remember them—decipher them. They reveal things if you know how to take them apart. When you dream, you are in the world of the spirits. You must see things as a spirit sees them.

Shedota had been a Powerful dreamer—a mide master. Only one other in all of the Ojibwa lands was considered her equal, and he had hated Shedota. Malsum had accused her of conjuring a spell upon his family. When Shanoka's aunt disappeared mysteriously, Shedota and Shanoka traveled to Nippising to confront the old man. That summer, Shanoka's life had changed forever.

Teota moaned and tossed. Shanoka set the prayer stone down to check on him. He felt feverish. She pulled the robe back and ran damp rabbit swaths over him. She felt the four long, scab-encrusted slashes on his calf, and moisture welled in the corners of her eyes. She kissed his forehead and then knelt down to nestle her head beside his. She shuddered at the terrible memory of Nippising. *Could the curse be real? Has it followed me here?*

Two-days' journey west of the Sunset Rivers, in the land of the Fire People, the palisades of Pokagon stood vigil over flat woodlands. The Mascouten controlled this territory. Their enemies called them Agwa. Most of the year the Mascouten lived in domed wigwams of reed and fabric tied over bent saplings. The wigwams were light and easy to transport where they were needed. In autumn, camps moved north to the marshy lakes in the land of the Winnebagoes to harvest wild rice. When winter threatened, the people continued north to hunt the peninsula between the lakes.

The tribes of the Fire Nation were blessed with abundance of deer, moose, bear, mink, and otter. Women of the tribes were masters at turning the pelts and skins into elaborately decorated clothing, pouches, and bags. Using quills, buffalo wool, basswood, and nettle fibers, they produced flowing geometric patterns in many colors.

With the arrival of spring, camp life ended. The Mascouten returned to their permanent towns to make maple syrup and prepare the fields for corn and tobacco. At Pokagon, the town was divided into Earth and Sky moieties. Clan houses were built of elm bark on a frame of supporting poles. Peaked roofs allowed ventilation and some relief from summer heat. In the lodge of the Bear clan, Kadona, chief of the Mascouten, spoke privately with an Erieehronon trader.

"You seem pleased, Dekari." Kadona tamped petun into his pipe and touched an ember to it, taking several long draws before continuing. "Your trading has been profitable?" He handed the pipe to the trader.

Dekari smiled as he contemplated his proceeds and what he would do with them. The Erieehronon peoples held a vast territory along the southern shore of Lake Iannaoa. It was a four-day journey by canoe from one end of the lake to the other. The Alhegalena River flowed four days south before leaving Erieehronon lands. Dekari's clan held a monopoly with the Attawondaronks and Wendats for all trade north of the lake and with the Fire People west of the lake.

The endless war between these nations made Dekari's father and Dekari wealthy men. All trade between the Attawondaronks and nations to the west passed through Dekari. Petun was in great demand with western tribes for its curative and spiritual Powers.

As Dekari accepted the pipe, there was a noticeable tremor in his left hand. At thirty-five summers, he was getting old for this life of constant travel. Blowing the first puff of pungent smoke to the earth, the second to the sky, he properly appeased the spirits of both worlds. "Your people value Attawondaronk chert almost as much as they value petun." Dekari closed one eye as he spoke. He'd had trouble focusing over short distances since the day a Minqua spear shaft glanced off his temple in his youth. His father made sure it was the Minqua's last mistake in this world. Kadona's jaw tightened at the casual mention of his enemies.

"You speak of the Petun people as if they are your friends."

"They're simply suppliers of items that other people want," Dekari answered cautiously. Trading with enemies was always a delicate matter.

Kadona nodded, his thick fingers accepting the long pipe. He didn't trust Dekari. Something strange always seemed to happen after he visited. Last cycle, a party of his men had been attacked on the Lake Between the Sunset Rivers while fishing for sturgeon. The only way the Petun people could have known where to find them was Dekari. "You said you had a proposition."

"Yes." Dekari hesitated, considering his words. "At summer solstice, I must travel to the City of the Ancients to complete a trade. I have been unable to obtain the goods that I promised." Dekari studied Kadona's stony expression, wondering whether he should just forget the whole thing.

"What does this have to do with me?" Kadona wanted to know.

"I have agreed to provide petun seed to someone, but the person to whom I promised it has cheated me. I know where I can get the seed, if you will help me, Kadona."

Kadona raised a bushy brow and folded his arms. "The Attawondaronks guard the seed with intent. How do you propose to obtain it?"

"I know their land well. I've been traveling it since I was a child." Dekari shifted his weight, leaning closer so he could whisper. "There is a small fishing camp on the lower reaches of the Tranchi. A man named Kadak and his woman are growing the best petun in all the land near that camp. If you and your warriors will escort me, we can take all the seed we want, and you will be able to grow petun here in Pokagon."

Kadona leaned back from Dekari's sour breath and stroked his chin. This was unexpected ... and convenient. He already had warriors on the Tadpole Island in the mouth of the northern Sunset River. They were preparing for a raid on Khioetoa, reprisal for the attack on his fishermen. "I've heard the Petun people are building a new chief town. Have you seen it?"

Dekari sat back, muddled by the shift in the conversation. "I haven't been there, but I know where it is. It lies in the middle of their peninsula, on the Tranchi, near the juncture of its north and south forks."

"First they drive us from our summer grounds, and now they encroach into the borderlands," Kadona muttered, pinching the flesh at an Adam's apple that looked as if it might burst. "Is Tsohahissen at this new town?"

"Yes." Dekari nodded, unsure where Kadona was going with this. "He rarely leaves now. He's very old."

"And Sannisen? He is there too?"

Dekari dipped an affirmative nod.

"How can you be certain of this?" Kadona casually tapped the cinder from the redstone bowl of his pipe, acting as if this was just a casual conversation.

"Because of these." Dekari held up his right hand. Only stumps remained of three fingers. "His woman did this to me."

Kadona reached out and examined the neat removal at the second knuckles. "How did she manage that?"

"She's a witch!" Dekari answered bluntly. "I met her once when she was a child, living with an old Sennikae named Togo. She was raised Midewiwin, of the Caribou People, and taken prisoner in a raid. Some of the Sennikae who captured her later vanished on hunts. They found one torn to shreds, his belly all eaten out. She escaped to the Attawondaronks before they could destroy her."

Kadona didn't want to believe that a woman of such Power lived among the Petuns. "Is she a conjurer?"

Dekari bobbed his head absently, his thoughts traveling back to a fearful memory. "I was headed home from trading with them last cycle. I made camp my first night in the shifting sand dunes on the north shore of Iannaoa. Something attacked me in my sleep. I stabbed it several times and drove it off, but it mangled my hand."

"You said the witch did that. Does she take the form of a bear?"

Dekari's eyes snapped back to the present He squinted at Kadona. "She calls upon the creatures of the underworld to do her bidding." He drifted off again. "I returned to their new outpost town, Tontiaton. Some of their shamans were there. They tried everything, but the black-skin spirits got into the fingers, and the shamans gave up."

Kadona's brows knitted together. "I've never heard of anyone surviving the black-skin sickness."

Dekari stared at his stumps before lowering the hand to his knee. "After the shamans left, the witch and her girl-child came. She said she had a potion that would save me, so I drank it." Dekari's face screwed up as the taste bit into his memory. "It made my vision hazy, and I started to sweat ... but the pain in my hand gradually subsided."

Kadona was growing impatient. "Our shamans can make pain go away too."

Dekari eyed Kadona as if he were a foolish child. "My spirit floated up above my body. I saw her open my eyelids and look in, to be sure that I wasn't in there. I was floating." Dekari rubbed at his stumps and started talking to the fire, his voice growing distant. Kadona leaned closer to hear. "She had a fur pouch—took out several items and laid them around me on the robes." Dekari stared deep into the shifting embers. "White shells, a bear claw, a bundle of knotted gray hair. Her-girl child sprinkled sand on my forehead." Dekari shuddered. "Then the witch laid a big egg-shaped crystal over my heart."

"She has a seer's crystal?" Kadona was shocked. He'd heard of them, in stories and myths, but had never heard of anyone actually seeing one.

"Yes," Dekari said, chewing on his lip. "Light shines right through it. It has a dark spot, like an eye, in its center. She thought I was gone, but I saw everything. She tried to draw my spirit into the crystal, and I was Powerless to stop her, so my spirit guardian pulled me from my body." Dekari's voice faded to a haunted rasp, and he started mumbling to himself. Kadona slid closer.

"When she realized that she couldn't capture my spirit, she asked her daughter for something. She pressed my hand onto a flat rock and, with three quick slashes, removed my fingers! My spirit jumped back into my body to stop her. I woke screaming, but it was too late."

"And you survived the black-skin disease." Kadona shook his head in amazement. He didn't like the sound of this woman, but Dekari's story presented an opportunity. Kadona studied the beads of sweat on Dekari's face, and he folded his arms, a sly grin thinning his lips.

"Is that when you told them where our men were fishing on the lake?"

"No, I told them when—" Dekari caught himself. He crabbed backward, expecting a deathblow from Kadona's club.

Kadona smiled. For the time being, he needed this unscrupulous trader. The Attawondaronks were growing far too arrogant and troublesome. "I will accompany you to this fish camp on the Tranchi. We will leave tomorrow."

A baffled expression rearranged Dekari's face. Slowly, he relaxed. Information had always paid better than trade, if you were careful. Perhaps Kadona had accepted this.

"Dekari …" Kadona's eyelids lowered; his face was inscrutable. "Do you think she captured any of your spirit with those fingers that she took?"

The shamans were not pleased to be shaken from sleep and summoned into the night. They were accustomed to the safety and tranquility of guarded palisades. Stumbling through brush in darkness was for hunters and fishermen, not the guardians of a nation's spirituality. Grumbling and moaning over cuts and scrapes, they seated themselves by rank around a ring of rocks that encircled a fire pit.

The shaman hierarchy was simple, determined by the number of people who fell under the influence of each chief shaman and the number of apprentices each shaman had managed to enlist. Most of these young men would never become full shamans. Enticed by the promise of wealth and status in this world and the next, it was always just beyond their grasp but close enough for the dream to survive. They provided the shamans with a troupe of helpers, adding mystique to ceremonies and rituals. Hiatsou's apprentices had already removed the grisly evidence of today's ritual.

Hiatsou moved to the center of the ring, scanning the gathering to be sure that all were seated as was proper. The shamans of Khioetoa, Kandoucho, and Teotonguiaton sat closest, wearing turkeyfeather robes. Lesser shamans from the outlying communities were wrapped in simple cloaks of rabbit hide. As chief of shamans, Hiatsou wore a finely crafted robe fashioned from the feathers of a gray fisherbird. He listened, for a heartbeat, to the muted grumbling about stumbling down here in the dark, and then he raised his arms for silence, waiting while the muttering died away.

"I was dismissed from council tonight! The time for discussion is over!" He had everyone's attention now. The fire sputtered, sending spiraling tracers of orange skyward and reflecting in twenty pairs of stunned eyes. "Our people have lost their way. We have no other choice but to save them from themselves. Since the day a warrior was named Tsohahissen, warriors have gained favor in the people's eyes, to the detriment of us all. Already the Land clans place more significance on the fleeting life of this world than in properly appeasing the spirit world. Today, the chiefs of Khioetoa and Tontiaton are Land clan warriors."

"Who will be named head shaman at Tontiaton?" Ayontat cried out.

Hiatsou scowled at the interruption but was obliged to answer. "I have decided we will not provide them with a shaman. We will withhold our protection and make an example of them." Hiatsou swung his eyes around the gathering. "We must convince the people that they cannot pick leaders who defile the sacred ways of our ancestors. We will show them that ignoring the shaman society is a sacrilege. A whirlwind of evil is about to descend upon our nation, and we are the ones who will save it!"

Hiatsou glanced from face to face. Heads bobbed in agreement. "We have already discussed the outsider woman who has infected our people. She contaminates their minds with her vulgar ways. We will deal with her, as we have discussed. When you return to your towns, set the plan in motion. Choose your most faithful follower for this task. Promise whatever is necessary to gain his cooperation."

The shamans started rising to leave. Hiatsou motioned to Shadaki, chief shaman of Khioetoa. "Something auspicious has occurred," Hiatsou whispered. "Council believes an Agwa attack on Khioetoa is imminent." Shadaki stepped back, his mouth dropping open and a horrified look altering the lines of his face.

"Don't worry," Hiatsou assured him. "I know that they only plan small raids this cycle."

Shadaki's eyes narrowed to slits. "How can you possibly know what is in the minds of the Fire People?"

Hiatsou was not about to mention the trader Dekari or the exorbitant price he had to pay in petun cakes when he balked at providing the seed originally promised. "It is sufficient that I tell you it is so. How many apprentices are with you?"

"Seven."

Hiatsou nodded thoughtfully. "That will be enough. Leave tonight. Travel fast down the Tranchi to Sucker Fish Camp."

Shadaki's face furrowed. He started to ask why he should be inconvenienced in this way but then thought better of it and clamped his jaw shut.

"Attack them while they sleep. Burn the camp and leave no one alive to talk about it."

3

"Mother ... I'm very hungry."

Shanoka's head snapped up from dreams of her ordeal as a prisoner of the Sennikae. Innocent brown eyes staring out from the sleep robes drew her back to Ounontisaston. "Teo ... Teota!" Her voice cracked from mental exhaustion brought on by a night of worry and fitful sleep. "Thank the deities!" She hugged the robes. Teota lay trapped and confused beneath the heavy skins.

Shanoka sat back on her heels, staring deep into Teota's eyes to be certain his soul was really back. "What happened?"

Teota pushed up on an elbow, rubbing a chubby fist into a sleep-swollen eye as he tried to decipher what it was she was talking about. "I went fishing with Ontarra ... I caught a big mooneye ..." He searched for more, but the memory was hazy. "Yadak helped me clean it ... then I left to bring it home."

Ontarra slid off his platform and knelt beside Shanoka. "Did you use the trail to the upper fields? You should have waited for me." Ontarra wanted to be annoyed but was too relieved.

"Teota, you're back!" Taiwa rushed between her mother and Ontarra, hopping on Teota's platform to smother him with a hug. Teota's eyes darted from face to face as he tried in vain to fathom all of the attention. "I just want something to eat." He pushed Taiwa back so he could wriggle out of the bedding. Pulling his leg out of the robes, he stared at a scabby row of gashes on his calf. Teota's eyes widened.

"Something attacked you on your way back from fishing." Shanoka brushed hair from Teota's eyes. "Try to remember."

Teota swung himself around, dangling his legs over the edge of the platform. He stared into the hearth fire and then shook his head. "I remember heading up the path. The fish and gear bag were getting heavy. I had to keep stopping to change hands."

"You didn't have the fish or my bag when the women found you in the fields," Ontarra said, trying to nudge Teota's memory.

Teota studied Ontarra with blank, tear-filled eyes. "I ... I ... don't remember."

"It's all right, Mosquito." Ontarra ruffled Teota's ratty hair to show that he wasn't angry. "Toutsou and I will have a look around. He's the best tracker of all the young hunters. I'll go get him, and we'll start now." He looked to Shanoka, and she nodded her assent.

"Taiwa, your father left before first light to prepare for a journey down the Tranchi. He will likely be in the canoe area or at Tsohahissen's lodge. Find him; tell him Teota is back." Shanoka watched as Taiwa trotted out the door to convey the happy news.

She turned back to Teota. Breathing a relieved sigh, she filled a wooden bowl with cracked corn and fish stew from the bark pot and watched in silence while Teota wolfed it down. Her mind flashed back to a young girl captured along with her when the Sennikae attacked at Nippising. The girl's spirit had eventually returned, but it was never whole again. That girl never remembered the massacre at the town, despite having witnessed all of the horrors while wrapped in Shanoka's arms. Shanoka pictured her mother's mutilated body—an image forever burned into her mind, and closed her eyes. It was a terrible way to have seen her for the last time. She wished she could be as lucky as that girl.

She recognized Sannisen's determined stride beyond the wall. He ducked inside, eyes settling on Teota contentedly chewing on corn cake. Sannisen crouched, wrapping Shanoka in a quick hug.

"He doesn't remember what happened," Shanoka cautioned.

"It's enough that he's with us." Sannisen smiled, accepting the bowl of stew that Shanoka handed him.

"How are your preparations going?" she asked.

"I picked ten of the best canoes and assigned some of Ahratota's men to check them over. We won't have time for repairs on the journey so losing a canoe will mean leaving two warriors to travel on foot. Half of the men will be my warriors, and Soutoten has agreed to accompany me with ten of his best bowmen."

Shanoka canted her head, her forehead furrowing. "Why are you taking hunters?"

"I expect to ambush the Agwa in their camp. If we find that we are outnumbered, it will turn into a running fight, with us doing the running. Soutoten's men have been using those new longbows wrapped in sinew. My men haven't mastered them yet. They require too much arm strength for a prolonged fight. We'll put a man with a long bow in the front of each canoe, and if we're attacked on the river, the hunters can return fire while the warriors paddle." Sannisen set his bowl down as he belched politely.

"Are you taking slat armor?" Shanoka asked.

Sannisen gave his head a shake. "Each man will have a wicker shield, but armor is too cumbersome for a fast-moving battle."

Shanoka let out a long breath, a grim look of acceptance thinning her lips. "If Soutoten has fresh intestine, I'll pack pounded meat and bear fat for emergency food."

"You stay and tend to Teota," Sannisen said, rising to leave. "Sounia is taking care of all that."

"Can you bring me back an Agwa bow, Father?" Teota spewed a mouthful of corn cake in his rush to get the words out.

Sannisen chuckled. "Seems he is unchanged by his experience. He—"

"Ho, Mother," Taiwa's voice interrupted. "I've brought a visitor." She scampered in, dragging Yadwena behind her. Sannisen stared at Yadwena's pretty young face, saddened to see the swollen red eyes and sallow skin. He turned back to Shanoka. "Perhaps Teota can come and help with my preparations." Teota jumped up, running to his father's outstretched hand. Shanoka studied Yadwena's pitiful expression, pursed her lips, and nodded. Sannisen and Teota ducked out.

"Come, sit at the fire, Yadwena." Shanoka motioned toward the mat across the hearth. Yadwena's downcast demeanor concerned her, and the glossy hair she was so proud of looked as if it needed a scrubbing. "Would you like some pine-nut tea?"

Yadwena accepted the bowl with trembling fingers. Yadwena was Sounia's age, but she seemed much older today. As a child she had been bubbly, always a favorite among her playmates and the women at the old town. By the time her moon flows started, many boys had tried to arrange a marriage, but the Killdeer clan rejected all offers. The boy Yadwena desired eventually gave up and moved to a nearby outcamp to share a hearth.

The actions of the Killdeer women were a mystery to everyone at the time. Shanoka suspected Hiatsou was somehow behind it all. He'd attained the highest status of any Killdeer clan member—ever. He had greatly increased the clan's prestige. In their quest to enhance the clan's standing, the Killdeer women tended to ignore that Hiatsou's strongest traits were all bad ones.

Shanoka scrutinized Yadwena's troubled face, deciding this would have to be a private discussion. "Taiwa, go help Sounia prepare the travel food."

Taiwa wanted to eavesdrop and had no desire to leave. "Go!" Shanoka commanded. Taiwa scowled but knew better than to argue.

Taiwa tromped out, and Shanoka brushed straggles of hair back behind her ears, pondering where she should begin. "Yadwena, have you been like this since your clan married you to Tsohahissen?"

Yadwena looked up from the coals for the first time. A tear slid down her face and perched on her lip. Shanoka noted that her eyes were sunken from crying, not from illness. "No, Shanoka, Tsoha' has been kind and asks little of me. I keep his belly full and warm his bed."

"Nothing more?"

Yadwena offered a thin smile. "He's tried, on occasion, but his baby-maker thinks for itself now, not at his bidding."

"I'm glad you can still smile." Shanoka brightened at the small success. "You know, because Tsoha' is old, you will someday remarry. You will have a baby of your own." Shanoka watched closely to see if she was interpreting the situation correctly. To her surprise, Yadwena slumped forward and started to rock, looking lost and defeated. Shanoka slid around the fire to sit next to her. "Yadwena," she said, lifting her chin and looking into her eyes, "you will have a man in your robes that loves you, and you will bear many children. Be patient; you'll see."

"You don't understand." Yadwena's hands flew up to her face as she broke into sobs. Shanoka wrapped a comforting arm around her. They rocked together until Yadwena settled enough to speak. "Shanoka," she sniffled, pausing for a breath, "my moon flow hasn't come. I'm having the morning sickness. I am already with child."

Shanoka pulled back with surprise. "Yadwena … that's wonderful! Tsohahissen will be so proud. It will add greatly to his esteem."

"No, Shanoka, the child isn't his. It's the child of a nether-creature! You have to help me be rid of it!" Yadwena's eyes were wild.

Shanoka's mouth fell open. She rose, moving over to a sleep platform to put some distance between her and Yadwena. "Not Tsoha's child?" Her mind reeled. "He will be disgraced." She looked at Yadwena with stunned eyes. *Tsoha' might order her killed. He will at least banish her, which is really just a slower way to die. Either way, the Killdeer clan will see it as a conspiracy against them, and …* Shanoka whirled. "How do you know it isn't Tsoha's child that you carry?" she heard herself snarl.

Yadwena leaned back, apprehension drying her tears. "Tsoha hasn't tried since autumn solstice," she sniffed. Perhaps she'd made a mistake coming here. Yadwena's eyes darted around the room like a squirrel trying to find a tree.

"Whose child is it then?" Shanoka demanded.

Yadwena started rocking again. "I … I can't tell you."

"Why have you come to me then?" Shanoka's voice quavered with anger, all feelings of pity washed aside by these sudden revelations and the implications they held.

Yadwena saw her last hope withering like parched corn. She broke under the strain of unrelenting worry and despair and wept uncontrollably, her body racked by sobs as tears tracked down her face. "Shanoka, please … make me a potion. Help me to be rid of it."

Shanoka was mortified. Never had she heard such repugnant words spoken before. To destroy a spirit that had returned to this world as an unborn child was a profanity. Shanoka fought to control her voice. "Yadwena, I am a healer, chosen by the manitos to heal sick and wounded bodies." Her hands tightened into fists as she tried to keep calm. "I would never do what you are suggesting. It would bring a curse upon our people that would destroy us. You must tell me who the father is."

"It's the child of a demon!" Yadwena sobbed. "I … I was in the sugar maple woods … checking the troughs. I heard noises down in the river flats. The sounds frightened me, but I had to see what it was. I crept to the top of the ravine. The brush was too thick to see." Yadwena closed her eyes, swallowing her fear.

"Tell me!" Shanoka demanded.

"I pushed into the undergrowth. There was a dog tied to a tree down below, its mouth bound shut. It was snarling and trying to break free. I turned to run … but the thing … it came up from behind and grabbed me." Yadwena buried her face in her trembling hands. She wiped away tears and continued. "It was horrible. Covered in fur but walking upright like a man." She closed her eyes. "Its breath was foul … huge claws …" Yadwena's voice cracked.

Shanoka couldn't believe what she was hearing. "What did the face look like?"

"It grabbed me from behind. I only saw the fur—the claws. It forced me down. Said if I turned around it would shred the flesh from my bones. It … it coupled with me, Shanoka … and it did this." Yadwena peeled her tunic up, twisting around to reveal four deep claw marks down each shoulder blade.

Shanoka reached out, running her fingers along the identical scars that Teota would carry for the rest of his life. "You said that it spoke to you?"

"At first it just growled. Then there was this terrible voice—half human, half animal." Yadwena clamped her eyes shut, but the memory remained all too vivid. "I think I've heard the human part before. I can't get it out of my head."

Shanoka's compassion returned tenfold as the awful burden Yadwena had been carrying sank in. She believed a monster was growing inside her. She could tell no one. Shanoka knelt down, wrapping Yadwena in her arms. "The baby you carry is a human baby, Yadwena. A spirit-creature would never allow its offspring to be born outside of the netherworld, for it would surely be killed at birth."

Yadwena wrenched free of Shanoka's grasp, eyes wide with horror. "You mean it will come back for me?"

"No, Yadwena. I mean it would never have let you leave in the first place. The child is of this world. We cannot harm it. Our concern now is how to convince everyone it is Tsoha's baby to avoid a clan war." Shanoka ran a hand over her face. "I have an idea that should work."

"Thank you, Shanoka." Yadwena sagged into Shanoka's arms. "I knew you would help."

Shanoka stared into the depths of the hearth fire. Something unspeakable was happening. She could sense it. With the clans already so deeply divided, she could tell no one of her suspicions—not without proof—not even Sannisen. She closed her eyes, shaking her head at the convoluted web this rape could weave. In her entire life, she'd only seen one person tether a dog ... *Poutassa!*

Ontarra and Toutsou found where Teota had veered onto a different trail halfway up the ravine. Toutsou scoured the brush for spoor, studying footprints and bent twigs. He pointed to marks on the ground left by the fish and the gear bag. Ontarra laid a hand on the scuffs, wishing they could somehow speak to him. "He still had everything when he was here."

They continued on down the trail, Toutsou in the lead, checking every leaf and every blade of grass. He stopped abruptly, scanning the shadowy forest ahead, his eyes searching down the hill and then swinging up the slope to his right. "Look here." He indicated several gouges on the path where clods of soil were dislodged. "There was a scuffle. Someone fell and then crawled up the hill through the brambles." He pointed to a patch of blackcaps and several broken stalks.

Ontarra bent down to trace a finger around the indistinct outline of a fish. "This is where it happened."

"What's this?" Toutsou moved a few feet up the trail, plucking something from the detritus of the forest floor. Ontarra peered over his shoulder as he examined it. Toutsou held it to a shaft of light filtering down through the canopy. "It's a patch of fur." Laying it on his palm, he compared it to his fingers and gave his head a shake. "Really long, and the shade is almost red. I've never seen an animal with fur this color." Toutsou scanned the area nervously and then held his hand up, cocking an ear toward the river flat. "Did you hear that?"

Ontarra held his breath to listen. Somewhere ahead, a faint sound rose from the deepening shadows—a low, guttural sound, like the snarl of a starving animal defending its kill.

Toutsou swung his head, locking baffled eyes with Ontarra. "Glouscap!" Toutsou always muttered the name of the trickster god when something startled him. "What is it?"

They crouched, moving cautiously down the path to a big oak. The sound filtered up through the trunks below. They eased down, backs against the tree, trying in vain to identify the uncanny sound. Reluctantly, Ontarra drew a deep breath and peered around. A clearing was hacked into the flats below, where a low stone wall wound around its perimeter.

Ontarra's gaze shifted left to where the strange noise seemed to be coming. In the dim half-light of the forest, he could make out the silhouette of a naked man kneeling beside a tree. His body was undulating in unison to primeval snarls and growls. The man shuddered, sagged forward, and went limp. It looked like a spell had just released its grip upon him. Ontarra's knee trembled; he slid back down beside Toutsou before his knee could give out.

"What is it?" Toutsou whispered. He saw in Ontarra's eyes that he wasn't ready to answer. Toutsou crabbed over him and craned his neck, squinting to see through the slanting shadows. A sacred Ring of Fire sat in a clearing below. Movement to the left caught his eye. A naked man climbed to his feet, tugging a breechclout over his buttocks as he glanced furtively around to be sure he was alone. The man turned, and a shaft of light played across his face.

"Poutassa!" Toutsou spat the name like an obscenity. Ontarra was beside him in a flash. A muffled snarl rose from the murky gloom as they strained to see. A dog was firmly tethered to a tree.

"Ho, Soutoten. It is Sannisen. May I enter?"

"Sannisen? Yes, come in." Soutoten's voice was heavy with sleep.

Sannisen brushed aside the doorskin and ducked inside. The lodge was identical to Sannisen's in layout and size, but the walls displayed the tools of a hunter. Bows of various thicknesses, mated to arrows with different-sized points, rested on pegs with their quivers hanging beside them. Lustrous hides gave the lodge a warm, friendly feel.

Sounia, looking fresh in a loose tan tunic, knelt at the hearth, adding cornmeal to a charred ceramic pot nestled in the coals. She flashed a smile and gestured to a mat at the hearth. "Have you eaten yet?"

"It is good to see you, Sounia." Crossing his ankles, Sannisen folded himself down onto a hemp mat. "I haven't eaten yet, and whatever it is you are making smells wonderful."

Sounia grinned and passed him a bowl. "I can't cook like Shanoka yet, but if you are very hungry, it should be fine."

Sannisen pulled an intricately carved spoon from his waistband and dipped into the steaming liquid, blowing to cool it as he watched Soutoten slide from his sleep platform to join them at the warmth of the fire.

"Are the canoes ready, Sannisen?"

"Yes, they've been checked over thoroughly." Sannisen raised the spoon to his lips, but yanked his head back and blew some more. Soutoten waited patiently as Sannisen slurped at the stew and then greedily dipped into the pot for more. He recognized the sweet taste of bear meat. "This is not your normal morning fare."

"We still leave tomorrow?" Soutoten asked.

Sannisen noticed that Soutoten had added a bird-bone whistle to his neck thong. One shrill whistle would bring every warrior in two arrow-flights running for the town. "Yes, we will leave at first light. I'll have the canoes loaded with four days of venison and cracked corn. Tell your men to bring their own weapons and shields. Each will need his own sleeping skin and emergency food too."

"Is Ontarra going with you?" Sounia tried to sound casual, but anxiety was evident in her voice.

Sannisen chewed on this a moment as he studied her across the hearth. "No, Sounia." He reached out, leaning across the bed of coals to lift her chin. His chest fluttered when he saw moisture in her eyes. He'd never noticed before just how much she looked like Shanoka—the same chin and heart-wrenching eyes. Unintentionally, his voice took on a fatherly tone. "Ontarra hasn't been successful on his vision quests. It's dangerous to go into a fight without your spirit guide. He will go with me soon but not this time." Sounia flashed an embarrassed smile, averting her eyes. For a woman to show weakness was as shameful as for a man.

Sannisen stood. Heaving a proper belch, he turned for the door. Soutoten motioned for him to wait and stepped to the back corner of the lodge.

He sliced something from a rafter with his skinning knife and tossed it to Sannisen—doe intestine packed with pounded meat and bear fat. Sannisen smiled and slid the delicacy into his leather waist pouch. "I may just eat this before we leave, Soutoten," he said with a wink. Offering a parting grin to Sounia, he sidled out.

The sun was breaking over the palisades in an azure sky. Ounontisaston was wide-awake. People milled everywhere, performing the various duties required to survive in a land that was often hostile and unforgiving. Sannisen walked with purposeful strides, alone with his thoughts. He'd already decided on the men best suited for this trip. All of them were Land clan. He absently rounded the corner of the Wolf clan longhouse and crashed headlong into Thadayo. The impact staggered them both. Sannisen instinctively drew his knife but caught himself.

"You're in a hurry this morning," Sannisen growled, rubbing his temple.

"Sannisen, I've been looking for you." Thadayo suddenly noticed the knife pointed at his throat and took a step back. "You must come to Tsoha's lodge. Shanoka is there. Hiatsou stormed in after her, and he is in one of his rages."

Sannisen's shoulders drooped. He jammed the bone-handled knife back into its sheath and ran his hand over his face. "Why is Shanoka at Tsoha's?"

"We'll talk on the way," Thadayo urged.

With a weary look of acceptance, Sannisen turned and headed back to the plaza. Thadayo led the way. "From what I overheard, Shanoka has a potion that she made for Yadwena. Hiatsou found out somehow and went after her."

Sannisen remembered Shanoka saying she was going to help Yadwena, but it never occurred to him that she might try a potion. Hiatsou bartered his potions to the relatives of sick and dying people for profit. To keep peace in the town, Sannisen insisted Shanoka not offer potions to anyone unless directly approached—and only in cases of serious illness. Even then, Hiatsou complained bitterly, but he couldn't stop people from requesting a specific healer.

As they neared Tsohahissen's lodge, Sannisen could here Hiatsou yelling. He didn't bother with asking permission to enter. Ducking in, he walked directly to Shanoka's side. Sannisen's sudden appearance set Hiatsou back.

The lodge fell instantly silent. Sannisen glanced at Tsohahissen, seated on his sleep platform with a bewildered look on his face. Shanoka's lips were pinched together tightly, her brows knotted, but in her eyes Sannisen could see her usual radiant self-assurance. It was obvious she held no fear of Hiatsou, only contempt. Hiatsou stood beyond the fire, arms folded, rocking back and forth on the balls of his feet, his perpetual scowl firmly in place.

Sannisen glowered at him. "What is happening here?"

Hiatsou's face stiffened. He waved an accusing finger at Shanoka. "Your woman has made a potion and offered it to Tsohahissen. She is purposely trying to undermine my authority in these matters."

"Helping people is not a matter of authority," Shanoka fumed. "Any person may use the knowledge they posses to heal another. I've prepared this at Yadwena's request." Shanoka handed a folded leather pouch to Sannisen. He opened the knot, spreading the swath out on his palm to reveal eight little balls that looked like rabbit droppings. His eyebrows arched. He looked to Shanoka for some explanation.

"I was explaining to Tsoha … before we were interrupted"—she shot a withering glare at Hiatsou—"that it is a Midewiwin potion. It is used for women who are without children, to make them fertile. Yadwena must mix one in her morning tea each day of her moon cycle. They always work," she added for Tsoha''s benefit.

Sannisen folded the pouch up and knotted it. "Tsoha', do you wish Yadwena to bring a child into your lodge?"

Sannisen watched his father rub at his furrowed face. He was silent a long time before looking up with a smile. "Yes, Sannisen. Yadwena would be happy with a child, and that would make me happy."

Sannisen nodded and handed the pouch to Shanoka. When she turned to give it to Tsohahissen, Hiatsou lost control. Lunging across the fire, he grabbed Shanoka's arm. She gasped as he twisted her arm, and the pouch dropped onto the hearthstones.

Before Hiatsou could bend down for it, Sannisen was on him. Sannisen wound a hand into Hiatsou's grimy hair, wrenching him up on the tips of his toes. With a quick sweep of his right foot, he kicked Hiatsou's feet from under him. The shaman hit the floor with a splat, like a fish just tossed from a canoe. Sannisen dropped to his knees, crossed Hiatsou's ankles over each other, and twisted. Hiatsou groaned and wallowed over onto his belly to keep his knees from dislocating. Sannisen slammed his knee into the small of Hiatsou's back. With his left arm curling around Hiatsou's neck, his right arm pulled the knotted legs up until they almost met the back of Hiatsou's head. Sannisen felt bones crackling under his knee, and he hesitated.

Tsohahissen grabbed Sannisen from behind. "Sannisen, don't do this! He's your brother … and my son."

Sannisen looked over at Shanoka. Her eyes pleaded with him to be rational. "I'm not hurt, Sannisen. The town will suffer if you do this."

He could never resist those eyes. Sannisen drew a deep breath, exhaling slowly. He unlocked his arms, and Hiatsou's face plopped into the dirt. He gurgled and coughed as his lungs struggled for air. Slowly, he pushed his knees under him and then rose silently, staggered over to the door, and placed a hand on the frame to steady himself. His lips curled into a vengeful sneer. He ducked out without looking back.

Shanoka plucked the pouch from the hearthstones, blowing the dust off before handing it to Tsohahissen. "Do you remember what Yadwena must do?"

"Yes." Tsoha' nodded, setting the concoction on his sleep platform. He touched Sannisen's shoulder. "Stay a moment and speak with me."

"As you wish." Sannisen's voice was calm, but his face revealed barely contained anger. "Let me arrange for Shanoka." He wrapped an arm around her, escorting her out to where Thadayo stood waiting. "See that she gets home safely, Thadayo."

"Certainly, Sannisen," he said with a smirk. "I think we'll avoid the Killdeer longhouse, though."

Sannisen pressed his lips to Shanoka's forehead before going back inside. He moved to the council fire and perched on his haunches, his thoughts turning inward as he stared at the coals. "Tsoha'," he began slowly, still gazing at some distant place in the glowing embers, "he is your son, and I have always tried to respect that, but he has never been a brother to me."

"He fears you, Sannisen," Tsoha' said softly. "You have all the skills and virtues that the people admire. All he has is what his shaman Powers can obtain. The people are turning more and more to Shanoka for healing and cures. I think he has grown more frightened of her than he is of you."

"His concerns about Shanoka are petty and trivial. She tries to help people and asks nothing in return. It's hard for her to repress her training when she sees a need." Sannisen let out a frustrated sigh. "If there weren't so many Bird clan to worry about, I'd drive him and his apprentices out of Ounontisaston for good."

Tsohahissen massaged his temples between a thumb and forefinger. "We can't banish people without a just cause. The Killdeer clan is in every town and village of the land. Hiatsou has brought them status. If we act rashly, the dissension will break the nation apart."

"I'm no longer willing to placate him, Tsoha'. If he ever touches Shanoka again, I'll open his fat gut and piss in his entrails."

Tsoha' wet a lip, nodding—that would have been his own response. "Did Shanoka ever tell you what she believes caused my illness last cycle?"

Sannisen lifted his eyes from the pulsing coals. "She said you had the coughing sickness."

"She thinks that I was poisoned." Tsohahissen and Sannisen held each other with their eyes. "And I believe that the shamans are up to something again. Soon, a majority of the people will want you as the next Tsohahissen. I think Hiatsou has decided to rid himself of the three of us before that happens. We need to find out what he's up to."

Sannisen looked at the fire and shook his head. "The next Tsohahissen cannot be named until you journey to the Village of the Dead."

"I was not intended to live so long, Sannisen. Our nation needs a leader who can go out and see what is happening in the land. I allowed the Bird clans to manipulate me. There are too many of them here. That is why things have spiraled beyond control. It is my responsibility now to correct that mistake. I will know when the time has come for you to take over, and I will gladly make the journey of the dead to make way."

Sannisen climbed to his feet, gently gripping Tsohahissen's shoulders. "I've been so caught up in my own concerns I've forgotten the problems you must face each day."

Tsohahissen wanted to change the subject. "You will be leaving tomorrow?"

"Yes, we're almost ready."

Tsoha' stared out past the doorskin. "There is an Erieehronon named Dekari who trades with the Fire People. He sometimes barters information about them for petun. He's untrustworthy but probably knows what they're up to ... and I have heard he owes his life to Shanoka."

Sannisen considered this a moment and then shook his head. "It's too late for that. We must get back to Khioetoa as fast as possible." Sannisen turned, leaving Tsohahissen's lodge with a heavy heart. He wished he could think of a better way, but he'd learned from Tsoha' long ago that one life meant little when you had to consider all of the people.

4

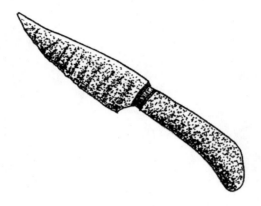

SUCKER FISH CAMP WAS A smoldering ruin. Elm-bark war canoes, barely visible in the murky half-light of a cloud-shrouded dawn, lined the bank of the Tranchi. Kadona silently gloated at how easily Khioetoa had been eliminated as a threat. After ambushing the Petun warriors sent to locate his camp on the Tadpole Island, young Tonqua had proposed a plan. He and his friend Watayon, dressed in their enemies' clothing, paddled a Petun canoe straight into the landing area of Khioetoa. Kadona and his warriors waited in the darkness downstream, watching with bated breath as the two young warriors beached their craft in the midst of their enemies' canoes. Four sentries who guarded the landing joined their ancestors before realizing there was any danger.

The canoes of Khioetoa were then shoved out into the current of the Lower Tranchi. Fists and clubs waved silently above the marsh grasses, jubilant at this early success. At only seventeen summers, Tonqua's first kills had marked him as a leader of men. When Tonqua and Watayon returned to Pokagon, they would carry themselves with the dignity of true warriors.

Kadona would have liked to burn the canoes, but he couldn't risk awakening the nearby town. The strong current would quickly carry the canoes out into the Sunset River and beyond reach anyway.

Kadona's men struck the shore at Sucker Fish Camp as the first hints of dawn lightened the eastern sky. The entire camp, believing themselves secure, was caught in their sleep robes. There was no thought of taking prisoners on a raid this deep into enemy lands. Swiftness and surprise meant everything now, if Kadona's plan was to succeed.

Kadona watched his warriors, searching for signs of survivors in the glowing heaps that had been a cluster of lodges. From where he stood, he counted thirty-eight bodies, many of them children. *Unfortunate, but necessary ... they're only Petuns.*

"Douse some of those fires before the sky lightens up!" he shouted. "We can't afford to have the smoke seen in daylight!" Kadona twisted around, scanning downriver for pursuers. A breeze was building, creating a light chop on the surface of the Tranchi. As far as he could see in the growing light, the river was empty. *They will discover the attack on their landing area soon, but they will have no canoes, and they will believe we've escaped out into Iannaoa.* A thought insinuated itself—perhaps he should leave some warriors here to ambush anyone who came up the river. Kadona gave his head a shake. *I need all of my warriors with me.*

He turned and walked up the path toward the town. This place would now and forever be a ghost town, haunted by the spirits of the dead that lay scattered around him. Souls of people who died violently could not travel to the Village of the Dead. They were doomed to roam the middle world forever.

Drops of rain spattered, sizzling on hot embers. Kadona surveyed the carnage. He had an uncomfortable feeling that he was being watched. He scanned around the area and then looked up at the sky. It was a solid layer of flinty gray cloud—the gods were with him. Rain would save time. He noticed a movement beyond the smoking debris and caught a glimpse of Dekari, pilfering the bodies. Kadona's chiseled face twisted into a scowl. His distaste for the trader was quickly turning to disgust. Dekari's eagerness to profit from the misfortune of others was reprehensible.

Dekari felt the cold stare and turned to see who was watching. With a sheepish grin he slipped a talisman and several charms into his waist pouch. Then he sauntered cautiously over to Kadona. "Just gathering a few trinkets," he said with a smirk. Kadona's stare was chilling. "The petun fields are not far from here." Dekari hesitated. He didn't like the look in Kadona's eyes. "After we get the seed, I think I'll strike out overland to Iannaoa … make my way home from there."

"Do you take me for a fool, trader? Your treachery knows no bounds. You would go to Khioetoa and have them attack us at the mouth of the Tranchi. Then you could return to Pokagon for your trade goods without me to worry about."

"I would never do such a thing!" Dekari said with an indignant arch of his brows. He screwed one eye shut to focus properly. "Haven't I done everything that I promised?"

Kadona crossed his arms, relishing Dekari's discomfort. "Do you really think I would risk the lives of my men so you can get petun seed? What I want is upriver, at their new town … and you are taking us there."

Dekari stepped back, horrified. He squinted toward the Tranchi. Kadona's warriors were already dragging the canoes over the weirs that spanned the river. "I … I can't take you there! Do you know what they would do if they caught me with you?"

"The same as they would do if they caught me or any of my men, I expect." Kadona scowled. "I thought you wanted to get even with that witch. What do you suppose she intends to do with those fingers of yours?"

Dekari's jaw locked. All of his life, his occupation had protected him. Traders were immune to the constant violence with which warriors lived. He'd never even considered how he might react to torture or the threat of death—he was above all that. If anyone harmed a trader, all traders would bypass their lands. Only once had he ever been attacked—by that crazy Minqua. "I can't take you any farther upriver. It's far too dangerous. Ounontisaston is their principle town, and I've seen Sannisen's warriors in action. They're ruthless and barbaric."

Kadona's eye's blazed. "What makes you so nervous, trader? You told me that town is lightly defended and the palisades incomplete. I warn you, if you've lied to me you will pay for it dearly. Have you forgotten that your trade goods are still at Pokagon?" Kadona could see he was getting nowhere. He turned away in disgust. "You will ride the remainder of the journey in the front of my canoe. If anything goes wrong, my arrow will shred your black heart."

Air whistled from Dekari's nostrils as he realized how hopelessly trapped he was. He stared at his mangled hand. It occurred to him that his spirit seemed to be intact. "My trade goods will mean little while Sannisen is dismembering me," he muttered. He glanced around nervously at the warriors all about. He'd have to wait for a better opportunity to make his escape. He started grimly toward the canoes.

A light drizzle began to fall. Kadona pointed to the front of his canoe, and Dekari teetered in. "The river is narrow here!" Kadona shouted to his warriors. "We will travel three abreast until it widens. If you see anyone, attack at once! I want no one to warn of our approach!"

The canoes slid off the rocks, surging into open water. Three at a time, they headed out. Kadona held back, watching the formidable array assemble upriver. As the last canoes fell into line, Kadona turned and ran his eyes over the ghost town a last time. Rain sizzled and spattered on the blackening heaps. A light mist rose into the air. The place was eerie and silent. Kadona couldn't shake the feeling that he was being watched. Hair bristled on the back of his neck as he scanned the shadowy treelines. He stepped into the canoe and shoved off with one foot. With Powerful strokes, the canoe sliced upriver.

"We should have taken the petun seed," Dekari muttered bitterly.

A faint grin curled a corner of Kadona's mouth. "When Ounontisaston is destroyed and Tsohahissen is my prisoner, we can take whatever we want at Tontiaton." Dekari's paddle dropped across the side rail. He pivoted around, staring at Kadona in stunned silence.

From the safety of the underbrush, Shadaki watched the Agwa war canoes disappearing upriver. Their sudden arrival had nearly been his undoing. If they'd shown up a few moments later, he and his apprentices would be lying among the corpses.

One of the minions whispered, "We might be able to run the trails and warn Ounontisaston."

"It is not our responsibility to save Ounontisaston. We must continue to Khioetoa; they may need us," Shadaki hissed at the young fool. He stared up the river, allowing an inward smirk. *Besides, if Hiatsou dies, I would be the next chief shaman.*

The lodge of the head shaman, in most of the towns, was larger and more pretentious than the dwellings of other chiefs. A shaman's life revolved around convincing others that he was a man of Power who could influence or even coerce the spirits and deities to do his bidding. Shamans did everything they could to create an image that commanded respect from the commoners. As men of ambition, greed, and little other ability, they had lived comfortably off others since the first humans fell into this world.

Hiatsou's lodge was a reflection of his vanity. Wider and longer than even Tsohahissen's lodge, it contained two rooms—an unprecedented extravagance in itself. Still, it didn't satisfy Hiatsou's craving for attention. He put the apprentices to work and pressured other people of the Bird clans to help. While he performed his daily chants and rituals, the elm bark of his lodge was painstakingly covered over with a veneer of willow bark.

Instead of the gray, earth-toned monotony of the rest of Ounontisaston, all eyes were immediately drawn to the large gold-colored lodge that sat on its own near the plaza. Hiatsou had demanded this location when he saw the security that the western palisades offered—so close to the bluff, they could never be scaled.

In the back room of the gold lodge, Poutassa knelt at his sleep platform, talking to himself—a habit he'd formed as a young child when he realized he was his only friend. "It is time for Poutassa to add to his trophy feathers." He pulled a wicker cage from the space below his platform, unfastened the gate, and reached inside. "Ah, yes, I can see that it hurts you," he murmured, slowly savoring the moment. "You thought when you came into this world, you would be happy, but this is not a happy place." He yanked again, plucking a finger-length feather from the fledgling robin's tail. Pink skin was visible where long wing and tail feathers had been. The bird had squawked itself hoarse long ago, choked wheezes the only sound it was capable of now.

"You think your mother might fly in and help you?" Poutassa thought of his own mother, and hatred swelled in his chest. He absently ran a finger over the lumpy scar tissue on his feet where Hiatsou had hurriedly removed a sixth toe when Poutassa was born. No one had seen Poutassa's feet since that day.

"My mother abandoned me when I was no bigger than you." He yanked the last two tip feathers from a wing and laid them on the sleeping skin, admiring their symmetry. He thought of Tonayata as he tied them to the thong around his scrotum. "The maidens think they can deny me. They are wrong."

"Poutassa! Where are you?" Hiatsou's angry voice called from the front room.

Poutassa locked the bird's wings behind its back and slipped a tiny hood over its head to stifle the wheezing before hiding the cage. "Father, you're back early." He hustled to the front room, stopping cold when he saw the angry expression on Hiatsou's face. "Is there a problem?"

Hiatsou ignored the question. "Why have you not cleaned this lodge?" Hiatsou's fat palm flashed by Poutassa's head, but Poutassa easily sidestepped the blow—he was always careful not to get within striking range when Hiatsou was like this. "I must do everything myself. I spend my time providing for us, while carrying the concerns of our entire nation on my back—and you live off me like a tick!"

Poutassa retreated slowly toward the back room, never taking his eyes from Hiatsou. He could see the tantrum fanning itself and wanted to be out of sight. He slipped back through the door and skulked over to his sleep platform. With shaking hands, he pulled a leather pouch from under the robes and removed the handsome dagger he'd found. He touched the serrated chert, wrapped his hand around the bone handle, and felt the weapon's Power tingle in his fingers—the Power to destroy. A giddy sensation aroused him, like forcing a woman to his bidding. "The feeling of authority," he muttered softly.

Hiatsou began throwing things. Poutassa cringed as a cooking pot flew through the door, splashing the contents across the floor. He looked at the knife one more time before hiding it under his leg. "If he ever hits me again, it will be the last time."

"Sannisen dares to threaten me!" Hiatsou shouted. "When I am chief of chiefs, I will have his whole family tortured! Do they believe that I would allow him to become the next Tsohahissen? He'd have to kill me first!" Hiatsou was about to smash his tortoise-shell rattle against a beam when his muscles locked—the thought had never occurred to him before. "Of course ..." His arm relaxed, and the tortoise shell fell to the floor. "They plan to kill me. That is why Tsoha' asked him to stay and talk. The Land clans think they can be rid of me like some vermin."

Hiatsou lowered himself to his tripod stool and stared at his reflection in the polished copper plate that he used to apply grease paints. The lodge fell silent as he reflected on events of the past cycle. Revelation upon revelation struck, like storm waves pounding the sand cliffs at Lake Iannaoa—the ridicule he'd been subjected to at council; the way Shanoka was gradually winning the people over. And the new town—it had been credited to Sannisen, rather than to Hiatsou, as was proper.

His protests against the site had been overruled. He realized he couldn't stop the move, so he held elaborate rituals for spiritual blessing of the bluff, but the entire nation still called it Sannisen's town. Hiatsou's mind quickly wove a web that fit his conspiratorial nature. He clenched his fists. "He and his outsider bitch will soon see!" He turned, staring at the door to the back room. "Poutassa, come out here."

After a moment of silence, Poutassa appeared. Standing cautiously in the doorway, he studied his father's demeanor and was relieved to see he'd switched to his guileful self. "I have been expecting word from Shadaki on a matter of grave importance," Hiatsou exhaled, "but as always, I must work around everyone's incompetence." He stared calmly at Poutassa, completely forgetting his earlier rage. "I've heard nothing from Teotonguiaton either, so we must make sure Sannisen does not leave tomorrow."

Poutassa relaxed and stepped into the room but was careful to keep the hearth fire between him and his father. "He needs Soutoten and his men for the raid," Poutassa said. He sucked in the corner of his lip and chewed on it thoughtfully. "Yes … I can make sure they are kept here." Poutassa's eyes narrowed to slits, his gaze settling on the fire as his mind worked. "The whole town will be in an uproar at dawn," he muttered softly, a scenario unfolding in his head. "Sannisen will be forced to wait at least one day."

"That's all we'll need." Hiatsou admired himself in the polished copper. "After that, too much will be happening for him to leave. Go and prepare while there is still enough light."

Poutassa pulled on a plain buckskin tunic to hide the body paints he always wore. When he stepped outside, the sun was dipping below the western horizon. He had just enough daylight left. Poutassa looked over at his dog tethered at the rear of the lodge. She bared her teeth with a low growl. A grin brushed Poutassa's lips, and he turned his attention to the town. Studying the activity around the longhouses, he decided it would be best to slip out the south entry and go down the bluff below the eastern palisade.

Poutassa skulked along the pathways, avoiding eye contact with the people he passed. Outside of the south entry, he shuffled slowly along the palisade, stopping occasionally to study a plant or bush and to see if anyone was watching him. Satisfied he'd drawn no attention, he slid around the corner and trotted along the eastern wall. Halfway down, he was dismayed to see several boys on top of the huge refuse pile. He sidled into a briar patch.

From his vantage point, he saw that the boys were trying to kill rats with little practice bows and blunted dead-head arrows. His jaw started working when he noticed Teota run around the front of the pile to hurl a rock at a dark blur skittering through the decaying filth. Poutassa had no choice but to force his way down the bluff through the brush. A shift in the breeze carried the overPowering stench of rotting fish. Poutassa had to lock his throat so he wouldn't gag. Holding his breath, he pushed down the hillside. When he finally had to fill his lungs, he stopped, gasping air through his mouth to avoid the reek wafting down on top of him. He'd wasted precious time but finally reached the hidden path the apprentices had hacked along the Entry River. He rested on his heels while his breathing settled. Then he straightened up and ran to make up for lost time.

He reached the clearing while the last shafts of light were still flickering through the canopy. Swinging his eyes around cautiously, he stepped out into the open. Poutassa was confident he was alone—even if a commoner stumbled upon it, he would never dare to enter such a sacred place. Poutassa moved to the Ring of Fire and slid a flat slab from the top of the rock circle. Reaching in, he reverently lifted the hide out and spread it over the rocks. He caressed the thick fur with slender fingers that had never known labor and lifted a paw to admire the huge hooked claws. The silver-maned bear was a creature of legend. Poutassa had never believed that such an animal actually existed until Hiatsou secretly obtained three hides from the Wendat traders.

He wormed out of his tunic and heaved the hide up over his back. The skull and upper jaw were still attached and sat comfortably on Poutassa's head, allowing him to see out through the big eye sockets. He slid his hands down through the sleeves, into the finger loops that gave him control of the paws and the wicked claws. He tied thongs at his waist and chest. The skin hung to mid-thigh, leaving his legs free. The only other hint of anything human was his chin jutting out below a row of jagged teeth.

Poutassa headed up the north path that led to the uplands. He nestled down in the brush where the forest met the vast crop fields. Women were heading back to the town, chattering about men and each other. Poutassa was always amazed at how trifling and meaningless their lives were. He waited as dusk settled across the land, and small groups of women passed safely beyond his strike zone. Poutassa knew that the attacks hadn't created the fear and rumors Hiatsou was hoping for. It was because of the rapes; his victims were afraid to tell anyone that they'd been violated by a spirit-creature.

The sound of a girl singing approached from his right. Poutassa squatted down. Through the branches he spotted Rona, the young wife of Dahtka. "She's pretty," Poutassa whispered to himself, feeling the familiar pull in his loins. No one else was in the area; she was alone. *Hiatsou will never know.* Rona gamboled past. Poutassa pounced, clamping a hand over her mouth and dragging her into the brush in the twinkling of an eye. Rona twisted and screamed. Poutassa swung a paw and delivered a stunning blow to her jaw. Rona sagged to the ground, but her eyes slowly refocused and flew wide with horror when she saw the terrifying apparition hunched over her. Poutassa growled menacingly and rolled her face down. Rona tried to scream, but her mouth was pressed into the dirt.

The chert dagger appeared in Poutassa's hand. He slit her dress from top to bottom, peeling it away to expose her bronze back and buttocks. Kneeling behind her, he pulled her thighs up to him, with his baby-maker probing. He felt soft, warm flesh part as he penetrated her. Rona screamed and tried to crawl away, but Poutassa was driven mad by his lust. He slapped the offensive female with a paw, laying her cheek open. Rona stopped struggling but groaned as he forced himself inside her. Poutassa rammed his hips back and forth, his excitement building as Rona's moaning kept rhythm with the sensations rising in his belly. His ecstasy grew in pace with the sounds of her suffering. As Poutassa's arms and legs started to tremble, the dagger slipped from his hand, clattering to the ground.

Rona's fingers groped for it and wrapped around the handle. She swung round, knocking the beast off of her. The knife arced up and slammed into the creature's left eye. Poutassa howled with pain. He raked Rona's face with another swat of his paw. Then he pushed the bear skull from his head and ran a finger down the deep gash over his cheek. Insane with rage, he rocked the knife out of the bear's eye socket.

"Poutassa!" Rona spun around and scrambled for the fields on her hands and knees.

"Filthy she-bitch!" Poutassa screamed. "You dare to try to attack me!" He leaped onto Rona's back, plunging the knife into her neck. Again and again, the chert blade struck, until Poutassa had to stop for breath. His senses slowly returned, and he saw the mutilated corpse beneath him. He stared in astonishment at the blood spattered over his arms and legs. His mind raced frantically. He saw what he had to do.

Sannisen's party was drifting down the Entry River when the bone whistles of the sentries began their shrill wail. The whistles could mean anything, from visiting dignitaries to an attack on the town. It was everyone's responsibility to stop whatever they were doing and find out what was happening. The canoes bunched up as paddles braked to a halt. Sannisen cocked an ear up the river valley to be sure what he was hearing. From the bluff top, the whistles shrilled again. Sannisen turned frustrated eyes to Soutoten.

"We'll have to go back!"

The canoes reversed themselves to return to the canoe area. The men gathered their weapons just in case and then fanned out over the pathways on the hillside. When they trotted in through the south entry, a large group was gathered in the plaza. Sannisen pushed through to the center of the crowd and took a horrified step backward. The shredded body of a young girl lay on a litter. Her flesh was torn, her abdomen laid open, with all the bowels and organs gone.

"By the deities!" Soutoten gasped, crouching on his haunches to study the corpse. He brushed the blood-tangled hair back to get a look at the face. "Who is she?"

"It's Rona," one of the women replied. "Dahtka's bride. She never returned from the fields last night. They didn't find her until dawn."

Ontarra appeared beside his father. "Dahtka is in his lodge. He's been unable to speak since we found her."

Sannisen was accustomed to brutality, but Rona's condition was shocking. "It looks like something … ate her."

Soutoten inspected the slashes that had shred the skin in so many places. They were undoubtedly claw marks. He poked a finger into the hole in her neck and slowly shook his head. He groped up into the body cavity. Pulling out the remaining large intestine, he looked closely at the way it had been removed.

"Ontarra, were there any tracks around her?"

"Toutsou scoured the area for spoor. It's all been cleaned up. She put up a fight—there's blood under her nails—but ..." Ontarra didn't feel comfortable saying more with so many people around.

Soutoten shifted his black eyes up, annoyed at being left hanging. "But what?"

Ontarra pulled a long breath. "We found no tracks of any kind."

The people in the plaza were already in shock, but Ontarra's words sent a murmur rippling through the crowd. Sannisen saw Shanoka pushing through to the front but couldn't move fast enough to stop her. She stared at Rona; her hand flew to her mouth as her breath escaped her. Sannisen stepped in front of her to block her vision, but she shoved past to kneel beside Soutoten. Shanoka ran her fingers over the claw slashes as moisture blurred her vision.

Sannisen gripped her shoulders and lifted her to her feet. "Come with me. There's nothing we can do here." He wrapped an arm around her, and the crowd opened to let them through.

"I was afraid something like this would happen!" Hiatsou's simpering voice caught them from behind. Sannisen and Shanoka turned to see him standing over Rona, arms crossed, a smug look on his face. "Do you intend to tell them what has happened here ... or shall I?"

Shanoka had known all along that this moment would come. At least this way, she could find out what he knew. She felt a twinge of fear for her family, but the smirk in Hiatsou's eyes replaced her fear with loathing. "I know you are somehow responsible for this, Hiatsou." Her tone was low and venomous. "Only you could be capable of something so depraved."

"You accuse me?" Hiatsou raised incredulous brows. "I spent last night at the Killdeer longhouse, tending to spiritual matters." He glanced at the Killdeer women in the crowd. They nodded obediently.

"Was Poutassa with you?" Shanoka shot back. "Where is Poutassa?" Shanoka waved her arm across the crowd. The people noted that Poutassa was indeed missing.

Hiatsou was taken aback. *How could she know?* He had to think fast. "Poutassa dreamed of a spirit-creature attacking our town in the night. He took an elixir and has followed the beast into the spirit world. He says that it came here from the land of the Caribou People."

Soutoten straightened and walked across the plaza until he was nose to nose with Hiatsou. The shaman couldn't stop himself from backing up. "Why don't you bring him out so we can see him?"

Hiatsou's scheme was coming apart. He pointed an accusing finger at Shanoka. "Why doesn't she tell us why she was banished from the Sennikae?"

The words hung in the air, and the plaza fell silent. Shanoka crossed her arms, and she glared but said nothing. She saw the flash of panic in Hiatsou's eyes, but he was an expert at looking indignant. He jabbed a finger at Shanoka. "She has been cursed by a Midewiwin conjurer!" Hiatsou scanned the wide-eyed expressions in the crowd. The finger stabbed again. "A pathway to the netherworld has been opened, and it flows through her! A beast known as Windigo appears wherever she goes. Its hunger can only be sated by human flesh!"

The people near Sannisen and Shanoka retreated backward, stepping on each other in their haste to distance themselves. "Wait ... wait!" Soutoten waved his hands for calm. "This is not the work of an animal! Rona was killed with a knife! The murderer tried to make it appear as if an animal did it!"

Hiatsou smiled as his plan fell into place. "The Windigo monster is half animal, half human. I have found out everything about it, so that I can destroy it. I had really hoped it would not follow her here, but it has. Now I must act. Our survival depends on it!"

"We will go out and track down whoever did this!" Soutoten shouted above the din of frightened voices. "And we will punish him accordingly!"

"You don't believe me?" Hiatsou raised his shoulders in an exasperated shrug. "Ask her if what I say is true."

Everyone stared at Shanoka, hoping she would deny the terrifying accusation. Soutoten couldn't keep from watching her reaction. Shanoka swung her gaze over the anxious faces. Then she spun on a heel and walked away. Sannisen ignored Hiatsou and looked at Soutoten. "I will be at my lodge." He turned and followed Shanoka.

Hiatsou was pleased with all the anxious expressions around him. He knew they wanted to hear more, but it would be far more effective to let them speculate—allow their superstitions to feed their fears. Her secret was exposed, and soon he would be called upon to save the town. Hiatsou stared down at Rona's lifeless body, shaking his head with a look of pity on his face. He adjusted his robe, turned, and ambled back to the gold lodge.

"You better show me where you found her," Soutoten whispered to Ontarra. He swung his eyes over the crowd, nodding to Toutsou and several of the hunters. They all slipped out of the plaza and through the north entry. Soutoten and Toutsou spoke in low tones as they walked; Ontarra had to strain to hear.

"It appears she was killed somewhere else," Toutsou said softly. "Her body was carried to where we found her, and all the tracks were brushed away with a branch or something when the culprit retreated." Soutoten frowned, rubbing his chin as he listened. "We didn't search beyond the immediate area before bringing her in," Toutsou continued, "but Ontarra and I believe we know where she was killed."

Soutoten stopped and crossed his arms, listening intently as Ontarra and Toutsou described the Ring of Fire and its location. The hunters milled around, pretending not to hear . . . growing visibly nervous and fidgety as they eavesdropped.

"We cannot enter such a place," one of them mumbled under his breath. Soutoten glanced over. His best men—men he'd always considered fearless—were already frightened by what they'd seen and heard today.

"Forget all this talk of monster creatures and curses," he said, scowling in disgust. "Rona was killed by a man with a knife. The sign will tell the story, as it always does, and you will feel like fools for listening to Hiatsou." Soutoten walked away with long strides, but his mind was troubled. "We will have to settle this quickly," he whispered to Ontarra. "If my men are frightened, imagine what the women are going to be like."

"Here's where we found her." Toutsou indicated a patch of sprouting corn near the treeline. Many of the shoots were bent and flattened. The hunters held back a few strides, scanning the area nervously. A breath of wind rustled the trees. Several of the hunters rushed to string their bows.

"Forget the weapons," Soutoten exhaled wearily. "Spread out and scour the area for tracks or any indication that something heavy was carried through here." The hunters sheepishly set their bows and quivers down to start a systematic search. Soutoten knelt where the body had lain. He poked at clumps of soil hardened by blood. "She was here most of the night."

Toutsou nodded. "She was already dead and disemboweled when she got here. There isn't enough blood for it to have happened here."

Soutoten rubbed his chin; his attention was still fixed on the soil. He noticed some scrape marks and followed them to the edge of the field, where they seemed to disappear. "A branch has been dragged across here to hide the tracks, but where did he go from here?" He straightened up, surveying the surrounding area. One of the hunters called out. "What is it?" Soutoten shouted.

"I think you better have a look at this." The man pointed to the ground. The other hunters joined him at the edge of the woods. They shuffled aside as Soutoten came up. A large paw print sank deep into the cultivated soil. Soutoten traced a finger over the pads to determine how old the track was.

"Bear," Soutoten murmured.

"Biggest bear I ever saw," one of the hunters grumbled, his eyes darting around anxiously.

Soutoten ignored him. "It has been placed here on purpose. It's too perfect. No soil kicked up to indicate motion." He swung his eyes over the landscape. "There's no other tracks or prints. It was pressed into the soil to throw us off."

"Or . . . whatever stood there . . . simply vanished," a young hunter stammered, trepidation in his voice as a breeze rustled through the trees again.

Soutoten stood, glaring at his men. "If you're frightened, why don't you run back to town and hide with the women?"

The silence grew as men looked to each other for support. "We think, perhaps ... the shamans might be better at this than us," one finally found the nerve to speak.

"Yes," another piped in, "I would like to make sure my family is all right. I can't do that if I'm out here tracking a Winged Deego." The men all nodded their agreement and, to Soutoten's chagrin, gathered their weapons and started back to town. He canted his head to Ontarra and Toutsou and rolled his eyes.

"People see what they want to see," Toutsou said with a shrug. "It seems to me that whoever did this must have come up the ravine to avoid leaving sign in the soft soil of the fields." He waited to be sure Soutoten agreed. "We should check the brush in the ravine."

"Which way is the Ring of Fire?" Soutoten asked, taking a frustrated final look at his men retreating into the safety of the palisades.

"It's an arrow-flight farther north," Ontarra pointed.

Soutoten nodded, glancing down into the tangled ravine. "Let's head toward it. I think we'll find what we're looking for on the way. Ontarra, go right down to the base of the hill. Toutsou, you take the middle of the ridge. I'll move along the top. Try to keep abreast so we can talk to each other."

Ontarra pushed through the heavy growth, tearing off vines that hindered him and ignoring the brambles that snagged at his leggings and tunic. At the bottom, he immediately found a path that had been traveled by many feet. He shouted to the others to join him. He studied the tracks while they crashed and cursed their way down the hillside. They broke out into the path ahead of him. Ontarra suppressed a chuckle as he watched Toutsou trying to extricate a branch that had punctured his leggings at the crotch. "That looks uncomfortable," Ontarra said, grinning at Soutoten.

Soutoten was trying hard not to laugh at Toutsou's predicament. "I think he's going to be preoccupied for a while." Soutoten tugged at a branch, noting the number of twigs broken off by bodies that had brushed by. "This is a well-used path."

"The Ring of Fire should be just ahead." Toutsou heaved a relieved sigh, retied his leggings, and headed out, ignoring the humor of the situation. At the clearing they all stopped. Only shamans were allowed to enter this place. Each, for his own reasons, had little respect for the shamans, but this was still a sacred place, and fear of the spirit world was inbred.

"We have to search it," Soutoten whispered. Taking a deep breath, he stepped out into the shadowed clearing. He moved a few steps and stopped, glancing around, waiting for something to happen. Wind swayed the treetops far above; two limbs moaned as they rubbed together and then a hush fell over the forest. The sudden silence was uncanny. Hairs bristled on Toutsou's neck as he and Ontarra watched Soutoten stepping closer to the circular stone wall. Something caught his attention. Soutoten stooped, running a finger over a slab of slate. He summoned them with a jerk of his head. They stepped out onto the sacred soil and padded cautiously to Soutoten's side. He held up a finger. "It's blood," he whispered with a shake of his head, feeling foolish for showing fear. "There's no one here but us," he said in a more normal tone. "Check for a blood trail."

They found a spot in the center of the circle where blood had stained a large area. Toutsou saw some turkey down, knelt and plucked up a scrap of hardened flesh. "Bird entrail," he mumbled. Soutoten canted a stare. "Looks like they've been reading turkey entrails," Toutsou explained.

A bloody thumbprint marred a flat rock, suggesting it had been lifted. They slid the stone back and found a storage pit. The cache was empty, but some animal hair was caught on the capstone. Toutsou held a few strands up to a shaft of light. "The same as what we found where Teota was attacked."

"Look here." Ontarra indicated a scuff mark leading toward the river. "Most of the sign has been swept clean. This is fresh." He bent down, following the scuffs in the direction of the Entry River. Where the brush began at the bank, some branches were broken. He slid down to the water's edge. "Someone stood in the mud, right here." Soutoten and Toutsou skidded down beside him. Soutoten immediately noticed a stone spackled with blood. There were several more in the area.

"Do you think she was killed here?" Toutsou wondered aloud.

"No," Soutoten answered slowly, picturing the cause of the blood spatters. "They must be throwing turkeys in the river after they kill them. We need to find the bear paw that they used so we have some—" Soutoten held a finger up for silence. "Wait ... listen!" In the distance they heard the bone whistles of the sentries.

Ontarra felt his heart skip. "What now?"

Soutoten dropped the stone in his hand and ran.

They used the shamans path. Soutoten knew it must go to the town. When they reached the top of the bluff at the south entry, Ontarra and Toutsou had to stop and catch their breath. The town wasn't under attack, but Soutoten huffed on and disappeared through the entry. People were gathered near the sick lodge. He saw Winona, grandmother of the Killdeer clan, heading for the gold lodge. Someone must be gravely ill.

Inside the gold lodge, Hiatsou was wrapped in his thoughts. He cursed the annoying bird-bone whistles—nothing but noise to him. He was surrounded by walls and warriors and had other things to worry about.

"Hiatsou," an ancient female voice rattled from beyond the door, "it is Winona. May I enter?"

Winona was the oldest woman of all the Bird clan moieties. She was constantly looking for ways to increase their status—and her own. She was Hiatsou's staunchest advocate and his accomplice in many schemes. "Enter, Grandmother. You are always welcome."

Winona bent at the knees and shuffled through, gripping the doorframe to straighten up, joints cracking and popping until she was erect again. She studied the mess from Hiatsou's fit the previous night. Then she shook it from her mind. The top of her head was bald now—only a few wisps of gray hung over her furrowed forehead and around her ears. She was old when Hiatsou was a child, and she'd lost track of her actual age long ago. Her eyes were still clear and alert, though, and her mind and tongue were as sharp as ever. "You must come to the sick lodge. The fishermen brought in a wounded man."

Hiatsou looked away so she wouldn't see his scowl. He hated the way she ordered him to do things. "Fishermen offer nothing but fish for my services. Get one of the apprentices."

"Not a fisherman. Kadak, the farmer who grows the sacred petun. Nadawa brought him in."

Hiatsou snapped around, his mouth hanging open. "Nadawa? He's alive?"

Winona shook her head impatiently. She saw Hiatsou for the lazy, self-centered man he was—a man whose strongest qualities were all bad ones. But he was cunning and ambitious, and she needed him. "Listen closely. Kadak is wounded. Nadawa and Watea came upriver with him." Winona spoke slowly, as if lecturing a child. "The fishermen brought them in. Shanoka has already examined him, but Tsohahissen has sent for you. The potential benefits of a healing ceremony tonight are timely, Hiatsou."

"I see." Hiatsou was flustered. He had to think. "You say that he's wounded?"

Winona rolled her eyes at the rafters in exasperation. "Yes, Kadak has an Agwa arrow in him."

"An Agwa arrow." Hiatsou nodded absently, wondering if Kadak saw who had fired it. "Has he said how it happened?"

"No, he's delirious." Winona was losing patience. "It was an Agwa arrow, Hiatsou. You remember—those people who try to kill us, and we them?"

"Yes, I ... uh ... see what you mean." Hiatsou's face brightened as he pictured the elaborate ceremony he could hold. As long as Kadak remained silent, the timing fit into his plans perfectly. "Well, let's go!"

Winona nodded and then creaked and popped her way outside again. Her frame was slightly bent, but she moved everywhere with a sense of purpose. She headed for the sick lodge with a steady gait, swinging her walking stick and not bothering to wait for Hiatsou. It galled him to have to trot at an undignified pace to catch up. "Grandmother," Hiatsou puffed, "a short time ago Sannisen threatened my life. He has insulted the Killdeer clan."

Winona wet her wrinkled lips to relieve the feeling that they might crack while talking. "I heard, but I've seen no advantage in it yet. We all need Sannisen right now, if the Agwa are in our lands."

"But they aren't. They …" Hiatsou caught himself. Winona would never approve of harming her own people.

Winona stopped mid-stride, squinting up suspiciously. "Is there something that you're not telling me?"

"No, Winona." Hiatsou forgot formality. "I just think that the shamans should be called upon to save us from the intruders."

Winona seemed satisfied and moved on. "You need only concern yourself with the healing ceremony. I will discuss the insult with the mothers of the Bird clans." She pushed through the throng of people gathered outside the sick lodge, amid whispers and speculation on what was happening. She stooped and shuffled inside.

The dim lodge smelled of wood smoke, petun, and death. Sannisen glared at Hiatsou, but Hiatsou pretended not to notice. This was fortuitous, an opportunity to impress. "Move aside. Give me some room," he demanded. Sannisen, Tsohahissen, Soutoten, Ounsasta, and another man moved to the back wall without interrupting their conversation. As Hiatsou's eyes adjusted, he realized the other man was Nadawa. Hiatsou strained to hear what was being said, while trying to seem engrossed with his patient.

Kadak was lying face down on a bench, with bloodied deer hides scattered all about. He was naked. The broken shaft of an arrow protruded from an ugly wound in his back. Hiatsou couldn't tell if the arrow was one of the ones he'd given to Shadaki. "What has happened here?" Hiatsou thoughtlessly pressed on the blue area surrounding the arrow in an attempt to appear busy. Kadak groaned.

"Our camp was attacked two days ago." Nadawa's voice cracked from exhaustion. "Only Kadak, his wife, Watea, and I are left. The rest are all dead." Nadawa clamped his eyes shut to keep himself from weeping. He slumped forward as if he might pass out. Sannisen gripped Nadawa's shoulders, trying to give him the strength to continue. Nadawa gulped a breath and straightened his back. "I'm sorry, Sannisen," Nadawa's voice was barely audible. He swayed slightly, but stood on his own again. "I left before dawn to take fish entrails over to Kadak. He puts them around his petun, so the spirits of the fish will enter the plants. The stench is horrendous, but his petun is the best I've ever seen."

Hiatsou pushed absently on the arrow shaft, as if he was unaware that there were nerve endings surrounding the point. Shanoka watched from a corner, closing her eyes as she felt the pain in Kadak's scream. "So you were away when the camp was attacked?" Hiatsou needed to know.

"They killed everyone in their sleep and then burned the camp." Nadawa's knee gave out, and Sannisen wrapped an arm around him again.

"Bring Nadawa to our lodge," Shanoka said, walking to the door. She ducked outside and raised her face to warm sunshine, trying to burn away the guilt that she felt. The only help she could offer Kadak now was to pray for him. Sannisen and Soutoten came out, supporting Nadawa between them. The crowd opened to let them through.

Hiatsou had heard enough to confirm that his plan was working. He left the lodge, pelted by questions he chose to ignore about Fire People and spirit-beasts. He had a performance to prepare for and no time to waste talking with commoners. *I might be able to save Kadak,* he reasoned, walking imperiously back to the gold lodge, *but what if he saw Kadaji?* He shook his head. *The risk is too great. He needs to die for the good of the nation.*

Nadawa's legs were failing him; Sannisen and Soutoten wrapped his arms over their necks to hold his weight. They jostled into Sannisen's lodge and settled Nadawa down onto a sleep platform. He'd already passed out.

Shanoka sat down on her mat at the hearth, her fingers absently caressing her prayer stone. Sannisen could see she was troubled. "It cannot be helped, Shanoka," he said. "We have to let Hiatsou perform a ritual for Kadak first. The atmosphere in the town is too tense for another confrontation with him right now."

"Kadak's wound is mortal," she said softly, closing her eyes to feel the prayer stone's Power. "If I so much as touched him, Hiatsou would blame me for his death." She opened her eyes and looked at Sannisen. "Did you see how everyone was avoiding me?"

Sannisen didn't want to admit that he'd seen the fear. The rumor had spread rapidly: Shanoka had brought a curse upon the town. He turned to Soutoten. "Did you find anything to indicate who killed Rona?"

"No, the tracks were carefully brushed away. We found one clean print, though … too clean." Soutoten rubbed his eyes and exhaled. "It was the biggest bear paw that I ever saw." Shanoka's head snapped up; she stared at Soutoten. He could see the question in her eyes. "It was carefully placed to confuse us," he assured her. "Unfortunately, my men believed some supernatural creature left it."

Sannisen sat down, rested his elbows on his knees, and steepled his fingers. "It must have been Poutassa or one of the apprentices. We'll need real proof before we can make an accusation like that."

"Well," Soutoten continued, "in the ravine below we found a Ring of Fire. Ontarra, Toutsou, and I went in and searched it. There was blood all over, but it seems to be animal blood, and we didn't find the bear paw."

Nadawa lurched upright, startling everyone. "Sannisen! The Agwa are coming here!"

Sannisen stepped over and crouched next to him. "How can you be sure?"

"Kadak and I … we were returning to the camp for more baskets of entrails. The forest was filled with smoke. We started to run, because it appeared that a lodge had caught fire. A warrior stepped out into the path ahead, and we saw that he was Agwa. We had no weapons, so we dashed into the brush. Kadak was hit. The Agwa started after us, but someone called him back to the camp. I could hear shouting and screams. I think I heard my Natia …" Nadawa choked and settled back.

Shanoka reached over to lay a hand on Nadawa's leg. "I think you should try to sleep."

Nadawa looked over at Soutoten and then back to Sannisen. Dirty streaks crawled down his cheeks as tears slid through two days' worth of grime. "There was nothing I could do. I helped Kadak down to the river and then I went for Watea, and we got their canoe. We headed upstream as fast as Watea and I could paddle, traveling day and night, only stopping long enough to warn people along the river."

"Did they follow you?" Sannisen asked.

"At the end of the first day, I waited at a bend in the river where I could see a long way back. I saw them coming." Nadawa's head sagged. Sannisen was afraid he'd pass out, so he sat down on the sleep platform, shaking Nadawa until his head lifted and his puffy eyelids parted.

"How many?" Sannisen demanded.

Nadawa held up a hand and stared at it, reassuring himself that there were five digits. "There were ten hands full. War canoes, Sannisen. Two warriors in each."

"How could they have gotten past Khioetoa's guards?" Soutoten murmured.

"They could never get by them—if they were alive." Sannisen bit his lower lip, the awful truth becoming apparent. "Fifty canoes with a hundred warriors could overcome Khioetoa if they surprised them. There may even have been more, and they left some behind to guard the mouth of the Tranchi."

"Then we are too late." Soutoten couldn't hide the defeat in his voice.

"They've heard by now that we built a new chief town." Sannisen delved into his enemy's mind, trying to divine their intentions. "With that many men, they must be planning to attack us here. They'll be stopping at night to keep the warriors fresh. So they should arrive tomorrow morning."

Soutoten shook his head bitterly. "I fear we have underestimated them, Sannisen. We believed ourselves protected by the outpost towns. We have been negligent. The people will hold us accountable."

"Perhaps," Sannisen reluctantly agreed, "but I have planned for this since I first saw this place." He stared up into the rafters, visualizing the coming fight. "We will defeat them, Soutoten. It is they who have blundered."

While Sannisen and Soutoten discussed a plan to defend Ounontisaston, two fishermen on the Tranchi strained to haul a heavy net into their canoe. "Feels like something big," the older man wheezed.

"Do you think a sturgeon could be this far up?" his son asked.

The father was too winded to answer. Slowly, an indefinite shape materialized. The son grabbed his spear, holding it ready. There was no movement in the net. The father hauled again, and matted fur broke the surface. "Glouscap! What is it?" He twisted the net. The upper jaw and teeth of a bear rolled into view. Shreds of intestine hung from a gaping hole where the bottom jaw had once been. The gory mass drifted with the current, pulling them along. The father grimaced. "Get your knife and cut the net."

"I just made that net!"

"Do you know what that's going to smell like if we pull it out of the water?" He took the knife from his son and sliced the net in half.

The bear skin and Rona's entrails hovered a moment and then slid back to the bottom of the Tranchi.

5

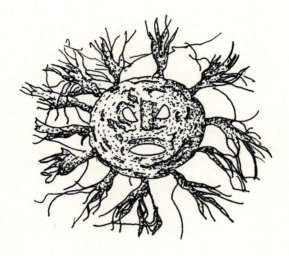

Clouds the color of the dark chert that tipped Manak's arrows churned in the sky. Rumbling thunder in the west threatened a deluge as the three trade canoes fought the currents of the Father Water. Matoupa, the head trader, knew the river well. He guided the craft through murky waters with an instinct born of experience.

The sun dipped below the clouds on the western horizon, splashing their bellies in a turbulent array of fiery orange. A large island hove into view, splitting the river into two channels. The right channel was completely blocked by brush and driftwood, apparently caught on a sandbar when the spring floodwaters had receded. Matoupa eased his strokes, the sun-circle tattoos on his fingers expanding and contracting as he studied the western shoreline. He slowly swung the canoe out into the left channel.

"Why do we stop?" Manak demanded, pulling up alongside. He followed Matoupa's gaze as it scanned the gumwood, poplar, and cypress trees bearded with moss. He saw nothing to cause concern.

"We've reached the land of the Quapaw," Matoupa said softly, hawklike eyes still fixed on the riverbank. The trees were in full leaf, obscuring any view beyond the shoreline, but Matoupa had been here many times. He knew that many eyes were watching.

Manak grew uneasy. "Are they not friendly to traders?"

"They're friendly if the proper gifts are offered. Otherwise, they just take what they want." Matoupa leaned into his paddle and started forward, moving with inbred caution. He glanced at the shoreline until he was aligned with the rocky outcrop he was using as a landmark. Stabbing his paddle deep into the water, he allowed the current to carry his canoe back downstream. Manak watched with a baffled expression. The paddle caught on something hidden below the surface, and Matoupa's muscles bulged as he strained against it.

A hemp rope tore from the water, snaking toward shore as it pulled taut. Matoupa released it, and the rope slithered back out of sight, swallowed up by the muddy current. Matoupa swung the bow toward shore as several warriors materialized at the treeline. A man in a heavy fur robe walked down to the water's edge. Warriors with nocked arrows followed.

"Are they dangerous?" Manak asked.

"Yes, but they realize that we know them," Matoupa answered from the side of his mouth, while signing a greeting to the man in the robe. "He is Chicopa, leader of the Buffalo clan. They block the eastern river channel each summer and collect a toll from everyone who passes."

Manak's wiry brows knitted. "This is how they live?"

"Only during trading season. In winter they join their other clans out on the plains, to follow the buffalo herds."

Manak studied the warriors. "We should have gone on by and not stopped."

"They would have given chase and killed us. They prefer it that way—much more sporting, and they get everything that we carry. You must pay to pass through their territory or die for your indiscretion. It has made them quite wealthy."

Manak spat on the water. "This is no way for men to live."

Matoupa shot a look from the corner of his eye. "Show respect, or our journey ends here." The dugouts skidded into shore, and Matoupa jumped out. Several warriors set their bows aside to help drag the heavy dugouts from the water. "Greetings, Chicopa," Matoupa spoke in a gibberish Manak had never heard before. "We are on a trade journey upriver, to the City of the Ancients."

Chicopa nodded, his leathery brown face a mask as he studied Matoupa's traveling companions. Matoupa turned, looking carefully at the men who accompanied him. They all wore long sleeves and leggings to cover their tattoos. He could see nothing to reveal that they might not be traders. He turned back to Chicopa, smiling to appear unconcerned. "We've have gifts, if you will allow us to enjoy some Quapaw hospitality for the night."

Chicopa snuggled the buffalo robe around his neck. He settled his dark eyes on Matoupa's face, taking note of all the scars. "My warriors will escort your men to our camp. Your trade goods will be safe down here."

Manak warily watched the warriors as they headed up the path. Feeling naked and vulnerable without his weapons, he stared longingly at his obsidian knife on the floor of the dugout. Matoupa stepped quickly to his side.

"Leave your weapons in the canoe and follow them now," he whispered.

Manak threatened Matoupa with a silent stare.

"Do as I say," Matoupa hissed. "He's already suspicious of you." Manak's jaw clenched. He began to say something but stopped as he glanced at Chicopa over Matoupa's shoulder. He pursed his lips and grudgingly started up the path. Matoupa walked to his canoe, hauled out a pack of trade goods, and slung it over his shoulder. He turned for the path, but Chicopa blocked his way. Chicopa's cold eyes cut through him like an east wind.

"Why do you come here with warriors, Matoupa?"

Icy fingers gripped Matoupa's heart. "What makes you feel that they are warriors?"

Chicopa crossed his sinewy arms, his eyes narrowing. "The way they carry themselves, the way their eyes follow every movement … and those weapons lying ready in the bows of your canoes." He tipped his head at the dugouts. "I've seen the big man with the angry eyes before, when your people made war on the Taposa. They called him Tattooed Panther."

Matoupa was mortified to hear Manak's war title. The only thing he could think of was the truth. "You are wise and observant, Chicopa." He looked away awkwardly, trying to think of a sensible reason for the deceit. "We are going to obtain something of great value to our people." Matoupa glanced at Chicopa's face for his reaction.

Chicopa's expression was inscrutable. "Go on."

"We deem it to be of such importance that we are taking warriors along to protect it."

"I have heard that the Tunica hereditary line to the great sun chief is broken. Is this what your journey is about?"

Matoupa was taken aback. He brushed some imaginary dirt from the beads on his dark tunic, giving himself a moment to think of a reply. "What you have heard is not correct. Our great sun is healthy and spry," Matoupa lied. "White Woman carries the unborn child of the Sun in the Sky. Our people are stronger and happier than ever before. You have been misinformed, Chicopa." Matoupa tried to sound convincing. "We travel upriver to obtain something of great value. That is all I can tell you now."

Chicopa reflected on this. Then he stepped aside and inclined his head toward the path. "I accept your answer, Matoupa, but if your warriors cause any trouble, I will hold you accountable." Matoupa nodded and started up the path. Chicopa fell in behind, smiling to himself. *We shall see what this treasure is when you return.*

When the camp came into sight, Matoupa noted that it had grown much larger since his last visit. Roughly ten hands of thatch-roofed huts, with their odd walls of willow wicker, sat in rows in the clearing. A throng of people had gathered to gawk at the strange men.

Manak was looking dangerously irritated. Matoupa made a show of handing out conch shells, freshwater pearls, and sharks' teeth to draw the crowd away from his companions. The situation seemed to call for generosity, so he gave away more than usual, finally presenting Chicopa with a large chunk of unpolished greenstone.

The people chattered over their new possessions as Matoupa folded up his empty pack. He joined Manak at a hearth fire in front of the visitors' lodge. Four logs protruded out from the fire, pointing to each of the sacred directions. They would be slid into the coals to feed the flame and replaced by new logs as they were reduced to ember and ash. To the Tunica, fire was a sacred entity, requiring careful handling. If anyone were to so much as spit in a fire, it would surely bring misfortune.

Women brought a catfish as big around as Matoupa's thigh and spitted it over the flames. A basket of freshwater clams was provided. The men tossed them on the coals, flipping them out with sticks as they steamed open. Manak watched a game of chunky in progress as he scraped a shell clean with his teeth. "These people are good with spears," he observed.

"The warriors are skilled and fearless." Matoupa nodded, his shell-bead bracelet flashing in the firelight as he gingerly twisted a chunk from the catfish and laid it on a rock to cool. "They have little respect for us. They use the Yazoo word, Tunica, when they talk of our nation." Matoupa stuffed some of the fish in his mouth. "Chicopa asked me if it was true that our great sun lineage is broken."

Manak stopped chewing. He gulped his clam down whole so he could talk. "If the rumor has traveled this far already, we are doomed. When the great sun dies, our enemies will attack us, and the Yoron will live only in legend."

"What we need is the Uktena Stone," a huge warrior named Mox mumbled, licking his fingers between fistfuls of meat. "We would be the most Powerful people in all the world."

"If I knew where to find the one-eyed serpent, I would go and slay him myself to get the stone," Manak muttered wistfully, staring off at the gray tones that bound the earth and sky in the west.

Matoupa fed some fish to the fire and listened somberly to the warriors and their futile delusions of supernatural intervention. "It's a foolish myth. No man has even seen the snake or its magic eye."

Manak pulled a stone pipe from his tobacco pouch and loaded it. The others followed suit. He tamped the mixture down and pulled a burning faggot from the fire to light it. Blowing smoke to the four sacred directions, he thought aloud. "White Woman is barren—no seed will live in her. Not even the sun in the sky can make something grow in fallow soil." He stared up at the darkening sky as the great bowl slid across the heavens, blocking out the sun's light. He contemplated the familiar patterns of twinkling lights as they started to appear, with the sun deity pushing its rays through the holes in the bowl. A revelation struck Manak. "The sun deity will have nothing to do with her ... because she's demented. So the sacred lineage *is* broken."

No one dared to agree out loud. Mox looked up, his meaty lips peeling back over a cavernous gap where his front teeth should have been. He broke the silence that had invaded the camp. "We are missing the Feast of Full Moon."

"I have a feeling there will be little feasting in Quizquiz while we are away," Matoupa pointed out. "There has been little to celebrate lately."

The men smoked some more and fell into a despondent silence. Manak decided he needed to be alone. He got up and disappeared into the hut. After settling himself down onto a sleeping mat, he rolled on his side to stare at the fire beyond the door. "I don't dare return without the sacred tobacco seed," he mumbled at the walls, "but nothing is going to help Fanacia provide a successor. I will have to think of something else if our people are to survive." He thought about Chicopa and wondered if Quizquiz would even exist by the time they returned.

If it falls upon me to save the Yoron, then I must buy us some time.

Hiatsou stared at his reflection in the polished copper. Women of the Killdeer clan applied grease paints to his naked body and tied beads to tiny braids in his stringy hair. He hated washing his hair. His first edict as chief shaman was to end the practice of washing hair for all shamans. It offended the spirits, he told them bluntly, without offering any other rational explanation.

As the women worked, trying their best not to get a whiff of Hiatsou's heady aroma, he ran the ceremony through his mind. He knew from cycles of experience which illusions played well to the imagination of his audience. He was a master of sound and supernatural effects. It was easy to deceive minds steeped in superstition.

It was unfortunate that his effort to save Kadak would appear to be a failure. That could easily be blamed on Sannisen, however, for letting the Agwa invade Attawondaronk lands in the first place. The second ceremony that Hiatsou performed would complete Sannisen's fall from grace. With the aid of the spirits, Hiatsou would ensure that the Agwa never arrived at Ounontisaston. He would conjure a spell and strike the Agwa on the Tranchi. "They will simply vanish from existence," he muttered without thinking.

"What did you say?"

Hiatsou jolted from his reverie at the sound of Winona's voice next to his ear. "Nothing, Grandmother. I ... didn't realize you were here." He admired his shiny copper image, congratulating himself with a smug smile. People would be singing his praises by this time tomorrow.

Poutassa busied himself by instructing the women on the proper colors of pigment to use. They carefully mixed the powders with bear fat before applying them to various body parts.

Winona waited patiently for Hiatsou to stand and greet her properly, but he made no effort to move. "I have the mothers of the Bird clan lodges with me." Her annoyed tone got Hiatsou's attention.

He jumped up to greet his collaborators, knocking one of the maidens aside in his haste. Her finger smeared a line of walnut-colored fat from his left nostril to his chin. Hiatsou nodded a greeting to each of the clan mothers, gracing them with a lopsided grin. With the smear of bear fat, it looked as if his nose was running.

"We've been discussing the current situation." Winona tried not to stare at the mucus-like green streak trailing from one nostril. "Sannisen has called the men together in the plaza to plan the defense of the town. Most of the people are out there now."

Hiatsou rocked back on his heels as if a blow had struck him. He'd been so pleased with himself that he'd forgotten—the men would be helping Sannisen all night. The sudden realization that they would miss his ceremony descended like a heavy weight. Worse still, he could see no way to make them stay.

Winona waited a moment for the vacant haze in Hiatsou's eyes to clear. The clan mothers couldn't keep themselves from staring at that green smear running from his nostril to his chin, each of them trying to decide if it was mucus or makeup. "It is our intention to demand a public apology from Sannisen in front of the whole town," Winona said, studying Hiatsou's face to see if she was getting through. "It will be a great embarrassment to him."

Hiatsou's mind cleared. "He'll never apologize."

"We think he will." Winona looked to the clan mothers. They nodded and murmured their agreement. "If he doesn't, we will withhold our consent for the men of the Bird clans to take orders from him. You will offer to lead them instead." The clan mothers grinned and bobbed their heads, quite pleased at their ability to wring an advantage out of any situation.

Hiatsou snorted in disgust. The clan mothers jostled back, before that sickening green glob landed on their feet. He almost berated the women for the notion that he should enter into a fight, but he stopped himself. *Sannisen believes that he needs all of the men right now,* he suddenly realized. *He would have to apologize or risk defeat at the hands of the Fire People. Between a public apology and the massacre at Sucker Fish Camp, Sannisen's stature would be greatly diminished.* Hiatsou unconsciously nodded his head as he realized the ramifications. The lines of his face spread into a wide grin, and the mucus-like line seemed to run into the corner of his mouth. Winona closed one eye, wiping her lips with the back of her hand as she imagined the salty taste.

Hiatsou jumped to his feet. "You are right, Winona. Let's go out now!" Before anyone could stop him, he was out the door. With long strides, he headed for the plaza. Poutassa and the clan mothers poured from the gold lodge, hustling to catch up.

Sannisen, Soutoten, and Ounsasta stood at the war post with the men of the town encircling them in irregular rows. Women and children stood behind as the men listened to Sannisen's plans. Hiatsou bulled his way through to the war post and was face-to-face with Sannisen before realizing that he'd left his backbone and political clout behind. Sannisen stopped mid-sentence. Everyone watched Hiatsou walk back to force an opening for the Bird clan mothers to enter the circle.

Hiatsou was completely oblivious to his ridiculous appearance—dressed in a breechclout, with only the left side of his body painted, his belly sagging over the confining waistband, and snot running from one nostril. Hiatsou scanned the crowd, his confidence growing as he noted that more than half the men were Bird clan. He was safe with all these eyes riveted upon him. His mouth twisted into an offensive grin. He crossed his arms and stared defiantly at Sannisen.

When it became apparent that he wasn't going to say anything, Winona stepped forward. "Hiatsou is here to demand an apology for your threats! You have insulted all of the Bird clans!" Winona was pleased with the commanding sound of her voice.

The plaza was dead silent as all eyes shifted to Sannisen. The muscles of Sannisen's jaw tightened as he worked to hold back an explosive outburst. The anger quickly evaporated, and his face relaxed into an amused grin. Sannisen closed his eyes as he rocked his head slowly.

Soutoten spoke first. "Why has Hiatsou picked this time of crisis for his petty posturing? Has he no regard for our current danger or the safety of our people? You seek to embarrass our war chief at this critical—"

Sannisen laid a hand on Soutoten's shoulder to stop him. He glared at Hiatsou and Winona. Winona felt herself cringe under the Power of those eyes. "Hiatsou can make demands of his minions," Sannisen said. "He can run to the Bird clan elders to whine and stomp his feet like a spoiled child, and he can order the camp dogs around if he wishes. But his feet will grow roots where he stands if he waits for an apology from me."

A murmur sifted through the crowd. The men of the Bird clans looked at each other nervously. Sannisen was their war leader, and they had great respect for him, but the clan mothers held more control over everyone's daily lives. The men might find themselves sleeping in their canoes if they weren't careful.

Hiatsou's arrogant smile vanished. A feeling of uncertainty crept over him. One eyelid developed a nervous twitch. He groped around for a suitable retort, but nothing was available. All the people were staring, waiting for him to say something—and wondering what that green stuff was on his lip.

The silence stretched, and Sannisen lost his patience. "I suggest that Hiatsou go and finish preening himself for his important duties," he said in a voice that dripped with sarcasm. "I think his brain is addled. He acts like a turkey that's been cracked on the head but is too stupid to fall down." Sannisen suddenly realized he was enjoying this.

Hiatsou's muscles knotted as he strained to formulate a clear thought. Fists clenched and unclenched at his sides. His arms started to shake. He never could think clearly when he was angry. *Insult piled on insult!* a voice raged in his head. He lost control. "Again, you insult the chief shaman and the Bird clans! I can turn you into a slug—crush you under my foot! I can call upon the spirits of our ancestors to haunt your sleep—to bring disaster upon your family! I ... I ..." His mind went blank.

Sannisen noticed Shanoka and Ontarra at the back of the crowd. There was a time when threats of spirits, sorcery, and dark magic would have cowed him, but Shanoka had convinced him long ago of Hiatsou's total lack of any real Powers. She smiled and nodded her encouragement. She mouthed the words *Get him*.

Sannisen stared over at Hiatsou and decided in the bat of an eye that the years of stifling his feelings for the good of the community had just ended. Sannisen folded his arms across his chest, mimicking Hiatsou's initial defiant stance to the amusement of everyone who noticed. "I have heard Hiatsou's threats before. I believe that if our chief shaman rolls all of his Powers together and shoves them into my right eye, they still would not bother me."

A ripple of laughter rolled through the plaza. Bird clan men forced their faces to remain blank as the clan mothers scanned the group for offenders.

Hiatsou was speechless. People were laughing at him. Sannisen was surprised at how good it felt to push the conflict into the open. An open Power struggle was more to his liking. It was encouraging to see that Hiatsou was not a match of wits. Sannisen knew he should end the confrontation now, but he didn't feel like it.

"If Hiatsou's Power is so great, why does he not turn himself into something other than a primping, self-centered fool?"

Hiatsou's lip started to quiver; a rage boiled up like bile in his gut. "The men of the Bird clans will take no orders from you!" he screamed, flailing his arms around as if bees were attacking. "All the men of the Bird clans will remain in their lodges for the next two days!"

Winona's eyes flew wide. "Hiatsou, this is not what we discussed," she whispered. "You must offer to lead our men and protect the town." Hiatsou didn't even hear.

The words fell like a thunderclap on Sannisen's ears. "Do you mean to say ... the men of the Bird clans will hide in their lodges like frightened puppies while the Agwa come to kill their women and children?" He swung his eyes from Hiatsou to the clan mothers and then to the Bird clan men in the crowd. They hung their heads, unable to meet his stare.

Ounsasta stepped forward, waving his war club in the air. "I am Owl clan. I will not sit idle while our enemies attack my people. I will lead any Owl clan men who will follow me!"

Thadayo pushed into the circle. "I will lead any Snipe clan men who have the courage to fight!"

Fear of being outcasts was still too much. The Bird clan men stared at the ground, at their feet, at the palisades—anywhere but at Sannisen.

Sannisen waited, but none moved. "Then we will fight the Fire People with the men who do have the stomach for it!" Sannisen yanked his club from his waistband and slammed it into the war post. Ounsasta and Thadayo followed suit. With whoops and hollers, all the men of the Land clans rushed forward. The pole rocked with the impact of clubs and knives as they all threw in with Sannisen. Ontarra and Toutsou rushed up to stand with the full warriors. Sannisen smiled. The Bird clan men glanced covertly from the clan mothers to the Land clan warriors, unsure what to do. Winona tried again to make Hiatsou relent.

"This isn't right, Hiatsou. You must offer to lead them or at least allow

Ounsasta and Thadayo. You will destroy their pride." She could see his mind was wandering its own path. *I might as well be talking to a rock.*

Hiatsou raised an arm for attention. "Any man of the Bird clans who leaves this town in the next two days will be cursed. Our men need not waste their time on Sannisen's foolishness. Let the Land clans pay for his incompetence. Tonight I will conjure a spell that will protect Ounontisaston from the enemies he has allowed to invade us!"

"So be it," Sannisen said calmly. Spinning on a heel, he headed for the south entry. One hundred forty-two men followed him. Slightly more remained behind.

Ounsasta surveyed the browbeaten knots of men; total disgust was etched into the lines of his bronze face. "Today is the first day of my life that I am ashamed to be Owl clan." He turned to scowl vindictively at Hiatsou and Winona and then slammed his club into the war post with such force that a piece the length of his forearm splintered off and landed at Hiatsou's feet. Ounsasta and Thadayo stomped out of the plaza to join Sannisen.

"You will pay for your betrayal—both of you!" Winona hollered.

Hiatsou remained rooted as the full impact of what had just happened dawned on him. The men of the Bird clans watched him with anticipation; their women waited in stunned silence. Winona touched Hiatsou's arm, saying, "I beg you to reconsider."

Hiatsou mustered his dignity, turned, and ambled back to the gold lodge without another word. *That worked out very well,* he tried to convince himself. *Now I will have more than half of the people here to witness my ceremonies.*

The men of the Bird clans gathered in whispering circles. An atmosphere of gloom had descended over the plaza like a storm cloud. The families of the Bird clan men began dispersing back to their longhouses. Even Poutassa, whose feelings rarely ventured beyond scorn and lust, felt their shame.

Ontarra and Toutsou held back to see what would happen. It was apparent the Bird clans weren't going to defy Hiatsou or the clan mothers, so they trotted for the south entry. Ontarra saw Yadak with other men of the Woodpecker clan and stopped. He was startled by the look in Yadak's eyes—not the shame or worry that animated the other men's faces. It was more like anger … or hatred. "Yadak, come with us," Ontarra prodded. Yadak scowled, spit on the ground at Ontarra's feet, and then turned and walked away.

The tattered fabric of Ounontisaston was torn apart.

The sun burned away the day's clouds before vanishing into its tunnel in the west. For a hand of time, the world was crowned with a radiant halo of color. The final crimson glow lasted for only a breath before melting away, an omen of the bloody day that awaited the sun's return. The heavens paled to lavender, and the deep blue of evening spread out across the horizon.

Ounontisaston was uncannily quiet. The day's events had cast a black mood. Only Hiatsou's apprentices were outdoors, preparing a bonfire for the nights rituals. Even the dogs were gone, drawn to all the commotion down in the river flats.

People from outlying camps drifted in to take refuge behind the palisades. All the Land clan newcomers went out to join Sannisen. The sound of voices floated up the bluff on puffs of evening breeze. Occasionally, the distinctive sound of trees falling could be heard. The palisades went unmanned. Hiatsou ordered the Bird clan men not to replace the sentries who had followed Sannisen.

Hiatsou finished his meal of baked fish and chewed bread. Food was provided to him each night from the Bird clan hearth of his choice. He belched and then berated Poutassa as he applied the final touches of paint to Hiatsou's belly, using a stick that rasped with each stroke. "That's enough! Check outside, and see how many people have gathered in the plaza."

Poutassa plodded over to the door, rubbing the knife-wound on his cheek as he scanned the area beyond the doorskin. "No one is out there." He sauntered back, settling down on a tripod stool with his back to Hiatsou to hide his smirk. He dabbed at his cheek with a damp swath to appear busy, but he listened to Hiatsou's breathing coming faster and shallower as his anger rose.

"Go to the Bird clan lodges and tell each of the clan mothers to assemble their people in the plaza!" Hiatsou ordered.

"I can't go out with this." Poutassa turned and ran a finger down the laceration beneath his eye.

"Come here." Hiatsou picked up a small bowl and wiped his finger around the rim. He swiped three red slashes under each of Poutassa's eyes, hiding the wound beneath one. "Now, go!" As he watched Poutassa trudge out, he reached for his ceremony bag.

Crossing his ankles, he lowered himself to a mat. After carefully balancing a table board across his knees, he spread out the bag's contents. He examined each item, picturing its effect on the night's ceremony. He returned some to the bag; others he dropped into his waist pouch. He kept the killdeer head fetish, a hollowed-out turkey-leg bone, his medicine bag, and a finger-shaped plug of sacred petun. He hung a small bag of finely powdered cornmeal and pine needles from his wrist. The turtle-shell rattle was indispensable, and a cornhusk mask suited the occasion nicely.

Hiatsou had learned much from his mentors, but his true talent lay in how he improvised to suit each situation. After this night he would be well positioned to be the next Tsohahissen—a title he should have held last cycle, if not for Shanoka. The thought of her made him fume. *How did she manage to hide her abilities from everyone for so long? I should have killed Tsoha' long ago, before Sannisen brought her here.* Poutassa ducked inside, interrupting Hiatsou's thoughts.

"The people are gathering," Poutassa announced.

Muffled sounds—grumbling voices, the bird clan mothers scolding—could be heard as people halfheartedly assembled in the plaza. Hiatsou took a last look at his reflection in the polished copper, scooped up his props, and went out. He wore deerskin leggings with bead-covered frills dangling at the seams. A beaver head hung over his waistband, appearing to grow right out of the bulging belly that strained to escape its confinement. His moccasins had wings sewn to the sides, suggesting that Hiatsou might be able to fly if he wished.

Hiatsou's bare chest had black crescents painted above and below the nipples. His upper arms were completely red, his forearms blue. A circle of red emblazoned each cheek. Around his neck dangled a string of human vertebrae tied together with hair—a relic that had been handed down to him. A turkey-feather headdress was perched delicately on top of his matted gray hair that hung in strands and clung to his skin wherever it touched. Three feathers pointed up, three down.

Hiatsou swaggered out into the plaza, studying the size of his audience. He waited for the chatter to die away, intimidating the crowd with his silence, so they would focus on his mystical appearance. A slow rhythmic hum rose from deep in his chest, like the droning of a striped-bee's nest. He started a shuffling dance. Turkey feathers materialized in each hand, slashing air as he gyrated and spun around the fire, every antic apparently necessary in summoning the spirits. The fire was strategically placed to cast an aura of light against the palisades. Hiatsou watched from the corner of his eye. He danced forward and then back, so his shadow contorted—shrinking and then growing to a monstrous size as it slithered across the logs in the palisade wall. He motioned to his apprentices without missing a step.

The air filled with a cacophony of grunts, moans, rattles, and whistles. An orgy of shadow people twined together on the palisade wall. The audience grew apprehensive. Souls of the dead lived on in their shadows until they were feasted and sung to the Village of the Dead. What if a malicious spirit leaped out from that wall? Would it enter one of them? OverPower someone's soul? One could never be sure about a shadow; it was only common sense to avoid them. People near the wall shuffled closer to the fire.

The plaza was filling up. Hiatsou saw some of the Land clan families watching from the darkness beyond the firelight. He gave a subtle sign to the apprentices. They danced out through the crowd to the sick lodge, disappeared inside, and then came out carrying Kadak by his arms and legs. They laid him face down in the plaza. Watea and Nadawa shuffled out of the sick lodge to join the circle of onlookers.

Hiatsou spun into a crouch beside Kadak. Shaking a rattle over the festering wound in his back, he placed a hand on Kadak's head and called to the sky in an ancient tongue, unintelligible to anyone but a shaman—or a spirit. The syllables were high-pitched and fast, like the angry chatters of a squirrel. People squirmed. The archaic words could only have meaning in another world.

Hiatsou smeared an ointment around the arrow shaft in Kadak's back. Despite his delirium, a tortured groan issued from Kadak's throat. Watea covered her face with her hands. Shanoka appeared at her side with a comforting embrace. Hiatsou leaped upright, his face to the heavens. He imitated Kadak's moans as if he had taken Kadak's pain upon himself. Hiatsou seemed to enter into a trance. An apprentice fastened the cornhusk mask to his face. It instantly took control of the shaman's mind and body.

The apprentices formed a wavering line that twisted and snaked around Hiatsou and Kadak. They sprinkled sand over Kadak's back. Everyone was captivated by the drama unfolding before them. They sat or stood in mesmerized groups, blank stares frozen to their faces by the awesome Power in the air around them.

"I call upon the spirits of our ancestors to help me heal this man!" Hiatsou cried out in a sepulchral voice. Throwing his head back, he raised his hands to the sky and howled, "Owoo-oo!"

From somewhere in the night, out beyond the palisades, an apprentice howled back: "Owoo-oo!" The spirit world seemed close at hand. Spectators gasped, huddling closer together. Hiatsou knelt to run a feather up Kadak's arms and legs. He dipped the feather in ocher and then drew a red circle around the wound, trapping the demons that infected the flesh. An apprentice placed the sacred calumet in Hiatsou's hand. Hiatsou put it to his lips, drawing his breath in hard. Petun in the bowl appeared to light by itself. He blew the smoke to the earth, the sky, and then onto Kadak's wound. Pulling the hollow turkey bone from his pouch, he placed one end over the wound.

Hiatsou sucked the demons out of the flesh and spat them into the fire. The night was utter darkness now, except for the halo of light around the fire. Grotesque silhouettes and haunting shapes flickered at the boundaries of the firelight. "Feel the ghosts of our ancestors. They are here!" Hiatsou cried, swinging his arm in an arc that encompassed the town. "Ayeee!"

"Ayeee!" the spectral voice beyond echoed back. The apprentices danced over to Kadak and rolled him onto his side. A rawhide strip was forced between his teeth, and a dozen hands restrained him. Hiatsou bent down and pushed on the arrow shaft with his thumb. Kadak choked; his body spasmed. Hiatsou increased the pressure. The arrow started moving through Kadak's flesh. An apprentice muffled the screams by holding Kadak's head between his knees. The skin near Kadak's navel stretched outward, snapping back in a crimson spray. Kadak's arms and legs flailed. Despite their efforts, two of the apprentices were tossed backward. A long, heartrending shriek blew the rawhide from Kadak's mouth.

Watea stifled a cry as Shanoka pulled her close. In a fluid motion, Hiatsou pulled a brand from the fire and pointed it to the southern sky, the direction of life and rebirth. He shoved it into the stomach wound he'd just inflicted. Putrid black smoke sizzling up into the air. Kadak's scream was much weaker this time. When Hiatsou finished, Kadak was moaning with every agonized breath.

At least he stopped the bleeding, Shanoka thought, as she struggled to keep

Watea from collapsing. Watea curled her head into Shanoka's shoulder and wept. Shanoka studied the faces reflected in the firelight. She had to admit, Hiatsou had the ability to impress people.

Kadak was carried back to the sick lodge. Hiatsou smiled behind his cornhusk mask as he scanned the faces—eyes fixed with vacant stares, heads bobbing with subtle nods of approval. With flawless timing, a howl rent the night. It was much closer now. An apprehensive silence smothered the plaza. Hiatsou turned in the direction of the howl, spreading his arms wide. "Spirits of our ancestors, you are with us now. I call on you and upon the manitos that reside in all things, living and dead. Help us! Cast a shield down around Ounontisaston! Protect us from our enemies! I wish for everyone who remains within the town to understand that you are helping me to watch over them!" Hiatsou put his clenched fist to his lips, subtly blowing pulverized corn and pine needles onto the fire. A flash of crackling flame and sparks burst into the air, tracing the swirling heat skyward.

"Owoo-oo!" The howl was frighteningly close, just beyond the palisade. Everyone held their breath. An apprentice craftily slid a hollow log packed full with hickory nuts into the fire. Hiatsou kept one eye on the log as flames licked up around it. He spun back to the fire, drawing the people's attention with him. He waved his hands over the fire in a motion that looked like he was shaking off water. His timing was off, so he chanted and tried again. The nuts started to explode, sending up another column of sparks. Hiatsou sprinkled petun on the coals to thank the spirits for answering his plea. The ceremony was over.

Hiatsou glanced again at the awed expressions. *So superstitious and gullible,* he marveled. He had to admit, the performance had been nearly flawless. His only disappointment was that he would receive no compensation for his efforts. He noticed Kabeza, grandmother of the Owl clan, trying to comfort Watea. An idea slowly formed in the back of his mind.

Hiatsou strutted across the plaza in their direction. Watea saw him coming. She wasn't at all certain she felt thankful to him, but she forced a feeble smile. Hiatsou lifted the mask and folded his arms across his chest. "Watea," he said, leering at her, "you are Owl clan, are you not?"

A wary frown wrinkled the corners of Watea's eyes. "Yes, Hiatsou, why do you ask?"

Hiatsou rubbed at his chin thoughtfully, staring at the ground with a look of concern. "I had a vision in my lodge today. It was revealed to me that if you wish ... uh ..." He pointed at the sick lodge as he tried to recall Kadak's name.

Watea glanced at the sick lodge and then back at Hiatsou. "Kadak?"

"Yes, that's it. If you wish Kadak to recover his strength, then it is necessary that you spend the night in the gold lodge."

Watea's jaw set tight, opened, and then clamped shut again. Moisture welled in the corners of her eyes. "But ... I must spend the night with Kadak. He needs his wounds bathed. He needs me to comfort him."

Hiatsou shrugged. "I cannot change what the spirits advise, Watea. I am only the medium through which they speak." He spun around and walked away, pulling the cornhusk mask back down to hide his lecherous grin. Guilt would drive her to him.

Kabeza looked at the tears rolling down Watea's cheeks and was outraged. *How could such a man have survived so long?* She shook her head. It was deplorable that the Bird clan's fortunes were tied to such a wretch! "Perhaps I can find a substitute from the Owl clan longhouses, Watea."

"N-no," Watea's voice cracked. "The spirits have requested me. I must go." She chewed on her lip to hold back the tears, turned, and ran to the sick lodge. Watea started washing Kadak's wounds, with tears rolling down her cheeks and dripping from her chin. Between sobs, she sang a heartening song of when the world began—when the goddess Aataentsic had fallen from the sky, landing on the back of a turtle that became this world. Kadak had always liked the song. When she could cry no longer, she bent and kissed Kadak's cheek and then stumbled out the door, wandering down paths through the darkness toward the gold lodge.

Kadak died alone in the night.

6

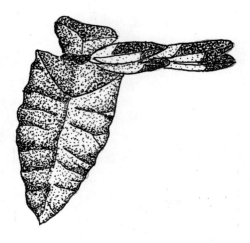

A CRIMSON GLOW BRUSHED THE eastern sky as the sun struggled to rise up from the bowels of Mother Earth. No trace of the ominous crimson shades from the previous evening had followed it through the underworld. From his position on the west bank of the Tranchi, Sannisen could just make out a solid layer of cloud as he squinted out through the beech and maple leaves. He'd carefully positioned his men an arrow-flight above the fork, where the south branch joined the main channel. The small island where the fishermen liked to set their nets was a stone's cast to his left.

The night had been a busy one for the men of the Land clans. Despite the lack of sleep, a nervous tension showed on their faces rather than any sign of exhaustion. No fires were allowed, in order to avoid detection. Tsohahissen even ordered the hearth fires of Ounontisaston extinguished. Sannisen had the camp dogs rounded up and barricaded in the Bear clan longhouse. He shuddered at the thought of facing the Bear clan women if he survived this day.

Trees had been burned through in three locations along the Entry River. The charred wood was gouged away with stone hand axes until the trees toppled across the waterway. If the Fire People got that far, they would be forced to continue on foot through open fields. Ounsasta appeared at Sannisen's side. "Many of the men are worried that their weapons and war pouches haven't been properly blessed." He kept his voice low; a voice could carry far up the river valley.

Sannisen stared pensively at the dark trench where the river flowed below him. "There isn't time—it can't be helped." He rubbed a gritty hand down his face to clear his mind. "I am more concerned about Ontarra and the other young warriors who have not yet found their spirit guides. They're all chafing for a fight. When the demons of war descend upon their minds, there will be no stopping them."

Ounsasta recalled his own youth, his chin bobbing in silent agreement. "They've just returned with the food you sent them for. They're passing it out now. Ontarra says the Bird clans refuse to post sentries on the palisade. I don't think we should leave the town unguarded like that."

Sannisen shifted his gaze from the river to Ounsasta as he considered the options. "No, we need all of our men here. The Agwa are running blind this deep in our territory. They must follow the Tranchi to find Ounon'. We will fight them right here. If the battle turns against us, we'll fight as we retreat to the town and draw them with us."

"What if they know the town's location, Sannisen?"

"How could they?"

"A prisoner, perhaps ... or a traitor."

Sannisen was silent for a moment. "Still, they must pass us here, and we must fight them here. Over half of Ounon's men are still in the town anyway."

"Hiding with the women." Ounsasta shook his head in disgust.

Sannisen laid a hand on Ounsasta's muscle-knotted shoulder. "Save your anger for the Agwas. Is everything ready upstream?"

"Yes, the warriors are well hidden. Soutoten has his men across the river. Everything is in place to entertain our guests." The brush rustled behind him. Ounsasta whirled, raising his club.

"We have some venison and dried fish, Father." Ontarra and Toutsou stepped into the cramped space between the trees. Ontarra bent to peer out through an opening in the leafy veil. There was just enough light to see the mouth of the south branch.

Sannisen didn't miss his son's wistful expression. "Be patient, Ontarra. They will arrive soon enough."

"I ... uh ... I was just wondering if any of our men are farther down and need food," Ontarra replied lamely.

"No." Sannisen flashed a grin at Ounsasta. "We're watching the forks. Everyone else is upstream where the banks are steeper. I have four runners downstream, but they're too far out. Go back to the warriors. Make sure they remain hidden."

Ontarra's shoulders sagged as he turned to leave. The sound of something approaching through the brush stopped him. Weapons appeared in everyone's hands as the four prepared to defend themselves. The brush parted, and one of the runners slumped in. Sweat glistened on wiry muscles as he doubled over to catch his breath. "They're nearing ... the forks," he gasped, his chest heaving in several gulps of air, "but ... there are only three hands of canoes." He forced himself upright on quivering legs. Ounsasta's eye locked on Sannisen.

"Nadawa said fifty." Ounsasta searched his mind for possibilities. "Do you think he miscounted?"

"Look," Ontarra whispered, pointing downstream. The bows of two canoes pushed cautiously out around the bend at the forks. The occupants paddled slowly to prevent exposing themselves as they gazed upriver.

Sannisen knelt, pulling a branch down to get a better look. Another runner stumbled in, startling everyone. He was breathing so hard, Ontarra wanted to muffle him. After several torturous moments, the runner jammed his fingers up under his ribcage and straightened up enough to talk.

Ounsasta lost patience. "Speak, man!"

The runner rolled his eyes up to Sannisen and gasped, "The first stream ... below the forks ... on the west bank ..."

Sannisen pictured the little feeder creek in his mind and nodded. "The one that runs north?"

The runner dipped his chin, lowering his eyelids in agreement. "Two hands of canoes ... went up that stream."

Ounsasta rolled his head and cursed. "That river points right at the town—they know where it is!"

Sannisen spun around, grabbing Ontarra's shoulders. "Take the young warriors and get back to the town! Warn the Bird clans that an attack is imminent!" Ontarra and Toutsou sloughed off their burden bags and sprinted into the brush. "How could they know?" Sannisen muttered, spreading the branches again to study the forks. Several canoes were probing around the bend now. There was enough light to see two figures sitting in each. He struggled to distinguish their features. "Ounsasta, I have to move upstream with the warriors. Take these men and go down where the fishermen are hidden. You'll be needed there."

Ounsasta smiled, smacking his war club in the palm of his hand before moving off. Sannisen took a last look downstream and then backed into the brush, stalking silently up to where his men were waiting. He'd placed the warriors on an inside bend that allowed a clear view of the island and the point where he'd just been standing downriver. The bank was steep there, half the height of the treetops in front. It was an easy shot to any point on the river.

The warriors saw by Sannisen's actions that something was happening. Without a word, they spread themselves out along the crest. Sannisen held a finger up to his lips for silence and then pointed his club toward the bend where the Agwa would appear. He glanced left at the island. Through narrowed eyes, he could make out three fishing canoes and six men hauling in nets. Smoke curled up from fires now being lit in the woods on the island. All signs gave the appearance of a fishing camp.

A warrior pointed. Sannisen swung his gaze to the right as several canoes poked out around the point; they fell back instantly when they saw the activity at the island. A few heartbeats later, three men in full buckskins appeared, crouching on the spit of land. Sannisen strained his eyes. The big one looked like Kadona, but he couldn't be sure. The man in the rear seemed familiar too. They were arguing. The man at the back shook his head and pointed inland to the northwest, where Ounontisaston guarded its bluff.

"I tell you, it's over there," Dekari hissed, pointing again.

"Then why is there no hearth smoke above the trees?" Kadona was angry and tense—this was taking too long.

Dekari shrugged, throwing his hands in the air, "I don't know. I haven't been there! It has only been described to me, but it should be right over there. Perhaps they know we're coming. All the lodges along the river have been empty since you destroyed the fishing camp."

Kadona chewed on his lower lip and twisted around. War canoes lined the shore; his warriors watched him with nervous intensity. It was no time for indecision. He glanced back at the men hauling nets. "We must draw the warriors out of the town before Watayon's men reach it. There has to be a canoe landing beyond that island. We will attack it, burn the canoes, and retreat downriver when their warriors arrive. They're bound to follow, and they'll have to chase us on foot."

"Come on ... come on," Sannisen muttered under his breath, shifting anxiously from one foot to the other. He looked over at his men. The tension was palpable. Finally, two canoes rounded the bend, paddling slowly upstream. No weapons were visible. The warriors tried to appear friendly, but their darting eyes said otherwise. Heads swung from side to side, scanning the shores for any movement. As they drew closer to the island and the towering banks on each side drifted lower, the men in the canoes seemed to relax a little.

Sannisen dropped prone, trying to melt into the forest floor as they pulled abreast of him. The men hauling nets suddenly drew the Agwas' full attention with shouts to identify themselves. The men in the canoes waved a friendly greeting and then leaned into their paddles to close the remaining distance quickly.

Sannisen climbed to his knees just as the suspicious fishermen abandoned their nets and retreated up into the woods. The Agwa canoes hit the point of the island at full speed. Warriors leaped out in hot pursuit.

Kadona watched the warriors splash from their canoes and race into the woods. After a few moments, muffled screams rang out. Kadona's grave expression transformed into a satisfied smile as his warriors trotted down from the woods and jumped back into the canoes. With three rapid curls of an arm, one of them signaled for Kadona to hurry.

The flotilla surged around the point. Sannisen counted twenty-eight canoes, running three abreast. The lead canoe slowed; the big warrior in back cautiously eyed the lofty terrain on each side. Sannisen looked down the line of men to his left. They were behind the brow and couldn't see the river. All eyes were locked on him. He patted his hand at the ground to keep everyone's head down.

Kadona marveled at how deeply the river had cut into the earth here. The banks were higher than any he'd seen before. They provoked a queasy feeling in his gut. As the riverbanks drifted down to half the height of the trees, he started feeling more confident. *Something still isn't right,* he cautioned himself, glancing around. *What is it?* He slowed to scrutinize his men on the island. They motioned again. He slowed his strokes even more, until he was just keeping the canoe in place against the current. A canoe thumped into him from the rear. His hand shot up for silence.

He listened intently as he scanned the shore with a practiced eye. *No sounds! No birds singing or flitting about, no squirrels—no activity at all!* A jolt of apprehension shot through his chest. Wildlife was everywhere just downstream.

Men in the canoes behind him started to murmur, growing fidgety as they sat in this exposed position. Kadona ignored the muted grumblings and studied the men on the island. The hair and clothing seemed proper. The weapons looked right. They started waving with unnatural urgency when they saw that the canoes had pulled to a stop.

Kadona rested his paddle across his knees and stuck his right arm straight up. He slowly curled his fingers into a tight fist, drooped it forward at the wrist, then the elbow, allowing his arm to slowly fall limp at his side. His stunned warriors went silent around him. The "withering penis" insult was so vile, it provoked men to extreme violence. The men at the island whispered to each other in confusion. One raised an arm and returned the insult.

"Get out of here! Go back!" Kadona cried, back-paddling as the still morning air erupted into noisy confusion. Canoes pounded and scraped together as they attempted to turn in too tight a mass. The rear canoes backed free from all the chaos before yawing around. Five near the center collided, rolling over instantly. Like wraiths from the netherworld, a long line of men materialized on the east bank. Drawing back on bows as tall as themselves, they launched a flight of deadly projectiles that arced up into the sky, reached their apex, hovered for a heartbeat, and then rotated down, accelerating as they descended upon the hapless jumble of elm bark and flesh. Screams echoed off the banks of the Tranchi. Jagged chert tore through muscle, shattering bone. Mortal wounds toppled warriors into the water.

Dekari paddled frantically for the west shore with the hiss of arrows terrifyingly close. He'd never been this frightened in his life. He heard a loud plop, like the sound of a rock dropped into wet mud, and turned to see the warrior in the canoe beside him clutching at an arrow shaft that protruded from his gut. Dekari froze, terror paralyzing his mind. He closed his eyes waiting for the arrow that he was sure would find him.

"Paddle, trader, you cursed fool!" Kadona screamed.

"Now!" Sannisen's voice echoed up the river valley. His men rose from the western crest above. The sound of Sannisen's voice flashed a premonition of horrible death through Dekari. His arms came back to life. Sannisen's men started firing straight down the bank. Kadona and his men found themselves trapped in a withering crossfire.

Canoes rolled belly-up as the dead toppled out. Survivors tried swimming downstream, but the arrows followed the bobbing heads. When chert and bone collides at high speed, the bone always loses. Men ran down both shorelines, chasing the eight canoes that had managed to break out. Sannisen led the way on the west bank, keeping his eye on the canoe that carried the leader.

Kadona and Dekari reached the bend where they'd gone ashore earlier. They drove hard to reach safety beyond the point. A net snaked up out of the water in front of them, spanning the entire river. Fishermen on the west bank reefed it tight around a tree. Dekari dropped his paddle to cover his face. The canoe plowed in, turned sideways to the current, and tumbled over. It slid slowly beneath the net as Ounsasta squinted from shore, watching intently as he waited for the men to surface, but they never came up.

"Lower it!" Ounsasta yelled to the fishermen. "It's not holding them." He scanned the river again, but there was no sign of the two men. He snorted a quick chuckle. "Swallowed by the Tranchi." Then he turned his attention to the next Agwa canoes, comically trying to stop before hitting the net. The warriors frantically slashed paddles and knives at the woven sinew and fiber, but the current relentlessly slid the canoes sideways and flipped them neatly onto their sides.

When the last canoe was hopelessly entangled, Ounsasta cut the main runners. The patchwork of nets strung together during the night dropped like a snare, slowly, inexorably, dragging men and canoes beneath the surface. Only three heads popped up, escaping the tangled web.

Dazed and battered, the three swam into the shallows. Ounsasta charged down the bank, meeting them in the knee-deep water. His club rose and fell, flashing in the morning light with vicious efficiency. The spirit of his weapon fed on Agwa flesh; water churned to red around him. Ounsasta was elated—he felt young again.

An upended canoe skidded into the shore just beyond the mouth of the south branch of the Tranchi. Two men crawled out from beneath it and slithered onto the bank. Dekari crumpled, still half in the water. After a few ragged breaths, Kadona reached up to grip a sapling and pull himself to his knees. Twisting around, he stared upstream at the carnage floating toward him. Bodies, canoes, paddles, and hundreds of arrows all mingled together like tangled flotsam after a flood. His head sagged down; he stared at his palms. "What will my people say?"

Sshwuck! An arrow buried itself in the mud where Dekari's fingers would have been, if they'd still been attached to his hand. A clutch of Soutoten's men appeared across the mouth of the south branch. Dekari willed himself to his feet as several more arrows sang past, slicing through leaves and branches that fluttered down around him. He saw some of the Attawondaronks throw down their bows as they jumped into the river to swim across. With renewed vigor, Dekari clawed his way up the bank, dragging himself on vines and brush when his feet could find no purchase.

Kadona watched Dekari scrambling up the root-woven slope. Petun warriors appeared on the opposite shore of the main channel now. Kadona resolved to die here with his men. It would be easy. Just wait a few moments … but Watayon might jeopardize his party by waiting for Kadona downstream.

Sssthwang! An arrow slammed into a tree beside Kadona's head with such force that it rattled the shaft. Kadona shook off his guilt and ran for cover.

Ontarra and Toutsou charged into Ounon' with four young warriors they'd picked up in the canoe area. Ontarra was yelling before he cleared the switchbacks. The Bird clans rushed from their longhouses. Edgy men scanned the palisades and entries in alarm, as women and children poured out of doorways. Frayed nerves and little sleep told on everyone's faces.

Watea peered out from the sick lodge, lost in her despair. Kadak had died of violence. She feared he was doomed to wander this world forever. If she had sung his spirit to Atiskein Andahatey at the instant it left his body, he might have found his way, but she'd been in the gold lodge.

Hiatsou, wearing only a breechclout, stepped out of his lodge to see what the commotion was. He saw Ontarra and folded his arms in annoyance. "What is the reason for all this?" he snapped.

"The Fire People are coming overland ... to attack the town from the rear," Ontarra gasped, hunching over to rest his hands on his knees while his lungs labored to catch up. Hiatsou swaggered over, hovering above Ontarra with a condescending scowl. "So, Sannisen has sent you young whelps to see if you can frighten us—to make the Bird clans doubt my Power to protect them."

Ontarra pushed upright, stepping to a hand's breadth from his uncle's nose. "I don't care about your so-called Powers or your petty posturing! They're coming! We have to barricade the entrances and prepare to defend ourselves!"

Hiatsou took a step back. Uncertainty flickered in his eyes, but he knew that there wasn't any real danger. He saw Bird clan warriors running into the longhouses for their weapons. Winona and other Bird clan elders surrounded Hiatsou, all talking at once. He threw his hands up in exasperation.

"No! Don't you see? This is all a ruse—a trick of the Land clans! The manitos are on our side! Return to your lodges!" He lumbered back into the imagined sanctuary of the gold lodge.

Ontarra rushed over to Winona. "Please, Winona! We must man the palisades!"

Winona could see that he was serious, but it was all happening too quickly. She never made good decisions under duress. She searched frantically for a reasonable solution, but there were too many ramifications, and everyone was waiting. "Perhaps *you* could apologize to Hiatsou for your father's insults." Ontarra couldn't believe his ears. He was seriously considering braining her with the butt of his knife when he felt the familiar touch of his mother's hand on his shoulder.

"Never!" Shanoka swung her gaze across the group of Bird clan elders, glaring at each one until they looked away. "These brave young men and the women of the Land clans will defend our town. You people can return to your longhouses and cower in the corners. Pray, if you want, that your shaman is not just a bag of wind!" Shanoka wanted to say more, but she sensed there wasn't time. "Ontarra, take your warriors and barricade the entrances. I'll get the women."

Ontarra and his warriors ran to the drying huts along the south wall and started tearing them apart. The new longhouse was dismantled next. When they were satisfied that the twisted piles blocking the entries would slow the Agwa enough, they began moving rocks up onto the parapets.

The Land clan women defied the women of the Bird clans, trouping right into each of the longhouses to take bows and armloads of arrows. They stacked the weapons at intervals in the moat of the north and west palisades.

Ontarra moved his warriors into the moat, spreading them out behind the outer wall. They picked openings that provided a good field of fire through the upper fields. The women took up positions on the parapet wherever rocks were piled. Ontarra motioned for the women to keep their heads down and out of sight. When everything was ready, he moved from warrior to warrior, smiling, encouraging them as he'd once seen his father do. Toutsou had his face pressed into a gap in the palisade, scanning his eyes in the direction of the Snake Creek ravine.

"Today we will be heroes," Ontarra said in a low tone.

Toutsou drew his head back, a wry grin on his face. "Dead ones, probably."

"Ontarra," someone whispered from the parapet above. He looked up to see Sounia peering down over the edge. She jabbed a finger at the palisade, pointing toward the creek.

Ontarra pressed his forehead to an opening. He saw a woman stalking along the edge of the ravine to the tree line, where she crouched behind a bush to stare down at Snake Creek. "It's Watea!" Ontarra gasped. "She sees them!" Slowly, Watea backed away from the ravine, slipping through the knee-high corn stalks to hide herself behind one of the blackened tree trunks.

A warrior not much older than Ontarra popped out of the foliage and sat on his haunches to study the town. Watea peeked out around the charred trunk less than ten strides away. The warrior seemed confused. *No fires, no people ... he thinks the town is abandoned,* Ontarra realized.

Watayon squatted in the field, surveying the Petun fortress. *An impressive stronghold,* he had to admit. *It appears to be completed.* He'd been led to believe that it was still being constructed. All he could see was a solid palisade wall. No entries were visible, and it was much too high to scale without sapling ladders. He'd heard the sounds of a fight on the river when he was beaching the canoes, so he knew where most of the people had gone. He had an uneasy feeling, but Kadona had given him the honor of leading older and more experienced men in this attack, and he didn't intend to let him down.

He moved out into the open field. A line of warriors emerged behind him. They hunched down as they stalked through the corn shoots, the hardened muscles of their arms rippling as they tightened their grips on menacing clubs. Heads swung from side to side, eyes scanning for anything that seemed out of place. They moved like predators but used all the cautious instincts of prey. The walls of the town loomed up ahead of them. Watayon stopped to study the palisade. "Kill as many as possible and then burn the town," he whispered. "Take no prisoners other than Tsohahissen. We have to be out of here before their warriors return."

Watea stepped out as the last Agwa moved past her. Raising a war club in both hands, she closed the distance on flying feet. The man sensed her presence and turned just in time to block the blow with his arm. The club glanced off his shoulder. She raised it again, but his knife was faster. Watea's mouth fell open, her arms jerked, her fingers relaxed, and the club tumbled to the ground. Watea slid off his blade and into a heap.

"Watea … no!" Shanoka covered the sound of her voice with her hands.

The Agwa warriors hunkered down, checking in all directions for another attack. Ontarra nocked an arrow and aimed.

"*Ahhg!*" The warrior behind Watayon went down, an arrow in his thigh. They were too exposed out here, Watayon realized as they sprinted for the palisade. Arrows spurted from the wall, and two more of Watayon's men went down before they reached it. With the element of surprise lost, Watayon knew he'd have to eliminate the defenders quickly. "Tonqua, take half the men that way! I'll take the rest around the other side! We have to find an entry and get inside!"

Rocks suddenly rained down, and three more warriors fell to their knees. Watayon didn't bother to look up as he charged along the wall toward the bluff. Arrows flew from cracks in front of and behind him, but the timing was off. Rocks thudded to the ground all about—he didn't dare stop.

"They're heading for the entries!" Ontarra yelled. His warriors all grabbed arrows and ran for the barricaded breaches in the walls. When they reached the south entry, Ontarra and Toutsou took positions behind each end of the first switchback. Brata was on the left parapet. Shanoka and Sounia crouched low and scampered along the right parapet. Sounia dropped an armload of rocks at Shanoka's feet and scrambled back for more.

Ontarra and Toutsou couldn't see any Agwa, but they knew they were out there. Brata and Shanoka started lofting rocks over the outer wall, to a chorus of surprised grunts and choked howls. Ontarra felt thuds under his feet when rocks missed their mark and slammed into the ground. Brata had to use both hands to lift a large chunk of granite. She rested it between the points on top of the palisade and peered over, waited a heartbeat, and heaved; the rock tumbled away. There was a sound like overripe squash hitting a tree trunk. Ontarra winced as he pictured the damage.

"Eeyaaaa!" Brata cackled, leaning over the palisade to shake a bony fist. "How'd that feel? Agwa maggot!" She ducked back as an arrow streaked past her nose.

"They're coming over!" Shanoka yelled, backing down the parapet and hurling rocks as she went. A head poked up above the tangled poles and bark that blocked the entrance. Ontarra leveled his bow and took aim. Before he could release, an arrow plopped into the right eye. The head disappeared, but another head sprang up. Ontarra glanced over at Toutsou.

Yours, Toutsou mouthed, grinning as he nocked another arrow.

Ontarra aimed and held, waiting for a larger target. Shoulders and a chest appeared, and he released. The arrow went a little high, slicing through the man's larynx. The Agwa's club dropped as he grabbed at the arrow shaft with both hands. He looked down at Ontarra, shock and horror twisting his mouth into a hideous silent scream. A frothy red spray spewed from the hole in his neck. He hung motionless in that instant before death came to claim him, and then he dropped into the devastation below.

"Ontarra! They're inside the north entry!" Sounia screamed.

He turned to see six warriors come out of the switchback, fanning out across the plaza. Tsohahissen was there by the war post, calmly nocking and firing. Two Agwa went down with two shots.

"Too many!" Shanoka yelled, still backing down the parapet and raining rocks on the attackers coming over the south entry. She threw the last one and jumped to the ground and then turned to help Sounia down. Ontarra grabbed each of them by an arm, and the three ran for the plaza.

Toutsou reached up to help Brata, but as she turned toward him, a bloodied arrow burst from her chest. She staggered back against the palisade, staring down at Toutsou with a grim look of acceptance. "Run, Toutsou," she said calmly. Brata slumped into a heap.

As they reached the plaza, Ontarra saw Tsohahissen take an arrow in his left leg. He dropped to his knees and began chanting his death song. Telling his life story, he asked for acceptance into the spirit world. Tsoha' finished his chant, shrugged off the pain, and nocked another arrow. Ontarra shoved Shanoka and Sounia toward the longhouse path. "Go to the Bird clan longhouses!" He turned and ran out into the plaza.

An Agwa warrior was almost on top of Tsohahissen. The man raised his club. Tsohahissen threw his bow over his head to fend off the blow. A rotating blur passed in front of Ontarra's face. Toutsou's throw-stick slammed the warrior's forehead with a satisfying crack that sent him sprawling. Ontarra and Toutsou reached Tsohahissen together and pulled their knives for the last-ditch effort. Toutsou sprang forward, piercing the large vein in the Agwa's neck to be sure he stayed down.

Agwa warriors flooded out from the switchbacks, forming a crescent across the plaza. Ontarra counted eleven. They moved forward slowly, eyes searching the town. Ontarra recognized the young one he'd seen earlier in the field. A grin spread across the young man's face when he realized there were only three defenders left. One of the Agwa got close. Ontarra slashed his chin for the indiscretion and then grabbed Tsoha''s club and prepared himself to die. Suddenly, a mass of armed men rushed out from behind the gold lodge.

The Bird clans had finally joined the fight. "A trap!" Watayon screamed. The warriors behind him turned and ran for the north entry. Watayon jumped forward, taking a quick swipe at Tsohahissen, but Ontarra parried the blow with Tsoha''s club.

Three of the Agwa were surrounded before they could reach the switchback. They circled, surveying the bristling wall of arrows that surrounded them. Two slowly dropped their clubs to the ground. The third swung, slashing air with his club, taunting with his weapon as he spun around the circle of men. "Come on, Petun! Come in here and fight me! I can take a handful of you at once!" It was a bad time for defiance. His body hit the ground, bristling with two hands of arrows.

As Ontarra's pounding heart slowed, a sound shifted from the back of his mind to the front. *Frenzied whining and snarling.* "The dogs!" he yelled to Toutsou. They ran to the Bear clan longhouse and started tearing bark and poles away from the door. The dogs rushed out through the debris, casting around the plaza for scent. The hair on their backs bristled as they whiffed blood. Savage, guttural snarls built in their throats when they picked up the alien scents leading to the north entry. The pack went over the top, slavering for a kill. With their bloodlust aroused, many of the Bird clan men scrambled up over the barricade and disappeared after the dogs.

Toutsou smirked at Ontarra as the sound of the pack faded away. "Not a good day to be Agwa, I think."

When Watayon reached the ravine at Snake Creek, an eerie sound—somehow familiar—touched his ears. He turned to see how many of his warriors followed. Only five of his original forty were sprinting through the corn. *What will I tell Kadona?* They caught up to him, panting, bleeding, and bruised. Watayon saw the source of the strange noise. A pack of dogs raced across the field. He heard vicious snarls but no barking—like a pack of wolves moving in on a wounded doe.

With sudden energy spawned by terror, Watayon spun, crashing headlong down into the ravine. Branches and thorns tore at his face and arms. His feet tangled in a vine, tumbling him hard into a creek. He rolled back to his feet and started up the other side. When he made the top, he heard screams as dogs dragged down the straggler. Several yelps rang out when the warrior used his knife in a final attempt to fend off the teeth that were tearing him apart.

Watayon covered his face and plunged into the brush, praying his direction was right. A heart-wrenching scream that sounded like death was abruptly choked short. Fear like he'd never known drove Watayon through everything in his way. He stumbled, sprawling out into a deer trail. It seemed to point west, so he took it. He ran in a crouch to keep below the branches that slapped and groped at him; his feet moved on their own now. His courage and resolve had fled—survival was his only concern.

When breath could no longer come fast enough and his heart was ready to explode from his chest, he staggered out into a flood plain covered in the withered chest-high weeds of last cycle. His terrified eyes flashed left and right in a desperate attempt to get his bearings. He saw the canoes. The sound of crashing brush behind him urged him on. He splashed out into the stream, dragging a canoe. Rolling into it, he paddled furiously for deeper water. Watayon saw his four comrades break from the woods and dash for the canoes. One waved for him to wait and almost fell from the effort.

The dogs appeared behind the men, heads bouncing up above the grass to catch sight of their prey, then disappearing, reappearing closer on the next leap. Without slowing, the warriors dragged canoes out into the water until they were waist-deep. Most of the dogs ran along the shoreline, but some followed into the water. Paddles glinted in the morning mist, slashing down on the heads of animals whose bloodlust had drawn them into an element where they were at a disadvantage.

"Cursed creatures!" The last warrior dealt a deathblow to every dog within his reach. The other canoes headed for the safety of the Tranchi, while he stayed behind to even the score.

Watayon reached the Tranchi. Swinging out into mid-channel, he headed downstream. Kadona was hiding on the opposite shore. He cupped his hands and hollered, but the only sounds Watayon could hear were the beating of his heart and the splash of his paddle. Three more canoes darted out of the feeder creek, running for home. Kadona waved his arms, screaming at them, but fear had blinded their senses.

How can they not hear me? Kadona wondered. It suddenly struck him—there was only one man in each canoe. "They're fleeing something," he muttered under his breath. Kadona ran along the shoreline and then jumped into the river to get around some fallen trees. When he was directly opposite the feeder creek, he sloshed back to shore and hid in the brush.

Troubled eyes scanned for the rest of his warriors, but none appeared. *Only four ... how can it be?* He glanced down the Tranchi at the only four survivors of his ill-conceived raid as they approached the first bend. *When Watayon gets back, all will know of this terrible calamity I have caused.* Kadona felt moisture building up in his eyes. He tore open the sleeve of his tunic, pressing his knife blade hard against the inside of his elbow. Beads of blood formed along the edges of the chert. Mournful chants floated to him across the water. *Death songs!* His warriors had stopped at the bend in the river. As he watched, a solid mass of war canoes seemed to emerge from the point of land that had hidden them from view.

Kadona strained his eyes but couldn't identify the craft. Whoops and hollers carried to him as the warriors of Khioetoa bore down on the last of his men. Kadona's head slumped forward. He lowered the knife. *Our disaster is complete.* Movement across the river caught his eye. Another of his warriors appeared on the feeder creek, pressing hard for the Tranchi. Kadona ran out from his cover, waving his arms. The warrior started backpaddling but stopped when he recognized Kadona.

Kadona gestured *Go back!* And then, pointing down the Tranchi, he drew a finger across his throat, and the warrior understood. He slipped to shore, hauling the canoe out of sight. Kadona sheathed his knife and slipped back into the brush. He tried not to look but couldn't stop himself. He was thankful the young warrior on the far shore couldn't see what was happening downriver. He wished that he couldn't.

Manak couldn't sleep. The traders and his warriors were sprawled around a tiny fire, enjoying their first sound rest since they'd fled the Quapaw—almost a half moon cycle. Chicopa's warriors hadn't stopped chasing them until yesterday. For several nights they hadn't dared to even stop. When they did pull in for short periods of rest, they had to take turns watching the river for the war party that was after them. When the landscape started to change, the Quapaw turned back. Matoupa said that the Quapaw were warring with the Kaskinampo, and this was *their* territory.

Manak had never known that a land like this existed. The red sandy soil and cypress trees draped in moss had gradually faded away and were replaced by deciduous trees and black crumbly soil that turned slick whenever it rained. The trees and brush apparently liked this soil. There were no bare patches of earth like the land around Quizquiz. Along the river he'd seen vast open plains, covered in nothing but lush green grass. Fat bushy trees grew leaves right from their bottoms to their tops, their dark bark lumpy, like alligator hide.

It wasn't the Quapaw or these strange surroundings that kept Manak from drifting off. His mind just wouldn't settle; thoughts constantly twined around the imminent calamity that his people faced. He rolled from his sleeping robe to sit on his heels by the fire. Dipping into his tobacco pouch, he pinched some off into the coals for the spirits. He wished now that he'd taken his spiritual training more seriously. Manak glanced at the tattoo on his shoulder. Marked as a warrior noble at birth, he was trained to fight, to kill without compunction. A noble-class warrior wasn't expected to understand the deeper meanings of the stories and legends that all other Yoron learned.

A cursory knowledge was enough. Until now, spiritual matters had held little interest to him anyway.

Their leader, the Great Sun, was dying. He was a living deity, brother to the sun in the sky. When the world began, the sun in the sky had placed his brother and sister on the earth, instructing his brother to rule the people of the middle world. The sun knew that earthly bodies would grow old and die, so he commanded his sister, White Woman, to take her mates from among the people and continue his hereditary line. From that day on, when the Great Sun died and returned to the spirit world, a new Great Sun was provided from White Woman's male children.

The line had continued unbroken from the time that the world began … until Fanacia. Manak had little faith that the Powerful tobacco seed they were after would ever make her fertile, but he had no choice now. She would have him killed on sight if he dared to return without it.

An idea slowly insinuated itself in the back of his mind. If he was to save his people, it would have to be by deceit. They'd passed people traveling and fishing on the Father Water. It surprised him that their skin was so much lighter than his own. Perhaps he could buy or steal a baby and say that the child was given to him by a Powerful seer—a child whose skin was light because it was touched by the sun. He knew he could get the stinkards to believe, and he could deal with Fanacia, if he had enough time.

His dilemma was that the hereditary line would still be broken. What would the sun in the sky do? Burn the land? Starve the people? Never return from his nighttime journey? Or would he understand his people's plight and nurture life in the world as he always had? Manak didn't know. Probably no one knew. It was troubling, but at least now he had a plan.

Manak heard a muffled sound from the direction of the river. He stood, cocking an ear in that direction. There it was again. He'd seen many new creatures lately; it didn't surprise him that he couldn't identify it. He moved into the brush, slipping silently toward the noise.

They'd made camp on a point of land where another immense river flowed in from the east to join the Father Water. The trade canoes were emptied, carried into the woods, and then covered with driftwood and branches. Matoupa insisted the trade goods be hauled even farther into the woods and hidden. Manak pressed himself up against a tree, searching the darkness ahead. Someone was out there, pulling the brush from the pile of trade goods.

Manak slid the ax from his waistband. He was Tattooed Panther now, moving with the stealth of the beast he was named for. The thief didn't hear his approach. The ax rose. There was a rustle beside him. Manak twisted and looked into the shocked eyes of a young woman.

She screamed a warning to the thief and ran. The thief whipped out a knife, but he didn't have a chance. Manak's first blow broke his wrist, and the knife flew off through the brush. The second blow broke his jaw. The third sent his spirit into the next world. The thief toppled like a cypress trunk into the trade packs that had cost him his life.

Manak sprinted after the woman. When he burst out onto the shoreline of the river, she was already pushing a small canoe into the water. Manak dropped to his knees, running his hand blindly over the ground while keeping his eyes on her silhouette over the moonlight water. His hand settled onto a rock the size of an apple, and he sprang to his feet. Twisting his head from side to side to get his range, Manak drilled the rock through the darkness that divided them. With a sickening, hollow thud, it took her square in the back of the head.

Mox and the other warriors exploded onto the riverbank, weapons ready. They spread out to secure the immediate area. Mox saw the body floating facedown and waded out to retrieve it. A spine-chilling wail drifted over the water. The hair on Manak's neck stood up.

Matoupa ran from the woods and stared at the anxious faces of the warriors. The chilling sound rent the darkness again. Manak fought back an urge to run. Matoupa splashed into the water and stroked for the canoe. Muscling it back to shore, he hauled it up onto the beach. Then he bent over and lifted out a cradleboard. The baby broke into hysterics. The warriors relaxed. Mox dragged the body onto shore and rolled it over—a young woman. Her skull was broken, warping what had obviously been a beautiful face. Manak joined him, staring down at her.

"She's Michagamea," Matoupa said. "We'll be in their lands tomorrow."

"What a waste." Mox slid a stone-headed maul into a strap at his waist and sighed wistfully. "Did you have to kill her?"

Manak shot a disparaging look, but didn't waste time with an answer. Instead, he asked, "How did they know we were here?" Manak paced up and down the shoreline, staring into the forest to see if their fire was visible. He noticed occasional flickers above the treetops but couldn't identify them. "What is that?" He pointed at the sky. Matoupa shuffled the wailing child to his left shoulder as he followed Manak's finger to the faint flashes.

"Bats," he answered. "They're catching insects attracted to the light of our fire."

"Bats?" Manak said, glowering. "Why didn't you warn me of this before?"

Matoupa patted the infant's back and scowled. "If you'd stop killing everyone we run into, we wouldn't have to hide all the time!"

"Did you expect me to let them rob us? I'm the one in charge of this expedition, trader. Don't you forget that!" Manak stepped up to Matoupa, watching his pathetic attempts to stop the baby from howling. "Give it to me," Manak ordered, grabbing at the cradle. Matoupa held on apprehensively, but the vicious look in Manak's eyes made him relinquish it. Manak untied the thongs and peeled the baby out, ignoring its screams. He held it by one arm and spun the cloth swaddle off. "A girl," he snarled with disgust. Manak turned and flung the baby out into the river. The terrified shrieks died instantly.

"No!" Matoupa jumped in, splashing around until he found her. After some sputters and coughs, the mind-numbing wails started up again, even louder than before. Matoupa stayed in the water, afraid to get within Manak's reach.

Manak crossed his arms. "Just what do you expect to do with it, trader? You aren't bringing it with us, and there's no one to care for it or feed it—unless you've grown breasts." The warriors chuckled. Manak looked over at Mox and shook his head. "He has shit where his brains should be. Take the men back; put out the fire."

The dark foliage swallowed up the warriors as they trotted into the shadows. Manak turned back to Matoupa. "You're lucky I need you." He reached around his back, tugging out the knife he always carried hidden in his waistband, and tossed it to the ground. "Stop that brat's caterwauling before someone else comes."

Matoupa looked at the odious black blade reflected in the moonlight—Manak wanted the reality of the situation to be clear. Matoupa cringed at the thought of using it on the child in his arms.

"Since you seem to have a better idea," Manak said, "you can dispose of the bodies. I'm returning to camp. You'd better render that brat quiet by the time I get there."

Matoupa watched him leave and then waded back to shore. He sat down with his feet in the water. Something made him think of sticking his finger in the baby's mouth. She tugged at it furiously. With her mouth busy, the crying ceased. Matoupa felt his tension ease. He smiled at the little cheeks pumping in and out, but his face fell when he saw the knife at his side.

The infant suddenly realized that no nourishment was in this finger. Frustrated little sobs started up. An idea came to Matoupa. He looked around, found the cloth swaddle, and wrapped her in it. When he set her down, the caterwauling started again with the ferocity of hunger. Matoupa rushed into the water, lifting the female up in his arms. Carefully, he laid her on her back in the canoe, with her head resting on the stern. He ran back and offered the baby his finger, but she wasn't falling for that again.

Matoupa grabbed the knife and returned to the canoe. Cold and tension made his hands shake. He sliced the woman's dress open from neck to hem and then folded it back. Carrying the baby down, he laid her gently on her mother's chest. The smell of Mother calmed her; the crying stopped. A dimpled hand groped for a breast. Lips followed, searching for a nipple. She found one and nuzzled in with contented mewing sounds. Matoupa pushed the canoe out into the current. He stood watching as its outline faded into the night. "I pray that the sun still shines on you tomorrow, little one."

7

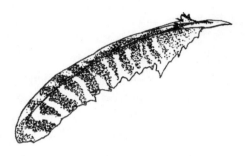

By midday Ounontisaston's dead were lying in the plaza. Kadak and Watea were at each other's sides, at peace in their final slumber. Brata's mate set a yellow daisy on her chest, as tears slithered down the cracks and crevices of his craggy face. One of Soutoten's men was carried in and lowered beside the young warriors killed at the north entry. The man's head was nearly severed from his body. The men were careful, not wanting it to become detached before the rituals could be performed.

Ounsasta was dragged from the Tranchi with a Mascouten arrow through his heart. The fishermen who had witnessed his death saw something they were not intended to see. While Ounsasta dispatched the Agwa in the river, Thozak, one of Soutoten's hunters, had appeared on the opposite shore. He ran out into the water, retrieved a Mascouten arrow, nocked it into his war bow, and fired, before hustling back into the brush.

It happened in an instant, but the three fishermen were adamant. Thozak had murdered Ounsasta. When Thozak learned that his onerous deed had been witnessed, he took refuge in the Killdeer clan longhouse, confirming his guilt. The Killdeer longhouse was a traditional sanctuary. Despite Thozak's treachery, he could never be removed by force. Thadayo and Winona were trying to resolve the matter with the Owl clan.

Hiatsou and Poutassa refused to leave the gold lodge. Not even Winona could persuade them to come out. Because the dead all died by violence, special rituals had to be performed if their souls were to have any chance of finding the pathway in the sky. With no shaman available, Tsohahissen suggested that Shanoka perform the rites. She refused—at first. She knew all of the Attawondaronk rituals, but her own beliefs told her that their fears were unfounded. Souls would find their way, as long as the bodies were whole and not desecrated.

She walked haltingly through the plaza, stopping to console wives and mothers. They didn't say it, but their eyes implored her to help. Their grief and foreboding invaded her conscience. Shanoka glanced from face to face and then stared down at the empty husks that had been her friends. She had little desire to perform the strange ceremony, but she was needed.

The bodies would not be taken to the burial platforms—allowing the flesh to decay from the bones, as was normal. Nor would the bones be retrieved, cleaned, and hung in the lodges, as a place for the soul to reside until it was released at the Festival of the Dead. Instead, the bodies would be cut up and the flesh burned from the bones, an appeal to the manitos so they would assist these souls in finding their way.

Shanoka was reluctant. In her own belief, there would be little chance of their being accepted to the Village of Dead after their bodies were butchered. It was much more likely that their ghosts would remain to wander the town at night, eventually entering another body. Perhaps an unborn baby would have the soul of Watea or Kadak, and they could redeem their chance to enter the Village of the Dead.

Despite the casualties, Ounontisaston's losses were minor compared to the defeat inflicted upon the Mascouten. The town wouldn't likely be attacked again by water. The warriors of Khioetoa had arrived, bearing the heads of the Agwa who'd escaped the dogs. Armloads more were hacked from bodies in the river. To Shanoka's disgust, the heads were being mounted on poles throughout the town.

Runners were sent to Tontiaton and Kandoucho to warn that enemy fugitives were being hunted in the land. Runners traveled faster than canoes. Trackers were following the Agwa who had escaped, but only a handful of trails could be found.

"Never have I seen so many dead Agwa," Kadaji said with a grin, slapping Sannisen on the shoulder as they watched the grisly trophies going up. Sannisen had purposely left the bodies in the river. He knew Shanoka hated this victory tradition. She found the macabre display revolting and would stop it if she could. Kadaji and his men felt differently.

Sannisen studied the Bird clan men who were celebrating with the Land clans. Although he found their actions over the past day reprehensible, at least they'd finally fought to save Tsohahissen. A spirit of camaraderie was everywhere. He decided it was best to withhold judgment for now. It was a time to rejoice, to reconcile. He couldn't spoil it. A light touch on his arm snapped him from his reverie.

Shanoka smiled up at him. "Soutoten and I have been discussing something."

"What have you been doing with my wife?" Sannisen asked, grinning and arching a brow at Soutoten as he walked up.

Soutoten chuckled at the inference. "We've done well today, my friend," he said, beaming. "People will sing of this for generations." He swung his eyes to Shanoka. She nodded for him to continue. "We felt that all other matters should be set aside today to let the people celebrate."

Sannisen shifted his gaze to the plaza. Men stood in huddles, recounting their prowess during the fight. Hands arced through the air describing flights of arrows; arms rotated around each other like canoes spilling their dead. Women of the Land and Bird clan moieties chattered, bubbling with pride for husbands and sons who'd saved the town with their brave deeds. Like the tug of a tumpline, Sannisen's eyes were drawn to the dead and settled on Ounsasta's face. It was difficult to be elated with his friend and mentor lying there with an Agwa arrow through his heart.

Soutoten squeezed Sannisen's shoulder reassuringly. "Ounsasta would want to see the celebration before he goes."

Sannisen looked into Soutoten's eyes. "You see into my thoughts again."

"The death rituals can wait for tomorrow," Shanoka said softly. "Their spirits need not hurry. They can celebrate with us tonight."

Sannisen rubbed at his temples. "If you are certain of this, I will ask Tsoha's approval for a victory celebration tonight."

Shanoka looked over Sannisen's shoulder as Hiatsou poked his head out of the gold lodge. Slowly, he stepped outside. He pulled a rabbit robe snug around his neck as if a chill was in the air. She thought she saw a faint smile when he noticed Ounsasta lying in the plaza.

"Go back in your lodge where you are safe!" an angry voice called out.

"You nearly had us annihilated!" another cried. A barrage of insults flew at him, and Hiatsou wilted beneath the onslaught. He slunk back into the gold lodge and hooked the doorskin firmly to the doorposts.

"Your spirit shield protects only the gold lodge!"

Shanoka studied the faces of the people hollering, observing that many were Bird clan. "Sannisen …" she said slowly, "I must also go to Tsohahissen's lodge to tend to his wound. See if you can locate the other chiefs. Bring them with you when you come."

"None of us have slept, Shanoka. Can't it wait?"

Shanoka stared thoughtfully at the gold lodge. "No," she answered flatly and started for Tsoha''s. At the door, she dipped her chin to the sentry, requesting permission to enter. Tsohahissen was sprawled on his sleep platform. Yadwena had his leg elevated on a luscious black-bear hide. The crackling hearth fire gave the lodge a cheery feeling. Despite his injury, Tsoha' was in a bright mood.

Shanoka started peeling away the rabbit swaths and tangle moss she'd applied to the knee earlier. "I'm pleased that you're feeling well, Tsoha." Shanoka leaned close to inspect the wound. "You're lucky—the arrow didn't hit any bone. It sliced the two large tendons behind your knee, though." She pressed her fingers around the wound. There was swelling and a huge blue-black bruise, but the flow of blood was staunched. "We shouldn't need to cauterize."

Tsohahissen pursed his lips, exhaling through cavernous nostrils. "Good," he grumbled. "I wasn't looking forward to that."

Shanoka looked to Yadwena. "I'll need warm water and more rabbit skin for bindings. Could you visit the longhouses and get me some?" Yadwena smiled as she turned to go. Shanoka followed her to the door. "Take your time," she whispered. Yadwena nodded and ducked out. *She's happy again,* Shanoka noted, watching the doorskin drop behind Yadwena.

Shanoka returned to her patient, laying her medicine bag down beside him. Untying the thong, she pulled out several small pouches and some bundles of soft hide and arranged them on the bedding. Unplugging a hollow corncob vial, she swiped a finger around the rim. The green paste inside was made from a mold she'd scraped off decaying squash rinds. Shanoka smeared it on and around the wounds. "Sinew heals very slowly. Sometimes it shortens, making it impossible to straighten the leg."

Tsohahissen studied the green paste with interest. "Are you saying that I won't be able to walk again?"

"I'll have some side braces fashioned," Shanoka laid a comforting hand on Tsoha's shoulder. "They'll hold the leg out straight. If your knee does lock up, at least you will be able to walk on it."

The sentry poked his head inside. "Tsoha, it is Sannisen. He has Soutoten, Thadayo, and Ahratota with him."

Tsohahissen gave Shanoka a puzzled look. "I'll ask them to return later."

"It's all right, Tsoha'. I asked them to come."

Tsohahissen seemed confused. He started to ask something but stopped himself. "Enter, Sannisen!"

The doorskin slid aside, and Sannisen and the other chiefs ducked in. Tsohahissen indicated the floor mats, and they folded themselves down. He nodded an informal greeting to each man and turned to Shanoka. "What is this about?"

Shanoka had misgivings about the magnitude of what she intended to say. She searched her mind for the best approach. The silence grew uncomfortable. Sannisen pulled out his petun pouch, offering some to the other chiefs and giving Shanoka time to think. By the time the pipes were lit, she'd decided how to begin.

"The Ojibwa tell a story of a long-ago time when people lived in a land between mountains of ice. The sun never set in this land, always riding on the horizon in a perpetual twilight. Plants wouldn't grow, because the soil never thawed. The only food came from animals that the men hunted. One day, people started getting sick. Many died.

"Some holy men appeared, saying that they'd come to save the people. If the people gave them lodging, food, and skins, the holy men would drive out the evil spirits that had fallen upon them. The men who hadn't fallen ill gave the holy men everything they asked for, until the people had no food to eat or skins to keep them warm. Still, the people grew sick and died.

"The hunters went to these holy men, asking for some of their food and skins back. The holy men laughed at them for their ignorance. When the hunters grew angry, the holy men changed shape, revealing themselves to be the monsters that lived beneath the ice. They chased the hunters but couldn't catch them. In their anger, the monsters hid the sun with snow and ice. The land grew cold and dark. The animals left. There was no food, except what the monsters had hoarded."

Shanoka swung her eyes across the bewildered faces of the chiefs but decided to push on. "The people prayed, and a seer came. His name was Master of Breath. He convinced the people to rise up, fight, and kill the ice monsters. Master of Breath told them to take back their food and skins and follow the animals. They would lead them to a bountiful land where food grew from the earth, and there would be trees to build shelters and rivers teeming with fish. When they reached this land, the sun returned."

"That is a good story, Shanoka," Thadayo sighed wearily, "but why are you telling us this?"

Shanoka wet her lips, wondering if she was handling this right. "I tell you this story, because the Attawondaronk shamans have become like those ice monsters of long ago. They've been allowed to become too Powerful, creating false beliefs in order to control the people."

"Shamans are held in high regard among all nations," Thadayo objected. "The ways of your people are just different."

"Since Sannisen took me as his wife, the Attawondaronk are my people," Shanoka shot back.

"I think perhaps they've heard enough," Sannisen said. He began to get up, but Tsohahissen stopped him with an outstretched palm.

"Let her finish, Sannisen."

Shanoka dipped her head in deference to Tsoha', then turned back, her face pensive a moment. "You are right Thadayo. Some shamans have real Powers. They commune with the spirit world—see the future—can even dream themselves into other times and places. Many cure sicknesses of the soul, and a chosen few, like my mother, have all of these abilities."

Shanoka looked from face to face. "The Attawondaronk shamans—our shamans—are all men like Hiatsou; men unwilling to hunt, or fish, or make things with their hands, so they've become shamans. They've kept your archaic beliefs alive to increase their own stature and bend the nation to their will." Shanoka turned, looking into Tsohahissen's eyes. "Yesterday, the clans were ready to fight each other because of them. Today, the manitos have granted us a reprieve and shown us a way out of this morass. The Attawondaronk must alter their destiny, or they will destroy themselves from within."

Tsohahissen steepled his fingers and stared at the floor. "Sometimes we dwell too close to our problems to see them clearly. You've lifted the fog that has obscured my vision." He rested his chin on his fingers, squinting at Shanoka with a conspiratorial grin. "You see a solution to this problem?"

Shanoka nodded. She explained her idea. She talked longer than she'd intended, but details kept occurring as she went. The men listened politely until she was finished. Her eyes settled on Tsoha' to see his reaction.

"I believe you should go now. Let us discuss what you have said." Tsohahissen was staring into the depths of the fire, lost in thought. He sounded to Shanoka as though he might be tired ... or angry.

"I hope I haven't offended by speaking this way. I know it is not my place to say such things, but I believe all that I have said to be true, and I fear this may be our final chance. Too much Power unlocks the monster that lurks in every human soul. The shaman society has grown into our greatest threat." Shanoka dipped her head, backed to the door, and ducked out.

When the sound of her footsteps faded, Sannisen broke the silence that pervaded the lodge. "I'm sorry, Tsoha'. I knew this would come up someday, but I expected to discuss it with you over time. She didn't mean to question—"

Tsohahissen raised his hand, cutting Sannisen short again.

"Don't apologize for her, Sannisen. I believe she is the smartest woman I have ever known."

Shanoka spent the rest of the day directing preparations for the victory celebration. She kept glancing over at Tsohahissen's lodge, but the chiefs remained in seclusion throughout the afternoon. She couldn't decide if the lengthy conference was good or bad, so she kept herself busy to allay her anxiety.

Several of Soutoten's men helped Shanoka move the bodies from the plaza up onto the parapet beside the north entrance. She seated the six bodies along the catwalk, covering them from the neck down with sleeping robes to fend off the night's chill. They would have a good view of the festivities and be out of the reach of dogs and creatures of the night.

The last of the winter stores were removed from storage huts. Corn, nuts, and berries, were hastily prepared for the night's feast. The warriors of Khioetoa decided to remain for the festivities. They carried in fourteen dead dogs from Snake Creek and the feeder creek as their contribution to the meal. Shanoka was thankful for the extra food. She had the dogs piled at the back of the plaza.

Sannisen's warriors were still scouring for any sign of enemy fugitives. Young warriors were sent back as the search area widened beyond the Tranchi. Shanoka saw Ontarra and Toutsou coming through the south entry and waved them over.

"Your mother wants us," Toutsou said, pointing and changing course for the plaza. "Do you think they'll find the rest of the Agwa?" Toutsou scrubbed his hands together, trying to remove the river mud caked on them.

Ontarra was distracted. Something he'd seen was nagging at him. One of the men who had escaped left a handprint on the muddy bank of the Tranchi. The hand had only one finger and a thumb. He had a vague recollection of a man with a mangled hand, but the memory eluded him. It slowly dawned on him that Toutsou had asked him a question. He met Toutsou's amused gaze with a blank stare. "What did you say?"

Toutsou snorted a laugh and shook his head. "I swear, sometimes you have the attention span of a shit fly."

The men who had built the new longhouse were busy sorting out poles and bark into usable and unusable piles. They griped good-naturedly as Ontarra and Toutsou walked past. With laughter and guffaws, the men belittled Ontarra and Toutsou for their wrecking skills and apparent lack of pride in their work.

"It came apart like a child's hut," Toutsou said with a grin. "Besides, we were in a hurry."

"Ontarra! Toutsou!" Shanoka called. "Get some help and dress out these dogs so they can be spitted!"

Ontarra and Toutsou traded a look, Ontarra's lips twisting into a lopsided frown. Toutsou's shoulder's sagged, and he threw his lower lip out in a comical pout. "I was just getting used to being idolized for my admirable exploits … and now this?"

Shanoka rolled her eyes at the sky and propped a hand on her hip. "Wallow in your vanity later. Right now, you'll have to settle for entrails."

They walked over to the dogs, muttering humorous epithets under their breath. Toutsou's mood changed abruptly when he saw his dog in the pile. He tugged him out. Tenderly stroking his muzzle, he pressed the eyelids shut. He studied the wounds and then checked a few of the other carcasses. "Head wounds—they clubbed them with their paddles." He twisted around, staring at the gold lodge, and then ran his eyes over the heap of dogs again. "Poutassa's bitch isn't here."

Ontarra glanced over and saw the tether hanging limp at the back of the lodge. "I hope her memory is short, and she forgets this place."

Toutsou looked down at his own dog and shook his head. "I hope her memory is long, and she returns with a vengeance."

The day went fast. Despite all of the work, Ounontisaston brimmed with bantering and laughter. Shanoka was on the parapet, adjusting Ounsasta's position, when the chiefs finally came out and split off toward their own lodges. She could see Sannisen was preoccupied as he negotiated the paths toward their lodge. Shanoka wrapped another robe around Ounsasta and climbed down.

She jostled through the bustling plaza to the pathway in front of the longhouses. Everyone smiled, greeting her as she passed. Bird clan men and women, who had avoided her in the past, now met her gaze with admiration in their eyes.

This is different, Shanoka thought, acknowledging the praise with quick dips of her chin. She had to admit that she liked it.

Shanoka ducked inside the lodge. Everyone was home. Sounia dabbed at cuts on Ontarra's cheek and shoulder as they spoke to each other in low voices and enjoyed each other's presence. Shanoka chuckled to herself when she overheard Ontarra asking Sounia if she could smell a foul odor emanating from his sleep platform. Sannisen stripped and shamelessly poached water from Sounia's bowl to clean away his own grime. Taiwa sat on the big sleep platform, shoving Teota to the back every few moments to keep him out of everyone's way. Shanoka turned Sannisen around once to check for wounds. She was pleased to find none.

"Do I pass inspection?" he laughed, pulling a breechclout from a pile on the floor.

"Yes," Shanoka said, tugging him to her. She rested her head on his chest in a loving embrace. "Did my ideas offend anyone?" She rolled her eyes up to see his answer.

"You're quite persuasive. They agree with you."

Shanoka rewarded Sannisen with a radiant smile. Breathing a relieved sigh, she lay her head down again. "I'm amazed at how little we suffered. When the Fire People got into the town, I thought we were finished."

Ontarra grinned at Shanoka as Sounia wiped at a gash on his ribs. "I think if you'd had more rocks, you could have finished them all for us."

Shanoka tossed Sounia the corn-cob vial. "Put some of this on the cuts."

Sannisen stared at Shanoka. "You did that? I counted six dead Agwa lying among the rocks at the south entry."

Ontarra chuckled. "Toutsou and I got a couple, but Mother busted a lot of heads with those rocks." He shook his head as he remembered the sounds. "I couldn't see the hits, but I sure heard them. It sounded like rotten squash were raining from the sky." Shanoka shot Ontarra a disgusted look that told him to keep his imagination to himself.

"It seems our lodge is full of heroes tonight," Taiwa bubbled, holding Teota back with one foot.

"I want to get down!" he whined, jabbing a foot back belligerently.

Ontarra started to pull on fresh leggings, but Shanoka stopped him. "We need to make a good impression tonight." She flashed a mysterious smile at Sounia, reached under the sleep platform, and pulled out a wicker basket. "I was saving this for your wedding."

Ontarra slid the lid off the basket. Speechless, he lifted out the identical leggings and tunic that she'd made for Sannisen many cycles ago. The buckskin was almost white; the tunic was covered in quill and beadwork, with long frills dangling at every seam.

Sounia held the tunic to Ontarra's chest. "You'll be so handsome," she said softly. Unable to take her eyes from Ontarra, she tilted her head toward Shanoka, asking, "How do you make them white?"

Shanoka's smile deepened. "It's a secret I learned as a child." She laid a bundle on Sounia's lap. "Open it," Shanoka said, dipping her chin at the package.

Sounia undid the thongs and folded the buckskin wrap aside. She gasped as she held up a white dress.

Shanoka's eyes sparkled with delight. "It matches mine."

It was difficult getting everyone dressed within the confinement of the lodge. Ontarra stepped on hot hearth stones more than once as he wriggled and cursed his way into the snug skins. Taiwa and Teota giggled from the safety of the sleep platform as they watched his contortions. Taiwa's laughter faded when she saw how striking her family looked together.

The men's tunics and leggings were an identical cut. When they raised their arms, tapered frills hung like wings. Geometric patterns of beads and quillwork on the chest slanted down and inward, suggesting the wood slat armor that the warriors sometimes wore. Shorter frills ringed the hem at mid-thigh. The leggings fell to the ankle, covering most of the thick hide moccasins that laced up to mid-calf, but the similarities ended there.

Ontarra's clothing was decorated in a green-yellow-orange combination, and the skins were fresh, with no wrinkles or stains. Sannisen was decorated in red-yellow-black. The elbows and knees were stretched and stained from use. The frills on his right arm and leg had locks of human hair tied to them. The right legging also had three red handprints, warning others that he'd purposely touched enemies three times without killing them. Turkey feathers were tied to the frills on the left arm, as symbols of specific exploits. Some had wedge-shaped notches cut out of them. On others, the tips were cropped off at various angles. Some were split down the center of the quill, and three had scalloped edges.

"What do they all mean?" Teota asked.

Sannisen held his arm up for Teota's inquisitive eyes. He pointed to the ones with a tip cut off. "Each of these shows that I killed an enemy. This one shows that I killed an enemy but was wounded. Here, I tracked an enemy and killed him for revenge. This split one shows that I was wounded many times in a fight but still managed to kill my opponent."

"You missed the best one," Ontarra said, beaming as he reached over and held up a feather with the tip cut off and three triangular notches out of one side. "No other warrior in our nation has this one. It means he was attacked by three men, killed them all, and wasn't wounded." Sannisen smiled as Teota puffed up with the pride he felt for his father.

"How do I look, Taiwa?" Sounia held her arms out and turned. The hem of the dress hung to just below her knees; a ring of frills swayed with every motion. Her moccasins laced up her leg to a hand-width below the frills, leaving just enough bronze leg showing to highlight the white buckskin. The sleeves were snug, widening out into loose cuffs just below her elbow. Finger-length frills where sewn into the seams on each side of the dress from cuff to hem.

Taiwa stared from Sounia to her mother and back again. The beadwork on the women's clothing matched their mates' in color and design. As the four stood together, the overall impression was one of a pride, confidence, and unity. For the first time in her life, Taiwa felt envious of someone's clothing. "You all look magnificent," she said softly.

"I wouldn't want to dress like this too often," Ontarra muttered, spreading his arms out self-consciously.

"Just often enough for people to forget how we look so they find it impressive again," Shanoka agreed. She motioned for Sounia to sit on a stool She began weaving a bead-studded braid into her hair. Shanoka tied the end with a hide lace and draped the thick braid over Sounia's left breast. Then she started braiding her own hair. "It's not vanity; it's symbolism. If you appear confident and Powerful, people will believe that you are."

Teota wriggled past Taiwa, escaping to cling to Shanoka's leg. "I want some clothes like that, Mother."

"When you and Taiwa stop growing, I'll make you some; I promise." She hugged Teota. "Tonight, I want you both to watch the ceremony with Toutsou's mother." Shanoka glanced over at Taiwa and held her eyes until Taiwa nodded reluctantly. "We'll be busy, and I don't want to be worrying about either of you."

"I'm not sure I want to see what they do to the prisoners anyway." Taiwa looked into the coals of the hearth fire, wringing her hands as she remembered another Agwa prisoner at the old town.

Shanoka lifted a brow and turned to Sannisen. "You took prisoners?" Sannisen exhaled wearily and rubbed at his eyes.

"The Bird clan men captured two in the plaza," Ontarra answered for him. "They tied them up and put them in the sick lodge, so the women wouldn't beat them to death."

"So they can do it themselves tonight," Shanoka said in a dejected tone, lowering herself onto a sleep platform. She looked up at Sannisen. He remained silent, turning to face the wall to avoid her eyes while he finished wiping his face with damp rabbit skin. "Sannisen, there's been enough killing this day. You should persuade the people to adopt them. They're brave young men. They'd be an asset to the community. The family of the Lynx clan warrior who died could adopt one, and the Owl clan could replace Ounsasta."

Ontarra shook his head. "We could never trust—" he began, but Shanoka shot him that look again, and he clamped his mouth shut. Sannisen held up his hand to stop her. "I can do nothing to prevent it. It isn't just the Bird clans that will want them tortured—it's everyone. They're Agwa; they killed our people. It is the way it has always been." Sannisen walked to lift Shanoka to her feet. "Perhaps someday we can make such changes. Tonight we will be concerned with other matters."

Footsteps padded down the outside of the lodge, and there was a rustling at the door. "Sannisen? It's Thadayo. May I enter?"

Sannisen looked into Shanoka's eyes. She forced a defeated smile. "Yes, Thadayo," Sannisen answered. "Come in." Thadayo lifted the skin and slipped inside, his eyes widening when he saw the stunning clothing. "What is it, Thadayo?" Sannisen demanded, uncharacteristically abrupt.

"The ceremony is starting," Thadayo said, "and the people are asking for you." He met Sannisen's eyes. "And I thought you might want to know about Thozak." Sannisen jerked a curt nod. "The Owl clan has demanded sixty gifts as retribution. Thozak can't pay, and he has no family. He's Turtle clan, but they refuse to pay for him."

Sannisen folded his arms. "Why did he do it?"

Thadayo canted his head, his face rearranging into a bewildered expression before answering. "It seems that Thozak believes Ounsasta was his father. He claims that Ounsasta bedded his mother but refused to marry her ... and he never acknowledged Thozak as his son." An awkward silence followed.

The muscles in Sannisen's face tightened. "This is unfathomable." He fixed Thadayo with a perturbed stare. "Is it true?"

Thadayo shrugged. "He obviously believes it. We don't know who his mother is, and Ounsasta can't tell us." Sannisen shook his head and stared at the floor. Thadayo studied the disturbed look on Sannisen's face, wishing he'd left this news for later. He decided not to ask for direction on the matter as he'd intended. "I'm sorry I troubled you, Sannisen. This can wait until morning." Thadayo turned to leave.

"Wait, Thadayo." Sannisen exhaled a long breath. "You must find a way to appease the Owl clan and bring this to an acceptable conclusion. We can't afford more internal conflict right now." Thadayo nodded and disappeared.

Sannisen eased down onto a sleep platform. He stared off at some distant place byond the wall, and shook his head. "A spurned mother rants to her child, and he mindlessly murders a great man."

The sun settled into its tunnel in the west with a fiery display, splashing a lofty row of fish scale clouds with streaks of crimson. Hundreds of eyes in the plaza were drawn to the heavenly spectacle that seemed to reflect the day's events. It lasted for only a breath of time, and then the splash of color sucked back into the horizon, inexorably drawn into a halo of dying light. The sudden curtain of twilight insinuated the fleeting nature of life in the minds of the prisoners, Tonqua and Huana, as they watched their last sunset through the cracks of the sick lodge.

The entire populace of Ounontisaston was crowded into and around the plaza. People from outlying camps had stayed for the victory celebration. Warriors of Khioetoa crowded together along the north palisade, anticipating a night of vengeful and entertaining torture. Enough food to feed the throng was spread out on skins near the skeletal remains of the new longhouse. Hiatsou and Poutassa remained hidden in the gold lodge. Sannisen instructed the apprentices to light the ceremonial fire. Excitement grew.

The two prisoners were brought out. Battered and already covered in cuts and bruises, their arms were tied behind them with tethers of rawhide. They were led on hemp ropes tied around their necks to prevent a sudden dash for freedom. They held their heads high, an attempt at bravery, but terror animated their eyes. They longed now for the ease of a sudden death in battle, wondering what weakness had allowed them to be captured.

Their captors dragged them through the crush of Attawondaronks. Women and children darted forward, brandishing sticks with ends heated to glowing ember in the fire. People poked, jabbed, burned, and beat them as they passed, using digging sticks, walking sticks, and hoes. By the time they were lashed to the war posts, their faces were covered with welts and burns that already were erupting into watery blisters.

The angry tumult of shouts and oaths diminished momentarily as the crowd cracked open, allowing the family of Sannisen to enter the plaza. The opening flowed shut behind them as they walked, appearing to press them forward into the circle of firelight. The babbling died away, replaced by awed murmurs of astonishment at the wondrous white clothing. Sannisen walked up and stared into the eyes of one of the Agwa.

The young warrior Huana stared back with frightened contempt. He felt a mixture of awe and fear as the Petun war chief who had planned Kadona's downfall peered into his soul. The big man was calm … serene. Huana could read nothing in his eyes, but the woman beside him held pity in hers. *Kadona was a fool to attack these people.*

Impatient voices in the crowd urged Sannisen to begin the torture. Sannisen turned his attention to the people who engulfed the plaza. He gripped Shanoka's hand in his, watching as Sounia and Ontarra joined hands. Together, they raised their arms in a show of unity and pride in the day's victory. The crowd went wild with shouts of joy, reveling in their imagined invincibility and the obvious superiority of their people and their leaders over all enemies. Sannisen raised his free hand for silence, waiting as the pandemonium died away.

"I thank you for the honor you bestow on me and my family. Today, we have proven that with courage and harmony, we can overcome all odds. I am proud of all the clans of Ounontisaston who have this day given us a great victory." The plaza exploded into cheers again. Sannisen waited. "Tsohahissen was wounded today by the intruders. He is old and weary. He tells me that with this wound he can no longer handle his duties. I ask you to let me shoulder this weight for him by taking on the responsibilities of chief of chiefs."

"This is not the way our chief of chiefs is chosen!" Winona forced her way into the plaza. "You cannot trick us and usurp control without the consent of the Bird clans. You insult us again with your scheming half-truths!" Winona shook her walking stick in the air. "Why is Tsohahissen not here to tell us this?" She waved the walking stick around the circle of spectators to prove her point. "Never will the Bird clans allow you to become chief of chiefs!" Winona spat on the ground at Sannisen's feet for effect.

In his younger days, Sannisen would have wrung her bony neck. Now, he returned an icy stare. "Then I must tell you tonight." He lifted his eyes from Winona to the crowd. "I have made a decision that saddens me. Everything that I have done in my life has been for the benefit of the Attawondaronk Nation. My family and I have decided to leave Ounontisaston to start a new town." The sudden silence was deafening. Stunned faces flickered in the firelight as people tried to understand the full import of his words. Sizzling hardwood sputtered and popped as sinuous flames twined sparks up into the night sky. The eerie screech of an owl rent the stillness—it came from up near Ounsasta on the parapet.

A Lynx clan warrior broke the spell. "Sannisen, this is the greatest town in our nation. Why do you wish to leave us?"

"I must leave, to end the conflict that has nearly destroyed us. This matter must be resolved here—tonight—or we will leave tomorrow to start a new town. I know a place. It will be stronger and some day more Powerful than Ounontisaston." Sannisen swung his eyes over the throng. "I cannot remain here and fight my own people. Those of you who wish to come with us are welcome."

People mumbled among themselves. Heated words were exchanged. Shanoka watched the animated discussions, noting that the Bird clan men were quiet, even as they looked gloomy and dejected. The debate raged. As the initial shock wore off, people began shifting left and right, breaking into Land clan and Bird clan groups. Soutoten walked out into the firelight. He raised his eyes, sharing a hopeful smile with Sounia and Ontarra before joining Sannisen. He turned to the townspeople.

"I follow Sannisen, wherever the path leads me, either as chief of chiefs or to a new town."

Ahratota and Thadayo walked in to stand behind Sannisen and Shanoka to show their support. Land clan warriors and hunters followed. Ahratota's men pushed through and crowded around their chiefs. In a rush, all of the Land clan families surrounded the family of Sannisen, prepared to follow him anywhere.

Shanoka scanned the Bird clan faces. Many seemed prepared to cross over, but none was willing to be first. As time stretched, her heart sank. The Bird clans outnumbered the Land clans. They would have to leave Ounontisaston unless they received more support. A woman stepped from the Bird clan group, cradling something in her arms as she sidled through the crowd. *Kabeza!* Shanoka allowed herself an inward smile as she watched the mother of Owl clan approach.

Kabeza walked straight to Ontarra, flashing a warm smile, before she turned so everyone would hear her words. "Owl clan wishes to honor Ontarra for defending Ounontisaston when others would not." The men of the Bird clan moieties sheepishly hung their heads at the pointed reference to their behavior. She turned to Ontarra and handed him Ounsasta's war club.

"Owl clan asks that Ounsasta's spirit be reincarnated into the body of Ontarra." Kabeza raised her arms to the twinkling stars, shouting it to both worlds. "Owl clan stands with Sannisen!" Astonished, Ontarra held the war club like a newborn child, afraid the slightest movement might damage it. Kabeza whispered to him from the corner of her mouth. "Hold it like a warrior, up above your head—the way Ounsasta would."

Ontarra waved the club in the air. With a sudden inspiration, he imitated Ounsasta's war cry. Owl clan men and women screamed their approval. They rushed across the gulf that separated them from the Land clans and were greeted by joyous hugs and back slaps.

A few of the unmarried Bird clan men inched toward the breach and then dashed across, joining their Land clan lovers. Some of the Bird clan maidens ran after them. The warriors of Khioetoa joined the Land clans—Kadaji wrapped his arms around Sannisen and Shanoka before stepping back to stand with the other chiefs. Winona watched in desperation, all her hopes and plans melting across the plaza in ones and twos. All of the chiefs and three-quarters of the people now stood with Sannisen.

"No!" she screamed. "You cannot fall for this! No one is to move until I return!" She spun around, stomping with amazing agility and amid a flurry of oaths, to the gold lodge, as her walking stick stabbed at spectral enemies all around her.

The blistering shrillness of Winona's voice rose from the depths of the gold lodge. The whole town listened as she vented her rage, sounding as if she was chastising an unruly child. In a hand of time she reappeared, herding a subdued Hiatsou ahead of her. As they passed through the Bird clans and into the plaza, Hiatsou molded a haughty visage. A hush fell as all eyes followed the pair. Hiatsou tromped up to Kabeza, throwing his face in hers in an attempt to intimidate. "What have you done?" he hissed.

Kabeza leaned forward, sticking her nose a finger's breadth from Hiatsou's. "Just saved us all from you, I think."

Hiatsou turned on Sannisen. "You cannot do this! It is not proper! The clans must propose a chief of chiefs, and the council must approve him!"

"I believe that has already been done," Shanoka said, waving her arm around the people standing with them.

Hiatsou's swept a caustic glare over the faces around Sannisen. Then he shot a glance behind him at the dwindling knots of Bird clan people siding with the Killdeer clan. When he turned back, his left eye had developed its twitch. "Fools!" he shouted. "You have fallen under the spell of this witch!"

Sannisen had been waiting for such an outburst. "So, you make unfounded accusations against my wife? What is your proof?"

Hiatsou searched his mind for something he could use, but anything he said could implicate him instead. His scheme hadn't had time to work yet. Sannisen waited, but Hiatsou was tongue-tied.

Sannisen folded his arms across his chest. "I am sick of all your blatant innuendoes," he said, fixing Hiatsou with a malignant stare that would chill the soul of even the bravest men in the plaza. "It is time we settle this—with personal combat." As Sannisen walked toward Hiatsou, Hiatsou pulled Winona between them. Sannisen's eyes narrowed, a contemptuous smile thinning his lips. "I haven't slept in two days, Hiat'. Perhaps you'll get lucky."

Winona yanked her arm free and tried to shove Hiatsou forward. "Fight him, Hiatsou!"

Hiatsou sidestepped, staring past Sannisen to the people who had turned on him. Rage boiled in his eyes. "Do you people *really* believe that it was Sannisen who saved this town? Do you think a few boys and women could have done this? Or do you see the work of the manitos in the Agwas' defeat?" Hiatsou scowled disparagingly and shook his head. "My appeal to the deities is what gave us this victory!"

People started mumbling and nodding their heads. It was miraculous that so few had died. The spirits had obviously been with them in this fight. Shanoka scanned the crowd for the warriors awaiting her signal. When she spotted them, she jerked a nod. They disappeared into the darkness.

To the right of the plaza, the crowd split apart. Four warriors carried Tsohahissen into the circle of light. He was seated on a stool that braced his back, so that his wounded leg could be held straight out in front of him. Sannisen could see Shanoka's skill in the braces and hide bindings that immobilized the leg.

The warriors set Tsohahissen down in front of Sannisen. People whispered among themselves, speculating whether Sannisen might have overstepped his bounds. Tsohahissen looked at Hiatsou and Winona. His eyes shifted, studying the number of people who had sided with their war chief. A hush fell over the plaza. Tsohahissen's normally stern expression slowly broke into a broad grin. He grasped Sannisen's hand and raised it to the crowd.

The plaza exploded with whoops and screams. Ontarra and Sounia couldn't hide their proud smiles as the joyous uproar reverberated through the town. Sannisen glanced up at Ounsasta seated on the parapet. He seemed to be smiling. Sannisen couldn't help but smile back. Tsohahissen had purposely withheld his show of support until it was clear that Shanoka's plan would work. If Sannisen had been forced to leave, Tsohahissen would need to remain, despite Shanoka's warning that his life expectancy would not be enviable under those conditions. Now the issue was decided … unless Hiatsou wished to fight.

Sannisen's family and all of the chiefs turned their attention to Hiatsou and Winona to see what the answer would be. The tumult died down. Winona stared at her feet in despair, leaning on her walking stick with both hands to support herself. An air of anticipation hung over the plaza. Hiatsou began shifting uncomfortably.

"I will not fight to save your miserable hides!" His voice was hoarse with anger. "Have you forgotten that this outsider woman has brought a curse upon us? Sannisen will not be able to protect you when the demons of the netherworld come and hunt you down!" Hiatsou spun around and stomped back to the gold lodge. Winona followed, hobbling back to the Killdeer longhouse, looking older than anyone could remember.

People in the plaza stared at Shanoka, wondering if they'd made a mistake. But it was done now, and only time would tell. Tsohahissen broke the tension by handing Sannisen a bag of trophy feathers, cut and notched by the Land clan women and then blessed by Shanoka. Sannisen studied Shanoka as she eyed a group of Kadaji's warriors who already were growing unruly, intoxicated by the days carnage and the prisoners at their mercy.

"We've already accomplished much," he whispered. "We should leave the rest for another time."

"No," she answered firmly. "We agreed that we must make changes. It should begin tonight." She held the bag up for people to see and called out in a loud voice to get everyone's attention. "I have the trophy feathers that have been earned by acts of courage and bravery this day! First, I will call upon Soutoten, our hunt chief!" Soutoten and four of his men pushed through the crowd, each carrying a large skin folded into a burden bag. The bulging hides were obviously heavy. The men stepped into the firelight and faced the gathering.

Sannisen dipped his chin, and the bundles fell open. Agwa heads, pulled down from the poles around the town, tumbled across the ground. The gruesome, bloodied, and broken faces; murky eyes fixed with empty stares; and mouths frozen in ghastly grins of sudden death got everyone's attention. Kadaji's men let loose with whoops and war cries that echoed off the palisades.

Huana was horrified. His friends and comrades were spread like gory refuse around his feet. He was shocked that so many had died on the river.

Sannisen picked through the heads until he found one that he remembered. He'd toppled the man from a canoe that morning with a well-placed arrow through the neck. Reaching down, he twined his left hand into the hair. With three quick slashes of his knife, he peeled off a patch of scalp the size of his fist and held it high over his head. "This will be our trophy of a kill in the future!" He shook the shock of hair at the bewildered warriors. "Smoke them over a fire, and add them to your war bundles! Or hang them from your waistband, if you wish! Never again do I want to see fetid heads brought into our towns to fester and rot and haunt us with their ghosts."

Silence hung ominously in the air. The crowd wasn't sure they liked this change of ritual or—more important—if the manitos would like it. Sannisen waited for a reaction that never came. He nodded to Ontarra and Toutsou, who had already removed the scalps of their victims. They started to dance, twirling around the fire with a trophy in each hand, and singing of their feats against the Agwa. They sang of their desperate dash to the town, of barricading the entries, of the fight at the south entry, and of the death of their enemies by their own hands.

The mood was infectious, and others joined in, happy to forget about curses and vengeful spirits for a while. Warriors began sorting through the heads to find their trophies. None would be taken unless the warrior was sure of his kill. To embellish upon one's feats would bring disgrace upon his entire clan. The warriors started dancing and singing, goading the prisoners by shaking the hair of their comrades in their faces. Knives were unsheathed. Tonqua and Huana were nicked and poked but not seriously injured, lest their senses be dulled before the torture.

"Did you think you could come here and defeat us?" a warrior sang as he slid his knife into an Agwa nostril, pulling slowly until the flesh separated in a spurt. "Did you think we would not capture you or torture you?" People laughed, clapped their hands, and started consuming the food that had been neglected during the standoff with Hiatsou. They chewed on dried fish and peeled succulent strips of meat from the spitted dogs. Sannisen kept a close eye on the heads as warriors skinned their trophies with growing zeal. When the mutilating ended and attention was focused on the prisoners, Sannisen gestured to Soutoten's men. They quietly removed the remains and trudged down to the Entry River to dump them.

Some of the older women pulled fagots from a fire and darted through the dancers to sear the flesh of the captives. The stench of burning hair and skin pressed the crowd back. Children, emulating their elders, ran in to swat and kick at the prisoners. A glowing firebrand was lofted through the air. It tumbled end over end, raining cinder and ash. Ontarra yanked Sounia from its path just in time. It smacked and clung to Tonqua's chest. Despite his frantic efforts to shake it off, it stuck, sizzling for several heartbeats before sloughing away with a swatch of fried skin.

People watched curiously as Shanoka had a heated conversation with the chiefs. The men apparently were disagreeing with her—they gave their heads abrupt shakes. Finally, they seemed to give in. Soutoten shrugged his shoulders and walked away, as if he wanted no part of it. Sannisen stepped over to the dancers, raising his hands to stop them. The warriors were ready for a rest anyway. They headed for the food.

Sannisen turned to the crowd. "Shanoka has a suggestion that she wishes you all to consider."

Shanoka strolled to the fire where everyone could see her. "My people!" she shouted above the din. "I want you to consider adopting these two young men into our community." Everyone stopped what they were doing; hundreds of eyes fixed on her with stunned disbelief. Shanoka swung her gaze over the slack-jawed faces. Everyone wondered if they had heard her right. For the first time all evening, Shanoka felt awkward and out of place. She decided to press on.

She raised her arms, quelling the murmuring that started to rise. "The clans that lost men in the battle can replace them!" she reasoned. "They would be an asset to our community!"

"They are Agwa!" someone hollered. "Are you crazy?"

"They'd murder us in our sleep!" another voice yelled. "Hiatsou was right—you will bring a curse upon us with all your crazy ideas!" Angry voices erupted from all directions. The mood began to feel menacing.

Shanoka shook her hands above her, but she'd already lost control. She could no longer be heard above the bedlam. Sannisen strode to her side. "You tried, Shanoka. It's just too soon—they aren't ready for this. Let's return to our lodge."

Shanoka looked up in frustration but realized that he was right. "Quiet them for me, Sannisen. Please." Sannisen looked into her pleading eyes, and sighed. He called for quiet several times. Gradually, the mob calmed down enough for Shanoka to be heard. "Do as you will!" she yelled. "I will ask no more of you tonight! But remember this …" She waited for the uproar to die down so she wouldn't need to yell. Then she swung her eyes across the shapeless faces. "All things are connected. Every life touches another. Anything we say or do comes back to us!" She put her arm around Sannisen's waist. They pushed through the crush of bodies without looking back. Ontarra and Sounia grasped hands and followed.

The doorskin of the gold lodge fluttered, and the edge peeled back a crack. The interior of the lodge was in utter darkness. Firewood hadn't been replenished since the Agwa attack. Wavering light from the ceremonial fire shimmered on bottomless black eyes and danced across a thin hooked nose. Other features of the face were hidden in shadow. The eyes darted around the activities in the plaza. People rarely talked to Poutassa anymore, because of those eyes. Something had been lost from them in childhood. They were cold and empty, seeming to draw anyone down into their depths, leaving a chilling impression that the soulless eyes of a weasel or ferret had been misplaced in a human face.

Poutassa listened to Hiatsou's heavy breathing in the bowels of the lodge behind him. Hiatsou had come back from the plaza, crawled into his robes, and escaped reality in sleep. Judging from past experience, Poutassa knew that Hiatsou would remain in his robes for days.

He watched Sannisen and his outsider bitch leave the festivities. His putrid cousin and Sounia followed. Sounia was the most beautiful girl he'd ever known. He felt the familiar urge and reached under his breechclout, caressing the trophy feathers dangling around his scrotum.

Someday I will add a feather for you, Sounia. He stared back into the lodge to where Hiatsou lay, oblivious to the world. *He can never stop me. I will take whatever I desire.* The doorskin dropped back. Poutassa picked his way through the darkness with uncanny precision, through the door, and into the back room. He skulked over to his platform and got into his sleep robes, succumbing to his rabid fantasies and the relentless craving in his loins.

The warriors of Khioetoa started the torture without delay. It was decided to mangle one of the Agwa and make the other watch. This approach had the added benefit of saving one for entertainment in the morning. Women and children were allowed to burn him with firebrands to see if they could break his will. Huana stoically resisted the pain until most of his skin was black; the acrid smell of burned flesh filled the air. When the warriors peeled his fingernails off, he could stand it no longer. Agonized screams rang through the town as each nail was torn away.

Sharp chert sliced ragged gashes into his biceps and thighs. Firebrands were thrust into the gaping wounds to stop the bleeding—and to agonize. An imaginative young warrior expanded on Sannisen's idea and removed the Agwa's scalp. The crowd roared with laughter at the ludicrous sight. Hot coals were laid on his skull. The pitiful wretch howled in agony.

When it appeared that he might pass out, water was poured over him to revive his senses. Hiatsou's apprentices used small sticks to locate nerves in the arm and leg wounds. With practiced precision, they slowly drew them out. When the nerves could stretch no farther, they snapped them with a quick yank. The creature tied to the war post no longer resembled a man. His head lolled on his chest, the strength to hold it up long gone. All that existed was pain.

Kadaji saw that the time was right. The Agwa watched in helpless horror as his abdomen was opened and several arm-lengths of intestine were drawn out. Kadaji began cutting out finger-length pieces and tossing them to the warriors, who popped them into their mouths and gulped them down, ingesting the man's Power and courage.

Shanoka sat at her hearth fire, softly caressing the prayer stone cradled between her palms, trying to close her mind to the ghastly sounds out in the plaza. The gruesome shrieks tore at her soul. She started to tremble, feeling each new horror. The family had fallen onto their platforms fully clothed, instantly dropping into the deep sleep of exhaustion. Ontarra and Sounia were wrapped in each other's arms on a platform meant for one.

Shanoka tried to concentrate as she prayed for the spirits of all the dead. Today would change so many things. Together, they would be a family of Power such that the Attawondaronks had never known—of that she was certain. Whether this was good or bad, she couldn't decide. She held no feeling of elation. Something still nagged at her mind—a vague concern, just beyond reach at the edge of her consciousness. She shook her head to rid herself of it. "Perhaps it will always be this way," she sighed wearily.

Suddenly, she realized that the torture had ended. All she could hear were ragged moans. He'd be left to suffer through the night and be burned at dawn, so the searing flames would drive his spirit away from the town. Shanoka felt the overwhelming anguish of her failure to save the young man from this horrible fate. Her eyes overflowed, tears tracking down her cheeks and dripping in soundless spatters onto her prayer stone.

8

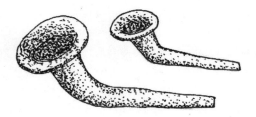

Low fog clung to the water, shrouding the three trade canoes in swirling eddies that flowed like the river itself. Manak was careful to keep sight of Matoupa in the lead canoe. Nothing seemed to exist beyond the murky mists. The only sound Manak had heard since dawn was the whirling sloosh of paddles drawing water, and the labored breathing of the men around him.

Cold beads of moisture dripped from his nose and chin, and his clothing was soaked through. Manak glanced up, surprised to see a clear blue sky above. The world still existed up there. Trees poked their branches up into sunlight that had burned the upper layers of mist away, leaving only the river valley trapped in ghostly vapors. Leafy branches seemed to float on the rolling white wisps. The sepulchral sound of disembodied voices drifted through the impenetrable haze up ahead.

Matoupa called out in the strange language that he used when they met people along the river. He canted his head, trying to hone in on the phantom sounds. *Thwack!... Thwack!* A sharp rapping came from the right. Matoupa swung his dugout toward it.

"What's happening?" Manak asked in a low tone.

"We've reached the City of the Ancients," Matoupa answered softly, his attention still fixed on the drumming sound guiding them in. Like a surprise attack, the shoreline was upon them. Despite their slow speed, the canoes pounded to a lurching stop, throwing everyone into the trade packs and brace rails. Shapes materialized from the mist, and the canoes were heaved up onto the bank.

"Greetings." Matoupa returned to the language of trade. Manak was always amazed at how much of this dialect involved hand movements, reinforcing the meaning of the clicking words. "We have come from far down the Father Water and request permission to enter the city."

As Matoupa babbled his gibberish, Manak took note of their surroundings. They were beached at the confluence of a small river that flowed into the Father Water from the east. As the sun worked at thinning the mists, Manak glimpsed the outlines of several strange canoes lining the bank upstream. He strolled up and inspected one. It was shorter and wider than the dugouts he'd known all of his life. Instead of being hollowed from a single log, it was fabricated from a thin white material molded over a frame, sewn with sinews and sealed at the joints. He lifted the bow and was astonished at how light the craft was.

"It's birch bark." Matoupa's voice startled him. "Kaskaskia. They strip it from trees in sheets and then wrap it around the frame. They build their lodges in the same manner."

Manak shook his head. "You'd never get me into one—too flimsy … dangerous." Manak stared past Matoupa's shoulder as two of the men who greeted them climbed into a canoe and headed up the tributary.

Matoupa shifted his head in their direction. "They're going to ask permission for us to come in."

Manak studied the warriors remaining from the corner of his eye. "There's only four left. My men and I could kill them in a heartbeat, and we can get on with it."

Matoupa covered his face with a hand and took a long breath. Rubbing at his eyes as if they suddenly pained him, he let out a weary sigh. "You've got to stop talking about killing people all the time, or you're going to get us killed. We are a long way from home, so try to be … prudent." A whistle shrilled in the distance.

One of Matoupa's men materialized from the mist. "We can continue," he said. Then he turned and melted away again. They returned to the dugouts and pushed off. Matoupa gave a final wave to the sentries guarding the river mouth and swung east up the stream. The fog was lifting rapidly now. As it dissipated, Manak was surprised to see a forest of dwarfed trees on both sides. The thick trunks indicated they'd reached maturity, but they weren't half the height they should have been. Large areas of marsh encroached into the miniature forest.

"What has happened to the trees here?"

"These are the old crop fields of the Ancients," Matoupa answered softly. "The holy men of that time were arrogant and boastful. They didn't bother to ask the spirits for fertile soil. When the crops stopped growing, they hoarded food for themselves. People took sides, warring on each other. The deities couldn't stop the killing, so they cursed this place. Everything has grown stunted since."

Manak glanced around at the eerie forest, suddenly realizing how cold he was. He started to shiver. "How much farther is it?" he asked anxiously. "I'm freezing."

"About two arrow-flights and we'll be at the old city. The trading town is just beyond."

They paddled in silence. Manak marveled at how far the old crop fields stretched. As they rounded a bend, a monstrous silhouette towered up over them. The base was barely discernible through the mists, but the top was so high that bright sunlight illuminated it. Manak's throat constricted as the shadow of the gigantic structure fell over him. Matoupa and his men grinned at each other, watching the awestruck faces of the warriors.

Mox craned his thick neck to see the top. "What is it?" he asked, unable to believe his eyes.

"It's the temple mound of the Ancients." Matoupa strained to suppress his grin. "The old city lies just beyond it, in ruins. The deities are reclaiming this place. One story says that there was a great reckoning. The people were all wiped out from this world, and their spirits are trapped in the mounds sitting everywhere around us."

Manak couldn't tear his eyes from the huge monolith. Its shape was distorted by saplings and brush growing from the sides and protruding from the top. The sheer size was overwhelming. It made his skin crawl. As he stared at the intimidating earthwork, Manak heard illusory voices. He thought he could hear dogs barking. The smell of ancient hearth fires struck him. An involuntary shudder ran up his spine, sending a chill through to his bones. Voices came again. "Do we need to go in there?"

"No," Matoupa assured him with an amused grin. "The new town is up ahead." He savored Manak's discomfort a heartbeat longer and then drove his paddle down and surged upstream. The voices in Manak's head grew louder. They rounded a bend, and a cluster of wattle-and-daub huts hove into sight. The town sat at the apex of a fork in the stream. People and dogs milled together over the entire area.

Manak was disgusted with himself for his apprehensions, studiously avoiding the eyes of his companions as the dugouts slid in to shore. He stepped out into knee-deep water and sloshed up the bank, instinctively scanning faces for any that had the look of trouble written on them. From where he stood he could see hundreds of people, busy chattering and dickering over piles of trade goods. This was clearly a place where any animosities were set aside. The only fighting was for profit.

Matoupa greeted some men with his bizarre hand signals. They grinned and helped him pull the dugouts to dry ground. Manak turned his attention back to the town. A temporary village had sprung up behind the permanent dwellings. There were curious domed huts made by bending saplings and covering them with hides. Others built in the same fashion had tall pointed tops with poles projecting out from a smoke hole at the peak. In the woods, simple lean-tos were erected. In several places, poles were lashed between two saplings, with a skin draped over and tied to form a simple roof shelter in case of rain. The shapes and styles of canoes along the river were as unique as the shelters.

Manak glanced over at Matoupa as he renewed friendships. Then he turned to study the old city. Across the river, the mounds were clearly visible now. The gigantic mound was surrounded by several smaller ones; all were eroded, succumbing to time and neglect. Even the smallest of them jutted well above the forest of stunted hardwood that surrounded them. He swung his gaze from horizon to horizon. There was no end to the old crop fields. Only to the west, across the Father Water, could he see where the dwarfed forest ended and a line of regular trees began.

Small clearings in and around the old city appeared to be ponds. They seemed familiar. It dawned on Manak that they were the borrow pits for the earthen mounds. The land around Quizquiz was peppered with similar holes, but at Quizquiz the holes were still raw—nature hadn't been given the time to reclaim them yet.

"Are you going to help with these packs or just stand there and gawk?" Matoupa yelled.

Manak took a final look, turned, and strolled back. He shook his head at Matoupa as he hoisted a pack to his shoulder. "They must have been giants."

"The legends say that all the people of the earth once lived here," Matoupa said as he walked toward the trade huts. "So many people that the whole city was built in one cycle. The few who escaped the wars and the Final Reckoning were scattered to the corners of the earth, becoming all the diverse peoples who now inhabit the world."

Manak's brow furrowed skeptically. "You mean that the people who once lived here were our ancestors?"

Matoupa dumped his packs against a post that supported the bark roof of the trading area. He turned to Manak and shrugged. "That's what the legends say." Matoupa strolled up into the trading area to view the goods on display.

Manak looked over at the old city again, gave his head a shake, and followed Matoupa. He was amazed at the quantity of items spread across the ground on skins. There were ornaments and jewelry of copper, highlighted with stones in colors he'd never known. There were stone carvings, pipes, weapons, and beads; splendid clothing with fantastic designs rendered in bead and quill; feathers of every size and color; and other exotic items whose purpose he could not even comprehend. Everyone was chattering and dickering at once.

Manak felt uncomfortably out of place here. There were too many people—he couldn't keep an eye on them at one time. People bumped and jostled into him, wandering behind him as if they thought he was harmless. He felt an urge to crack a few heads and end this mind-numbing babble. His temples started to throb as his jaw muscles locked up. He saw Matoupa beckoning from the next hut. Manak rammed, jarred, and elbowed his way through the chaos, relieving a bit of his tension.

The second hut held larger items—huge skins from animals bigger than Manak had ever seen before, woven baskets, pottery with strange designs, and piles of tobacco bricks. Manak tried to hear what Matoupa was saying but could barely understand a word above the din. He was in a heated discussion with another trader over tobacco. The trader listened attentively to Matoupa, trying to calm him down while squinting suspiciously at Manak. The man was tall but poorly muscled. His shifting eyes made it obvious that he didn't like the look of Manak. Manak disliked the man instantly.

"He's with me," Matoupa assured the stranger. "Let's go some place quiet and discuss this rationally."

The three walked out into sunshine and strolled toward the temporary village of travel huts. As the racket died away behind them, the trader began talking to Matoupa in a language that Manak hadn't heard before. He'd recently begun to understand a bit of the trade language; it irked him to hear a new one. "What are you speaking?" he demanded.

"We each know enough Tuscarora to talk to each other," Matoupa answered. "The trade language is too restrictive to express yourself properly." They reached a lean-to, and the stranger gestured for them to be seated at a small fire that was smoldering. They folded themselves down around it. The trader perched on his haunches, stirred the coals, and added some wood. He pulled a pipe from his tobacco pouch and tamped in a dark wad. Lighting it with a stick from the fire, he drew too hard. The pungent smoke caught in his throat. When he finished coughing, he blew smoke to the sky and earth and then sprinkled some tobacco on the coals for the spirits. He handed the pipe to Manak, watching warily as he copied the ritual. Squinting at Matoupa, he asked, "Your friend is also Tunica?"

"The word is Yoron," Matoupa said flatly, taking a draw and handing the pipe back to the trader. Manak noticed that the man had three fingers missing. "Manak," Matoupa said, inclining his head, "this is Dekari." The stranger closed one eye, dipping a curt nod of greeting as he passed the pipe across the fire. "He tells me he has been unable to obtain the seed that he promised me," Matoupa continued. "He does have twenty bricks we can have." Manak glared at Dekari, his hand dropping to the knife at his side. Matoupa grabbed Manak's arm. "We can obtain enough to last a long time."

"Twenty bricks is not enough to pacify Fanacia!" Manak shouted. "She wants seed, so we can provide for ourselves. You've dragged me all the way to this cursed, forsaken place for nothing!" Manak fixed Dekari with a deadly stare. "And this pissant is going to pay for his deceit!"

"Let me talk to him some more. We may be able to work something out." Matoupa glanced at Dekari across the fire. Dekari's eye was jumping nervously from the knife to Matoupa, wondering what he'd gotten himself into. "We were counting on you, Dekari. My companion thinks he should put an end to your miserable existence. Are you certain … that you cannot obtain the seed?"

Dekari realized he would have to make the Tunicans understand. "The people who grow it guard it with great tenacity. I almost died trying to get you that seed. Is it worth risking one's life for?"

"We've already risked our lives for it, many times over." Matoupa felt a surge of anger. He considered letting Manak have his way. "It is of great importance, Dekari. Can you get it or not?"

Dekari glanced at Manak. The venomous eyes sent a cold chill through him. For the third time this season, he was gripped by the feeling that he might not live out the day. His mind jumped to Pokagon and the losses he'd incurred in the spring. He was getting too old for the demands of this life. Being a trader wasn't as safe as it used to be. No one could be trusted anymore. He sighed and looked over at Matoupa. "The nearest place that we can get the seed is a half moon cycle journey overland. Do you really wish to endure such a long trek?" He shifted his gaze to Manak as Matoupa translated. Manak nodded without hesitation.

Dekari saw by the lack of discussion that the seed was of great value to them. Despite his precarious position, he had to ask. "What will I get in return for taking you there?" He listened intently while Matoupa spoke in Tunican. Manak shot a disgusted look at Dekari. He stood and walked away. "Your friend is not an easy man," Dekari muttered in Tuscarora. "Why are you traveling with a warrior?"

Matoupa eyed him. Was Manak's character so readily apparent to everyone? "It's a long story," he sighed, rubbing his temples between a thumb and forefinger. "And it's been an even longer journey. He's a strange one, all right. He even makes me nervous. I would prefer to go back, but if Manak wants to continue, I'll have to go along."

"Why did he leave so suddenly?"

Matoupa shrugged. "I don't know. His thoughts are as elusive as the Uktena Stone."

Dekari raised an eyebrow, closing the other eye to focus. "What is an Uktena Stone?" he asked, trying not to sound overly interested.

For lack of something better to do, Matoupa explained the legend of the giant horned serpent, whose single eye was a yellow crystal that could bring any wish to the man who had courage to take it. Manak returned, interrupting the story. He was carrying four packs and laid one at Dekari's feet.

"Tell him that if he takes us to the seed—and we obtain it—that one is his."

Dekari listened to the translation. He reached down, untied the knots, and folded the skins back. His bad eye screwed shut; his good eye widened to a saucer shape. Dekari exhaled in a long wheeze. Two hands of greenstones, some as large as robin eggs, were lying on top. He unfolded a bundle full of black, razor-sharp teeth, shaped like arrowheads. There were beautiful pink shells the size of his fist, and a handful of long, black points flaked from obsidian. Another bundle was full of feathers in fantastic shades of green, blue, and pink. On the very bottom was a black-stone ax, its head and handle carved from a single piece of slate. It was more wealth than Dekari had obtained in his last three cycles of trading!

As he eyed the other three bundles, his greedy imagination ran wild. "Only four of us would be allowed to enter their territory at one time. We'd have to strictly abide by their customs," Dekari said softly, mesmerized by the bulging trade packs.

Manak listened to the translation and dipped his chin affirmatively. "We'll take Mox and send the others back with the tobacco bricks."

Dekari looked from Manak to Matoupa. Then his eye was relentlessly drawn back to the riches at his feet. "When do you wish to leave?"

Matoupa sighed and spoke to Manak again in Tunican.

A moon cycle had passed since the victory celebration. The people of Ounontisaston now referred to that night as the hair dance. The entire town was shocked and dismayed the following morning when they discovered that the tortured Agwa's throat had been cut during the night. The second Agwa had disappeared completely. Even the tethers that bound him were gone without a trace. Frightened speculation grew, in whispers and hidden conversations, that Hiatsou's dire warnings were already coming true.

Sannisen quickly quelled the rumors. He ordered a meeting of the new clan council. His warriors had discovered an abandoned canoe on the bank of the Tranchi opposite the stream the Fire People had used to approach the town. The spoor of two men led from the Tranchi to the shore of Lake Iannaoa, where a fisherman was found with his skull split and his canoe missing. Apparently, one of the Agwa returned to the town to cut his companion free.

The handful of days in spring on which the community had been disrupted had created extra work for everyone. The petun seedlings hadn't been planted on time. Weeds, which always grew better than the crops, were choking the young corn sprouts, and the sunflowers had to be hoed at once. Weeds sucked up precious moisture from the soil that the sister crops needed to survive. All the women of the community worked the fields from dawn to dusk for a hand of days, just to catch up.

The nets used to trap the invaders on the river had to be destroyed and new ones made to replace them. No one considered repairing the old nets. It was well known among the fishermen that any new nets would be jealous of nets that had captured men. They would refuse to simply catch fish. The tedious chore of weaving nets from sinew and hide caused the fishermen to miss the spring spawn when the fish were in shallow water. They would have to work diligently all through the short season to provide adequate stocks for winter.

Arrows and other weapons lost in the fight had to be replaced immediately in case there was a sudden reprisal. The Fire People's arrows were used only as trophies or as occasional schemes to make other enemies believe the Fire People had attacked them. The wrecked drying huts and longhouse had to be rebuilt. The common goal of putting the community back in order made everyone come together, and Ounontisaston was a happy place.

The first significant change that Sannisen made to the town's social structure was to create a clan council. Shanoka had seen this system when she lived among the Sennikae. A man was selected by the clan mothers to represent his clan at the new council. Meetings were held around a fire in the plaza every six days. Lively discussions animated the first councils, but rules of conduct were soon established. Every clan now had a voice and a means to solve disputes before they degenerated to infighting or personal animosities. Everyone liked this new system of decision making, and a spirit of cooperation quickly wound its way through all aspects of daily life.

The clan council reported to the tribal council through Thadayo. Tribal council remained unchanged; Sannisen's new status, undisputed. Thadayo's first report to the tribal chiefs was that the clans wished Sannisen to take over all the duties of chief of chiefs. They quickly approved Sannisen's idea to separate the duties of shamans and healers; this edict to be enacted immediately.

Shanoka avoided the first clan councils, fearful that she might be accused of interference. She attended the third and was granted permission to address the clan leaders. She made an impassioned speech in favor of adopting prisoners rather than torturing them, and finished with a second request—that the practice of killing all animals encountered during hunts be ended. She wasn't openly criticized, but a clear message was sent when the council unanimously rejected her pleas. No one, especially an outsider, would be allowed to meddle with the nations' long-held beliefs and traditions.

Word came in from Teotonguiaton. A girl had been attacked and partially eaten by a strange animal. Sannisen sent warriors to all of the towns that had shamans. If there was another attack of this nature, Sannisen would hold the head shaman of the town responsible. The attacks ended.

Hiatsou was forbidden to attend tribal council. The decree met with little opposition, since he'd rarely been seen since the night of the hair dance. Poutassa took up the daily rituals of greeting the sun and communing with the spirits. The rush to put the community back together made it necessary to cancel the summer solstice ceremony. Poutassa and the apprentices still made a big show of blessing the crops and thanking the manitos for fertile soil.

In deference to Ounsasta, no one was appointed Keeper of the Wampum. Tsohahissen agreed to perform the duties for the time being. Ounsasta's spirit would be reincarnated into Ontarra, and so, to Shanoka's relief, Ounsasta's body was not cut up and burned. He was taken out to a burial platform, which allowed the flesh to cleave from his bones in the normal manner. His soul could wander the town until the Naming Ceremony allowed him to enter Ontarra's body.

The Owl clan received no restitution for Ounsasta's murder, so they devised a novel punishment. A post was planted in the ground beneath Ounsasta's burial platform. Thozak was seated with his arms and legs wrapped around the post. He was lashed in that position and left. The summer sun quickly bloated and blackened Ounsasta's body. The stench was unbearable. Thozak wouldn't have drawn a single breath if he could have stopped himself. On the fourth day, the body burst. Putrid black liquid and decaying slime oozed and dripped onto Thozak.

A plate of food and some water were provided each day, but the bowls immediately filled with filth and corruption exuding from the corpse. Thozak tried, but he could keep nothing down. The food went untouched. As he neared death from thirst and starvation, the Owl clan relented. He had served his punishment—his tormentors had their retribution. They offered to adopt him into the clan. Thozak was a free man, but the indignity had been too much. Thozak left Ounontisaston forever.

The cool, unpredictable days of spring transformed into the sweltering humidity of summer. Corn was belly-high in the fields. Many people were sleeping on mats outside to avoid the stifling heat of the longhouses.

Shanoka pegged the doorskin back, happy for the slight air movement it allowed. She would have preferred to eat cold food outside tonight, but the whole family was coming to feast on a baked mooneye that Teota had caught. He'd become a very successful bait fisherman in a single moon cycle. He fished every day, rarely coming home empty-handed. With quick strokes of her palm blade, Shanoka removed the head and fins and then laid the big fish on the ground.

With a ladle, she scooped a hole in the center of the hearth fire, heaping the glowing embers off to the sides. She uncovered a flat rock that was buried a handspan down, widened out the opening to accommodate the fish, and then covered the rock with fresh corn leaves that Taiwa had liberated from the Killdeer clan's plot. Shanoka stuffed the mooneye's cavity with corn bread, leeks, and heads of clover, and then lowered it onto the hot slate. She covered the fish with soaked corn leaves and a layer of fresh earth before leveling the hot coals back on top.

Shanoka sat back from the heat of the fire and wiped her hands on a rabbit hide. She studied Taiwa, who was absently scratching marks in the dirt floor with a stick. Taiwa was taking more interest in her appearance lately. She was bathing regularly and combing the ratty tangles from her hair. She still dressed sparingly, but her breechclout was clean, and she always wore her moccasins.

"You're quiet, Taiwa. Is something troubling you?"

Taiwa's eyes snapped up with a start. She turned her attention back to her floor art. "I hardly see Sounia anymore." She made several agitated strokes in the dirt. "She's always with Ontarra."

"They are promised, Taiwa. It is the way of things." Shanoka laid a comforting hand on Taiwa's shoulder, glancing down curiously at the symbol repeated over and over on the floor—a cross within a circle. "She'll be here for evening meal ... what is that you're drawing?"

"I'm not sure." Taiwa exhaled a long breath. "It's in a dream I've been having. There's a man standing in the shadows, in the forest. I can't see his face. I ask him why he's watching me, but he won't answer; he just keeps staring. Some sunlight flits through the trees and flashes across this symbol on his shoulder. What do *you* think it means?"

Shanoka pondered the circle and lines and shook her head. She'd been trying to help Taiwa find the meanings in her dreams, but they were always so strange that she found them baffling. "Perhaps it is the four sacred directions, and he guards them," she mused. "Maybe he is Pierce Head, waiting to suck out people's brains on their way to the Village of the Dead."

Taiwa took a last look at the symbols and swept her hand across the dirt, obliterating them in frustration. "I don't know, but he frightens me. I wish he'd stay out of my dreams."

Shanoka chewed on her lip, ruminating as she watched Taiwa's troubled expression. "I have something I've been saving for you, Taiwa." Leaning under the storage area, she pulled out her wicker basket, found her mide bag inside and laid it on a floor skin. Gently untying the otter-head closure, Shanoka probed inside with two fingers until she located what she wanted. She laid it on her palm and held it out to Taiwa.

"Oh! It's beautiful!" Taiwa cradled the stone talisman on her fingertips. It was a thunderbird carved from dark stone, almost black, with two white buckskin thongs threaded through holes on each side.

"It belonged to my mother. I've been saving it for you. It protects its wearer from harm." Shanoka smiled, watching Taiwa tracing her fingers over the finely etched lines. "Here, let me put it on you." She wrapped the braided thongs around Taiwa's neck, tying them snug, so that the thunderbird nestled into the hollow of her throat.

Taiwa closed her eyes, running her fingers down the leather to the stone. She rubbed the thunderbird between her thumb and forefinger. "I can feel its Power," she said in a soft, enchanted voice.

Shanoka had the eerie sensation she'd seen this before. Had she dreamed it, or was the circle of life repeating itself? The image threw her back in time to Amikwe. She saw her mother deep in thought, rubbing the stone in the same way. Shanoka snapped back as Ontarra and Sounia came in.

"Sounia!" Taiwa jumped up and gave Sounia a hug that made her gasp. Ontarra pretended to pout. "Don't I get one?"

"Hmmph! You steal my closest friend, and you expect me to be nice to you?" Taiwa folded her arms, thrusting out her lower lip to pout in return.

"You may someday wish that you were nicer to me," Ontarra chuckled, settling down on his sleep platform and pulling Sounia down beside him. "Glouscap!" Ontarra screwed his face up. "What … is that smell?"

Sounia sniffed the air but then noticing Taiwa's choker, she asked "Where did you get that?"

"Mother gave it to me. It's my grandmother's protective talisman." Taiwa smiled and stepped closer so Sounia could admire it.

Shanoka looked over at Ontarra as she added more wood to the coals. "Your father says that you've been released from sentry duties until after the Naming Ceremony. Are the other young warriors angry about the extra duty?"

"No … except for Yadak. He hasn't spoken to me since the Bird clans refused to fight."

"He's just jealous of your new hero status," Sounia said with a scowl, "but he'll get over it." She glanced over at Shanoka. "Something else has been troubling me. When Ontarra receives Ounsasta's spirit, do you think it might … change him?"

"He won't change in a way that anyone would notice. Ounsasta's courage and skills will simply enhance his own. He'll take Ounsasta's name as an additional name, but we can still call him Ontarra. It isn't like the chief of chiefs, who always receives the spirit of the previous chief and then takes the name Tsohahissen."

"Will it hurt?" Ontarra blurted and instantly regretted it.

"Some say they can feel presence, but he's not going to talk to you, or control your thoughts, or make your legs move. It's a very simple ceremony and a great honor." Shanoka swung her gaze to Taiwa."I think Taiwa should perform the ritual. She's ready."

Taiwa rubbed the talisman between her fingers, an impish grin spreading across her face. "Yes, I will perform the ritual, and you have my word, Ontarra … you won't feel a thing."

Footsteps approached. Sannisen appeared at the door. "I have brought a visitor," he said, grinning at Shanoka as he ducked inside. Teota pranced through the door with a tall thin man in tow. The man straightened up, flashing a bright smile and nodding to everyone present.

"Togo!" Shanoka rushed to hug her stepfather, knocking her wicker basket into the hearth, where Sannisen rescued it from the flames. "I thought I'd never see you again!" She buried her face in rabbit-fur strips sewn into the chest of his tan tunic. She squeezed him in a tight embrace, rolling her head back to study him. "How did you get here? Why have you come?" She wiped tears from the corners of her eyes. "Here," she said, pulling a stool across the floor, "sit down."

Togo laughed and wrapped an arm around her shoulders. "Slow down, Shanoka. I haven't even met my grandchildren yet, except for the little fisherman here."

"I'm sorry, Togo … I just …" Shanoka palmed moisture from her eyes again.

"This has to be Taiwa." Togo reached out exceedingly long fingers, lifting both of Taiwa's hands to admire her. "She has her mother's beauty."

"She has her grandmother's beauty," Shanoka corrected.

Taiwa's initial embarrassment melted when she saw the twinkle in Togo's eyes. She dropped her hands and hugged his bead-covered waistband. "Togo, I've always wanted to meet you."

Togo eyes shifted to Ontarra and Sounia. He pried Taiwa off and made a fist with his right hand. Tapping the fist to his left shoulder, he opened the hand, palm down, and swung it in a level arc, left to right. "Ontarra, hero of the Attawondaronks, I greet you." Ontarra raised his eyebrows, looking askance to Shanoka.

"It's a warrior's greeting of the Sennikae," she explained.

Ontarra nodded, solemnly rose, and repeated the gesture. "Togo, trader of the Sennikae, holy man of the False Face, I greet you."

"He learns quickly," Togo said, flashing a toothy grin to Shanoka. He turned his attention to Sounia, who suddenly felt like an outsider with this stranger in their midst. "Sounia … Sannisen told me his son was promised to the second most beautiful woman in Ounontisaston, but now that I see you, I believe that your beauty rivals Shanoka's."

Sounia admired Shanoka over any other woman she'd ever known. Her face cracked into a skeptical smirk, but the compliment put her at ease. "I thank you for your kind words, Togo."

"Togo, sit." Shanoka hauled him to a sleep platform and forced his lanky frame down onto it. "We have a feast of baked mooneye ready. You can tell us of your travels." Sounia started brushing the coals back to open up the hearth. The fire was uncomfortably hot, so Shanoka and Sounia decided to serve the meal rather than letting people help themselves as was customary. Shanoka folded the corn leaves back and with a quick tug of her rock tongs, she peeled the skin off, revealing steaming white meat that flaked apart when it was touched. Shanoka ladled generous portions into wooden bowls and handed them to Sounia.

Everyone retreated to the sleep platforms. The lodge grew quiet as they gorged themselves on the savory meat and tangy stuffing. Teota's pudgy face radiated pride as he watched the enjoyment his meal provided. Shanoka refilled bowls as they emptied. As she handed Togo a second portion, she noticed a thick white streak of hair behind his left ear that she'd never seen before. His roguish eyes met hers for a brief instant. "A dog took offense when I saved a fox kit from its jaws. When the torn scalp finally healed, I was left with this white patch." He pulled it away from his ear for everyone to see. "It reminds me not to interfere with nature's ways."

Shanoka grinned, suddenly realizing just how much she'd actually missed the old scoundrel. "Togo, I calculate that you are fifty-two winters now. You're a little old for such journeys. Why are you here?"

"Age is a state of mind, Shanoka. I still retain the vigor and mostly black hair of my youth, and I credit the Attawondaronk petun for that. I smoke it daily to keep my mind clear and my body young." Shanoka's smile deepened, and she shook her head. He still had his penchant for exaggeration, embellishing every story. "We heard of a strain of petun being grown by a farmer named Kadak," Togo went on. "It was rumored to be of such potency that it was only used for religious and ceremonial purposes. The False Face Society sent me to see if I could obtain some. I tried Kandoucho, but they wouldn't trade the little that they had. They sent me on to Tontiaton."

The mention of Kadak saddened Shanoka, and her eyes fell to the floor. "Kadak is dead. His fields lay untended now. I fear that strain of petun will be lost to us forever."

Togo nodded. "Yes, I heard. I managed to get three bricks at Tontiaton. Sannisen tells me there may be more at Khioetoa, but I can't stay that long."

Everyone had eaten more than enough, but the smell of mooneye lingered in the air. They couldn't stop themselves from returning to the hearth and plucking juicy morsels that caught their eye. Sounia dug under a platform and found a fly whisk. She shooed flies from the meat as Togo rubbed his chin thoughtfully and then said, "At Tontiaton, they sang a song of Sannisen and Ounsasta, who massacred a war party of Fire People." Togo glanced from Shanoka, to Sannisen, then to his newfound grandchildren with pride in his eyes. "The ghosts of the invaders were condemned to the depths of the Tranchi, imprisoned with the okis for all of eternity. Ayontat told me that the family of Sannisen was now the chief family of all the Attawondaronks. He said the manitos have blessed this family and that the Attawondaronk Nation was destined to become the greatest of all peoples."

The lodge was silent as everyone contemplated what the future might bring. "It is good to hear what is being said and that the words are favorable." Sannisen steepled his fingers, trying to see ahead through time. He pulled his feet under him and straightened up. "I'm sorry, Togo, but I must return to Tsohahissen's lodge for a council meeting." He glanced at Teota's expectant face. "That was a great meal, Teota." Sannisen brushed himself off, belching politely before returning to his duties. The resounding belch put a proud grin on Teota's face. Everyone watching for his reaction grinned along with him.

"I'm sorry, Togo," Shanoka apologized. "He's been very busy."

Togo shrugged. "It's the price that comes with responsibility."

Shanoka nestled down next to Togo, hugging his arm. "You must stay a while and help to celebrate Green Corn with us."

"Yes," Sounia agreed. She felt she'd known Togo forever now. "Ontarra will be given Ounsasta's spirit."

"Oh?" Togo shot a quizzical glance at Shanoka.

"It is a custom," she answered simply.

Togo saw she didn't want to discuss it any further, so he changed the subject. "Taiwa," he said, looking at the talisman, "the last time I saw that was on your mother when we visited the chert mines at Ouaroronon."

Taiwa's face lit up. "Oh, tell us about the great cataract of Onghiara."

Shanoka gave Togo a disgusted look. "Well, I'm afraid we never saw it," she said.

Taiwa's face fell. "But you told us you went on a trading journey with Togo so that you could see it."

"Yes, but Togo insisted we get the chert first. While he was completing the trade, another group of Sennikae arrived, and they were very unfriendly." She shot another irritated glare at Togo, and he burst out laughing.

"I must say in my own defense that I believed those traders were in the west with the Mingo at the time. Besides," he said, smirking as he swept his arm around the room, "look at the wonderful family my little mistake created."

"Little mistake? You are insufferable!" Shanoka shook her head as she rolled her eyes at Taiwa. "It seems the Sennikae clans hold monopolies to trade with certain nations, and they will kill to protect their livelihood."

"They wanted to kill you?" Taiwa gasped.

Shanoka nodded. "They would have too, but the chert diggers stopped them. The death of Sennikae traders in their territory, even at the hands of other Sennikae, could cause a war, so they escorted us to Kandoucho for our own safety."

"I got to keep the chert too," Togo added with an impish grin.

Shanoka looked away, forcing herself not to laugh before continuing. "It was a tense situation, so Kandoucho sent us on to Ounontisaston, the old town, under the protection of Tsohahissen. We had to winter there."

Togo cut in, "There was a young warrior named Sannisen, who was very smitten by you, as I recall; created a lot of jealousy among the maidens."

Shanoka shot Togo a withering look. "What really upset them," she explained to Taiwa, "was that I remained aloof. The more he tried to impress me, the more I ignored him."

"Why?" Sounia asked, puzzled.

Shanoka's eyes took on a faraway look. She unconsciously caressed her lips with her fingertips as her mind drifting back to those days. "My mother's crystal rarely works for me, but it was quite clear about Sannisen—he was the one for me. As he was the son of Tsohahissen, I knew there would be opposition to his marrying an outsider, so he had to desire me above all others."

Togo looked at Shanoka with mock disgust. "So she tormented him all of that winter."

Shanoka was still staring into the distance. "It worked—he asked me to stay and share his lodge. Togo went back to Joneadih."

"I, for one, am glad that the deities have brought us all together," Sounia said. She stood, pulling Ontarra to his feet. "Come on, let's go for a walk."

Togo admired the happy couple as they slipped out into the twilight. He turned back to Shanoka. "What is this about putting Ounsasta's spirit into Ontarra?"

Shanoka looked tenuously at Togo and then at Taiwa. "Why don't you go to the Lynx clan lodge. One of the hunters has injured his hand, and he needs new dressings."

"But I want to stay and talk to Togo!"

"We will have plenty of time, Taiwa," Togo assured her. His spindly fingers gave her hand a squeeze. "I'll stay for Green Corn, so I can watch your ritual." He stood, grasping both her hands in his. "May I kiss your forehead, Granddaughter?"

Taiwa's face brightened; she leaned forward.

"Take Teota with you," Shanoka said softly. "Togo and I want to talk for a while."

"I knew she was going to say that," Teota said peevishly as he climbed down from his hiding place at the back of the big sleep platform.

When Shanoka and Togo were alone, Shanoka absently added more wood to the coals as she mulled over her thoughts. "The Attawondaronks believe that a soul can be reincarnated into another person after death," she explained. Her eyes remained fixed on the hypnotic shadows pulsing through the embers.

"Ounsasta is probably already at the Village of the Dead," Togo said, following her gaze to the coals. "It's strange to think he would wish to remain here."

Shanoka pulled her legs up and rested her elbows on her knees. She sighed, "Each nation has its own Village of the Dead and its own beliefs on how you get there—this is what they believe."

"Is it true that they kill any animal they come across, as if it were a spy?"

Shanoka nodded. "And they refuse to adopt prisoners taken in war." Shanoka reached for her prayer stone, positioning it on her palm as she talked. "They torture them all … even the women and children."

Togo thought about this as he assembled a long-stemmed pipe and tamped the bowl full. "I can see how these ideas would trouble you," he said as he lit the petun with a stick from the fire, "but it strikes me that you are well positioned to change some of this now."

Shanoka picked up Togo's lighting stick and stirred the embers with it. "I have already had some successes. Sannisen is on my side, but how long does it take to change the things people have believed in all of their lives? A generation? Two? It will take a very long time, I fear."

Togo blew smoke to the earth and sky. "You still have your prayer stone, I see."

"It's still my most precious possession; it comforts me." Shanoka propped the lighting stick between the hearth rocks and the coals to keep it glowing.

Togo could see that their discussion had saddened her and that she wished to be alone. He rose to go. "I will stay at Tsohahissen's tonight. He asked that I stay with him and Yadwena while I'm here." He turned back hesitantly when he reached the door. "Tell me about this baby potion."

Shanoka twisted to look at him. "Sometimes small deceits can correct great wrongs," she said softly. "Go along with it, Togo."

Togo nodded and ducked out into the night.

Poutassa sat cross-legged outside the gold lodge, his back propped against the wall, as he peeled the skin from a spotted frog. He liked the way the skin came off in long strips, and it was amusing to see the frog hopping around naked. Poutassa watched the people streaming from longhouses with their sleeping mats to escape the heat. Most would spend the night within the palisades. Well-armed younger warriors and hunters wandered out the north and south entries, heading for the privacy and solitude of the fields. Maidens normally would have followed, but they'd been ordered to remain in the longhouses since the attack on Rona, a precaution that Poutassa was finding stressful and irritating.

Absently tapping a finger on the point of his dagger, he tapped too hard and pierced the skin. He squeezed the fingertip and a droplet of blood formed. His mouth angled into a crooked grin. He rotated the knife and stabbed it into the ground, popping out a chunk of hard-packed soil. Hiatsou's gurgling snores started up again, intruding upon his thoughts.

Hiatsou had been in a daze since the Agwa attack. Poutassa liked it that way. He seemed to be accepted as a full shaman by the people now, at least for all the mundane rituals. He could make the plan work without Hiatsou.

It would be exciting. Sinister images threaded the twisted pathways of his mind. He could feel it—his time was coming.

He heard footsteps. Darting black eyes probed through the twilight. Two forms took shape, moving toward him. He drove the blade down, popping another chunk of soil ... waiting ... watching.

Ontarra and Sounia clasped hands as they strolled, careful to remain on the pathways to avoid the slumbering heaps scattered throughout the town. "Let's go down to the canoe area," Sounia suggested. She pranced ahead, straining to drag Ontarra along.

Ontarra tugged back. "Slow down. We don't want to stomp on someone." Sounia came to an abrupt halt and Ontarra thumped into her. He was about to ask what had startled her, then followed her gaze and saw Poutassa silhouetted in the filaments of moonlight that highlighted the gold lodge. "Come on," Ontarra urged her. "We'll go this way and won't have to walk past him." Ontarra turned down a path toward the south palisade.

When the path widened out enough so that they could walk abreast, Sounia pulled her hand from his and folded her arms across her chest. "I don't like how he looks at me."

"What do you mean?"

"He never speaks to me, but sometimes I catch him staring. It's like ... how a lynx looks at a rabbit before he pounces."

Ontarra snorted a laugh. "How would you know what a lynx looks like when he attacks a rabbit?"

Sounia caught herself. "Never mind. I don't want Poutassa spoiling our evening."

They exited the south entry and walked along the crest of the bluff. A three-quarter moon cast ephemeral light over the fields below. Cool evening air drew a mist from the Entry River. Wispy tendrils drifted through the trees, snaking through the sea of corn tassels and around the ghostly blackened trunks of the sentries. A whiff of river-scented air drifted up the bluff, rustling the leafy canopy overhead. Silvery moonbeams shimmered through a gap in the leaves, dancing across the hillside. The chirping of frogs and thrumming of insects filled the scented air. After a few moments, Ontarra's ears ceased to distinguish the sounds, and they became the rhythms of the night.

Sounia inhaled the fragrant air, perfumed with the heady smells of summer. "I love warm summer nights."

Voices of men, night-fishing out on the river, drifted on mellow puffs of air coming up the valley. Torchlights twinkled, flashing like giant fireflies through the treeline near the Tranchi. Sounia pointed to the star-splattered sky. "Look at the Pathway of Souls," she whispered. "It seems brighter than I remember."

Ontarra followed the hazy band that stretched across the heavens. "Atiskein Andahatey," he murmured thoughtfully. "It grows brighter each cycle as more and more souls tread upon it."

Sounia snuggled her beaver cape around her shoulders. Ontarra was about to ask why she had brought it on such a warm night, but her next words shifted his thoughts. "I wonder what the world looks like from up there," she murmured dreamily.

Ontarra smirked. "I believe I can wait to find that out. Let's go down to the river."

They picked their way down the bluff, trying to avoid trees and drying huts that suddenly loomed in the inky darkness. Sounia tripped over a shapeless lump. To her embarrassment, it grumbled and cursed her.

At the canoe area, some fishermen were unloading their catch before heading back out to the Tranchi. They tossed in more kindling for the basket torch, which extended from the bow to light the water and drew fish into range of their spears. The men pushed off and headed down the Entry River just as another canoe pulled in to repeat the process. The fishermen's wives were gutting fish and hanging them on smoke racks. Night-fishing would carry on all summer to make up for the missed spawning run.

Sounia folded her fingers around Ontarra's arm. "It's too busy here. Come with me; I want to show you something." They walked along Snake Creek, alone with the droning sounds of the night and their own whispers and laughter. The men's voices were soon lost in the hum, replaced by the gurgling flow of water rushing around rocks.

"Ontarra ... I don't want to wait any longer. We should be mated. I know that your spirit guide hasn't revealed himself yet, but we can't wait forever."

The mention of his spirit guide shattered Ontarra's mood. He felt guilty, as if somehow he was to blame. "Until I have full warrior status, I cannot support us," he muttered wearily. "We would have to live with your father or in the Wolf clan longhouse. I can't even use the community food stores. We have to wait."

"I know," she sighed, "but it's hard." Sounia looked up at the night sky. "We will need to build a lodge when we join, and the town is already filled. Where will we go?"

Ontarra brightened. He squinted toward the skyline in the southeast, but it was hidden by trees. "Let's cross the creek," he said. They slipped off their moccasins and stepped carefully through the calf-deep water, sliding on the moss-covered stones. Sounia shrieked when her foot settled on a crayfish. Ontarra clambered up the bank, hauling Sounia up behind him. When they sat to tie their moccasins, Sounia leaned over with a kiss so passionate that Ontarra almost forgot his purpose.

They pushed through chest-high sunflowers as Ontarra scanned the area to the southeast. Then they continued deeper into the crops. Ontarra stopped and pointed when they reached the center of the field. "There," he said, indicating a hulking shadow, like a giant turtle, on the far side of the Tranchi. "It's the hill at the bend in the Tranchi. The river wraps right around it."

Sounia leaned forward, studying the dark silhouette outlined against the blue-black sky. "It's the hill opposite the mouth of the Entry River. Taiwa says … a society of holy women will live there someday in a massive lodge carved from stone."

Ontarra dropped his arm to stare at Sounia's silhouette. Luckily, the dumbfounded look on his face was hidden in darkness. "Carved from stone? Well … I think it will be okay for us to live there until they arrive to contest our presence."

Sounia detected the sarcasm in his voice and wished she hadn't brought it up. "Would we be safe out there by ourselves?"

"Some of the young warriors and hunters have agreed to join us. There's room for several lodges and good fields for the crops. We can see Ounontisaston from up there too, and we'll be close enough to visit anytime we want."

"It sounds wonderful. Can we go and see it tomorrow?"

Ontarra rolled his eyes to the heavens with mock exasperation. "You're so impatient!"

Sounia walked farther into the field, ignoring the dew that soaked through to her skin. "I wonder what our children will be like," she whispered dreamily. "Ontarra, we can't marry and have our own lodge yet, but why don't we perform our own ceremony, right now? At least *we* will know that we are mated, even if no one else does."

Ontarra felt the guilt return. It was his fault that they couldn't marry. Now, Sounia was willing to accept a pretense of marriage. His shoulders sagged and his head drooped for a moment. Ontarra sucked a long breath, exhaling slowly.

Sounia turned him so that he faced her. Gripping her chest with one hand, she closed her eyes.

"Is something wrong?" he asked.

"No," she said softly, "just stand still. I give you my heart … to keep and do with as you may, as long as it resides in this world." Sounia pulled her hand from her chest. Extending her arm, she placed her open palm over Ontarra's heart. Ontarra felt a wave of emotion. He pulled her close for a kiss. Sounia tilted her head back, staring up expectantly. "Now you do it."

He didn't get the words quite right, but it was close enough for Sounia. She laid her hand over his when he placed his heart in her chest, a mischievous grin in her eyes. She turned and sauntered off as if nothing had happened.

"Wait—where are you going?" Ontarra asked.

"I wanted to show you something, remember?"

"It may not be safe out here. I didn't even bring a knife!"

"What? The hero of Ounontisaston is afraid of the dark?" Sounia snickered. "Did you know that people are calling you 'Bold Face'?"

Ontarra laughed. "Yes, because of that Agwa whose face I slashed. And they're calling Toutsou 'Silent Death,' because he's so lethal with that throw-stick of his."

Sounia perched her hands on her hips. The moonlight revealed every muscular curve under the damp buckskin dress. "So, Bold Face," she teased, "are you coming with me or not?"

Ontarra looked out across the fields. There was nothing threatening in sight. The only sound was the buzz of insects and a light rustling of sunflower leaves in the breaths of air. "All right."

They threaded through the field, careful not to damage any of the crop. When they reached a steep hillside, Sounia stopped and studied it. "Right here," she said, shoving some branches back.

"You want to climb up through this mess?"

"There's a path." She grabbed his hand and slipped into the brush. They climbed with their heads tucked down to avoid the grasping branches. In two fingers of time, they popped out onto a small ledge tucked into a boulder-strewn ravine that ran down from the crest above. "Look," Sounia said, pointing out over the valley.

Ontarra turned, and his breath escaped him. The towering palisades of Ounontisaston were clearly outlined against the star-dusted northern sky. To his right, he could see the hill on which he'd promised to build a lodge, with the basket lights of the fishermen reflecting off the Tranchi below. "It's beautiful. How did you find it?"

"Taiwa found it." Sounia suddenly felt a bit deceitful. "Don't tell her I brought you here; she wants it to be a secret."

Brush above the tumble of boulders rustled. An owl screeched in the depths of the forest beyond the brim and then burst into the air with a flurry of wings. Ontarra gripped Sounia's arm and squinted up the tumble of boulders. Sounia followed his eyes, half-expecting to see Slammer and wondering nervously if she had erred in bringing Ontarra here.

"It's nothing," she said as she laid her cape on the ground with the glossy fur up. "Just a raccoon or something." Sounia tugged her dress up over her head, and Ontarra forgot about the night sounds. Settling down on the fur, she gripped his fingers and pulled him to her. She peeled his tunic off and kissed his neck. He folded down beside her, caressing the sculpted curve of her hip and running a hand down her thigh. His fingers traced up along the big muscle of her inner thigh and explored the triangle of hair at the top. Sounia moaned, pressing herself against him. Her silky feel and musky smell intoxicated him, sending a shudder along his spine. Ontarra lost himself in her embrace.

He didn't notice the movement in the brush above this time. Poutassa leered at the two lovers below, a dagger rotating in his left hand.

Sounia fumbled at the cord that held Ontarra's leggings; he helped her get them off. She ran her hands over his chest and shoulders, sighing at the warm glow that seemed to emanate from the pit of her stomach. Ontarra pulled back suddenly. "We can't chance a baby right now."

"Shanoka gave me something to prevent a new spirit from entering," Sounia whispered.

Ontarra wondered how that could be but didn't have the will to argue. The night sounds faded as their senses turned inward. They thrilled each other with unexpected pleasures. Their excitement grew; their bodies merged in a rush of desire. Nothing existed beyond the frantic rhythms of their own flesh. In writhing spasms, they climaxed together and then lay breathlessly entwined in the warm afterglow.

Poutassa's breath came in ragged gasps. His pupils had widened to empty black holes and turned glossy and fixed. He shuddered, and the dagger tumbled to the ground. His seed dribbled out between his fingers, a glutinous strand oozing onto the chert blade in the grass. One of his headaches exploded in his brain. He fell on his side, muscles contorting in spasms as the world went black.

9

LUSH GREEN CORN STALKS, AS high as a man's head and draped in squash and bean vines, were a beautiful sight. For the women, the fields were a great source of pride. They bickered light-heartedly over whose plot had the tallest stalks and straightest rows. Green Corn ceremony would thank the deities for blessing the earth with fertility and providing the first fresh crops of the cycle.

From this time forward, the women's duties in the fields would change. Tilling and digging tools were stored away, replaced with hollow sticks, rattles, and skins stretched tightly over hoops—anything that could be shaken or hit to make noise. Constant vigil would be required to guard the crops from the hungry vermin sent by Glouscap, the trickster god.

Rabbits, squirrels, and raccoons would raid the fields nightly, stealing the budding ears of corn and tender bean pods. To deter the bandits, women would roam in squads, day and night, until the crops were safely harvested. Deer couldn't resist the smell of the corn. It overrode their inbred fear of man. They destroyed large sections of the fields if they weren't stopped quickly enough. When the women found an area invaded by deer, the hunters were summoned. Blinds were erected. Despite the scent of man everywhere, the unrelenting aroma of the corn lured the deer into the trap. They were usually ambushed the first night. Enough deer would be taken this way to keep fresh venison roasting in Ounontisaston for the remainder of summer.

In three more moon cycles, when the crops reached maturity, birds would become the main threat. Marauding flocks of blackbirds, crows, ducks, and even the black-head geese were drawn to the ripening kernels of corn and sunflower seeds. All the women took to the fields as harvest approached.

Green Corn ceremony was spread over three days. The first day was devoted to various clan dignitaries. They made speeches thanking the manitos for past, present, and future blessings. The second day was a day of dancing and fertility rites. Unmarried young men and maidens shuffled, twirled, and sang before wandering out the entries in pairs for a private liaison. Married men and women ate and gambled as they watched the choices of the young people. Future clan alliances were quickly approved or disapproved when the desires of the young people became clear.

The third day of Green Corn dawned beneath a hazy blue sky. The air was motionless. Smoke from the fires of Ounontisaston twisted and curled in a hundred pillars straight up into the sky, spreading out as the day progressed and forming a stationary gray slab the color of the slate cliffs near Teotonguiaton.

On this day, Togo was invited to sit with the families of the chiefs. He added to everyone's enjoyment by regaling his listeners with tales of strange places and escapades from his travels. He enjoyed his petun more than anyone Ontarra had ever known. His pipe was a palm-sized clay bowl with an effigy of an ugly man that stared down the stem at the smoker each time he took a draw.

The long wooden stem puzzled Ontarra. "How did you ever hollow out a wooden pipe stem the length of your forearm?" he marveled, absently leaning sideways to scratch his butt.

Togo glanced curiously at the scratching, shook his head, and decided to ignore it. "I've made these for years. It's something I learned by accident." Togo smiled as he tugged the stem out of the bowl so Ontarra could have a better look. It was slightly thinner than an arrow shaft. When Ontarra held it up to his eye, he could see light from end to end. The hole was dead straight.

"That's amazing." Ontarra gave his head a shake and handed it back. He started scratching again. "How do you do it?"

Togo's smile deepened. "You would have to *see* the process, or you'd never believe me. Many things in this world are not nearly as difficult as they first seem, Ontarra." Togo frowned. "Why do you keep scratching like that?"

"Mosquito bites."

"How did you get mosquito bites on your rear ... oh." Togo chuckled tactfully. He pushed the stem back into the ugly man's chin and touched a glowing twig around the petun in the bowl. "I like a long stem; it cools the smoke." He belched out a huge cloud that looked to Ontarra like it might block the sun.

Shanoka and Taiwa returned from a rehearsal of the reincarnation ceremony. "You're dressed formally for a change," Shanoka said, admiring Togo's clothing.

"Yes, I had to wear this outfit at least once, or I'd have carried it all this way for nothing." Togo stood and stretched his arms out to show off his tunic. It was made from buckskin. The hem dangled below his knees so that no leggings were required. It had no arms, just large openings at the shoulders, allowing air to move freely. Fabulous quillwork covered the entire front. A cap of black feathers crowned his head—not the long tail or wingtip feathers used as trophy feathers but short body feathers, with downy feathers intertwined. It was all very elaborate, but it had a far too female look for him, and Ontarra had to suppress a laugh.

The dancing started, and everyone's attention turned to the plaza. At regular intervals various male elders walked out, interrupting the dancers to give a personal speech of praise to the manitos. After several of these interruptions, Togo started to chuckle. Shanoka jabbed him in the back with her toes. He leaned over to Tsohahissen. "Sorry," he said, "it all seems just a little unorganized."

Shanoka shot Togo a good-natured scowl as she folded herself down into the line of women seated in front of the men. "Actually," she told him, "it is quite carefully planned to give the impression of spontaneity."

"Why have you and Taiwa been absent from the festivities these past two days?" Tsohahissen asked her as he slid his stiffened leg into a more comfortable position.

Shanoka turned so she could whisper. "It's the fleas and ticks. Anyone who's been sleeping on the ground is infested. We've been mixing lye made from corn ashes with bear fat and sumac. It irritates the skin but drives the parasites away."

"I think I'd sooner have the bugs," Ahratota whispered in Tsohahissen's ear, gingerly scratching at an angry rash running up his legs and into a loose breechclout. Togo choked on his smoke trying not to laugh and broke into a coughing fit instead.

Ontarra caught a whiff of the sickly-sweet aroma and screwed up his nose. "That is strange smelling petun."

"It's … uhuhhm … uhuhhm … called … hhmph … poquital," Togo choked out. "A blending of tobacco and other plants from a people that live far to the south, called the Konis, or Kohanis, or something. Some traders brought it last year. I'm growing my own from the seeds I found in the mixture."

"It stinks!" Taiwa held her nose with disgust.

Togo ignored her and puffed again. "I believe it has medicinal qualities."

Women arrived with baskets full of fresh green cornstalks cut in lengths of a man's forearm. Everyone grabbed a couple and started munching the stalks to get at the juicy pith in the center. "Your corn is almost as good as your petun," Togo said, grinning at Tsohahissen. He spit a fibrous green wad on the ground and chewed some more. The chattering of voices and songs died away as attention suddenly turned to the gold lodge.

Poutassa emerged, dressed in the regalia of a full shaman. He studied the crowd and then strode haughtily out into the plaza, aware that all eyes were following him.

"He has Hiatsou's turtle rattle and feather fans," Taiwa said in a hushed voice.

"It seems he's promoted himself," Sannisen grumbled caustically, starting to climb to his feet.

"Wait," Shanoka said, tugging him back down. "Everyone is just as curious as we are. Let's see what he does."

Poutassa wasted no time. He started dancing and gyrating around the plaza. People had to move back to give him room. He expressed his gratitude to the entire pantheon of spirit forces. He thanked the earth, the sky, the sun, the moon, and the wind, rain, and water. The other dancers seated themselves when he showed no signs of letting up.

He thanked the trees, the grass, the plants, and the flowers; he thanked insects, birds, fish, and animals. When it mercifully seemed that there was nothing left, he worked his way through the various manitos. Then he stopped and walked back to the gold lodge without explanation, leaving everyone bewildered and shaking their heads—but the entire town had just witnessed Poutassa as a full shaman, without objection. More important, everyone would recall exactly where he was today.

"He puts on quite a performance," Togo chuckled, tapping out his dottle and packing more poquital into the bowl. Sannisen shot Tsohahissen a sidelong glance and shook his head in disgust.

Tsoha' shrugged. "How his mind works is a mystery."

The chatter started up again while everyone waited for the ceremonies to get back on track. Shanoka nudged Taiwa. "This would be a good time." Taiwa looked over at the large crowd with reluctance. The number of people was intimidating. With a resigned look of acceptance, she rose, brushed off her dress, and pulled Ontarra to his feet. Hauling him along to the plaza, she plodded out to the war posts and turned to face the gathering. Shanoka held her breath.

Taiwa nervously rubbed the talisman around her neck but then raised her arms up to the sky. "Ounsasta!" she cried, pausing as if waiting for him to answer. "We know you are here among us! It is our desire that you enter the body of Ontarra, a hero of Ounontisaston! We ask that your skill and courage remain with us, to guide Ontarra and our people with the knowledge and wisdom of your accomplishments!" Arms still upraised, she whispered to Ontarra from the corner of her mouth. "Prepare yourself."

Ontarra's eyes darted around the plaza, but he saw no spirits nearby. Taiwa nudged him with her elbow. He tilted his head back and closed his eyes, raising his arms slowly until they canted at a stiff angle at his sides. He rotated his wrists until the palms faced forward.

"He looks like he's waiting for an arrow through the heart," Togo mumbled with a soft chuckle. Shanoka twisted around and glared at him.

"Ounsasta!" Taiwa called to the sky. "We ask that your spirit now come to reside in Ontarra! Return to us!" She bent and placed her right palm on the ground. Ontarra held his breath, locking his jaw to prevent any possibility of a sound escaping. Taiwa slowly drew her hand from the ground, raising her arm as if a great weight hung from her palm. Turning, she lowered the hand onto Ontarra's head and counted ten heartbeats. "Ounsasta ... we welcome you!" Taiwa yanked her hand away.

A tense silence enveloped the town. A crow called from the trees out on the bluff. Ontarra opened one eye a crack, squinting at Taiwa. "That's it?" he whispered.

Taiwa glanced at all the people watching. "Yes, that's it, you idiot ... do something."

The anticlimax confounded him, but Ontarra managed to mimic Ounsasta's war cry. To Taiwa's relief, the crowd applauded her success. Taiwa and Ontarra returned to their seats and the dancing began anew.

"Very nice ceremony, Taiwa," Togo rewarded her with a long hug.

Sounia leaned forward, searching into the depths of Ontarra's eyes. Relieved that he was still in there, she sat back and wrapped an arm around him. "What did it feel like?"

Ontarra shrugged. "I didn't feel a thing."

"As with your spirit guide, Ounsasta will pick his own time to reveal himself," Shanoka said, trying to sound reassuring. The look on Ontarra's face at the mention of his spirit guide made her wish she'd said nothing.

Men and women broke into groups around the town to begin gambling. The men used six bone chits, colored white on one side and charred black on the other. They shook the chits in a bowl and tossed them, betting on who could land the most white sides up. The women played a similar game but used a ground skin to toss the chits in the air.

Togo watched with greedy fascination as the piles of items bet on each toss grew larger. He dismantled his pipe and rose to join in the wagering. "I think I'll wander around a bit," he muttered and headed straight for the richest game. As was customary, each of the chiefs joined one of the games, a deterrent to the unruly disputes that inevitably developed.

Sounia and Taiwa left to help with the food for the feast. Several fires were surrounded by half-grown ears of corn waiting to be roasted. Fresh strawberries lay on ground skins, tempting everyone. Succotash was simmering in huge ceramic pots nestled into the hearthstones. Smells of venison roasting, corn cakes, and fresh fish spread tantalizing aromas through the town.

Shanoka didn't like to gamble, but she enjoyed watching the wealth changing hands and the mood swings of the players as coveted treasures were won or lost. Mostly, she loved the respite from daily routines and the pleasure it brought everyone. As she surveyed all the activity, she found herself staring at the gold lodge, wondering what Poutassa was up to. Hiatsou hadn't been seen in days.

Ontarra hadn't moved since the reincarnation ritual. He sat with a distant look in his eyes, lost in thoughts of the spirit world and his distressing inability to make any form of contact with it. It seemed he was not intended to be a warrior. It was time he made a decision.

When the sun was in the middle of its descent toward the western horizon and the smell of food was driving everyone mad with hunger, the feast was ready. Each person was expected to help himself or herself, which always created a frenzy. The beginning of a feast with the Attawondaronks reminded Shanoka of field dressing a deer when the dogs were around. The chaos grew more relaxed, however, as ravenous appetites were sated, and people remembered a few social amenities.

Shanoka noticed Ontarra was still brooding, so she loaded a bowl with roasted corn and venison and sauntered over to sit with him. She offered him the bowl. He accepted but with little enthusiasm. Crossing her ankles, she folded down beside him. "You shouldn't worry so much about the spirits," she said, reading his thoughts. "Only they can know when the timing is right to manifest themselves."

Ontarra nodded absently as he picked at the roasted meat. He noticed Teota coming through the south entry with his tubby friend, Toad Belly. Teota had skipped the ceremonies to fish the mouth of the Entry River while there was no canoe traffic. Teota's face cracked into a broad grin when he saw Ontarra and his mother. He raised his arm up high, showing off two small mooneyes and a nice wolf fish. Teota flopped the tether of fish on the ground for Ontarra's appraisal. "They liked the wooden minnow today," he huffed, still trying to catch his breath from the climb up the bluff. Teota stared down greedily at the venison.

Ontarra smirked and handed him the bowl. "You have flawless timing."

"Toad Belly always knows when there is food that needs to be eaten,"

Teota said. He peeled off a chunk of meat and crammed it into his mouth. Then he passed the bowl to Toad Belly.

"Look ... strawberries!" Toad Belly's eyes took the shape of saucers as he ogled all the food spread around the plaza. "Let's get some strawberries." He tugged Teota's arm.

"Wait a hair," Teota said, pulling his arm back and laying the fishing gear beside the fish. "Is the Naming Ceremony over? I figured it must be when I saw Taiwa and Sounia down at the creek." He bent and stared into Ontarra's face. "You look the same to me."

Shanoka grabbed Teota's arm with sudden apprehension. "Where did you see them?"

"They were crossing Snake Creek into the fields." Teota pointed toward the south entry as he spoke. "I don't know why. No one is out there today. Everyone is up here. I hollered, but they didn't hear me."

"Poutassa is out there," Toad Belly mumbled absently, his mouth full of venison. He eyed the strawberries again and tugged at Teota's arm.

"I didn't see Poutassa," Teota said.

Toad Belly was getting impatient. "I did. He was gathering corn, I think." Toad Belly couldn't stand this any longer. He gave up on Teota and beelined for the strawberries.

Shanoka and Ontarra locked eyes, momentarily frozen by unspoken fears. Shanoka thought of Yadwena; the image of Rona's mutilated body flashed through Ontarra's mind.

"Ontarra—run!" Shanoka cried.

Ontarra jumped up, knocking the bowl out of Teota's hands. "I know where they're going!"

Toutsou was watching the gambling when he saw Ontarra running flat-out for the south entry. Ontarra stopped long enough to yank a knife from the belt of a young warrior and then disappeared into the switchbacks. Toutsou dropped his food and tore after him. Sannisen loped across the plaza to Shanoka with a look of concern.

Toutsou didn't catch up to him until they were charging across Snake Creek in a burst of spray and foam. Ontarra explained his fears on the run. The sense of urgency had him rattled. Sharp corn leaves tore at their faces. As they neared the hill, Toutsou grabbed Ontarra's arm, stopping his headlong dash. "Wait … you have to tell me … what we're dealing with." Toutsou managed between gasps. "Let's get our wind … approach this cautiously."

Ontarra stared up the hill and then nodded to Toutsou as he rested his hands on his knees.

Taiwa slipped the fresh-baked mooneye from her carry bag. She climbed up the rocks to lay it on the top boulder and backed herself down again. "Come on, Slammer. You're going to love this!" With her tongue and teeth she made a sound to which the cat had learned to come. "*Sshuck-sshuck.*" She turned to whisper to Sounia. "I haven't been able to come here for two hands." Sounia looked away, feeling guilty about bringing Ontarra to Taiwa's secret spot.

Brush at the top of the tumbled boulders rustled. Taiwa grinned at Sounia. The bushes suddenly erupted. A lanky man gamboled down the boulders onto the ledge between the two girls. Taiwa screamed and stumbled backward. Her fright transformed instantly to anger as she realized that it was Poutassa. "You followed us! You despicable creature!"

"I need not follow people," he sneered. He waved a chert dagger under Sounia's nose, forcing her to lean back. "I am shaman. I know everything."

Taiwa's anger flared. "Shaman? *Phewf.*" She spat on a rock. "You're as phony as your father." She saw the dagger, and her eyes widened. "What are you doing with that?"

Poutassa pranced across the ledge to block their route of escape. He waved the dagger back and forth, pointing it from Sounia to Taiwa, a repugnant sneer on his face. "I've come to add to my trophy feathers." He knew they wouldn't understand. Smug snickers issued from his throat. "You will understand my Power when you're perched on my spear." He tore his breechclout away, exposing his member. A ring of tiny feathers dangled around his scrotum. The appalled look on Taiwa's face sent a thrill through his gut. He spun to face Sounia, hoping for the same reaction. Sounia's face tightened as she pictured Poutassa groping at her. She forced herself to look at his face, but her eyes were slowly drawn down to the paltry appendage he was swaying back and forth for shock effect.

Sounia howled with laughter. "You think you can threaten us with that?" She pointed at his groin and the disgusting swaying stopped instantly. Sounia's eyes searched the ground around her. She bent, plucking up a slender twig and snapping it off short. "Here—use this." She threw the twig and bounced it off his chest. "At least with that, I can tell Ontarra in honesty that I was violated."

The brazen smirk on Poutassa's face fell away, and his serpentine black eyes burned with rage. His back was turned to Taiwa, and she started inching toward him. He spun, jabbing the dagger at her, backing her toward the rocks until both girls were standing together. Sounia was still laughing, but Taiwa could see no humor in the situation. "You'll have to kill me first!" Taiwa screamed.

"I thought killing you *afterward* would be exciting," Poutassa said, "but *first* is an interesting idea." He saw fear flicker through Taiwa's eyes, and his cruel grin returned. "Let's see now ... who shall be first?" He waved the dagger back and forth, bending to pull hide bindings out of a pouch lying beside his breechclout. A twig snapped in the brush above. Poutassa lurched upright.

Sounia and Taiwa locked eyes. An idea occurred to Taiwa; her eyes narrowed. "I'll show you who has Power," she spat out. "Here, Slammer! *Sshuck-sshuck*. Come on, Slammer. *Sshuck-sshuck*. We need you, Slammer!"

Poutassa thought he heard a movement behind him. Whirling, he slashed the dagger at the rocks above him, but nothing was there.

"Come, Slammer. *Sshuck-sshuck*."

"Quit that!" Poutassa snarled. He sprang at Taiwa, slamming the butt of the dagger into her temple. Taiwa collapsed to the ground. Poutassa scanned the rock pile above him. He turned and trotted to the crest of the ledge, staring into the brush below. His nerves settled a bit, and he stalked back to Sounia. "Take that dress off!" He swept the dagger past her nose.

Sounia backed away until the boulder pile stopped her. "Ontarra will have your head," she hissed.

Poutassa moved in close so she had nowhere to go. Grabbing her dress by the ruff, he ripped. Sounia held her dress on with one arm, flailing at him with the other. "Get it off!" he demanded, ripping it again. The dress shredded and sloughed to the ground. Sounia glanced down at the torn buckskin. Then she took a deep breath and lowered her arms to reveal her nakedness. Poutassa ran his tongue over his quivering lips, leering at her stunning legs and thighs. Pert nipples poked slightly upward from large brown areolas on her ample breasts. The light copper tone of her skin was tantalizing. Spellbound, Poutassa lowered the dagger.

Sounia studied the gaping stare as she ran her hands over the rocks behind her. She found one that fit into her palm and swung with all the force she could muster. She felt Poutassa's nose break with a crunchy splat, like walnuts under a pestle. Poutassa screamed, dropping the dagger to grab his nose with both hands. Blood spurted out between his fingers.

"She-bitch! I'll kill you for that!" He lashed out blindly with the back of his hand. Sounia grabbed a fallen limb and started pounding him mercilessly. Fear enhanced her strength, speed, and agility. Poutassa couldn't even get his head up long enough to find her.

He screamed, wrapping his arms over his head as he backed up, until he finally got a hand on the branch and yanked it away. He backhanded Sounia across the cheek, and she sank to her knees. Little lights flashed behind her eyelids. Her stomach heaved. Poutassa got a clear look at her through the blood in his eyes. He raised the branch in both hands but then, hearing a sound, he whirled.

He found himself looking into enraged yellow-slitted eyes. The lynx peeled its lips back in a menacing snarl. Saliva dripped from a curved fang, less than an arm-length from Poutassa's face. Poutassa leaned backward, preparing to spring from its reach. The cat crouched, planting his rear paws with a quick twist of the hips. The murderous look in those slitted eyes paralyzed Poutassa with fear. He didn't hear the crashing of brush coming up the hill behind him, but the cat heard.

The lynx relaxed his muscles, backing up a step. Poutassa was too terrified to move. With the blinding speed of rock-hard muscle, the left paw lashed out. Razor-sharp claws unsheathed, four of them tearing through the right side of Poutassa's face. Flesh and bone separated from each other, as one claw rattled along Poutassa's clenched teeth. Then the cat was gone. Poutassa toppled backward, screaming in agony.

Ontarra burst into the clearing, landing in a crouch. His knife swept ahead of him, searching for something to cleave. He saw Poutassa writhing and wailing on the ground, clutching at his face, his naked body spattered with blood. Sounia was naked too, bending over Taiwa's limp form. He could see an angry lump on Taiwa's temple.

Toutsou loped down the boulders from the crest above, spoiling for a fight. He stood on the last boulder, holding his throw-stick like a club, but as he cast his baffled eyes around the ludicrous scene, he slowly lowered the throw-stick to his side.

Ontarra trotted over to Sounia and lifted her up. A red welt marred her left cheek, but there were no cuts. He turned her around and found a shallow knife slash on her left shoulder. "I'm ... all right." Sounia's voice was gravelly and weak, her earlier defiance all but drained away. "He hit Taiwa really hard." Ontarra bent and picked up the shredded dress, looking at Sounia with questioning eyes. "No ... he didn't ... but only because you arrived in time. I tried to fight him. He was too strong." Tears filled her eyes. She buried her face on Ontarra's shoulder.

Ontarra sat Sounia down on a boulder, gently prying her fingers from his neck. Ontarra's eyes narrowed to murderous slits as he visualized what had occurred—and what could have happened. Wrinkles creased his brow, and the muscles in his jaw worked as a smoldering rage boiled up from his gut. Sounia fell silent as the concern on Ontarra's face transformed into something she'd never seen before—the cold, ruthless look of a warrior, about to take a life. The sudden change was uncanny. An eerie chill swept over her.

Ontarra whirled on one heel and launched himself through the air. He landed on Poutassa with both knees, ending the pathetic whining in the instant it took for all the air to blast from Poutassa's lungs. Toutsou jumped down, kicking the dagger out of Poutassa's reach. Ontarra wrapped his hand into Poutassa's hair and hauled him upright. "You sniveling maggot!" Ontarra's right hand snapped up and back, a chert blade poised for a slam to the windpipe. It hung there. Slowly, he lowered his arm, straightened, and glanced at Toutsou in stunned disbelief.

Toutsou moved up beside him and took a look. "Glouscap! What happened to his face?"

Poutassa was still in shock. Until this moment, he was hardly aware that Ontarra and Toutsou had arrived. His beady eyes widened with terror as the reality of his plight finally dawned on him. Poutassa saw the knife in Ontarra's hand. He gasped and rolled to his knees, starting to shuffle backward and holding the ribbons of flesh to his face with one hand. His eyes darted around for an escape but saw none. The eyes grew wild, like a deer driven into a trap. Poutassa jerked his chin. "It was them! They called up a creature from the netherworld to attack me!" He forgot himself and started to point with the hand that held his face. A strip of flesh sagged from his cheek, exposing his upper teeth. He wailed and tried to tuck it back in place.

Ontarra twisted around. "What happened, Sounia?"

Sounia wiped moisture from her eyes. "I think it was me who mushed his nose, but when he got over near those rocks, something took a swat at him." Sounia shifted her eyes to the top of the boulder heap as she spoke. She knew Ontarra would see if she lied; a half-truth didn't seem so bad.

Toutsou padded over to Poutassa, raising his throw-stick. "Move, and I'll crack your skull." He grabbed Poutassa's wrist, pulling his hand away to inspect the wounds. Poutassa tilted his head to the left in an effort to keep the flesh on his face. Toutsou stood up and backed away with no attempt to hide his disgust. "A cat got him."

"Well ... divine retribution." Ontarra moved in closer, repositioning the knife in his hand. "I'm glad he's had a chance to suffer." Poutassa held his free arm up in an effort to protect himself. Ontarra noticed something, and with a quick snatch, he grabbed the lacing of robin feathers. Poutassa yelped as they snapped from his scrotum. Ontarra looked over his shoulder at Sounia. "Why are these things hanging from his grapes?"

"He said they were his trophy feathers. He was going to add one for me and one for Taiwa, when he was finished with us."

Ontarra pictured the dog at the Ring of Fire and threw the corrupted feathers in Poutassa's face. "He's too pathetic to kill! Stand him up, Toutsou!" Toutsou hopped behind Poutassa, wrapped an arm under his chin, and lifted Poutassa to his feet. Ontarra shoved the point of his knife in Poutassa's nostril and backed him up, bending him over a boulder. He pressed a knee into Poutassa's chest to hold him there.

"What are you doing?" Poutassa looked down in horror as the blade slid down his ribcage, over his belly and stopped at his groin. He tried to struggle, but it was too late. *"Aarhgg!"*

In the next instant, Ontarra held a bloody penis up by its foreskin, dangling it in Poutassa's face. The severed arteries disgorged themselves, oozing crimson blobs. Poutassa stared in horror at his member, which shriveled up until it was a ghastly, wrinkled lump no bigger than Ontarra's thumb. Ontarra studied the horror in Poutassa's eyes with grim satisfaction. He glanced at the withered, offensive thing on which Poutassa's eyes were fixated. Then he straightened and stepped back. Ontarra held the penis out, as if he'd just noticed it for the first time. He screwed up his face in mock disgust and, with a flip of his wrist, tossed it down the hillside.

Poutassa howled, ran across the ledge and went crashing down the hill, forgetting his face entirely as he clamped both hands over his groin.

Toutsou watched Poutassa's flank steaks disappearing into the brush. If so much hadn't just happened, it might have been laughable. He raised a questioning brow to Ontarra. "He'll bleed to death before he gets halfway across the fields."

Ontarra shrugged. "Good. Let him watch his miserable life ooze away."

The fishermen who found Poutassa carried him into the town before they heard what had happened. If they'd known, they might have just rolled him into the Entry River and never said a word. To everyone's surprise, he was still alive. He'd somehow gathered his wits enough to pack clay on his wounds, slowing the bleeding enough to make it into the canoe area before he collapsed. Shanoka had never refused treatment to anyone, regardless of her feelings, but "Let him rot!" was all she had to say about Poutassa.

Like a raging wildfire, word spread of his attempted atrocity. Poutassa was carried to the gold lodge and left with Hiatsou. Hiatsou's healing knowledge was limited, but he knew how to cauterize wounds—he even enjoyed doing it. Poutassa's agonized screams reverberated through the town well into the night. He spent most of the next day, screaming again as he tried to pass water.

The councils spent that day in discussions. Several Land clan maidens came forward with tales of attacks in the fields and woods. Tribal council wanted Poutassa put to death. Clan council was fearful of the disgrace this would bring upon the Bird clans. The decision was made: if Poutassa survived, he and Hiatsou would be forced into exile—to Tontiaton, if they'd take them.

Messengers were sent to Ayontat. He agreed to accept them as shaman and apprentice, despite all the trouble they'd caused. Assurances were given to Sannisen that they would be kept on a short tether. Ayontat sent three canoes with six warriors to escort them back.

Poutassa and Hiatsou were led from the gold lodge with only what they could carry. All of their other possessions were forfeited to Rona's clan. The people of Ounontisaston lined the pathways, watching the solemn procession. Poutassa's wounds were still tender. He walked in slow methodical steps.

Hiatsou scowled vindictively at the faces he passed. He stopped and turned to the crowd. "I have warned you of the curse you have brought upon yourselves." Shanoka appeared from nowhere. She held a seer's crystal inches from his nose, tilting it so sunlight blinded his eyes. Hiatsou was stupefied. "Where did you get a seer's crystal?" he gasped, flinching backward.

"It has come down to me through my ancestors," Shanoka hissed through clenched teeth. "It holds great Power. And I am warning you both." She glared pointedly at Poutassa, who was leaning himself against a pole, holding one leg out in obvious discomfort. "If any harm comes to my family or to anyone else in this town, and I think it is because of you"—she turned her venomous eyes back to Hiatsou—"I will suck the life forces from your bodies, trap your essence in this crystal, and throw it to the bottom of Lake Iannaoa!" Shanoka extended her arm to touch Hiatsou with the crystal. As she expected, he backed away.

Two of Ayontat's warriors stepped between Shanoka and Hiatsou. Shanoka nodded for them to continue. The warriors grabbed Hiatsou's arms and walked him toward the south entry. Tontiaton's war chief, Satwani, stood at the switchbacks, talking with one of his men as he waited to take up the rear of the procession. Their conversation stopped as Poutassa hobbled by and they got a good look at his face. The warrior grimaced. He had to look away. "Whewff! Not even a she-bitch would have anything to do with him now."

Satwani smirked, shaking his head. "He isn't going to be doing much coupling, from what I've heard." They both laughed. The warrior mimicked Poutassa's hobble as they followed him out.

Sannisen ordered the gold lodge burned to the ground that night. As the town watched the spectacle, Shanoka sat at her hearth, caressing her prayer stone and talking with Togo. "Do you really have to leave tomorrow?" she asked sadly.

"Yes, I should have been back by now." He spoke in a low tone so he wouldn't wake Taiwa. She'd recovered quickly from the blow to her temple, but she was having headaches and sleeping a lot. Togo got up and checked to be sure that she was comfortable. He moved over to Ontarra's platform and rolled him onto his side to stifle the snoring before sitting down beside Shanoka again. Togo studied the worry lines around Shanoka's eyes. "Ounontisaston should be a better place now, Shanoka."

"It should," she agreed with a tight smile, "but I keep having this feeling that something isn't right or is about to go wrong. It's probably because we've had so many troubles. I don't know—I can't explain it."

Togo nodded and propped a lighting stick in the coals. "I think I may have an insight for you," he said, rolling the end of the stick in the embers thoughtfully. "Remember our discussion about each nation going to their own Village of the Dead?"

Shanoka scrutinized Togo across the fire, her expression puzzled. "I remember."

"Well, let me ask you this." Togo lit his pipe and blew a cloud at the sky. "Which one will you go to? The Ojibwa? The Sennikae? Or the Attawondaronk?"

Shanoka stared at her prayer stone, rotating it between her palms. "I want to be with my family."

"Which one? Your old one or your new one?"

Shanoka nodded as she digested this. "Both," she finally replied.

Togo raised a brow. "How would you do that?"

"I can't," Shanoka sighed. "You think I must decide, for this feeling to go away?"

Togo got up and stepped around the fire. He bent, pecking Shanoka on the forehead. "I think it is a decision that would trouble anyone." He straightened up and moved over to the door but then turned back. "I'll say good-bye in the morning," he said before ducking out.

Ontarra dreamed of Ounsasta that night. Ounsasta stood knee-deep in the waters of the Tranchi, staring at an Agwa arrow in his chest. He wrapped his fingers around the shaft and tugged, but it wouldn't budge. He looked up with weary resignation, his good eye settling on Ontarra, who was watching from the bank. *Never leave an enemy behind you, Ontarra.*

Ontarra lurched upright, sleep robes scattering to the floor. He pushed back the hair matted to his forehead and then dropped his hand and stared up into the darkness.

"I should have killed him."

Days were growing shorter; the sun rose a little farther south each morning.

Its benevolent rays had worked their miracle, caressing the earth and nursing the three sister crops to maturity. The corn was so tall, the women could no longer see over it. Men stole out into the fields in the evenings, waiting until the women weren't watching, to pilfer ground leaves from the petun plants.

Blackcaps had come and gone. Adolescent girls brought in basket loads for several days, and everyone gorged themselves on corn cakes piled high with berries and smothered in maple syrup. Black cherries were almost ready. A close watch was kept on the wild grapes in the surrounding countryside.

The tranquil days of summer had flown by, as always. It was three moon cycles since Hiatsou and Poutassa had been exiled to Tontiaton. The men spent the summer hunting and fishing. Many of Sannisen's men joined with the Khioetoa warriors on raids into the Fire Nation. They dressed as Mascouten, using the captured Agwa arrows. The Fire People were too busy fighting amongst themselves now to cause any trouble for the Attawondaronks.

Young warriors remained at Ounontisaston to protect the town and help the women patrol the fields. Turkeys, pheasants, grouse, and flocks of grackles and crows were a constant threat. Corn husks and strips of hide were tied to the blackened trunks of the sentries to rustle and flap in the wind. Crows were shot and hung up by the legs as a warning to others. Stands were erected in strategic locations so the women could get up above the corn, where they would yell, wave, and bang on their skin hoops. The fields were alive with activity. The women were so vigilant and boisterous that the flocking birds had to leave the area just to land and rest themselves. Working together all summer created a sense of harmony that Ounontisaston had never known. It was to prove a fleeting respite; change is always resisted.

The shaman society intended to fight back. They met at Tontiaton, unanimously condemning the changes taking place at Ounontisaston. A legend was resurrected—or invented, in Shanoka's opinion. It told of an eccentric but Powerful shaman who had lived in the time of the ancients. His extraordinary Powers derived from the fact that he was a eunuch. He'd saved the people many times from witches, demons, and creatures of the netherworld. The legend foretold of his return in the time of his people's greatest need.

Troubling rumors filtered back to Ounontisaston. Poutassa claimed to be this ancient shaman, reincarnated. He'd suffered his terrible wounds when killing the Windigo monster at Ounontisaston. Hiatsou and Poutassa rapidly gained a large following at Tontiaton. One morning, the apprentices at Ounontisaston were gone. Many of the Bird clan men and women followed them to Tontiaton, preferring the comfortable familiarity of their old ways to the constant flux of change.

With no shaman, Ounontisaston was helpless to perform even the simple tasks, like welcoming the sun or blessing the soil. Tribal council sent word to all the towns: Ounontisaston required a shaman. They would reward him handsomely upon his arrival. The shaman society thumbed their noses. No shaman would live at Ounontisaston with his Power and prestige reduced.

A shaman had to be found before winter solstice, to call the sun back from its journey south. People started to worry. It was suggested at clan council that Shanoka and Taiwa perform some of the shaman duties. Wild arguments erupted, until Shanoka politely declined, pointing out that the Attawondaronk shamans were traditionally male. The situation went unresolved.

Ontarra and Toutsou were relieved of sentry duties for the summer. Their new hero status made them the ideal choice to begin the training of adolescent boys in hunting skills, use of weapons, and fighting. Each morning, two hands of excited boys gathered at the canoe area, or the plaza, or Snake Creek ravine for practice. Toutsou ignored bows, since the boys had all used bows from the day they could walk. He demonstrated the throw-stick, the bola, and even his blowgun.

Ontarra taught the boys to fight with knives and clubs. They learned to feint, to parry a blow, and which critical points of the body to hit and which to protect. They learned to catch a marmot by building a fire over his hole. They set snares and built a deadfall. Toutsou obtained permission from the women for a rabbit drive through the upper fields. Nets were strung along one edge of the field. Half the boys drove, while the other half manned the nets. So many rabbits, grouse, and turkeys burst from the field and tangled in the nets that many escaped before they could be clubbed or have their necks wrung.

Today was the final lesson. Ontarra and Toutsou followed the boys through the north entry, listening to them chatter about their first big deer drive tomorrow. Teota was dragging a marmot from the bounty of the upper fields; it was so fat, its feet seemed to grow directly from its body.

"You mean that your spirit guide came to you on your first vision quest?" Ontarra asked in disbelief. Toutsou nodded. Ontarra sighed and shook his head, watching in forlorn silence as the boys broke up and headed for their longhouses. "Your spirit guide is a man?" he asked, his tone dejected.

Toutsou bobbed his chin. "He said his name is Pathfinder. He wore the skin of a huge white bear, like a cloak, and he carried a spear with a stone point as long as my hand."

"It's strange for a spirit guide to be a man. It's usually a spirit animal."

Toutsou nodded thoughtfully. "Pathfinder told me that he saved his people many times by leading them to the animal herds. He will come to show me the proper path, when I need his direction."

Ontarra chewed on his lip, staring up at the sky. "It would be a great relief to find my spirit helper."

"You said Ounsasta came to you. Perhaps he is to be your helper."

Ontarra brightened. "Yes, just after the Naming Ceremony."

"What did he say?"

Ontarra's face fell again. "He said that I should have killed Poutassa."

Toutsou shook his head in disgust. "I thought you did. I didn't think he'd make the cornfields. I hear that they're regaining their status at Tontiaton. It's hard to fathom."

They reached the lodge just as Shanoka was coming out. "Ho, Toutsou." She smiled, and turned to Ontarra. "I'm going to Tsohahissen's lodge. He has asked to speak with me. There's stew in the pot—help yourselves." Shanoka started up the path. The town was busy today. Drying huts and storage pits were being prepared, and a steady stream of people flowed in and out of the entries.

Tsohahissen greeted her outside the lodge with a warm smile and a hug. They ducked in. Hobbling over to his sleep platform, he indicated a tripod stool for Shanoka. He held his leg out straight and rested it on the heel. The wounds had healed well, but his limp was pronounced and permanent.

Shanoka glanced around the lodge. "Where is Yadwena?"

"Yadwena has begun to have the cramping pains. She likes to walk to relieve them."

Shanoka was pensive but then said, "She's very big. It isn't unusual to be uncomfortable in the final stages. I'll see her if you wish."

"No, Shanoka, that's not why I have asked you to come." Tsohahissen looked into the fire with a sad expression. "The chief of Tontiaton has died."

"Ayontat? Dead? How can that be? He was fine just three moon cycles ago."

"He became sick and grew progressively worse. Apparently, he died in a matter of days. They have picked Satwani as their new chief."

Shanoka nodded. "Satwani is a good choice. I remember him well from the old town."

"And he remembers you. He has asked that you perform the Naming Ceremony at the Festival of the Dead, to reincarnate Ayontat's spirit into him."

Icy fingers clutched at Shanoka's chest. "It is Hiatsou's responsibility. Why would he ask for me?"

"Hiatsou was with Ayontat when he died. He says that Ayontat asked for you. Satwani believes this, because neither he nor Ayontat trusted Hiatsou. He also feels that it's a good way to show Hiatsou he's not indispensable, and it will show the people that there is no animosity between our towns."

Shanoka stared into the distance. She didn't like this. "Does Sannisen know?"

Tsoha' nodded. "He doesn't think we should offend Tontiaton by refusing, but he wants the decision to be yours. He asked me to discuss it with you."

Shanoka sighed, a look of acceptance softening her face. "I will go, then."

"I knew you would," Tsohahissen said solemnly. He started to rise to escort Shanoka to the door, but she gestured to remain seated.

"Rest your leg, Tsoha'," Shanoka said. She excused herself and ducked out.

She absently negotiated the pathways home, searching her troubled mind for what Hiatsou and Poutassa might be up to. She didn't relish the idea of seeing either of them again, but Satwani would make sure she was well protected. Her anxiety subsided when she entered the lodge to the smell of marmot roasting. Shanoka had to smile when she saw the purple smears of blackcap juice on Teota's face.

"You have talked to Tsohahissen?" Sannisen asked.

"Yes." She shot him a perturbed look. "I wish you would have warned me."

"I thought it would be best if you didn't have time to brood over your answer," Sannisen replied, wondering how she always managed to make him feel guilty. "I wanted you to make your own decision without influence from me." He eyed her. "What was your answer?"

"I agreed to perform the Naming Ceremony. I think I'll take Taiwa and let her do it." Shanoka folded herself down at the hearth, exhaling wearily. "I fear Hiatsou is behind this, planning some embarrassment."

Sannisen rubbed at his chin. Squatting down, he sat on his heels to stir the coals with a stick while he thought. Angry footsteps stomped down the side of the lodge, and Taiwa burst through the door in a huff.

"Why can't they understand that what they're doing is wrong?" She crossed the lodge in three strides, dropping on her sleep platform to stare at the coals. She folded her arms across her chest in angry frustration. "They worry that the animals will talk and avoid us, so they kill them all and destroy the cycle of life! What will happen when there are none left to mate?"

"Taiwa, I asked you to say nothing more to clan council about this, at least for now." Sannisen was more annoyed with her noisy intrusion than her disobedience.

"I had to, Father. The deer hunt is tomorrow. The spirits of the animals are all around us. They're haunting my dreams! They say that no other people do this and that we are evil!"

"She's right, Sannisen," Shanoka said softly. "It is an offense to the manitos to kill more than we need. All the killing is just a ploy, instigated by the shaman society, so they can get the extra meat and hides. The practice has to stop, or the manitos will punish us, and there will be no game left to hunt."

"Have you ever heard of that happening?" Ontarra rolled on his sleep platform to see her answer.

"I've seen it," Shanoka replied bluntly.

Sannisen stood to relax his legs. "It's too late to do anything about tomorrow's hunt. We'll see what can be done next cycle." He looked over at Ontarra lying on his back again, entranced by the shadows flickering across the arched ceiling. "Ontarra, the Festival of the Dead is only a half moon cycle away. So many of the warriors and hunters will be gone that I will need to remain here. You will have to go to Tontiaton with your mother and Taiwa to be sure no harm befalls them."

"Can I come, Mother?" Teota's chirpy voice rose from his hiding place at the back of the big platform.

"It's too long a trek for you," she replied.

Ontarra sat up, dangling his legs over the edge. He studied Sannisen pensively. "As you wish, Father. I'll take Toutsou. As soon as I return, though, I must leave on another vision quest. I'd like to use your hunt camp."

Sannisen studied him curiously. "Why so far away?"

"I need to be secluded—far from other people—and I like that place. No one ever goes there."

"It will take two days just to get in," Sannisen pointed out. "Do you really think it's necessary?"

Ontarra thought about Sounia and the lodge he'd promised to build on the hill across the Tranchi.

"Yes, Father, it is."

Soutoten's men organized the annual deer drive. A multitude of considerations had to be taken into account, and the hunters understood their quarry best. Deer were extremely cautious creatures. The male protected himself with instincts bred through eons of being preyed upon. Does were free to graze or tend to their fawns, while the buck remained vigilant for any danger. Most of the year, they roamed the deep forest, only coming out at night to graze in the river flats and drink from the creeks and streams.

In autumn, the situation changed. Meadow grass and vegetation in the forest lost its nutrition after the first frosts. River valleys supported growth later in the season, and the ripening crops were an insidious draw. Movement of the herds from the deep woods coincided with the rut. The buck's survival instincts were blinded by his drive to mate.

Autumn was the time to hunt deer. The Attawondaronks learned to take full advantage of the fatal flaw in the buck's seasonal cycle. One successful drive provided enough venison and hides to last the winter. On a bluff above the Entry River, an arrow-flight north of Ounontisaston, Ahratota and his men constructed two angled walls of a palisade. The walls were concealed just inside the treeline. At the apex of the two walls was an opening that funneled the deer out onto a point. Precipitous banks on each side dropped to the river below.

The top of the point was cleared, opening a field of fire. Any animal driven up to the walls would try to escape the trap through the opening at the apex. Beyond the opening, Soutoten's best bowmen waited in blinds. When the deer bounded out onto the bluff, there was nowhere to go but down. The animal froze momentarily. Before it could decide where to go, it was cut down by sharp chert tearing into vital organs. The unfortunate creature usually lived long enough for one leap, over the precipice, and then tumbled down the hill to the women waiting below. Animals were quickly dressed out, skinned, quartered, and sent in canoes downstream to the town.

A glimmer in the eastern sky hinted that daylight was approaching as the men assembled in a clearing near the deer trap. Soutoten quietly assigned positions to the hunters. All the town's men who were not too old or away raiding had turned out. Warriors were not obliged to hunt, but none could resist the excitement of a deer drive. The knot of hunters broke up; one approached Ontarra and Toutsou.

The hunter motioned to several other men to join them. "This is the plan." He scuffed a bare patch on the ground with a moccasined toe and began scratching lines in the dirt with a stick. "The river is here … the trap is here. The boys that Ontarra and Toutsou have trained as drivers are four arrow-flights to the west of us. They'll begin the drive when the sun clears the horizon. Soutoten wants to alternate the hunters and warriors in two lines, here, and here." The hunter scratched lines north and south of the trap, running them inland from the Entry River along two feeder creeks.

"The men along the south creek must be our best bowmen. Any deer that gets through our line in that direction will charge right through the upper fields." The hunter swept his eyes over the faces around him. "If that happens, the women will castrate us in our sleep." The men winced and groaned, casting pained expressions at each other. "Six of the best hunters are across the Entry River"—he pointed toward the sunrise—"in case any deer escape down the bluff. Eight of Soutoten's best men are going to be in the blinds, where the deer exit the trap." The hunter flashed a smile to Toutsou. "Soutoten has asked that Toutsou go in the blinds." Toutsou's face cracked into a wide grin. Ontarra clapped him on the back before he trotted off.

Ontarra took a position along the south creek. Eyeing the hunters on his left and right, careful to keep each one in sight, he decided on a spot and poked his arrows into the ground ahead of him. He glanced at the hunters again. They nodded their approval. Sounds of the drivers rose from the forest to the west. Ontarra took a few deep breaths to settle his nerves. He strung his bow and then knelt down to hide his silhouette in the shadowy half-light of early dawn. Frosty dew started to curl from the ground, creating a light mist that hung suspended at waist level. There was a constant rustle of leaves spiraling down and scattering across the forest floor.

Through an opening between the tree trunks, Ontarra could make out Toutsou and the other hunters crouching in the blinds. The drivers were closer now. Other noises began filtering through the dim woods. Something was running toward them. The sound of dry leaves crunching under fleeting feet was unmistakable. Ontarra canted his ear. It didn't sound like deer—it was something larger. He nocked an arrow, trying to picture what animal could make so much noise.

Ontarra peered out into the depths of the forest, tensing as the crashing grew louder. It was driving right at him, but he still couldn't see it. He scanned the slanting shadows, certain a large animal was almost upon him. "Bear," he muttered under his breath. He stood and drew his bow. His hand started to shake. He waited, holding—it was almost upon him. He caught a blur of movement on his right and swung. Brown fur flashed on his left. His heart jumped, and he swung back. Ontarra shuddered and backed into a tree, slowly releasing the tension on his bow as he sagged against the trunk. He rested a hand on a shaky knee and waited for his breath to return.

Hands upon hands of rabbits darted and bounced around him, leaping the feeder creek to his rear in a headlong rush to escape the frightening racket descending upon them. The hunters on his left and right held their stomachs, trying in vain to stifle the sound of their sidesplitting laughter. One dropped to his knees, laying his bow down while his body rocked and tears rolled down his face. Ontarra's nerves settled. He shook his head with an embarrassed grin, moving his arrows ahead to a safer position, where he had a tree between him and whatever came out of the woods next. He rocked his head again, chuckling to himself. *Hero of Ounontisaston, frightened by rabbits.*

Birds came streaming out of the molting canopy above. The man to Ontarra's left swung his bow in an arc and released. Ontarra saw a big cock turkey tumble across the ground. A raccoon scurried out of the brush beside Ontarra. He brained it with a rock. The drivers were getting close. Ontarra squinted at the trap through the opening in the trees. A big buck burst out onto the point, skidding to a halt in confusion when he saw there was nowhere to go. Four arrows appeared in his side and chest, but he seemed not to notice. With two magnificent leaps, he disappeared over the brow.

Two does and a fawn cantered out onto the point and then tumbled to the ground, hooves stabbing the air. Hunters rushed out, clubbed them, dragged them to the crest, and rolled them over. Four deer appeared at once. The hunters dropped, hugging the ground as arrows flew over their heads. Three of the deer stumbled off the bluff, and the hunters clambered to their feet and tossed the fourth.

The sound of hooves came crashing through the forest ahead, turning Ontarra's attention back to his immediate surroundings. Men up and down the line stood up, stretching their bowstrings back. A buck appeared in front of the hunter to Ontarra's right. The man jumped at it, screaming, arms flailing, hoping to turn it back toward the trap. The buck stopped, swinging his head to look up the line of men, so the hunter nocked and fired. The buck leaped sideways toward Ontarra and landed, legs quivering. He settled to his knees before Ontarra could draw down. Ontarra ran out and slit its windpipe.

A doe and her fawn appeared next. They spun, bouncing back into the trees when they smelled death. Shouts and cries extended up and down the line as animals beyond Ontarra's vision were turned or dropped. Ontarra glanced at the trap again. Deer were piling up faster than the hunters could remove them. More hunters abandoned the blinds to help throw the carcasses down to the women.

A buck took Ontarra by surprise, appearing like magic on his left. His aim was fast and true. The arrow drove deep into the animal's chest. The buck faltered, took two steps, and dropped on his side as his legs buckled. The slaughter went on for three full hands of time, and still the deer kept coming. No one had ever seen so many. There was already more meat than the town could use. Ontarra saw the drivers pull to a sudden stop as deer approaching the trap smelled blood and came charging back at the line of boys and old men. Many of the boys broke and ran, but the men managed to turn the deer back.

Toutsou lowered his bow, staring in disbelief. Taiwa came climbing up onto the point from the river below, waving her arms frantically. "Too many!" she hollered at the hunters. "We have too many! Stop killing them!" The hunters looked at one another as if she was insane. Taiwa saw Toutsou and ran out across the killing ground.

"Get out of there!" Toutsou screamed. "You're in the kill zone!" Toutsou saw a blur pass across the ridge. Taiwa grabbed at her neck and crumpled to her knees. Toutsou spun around to see who'd fired. None of the men with him had taken the shot. His eyes searched the trees across the ravine. He saw no one. Running out, he grabbed Taiwa by the arm and dragged her to the blinds, just as a six-point deer dashed into the open and a hand of arrows cut him down.

Toutsou pulled Taiwa's hand away to see the wound. "Something stung me!" she gasped, staring in shock at the blood on her hand. The arrow left a long slit in the skin but didn't cut the vein.

"Something stung you, all right!" Toutsou scanned the trees across the ravine again. "Come on, we're getting out of here!" He grabbed her wrist, pulling her along the outside edge of the palisade so they would at least be safe from charging animals.

The men in Ontarra's line started closing toward the trap. The Entry River blocked their way as it swung into a ravine between them and the trap. The entire line shifted left, bunching up to avoid the defile. They held their bows at the ready as they moved in. Two more deer were taken along the line. So far, none had escaped. Men nodded and grinned to each other as the drive neared its climax.

Ontarra could see the walls of the trap through the trees ahead. The smell of blood, entrails, and feces struck him. His eyes swung in the direction of the stench, staring down into the ravine. He froze, shocked at the number of deer strewn down the hillside and heaped on the riverbank. He thought he heard Taiwa's voice. His gaze swept up again in the direction of the trap. He saw Toutsou pulling Taiwa along the palisade.

Ontarra broke the line. Running forward, he cupped his hands to his mouth, calling out, "What's wrong?" He could see Taiwa crying. Toutsou gestured for him to come. Ontarra broke into a trot and then slid to a stop. A buck, with a rack larger than Ontarra had ever seen, was staring at him from the brush, only a stone's cast away. Ontarra pulled an arrow to his cheek, sighting down the shaft.

"No!" Taiwa screamed. "Don't kill it, Ontarra! We've killed too many already!" Her voice was frantic. Ontarra hesitated. The buck stared down the arrow at him.

"Drop him!" a man yelled from behind. "Shoot!"

The buck charged ahead. Ontarra swung to fire but caught the chert point on a sapling and snapped it off. A hunter ran to plug the opening that Ontarra had left in the line. The man shouted, jumped and waved his arms to turn the buck, but it had no intention of going back. It leaped to clear the man's head, but its rear hooves slammed into the hunter's face before he could duck out of the way. Arrows flew after the buck, but none found its mark. The buck plunged through the feeder creek, and the brush swallowed him up.

Ontarra ran to the injured man. It was the hunter who had laughed so hard when the rabbits came through earlier. His face was splayed open from his left temple to below his right ear. The nose was mashed, the lower half dangling from his lip. Hunters and warriors crowded around. He was still alive, so they commandeered a canoe and rushed him back to town. The hunter died.

Clan council was called that night. Foolishly causing a man to be injured and killed was bad enough, but the big buck smashed a huge swath through the upper fields, destroying valuable crops. Sannisen listened to the angry voices out in the plaza, trying to control his own anger. He glanced over at Shanoka as she tended the wound on Taiwa's neck. His jaw tightened. He turned to Toutsou, sitting on Ontarra's sleep platform. "You're sure it wasn't an accident?"

Toutsou gave his head a negative shake. "It was no accident. The arrow flew straight and fast. A stray shot couldn't have cleared all the trees in the woods and still carried so much speed. Someone fired from the treeline across the ravine."

Shanoka looked up from the platform where Taiwa was lying, her luminous eyes wrinkled at the corners with worry. "Who could it be?"

"Someone on clan council, probably. Bird clan for sure." Sannisen folded his arms across his chest and started pacing between the fire and the door. He knew he should try to calm himself, but he was finding it difficult.

"It's my fault that the buck escaped, Father," Ontarra mumbled at the floor, his voice bleak. "That's what they're arguing about out there. If it is their intention to punish me, I should go and address them."

Sannisen stopped pacing and dropped his arms. "All of you remain right here. I'll speak to the clan council." He spun and ducked out.

"You did the right thing, Ontarra." Taiwa tried to sound reassuring, but she realized that she was probably the only person in Ounontisaston who truly believed he'd done the right thing.

Sannisen walked straight into the plaza with a purposeful stride. Angry voices subsided as he approached the fire. He swung his gaze from left to right, taking note of each friend and foe. His eyes settled on Thadayo. "What is being discussed here, Thadayo?"

Thadayo stood, pursing his lips. He could see the anger in Sannisen's stance and was not looking forward to this. "Sannisen, a man has been killed, crops destroyed—"

"And my family will make restitution for this," Sannisen said, cutting him off. "What else?"

Thadayo glanced around furtively at the council members. They were studying their feet, looking at the sky—looking anywhere but at Sannisen. He took a deep breath. "The argument has been made that there will be no deer here for next autumn's drive. The vote was slightly in favor of banishing Ontarra … and Taiwa."

Sannisen glared from face to face. The Bird clans had one more voice at council than the Land clans. "I think I can guess who is asking for this. Do you really believe that I will allow a member of my family to be banished? I have the warriors; Soutoten has the hunters. I'm warning you all right now, if anything unusual happens to my family, we will remove every Bird clan member from Ounontisaston beneath a solid line of war clubs." He waited in silence to be sure his words were fully understood. "I believe the deer will be here next cycle. If they are, we've been slaughtering them for nothing. Things have changed, and there will be more changes." The threatening tone of Sannisen's voice and his withering stare left no doubt that he meant what he said.

10

THE MORNING AIR WAS CRISP. A frosting of white coated the ground, but the clear sky promised a warm fall day as the people of Ounontisaston assembled in the canoe area. A light breeze stirred the trees. Vibrant leaves fluttered down into the canoes, pattering across the current of the Entry River and spiraling downstream in the swirling eddies.

Bones of loved ones, tenderly cleaned and colored with ocher and charcoal, were wrapped in the finest skins. Men carefully loaded them in the canoes for their final journey. Brata's mate, Sakawa, far too old to make the trek to Tontiaton, had asked Shanoka to take her. She laid Brata down in the center of the canoe while Ontarra held it steady against the shore. Shanoka stepped lightly over Brata and took her place in the bow.

It had been seven cycles since the last Festival of the Dead. All of Ounontisaston's families had lost someone. Soutoten and his men were away on a hunt. Sannisen had expected them to be back by now. With many of the warriors still off on raids, he ordered the young warriors and hunters to remain in the silent town as sentries. Sounia reluctantly agreed to stay and prepare meals for the young men. Fewer than a hundred people would be in Ounontisaston for the coming three days.

Ontarra waited while several Bird clan families pushed off. They studiously avoided any eye contact with him. Since Sannisen threatened the clan council, the old atmosphere of animosity had returned. Taiwa grinned, waving to someone up on the bluff. Ontarra looked up to see Sounia on the hillside, watching the exodus. She placed her hand over her breast and shot her open palm out at Ontarra, throwing her heart to him. Ontarra threw his back. Taiwa giggled.

"I wish Toutsou was here to see that," she snickered. Ontarra's lips curled into an embarrassed grin.

Toutsou had left for Tontiaton the previous day. He'd convinced Ontarra that the present circumstances demanded the trail be scouted ahead. Ontarra felt a bit uneasy that Toutsou wouldn't be around to watch their backs along the river. Taiwa settled herself down on a travel pack in the center of the canoe. Ontarra stepped in back and pushed out into the current before seating himself. He laid his bow and several arrows on Brata, where he could reach them fast.

Shanoka was as skilled with a canoe as any man. Stroking into turns, ruddering around bends and rocks, she guided them down the Entry River, swinging the craft hard right when they reached the Tranchi. They passed the island where the battle had begun. Cutting silently through the ambush site, Ontarra pictured enemy warriors lining the banks on both sides, He shuddered at the thought of being caught in such a vulnerable position.

At the forks, a long line of canoes cut out from the lower branch, carving left into the main channel. People of Kandoucho and Teotonguiaton waved, shouting greetings to friends and relatives they hadn't seen in many cycles. The boisterous yells died away. People pointed and whispered in low tones when the new chief family of the Attawondaronks was spotted. Ontarra attempted not to notice all the eyes riveted on them as they passed. Shanoka smiled and nodded to everyone, but leaned hard into her paddle to propel them past the gawkers.

The sun was rising above the treetops when they reached the landing that marked the overland route to Tontiaton. Warriors skidded and slid down to the water; they pulled canoes up the high banks as they arrived, in case of high water while they were left untended. Men from Tontiaton loaded packs onto pole sleds harnessed to dogs, to help ease the burden of the older people. Many of those milling around the landing had blackened their faces to show they were still in mourning.

Because the dogs would travel faster than the people, the animals were started down the trail first. Ontarra scrutinized the area, looking for anyone who might pose a threat. He was relieved to see Toutsou coming down the trail with another of the young hunters at his side. He recognized the young Doe clan hunter, Taskinao. Ontarra could see Toutsou's prudence and foresight in their accoutrements. They were deep in conversation as they stepped absently to one side, letting the dogs pass. Toutsou and Taskinao each had a knife and throw-stick in their waistbands. On the lower left side of their leggings, an elongated pouch was loaded with arrows. If they had to kneel down for cover under fire, their arrows would be right in front of them. Their bows were already strung and hanging over their shoulders. Each of them leaned on a tall walking staff that seemed innocuous enough to onlookers but would be highly efficient at quickly rendering an opponent passive in a close fight.

Taskinao saw Ontarra and dipped his head in a quick greeting. Toutsou looked over, beckoning with a sweep of his arm before turning back to the conversation with Taskinao. He pointed into the forest, chopping with his hand toward the south. Taskinao dipped a curt nod and headed off into the brush.

"Ho, Toutsou," Ontarra said, gripping Toutsou's shoulder. "What have you found?"

"We've checked the entire trail. There's no sign of danger. We've been over the immediate area for three arrow-flights in all directions. Now we're going to travel back to Tontiaton on each side of you, just beyond sight of the trail, so that no one gets curious about what we are up to."

Ontarra scanned the faces in the landing again as he listened. "How does the town look?"

Toutsou leaned on his walking staff. Ontarra noticed that a sharp point had been charred on the top. Toutsou chewed on his lower lip before answering, "There are more people at Tontiaton than I have ever seen in one place. If we have any trouble, that is where it will be. I've explained our concerns to Satwani. He's sending two warriors out to meet you at the Tonti and escort you into town." Toutsou looked over Ontarra's shoulder; Ontarra followed his gaze.

More canoes were arriving. Men began to trample down the huge golden weeds and purple-topped nettles to make more room. People started moving out in small groups. Ontarra didn't want any more potential threats ahead of him than necessary. "We'd better get moving."

"Don't worry," Toutsou said, flashing a quick grin. "We've got you covered while you're on the trail." He turned and threaded off into the forest.

Ontarra tied Brata to the travel pack and hoisted her to his shoulder so Shanoka and Taiwa could walk unfettered. The path to Tontiaton was well worn from two cycles of continuous use. The forest floor was a carpet of bright colors, with crisp leaves crunching underfoot. Sunlight sifted through the dying canopy of the forest, splashing its warmth over faces and raising everyone's spirits.

Adults talked and laughed as they trudged along. Children scampered into the woods to investigate everything. Bright yellow crab apples began to appear as boys brought armloads from a tree they'd located. Land clan people made a point of talking to Shanoka and Taiwa. Bird clan men and women moved silently off the path when Shanoka and Taiwa approached. "It's started again," Shanoka murmured through tight lips, shaking her head sadly.

Taiwa decided to describe another of her dreams to divert her mother's attention. Ontarra was wrapped in his own thoughts, only half-listening. "A red snake and a white snake meet in the forest. The red snake is suspicious of the white snake, because he has tried to hide his color under dark clothing. The white snake finally convinces the red snake that he is a friend. When the red snake isn't watching, the white snake devours him."

"Your dreams have become more and more bizarre, Taiwa, ever since Poutassa cracked you on the head. I wish we could talk to a real seer, so we could decipher their meanings."

Taiwa heard the concern in her mother's voice and rested a comforting hand on her shoulder. "The dreams no longer trouble me, Mother. I dream whenever I'm asleep now. I've learned to observe like a spectator and not be a part of them. I've even begun to see how things in my dreams relate to life in this world. Remember the man with a cross inside a circle on his shoulder?"

Shanoka glanced over, thinking back. "Yes ... the one who frightened you."

Taiwa pushed errant strands of glossy black hair back from her face. "I dreamed he was standing in the shadows again, but this time another man was with him. I moved closer and saw that the other man was Poutassa. Now I know that this man is my enemy, and I must avoid him." Taiwa's revelation did nothing to lighten Shanoka's spirits. They walked on in silence.

By midday, the skeletal leaves on the trail had been pounded into a fine powder. It hung like mist in the air and caught in the throat. People began coughing and hacking. They wandered off the trail into the woods to clear their lungs. Many sat on fallen trees, wolfing down travel cakes or jerked venison. Occasionally, in the distance to his left, Ontarra heard the sharp *Ka! Ka! Ka!* of a crow in distress. It was quickly answered from the thick forest to his right, and he knew Toutsou and Taskinao were nearby. He hadn't discussed any stops with them, so he dug into his travel pack for the smoked mooneye Teota had provided.

They tore and gnawed on the hickory-flavored meat as they walked. A small amount quickly filled the belly as it mixed with stomach fluids and expanded. Ontarra noticed that the unusually flat land they were traveling over was gradually beginning to dip and roll. He couldn't see the change, but he felt it in his calf muscles as they strained up the slight inclines. He knew they were getting close to the Tonti, when the trail began crossing deep ravines cut by feeder creeks. The sun was halfway through its descent when they reached the crest of the ravine that overlooked the Tonti. Ontarra caught glimpses of the palisades of Tontiaton through gaps in the trees on the far ridge. A warrior fell in with them on each side when they reached the river.

They crossed over on logs that had been laid as a footbridge. Ontarra was surprised at how much smaller this river was than the Tranchi. Only nine paces across the bridge, but it was deep enough for canoes, and Lake Iannaoa was only a half day downstream. They approached Tontiaton from the north. It seemed to Ontarra that its walls were continuous. As they moved closer, he noticed that a small entry on the northeast side had been temporarily blocked for security.

Rather than the odd irregular shape dictated by the bluff at Ounontisaston, Tontiaton was almost round. The uplands east, west, and south of the town were perfectly flat fields; the forest had been burned away to make room for crops. Domed travel lodges that could accommodate four people within their bark-and-skin coverings surrounded the palisades. People had been arriving for days, from all of the twenty-eight towns and villages of the Attawondaronk Nation.

Ontarra bent over to scoop up a handful of soil from the path. It was a lighter color than at Ounontisaston. He realized it was full of sand. The trees were more varied here. A mixture of maple, elm, oak, beech, and walnut. As they passed around to the south side of the palisade, Ontarra saw that the ossuary was set out away from the town, across a large open area where the festivities would be held. Shanoka headed directly for it. Taiwa and Ontarra followed. People milled everywhere. Women were preparing all sorts of food, while boys rushed around playing hoop. On the southwest corner of the palisade, a black bear paced back and forth in a cage. He'd been fattened all summer to provide meat for tomorrow's feast.

Ontarra ignored the stares as he carried Brata to the ossuary. He'd seen one once before, at old Ounon. A round pit was gouged into the earth; the soil was hauled aside in baskets. Ontarra estimated that the gaping hole was twenty paces across and deeper than the height of his head. A palisade was erected around three sides of the pit, leaving the north face open so that the dead would have a good view of the town and the festivities to come. A platform suspended around the inside walls, at eye level, was already crowded with bones.

The dead would be at the center of the festivities. They could sing and dance with the living one last time before their souls were released for the long journey to the Village of the Dead. Food and petun lined the pit, so the spirits of the dead could enjoy the pleasures of this world before leaving. Ontarra solemnly laid Brata near the front of the platform, where she would have a good view. Shanoka nodded, turned, and strolled with a confident air back toward the town. Ontarra and Taiwa stayed close. Ontarra spotted the two Tontiaton warriors, shadowing their movements at a respectful distance.

Mouth-watering aromas filled the air. Deer and dogs were skewered over beds of coal. Ontarra saw piles of the silver finger-fish that were netted in unbelievable numbers at Lake of the Okis each spring. He studied the piles spread out on ground skins, recalling a time when he was a young boy. He'd watched fishermen as they hit the water with their paddles, sending basket loads of the tiny fish flying up onto shore.

Roasting corn was heaped around the fires. Baskets of apples, pears, and nuts lined the palisade. Stinking corn was fermenting in bark containers. Several maidens were chattering and laughing as they chewed corn from cobs, spitting the pulp and saliva into bowls to make chewed bread. They flashed toothy yellow grins at Ontarra as he passed. He grinned back, forcing himself not to laugh.

A man hailed Shanoka from the south entry. Satwani greeted her formally by gripping her shoulders. Ontarra hung back, admiring the town's defenses.

It lacked the natural bluff that protected Ounontisaston but made up for it in other ways. The double palisade was built around a freshwater spring. It bubbled up between the walls at the southwest corner, cutting a deep trench all the way to the northern end, where it passed out beneath the protective barrier. It was dammed outside the north palisade, creating a moat and water supply for the town. Anyone who scaled that wall at night was in for a sudden surprise.

Inside the fortification stood eleven longhouses; several individual lodges accommodated visitors and dignitaries. Most were lined up in neat rows, but several sat askew, conforming to rolls and dips in the terrain. Two huge longhouses ran the entire length of the west wall. Ahratota and Dahtka were inspecting the design and marveling at their size. The plaza started at the south entry and bent through the center of town in the shape of a war club. The men had taken over the plaza with gambling, smoking, and telling tales of days gone by. People stopped whatever they were doing to eye the family of Sannisen as they strolled through.

The Rakarota of Kandoucho was in the middle of the story of First Man and First Woman, passing on the legends of the Attawondaronk People to another generation of fervent young faces staring up at him. He stopped mid-sentence, leaving the spellbound children hanging as he stared at Shanoka approaching. A smile of recognition slowly spread across his face. The old man jumped in front of her with his arms spread wide. "Shanoka! I haven't seen you since you were a young maiden."

Shanoka submitted to a quick hug. "Ho, Jik. You have been telling the stories for many cycles now. Have you no one yet to help you?"

Jik's smile faded and he shook his head. "Alas, all the young men wish to be warriors and hunters now. I fear that I must keep the stories alive until the flesh has fallen from my bones."

"Have you considered training one of the maidens?" Shanoka could see by the look on Jik's face that he hadn't. "Jik, I need to speak with Satwani right now," Shanoka said, apologizing with her eyes. "I will come back and talk more with you later." Jik nodded absently, staring past her as if he'd just had a sudden revelation.

They pressed on through the town. Ontarra's eyes swept left and right. He noticed some men milling around a lodge near the northeast palisade. One of them pointed as he whispered to strange-looking men with dark skin and shaved heads. Ontarra squinted, closing his left eye to the slanting sunlight. Hair bristled on his neck, and his face twisted into a scowl. "Poutassa," he spat out under his breath. His hand instinctively dropped to the knife in his waistband, resting on the hilt as he thought. He decided to say nothing and pretended not to see them.

Satwani led them to a small longhouse near the north wall. The two big longhouses sat to its right, making it seem tiny. "I've made room for you in the Lynx clan lodge," Satwani said. He directed them to the rear of the longhouse, where a space had been separated off by hanging hides from the rafters. "I'm sorry there was nothing more private available," Satwani apologized.

Shanoka's eyes were already watering from the smoke, but she was gracious and managed a smile. "Why have you requested our presence here, Satwani?"

Satwani took a deep breath and exhaled slowly. "You've probably already guessed that I don't trust Hiatsou and Poutassa. When they arrived here, they spread a story that Poutassa had killed a Windigo monster—that his face and body had been mutilated in the fight."

Shanoka shook her head and looked away in disgust. "And your chiefs believed that? Don't you know what happened at Ounontisaston?"

Satwani hunched an awkward shrug. "We knew, but we needed a shaman. We didn't feel it mattered if they embellished their Powers a bit, and Poutassa is certainly no threat to the maidens anymore." Satwani glanced pointedly at Ontarra.

"I wouldn't be so sure of that," Shanoka fumed with a cutting stare.

Satwani nodded as he rubbed a gnarled hand across his face. "Well, the shaman society met here for summer solstice. Hiatsou cajoled them into agreeing that no shaman would go to Ounontisaston. Ayontat urged them to reconsider, but Hiatsou and Poutassa held sway with horror stories of their persecutions at the hands of the Land clans. Now, Hiatsou has convinced a lot of our young people that Poutassa is the greatest shaman the Attawondaronk Nation has ever known. I think Hiatsou has actually come to believe it himself."

"I'm sure he does," Shanoka said. She made no effort to hide her bitterness. "He's crazy—they're both crazy. If you want my advice, you should go out there and kill them right now."

Satwani shook his head. "It's no longer that simple. As soon as the apprentices arrived from Ounontisaston, Hiatsou elevated their status and privileges. They're all full shamans now. Their only goal since arriving here has been to convince the young people that Poutassa can gain them Power and wealth and that he will protect them in this life and the next."

Shanoka rolled her eyes. "Never mind. Tell me how Ayontat died."

Satwani rubbed at his chin, staring at some distant place in the hearth flames. "I've never seen anything like it," he said slowly. "He got sick. His skin grew pale, and his eyes seemed to turn … yellow. The third day of his illness, he called for me. He tried to tell me something about Hiatsou, but he died before he could explain. Hiatsou told me that Ayontat just wanted to be sure it was you who performed the reincarnation ceremony. Frankly, I would have asked for you anyhow."

"That's exactly the same sickness Tsohahissen had last cycle," Shanoka muttered, more to herself than Satwani. "Tragedy follows wherever they go. Those two are going to be trouble for our people as long as they live. It seems we have slain the monster, only to find ourselves in a world filled with venomous snakes."

"Who are those strange men I saw with them?" Ontarra wanted to know.

"The Erieehronon trader, Dekari, brought three men here from the west. They have asked to trade for petun seed. Because they are from so far away, council is considering the trade."

Shanoka grimaced. "Dekari is a despicable man. Why are these strangers with Hiatsou?"

"They seem to be interested in our rituals," Satwani answered. "They've asked to stay and observe the festival. Hiatsou offered to share his lodge while they're here."

Shanoka gave her head a dubious shake. "Hiatsou never helps anyone unless there is something in it for him. I want them all kept away from us, Satwani." She rubbed her temples between a thumb and forefinger. "Let's get the ceremony over tonight. I want to leave at first light."

Satwani steepled his fingers thoughtfully. "As you wish. There is a stickball game being organized now. After that, we will feast and begin the ceremony."

"If it's all right with you, Satwani, I'd like Taiwa to perform the ceremony. She knows it well, and I want to keep my eyes on Hiatsou."

Satwani smiled at Taiwa. "I've heard of Taiwa's abilities. I would be honored; so will Ayontat." He turned back to Shanoka. "I will instruct the two warriors to remain with you while you're here." Satwani pushed the skin partition back and sidled out.

Shanoka sighed softly and started untying the travel pack. She removed her ceremonial dress, spreading it out on a sleep platform, and then dug in the pack again and laid an identical dress beside hers. Taiwa's breath caught in her throat. She snatched up the dress, holding it to her chest.

"Mother! It's beautiful!"

Shanoka smiled for what felt like the first time that day.

Ontarra would have liked to join in the stickball game, but his duty lay elsewhere. He wondered about the strangers with Hiatsou and Poutassa. His mother's obvious concern about them was troubling. He thought about how he would feel if his mother or Taiwa were hurt. Ontarra pulled his knife, running a thumb across the edges and feeling a flash of anger at his spirit guide for eluding him so long. A thought insinuated itself in the back of his mind. *You are a warrior when you believe that you are a warrior.*

Ontarra sheathed the knife and dug into his travel pack. He removed Ounsasta's war club, holding it straight out with his right arm. It felt lighter now—more natural. He wasn't allowed to carry a war club until he had full warrior status, but he didn't care anymore. Defiantly, he hung it from his waistband. He searched through his travel pack until he found his trophy feathers. He tied them to his headband so they hung down over his right ear.

Shanoka and Taiwa finished dressing. Shanoka turned, and her heart caught. Seeing Ontarra as a man for the first time, she felt a heady mixture of pride and loss. The knot in her throat embarrassed her. Ontarra expected her to be annoyed, so he was surprised to see moisture brimming in her eyes. Shanoka managed a smile and brushed past him, shoving the hides aside without saying a word.

The two warriors who had met them at the river yesterday were guarding the door to the longhouse. They fell in on each side of Shanoka and Taiwa; Ontarra took the rear. They were a Powerful-looking group as they strolled through the town. People couldn't keep themselves from staring. Shanoka deliberately plotted a course past Poutassa and Hiatsou, daring them to approach her. Her eyes blazed vindictively as she walked slowly past them.

Hiatsou returned her stare. It was apparent that his old arrogance had returned.

They threaded through the plaza, greeting people, nodding, and then exiting the south entry just as the stickball game was about to begin. Shanoka picked a sunny spot along the south wall where they could sit and enjoy the competition. The Land clans had challenged the Bird clans. Opposing teams, each with about eight hands of players, paraded around the goal posts with their web-pocketed sticks held high. Like a war dance, they chanted and sang of the feats they were about to perform.

Off to one side, near the center of the field, people were tossing personal treasures into two piles, wagering on the outcome of the contest. The Bird clans, taking no chances, called upon Hiatsou and Poutassa to use their influence with the spirits to strengthen their team and bring calamity upon the Land clan team. The Land clan players responded by calling on Shanoka to do the same. They coaxed her to her feet. Shanoka spread her arms to the sky and sang a short song, imploring the manitos to play on the side of the Land clans. An old man threw a skin-covered ball out onto the field, and the game was on.

Anything was allowed in the frenzied chaos to control the ball. Stomping, hitting, kicking, tackling, tripping, and biting each other caused all types of injuries. Players ran and leapt over each other, violently foiling their opponents until the ball was finally cast between the goal posts, and a point was scored by the Land clans. The Land clan players mocked the Bird clans with insults, gobbling like turkeys and waddling like ducks, to goad them.

The game lasted until late into the afternoon. Players left the field with cuts, gashes, broken bones, and missing teeth. One young man was carried from the field and laid by the palisade so the game could continue—his head was cocked at an odd angle. Shanoka went over to offer some comfort, but he was gone before she reached him. When the sun settled into the treetops to the west, the Bird clans scored their final goal, winning with ten goals to the Land clans' nine.

The feast began immediately, massive quantities of food quickly disappearing. Full bellies soothed the spirits of the disgruntled Land clans. People scooped their bowls full of whatever appealed to them, greedily stuffing themselves. If people had no bowls and food was too hot to hold in their hands, sunflower and burdock leaves were provided.

Ontarra went straight for the sun-dried finger fish. He bit off the heads, spitting them on the ground for the dogs. The rest he gobbled down, bones and all. Some people ate the heads as well; others tossed the fish on the coals, flipping them out again with a stick and then laying the hot meat on chewed bread covered with fresh leeks. Ontarra turned, searching the area with keen eyes while he ate. He hadn't seen Toutsou since leaving the landing at the Tranchi. Choruses of belches brought smiles to the women's faces. It was pleasing to hear the noisy compliments after so much work preparing food. It also made room for one more bowlful.

Hiatsou and Poutassa paraded through the south entry, draped in beaver robes. Three hands of young acolytes followed, wearing breechclouts and with their bodies painted in fantastic designs. They strutted across the playing field to the ossuary. The retinue started to dance, reciting incantations as Hiatsou and Poutassa made a show of sprinkling ashes over the bones. The shamans of Kandoucho, Khioetoa, and Teotonguiaton joined them to personally attend the dead from their own towns. The dancers gathered food that was left over and tossed it into the pit for the spirits.

A melancholy rhythm from log drums and bone whistles rose and fell. People with family members on the platform joined the dance. The dead could feel comfortable about leaving, now that they were properly feasted and honored. Tonight was their last night in this world. Tomorrow, their bones would be interred, the pit covered over, and a great bonfire would be made of the ossuary palisade. Spirits would be released from the bones by the intense flames and would rise up with the smoke on their way to the heavens. The bear would be roasted over the coals for the entire day.

Satwani strolled over, bending to whisper in Shanoka's ear. She stood, brushing herself off, and then motioned for Ontarra before walking to the edge of the playing field. Ontarra popped a last fish into his mouth and ambled over.

"Taiwa will perform the Naming Ceremony," Shanoka whispered. "Stay near us." She walked out onto the field, raising her arms for attention. "Quiet, everyone ... quiet!" She took in the crowd with a sweep of her eyes. "Tontiaton has a new chief! The spirit of Ayontat waits to join us in his new body!"

Taiwa stepped up, grasping Satwani's hand. "Prepare yourself to receive his spirit," she instructed. Satwani tipped his head back. Closing his eyes, he held his arms out to his sides and rolled his palms forward. "Spirit of

Ayontat!" Taiwa cried in a voice that could wake the dead. "We know you are here among us! We ask that you join us now, in the body of Satwani! Come! Continue to guide us with your wisdom and knowledge!" Taiwa bent at the waist, pressing her palm flat to the ground. Lifting it slowly, she pulled Ayontat from the earth, and lowered him into Satwani's head.

Matoupa and Manak stood near the ossuary with Hiatsou. Matoupa listened to the muffled voices around him. He'd begun to understand some of their language. It was similar to Tuscarora, but they spoke it crooked. "What are they doing?" Manak asked, dumbfounded.

"She's putting the spirit of the dead chief into the new chief," Matoupa whispered, eyes still glued to the ritual. Matoupa leaned to Dekari. "Can she really do such a thing?"

Dekari, mesmerized by the reincarnation, didn't answer for a moment. He shot a sidelong glance. "Look at the faces of the people," he said, jerking his head. Matoupa studied the hypnotic stares. People were enthralled; they witnessed this supernatural occurrence in slack-jawed silence.

"I feel your spirit, Ayontat!" Satwani shuddered and slumped forward. For a heartbeat, it seemed he might topple, but suddenly he straightened. "I have returned," he cried in an unnaturally thick voice, "to help Satwani guide our people!" The crowd applauded Taiwa's mastery of the ritual. Yells and war whoops rolled across the fields of Tontiaton.

Satwani opened his eyes, holding his hands high to silence the crowd. "I have something to tell you that will be of interest to many. Shanoka can provide a potion that will plant the seed of a child into a barren—"

"What? No!" Shanoka grabbed Satwani's arm to stop him. "Who told you that?" Shanoka's uncharacteristic outburst took Satwani by surprise. His bewildered eyes stared down at her; his mouth was agape. Shanoka lowered her voice, turning him away from the onlookers so they could talk without being overheard.

At the ossuary, Manak whispered to Matoupa, "Tell the shaman it is time to prove that what he has told us is true."

Dekari listened as they spoke, and when Matoupa signaled, Dekari leaned toward Hiatsou and said, "They want you to show them."

Hiatsou raked stained teeth over his lip. Nervously wiping sweaty palms on the beaver fur, he searched for the courage that he was about to need. Shanoka and Satwani were in a heated conversation. The baby-potion ploy had created the diversion he'd hoped for, and their backs were still turned. Hiatsou sucked a deep breath, stood, and walked straight to them.

"Poutassa has just advised me that the baby potion is a hoax!" he bellowed so everyone around would hear.

Shanoka spun around and stepped back with a start. Her initial shock at Hiatsou's unexpected presence exploded into anger. "Get away from me!" she snarled through her teeth. Hiatsou slid closer. Shanoka retreated a step. Like magic, the seer's crystal was in her hand. She thrust it in Hiatsou's face, rotating it between her fingers so sunlight refracted into his eyes.

Hiatsou rocked back onto his heels. He didn't want that thing to touch him. Stumbling backward, he jostled into Manak, who was peering intently over Hiatsou's shoulder.

"The Uktena Stone!" Manak gasped. There was no doubt—the eye of the Great Horned Serpent had been described to him all of his life. Sunlight danced through the yellow crystal; a dark pupil stared out from its center. Manak could feel its Power. Hairs on the back of his neck bristled.

Taiwa grabbed her mother's arm, pulling her backward. "Mother," she gasped, her voice tinged with fear, "it's him—the man in my dream!"

Manak couldn't help himself. He lunged, grabbing Shanoka's arm to get a closer look at the sacred stone.

Ontarra was folded up tight and airborne when he slammed into Manak with both knees. The bone-jarring impact emptied Manak's lungs. He flew sideways, crashing to the ground. Before Manak could draw a breath, Ontarra was on him. They tumbled twice and came to their knees in a grapple, knives straining for each other's throat. Most men could never have fought back after such a blow, but Manak had forced his lungs to start working again sometime during the tumble.

Toutsou came in from nowhere, launching himself to slam a foot into Hiatsou's chest. The shaman was too stunned to move out of the way. When he opened his eyes again, he was bent backward over Toutsou's knee, a skinning knife pressed against his windpipe.

Manak was primed now, his size and strength starting to tell. With a violent twist, he rolled Ontarra onto his back. Muscles strained. Manak's knife descended toward Ontarra's throat. Ontarra's knee came up hard, finding Manak's groin. The man barely blinked. Muscles rippled and bulged, and the point of the black blade poked Ontarra's throat. Ontarra felt his skin pop; a warm trickle slithered down his neck.

A foot drove into Manak's diaphragm, his lungs voiding themselves for the second time in a matter of moments. He went limp and fell to his side, choking for air, eyes blazing up at Ontarra. Manak rolled to his knees to protect himself and then saw the ring of chert points penning him in. One of Shanoka's guards kicked the knife from his hand and hauled Manak to his feet.

Satwani shoved through the ring of bowmen, staring angrily at Manak, and then turned a menacing scowl on Hiatsou. "Let him up, Toutsou!" Toutsou wiped his blade on Hiatsou's beaver robe and sheathed it. He straightened abruptly, and Hiatsou fell, his head cracking on the hard-packed soil. Slowly, Hiatsou pushed up on his elbows to face Satwani's wrath. "I'm s-s-sorry, Satwani," he stuttered. "I was just—"

"Silence! Take these strangers back to your lodge and give them whatever they arrived with! They leave our lands tonight!"

In Hiatsou's lodge, Manak and Matoupa huddled together near the back, talking in low tones. Manak was still quivering from the altercation and the thrill of seeing the Uktena Stone. "Did you … see it?" he whispered in a shaky voice. "These people don't even realize what it is."

"The woman knows," Matoupa cautioned. "You saw how she used it to defend herself."

Manak nodded, his knee bouncing with adrenaline as he pictured the crystal again. "Yes, she has Power. I could feel it." He glanced across the hearth at Hiatsou and Poutassa. Poutassa's face twisted into a smug grin as he finished explaining something to Hiatsou. "Get Dekari," Manak ordered, still eyeing the pair. Matoupa left, returning a few moments later with the trader. "Ask him if he believes these two," Manak instructed. Dekari listened to Matoupa in silence, squinting at Hiatsou and Poutassa for a long time before answering. He didn't want to get himself killed over this. The hesitation angered Manak. "Answer me trader!" he snarled in Tunican.

Dekari turned and perched on his heels. "I believe they can be trusted. I've never had much use for Hiatsou in the past," he said softly, "but he has control of their shamans." Dekari glanced over to be sure the two weren't listening. "The young one is cunning"—he tapped his head in the direction of Poutassa—"and the fat one listens to him. Their young people and the

Bird clans seem to believe what they tell them and are willing to do whatever they ask."

Manak nodded thoughtfully, staring out beyond the doorskin as he listened to Matoupa's translation. He bent down and pulled three burden packs from under the sleep platform he was sitting on. Dekari's heart sank when he saw all three. Manak walked around the fire, handing one to Hiatsou and one to Poutassa. He returned for the third and hoisted it up, hesitating a moment to enjoy the look of anguish on Dekari's face. "This one I will keep for you, trader." He shoved it back under the sleep platform. Dekari sighed with relief.

Hiatsou and Poutassa unfolded the packs, spreading the trade goods across the floor. Hiatsou held up a cape made from bright green feathers and then wrapped it over his shoulders. There was a matching headdress. He found two hands of light green stones with little whorls of silver and brown spun through them. Untying a parfleche, he poured out lustrous white beads that sparkled in the firelight like the inner shell of a river clam. At the bottom of the pack, something was wrapped in a thick hide that was covered in lumps and knots. Hiatsou ran his hand over the rough hide. It was definitely a skin but had the texture of walnut bark. He laid the bundle on his sleep robes and spread it open to reveal a black ax, the head and handle carved from a single piece of stone.

"It is a symbol of Power among our people," Matoupa said, answering the questioning look in Hiatsou's eyes. "Any man who wears one is omnipotent."

Hiatsou smiled and shoved the ax into his waistband.

Poutassa found a pair of shell-bead armbands and slid one up above each elbow. He tried on a silver ring that wrapped twice around the finger, ending on top in a coiled serpent's head. It was too big. He handed it to Hiatsou. A bag was packed full of vibrantly colored shells. He opened a carefully folded swath of white fabric and gingerly lifted out a sheet of hammered mica. It was pounded wafer-thin, painstakingly shaped to portray the taloned claw of a huge bird about to snatch its prey. Poutassa traced his fingers along the hideous scars on his face.

Hiatsou pinched his lips, trying to hide his elation at receiving such amazing treasures, his mind already refining Poutassa's plan. He cast a dark smirk at Dekari. "Tell them that we have a trade."

Satwani posted fresh guards at the Lynx clan longhouse. Still, Ontarra found it impossible to sleep. Being confronted by an apparition from her dreams had left Taiwa badly shaken. The dark-skinned warrior hadn't exactly endeared himself to Ontarra, either. Something troubling him suddenly revealed itself—*the man is a warrior, not a trader.*

Ontarra stepped lightly through the longhouse to check on the guards again. Heavy breathing and occasional snores punctuated the darkness. He had to step carefully over sleeping dogs and people. The guards were still there. The first streaks of dawn splashed the bellies of low ribbons of cloud in the eastern sky. Ontarra relieved the guards so they could get something to eat. Then he settled himself down on a stool and rested Ounsasta's club across his knees.

Beyond the north palisade, the sounds of lodges being dismantled rose in the chilled morning air. Fishermen wanted to get back to their nets, and the women were anxious to finish the harvest before the weather turned. The fishermen were mostly Bird clan, and their families would have to leave with them. Ontarra chuckled, listening to the Bird clan women griping at the men over being forced to miss the final day of feasting, while the Land clan women could remain behind.

The festivities had lasted long into the night. No one within the town was up yet. The arguing and bickering beyond the north palisade finally got some faces poking from doorways, but the sun was well above the trees before the first aromas of morning meals began sifting through the town. Ontarra noticed two men crossing the plaza. He held a hand up to shield slanting rays from his eyes. They were armed to the teeth. He jumped up, club in hand, scrutinizing them closely. He relaxed when Toutsou waved a greeting.

"Ho, Ontarra." Toutsou's face cracked into a patronizing grin. "You know, I really don't think you hit that skinhead warrior hard enough."

Ontarra snorted a laugh, giving his head a bewildered shake. "I really didn't expect him to get up again." Ontarra's smile faded. "You noticed that he was a warrior too?"

Toutsou nodded. "I watched the strangers a long time yesterday. Two are traders, but the big one with that weird earlobe plug and the one you bowled over are definitely warriors. You can see it in their eyes and the way they carry themselves."

"And in the way he fights," Taskinao said with a smirk. "I got a good look at that earlobe plug," he added. "It's a neck vertebrae—human."

Toutsou gave his head a shake and looked to Ontarra. "When do you expect to leave? We want to move out ahead of you."

"I expect we will be ready by—" Ontarra was interrupted by a rumbling crash beyond the south entry. Women screamed; some men started yelling. Toutsou scanned the area behind him and turned back to Ontarra with knitted brows. "Sounded like a tree falling," Ontarra speculated.

Female voices began to keen. As the commotion grew louder, Ontarra felt a need to investigate, but he didn't dare to leave Taiwa and his mother unguarded. "Toutsou, wait here. I'm going in to wake them." He turned just as Shanoka ducked out.

"What's happening?" She was already dressed in her traveling clothes. Taiwa popped out behind her, dragging the travel pack.

Ontarra shrugged. "Something fell." They stared out across the plaza, listening to the mournful cries. Satwani walked rapidly around the end of the big longhouse, with two of his warriors hustling to keep up. Satwani was clearly agitated. He didn't waste time on formalities.

"Shanoka, you must come at once. The ossuary collapsed. It's a terrible omen." Satwani wrung his hands. "Everyone is frightened—we have to get them calmed down." Satwani sounded out of breath.

"We're ready to leave, Satwani. I want to get back while there is still some daylight." Shanoka could see how upset he was, but she didn't dare meddle with all of the shamans here. She laid a comforting hand on Satwani's shoulder. "Satwani, it is the shamans who must deal with this."

"The shamans aren't here, Shanoka. They've gone off with all the apprentices to perform some idiotic ritual, at the only time I can ever recall really needing them!" Ontarra and Toutsou traded a suspicious look. Shanoka rubbed her cheek with her fingers and stared at the ground. "All right," she sighed, "I will try to put everyone at ease." She pushed past Satwani, heading for the south entry. Taiwa ran to catch up.

Ontarra disappeared into the longhouse, calling over his shoulder to Toutsou, "Stick with them while I get my things."

Shanoka started shouting orders as she crossed the stickball field. Two of the ossuary walls had collapsed into the pit, scattering the bones of the dead into a jumbled mass. "How could this have happened?" Taiwa whispered.

"I don't know," Shanoka muttered, staring down at the hopeless tangle of wood and skeletons. She leaned down and pulled out two sturdy saplings about three paces in length and set them to the side. "We must act like nothing is wrong—like we've done this before," she whispered. "Push the rest of the walls into the pit!" Shanoka yelled to the people standing in anxious knots. In a hand of time, the ossuary was heaped to its brim with wood, and all the bones were hidden from view.

Shanoka walked calmly to a cooking fire and pulled out a burning log. She started a low chant. Walking to each side, she set the tinder afire. When four good blazes were started, she tossed the burning log to the center. Shanoka whispered instructions to Taiwa. Together, they sang a psalm to raise the souls of the dead to the heavens. Other women gradually joined in, their anguish over the calamity quickly fading in the comfort of prayer.

Roaring flames licked skyward, tongues of orange leaping away and disappearing in a spiraling vortex of cinder and ash. An old woman pointed to the spirit of her mate, departing in a wispy flare of orange. Others saw their loved ones higher up in the billowing gray column of smoke. The pyre moaned and caved in on itself.

Shanoka nodded to Taiwa. They picked up the two saplings and moved to opposite sides of the pit. Shanoka swung her gaze over the puzzled faces of the mourners and then closed her eyes and lifted her face to the heavens. "Creator of all things! We mingle the bones of our families, so that in death, they will bind our people together!"

Shanoka and Taiwa walked around the ossuary, probing into the embers and mixing bones and the ancestors of the nation together as one. Shanoka offered the sapling to the old woman whose mate had embarked on his journey in a tongue of flame. She hesitated but then took the charred pole, hobbled over to the pit. and stirred as tears slithered down her creviced cheeks. A woman with her face painted black stepped over to Taiwa. Taiwa surrendered her sapling and backed away.

Ontarra watched from the south entry, shifting his gaze between his mother and Taiwa and several maidens bathing in the ditch between the palisades. At Ontarra's request, Satwani had assigned two warriors as escorts for the trek back to the Tranchi. Shanoka approached, casting a questioning eye at the warriors and then to Ontarra.

"I don't want to run into those strangers on the trail by myself," he answered simply. Ontarra nodded to Toutsou and Taskinao at the southwest corner. They turned and headed out. "I'll take the lead," Ontarra instructed the warriors. "You bring up the rear. Keep your clubs ready." He looked to his mother. "One of you will have to carry the travel pack this time." Shanoka heaved the pack to her shoulder, sliding the tumpline onto her forehead. Ontarra moved out. Shanoka could hear the warriors talking quietly behind her.

"He's dressed as a full warrior again. Something should be said."

The other warrior snickered. "Did you see him drop that darky yesterday? You can censure him if you want. I'm not saying a word."

Shanoka and Taiwa traded a grin as they listened to the exchange.

The trail was busy, but the morning slipped away uneventfully, and Ontarra began to relax. The hush of early autumn was broken occasionally by crows in distress, assuring Ontarra that Toutsou and Taskinao were close by. People started breaking off into the woods for a midday meal. Shanoka dug out some finger fish, passing them out so they could eat on the move.

When they reached the Tranchi, a lot of the canoes had already left. Some were out on the river, leisurely making their way upstream, their occupants enjoying one of the last warm days of the cycle. Ontarra felt a little foolish as he thanked the warriors for wasting their day on a fruitless trek.

"There is no such thing as too much caution, Ontarra," the older one said, smiling. He helped Ontarra drag the canoe down the bank, clapped him on the shoulder, and headed back.

At the forks of the Tranchi, Ontarra turned the canoe in to shore. Shanoka and Taiwa hopped out, helping him pull a canoe full of provisions from the underbrush where Sannisen had hidden it the day before. Everything he needed on his vision quest was there. He looked from his mother to Taiwa, uncertain what to say. Shanoka broke the silence with a hug. "Be careful."

"Sounia is going to be miserable until you return," Taiwa said.

Ontarra drew in a deep breath and glanced up at the sky. "She knows that I must do this." He noticed it was one of those rare days when the moon was visible in the daytime sky. Staring at the lopsided disc, a thought came to him. "Tell Sounia to look at the moon each night as it rises, and that I will be watching back from the other side." Taiwa tried to keep a straight face but couldn't. Ontarra's lips thinned as he shot her an exasperated scowl. "Just tell her I'll be back when the moon is full then!"

Ontarra had an uneasy feeling about letting them carry on alone. He was relieved when he saw Toutsou and Taskinao pull in and wait on the opposite shore. With no further reason to remain, he climbed in and started up the south branch. At the first bend, he twisted and stared back. They were still watching him from the forks. He waved, slipped around the headland, and disappeared from their sight.

The Tranchi's south branch was only half the width of the northern channel. At first, the high banks towered above him, falling in a precipitous decline to the river's edge. Over eons, water had twisted and flowed around the moraines and ridges, cutting a deep trough through the landscape. Loops and wild course swings made for slow progress. Tall trees covered both banks, their branches reaching across, trying to touch but not quite able to. In summer, the river here was an eerie trench of twilight and shadows. Today, the trees were nearly bare. Ontarra was soon sticky with perspiration from sweltering sunlight beating on his back.

Gradually, the high banks eased down, angling inland away from the river. The tight valley opened onto a broad floodplain and straightened into an easterly flow. The banks sank down to chest height, allowing Ontarra a clear view into the naked forest. Shadows of trees darkened the waters near shore, leaving a glittering path of sunlight midstream. Brilliant flashes danced off the ripples, stabbing Ontarra's eyes. He tried to navigate with his head turned to the side and one eye clamped shut.

Elm, maple, ash, and oak grew thick across the river flat. Marshy areas created huge gaps that plunged deep into the forest. Willows grew along their edges. Only marsh grasses, cattails, and bog willow took root in the black muck. A red-winged blackbird burst from the tawny stalks, hovering just out of Ontarra's reach. In spring it would have dove and feinted aggressively, chasing Ontarra an arrow-flight upstream from its nest, but the season was late and the instinct dim. Ontarra taunted the feisty bird with his paddle. The red-wing broke off his attack to perch on a swaying cattail—still defiant but from a distance.

In places the river was shallow. Lily pads and raccoon weed clogged the channel. The canoe plowed over them with little effort. Where the banks were high enough to remain dry all summer, stinging nettles and flower thistles grew taller than a man could reach. Numerous feeder creeks flowed into the main river from the north and south. In the silt plugging their mouths, stinking cabbage grew in thick, sprawling patches.

The floodplain began to rise and fall in gentle hillocks. At some of the larger creeks, fields were carved into the forest. People ran out, waving, urging Ontarra to visit. He briefly explained the purpose of his journey as he drifted by and politely declined their generosity. Most of these people would winter at Teotonguiaton, a day's journey farther up the river. The small town guarded the overland route from the Tranchi to the Kandia, the other great river of the Attawondaronk territory. The Kandia began in the land of the Wendats, flowing south to empty its waters into Lake Iannaoa. Kandoucho sat on its western bank, a half day above the lake.

Ontarra recognized a large stream joining the Tranchi from the southwest. He twisted around, shielding his eyes to squint at the hill an arrow-flight up it. In the shadows of the trees, poking above the veil of brush, he could just make out a few remaining posts of a rotted palisade. His father had taken him there as a child to see an ancient village of their ancestors, long abandoned.

Ontarra closed his eyes and rolled his head back, basking in the illusion of solitude the river provided. He was never really alone—wildlife was everywhere. Ducks with green heads, red heads, and brown heads exploded in a flurry of wings at every bend. The little ducks with the puffy black heads brought a smile to his lips as they raced ahead of the canoe, dove below the surface, and reappeared an amazing distance behind him. He heard the mournful cry of loons in the distance, but he never did see one.

Noisy flocks of black-head geese were flying their arrowhead formation, haunting cries urging each other on as they followed the sun to its winter home. Slanting rays of sunlight painted a lonely row of fish-scale clouds high above the geese. He wondered what it would be like to travel the world with the ease of a black-head goose.

The canoe sliced silently on. Ontarra saw a pair of the huge gray fisherbirds ahead. They patiently stalked the water's edge on their spindly legs, watching for any movement below the surface. One froze, aimed his long beak, stabbed, and flipped his head back. A minnow wriggled and squirmed through the air and then disappeared down the bird's gullet. Ontarra laughed, startling the birds with his presence.

Fisherbirds normally flew away from an intruder, but a sharp bend upstream put the treeline too close to clear. Their huge wings struggled to lift them skyward. Ontarra held his breath, silently praying as they passed over. The indignant male emptied his bowels in a long white stream that trailed across the water, splattering over Ontarra's travel pack. Ontarra winced. Without thinking, he scraped some of the slimy paste up on a fingertip and sniffed. The combination of feces and fish made his stomach roll over. He screwed up his face in disgust, deciding in a single dry heave that fisherbirds were filthy creatures. He splashed some water on his travel pack to keep the smell down and flipped it over.

The sun was slipping below the treetops when Ontarra found the mouth of the river he wanted. It flowed into the south branch from out of the north. The river was small, only two canoe-lengths wide. The mouth was flanked on each side by high banks. A deteriorating farm lodge peeked over the crest of the northwest ridge. Ontarra guided the canoe between the headlands and pushed upstream.

He'd only been here once, but he liked this little river. The trees on each bank mingled their branches overhead like the arched roof of an endless longhouse meandering through the wilderness. No one lived along this river. Shallow rapids that canoes had to be dragged over interfered with travel. Sannisen had located his hunt camp on it for the isolation it provided.

Ontarra saw striped sucker fish darting off the bottom as the shadow of his canoe passed over. Several times he was blocked by tumbles of stony rapids, forcing him to climb out and haul the canoe over the slippery rocks. He had to go under or around trees that had fallen and straddled the stream from bank to bank. He was tired and soaked when the light of day failed him, only halfway up the river to the camp. Stiff and sore, he lifted the packs from the canoe and dragged it up onto high ground. Winter was in the air. Curling mist was already rising off the water in the evening chill. Ontarra rolled the canoe onto its side and spread his sleep robes beneath its meager shelter. He gathered wood, sparking a flame with his firestones, and then rolled into his robes and watched the sinuous orange tongues take hold. He tried not to think about food—he was determined not to eat again until he met his guardian spirit.

Ontarra's stomach woke him before dawn. Churning and growling, it felt like it had begun to digest itself. His legs were unsteady. He had to fight a whirl of dizziness before bending to the river for a drink. The canoe and pack seemed heavier than yesterday. His joints ached with every stroke as he pushed upstream. The river was getting smaller and shallower. He spent more time muscling the canoe over and around obstacles than he did paddling. He stopped long enough to attach a hide tether to the bow, so he could pull the canoe over rapids without bending his back.

At first his teeth chattered from the chill in the air and the frigid water. But by the time the sun was directly overhead, he was soaked with sweat. He had to stop for rest. A watery blister had erupted in the hollow between his thumb and forefinger. Ontarra cursed his carelessness as he gingerly peeled the pasty skin away and wrapped a swath of rabbit hide over the raw flesh.

He scanned upstream for something that would touch a memory; he searched for anything that might give a hint where he was. His eyes settled on the leaning trunk of a dead elm. Ontarra jumped to his feet. Hands shaking with excitement, he dragged the canoe through the rapids and then jumped in and paddled to where the ancient trunk canted out over the water. He recognized the gnarled scar that Sannisen had gouged many cycles ago, and he let out a whoop.

Ontarra glanced at the sun—it was almost in the treetops. He got his second wind and paddled on with a sense of urgency. The rapids were so shallow now. He had to remove his packs, setting them on shore while he eased the canoe over rocks. He paddled furiously through the deeper water, leaning forward anxiously at each bend to gaze upstream. He started wondering if he'd gone too far when he spied a clearing up ahead. In a shadowy grove, he saw the arched roof of a bark lodge. Ontarra sat back, exhaling with relief, and then forced himself on.

The little valley around the lodge was a forest of walnut trees. They'd spread out over the entire area. A lazy creek wound its way through the valley. Where its progress was hindered by walnut roots, the whirls and eddies of spring floods had carved out deep pools and lopsided ponds. A stone's throw west of the camp, the little creek spilled into the main river.

Ontarra walked the creek's bank, pulling the canoe by its tether. He'd forgotten how unusual this place was. Toxins from walnut husks permeated the soil of the grove. Nothing could grow beneath the trees except a strain of grass that was only knee-high. Instead of the impenetrable brush that normally clogged the woodlands near rivers, a wide expanse of open area spread out in all directions. From where Ontarra stood, he could see out through the trunks past the river an arrow-flight west, to the low hills on the opposite side of the valley.

He hoisted his packs from the canoe and hauled them up out of the creek. Resting against a walnut trunk, he studied the lodge. It was similar in size and shape to their home at Ounontisaston—nestled into the elbow of a steep ridge that angled off to the north on one side and to the west on the other. In some ancient time, detritus had washed out of the crook where the ridges joined, leaving a ragged ravine and forming a low saddle that pointed like a finger out into the grove. The lodge was tucked to the rear of the saddle, safe from flooding and sheltered from the winds by the ridges on each side. Its door faced west across the valley.

Ontarra hefted a pack, huffing wearily up to the lodge. The roof was sagged in the center. Rotted hide bindings had dropped some of the bark sheets inside. He ducked in to survey the damage. A low growl threatened him from the darkness in the back. Ontarra pulled his knife in one fluid motion and retreated. He backed slowly away from the lodge until he felt his travel pack behind him. Eyes fixed on the door, he groped around for his bow, bent it beneath his armpit, strung it, and pulled three arrows. He gathered twigs and deadfall and managed to spark a fire, still watching for any sign of movement. Wrapping some dry grass around a sturdy limb, he set it ablaze. With knife in hand, he stuck his torch through the door.

Two eyes glowered at him. Ontarra exhaled a long breath, leaned against the doorpost, and burst into laughter. "You are going to have to find yourself another lodge," he said as he walked to the back and jabbed his torch at the raccoon. It arched its back and hissed, but the fire was too much. It sidled past, swaggering indignantly through the lodge and out the door. Ontarra followed, watching the furry freeloader shuffle and sway to the creek before turning a perturbed stare to Ontarra from what seemed a safe distance.

"Are you going to tell the other animals about me? Warn them away?" Ontarra looked over at his bow leaning against a tree, smiled, and shook his head. "I feel that I must warn you not to make trouble." Ontarra pointed his knife for effect. "I have killed a lot of your relatives." The raccoon humped over the bank and out of sight.

Ontarra went back inside. The lodge was littered with raccoon and squirrel droppings. He checked the bottoms of his moccasins, realizing with disgust that the turds weren't all dry. He located some cedar trees out on the ridge and snapped off several boughs to sweep the floor. He piled some firewood in the rear and then went down to the creek, where he gathered rocks to rebuild the hearth. By the time he finished repairing the roof, it was dark. He hung a sleep robe over the door to replace the tattered skin chewed away by animals and eased himself down on his haunches.

His stomach ached. Ontarra propped his travel packs along the back wall, spread his robes, and folded himself in. He watched the fire a moment but then fell into an exhausted sleep. In the night he grew too warm and kicked his robes off to let cool air wash over him. Later, he started to cough. His senses slowly returned to the real world. He found himself drenched in sweat, with an overPowering thirst.

Ontarra staggered outside, stumbling through utter darkness down to the creek. He drew long gulps and splashed water over his face. He started coughing uncontrollably, raising mouthfuls of slimy mucus. He caught his breath, lungs wheezing. Another coughing fit struck, leaving him gasping for air.

Ontarra stumbled back up the saddle to the lodge. Adding wood to the fire, he recited a prayer his mother used to ward off dark spirits. Pulling a cedar bough from under his sleep robes, he laid it in the flames so that its healing fragrance would fill the lodge. Ontarra crawled back into his robes, wrapping them around him as best he could. He dropped into a fevered sleep.

When he woke to dawn's early light, he couldn't remember where he was.

11

Shanoka and Taiwa struggled up the bank into the canoe area, heaving the canoe between them. Shanoka paused, stretching her aching muscles and working the stiffness from her joints. Taiwa shaded her eyes against the setting sun as she stared up at the fortress pouting defiantly down from the crest. With so many people still away, the normal hustle and bustle along the bluff face was strangely absent; the worn pathways were empty and silent. She was struck by the eerie stillness, and a feeling of apprehension crept over her.

Shanoka saw the look on Taiwa's face. "Strange to see it so quiet, isn't it?"

Taiwa's eyes were riveted to the empty bluff. "It looks like no one is here."

Shanoka groaned as she shouldered the travel pack, thankful that Ontarra had taken the big one. "Everyone is weary from the trip. Don't worry; look at how many canoes are here, and there are hearth fires burning. Let's go up; your father will want to hear about Tontiaton." Taiwa hadn't noticed the comforting smoke of the hearth fires. She shrugged off her anxiety and started up the main path.

As they trudged up the bluff, another canoe thumped in. Toutsou waved;

a fawn he'd taken downstream was draped across the bow. Taiwa grinned and waved back, but she was too tired for conversation. They forced their legs to carry them up the slope, one step at a time, in breathless silence. Despite her lean, flat muscles, Shanoka had to ask Taiwa to stop while she caught her breath. She generally didn't dwell on such things, but at twenty-nine summers, she was starting to feel her age.

Shanoka pressed on to the top without stopping but had to pause again at the south entry. She sat on her pack while Taiwa stood over her with an annoying smirk on her face. Shanoka smiled to herself, taking a last breath before standing. She shoved the travel pack into Taiwa's chest and took a half-hearted swat while Taiwa's hands were full.

Taiwa stepped back, easily avoiding the open palm. "I didn't say anything!"

They rounded the switchbacks and entered Ounontisaston. As she stepped into the open, Shanoka's legs were kicked out from under her. She couldn't get her hands out in time, and she hit the ground, face first, with an impact that stunned her. An instant later, Taiwa landed hard beside her. A heavy foot pressed between Shanoka's shoulder blades. Rough hands yanked her arms back behind her, binding them at the wrists.

Shanoka's head was still reeling when she was yanked to her feet. She had grit in her eye and debris hanging from her lips. Wincing painfully, she tried to rub her eye on her shoulder. She caught a glimpse of a man in a gaudy green cape and headdress, but she couldn't get her focus. "What ... is the meaning of this!" Shanoka choked, coughing up some dirt. She tried to blow the debris from her lips, but a hand shoved her forward three steps and then yanked her head back.

"We've been waiting for you." Hiatsou's repugnant sneer was in her face. Poutassa strutted up beside him.

"You are banned from this town!" she sputtered. "How dare you come here?"

Hiatsou steepled his fingers under his chin, savoring the moment with a smug grin.

Shanoka noticed people gathered in the plaza and along the pathways. She twisted, trying to squirm free of the hands restraining her, but they wrenched her back mercilessly. "Why are you all just standing there?" she called to them. "Get them out!" Shanoka heard the panic in her voice, like a distant echo.

"They have a little dilemma," Hiatsou said, smirking. "Hiatsou and Poutassa are dead and gone. I am Feathered Serpent, and this," he added with a flourish of his hand, "is Windigo Killer." Poutassa turned a circle on one foot, displaying his frilled buckskins. A silver eagle's foot adorned the front of the tunic. "Bring them to the plaza!" Hiatsou instructed as he turned and walked off.

The name Feathered Serpent felt familiar to Taiwa. She'd heard it before—or perhaps she had dreamed of this moment. She searched her memory but couldn't recall. As she struggled to her feet a revelation slowly unraveled in the back of her mind—*my dream of the snakes!*

Young Bird clan men from Tontiaton surrounded her, arrows nocked and ready. Taiwa saw the apprentices scattered among the crowd. They'd all been elevated to full shamans. Heavily armed with clubs and knives, they appeared to be chafing to use them.

Shanoka searched desperately for Sannisen. She saw his young warriors. They'd been disarmed and herded in among a few Land clan women and children who had remained behind. The shamans from Khioetoa and Kandoucho were with the throng of Bird clan men and women. They spoke to Winona in subdued, conspiratorial tones. "Where is Sannisen?" Shanoka hollered to the young warriors. "He'll have your heads for this!" The warriors' distress was evident in the defeated expressions on their faces. They looked away from Shanoka's accusing eyes.

"We are in the sick lodge, Mother!" Teota's frightened voice called out. Shanoka twisted around. The door of the sick lodge was barricaded and guarded by zealous young shamans.

"Move!" a male voice commanded. Shanoka hesitated a heartbeat too long. A kick in the back staggered her forward.

"Sannisen isn't feeling well today," Poutassa hissed in her ear, sharing a smirk with Hiatsou.

Hiatsou turned around at the center of the plaza. Folding his arms across his chest, he ordered, "Tie them to the posts." Young men from Tontiaton shoved Shanoka and Taiwa down on their butts with their backs to the war posts. Poutassa elbowed in, grabbing the hide bindings away from one of them. He yanked Shanoka's elbows back on each side of the post, forcing her to hunch forward or lose her shoulder joints.

"Where is Ontarra?" Poutassa growled, reefing the knot so tightly that it bit into her flesh.

"He's at Tontiaton," Shanoka lied through gritted teeth.

"Guard the entrances!" Poutassa yelled, moving to Taiwa's post. Several of the new shamans ran to take up positions on each side of the entries. Poutassa quickly cinched Taiwa's arms behind the post and then shuffled around sideways, still perched on his heels, to be sure that his order was being followed. Taiwa leaned over and sank her teeth into his arm. "Argh!" he cried as he backhanded her. He yanked a dagger from his sash, and his arm arced upward. Hiatsou grabbed his wrist before the blade could make its plunge.

"We still need her," Hiatsou reminded him. Poutassa scowled and slowly lowered the knife. Shanoka searched the onlookers for a friendly face. "Why don't you people help us?" She saw Kabeza peering over someone's shoulder. "Kabeza, get Tsohahissen. We need him." Kabeza started to say something but thought better of it. She turned and walked away.

Hiatsou snorted derisively. "No one here will help you, now that they know."

Shanoka craned her neck to see him. "Know what?"

A dark cloud seemed to descend over Hiatsou's face. His jaw locked, and his eyes narrowed to dark, malicious slits. "That you are a witch!"

Shanoka's mouth dropped open. She looked at all the Bird clan faces staring at her and realized that she was being judged. "Wh-what?" she stuttered, tripping over her tongue. "What ... is your proof?"

"Hah!" Hiatsou turned, raising his arms to the crowd. "She doesn't bother to deny it—just asks what proof we have uncovered. I warned you all what would happen if you allowed an outsider to live among us." Hiatsou crossed his arms behind his back, gloating at Shanoka's poor choice of words. Playing to his audience, he started to pace. "Watea ... Kadak ... Brata ... all dead! Ounsasta murdered, and Rona eaten! Now, Tsohahissen is suddenly sick and dying!" Hiatsou spun to look down at Shanoka, savoring the stunned look on her face.

"What have you done to Tsoha'?"

"Don't insult us by feigning ignorance, witch! We are here to discover what you have done to him. Perhaps if you tell me, Windigo Killer and I can still save him. Do you think these people are going to believe that all of these calamities are pure coincidence? Does Ounontisaston just happen to be very unlucky?"

"How can you listen to someone so twisted and evil!" Shanoka screamed at the people watching. She tried to stand but the bonds were too tight. She couldn't get her feet up under her. "Most of those people were my friends. They died protecting our town! You all know it was Poutassa forcing himself upon the maidens. You saw what he did to Taiwa and Sounia. Now they've poisoned Tsohahissen like they poisoned Ayontat!"

Hiatsou started to strut. "Explain to us how the Agwa knew where to find the town. How the prisoners disappeared from these very war posts." He beckoned to Winona. "Winona, tell us of Tonayata."

Winona hobbled out and turned to face the people. She'd known all along her time would come, and she intended to make the most of it. "Tonayata was found yesterday, in the middle of one of the upper fields. Her body was torn open. She was with child when she was killed." Winona was pleased with the shock effect of her words and wanted to bask in the afterglow, but Hiatsou pushed her back into the crowd.

"Yadak, come here." Yadak jostled his way to the front. "You and Tonayata were promised?"

"Yes."

"Was this your child she carried?"

"No!" Yadak called out for everyone to hear. "It was Ontarra's child!"

"That's a lie!" Taiwa screamed. "Ontarra hated Tonayata!"

Hiatsou smirked. "Judging from her condition, I'd say he hated her very much." Hiatsou clapped his hands. There was a commotion from inside Soutoten's lodge. Shanoka twisted around as Sounia tumbled out of the doorway. Two of the new shamans ducked out and lifted her up. Her hands were bound with a long hide tether. The shamans used it to haul her toward the plaza. Sounia offered no resistance until she stumbled and fell. The irritated shamans grabbed her under the arms, dragging her the rest of the way and planting her on her knees in front of Hiatsou.

Sounia's shoulders slumped; her head lolled on her chest. A dry cough rattled up from her throat. Shanoka could see crusted blood at the corners of her lips. Poutassa stepped close, hovering over her, his mouth twisting into a cruel grin. "Tell them!" he demanded. Sounia remained silent. Poutassa kicked her in the ribs, buckling her forward and causing her to gasp for air.

Poutassa wrapped his hand in her hair and sat her back, pulling her back until her face was to the sky. One eye was swollen shut. and a blue-black color was spreading across the side of her face.

"Tell them!" he screamed. Sounia winced as his saliva spattered on her face. She started to say something, but it caught in her throat. Poutassa gave her a violent shake.

"Taiwa ..." Sounia mumbled. "Taiwa ... talks to animals."

"Louder!"

Sounia closed her eye and choked out the words. "Taiwa talks to animals." An astonished murmur swept through the crowd.

Poutassa sneered and gave her hair a sharp yank. "Have you seen her do this?"

"Yes," Sounia sniffled, "I've seen her do it." Her good eye rolled down to Shanoka and Taiwa, tears tracking down her face. "I'm ... sorr ..." Her voice cracked.

Poutassa released Sounia's hair. Sounia's head drooped and her shoulders shook with silent sobs. Poutassa wiped his hands on his leggings as if he had just handled something filthy. "Tie her to a post!" he ordered.

Shanoka's eyes brimmed with moisture. "Release her. She has done nothing."

One of Sannisen's young warriors found his voice and agreed. "Sounia is innocent. Let her go." Others joined in with shouts to release her.

Hiatsou scanned the faces in the crowd. He leaned in to whisper to Poutassa. "We need the people's support. It won't be well received if we harm her. She can cook for us."

Poutassa started to protest but a wicked smile slowly rearranged the lines of his face. He motioned to the new shamans. "Take her back to the lodge; she will be our servant." Sounia was lifted up and led away.

Hiatsou folded his arms, strutting again for his audience. "Last night, I dreamed that we must come here to save our people. I saw a great evil that had invaded Ounontisaston, threatening its very existence." Poutassa clapped his hands. Two of the new shamans carried a heavy buckskin bag into the plaza. Poutassa reached into the bag and lifted a dead lynx up by its hind legs. Blood still oozed from an arrow in its chest. He held it aloft for everyone to see and then turned and showed it to Taiwa.

"Slammer!" Taiwa cried, "You've killed Slammer!" She slumped in her bindings with mournful sobs. Shanoka looked at the dead lynx and then at the tears running down Taiwa's face. Poutassa pulled his dagger. Slicing something from around the cat's neck, he held it up, and Shanoka's heart sank—a Midewiwin armband ... her mother's.

"Did the little witch enslave the animal's spirit with this?" Poutassa held the armband up. "Or is this creature another of their Windigo monsters in its daytime form? Have they summoned it here with dark rituals to kill more of our maidens?" The plaza fell silent as the terrible implications of such an evil in their midst registered in the minds of the mortified onlookers.

"My son was killed by a deer that Ontarra allowed to escape during the hunt!" a woman wailed.

"My mate was bitten by a fox with foaming-mouth disease last winter!" A panic surged through the crowd. People started remembering all forms of black sorcery that had occurred over the years. Some of the voices began shouting oaths, demanding retribution.

Hiatsou waved his arms. "Quiet, my people, quiet!" When the ruckus died down, Hiatsou put on his sanctimonious face. "In my vision, I was told that Windigo Killer and I must hurry here, to Ounontisaston. Because of the malignant nature of this evil that has come among us, we brought with us the most Powerful men of our nation." Hiatsou included the shamans with an encompassing sweep of his arm. They puffed themselves up, nodding to each other in agreement. "We rushed here immediately, but I am saddened to say, we were still too late to save Yadwena."

Poutassa reached in the bag again and held up a bloody human fetus. He held it high, letting it swing by one arm. "This demon child that the witch planted in Yadwena has devoured her." Hiatsou shook his head sadly. "You all saw how ill she became, and look"—Hiatsou held a tiny foot up and spread the toes—"the creature has six toes!"

Shanoka's stomach rolled over. She retched. Bile ran down her chin, and she couldn't wipe it away. She rocked her head, trying to shake off the nausea. "You vile creatures," she sputtered, choking on her vomit, "you've killed Yadwena and her baby!" She sagged forward, hanging from the bindings at her elbows, defeated. Shanoka rolled her head up, looking at the Bird clan people in despair. They were mortified; any doubts they'd harbored about Shanoka's guilt were rudely ripped away by the abomination Poutassa was dangling in front of them. It told in their faces—Shanoka was a sorceress, an evil conjurer in league with the forces of the netherworld.

"Don't listen to them!" Taiwa cried in desperation. "If you are foolish enough to believe them, they will destroy you, like a snake swallows its own young!"

"Listen to the little witch trying to save herself," Poutassa jeered.

Winona saw her chance to incite the crowd. "We must kill them! Stone them so we can rid ourselves of the troubles that have plagued us." Angry voices shouted in agreement. Shanoka was rattled and dazed, unable to formulate her thoughts. A stone lofted through the air and grazed Taiwa's cheek. Some of the new shamans edged in closer, brandishing rocks and knives. Shanoka decided to accept the role she'd been given.

"If you harm her, I'll curse you all," she growled menacingly, fixing them with a cold venomous eye. The young men stopped in their tracks, and a hush fell over the plaza. Shanoka had transformed in front of their eyes. She was either touched or possessed. "Get back! All of you!" she snarled in a sinister, unnatural voice.

"Wait!" Hiatsou stepped between his captives and the new shamans. "This must be done properly. Only fire can cleanse such evil. Put them in the sick lodge. We will destroy them all tomorrow. Windigo Killer and I will spend the night in their lodge to purify it." Cutting the hide tethers from Shanoka's arms, he stood her up. Hiatsou groped at her mide bag, tearing it free. She squirmed and twisted away. Hiatsou's arm bent at an odd angle. His elbow cracked, sending a jolt up his arm. "Argh!" He dropped the bag on the ground, staring at it in slack-jawed silence.

Poutassa quietly ordered the new shamans to remove the witches, watching as they were led off. He looked over at Hiatsou who still stared lamely at the mide bag on the ground as he rubbed at his arm. Poutassa studied the bag apprehensively. He beckoned to a young Tontiaton warrior. "Take it and hang it in the witch's lodge."

The makeshift barrier on the sick lodge was pulled aside. Shanoka and Taiwa tumbled in. Teota ran to his mother, burying his face on her chest. Shanoka tilted his head back to get a good look at him. His eyes were red and swollen, and tears tracked grimy streaks down his cheeks, but he seemed to be unharmed. "Why are they doing this?" he sniffed.

Shanoka didn't know how to answer him. "How is your father?"

"I'm ... all right," Sannisen's groggy voice answered from the darkness. Shanoka sat Teota off to one side, moving over to kneel beside Sannisen. She used her shoulder to move Sannisen's head, so that a shaft of light sifting through a crack was cast across his face. He had a nasty gash on his forehead. "We've been trying to untie the cords on our wrists. Mine are loose—see if you can get them." He slid around so their backs touched. Shanoka fumbled at the rawhide.

"They plan to burn us in the morning," Shanoka whispered, feeling a pang of guilt.

"I heard," Sannisen grunted. "My warriors won't be back for days. Soutoten could be longer. He and his men are helping with a deer drive at Khioetoa. Khioetoa's hunters have been out raiding all summer, and their meat supply is low." Sannisen felt the cords release and wriggled his hands free. He rubbed at his wrists and then started untying Shanoka. "Has Ontarra gone to the hunt camp?"

"Yes."

Sannisen shook his head. "He'll walk right into this when he returns." He tiptoed over to a crack near the door. The guards were out there, waving their arms in an animated conversation, but he couldn't make out what was being said.

"How many?" Shanoka asked, moving to untie Teota and Taiwa.

Sannisen put a finger to his lips, shushing her. "It sounds like three, but someone else is coming." He hustled back to the spot where he'd been bound, and they all sat as if their hands were still tied behind them. Keeping his eyes on the door, Sannisen leaned to Shanoka. "We'll have to try to escape."

Shanoka shook her head. "How?" she whispered. "They'll kill us before we reach the switchbacks."

Sounia's voice carried from beyond the wall. "I've brought them some food. Let me go—they need to eat!"

"Ha! They don't need food where they're going!" one of the new shamans snorted. Deprecating laughter followed as his companions shared the joke. The snickering stopped as suddenly as it had begun. "Give me the food, and get out of here!" the shaman ordered. "I'll see that they get it."

"She betrayed us," Taiwa muttered in a dull monotone.

"They frightened everyone terribly," Shanoka said sadly. "Nothing Sounia did made any difference. It makes no sense for her to die too."

Sannisen stood and started pacing, squinting up at the lodge's construction. "I could crash through these walls and—"

"And go where?" Shanoka sighed. "We'll have to wait at least until the middle of the night before we do anything. Perhaps they'll let their guard down long enough to try something."

Sannisen exhaled his frustration. "You're right. I just can't take sitting here."

As the night wore on, Sannisen found a loose rafter and patiently began working on it. Shanoka was overcome by her exhaustion. She nodded off in short bouts, but anxiety woke her with a start every time. As the night waned, she became aware of painful groans coming from outside. She shook herself awake. Slipping over to the door, she peered through a crack. Sannisen stepped in beside her.

"Are they getting tired?"

"No," she answered, "they're holding their bellies. One's hopping from foot to foot like he's performing a ritual."

"Keep an eye on them for me," Sannisen said softly. He moved back to the center of the lodge, reaching up to the rafter he'd been working on. It came free with a sharp crack. He cursed under his breath and scampered back to the door with the rafter raised above his head.

"They didn't hear," Shanoka muttered, her face still glued to the wall. "I see one running toward the south entry. Perhaps someone is coming in." Sannisen stepped into the center of the lodge, swinging his club back and forth to test its balance. Shanoka stepped lightly over to Taiwa, gently shaking her awake. "Get Teota up—it's time." She stalked back to the crack, twisting her head from side to side, trying to see through the darkness. "Everyone, quiet!" Shanoka hissed, backing away from the wall. "Someone's coming!"

The brace poles on the barricade dropped to the ground. Sannisen slid along the wall to the door and raised his club. The barricade rocked sideways. A shadowy head poked in. Sannisen tensed, aiming his blow. "It's me," Sounia's voice squeaked.

Sannisen caught himself just in time, emptying his lungs in a rush as he lowered the club. "Where are the guards?" he asked.

"Outside the palisades, relieving themselves," Sounia answered mysteriously. "I put purge root and pointed mushroom caps in their stew. Kabeza got them for me. I gave some to the men at the entries too."

Shanoka hugged her. "We'll have to hurry," Shanoka whispered. "They'll be suspicious when they realize that they're all sick."

Taiwa jumped up, hugging Sounia so hard she let out a yelp. "Sorry," Taiwa said, letting go. "I knew you couldn't turn on us." Taiwa's tone turned somber. "The pointed mushrooms will kill them, you know."

"They would have killed us," Sounia answered bitterly. "Besides," she continued, her voice brightening, "I was listening to them for a long time. They're quite uncomfortable. Death will probably come as a relief."

"I need my mide bag and prayer stone …" Shanoka's voice trailed off as she considered the risk. "No … it's more important that we save ourselves."

"I'll get them!" Teota squirmed past and was out the door before Shanoka could get her hands on him. She jumped out after him, but he was already disappearing behind the next lodge. Sannisen appeared beside her.

"Sannisen get him!" she hissed.

Sannisen scanned the area for guards. "We can't all go, and I'm not leaving you here unprotected. We'll have to wait for him. You watch the front; I'll take the rear." He handed Shanoka the club.

Sounia produced a knife. "Take this."

"Good girl," Sannisen said thankfully. He trotted to the back and knelt in the shadow of the palisade. The sound of foul liquids being voided, followed by pathetic moans, rose from just beyond the wall. Sannisen clenched his lips to stifle a chuckle.

Teota crept from lodge to lodge, the way he'd learned by playing warrior with the other boys. He couldn't see any guards on the parapets. The lodges were silent. He squirmed along the ground to get past doorways, darting from shadow to shadow until he reached home. Crouching beside the door, he listened to Hiatsou's snoring. He peeked inside, but the hearth fire was low—he couldn't tell if Poutassa was asleep or even in there. Groping around on the ground, he found a pebble and tossed it in. It pattered across the floor, bouncing off the back wall. Hiatsou's snoring skipped a beat but fell back into rhythm. There were no other sounds.

Teota sucked in a breath and rolled to his belly in the doorway. Slowly, he inched himself into the lodge. The dying embers cast a faint glow. He could see Hiatsou's arm dangling from his parents' sleep platform. He snaked his way under the platform between the support leg and the hanging appendage. Feeling around the storage area, he found the wicker basket and tugged on the lid. It made a grating sound and then finally scuffed off. Gently touching each object inside, Teota felt the curved surface of the prayer stone. It filled his chubby hand and he had to clamp his fingers down hard to get enough grip to raise it. He managed to lift it to the brim, then held his breath as he rolled his hand over so he could cradle it safely on his palm.

The effort made his heart beat wildly. He wanted to gasp in air. Fighting the urge, he controlled his breathing. With his elbows and toes, he started backing himself out. Hiatsou stirred, and the snoring stopped. Inquisitive fingers slid across the back of Teota's tunic. Teota froze. The fingers stopped moving and rested between his shoulder blades, slowly relaxing as Hiatsou's nostrils snorked back to life. Teota slid sideways until the hand flopped off. He rolled onto his back and waited for his legs to stop shaking. Swinging his gaze around the lodge, he searched for the mide bag. *Where would they put it?*

As his heart slowed to a patter, he noticed the fuzzy outline of something hanging from the post of Ontarra's sleep platform. He pushed up slowly, terrified that his knees might crack. Placing a foot, he felt the ground through his moccasin before leaning his weight onto it. Three silent steps—and he had it. The furry hump on the bed was probably Poutassa. Teota bent down slowly and shuffled something out from under Ontarra's bed. Eight agonizing steps, and he was outside again. Teota tied the mide bag to a loop on his tunic.

He'd taken too long. He dashed through the moonlight to the row of longhouses and then darted along the backs to Ounsasta's old lodge. Sliding along the wall, he scanned the darkness ahead for the outline of the sick lodge. He was close—and then a hand grabbed his arm, lifting Teota until his toes just touched the ground.

"Why are you out here, boy?" Even in the dark, Teota instantly recognized the gruff voice and rancid smell of the head shaman of Kandoucho. "Everyone is confined to the longhouses tonight!" the shaman growled. "Answer me!" He twisted Teota's arm. Teota fought his impulse to scream. The man hadn't recognized him yet.

Teota hung his head, whimpering pathetically. "I had to help my mother," he squeaked in a tiny voice, so low it was completely inaudible.

"Speak up, you little whelp!" The shaman shook Teota savagely, leaning closer to hear him. Teota swung with all of his might. The prayer stone would have sailed right over the palisades and out of Ounontisaston—if it hadn't come to a sudden stop on the shaman's left temple. A fetid rush of air blew from his gaping mouth. The shaman hung there a heartbeat, quivering … and then his legs buckled, and he went straight down.

As he knelt to pry the man's fingers from his wrist, Teota whispered into a deafened ear. "I said, I had to help my mother."

"He's coming," Shanoka called softly to Sannisen. She held her arms out, and Teota ran into them.

"I got them," he said proudly, handing her the prayer stone and mide bag. Shanoka crammed them into her waist pouch and hauled Teota along behind her to the back of the lodge. The five edged through the shadows of the palisade until they reached the switchbacks of the south entry. There was no sign of guards, so they continued on through. Sannisen poked his head outside. From the darkness to his right and left came the unmistakable sounds—and smells—of angry bowels.

Sannisen leaned back in. "Give me the club." Shanoka handed it to him. He gave her the knife. "Everyone, quiet now. Follow me." Sannisen straightened to his full height and, at normal pace, walked straight to the main path down the bluff. He stopped in the shadows of the trees to be sure they all made it across. No one saw—at least, no one challenged—so they quickly moved on and were soon in the canoe area.

Sannisen picked out two canoes and dragged them to the water's edge. The women searched the area for anything that might be of use. They threw nets, dried fish, and rawhide tethers into the canoes. Shanoka found a canoe prepared for a journey and hauled out the travel packs. Sounia helped pull them over to Sannisen.

"Shanoka and Sounia, take that one," Sannisen said, indicating a canoe. "Taiwa and Teota, ride in front of me. If anything happens, we'll meet at the forks."

Suddenly, a voice barked from the darkness. "Who's there?"

Sannisen slid the bow of his canoe back up onto the bank and grabbed a paddle. His mind raced. A figure moved cautiously out of the murk, a bow drawn taut in his hands. He seemed to be alone.

Sannisen searched his mind for someone he might be able to imitate and had an unlikely thought. "It's me, you fool—Windigo Killer," Sannisen answered in a hoarse voice.

The figure hesitated and then relaxed and moved a little closer, rocking his head from side to side, trying to focus through the pitch. "Oh, I thought maybe—"

Shhwack! Sannisen swung the paddle. The man flew backward. Shanoka was on him in an instant. She lifted the man's chin, expertly piercing both the big veins under his jaw. She waited a few heartbeats for the gurgling to start and then wiped the blade on his tunic and slid it into her waistband.

The rushing current spilled over itself in crests and troughs, carrying Ontarra along with it. He forced himself to stroke for shore, but he was cold—so cold. He couldn't feel his feet. Numbness crept up his legs, sapping their strength. He felt the tug of icy fingers groping at him, pulling him under. It was quiet and peaceful beneath the surface. The terror he'd felt only moments before had mellowed to a tranquil serenity.

His chest grew heavy. A voice called from somewhere in the void. *Liquid is in your lungs! You're drowning!* Ontarra's arms flailed desperately for life. He broke to the surface, coughing and choking, trying to clear the fluid from his lungs. His head ached; thoughts were distant and foggy. He had to get himself to the shore before it was too late.

A figure appeared on the bank. The man seemed familiar. His arm curled up slowly, encouraging Ontarra on. "Fight it! You must not give up!" he called out in a voice that seemed farther away than the distance separating them.

Ontarra tried, but his legs wouldn't work. The effort drained him. He felt himself sinking again. *So easy to let go … drift down to oblivion. Mother? Is that you? Why is Sounia crying? No!* He clawed his way back to the surface. Fluid spewed from his tortured lungs. The man on shore knelt down, speaking into the tall grass and pointing to Ontarra. An animal leaped into the river and started swimming. Yellow eyes bobbed intently toward him, striking fear into Ontarra's soul. A lynx, so cunningly adept at slaughtering wounded prey, was coming to finish him.

The cat swam around him once, eyes talking to him, calming his fear. Around its neck was a Midewiwin armband—his mother's! With the last of his strength, Ontarra reached out and slowly closed his trembling fingers around the mide band. The lynx was small, but it pulled him to shore with Powerful strokes. Ounsasta hauled Ontarra up the bank. "Ounsasta," Ontarra chattered, shivering uncontrollably, "have I … passed over?"

"Death is close," Ounsasta answered gravely, "but you are needed here, more now than ever before. The upper and lower worlds are at odds over the path that the middle world will now take. Our nation teeters on an abyss of torment and despair. You have the Power to change this, Ontarra. You can alter the balance."

Ontarra tried to make sense of Ounsasta's words, but his mind was numb. His eyes wandered to the lynx. "He wears Mother's armband."

"He is your spirit guide and my friend." Ounsasta knelt down, running his fingers along the cat's back. The lynx arched up, a curious grumbling noise emanating from his throat. "We will watch over you, young warrior, and come to you if you should need us." The cat pranced into the brush. Ounsasta straightened up and followed him.

Ontarra tried to sit up, but his muscles wouldn't obey. The feeling of helplessness shot a surge of panic through him. Yellow eyes flashed into his mind again. An ethereal voice spoke a long-forgotten language inside his head. The words were primeval, gibberish, but somehow he understood.

It is your choice now ... stay here where you are needed ... or give up, and come with us.

Ontarra searched inside himself, but his limbs just wouldn't move. He concentrated on screaming. By sheer force of will his mouth moved. "*Aaaaaah!*" He lurched upright to find himself in a dark lodge. His teeth were chattering, and thick mucus covered his face and sleep robes. He realized that he was naked, and he wrapped a robe over his shoulders. The hearth fire was out; the lodge was cold and empty. A raccoon lumbered from the back of the lodge and out the door. Ontarra was too dazed to be startled. The animal reminded him of something ... he couldn't remember what.

Ontarra struggled to the door and pulled the skin back. The valley was dusted a powdery white and sparkling in gossamer moonlight. Where were the people—the town? His head reeled, and he dropped to his knees, hacking up more mucus and phlegm. He gagged, then retched, and fell onto his side, where he lay gasping for air until the fit was over.

Crawling back to his bedding, he pulled the cedar boughs from under the robes, snapped off the driest twigs, and arranged them in the hearth. There was no tinder to start the fire. Hands shaking with cold, he dragged the travel pack over and dug for his knife. Kneeling over the hearth, Ontarra clutched a handful of his hair and sliced it off. As he arranged the hair beneath the wood, he was overcome by a sudden swoon and slumped forward onto his forehead. The world was spinning so fast, he had to spread his arms out to brace himself. He felt like passing out, but he couldn't allow it.

He searched through the travel pack for his firestones. They weren't there. Groping around on the floor, he finally found them under his sleep robes. Ontarra held a stone in each trembling hand ... and struck. *Crack!* The spark missed the hair and fizzled out. *Crack!* Another miss. *Crack!* The sizzling chip landed on the hair and started to smolder. Ontarra blew. A tiny flame curled to life. The pungent smell of burning hair struck him. He added twigs and then branches.

When the flames took hold, Ontarra collapsed on his sleep robes. He knew he should eat something, but he didn't have the energy or the desire. He closed his eyes, drifting back into delirium. He was a small boy again, at the old town. His mother had just discovered he'd given his practice bow to his friend, because Toutsou didn't have one yet. She stared down at him, arms folded. He waited for a scolding, but her face broke into a heartwarming smile. She bent and kissed his forehead.

"Is this it?" Shanoka asked, balancing to hop from the canoe onto the riverbank.

Sannisen pulled the canoe halfway out of the icy water, before turning to scan the valley again. His forehead wrinkled with concern. "This is it, but it appears deserted." He grabbed the paddle Taiwa shoved at him and pulled her in to shore. Shanoka shielded her eyes from the glaring snow. No smoke, no footprints, no sign of human presence.

"He camped for a night downstream," Sannisen said. "He must have made it here." With a skilled eye, Sannisen surveyed the entire area. Something was amiss. He turned his attention to the small stream twining through the walnut grove. There was a hump in the snow that looked out of place. A canoe! He swung his gaze over to the lodge nestled into the crook of the hill. A new doorskin hung on the entrance. "He's here!"

Shanoka saw the doorskin at the same instant and knew something was wrong. A rush of dread carried her across the walnut grove at a dead run. Sannisen ran after her. Shanoka slipped twice in the slushy snow as she went up the saddle, and Sannisen caught up. "Let me go in first," he said, jerking the knife from Shanoka's waistband and ducking inside. Teota ran up the saddle, Shanoka wrapped her arms around him to hold him back. Sounia and Taiwa slipped and clawed their way up, reaching the top just as Sannisen cried out, "Shanoka! Hurry!" They all rushed inside. Sannisen was kneeling over a motionless hump of sleeping robes. The hearth was out; the air in the lodge was colder than the air outside. Shanoka pulled the furs from Ontarra's face. His sallow skin frightened her. She ripped the covers back and pressed her ear to his chest.

"Is he dead?" Sounia asked through her fingers, her voice choked.

"His heart is beating, but his lungs are full of fluid." Shanoka sat back on her heels, resting a palm on his forehead. Despite his clammy complexion, he was burning up with fever. She'd seen this many times. "His spirit fights to remain with his body," Shanoka said softly, trying to keep any sign of panic from her voice. *I must be analytical. Keep my thinking clear. He still has a chance.*

Teota squirmed away from Taiwa and dropped down at Ontarra's side. "He looks dead." Tears welled up in Teota's eyes. "Look at his hair."

Shanoka rolled Ontarra's head to the side. His long ebony hair was hacked off in crooked chunks above his ear. Shanoka shook her head. The answer could wait. "Sannisen, get a fire going." Shanoka reached over and took the knife from Sannisen, tossing it to Taiwa. "I need willow bark for tea, and yellow weed seeds for a poultice. Sounia, see if you can find wintergreen and algae at the creek. Teota, there should be tangle moss under the snow in the flats."

Taiwa knelt down to grip her mother's arm. Their eyes met for a brief instant. "We'll save him, Mother," Taiwa whispered and then jumped to her feet and rushed out. When everyone was gone, Shanoka could hold back no longer. For the first time in many cycles, she allowed herself to cry. Tears rolled down her cheeks and dripped from her nose and upper lip.

Everyone was busy until dusk. The lodge was finally warm, with a lively fire crackling in the hearth and a supply of wood piled against the back wall. Sounia managed to find some wintergreen, and Teota had hauled in an excessive amount of moss. Taiwa found willow bark and even some red sumac clusters, but she couldn't locate any yellow weed. In desperation, Shanoka decided to improvise. She ground walnut husk and cedar leaves into a paste. Setting a flat rock on the coals, she kept grinding and adding water until the temperature and texture were exactly right. She smeared the dark green mess over Ontarra's chest and then covered it with the moss. Shanoka finished by wrapping his chest with strips of hide cut from one of the travel packs. *It might help, or it might kill him,* she thought, but she had to do something.

Taiwa sat by the hearth, laying cedar boughs on the embers. They hissed and crackled, and the air filled with their aromatic fragrance. She alternated every second bough with a cluster of sumac and then a pinch of petun for its curative Powers. Ontarra's wheezing gasps for air seemed to ease as the night wore on. Sannisen couldn't sleep. He craved a smoke, but sacrificed the last of his dwindling supply of petun to help Ontarra.

"I'm going to watch the river to be sure we weren't followed," he said, grabbing Ontarra's bow before he ducked out to be alone with his thoughts. He walked along the riverbank, wondering how so much could change so quickly. Perhaps if they'd arrived sooner ... but they could only risk traveling by night, so it had taken three days.

Last night they'd stayed in an abandoned farm lodge perched on a high bank overlooking the confluence of this stream and the south branch of the Tranchi. Two canoes full of young warriors had passed in the middle of the night, searching for them. They'd been close enough for Sannisen to hear their conversation. They believed Sannisen and his family would run to Tontiaton for the protection Satwani could provide. The careless lack of stealth indicated that they believed they were wasting time in this direction.

Can the shamans muster enough support to hold Ounontisaston? Sannisen wasn't sure. *What will happen when Soutoten returns?* Sannisen shrugged off his rambling thoughts. *Tonight I have my family to worry about.* His jaw set with determination, and he pressed on into the darkness.

Shanoka massaged her temples between a thumb and forefinger. She could think of nothing more in the physical world that could help Ontarra. Slipping her hand into her waist pouch, she slid her mide bag out, undid the closure, and dipped two fingers inside. She had to be gentle or the old roll of birch bark would crumble. Laying the sacred memory scroll on Ontarra's chest, Shanoka rolled it open. Her mother's teeth marks recorded the ritual, if she could only decipher them.

Shanoka studied the pattern of the bites, bits and pieces coming back to her. She arranged the items she would need on the ground in front of her and then pulled the sleep robes down to expose Ontarra's chest. Holding the mide bag upside down, she shook the last few grains of her red onaman sand onto the poultice. She set a bear claw in the hollow of Ontarra's throat. Studying the memory scroll again, she started the ancient ritual. The meaning of the words escaped her, but she remembered the cadence. The guttural, single-syllable sounds had an archaic quality that sent a chill through Sounia.

Shanoka set her seer's crystal on Ontarra's forehead, hoping it would tell her something. It revealed nothing, so she set it aside and picked up the hollowed-out leg bone of a crow. She tried to suck the sickness from Ontarra's chest, ears, and mouth and then set the seer's crystal on his forehead again. After a hand of time, she hung her head and set the crystal on the robes.

Teota lay with his chin propped on Ontarra's legs, entranced by his mother's display of supernatural Power. Sounia cradled Ontarra's head, bathing his face with a damp skin and then dabbing the perspiration from his eyelids. He rasped and hacked suddenly. Shanoka set her mide bag on the floor, rolling his head to one side to clear the yellow mucus out of his mouth. His breathing seemed to stop. Their hearts pattered with dread, until he finally choked and gasped for air again. There was only one thing she could do now. Shanoka cradled her prayer stone between her palms, praying to Ontarra's soul, begging it to stay with his body. And they waited.

The night waned. Sounia's exhaustion caught up to her. Her head drooped, lolling onto her chest. "Ounsasta, wait!" She jolted awake. Ontarra's eyes fluttered open. He stared up at Shanoka. "I'm not ... feeling well, Mother," he faltered in the voice of his childhood.

Shanoka bit on her lip, moisture forming in the corners of her eyes. "I know. Try and rest."

Ontarra's eyes drifted shut but then snapped wide again for an instant. "I'm sorry I broke your hair comb," he said softly.

Shanoka smiled. "Never mind. Just try and sleep." Ontarra's eyelids faded down again. Everyone was silent until his breathing took on a rhythm.

"What was that about a hair comb?" Sounia whispered.

Shanoka wiped the corners of her eyes with a thumb. "He thinks he's at the old town. When he was Teota's age, he hafted my hair comb to a pole and tried to spear fish with it." Shanoka chuckled, but her voice cracked. She covered her eyes to hide the tears. Sounia slid over, wrapping her arms around Shanoka's shoulders. Tears tracked down Taiwa's face as she watched in silence, still diligently adding sumac and petun to the fire. "I'm sorry,"

Shanoka sniffed, ashamed of her weakness. She forced her feet under her and straightened up. "I need to go out—to get away from this smoke."

Sannisen returned at dawn, a cock turkey slung over his shoulder. Taiwa welcomed the chance to go outside. She soon had the bird skinned and gutted. Sounia spitted it over the fire. "It's going to taste like cedar and sumac," she warned.

"It will be good," Sannisen said from the side of his mouth, unable to take his eyes off Ontarra.

"We need to take stock of our supplies," Shanoka said solemnly. "How many skins do we have?"

Sannisen rubbed his eyes. "I've already checked. There are four in the travel packs; Ontarra had two."

Shanoka drummed her fingers on her leg as she thought. "We'll have to sleep in pairs then. Food and clothes are going to be our immediate concerns."

"We can take the nets apart for sewing and use the travel packs to make heavy boots for everyone," Sounia suggested. "I'll make a thread puller and start today," she added, rotating the turkey. "We'll need a cooking pot too. We could use bark from one of the canoes."

"No. We're going to need the canoes," Sannisen cautioned. "We have two knives, one bow, and eight arrows." His eyes swung back to Ontarra. "We can make another bow, but we'll have to dry the wood over the fire. It'll take a while."

"How many people know of this place?" Shanoka asked.

"Only Ounsasta and Soutoten have ever been here, and Soutoten would never say anything."

"I wish we could warn him somehow," Sounia sighed.

"He'll know something is wrong as soon as he gets to the canoe area." Sannisen smiled to allay her fears. "He'll be all right." The lodge fell silent. They all watched the turkey sizzling as they considered their new realities.

"He's awake!" Teota cried.

All eyes locked on Ontarra. He stared back, mystified, from under his covers. "What are all of you doing here?" he asked in a gravelly voice. Sounia flew around the fire. She dropped on her knees to hug him but quickly sat back with an offended look as Ontarra exclaimed, "*Yech!*" Ontarra pulled his hand from under his robes—it was covered in glutinous green paste. "What is this stuff?" He screwed up his face. Ontarra's disgusted expression set off chuckles of relief. He looked from face to face as if they'd all lost their sanity. Slowly, he smiled and shook his head. "Get this putrid crap off of me." He tried sitting up, groaned, and fell back. "I'm awfully thirsty."

Taiwa wiped the tears of laughter from her cheeks and filled a wood bowl with water. Sannisen handed it across, watching as Ontarra drank. Ontarra slid the bowl back and then lay back to stare up at the rafters. "My spirit guide came to me," he mumbled in a dreamy voice. "He's a lynx. He wears a Midewiwin armband around his neck … just like Mother's." Shanoka's jaw dropped, her eyes swinging to meet with Taiwa's.

Taiwa sat back on her heels. "It's Slammer!"

"What did he look like?" Sounia asked in astonishment.

Ontarra glanced up, his eyes wrinkling. "What do you mean, what did he look like? He's furry, with spots, yellow eyes, stubby little tail—he's a lynx!" Ontarra chided playfully.

Sounia looked away, embarrassed. "Well … was he big? Small? Fat?"

"He's small … for a lynx," Ontarra answered thoughtfully. "And he wears an armband around his neck, like Mother's."

Shanoka steepled her fingers. "This is amazing. It seems the manitos expect a lot from you." She started removing the poultice, explaining the events of the last few days while she worked. With each new revelation, a burning hatred grew in Ontarra's soul. He was furious with himself for the near calamity he'd helped to create by letting Poutassa survive.

"So that's what Ounsasta was trying to tell me," he said under his breath.

"What?" Shanoka stopped what she was doing to be sure she'd heard him right.

"I should have killed Poutassa when I had the chance. Ounsasta told me that. I vow to you all"—Ontarra struggled with the rage inside him, measuring his words carefully. An oath was no idle matter—"Poutassa and Hiatsou will die piece by piece for what they have put you through."

"We have to survive this winter first," Sannisen pointed out. Taiwa handed a bowl of willow-bark tea to Shanoka. Sounia lifted Ontarra's head so he could drink the steaming brew in short sips.

They attacked the turkey with gusto. The hint of cedar and sumac didn't bother anyone as they filled their bellies for the first time in days. There was enough left over for a stew and soup, so Sounia and Taiwa left to slash bark for a pot. Ontarra nibbled at the meat, but wasn't ready for much solid food. The willow-bark tea made him drowsy, and he dozed off again.

Teota stood, wiping his hands on his leggings. "I'm going to check the river for fish." Pecking Shanoka on the cheek, he trotted out. He ran to the creek, starting there and gradually working his way to the river. He inspected the holes upstream and downstream as if his family's lives depended on it—which they did. He returned with a befuddled snapping turtle, snatched from his winter sleep. Tossing it on its back in the coals, he held it down with a stick until it stopped struggling and then flipped it out on the floor.

"It will make a good stew," Shanoka said, smiling.

"And a good bowl," Teota added proudly. "There are only minnows in the creek out front, but there are plenty of big sucker fish in the river. It's shallow," he added thoughtfully. "I think I'll build a weir with rocks." He nodded to himself, already designing it in his head.

By the following day, Ontarra could sit up and move around enough to be a nuisance. His appetite returned. Sounia batted playfully at his hand as he stole morsels from the turkey stew she was concocting in the new bark pot. Outside, winter was taking hold. Ice began to crust along the edges of the creek and river. The sun shone brightly in the afternoon, so Ontarra wrapped himself in skins and sat outside with his back to the wall, enjoying the warm rays while he watched Teota building the weir.

Ontarra noticed the raccoon staring down at him from a hole in a walnut trunk. He'd finally found himself a new dwelling. One human in his lodge was bad enough, but six was intolerable. Sannisen hove into sight, walking along the bank downriver. He strode through the grove and up onto the saddle.

"I've found a spot just beyond the first bend where we can set a deadfall. There's a tree already teetering on the bank in just the right position. I'll need your help to set it, though."

Sannisen saw that Ontarra was only half-listening, and he followed his gaze to the masked face up in the tree. He pulled an arrow and nocked it, but Ontarra's hand fell on his father's wrist.

"No. He's my friend."

Sannisen lowered the bow, cocking his head with a baffled look. "This is becoming endemic. We need the meat and skin, you know."

Ontarra bobbed his chin, eyes still fixed on the raccoon. "We'll eat him if we have to, but only if it becomes imperative." Shanoka stepped out at the sound of Sannisen's voice. Sannisen shot a bewildered look from Ontarra to Shanoka and then slowly unstrung his bow.

"Must be some kind of Ojibwa thing," he grumbled.

Shanoka missed the meaning of the statement, so she skipped to what was on her mind. "We need another lodge. We can make an Ojibwa travel lodge quickly." She watched Ontarra from the corner of her eye. "We have a marriage to perform."

"You let them escape, you ignorant fool!"

Hiatsou didn't understand the words, but the anger was clear. Fear knotted his stomach as Manak's hand, trembling with rage, dropped onto the hilt of that big black knife in his waistband. But this was Hiatsou's town, his people. He knew how to deal with these outsiders. He clapped his hands. Four young shamans burst through the door with clubs readied. Hiatsou held out a palm to restrain their youthful zeal. They spread themselves out around the strangers.

Manak scowled condescendingly at each of them. Their faces showed no fear. It was their only good quality. He could kill every one of the young pups in such a restricted space before they could land a single blow. And he felt like proving it. Manak didn't suffer fools lightly, and he wasn't accustomed to controlling his anger, once it was aroused. It was the hardest thing he'd done in cycles, to take his hand from his knife and cross his arms. He forced his lips into the closest thing to a smile that he was capable of. "Ask the fat slug if he knows where they went," Manak said. Every word was a sinister monotone, but Manak kept the half smile firmly fixed to his face.

Hiatsou tried not to smirk, but he just couldn't stop himself when he saw how easily the big warrior backed down. Matoupa leaned over, whispering to Dekari. Dekari took a deep breath and settled himself down on the sleep platform across from Hiatsou. "Forgive his outburst, Hiatsou. It is difficult for him when he was so close. He asks if you know where they went?"

Hiatsou shrugged with a weary sigh. "It's a tense time for all of us," he grunted bitterly, trying to ignore Manak. "The witch conjured a spell. Four of our young shamans and one young warrior had their spirits ripped from their bodies through their rectums. The chief shaman of Kandoucho still breaths, but his spirit is gone too."

Manak listened scornfully to the translation. Holding the smile was too much effort; his lips settled back to a brooding slit. "Tell the imbecile to save his superstitious babble for his minions." Manak stared pointedly at Hiatsou's bodyguards. "I saw that pitiful wretch at the canoe landing—they fought their way out of here. Does he know where they went or not?"

Dekari lifted his eyes nervously to the overeager young shaman hovering next to him, tapping a war club against his leg. His gaze shifted back to Matoupa, pleading with him to calm Manak down. Matoupa laid a hand on Manak's shoulder. "Careful. He may begin to understand your words," Matoupa whispered. Manak yanked his shoulder away with a dark glare.

Dekari didn't wait for Matoupa's translation before turning to Hiatsou again. "He says that he understands how dangerous the woman is, but if you know their whereabouts, he and his men will go after them."

Hiatsou stood and started pacing. "They took two canoes—probably headed downriver to get away as fast as possible. We have men searching the river and trackers combing the banks for any sign of them. We'll find them," he mumbled at the floor, more to convince himself than Manak. He shuddered, unconsciously pulling his feather robe tight as he thought about how much support Sannisen would be able to raise in the outlying towns and villages. He had to find them—and quickly. He glanced over at Dekari. "Tell them you are welcome to remain here until we locate them. We've prepared the sick lodge for your use."

Manak listened to the translation with fire in his eyes. He couldn't abide the thought of remaining in this land any longer. The flimsy construction of their towns and the bark shanties they lived in—it was too depressing. And this was the coldest place he'd ever known. He looked to Matoupa for some direction.

Matoupa shrugged. "It seems there is no other choice."

Manak shot a look across the lodge to Hiatsou, resigning himself to the situation with a heavy sigh. "Make him understand that we have no deal until I have the woman." Manak forced the unnatural-looking smile again; Hiatsou smiled back. "When I finally have the woman, you fat maggot," Manak said, "I will come back here and cut that smug grin from your face." Matoupa held his breath, watching to see if there was the slightest glimmer of understanding in Hiatsou's eyes. Hiatsou smirked, nodding profusely. Manak spun around and ducked out. He took several deep breaths while he listened to Matoupa and Dekari lying about what he'd just said.

They came out and joined him, walking slowly along the path toward the sick lodge. "I hate this place," Manak railed. "They live in squalor. There are no temples. Their barrier walls are nothing but saplings stuck in the ground. We must get that woman and get out of here!"

Dekari rolled his head back, trying to rub tense knots out of the muscles in his neck. He stopped in his tracks, staring up at the sky. Matoupa followed the Erieehronon gaze to the sun deity directly overhead. A hazy rainbow encircled it—a sun dog. He shielded his eyes to scan the horizons. A dark line of clouds was building in the west.

"I fear we've waited too long," Matoupa said, exhaling bleakly. "The rivers are about to ice over."

Manak swung a blank stare from Dekari to Matoupa. Puzzled wrinkles tracked out at the corners of his eyes. "What ... is ice?

12

When Soutoten and his hunters arrived in the canoe area of Ounontisaston, they knew something was amiss. The few people they saw on the bluff and out in the fields ran into the town, shouting warnings. Soutoten's men spread out, hunkering down to move up the bluff. The entries were barricaded. Unfamiliar young warriors appeared on the parapets, shouting insults and taunts, flagrantly daring Soutoten to attack them. It was apparent there were too many defenders to risk a direct assault on the walls. Soutoten surrounded the town to wait until their water ran out.

The reckless lack of fear among the young fanatics on the palisade amused Manak and Mox. They wandered along the walls several times each day, egging them on with shouts of encouragement and war cries. Mox enjoyed waving his stone-headed maul in the air, inciting the young fools into exposing themselves. "I can't believe they aren't picking the idiots off when they do that," he said, shaking his head at Manak with a big gap-toothed grin.

"Apparently, the ones outside hope to resolve this without too much bloodshed," Manak replied. "After all, their families are trapped in here with the rest of us." Manak rubbed his chin as a thought occurred. "Come on. I need to talk to the head moron."

Sannisen's men began arriving in small groups from their raids on the

Fire Nation. Soutoten used them to plug gaps in his line. On the third night of the siege, Winona and several of the Bird clan women climbed up on the parapets, trying to convince their men to cross over. They went to great lengths, explaining how Feathered Serpent and Windigo Killer had saved the town from the witch.

On the fourth night, Land clan women halfheartedly called out from inside the town to their mates and sons, asking for permission to get water at Snake Creek. Soutoten flatly refused. The men were clearly worried about their families inside. They started grumbling anxiously behind Soutoten's back. The next day, a blanket of snow covered the ground, and the defenders had all the water they needed.

Soutoten found that half of his men had defected during the night to join their families inside. It was a hopeless stalemate. More men crossed over the next night. Before dawn, Soutoten called in the few remaining hunters and warriors who had remained faithful. The ragtag group fell back from the bluff and the upper fields into the canoe area. Soutoten realized bitterly that only the young unmarried men remained. He stared up at the fortress that he'd helped to build one last time before leaving. *I'll be back, Hiatsou,* he promised. *I'll fry your black heart and throw your body to the fishes in the Tranchi.*

A handful of canoes shoved off, heading down the Entry River. Soutoten felt it was likely that Sannisen had gone to Tontiaton. He swung out into the Tranchi, surging downriver, furious at his sudden impotence. He wanted to lash out, to get even. His rage was evident in the set of his jaw and the driving thrusts of his paddle. The young men in the canoes around him didn't dare say a word.

Something alerted Soutoten to danger. He froze with his paddle in midair, searching the naked trees that lined the lofty snow-covered banks with the piercing eyes of a predator. His skin tingled as the cold breath of imminent danger wafted over him. A net snaked out of the water. Soutoten's eyes shot up as flights of arrows traced an arc skyward and then seemed to suspend for a heartbeat directly overhead. The doomed young hunters and warriors watched in helpless dread as the murderous chert points nosed over.

Sudden death rained down upon the Tranchi.

Snow was falling at the hunt camp. It had snowed every day for half a moon cycle now and showed no sign of letting up. They were all anxious over the lack of preparation for winter. Time could not be squandered. They needed food stored away, and they needed it now. So they worked on through the foul weather. The walnut valley was frantic with activity.

Ontarra tried, but he wasn't much help at first. He could only walk a stone's cast before a coughing fit seized him, doubling him over and leaving him panting for air. Shanoka made him chew petun to clear his lungs and restore his vitality. Ontarra had never learned to enjoy smoking petun. He was mystified when he found himself beginning to crave the bitter, burning juice. It seemed to invigorate and refresh him. Gradually, his stamina returned.

Ontarra spent two days burning out four rockwood trunks from a stand in the ravine above the saddle. Rockwood was so hard, even a slate adze wouldn't mark it. Only fire could gradually wear it down. When he finished, he had four rockwood clubs as tall as his shoulders and as big around as his wrist.

With Shanoka's guidance, Ontarra and Teota built a domed Ojibwa travel lodge adjacent to the main lodge. The frame was constructed of saplings bound together with cords from the nets. Bark was stripped from two maple trees on the uplands east of the camp. It was tied in position and then held in place with a second exterior frame of saplings. Cedar boughs were spread over the floor, creating a cozy little nest for Ontarra and Sounia. Sounia made a crude dream-catcher, proudly hanging it from a rafter over the door.

The canoes were carried up off the floodplain and lashed together around a tree on the hillside, so a sudden flood wouldn't carry them off or so a winter wind wouldn't smash them into kindling. Everyone helped to build the deadfall downstream. The river was blocked by felling a walnut from the south ridge. Anyone traveling upriver would be obliged to go around it on the flats. When they did, a huge teetering oak trunk would give them a nasty surprise—and warn the camp of intruders.

Sannisen scouted the area every day for deer trails. He found two on the uplands behind the camp that seemed promising. For three days, Ontarra waited in ambush, while Sannisen drove deer through the forest. No matter where Ontarra positioned himself, the deer passed out of range. The thought crossed his mind that the raccoon might have warned them. On the fourth day, in frustration, Ontarra stood and fired on a buck pushing two does out in front. His arrows fell short, only serving to make the buck more wary.

Sounia and Taiwa gathered walnuts, piling them behind the main lodge. They pulled armloads of cattail roots from the creek—they'd be tough but nutritious. On one excursion, they came across an area littered with acorns, so they slipped their dresses off and filled them full before the shivering walk back to camp.

Shanoka found leeks, parsnip, and rattlesnake root. She and Teota pried them from the ground with sticks, storing them with the other tubers in the storage pit at the back of the main lodge. A tree of scabby apples was located. Apples that hadn't already fallen were picked and added to the cache in the lodge. What they really needed now was meat.

Sounia sprinkled pounded acorns into the bark pot to add some body to evening meal. She longed for even a hint of meat to mix with the cattail roots and wild carrot.

"Here, add a bit of this." Shanoka offered a small packet of powder from her mide bag. "It's for head pain, but it's full of flavor."

"I hope Father and Ontarra got us a deer," Taiwa said wistfully, holding her frigid hands up to the flames. "My belly craves venison every time I think of it."

"Don't think of it," Shanoka said flatly.

Teota sat with his back to the wall, only half-listening to the women around him. The sucker fish had eluded all his best efforts to catch them. The river was icing over, and soon it would be too late.

"Ho." Sannisen and Ontarra ducked inside, followed by a swirl of white flakes. They let the sleep robes slide from their shoulders, giving them a shake to remove the snow before hanging them from pegs on the rafters to dry.

"Any luck?" Taiwa asked hopefully.

"No," Sannisen sighed. "They realize that we're after them now." Ontarra slumped down at the hearth, rubbing his hands over the coals. He stared into the fire in silent disappointment.

Shanoka chewed on her lip. "We need meat. The snow is already up to my knees. We'll be confined to the trails around camp soon."

Sannisen sat on his haunches to let the heat waft over him. He steepled his fingers, thinking out loud. "We'll have to move to another trail farther back from the camp." Ontarra's head drooped slightly, disgusted with himself for attempting an impossible shot and alerting the deer to their presence. His impulsiveness may have sealed their fate. Teota could feel Ontarra's shame.

He knew better than to ask what had gone wrong, so he directed Ontarra's thoughts elsewhere.

"Ontarra, I've tried everything on the sucker fish—nothing works. Can you think of anything?"

"Well ... they're bottom-feeders, so bait won't work." Teota knew that but remained silent. "The nets might have caught them, but we've torn them up too badly for bindings. Have you tried spearing them?"

Teota shook his head. "They're too fast, and they lay on the rocks, so I'm always breaking my points. I've even tried throwing rocks on them, but they're so quick, it's impossible to hit one."

Something Toutsou had once explained slowly came back to Ontarra. A smile spread across his face as he ran the conversation through his mind. "How deep is the water?"

"Only up to my waist," Teota answered. "It's way too cold now to build another weir, if that's what you're thinking. Besides, I tried that; they won't go in."

Ontarra heard the defensive tone in Teota's voice. "You're right, Mosquito. I know you would have considered that. We would surely freeze before we caught them. I have an idea, though. Something Toutsou once told me." Sounia handed him a helping of stew on a bark scoop. Ontarra ran the idea through his mind as he chewed.

The root stew was simple but filling. The meager fare tasted surprisingly good on an empty stomach. Sounia smiled at the complimentary belches. "That taste is an herb that Shanoka gave me." The problem was, they'd all be hungry again in a hand of time without protein or fat to sustain them.

"Sounia has the matrimonial lodge ready," Shanoka said. She studied Ontarra as she added more wood to the fire. "It's time for you two to move out and give us some room in here."

Ontarra and Sounia beamed at each other, but Ontarra's expression turned serious again. "I want to wait until we have some meat." Sounia threw a mushy cattail root across the hearth. It hit Ontarra's cheek and slithered down to his chin before sloughing to the floor.

"You're always going to have an excuse!" she fumed with a playful grin. "Do you think you can just keep me waiting forever?"

"Look at what I'm going to have to put up with," Ontarra said. He shook his head, wiping the slop from his face. The chorus of laughter relieved the anxious mood in the lodge.

The women laid out the sleep robes. It was best to sleep as much as possible through the long nights, conserving heat and energy for the necessary work of survival. Ontarra and Sounia would not sleep together again until they were joined, so Teota crawled in next to Ontarra.

At dawn, Ontarra and Teota wrapped their sleep robes around them and slipped out. For the first time in a long while, it wasn't snowing—the sky was clear. They trudged along the trail that Teota's busy feet had pounded through the snow to the river. An arm-length of ice clung to both banks, leaving only the main current open out in the middle.

"They're stuck in a hole between this rapid and that one." Teota pointed to a rock-strewn tumble of water a stone's throw downstream.

Ontarra crawled out on the ice. It cracked, groaning under his weight. He spread his arms out, peered down into the water, and saw several sucker fish the length of his forearm resting on the bottom. He crawled back to shore, the plan already forming in his mind. "They could escape through those rapids down there if they really wanted to," he thought out loud, "so we'll use the canoes."

By midmorning everyone was at the river. Sannisen listened skeptically as Ontarra outlined the plan, but anything was worth a try. They loaded a canoe with walnut husks scavenged from the pile behind the lodge. While that canoe was being skidded to the river, Ontarra snapped off exposed walnut roots at the creek bank and filled a second canoe.

At the upper rapids, they used the paddles to scoop a trough into the rocky bottom. The husks and roots were dumped into the trough. The men began pounding the pile into a pulp with the rockwood clubs while the women slid the canoes down the ice to the lower rapids. They positioned the canoes across the stream and then sat in them to keep them from floating away. The girls laid the paddles across their knees, ready for any fish that tried to break through.

Teota started shoving pounded pulp and roots out into the current. The swirls and eddies turned black and then spread out under the ice in a brackish green stain. They kept pounding until the pile was mush and the water downstream was an impenetrable murk. The men stopped to watch as the cloud drifted toward the lower rapids.

Shanoka raised her paddle and stabbed down at something in the water. "They're running ahead of it!" she yelled, stabbing again. Sounia and Taiwa jumped up and started pounding the water around them. The canoes tipped and teetered as the women fought to keep their balance while frantically swinging the paddles. The men roared with laughter at the comical scene, but the girls were too busy to notice.

A silver belly rolled up, flashing just below the surface. Another drifted up beside it. Teota let out a whoop and ran down the bank. Ontarra and Sannisen followed. Teota jumped right into the icy shallows, throwing a stupefied fish up onto the shore. "It worked!" Teota hopped up on the ice and slapped Ontarra on the leg before splashing back to toss out more fish.

Ontarra looked at all the fish flopping around him, his lips curling into a broad grin. "Toutsou told me that walnut roots and husks would stun them, but I've never tried it before. When I see him again …" Ontarra's voice trailed off.

Sannisen caught the inflection. He tossed a fish up on the bank and looked over at Ontarra. "We'll see him again."

Four hands of sucker fish were caught—a moon cycle's worth of stews and soups. They smoked the meat all afternoon in the lodge, except for two that got chunked and went right into the bark pot. Evening meal was a feast. Ontarra's belly hadn't been so full since the Festival of the Dead. When he felt his capacity waning, he stabbed into the pot with his knife, pulling out a stewed head. He chewed the delicate white meat from the cheeks and then sucked out the eyes, tossing the rest on the fire for the spirits.

Next morning, Ontarra and Sannisen left while it was still dark to make another try for a deer. They forced their way through the underbrush of the upland forest behind the camp. The sky was brightening in the east when they reached a depression that cut from east to west through the forest. The trench appeared to be a dried-up riverbed, or wash, that had grown in. Along the bottom of it was a well-worn deer trail.

"The river is that way," Sannisen said, pointing to the west. "They're probably down there drinking now. They'll be back to bed down before the sun rises much higher. I'll wait here. You go farther downwind. Don't cross the trail, or you'll give us away."

Ontarra bristled at being told something so obvious, but he understood his father's concern and moved off without comment. He found a fallen tree and worked his way into its branches before realizing that a huge oak farther down blocked his view. Studying the oak's shape, an idea occurred to him. He extricated himself from his hiding place and moved silently down through the slanting shadows of dawn. Nothing was on the trail yet; the forest was a ghostly silence. Ontarra reached up, hanging his bow from a branch, before swinging himself up onto the lowest limb. He crawled out, perched himself in a fork, and then hauled his bow up. He was closer to the trail than he would normally dare, but deer didn't look for danger in trees.

Ontarra heard a whisper of sound. He listened intently and heard it again—snow and leaves crunching under splayed hooves. It wasn't from the west, though, but from behind him. He slowly turned his head. From the corner of his eye, he saw a doe, nose in the air, ears flicking back and forth warily. Ontarra prayed that his smell was above those nostrils.

He tried not to breathe, but his heart was racing. The doe moved cautiously down the slope, stopping every few steps to scan her surroundings, her nose testing the air. She passed directly under Ontarra's dangling feet. Ontarra thought his lungs would explode. The doe moved down onto the trail. Ontarra allowed himself to breathe again. Calming himself, he drew back on his bow, waiting for a side shot.

Something moved beneath him. Ontarra rotated his head, gazing down over his left shoulder. A big buck was following the doe's lead. Ontarra froze. If he moved now, he'd spook them both. He remembered Toutsou telling him once that a deer could hear a hunter's thoughts. He tried to clear his mind by concentrating on his breathing. The tension of the bowstring made his arm shake. He backed off slowly, muscles screaming at the effort. The buck continued down into the trough.

Ontarra's right arm ached from the strain. He watched the buck turn toward the river, lowering his nose to check the trail for scent; the buck knew that something wasn't right. Ontarra took a deep breath, exhaled half of it, and drew the arrow to his cheek. The deadly missile hissed through the forest, striking the buck between two ribs and burying itself halfway to the fletching.

Ontarra wanted to scream with joy, but he didn't budge. The razor-sharp chert had cut so clean and fast, the buck wasn't sure what happened. His head snapped up, eyes searching from side to side for the cause of the sound and the burning discomfort in his chest. He took a step. A leg trembled. Another step, and his knees bent, slowly sinking him onto his belly. He lowered his nose to the ground, the snow turning red around his nostrils.

The doe was confused. She stepped over the buck, nuzzling at his neck. Ontarra let fly with a second arrow. The intoxicating rush of a successful kill affected his aim. The shot wasn't as clean, taking the doe in the big muscle of her neck. Deer rarely made a sound, but the doe leapt straight up in the air with a terrified bleat, landed, and then bounded up the slope, disappearing over the crest. Her pathetic cry sent a pang of guilt through Ontarra, but the joy of saving his family from starvation pushed it aside. He let out a whoop that shook the forest, ending any further hope of hunting for this day.

Ontarra dropped from the tree and ran to the buck. He sliced the throat to let it bleed. Cutting carefully around the anus, he pulled out the rectum and knotted it so feces couldn't taint the meat. With a quick slit, the belly burst open, sloshing bowels and organs over the snow. Ontarra cut down through the muscle along the arrow's shaft, slowly sliding it out with minimal damage.

When Sannisen came trotting up the wash, Ontarra tossed him a chunk of warm liver. They congratulated each other with bloody, satisfied grins, as they devoured the delicacy. The rest of the animal would be shared—fresh liver was the hunter's reward. Sannisen noticed the doe's tracks. His eyes followed them up the slope to red speckles frozen on the snow. He raised an eyebrow, unable to believe in such good fortune. "Two?" Ontarra flashed a crimson smile.

They hauled the carcasses back to the grove, leaving the entrails behind for the scavengers. It was dusk when they came shouting and screaming down the hillside into camp. Everyone was ecstatic. The two deer were not just food; they were life—the gift of hope and the means to carry on. Sounia carved a huge roast from the buck's rump, laying it right on the coals. The animals were then quartered before hanging the meat in the matrimonial lodge. Sounia didn't even complain.

With meat in camp, predators would be a problem. Ontarra and Sannisen would sleep in the travel lodge tonight, but the meat would have to be cut into strips and then smoked and dried tomorrow. It wouldn't be safe until it was cached in the storage pit. Shanoka carried the hides into the main lodge, giving them their first scraping before tying them to the walls to begin drying.

"I can make two winter leggings and perhaps have enough left to make a heavy tunic for Teota," she said, seating herself next to Sounia.

Sounia grinned. "We have enough meat for two moon cycles now."

The smell of venison roast brought everyone inside to enjoy the wonderful aroma. Shanoka reached for her prayer stone. The chatter and laughter stopped while she prayed for the animals' spirits, thanking them for giving their lives so that her family might live.

Everyone waited somberly until she was finished and then they greedily attacked the roast. Shanoka loved the crisp, smoke-flavored outer crust. She tore off a big strip, clamping one end between her teeth. With a slash of the chert blade in her free hand, she severed a piece that filled her mouth. "So, tomorrow we will be having a wedding ceremony?" she asked, raising a questioning brow to Ontarra. Ontarra chewed thoughtfully on a bloody chunk cut from the center as he studied Sounia across the fire.

"You've caught me off guard, Mother. Give me some time to think up a suitable excuse." Sounia's lips pinched together, her eyes narrowing to venomous slits. She didn't need to say a word. The lodge rocked with sporadic bursts of laughter that evening, until the roast was gone and the men had to leave to guard the meat. With concerns for survival temporarily averted and bellies full of venison, the atmosphere of the hunt camp changed—from hideout to home.

The next morning was spent cutting meat and preparing a smoke rack. Sannisen noticed Shanoka staring out through the walnut trunks at something across the valley. He set his knife down and went to stand beside her. "What is it?"

"Look." Shanoka pointed across the river flats to the opposing hill. It was spackled with gray and white lumps. "The gulls have come inland from the lakes," she whispered ominously. "There's a big storm brewing."

When all the meat strips had been hung over a glowing firebed, attention turned to the simple Attawondaronk wedding ceremony. Sounia began by entering the matrimonial lodge. After a few moments, she set a bowl outside the door, tipping her head to her guests at the smoke rack before going back inside to await her suitor.

Ontarra stepped from the main lodge. His leggings and tunic were spattered with blood, but they were the best he had. He bent low in a mocking bow to the guests. With a roguish grin, he strutted over to the travel lodge.

All he had to do to consummate the union was accept the bowl of hot stew and step inside. When he picked up the bowl, the cocky smile disappeared. With a bewildered expression, he showed Shanoka that the bowl was empty.

An empty bowl was a polite rejection, telling the suitor he was not acceptable. Ontarra was now obliged to walk away with his tail between his legs. Instead, he stood there, paralyzed by indecision and looking like an idiot. Sannisen and Shanoka glanced at each other.

"What can this mean?" Sannisen wondered out loud.

Sounia's arm shot out of the doorway, a steaming bowl of fish stew in her hand. The guests howled with laughter at Ontarra's expense. He sheepishly ducked inside.

Sounia's dress was tattered and filthy, but she'd spent most of the morning combing her hair out. The clothes didn't matter to Ontarra. She was breathtaking. Sounia led him to the sleep robes and pulled him down beside her. They didn't come out of the travel lodge until evening meal. They were bound together forever, unless Sounia ever decided otherwise, in which case she could kick Ontarra out, keeping the lodge and everything in it for herself and her next mate—an arrangement that induced men to be good providers.

The meal that night was a celebration. They munched on dried venison strips while Shanoka worked on a fish stew, adding everything she could think of to the pot. Teota dug down in the back of the storage pit for a shelf fungus he'd hidden for this occasion. Shanoka sliced away the outer skin, adding the pith to the mixture. Taiwa offered her choker as a wedding gift, but Sounia couldn't bring herself to accept it.

"It's of your lineage, sister." She embraced Taiwa, and sat back. "I cannot."

Teota went back to the storage pit, returning with something rolled up in a swath of rabbit hide. He handed it to Sounia. She cradled it on her palms with a questioning look. Teota's eyes sparkled with anticipation. "Open it."

Sounia set the skin on the floor and undid the ties, rolling it open as if she was rolling corn bread. Bending down, she scrutinized the contents—a lumpy object on a stick—and sat back with a start.

Ontarra leaned over her shoulder to see but couldn't quite make out what it was. With a thumb and forefinger, he gingerly lifted the stick, holding it close to his puzzled eyes to be sure of what he was seeing—the shriveled, mummified remains of two frogs caught in the act of mating and skewered with a stick. His face rearranged into a pained expression. Ontarra exhaled slowly. ""Phewee! What a way to go."

"It's an Ojibwa custom," Shanoka said. "As long as they remain together, your marriage will last. I told Teota in the spring that it would make a good wedding gift."

"I dried them all summer." Teota beamed with delight. "I kept them under Ontarra's sleep platform. He never cleaned the mess under there, so it was the safest place."

"*That's* what the disgusting stench was that no one else ever seemed to notice." Ontarra shook his head. A thought occurred. "How did you get them here?"

"I got them when I went for the prayer stone and mide bag," Teota answered proudly. "They fit in the bag, so I brought them. I figured if they made it, we'd all be okay. If they didn't"—he shrugged—"oh, well." Ontarra had to chuckle at Teota's bravado.

"You must handle them carefully," Shanoka cautioned, taking the frogs from Ontarra and setting them back in Sounia's hand. "Put them in a safe place. Your happiness may depend on it."

"Well … thank you, Teota." Sounia dipped her head. "And to you too, Shan … Mother. I'll … treasure them always." Sounia wrinkled up her face and looked around for somewhere to put them.

No one wanted this day to end. They laughed and joked well into the night. Heads began to nod, and the talk grew more serious. Sannisen's petun was long gone, so he filled his pipe with bark and sumac. He puffed away on the unsatisfying mixture, pondering a return to Ounontisaston.

"How can we ever trust them again?" Shanoka fumed. "We'd be better off going to live with Togo. The Sennikae are honorable and trustworthy."

"We have to go back." Ontarra's mood had turned sour. "I have unfinished business."

Sannisen laid a calming hand on Shanoka's arm. "We can take back control by force and punish everyone responsible," he said softly. "They're our people; they need us."

Shanoka shook her head; she saw a murky future. "There will be deaths, and then there will be reprisals. We'll spend the rest of our lives waiting for an arrow to find us when we're not looking—and for what?" Taiwa bobbed her head in sad agreement, unconsciously tracing a finger over the scar on her neck. "I'm sorry, Sannisen," Shanoka sighed. "I know this is hard for you, but I have no desire to live with people who've tried to kill us. We would need to annihilate half of the nation, just to feel safe. I'll never be able to believe the Attawondaronks are my people after all this."

Shanoka's eyes glistened with moisture, and Sannisen's heart melted. "We are safe here until spring. We can decide then," Sannisen said thoughtfully. "Perhaps things will be different by then. Soutoten and Satwani won't be taking this lightly."

"Sannisen," Shanoka said slowly, "I've been thinking about this for a long time. When I die ... it is my wish to go to the Ojibwa Village of the Dead." Sannisen lowered the pipe from his lips to say something, but Shanoka held up her hand. "Hear me out, Sannisen. I have no desire to spend my afterlife around people like Hiatsou or Poutassa. There are many people from my childhood that I long to see again. No matter what we decide in the spring, will you agree to go there with me?"

Sannisen reached over, taking both of Shanoka's hands in his and smiling gently. "I will go wherever you go."

Shanoka's eyes flew wide. "Just like that? I never thought you would even consider it."

Sannisen puffed on his pipe, smiling with his eyes. "Togo and I talked about it. He felt compelled to say something, thinking that you would never bring it up. It bothered me at first, but frankly, there are some Attawondaronks I'd rather not see again. I'd like to meet your relatives, and I'm sure the Ojibwa Village of the Dead is a beautiful place."

Shanoka shuffled over on her knees and put her arms around him. Sannisen had to unclench his teeth, letting his pipe tumble to the floor to keep from burning her. He smiled and kissed her forehead. "I go where you go," he stated simply. Shanoka felt a great weight lifted from her. The lodge was silent for several moments.

"I also go where you go, Mother," Taiwa said.

"Me too." Teota yawned from his robes.

Ontarra and Sounia looked into each other's eyes. Sounia was unsure for several heartbeats. Slowly, she smiled, and nodded. "Us too."

Four days of snow kept everyone close to camp. Fat flakes swirled down through the walnut branches, so thick at times that they hid the creek, only a stone's cast away, behind a wall of white. Wolves followed the trail of blood to the camp. They prowled the crests of the ridges, peering down at the lodges with ravenous eyes. The stench of fire and humans kept them at bay, but they ventured closer each night, irresistibly drawn to the smells of a fresh kill. Sannisen wouldn't allow Teota or the women to go outside without him or Ontarra to provide protection.

Ontarra wore Ounsasta's war club everywhere now. He began practicing each morning to become familiar with the big weapon. The sight and sounds of a man wielding a war club also served notice to the wolves that the humans would not be easy prey. Sannisen came out to watch one morning and was struck by how similar Ontarra's movements were to Ounsasta's style.

When the snow showed no sign of letting up on the fifth day, the idle tension became too much. Sannisen and Ontarra decided to try another hunt. Everything in the travel lodge was moved to the main lodge. They had to take the bows, so Sannisen placed one knife and the rockwood clubs by the door. Crouching down on his heels, he gripped Teota's shoulder. "You must protect the women while we are gone." Sannisen saw a flash of fear in his son's eyes, but Teota quickly forced it aside, accepting the responsibility with a firm set of his lips and a resolute dip of his chin.

The wolves didn't appear at the camp that day, choosing instead to track Sannisen and Ontarra and waiting for the men to split up or make some other mistake. Sannisen realized immediately that the wolves were out there. Many times through the day, he stopped, holding a hand up for silence. The faint sound of paws padding through the snow, just beyond the veil of white, was nerve-wracking. Ontarra knew he would always remember this. He didn't care for being hunted.

They had to give it up well before dusk. Even if they could have brought down a deer, the wolves would never let them get it back to camp. Ontarra ducked into the travel lodge, followed by a swirl of white. He shook himself off and began building a fire. Sounia popped in with their sleep robes, tying the doorskin tight behind her. The kindling caught; a weak flame licked up around the damp twigs.

"This is no ordinary storm," Ontarra chattered. "The animals are all hunkered down, no tracks anywhere—even the birds are hiding."

Sounia listened from the sleep robes, pulling them tight around her shoulders to lock out the chill. "We have plenty of food and wood. It will be cozy."

"That depends on how long this lasts." Ontarra tossed moisture out of his lopsided hair with a flip of his hand. "We better bring enough food from the main lodge for several days." He glanced over at Sounia with a playful grin. "I think we will be spending them in our robes."

Sounia's luminous eyes smoldered with desire in the flickering light. "I'm not hungry right now. Are you?" she asked in a husky voice.

Ontarra stripped off his clothing and crawled in beside her. They wrapped themselves around each other for warmth. Ontarra traced his fingers up the inside of her thigh, moistening his lips with his tongue.

They stayed inside the lodge for two days, except to relieve themselves. Ontarra scampered in from a sudden urgent call of nature, naked and covered in white, cursing under his breath. In the twinkling of an eye, the flakes disappeared, leaving a glossy sheen on his skin. Sounia giggled from under the robes as he hunched over the fire, his swollen member bobbing dangerously close to the hearthstones.

"Please be careful. That belongs to me now."

Ontarra grinned and hopped over to their robes. Sounia's arm shot out, her fingers wrapping firmly around his maleness. Ontarra gasped, held motionless, every nerve in his body focused on her gentle caress. She pulled him down into the furs, folding herself around him. Sounia guided him to her; the storm and the cold faded away. The feeling of her sent a shudder through every fiber of his being. Their souls melted together in writhing spasms, floating higher, ever higher, until nothing existed beyond passion and desire. They lost control together in a rush of ecstasy, reluctantly drifting back down to reality, each holding on to a piece of the other's spirit for all of eternity.

"How long have we been here?" Sounia whispered softly, her energy spent.

"I don't know ... it's dark now."

"I wish we could stay like this forever," she sighed dreamily.

Ontarra was awakened during the night. An east wind howled off the uplands, shrieking and moaning through the treetops. He scampered over to the doorskin and untied it. The doorway was blocked by a crusted wall of white. He wrapped a robe around himself and crashed through it. Wind and snow blasted in, instantly robbing the lodge of its warmth and extinguishing the fire in a burst of steam.

"My brilliant warrior!" Sounia yelled from beneath the robes.

Ontarra came back in and grabbed her. The snow was waist-deep with drifts higher than their heads. White powder blasted off the top of the ridge, swirling down through the walnut trunks to settle on the lodges on the lee side of the hill. Gusts created rotors laden with snow, cascading down the hillside like swollen cataracts. Ontarra could barely make out the main lodge. "Come on!" he hollered over the din. "We have to get into the main lodge before we're completely snowed in!"

They leaned into the biting onslaught, plowing through the drifts. Ontarra dug down through a white mound until he found the doorskin. He tumbled inside, his body trembling with cold. Sounia crawled in behind him. Sannisen sat up in his robes and snorted a laugh. "Water rats in search of a lair." Shanoka had a tea steeping on the fire. She picked up the pot by its brim, offering it to Ontarra.

Ontarra sipped and passed it over to Sounia. "It's terrible out there," he gasped, moving closer to lean over the fire and rub some circulation back into his fingers. "We're going to have to stay inside until this is over." He glanced over at the dwindling woodpile. "We'd better start rationing the wood, finding more under all this snow will be impossible."

Sannisen stood up, his robe still wrapped around him, looking like a bear coming out of hibernation. He sat on his heels next to Ontarra. "We should bring in what we can now, before the door is blocked again."

Ontarra looked tentatively at the door and shook his head. "It's too late for that. The back of the lodge is buried. We'd freeze before we got to it. All the snow will keep the lodge warm without much wood. We'd better wait it out."

"What about relieving ourselves?" Shanoka's brows knitted sourly at the obvious oversight.

"Well …" Sannisen said, glancing around the lodge.

"Oh, no." Shanoka shook her head in disgust. "I'm not living in a fecal pit."

"Here." Teota's hand extended out from his robes, offering his prized turtle-shell bowl.

"That is quite a sacrifice, Mosquito." Ontarra pinched his lips together to keep a straight face. "We'll make sure you get it back when we're done with it." Teota screwed up his face and disappeared back into his robes. Ontarra chuckled and looked over at his mother. "How long is our food going to last?"

"About one moon cycle, if we're careful." She passed the tea around for everyone to sip before setting it back on the coals. "We'll be fine. We're safe, and we are all together."

"We should set some snares," a faint voice chirped from Teota's bedding.

"I believe he is actually enjoying all this," Ontarra mused. It dawned on him suddenly that despite the worry and hardship, he liked it here too.

"I love this place," the muffled voice answered. "There's more animals and birds than I've ever seen before. Fishing is kind of weird, though."

"We will always have fond memories of this place, Teota most of all," Taiwa muttered in a faraway voice as she focused on something in the coals.

Shanoka shot a sidelong glance. "Dreaming again?"

"Whenever I sleep, Mother. Gibberish, mostly. Some things seem relevant, though."

"How long will we be here?" Ontarra wanted to know.

"I'm not sure," Taiwa answered slowly. "It's all very vague. Sometimes I think a short while. Sometimes I get the feeling that we might decide to stay forever."

"It's time we performed the Midewiwin rites," Shanoka said firmly. "My mother will be proud to know her granddaughter is a dreamer."

Sannisen rested his elbows on his knees, twining his fingers together. "Spiritual Powers have brought us nothing but grief."

"Only because they've been used for personal gain by some people," Shanoka shot back. She calmed herself. "I will leave the decision up to you then, Sannisen."

Sannisen looked from Shanoka to Taiwa. Taiwa's eyes implored him to be fair. Sannisen sighed. "And I will leave the decision to Taiwa."

"Thank you, Father." Taiwa scrambled from her robe to give him a hug that squeezed a smile to Sannisen's lips.

A dull glimmer of light through the smoke hole was the only indication that night had turned to day. They sat huddled in their robes, reminiscing about the good times at old Ounon and even a few at the new town.

Shanoka filled in pieces of the puzzle surrounding her childhood on the north shore of the Sweet Water Sea. She told of the time when she was living with Togo. A hunter was found torn apart in the woods, partially eaten. "The False Face Society of that village came to question me about Windigo monsters and curses," Shanoka said, her voice turning serious at the memory. "Togo saw them coming, and he knew it meant trouble, so he started dancing and chanting. When they walked in, he fell to the floor in a fit. He writhed and thrashed around, making horrible noises. It frightened those men so badly, they left Joneadih and never returned."

"What happened to Togo?" Taiwa asked, caught in the suspense.

"He opened one eye, asked if they were gone, and then got up and ate his morning meal."

Everyone chuckled, shaking their heads.

Constant darkness in the lodge made it impossible to keep track of time. They slept for short periods and then just lay in their robes, discussing the past and the future. Ontarra and Sounia couldn't be this close to each other without making love. They tried to be quiet but always lost themselves in their passion and couldn't remember what they'd said or done. No one objected, but Sounia was thankful for the darkness.

When it seemed they'd been stuck in the lodge forever, Ontarra awoke with the feeling something had changed. He cocked an ear toward the door. The sound of the wind was diminished. He dug a tunnel to the world outside. It was daylight, but the storm still raged. The lodges were little crests in a sea of white. The thick snow had simply muffled all the sounds. He leaned against a tree, surveying the white wasteland around him, wondering if his little raccoon friend could survive all this.

Out in the murk of flying snow, Ontarra caught a movement. Shielding his eyes to the onslaught, he squinted into the stinging blast. Were his eyes playing tricks? A dark face and urine-colored eyes stared back at him from behind a tree in the river flat. He glimpsed flashes of gray in the swirling white. *The wolves!* Close to the lodge and dangerously thin. Ontarra dropped to his tunnel and scrambled back inside. He groped in the corner and grabbed a bow.

"What's wrong?" Sannisen lurched upright, scattering the sleep robes and rudely awakening Shanoka.

"The wolves are skulking around in the river flat. I'll teach them a lesson."

"We only have four arrows," Sannisen cautioned. "We can't risk losing any. I'll cover you with the bow. You drive them off with a club."

"All right," Ontarra tossed a club out the tunnel and disappeared after it. The black wolf hadn't budged. Ontarra counted eight—perhaps nine—skulking around in the trees behind him. Sannisen popped out. He jabbed the arrows into the snow in front of him. Ontarra rested the rockwood club on his shoulder and plowed his way down the slope.

The black male curled his lips back in a menacing snarl that bared all of his teeth. Ontarra was unimpressed. He halted, swinging the club back and forth. "This is our den!" Ontarra bellowed in a voice that the wolf would understand to be a threat. Ontarra moved closer, swinging the long club again, "Go! Or I will smash every bone in your body!"

The black wolf shot a look behind him to be sure his pack was with him. He tried threatening Ontarra with another snarl. Then he lifted a leg and marked the tree with his scent. Ontarra pushed forward, swinging and hollering. The wolf pulled his head back, starting to give ground. Ontarra jabbed at his muzzle. The wolf kept just out of range. When Ontarra had backed him off several paces, he rammed his club into a drift and untied the cord on his leggings. Ontarra emptied his bladder against the tree, obliterating the big male's scent.

Ontarra yanked the club from the snow, slamming it against the tree trunk with such ferocity, the startled wolf jumped backward. Ontarra retied his leggings and retreated. The wolf advanced slowly, keeping his eyes on the intimidating human as he dropped his nose to the yellow stain. His head snapped back, eyes screwing shut, lips curling upward and quivering until his muzzle was a mass of wrinkles. A fit of violent, head-snapping sneezes followed, blinding him. He had no choice but to back off. The big black spun around and loped up the hill into the wall of flying snow.

"Apparently, you don't smell very good," Sannisen said. He clamped his lips together, trying to appear serious. "Does Sounia know how territorial you are?" He fought to keep a straight face but burst into laughter.

The storm's fury seemed to grow with each passing day. Food was running low. Moods were turning gloomy; laughter and light spirits were a thing of the past. The long imprisonment in the lodge played tricks with the mind. Joints stiffened painfully from lack of use. None of them could move without annoying someone. Nerves started to fray. They all worked hard to keep tempers under control. And then the meat ran out. Shanoka began boiling deer bones to get the marrow out for broth. She started holding her prayer stone, muttering psalms under her breath to keep awake while she cooked. Ontarra found it unsettling listening to her.

Teota started whimpering in his sleep. Taiwa was talking to people only she could see. Sannisen wanted to pace to burn off some of the tension, but he couldn't even do that. He started singing old songs from under his sleep robes instead. Ontarra and Sounia were finding the cramped quarters and lack of privacy unbearable. Shanoka realized they were all getting bush fever from the long confinement, but there was nothing she could do but pray.

The firewood was running out. They let the coals almost fade away before adding one more stick. Sannisen was smoking bark to stave off the hunger. Debilitating worry gnawed at their sanity. Time was their enemy now.

Then it happened. There was no longer enough heat to keep the smoke hole open. Snow covered the hole while they slept, and the lodge filled with deadly fumes. They choked and coughed, but no one awoke, and they fell under the deadly spell of the smoke. A trickle of water slithered down a rafter from the smoke hole, dripping on Shanoka's cheek. Another hit her forehead. Shanoka saw herself walking in fog, wondering how she'd lost her way. Something was wrong, but she didn't know what—if she could just get beyond this mist. Water splashed on her neck. She opened one eye to utter darkness, trying to recall where she was. Water dropped in her eye with a shocking jolt. *The hunt camp!*

She called out to Sannisen. He didn't respond. Groping along the floor, she found Sounia and Ontarra but couldn't wake them. Shanoka's lungs seared with every gasp of heavy smoke. Fumbling around at the door, she felt a rockwood club. She forced herself to her feet as the darkness whirled around her. Stumbling to the center of the cold hearth, she jabbed upward with all of the strength she could muster. Snow crashed down, forcing her to her knees. Fresh air rushed in.

In a hand of time, Shanoka had everyone sitting up and coughing and hacking to clear their lungs. She used the bark pot to scoop snow out of the hearth, piling it at the door. Everything was soaked. Despite their best efforts, they couldn't get another fire started.

Ontarra recovered enough to dig out. He came back with cedar boughs from the travel lodge. While Sannisen worked at getting them lit, Ontarra went back to smash sections of bark from the walls. It took the entire day to get a fire going and dry things out. The effort sapped vital energy that they needed for survival. Shanoka managed to scrape enough marrow from some well-used bones to make a weak broth.

Huddling in a group on the driest side of the lodge, they wrapped all the robes around them to retain body heat. Just enough wood was added to the hearth to be sure it kept burning. Total exhaustion gripped them all. Cold, hungry, wet, and miserable, Ontarra tried to fight off sleep. No one said it, but they all realized this was the sleep from which they might not wake. Occasionally, a hand popped out to add a stick to the fire.

Try as they might, they couldn't hold off sleep forever. For Ontarra, it came and went in hypnotic flashes, until he could no longer tell what was real and what he'd dreamed. He woke, trying to remember something he'd seen when he first arrived. The memory slowly worked its way up from the depths of his muddled mind. He crawled to the door and dug his way out.

No one missed him until he struggled back in, trembling with cold. He set a gray lump next to the hearth, feeding the few remaining sticks to the coals. Ripping the wasp nest apart, he dumped yellow pollen into the bark pot. His shaking fingers removed the combs holding the larvae and packed them down into the pot. He filled the pot with snow, pressed it down into the coals, and crawled back into his robes, falling asleep instantly.

The mush in the pot was bland but life-giving. Passing it around, they sucked the gruel off their fingers. Shrunken stomachs wanted to heave back every mouthful.

"If it is our destiny to die here, I am ready." Shanoka set the empty pot down, her voice calm but bleak. "I've known more joy than sorrow … and we will still be together."

Ontarra could think of nothing encouraging to say. He gently lifted Sounia's chin. Her eyes fluttered open. A flash of recognition passed over them when she saw him. She managed a weak smile. He felt for her hands under the robe and lifted them up to his face. Her fingers felt spindly and withered. He pressed his cracked lips to her knuckles, brushing his cheek across them tenderly. Sounia rested her head on his shoulder, and they nestled down together to await their doom.

Ontarra forced his eyes open at the sound of his mother's voice in the distance. He'd lost all track of time. Shanoka held her prayer stone pointed north–south; she was chanting softly. He heard Taiwa's voice from somewhere. "Mother, is it true that spiders taught us to make nets?"

When he woke again, Shanoka forced a hide strip into his hand. "Eat it," she said in a gravelly voice. "It will keep your spirit with your body." Ontarra and Sounia chewed on the piece of doorskin until it was gone. Ontarra wondered vaguely if the effort of chewing the tough hide was worth it.

The wood was gone. Ontarra had no energy to go out for more. On hands and knees, he struggled to the storage pit and groped around, pulling out several boiled deer bones. He lifted a misshapen rock and dropped it back; then he felt for it again. He held it up to his face—it was a gristly chunk of deer meat that had been missed. He tried biting into it, but it was frozen solid. Ontarra crawled back to the hearth and laid the deer bones on the coals. With luck, they would burn for a day. Setting the frozen gristle on a hearthstone, he bundled back into the robes.

Ontarra had no idea how long he slept. A vaguely familiar sound from the distant past woke him … sizzling fat! The fat from the chunk of gristle was melted over the hearthstones. Ontarra stuck his foot out, shifting the chunk onto the floor with his toes. The sizzling died away as another sound, or lack of sound, insinuated itself on his mind. He couldn't hear the wind. He listened closely to the shallow breathing around him. He could make out everyone but Teota.

Ontarra thought about tunneling out but couldn't muster any energy. He heard a scratching, scuffing sound at the door. A faint circle of light appeared in the wall of snow. The little raccoon pushed through. The silhouette of his face turned up to Ontarra and then shifted to the ball of gristle on the floor. "The smell of fat was too much for you," Ontarra croaked. He ran his tongue over his lips, unconsciously checking the painful cracks.

His mind was blurry. Reaching out, he lifted the half-melted lump of food, looked at it a moment, and then set it on the floor, offering it to the coon. The coon took a step forward and tilted his head up, looking at Ontarra again. "Go ahead, little one. It's too late for us." His mind made up, the coon waddled forward and sank his teeth into the juicy morsel, He turned to make his escape—and the shinbone of a deer slashed down, shattering his skull.

Ontarra found his knife and slit the animal's belly open. Fingers barely working, he clawed the steamy organs and entrails into a pile on the coals. He spread them evenly with his knife, fighting to keep himself awake. When they fried to a solid mass, he flipped the pile over. It smelled delicious. He poked the knife blade into the sizzling lump and slid the pile onto the hearthstones to cool.

"What's that smell?" Shanoka squeaked.

"It's over," Ontarra croaked. "The storm … is over. I have some meat. Is Teota alive?" There was a long silence.

"He's breathing," Shanoka's voice came back.

13

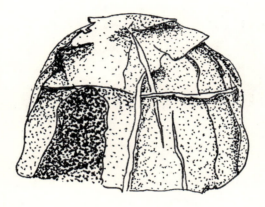

They shared the raccoon's organs, tentatively chewing and swallowing, waiting cautiously to be sure it stayed down. It wasn't much food, but it was all their stomachs could handle anyway.

Teota wouldn't wake up. Shanoka picked up the fat-covered hearthstone, swiping some over Teota's lips before passing it around. She cut the coon's intestines into finger-length strips. Squeezing the partially digested contents onto her palm, she used her finger to wipe the fecal paste on Teota's tongue and gums. She could see his cheeks working in and out, unwittingly sucking down the nourishment. As their metabolism turned to digestion for the first time in hands of days, it sapped the little strength they had, lulling them into the world of dream again.

When Ontarra awoke, he mustered enough energy to tunnel out. Puffy white clouds scudded across a clean blue sky. A few fat flakes drifted down, but it was over. Ontarra's breath hung like river mist in the crisp air. Snow was heaped in tall mounds throughout the grove, climbing halfway up the walnut trunks in places. He dug down until he found the short grass that covered the ground. Pulling several handfuls, he went back inside. The others were still asleep.

Ontarra found the bark pot and loaded the grass into the bottom. His fingers wouldn't work right; they fumbled at the simplest task. Luckily, the coon's skin peeled off like a glove. He cut off the hindquarters, adding them to the pot, and then filled it to the brim with snow and rocked it down into the coals. Crawling into the robes behind Sounia, he wrapped his arms and legs around her to hold her close and then promptly fell asleep.

By using every scrap, they turned the raccoon into four small meals. Teota woke in time to share the last pot. Ontarra's thoughts wandered back as he watched Teota chewing the meat from a tiny paw. Sparing the raccoon's life had eventually saved the lives of his family. Clearly, taking the life of an animal when it wasn't necessary was wrong.

Ontarra and Sannisen tore some more of the travel lodge apart for fuel. Their legs kept failing them. Falling all the time made doing anything outdoors tedious and exhausting. At Sannisen's request, the women unraveled more of the net to provide sinews for snares. Sounia melted snow to water in the bark pot, while Shanoka tied a hand of sinews into sliding nooses, dropping them into the pot one at a time to soak. Sannisen and Ontarra tied the waterlogged sinews to the rockwood clubs, spreading the nooses into perfect circles by packing them full of grass. Ontarra took them outside, angling the clubs down into a snowbank so the snares would freeze in place.

The squirrels were already busy searching the walnut grove for the nuts they'd hidden. Their tracks crisscrossed from tree to tree. Walnut husks lay in tatters around all of the trunks. Ontarra dug down behind the main lodge until he found the walnuts they'd stored before the onslaught of snow. Studying the squirrel tracks carefully, he picked the trails that showed the most use. He inclined the rockwood clubs against the tree trunks so the squirrels could scamper down to where the frozen noose sat waiting for them. Below the noose he laid several nuts in plain sight. Squirrels spent their lives scrambling around through tangled limbs and holes. They would be totally unconcerned about sticking their heads through the noose for the walnuts; their tapered bodies would fill the noose and melt the ice. The more they struggled to free themselves, the tighter the snare would hold them.

During the night, Ontarra heard the angry chatter of squirrels trying to get loose. In the morning he collected three blacks and one gray. "We have to try for a deer," Ontarra muttered, watching the squirrels fry over the coals. "We'll use up more energy getting small game than it's worth."

"I know," Sannisen agreed, "but the snow is too deep. We'll never make headway."

"We could try the trails just over the crest," Ontarra suggested. "That's not too far."

"I'm not sure I am up to it yet," Sannisen mumbled.

Shanoka lifted one of the spitted squirrels and slid it into a waist pouch. "You have to try—squirrels won't keep us going forever. Both of you rest for today. We'll save one squirrel to give you energy while you hunt tomorrow."

Sannisen and Ontarra spent the remainder of the day in their sleep robes. While they rested, the women went out for the first time since the storm began. "What part of the cycle do you think we are in?" Sounia asked. Shanoka looked at the snowy wasteland around them and then to the sun.

"I have no idea," she said, shaking her head. "It's still winter; that's all we need to know for now." She scanned north up the creek to where a big willow tree leaned out from the bank—a stone's throw in summer; a half-day's journey now. "We need willow branches," Shanoka said, pointing to the leaning tree. "We had better get started; this is going to take a while."

Sannisen woke to the sounds of the craftswomen chattering and laughing beyond the south entry. He sat up in confusion, staring around the lodge. Shanoka and Sounia sat at the hearth, tying willow branches into round hoops. Taiwa and Teota cut handspan-lengths of cord from the net, handing them over as they were needed.

"You look lost," Taiwa said with a smirk.

Sannisen ran a hand over his face. "Having a dream, I guess. What are you making?"

"Snow-walkers." Shanoka held up a distorted hoop with a weave of willow branches crosshatched through its center. "Ojibwa hunters use them all the time," Shanoka said proudly. "You can walk on top of the snow with them."

Sannisen pulled it from her grasp and inspected it. The outer frame was a branch the size of his thumb; the webbing branches were about the size of an arrow shaft. "I've heard of these." Sannisen handed it back, "I never thought I'd have to learn to walk on them."

Before evening meal, Ontarra and Sannisen went down to the river flat to practice. The girls came out to shout encouragement, poking fun as they stumbled, fell, and cursed. "Sweep your feet out to the sides," Shanoka yelled, "so you don't keep stepping on them!"

The girls burst into laughter as Ontarra tripped, wiping out Sannisen on his way down. They persisted, despite the ridicule from the womenfolk, until they could move at a reasonable pace without falling. When they came back in they were both exhausted. "I'll have to eat all the food we have left just to get my strength back," Ontarra grumbled.

Morning dawned bright and clear. Sannisen and Ontarra dressed for the cold, crawled out, and slung their gear over their backs. They forced their way to the crest of the hill. At the top, they tied the snow-walkers to their feet, snapped a quick wave to the girls watching from below, and disappeared.

The forest looked entirely different. The sunrise side of every hardwood tree was encrusted in a palm-thick layer of snow. A cluster of white pines on the west ridge sagged to their breaking points under heavy mantles of white. White hills and troughs rolled through the forest like waves on Iannaoa. Two chickadees, always the first creatures to venture out, flitted by—a hopeful portent. Ontarra scanned for deer sign as he struggled up a drift. "I don't think they've started moving around yet," he said, each word floating in the air in front of him.

Sannisen leaned against a crusted trunk to catch his wind. "What worries me is losing our arrows in all this snow. We have two each and no chert for new points." Sannisen bent down to see below the pine branches ahead. "Something's moving in there," he whispered. Ontarra bent low, peering into the slanting shadows. They saw them at the same time.

"Glouscap!" Ontarra shouted. "The wolves!" He straightened, checking to the rear to see if any were between them and the camp yet.

"Look at them," Sannisen hissed, a tinge of fear in his voice. "They're starving."

Ontarra ducked down to get another look. They were an arrow-flight into the woods, bounding up and down to plow through the deep snow, coming straight on, stealth and caution driven aside by the insatiable craving in their bellies.

"Let's try to make it back to camp!" Sannisen shuffled around, running in a waddle down the drift. At the bottom, his foot punched through the webbing of one of the snow-walkers, sending him sprawling into a bank. Ontarra rushed down, slashing the snow-walkers from his father's feet.

"Come on!" Ontarra yelled. "We can still make it!"

"I don't think so," Sannisen warned, staring up the drift. Ontarra spun.

The black male was crouched on top, jowls slathering, every rib showing through his pelt. A gray appeared beside him. Ontarra glanced to his rear. The wolves had already circled them. The gray crept down the drift. Ontarra swung his bow like a club. A sound behind them whirled Sannisen around; two were creeping in almost ready to lunge. Sannisen pulled an arrow. His breath caught—the shaft was snapped. He pulled his last arrow—broken.

The gray made a rush at Ontarra. Ontarra kicked, catching him on the nose. The gray jumped backward, lashing blindly in a fury of snaps and snarls. Ontarra pulled Ounsasta's club. The gray dashed in again. Ontarra knew he would land only one blow. *Yaark!* The club smashed the gray's left shoulder. The wolf dropped to his chest in the snow, still full of fight but unable to move.

A silver muzzle studded with teeth darted in beside Sannisen. He swung his bow, and the wolf jumped out of range. Ontarra fumbled at his waistpouch with his free hand, swinging the club with the other. Sannisen glanced at Ontarra from the corner of his eye. "I don't think pissing on them is going to work this time!"

Ontarra pulled the roasted squirrel from his pouch. Setting it on his knee, he rammed his knife blade up through the mouth and into the skull. With a quick snap, he broke the point off inside the squirrel's head and lobbed it to the wounded gray. The wolves that Sannisen was dealing with rushed right through the two men with no concern for their own safety. Crazed with hunger, they attacked the gray. He couldn't fight back, but he would never relinquish the squirrel while blood still flowed in his veins. He clamped down tight. The chert point pierced his tongue and punched out through the bottom of his mouth. Blood spurted onto the snow. The smell of the blood brought the entire pack down on him. Fur and shreds of flesh flew into the air. Blood sprayed over the snow in a horrifying frenzy that drowned out every other sound.

Ontarra cut the snow-walkers from his feet and backed away. The wolves forgot the humans, attacking each other in a mad, hunger-driven fury. Ontarra and Sannisen stumbled up the drifts, struggling over the tops and rolling down the back sides, fear driving them on. It seemed they were never going to make the crest above camp. When they were only a stone's cast from the ridge, the wolves remembered them.

Ontarra thought his lungs would burst, but survival kept him running.

When they reached the crest, Sannisen fell. With a blinding dash, the black male was on Sannisen, clamping his foot. "Run, Ontarra! Save yourself!" Sannisen pulled his knife, trying to regain his balance so he could use it. The black yanked him flat every time he sat up. Ontarra nocked an arrow, aimed, and loosed it. The wolf threw himself backward with all four feet and landed on his rump, instantly falling to his side in the snow. He quivered once and went limp.

Sannisen tried to stand but fell when he put weight on the mangled foot. Ontarra struggled over and wrapped an arm around his father, supporting him until they reached the brow above the camp. The women were coming up the hill with the rockwood clubs. "Take him down and get him inside!" Ontarra hollered. "Where's Teota?"

"Here!" Teota stood in front of the main lodge, waving.

"Teota, set fire to the cedar boughs in the travel lodge—hurry!" Ontarra looked back at what was left of the wolf pack. He counted six, torn and bloody but still alive. He judged the distance to the closest one. His aim focused by desperation, he planted a chert point in the wolf's chest. The pack attacked him. Ontarra inched his way back to the dead male. Grabbing the tail, he pulled it to the crest, swung with both hands, and tossed it down the hill into camp.

The dry cedar boughs roared to life just as Ontarra got there. Vicious snarls interspersed with yelps and howls gradually faded. Bloody faces with wild eyes stared down at the humans standing around the safety of a huge fire. A column of smoke rolled up the hillside into the wolves' faces. Their manic craving for food was satisfied. Pain from self-inflicted wounds overwhelmed the packs desire to kill again. They'd had enough.

The fire consumed the travel lodge to the snow line. Melting snow slid down what was left of the bark walls, snuffing out the flames. Water trickled through the door, drowning the embers left by the cedar boughs. In a hand of time the fire was out, leaving a charred skeleton where the matrimonial home had stood. As they watched the dark gray smoke billowing skyward, Ontarra bent down, plucking up the smoldering remains of a dream-catcher. Tears ran down Sounia's cheeks.

Shanoka untied the thongs of Sannisen's tattered moccasin and gently tugged it from his foot. Sannisen gritted his teeth to hold back the pain. Blood spilled out on the snow as Shanoka freed the foot. She quickly checked the wounds and then put snow in the moccasin, sliding it back on to slow the bleeding. "Ontarra, help me get him inside!"

Sannisen clamped his jaw tight as they laid him down on his sleep robes. Shanoka lifted the injured foot, shoving a travel pack under to hold it up. She wasted no time. "Teota, salvage all the wood you can from the travel lodge. Sounia, try to build a decent fire. We need to boil water. These wounds have to be cauterized."

"Oh, great," Sannisen groaned, dropping his head back in despair.

Shanoka looked down at him, wishing she could say something comforting. "Quit feeling sorry for yourself," she said with a smirk. Sannisen opened one eye with amused annoyance. Shanoka turned to Ontarra. "I need slippery bark from a willow. Taiwa can't go with wolves prowling around—you'll have to get it." Ontarra nodded and ducked out. "Taiwa, drag that wolf in here before the smell of blood brings the others back. I want you to dress him out. Cut me several arm-lengths of gut to use for wrappings." Ontarra plopped the wolf inside the door just as Shanoka finished.

"Save the arrow," he instructed."

Ontarra plowed his way to the top of the hill. Sitting just below the ridge, he poked his head up, scanning the area beyond. Blood, gore, and bones were spread over a wide area. The wolves were gone. He stood to make his way out onto the uplands, searching the bloodied snow for the arrow that brought down the wolf. All he found was torn fletching. He stared off into the woods.

Pulling Ounsasta's club, he took a deep breath and pushed on, following the trail they'd left when escaping the pack. He stopped every few steps, checking for movement in the forest around him. Between the snowdrifts where the wolves first surrounded them, he found two broken arrows and one good bow. As an afterthought, he went back, picked up the two best snow-walkers, and tucked them under his arm.

When he reached the camp, he heard Sannisen scream. Hot brands were being pressed into open wounds. Ontarra had known that agony only once. He closed his eyes at the recollection, trying to squeeze the memory from his mind. He had to get slippery bark.

When he returned with the bark, Sannisen was unconscious. Ontarra's stomach rolled over at the smell of burned human flesh. He sat down at the hearth to begin the painstaking task of stripping the slick inner layer of bark away from the tough outer layer. "Will he be all right?" Ontarra asked, rocking his broken knife blade between the layers of bark to peel them apart.

"The bleeding has stopped," Shanoka whispered, sitting down next to him to lend a hand. "We have to wrap the wounds with the bark quickly to keep the festering spirits from getting in." Shanoka used Sannisen's knife to get the slippery layer started and then peeled it back slowly with her fingers. "The big sinew at the back of his foot is punctured. It will be very painful and slow to heal."

Ontarra glanced over at Taiwa, who was skinning the black wolf. "Will we be safe eating it?" Ontarra asked in a low tone.

Shanoka leaned closer so only Ontarra would hear. "I have heard of people eating predators in extreme emergencies," she said softly. "That creature has devoured so many animal spirits …" Her voice trailed off. Shanoka cursed under her breath as the strip of slippery bark tore the wrong way, leaving her with a useless fragment. She rested her hands on her knees to calm herself. "If you cannot bring us any other meat tomorrow, I would consider this an extreme emergency. I will ask the spirits of all the dead animals to forgive us. We don't have any other choice."

"There's only one good arrow left." Ontarra reached back to his robes for the broken arrows. "We'll have to make new shafts." Shanoka rolled the arrows between her fingers, inspecting the points and fletching.

"We can make new ones from these. We'll work on them while you hunt."

Ontarra saw nothing but tracks the next day—wolf tracks, fox tracks, predators like himself searching for game that still hadn't ventured out from snowy hideaways.

Wolf meat should have tasted as good as dog, but the thought of eating it was disturbing. They picked slowly, forcing each mouthful, holding it down for a heartbeat before hazarding another bite.

Hiatsou hated winter. At least the storm was finally ending—the worst he could ever remember. Three storms, back to back, with only a day of relative calm between them. The final blast roared in from the east, howling up the bluff and over the palisades in a maelstrom of whirling vortexes, burying Ounontisaston beneath a mountain of white. Hiatsou hadn't ventured beyond the door for at least a moon cycle. Waiting out the long season was hard on the nerves; he wished he could sleep through it like the bears and marmots.

Short bursts of sunlight lit up the white ditch beyond the doorskin. Fat, fluffy flakes drifted down during the intervals when the sun disappeared, swirling inside when the wind kicked up, sacrificing their souls to a muddy puddle on the floor. Hiatsou watched each one fade from existence with a morbid fascination. Harsh winters like this put life on hold. Ounontisaston was secure until spring.

When Tsohahissen died, Hiatsou had appointed himself chief of chiefs. He wasn't popular with everyone, but he was leader. He preferred simple obedience to respect anyway.

Sannisen was his main concern. It was mystifying how they could have disappeared so completely. Young people defecting from Tontiaton assured Hiatsou that Sannisen wasn't there. Word arrived from the shamans of all the towns and villages. There was no sign of Sannisen or the witch. Hiatsou shook his head and stared at the floor. *Well ... if Sannisen isn't at Tontiaton,* he brooded, *we can proceed with Poutassa's plan to take the town during spring solstice.* Hiatsou listened to footsteps crunching past his head beyond the bark wall.

"Ho, Feathered Serpent, it is Dekari and Matoupa. May we enter?"

"Enter." Hiatsou leaned down to add some wood to the fire. He sat back and pulled Tsoha's bear skin tight around his shoulders to keep out the icy chill that was sure to follow them in. They ducked inside and shook themselves off. Hiatsou gestured to the tripod stools, still watching the door to see if Manak was with them. "Where is the angry one?" he asked Dekari.

Dekari and Matoupa looked at each other. Dekari dipped his chin for Matoupa to answer. "In ... lodge ... he stays." Matoupa had been practicing, but the slant of the Attawondaronk words was difficult. Hiatsou looked to Dekari for clarification.

Dekari gave his head a shake, throwing his hands up with frustration. "He has the fever. He just sits at the fire, wrapped in skins. He shakes and shivers, complaining that he can't get warm. When we left, he was muttering about being trapped in the netherworld—a place where white flakes fall from the sky, smothering the earth like dead skin; where rivers turn to crystal; and where his only protection is tree bark tied to poles. He's been ranting like a madman for days. He doesn't even go outside to relieve himself."

Hiatsou snorted, canting his head to Matoupa with an amused grin. "This is your greatest warrior?"

Matoupa let out a weary breath. "Everyone fears … fear."

"Manak told us to see you," Dekari continued. "He thinks if he can locate the woman, we can try to walk out of here. He won't listen to us anymore. I don't believe he can last two more moon cycles."

Hiatsou glanced out at a brief interlude of sunshine, his mind working. "Some people never recover when they get it that bad." Hiatsou probed a nostril with his thumb while he thought, studying what he found with casual interest before flipping it into the fire. "So let him leave. He won't last two days out there."

Dekari had anticipated this kind of answer. "You accepted his trade goods, and the bargain is not fulfilled. Are you willing to give them back?"

Hiatsou considered this for a moment. "Matoupa, I wish to speak with Dekari alone." Matoupa got up reluctantly and went out into the cold. Hiatsou watched him leave and turned back to Dekari. "I could just kill them and keep it all," he simpered in a hushed voice.

Dekari glanced warily at the door. He knew how Hiatsou's mind worked. If he wanted to carry his own burden pack of treasures out of here, he was going to have to be convincing, or Hiatsou would get him next. Dekari leaned close to whisper, "If you do, word will spread that traders came here and never left. No trader would ever come again. Besides, they want Sannisen's woman. Who do you have who is capable of beating him in a fight? Certainly not your young fanatics, and the older warriors will side with Sannisen, not fight him. Manak and Mox are the ones you need, when you find them."

Hiatsou brushed his hand across his chin. "You're right. I've been worrying about that."

Dekari sat back, relieved. "What we have to do now is get Manak straightened out before he's permanently touched. You need to talk to him, give him something to make him sleep, or make him unconscious for a while."

"The storm is ended. The thaw could start in one more moon cycle." Hiatsou looked out the door as if he could see the melt coming. "You're going to have to convince him to stay that long, at least."

Dekari rolled his eyes. "Hah! You go tell him. He's ready to blow and kill someone, and I'd rather it wasn't me."

"Why must I always do everything?" Hiatsou sighed. He pulled a bag from under his sleep platform, rooted around inside a moment, and came up with a willow-bark container. "Tell Matoupa to put a pinch of this in his food. He'll soon start sleeping most of the time."

Dekari pulled the wood stopper and shook some of the brown powder onto his palm, poured it back in, and capped it. He stood to leave but then crouched back down to Hiatsou's level. "Do you think I could stay in your lodge for a few nights?"

Their bellies cramped and churned for two days after eating the wolf. Sharp spasms doubled them over, sending everyone running time and again for the skeletal remains of the travel lodge to relieve themselves. Sannisen's plight was pure misery. Unable to stand, he had to endure the humiliation of arching his body while Shanoka slid Teota's turtle-shell bowl under him. He cursed his luck, the wolves, the weather, and anything else that came to mind. Taiwa said that the spirits of all the animals trapped in the wolf's flesh were now anxious for their freedom.

When Ontarra recovered from the scours, he hunted. For two hands of days, all he got was a few squirrels, pierced through with his last arrow while they brazenly scolded him for being there. Finally, he brought home a rabbit. The next day, Ontarra carried a small doe down the hill into camp, careful not to leave a trail of blood for the wolves to follow this time.

Winter seemed to have blown itself out on the monster storm. Days grew longer. The big drifts started caving in on themselves in the afternoon sunlight, packing to a firm crust beneath their own weight. If Ontarra stepped softly when he hunted, the snow would carry him. When he got careless, he crashed through, forcing him to kneel on his free leg in order to pull the trapped one out.

Today was the first truly warm day of the cycle. Sannisen needed to be outside. He hobbled through the door of the lodge, leaning on a rockwood club while trying not to put weight on his injured foot. Settling himself down on the log Ontarra had dragged up from the flats for him, he watched Shanoka filling the bark pot in a hole she'd chopped in the ice of the creek. He looked past her at the sunlit hillside across the valley, allowing his mind to wander.

Shanoka struggled up the saddle, trying to keep the pot and herself upright. She sat down next to Sannisen to catch her breath. "We could make maple syrup if you carved us some taps." Sannisen stared silently out across the valley. Pulling out his pipe, he absently packed bark shavings into the bowl before realizing he had no way to light it.

"Tonight would be a good night for Taiwa's mide ceremony," Shanoka said, following his gaze. "I'm going to ask the girls and Teota to start gathering wood for a bonfire." Shanoka waited for a response. Sannisen had a distant look in his eyes, obviously lost to his own thoughts. Shanoka jabbed a finger in his ribs. "Perhaps I should go talk to one of the walnut trees."

"Hmm?" Sannisen cocked his head as if he'd just noticed her.

"Bonfire ... mide ceremony." Shanoka rolled her eyes to the sky in exasperation. "Where is your head?"

Sannisen looked into the distance again, to where Ounontisaston sat two days away. "I was thinking ... that Ontarra and I could ride the spring flood to Tontiaton. We can join up with Satwani and Soutoten ... maybe send runners to Khioetoa for Kadaji's warriors."

"With your foot like that?" Shanoka blurted. "Be realistic. Even if you got past the forks of the Tranchi without being spotted, how would you make the overland trek into Tontiaton? And do you really think they're going to want to drag a gimp around with them while they attack the strongest town in the land?"

Sannisen's face fell, and Shanoka regretted her words instantly. She sighed and cupped her hand over his. "What are you going to ask them to do? Raze Ounontisaston? Kill everyone inside?"

"To kill a snake, it is only necessary to cut off the head."

Shanoka had never heard hatred in Sannisen's voice before. It frightened her. She looked up into his eyes, forcing him to meet her gaze. "This snake has many heads." They sat in silence for a few heartbeats. "You can't go anywhere until that foot is healed," Shanoka said softly. "For tonight, let's think of life. We have much to be thankful for. It's warm, we have meat, and Taiwa is ready for her initiation."

Sannisen patted her hand and managed a thin smile. "What do you want me to do?"

First, they piled wood for the bonfire. Then they stomped down the snow around it and laid down a mat of cedar boughs. The smattering of cedars around the edges of the grove was nothing more than spindly trunks now.

The activity put Sannisen in better spirits. He teetered around on the cedar mat, smacking down unruly branches with his rockwood club to flatten things out.

At dusk they lit the blaze. A hindquarter of venison, boned out and tied around a forked limb, was leaned against a tree next to the fire to slowly roast in its own juices. Teota couldn't resist throwing more and more wood on the tall blaze, until Shanoka finally stopped him with a firm hug. "We don't want to run out."

When it was time, Ontarra and Sounia went up to the lodge to bring out the novice. They each held her by an arm as if she was a prisoner being led to execution. Walking her out onto the cedar mat, they turned her to face her mentor. Shanoka pointed her mide bag at Taiwa's stomach. Taiwa staggered as every known sickness invaded her body. She sagged and doubled over, falling dead on the cedar boughs.

The walnut valley was silent except for the crackling of the fire. Sparks spiraled skyward in the column of heat from the flames. Slowly, Taiwa crawled to her knees and pushed to her feet again. She spat the sickness and demons from her body onto her palm, in the form of a white cowrie shell. Taking two steps forward, she touched the tiny cowrie shell to Shanoka's chest. Shanoka recoiled, jarred by the Power imparted upon the shell. Shanoka smiled and held out her mide bag. Taiwa dropped the shell inside.

Shanoka hugged her. "Now you will know the wisdom of the ages. You are Midewiwin, my daughter." They all gathered round, congratulating Taiwa. Sounia hugged her while Teota hung off her waist. Sannisen avoided the group hug by rotating the meat. He wasn't at all certain it was a cause for celebration, but he acted happy anyway.

When the roasted side of the meat stopped sizzling, they slid up behind the tree one at a time, using the trunk to shield them from the licking flames. Reaching an arm around, they could peel off succulent strips of the crisp outer layer. When the flame-charred meat was cleaned away, Sannisen rotated the rump again. They could eat all night this way, while never feeling too full. Taiwa chewed contentedly as she watched her father across the fire, struggling to keep his balance on one foot while turning the roast.

"Is he going to be able to walk normally again?" she asked Shanoka from the side of her mouth.

Shanoka stared over at Sannisen with tender eyes, turning to face Taiwa so no one else would hear. "No." Taiwa stopped chewing. Shanoka gripped Taiwa's arm. "It's all right. The manitos have taken away your father's foot so that we may keep the rest of him."

Taiwa settled sorrowful eyes on her father, still fighting with the roast. "He'll never understand."

Beyond the firelight, the night deepened. The sky was an all-encompassing black canopy dusted with stars that spread out across the heavens. The northern horizon began to throb with an eerie green radiance. Shanoka was the first to notice. She walked out beyond the circle of light to let her eyes adjust. Spectral shafts stabbed upward into the night, touching Atiskein Andahatey and then fading back as others shot up beside them. "Look ... it's the night lights," Shanoka marveled. "I haven't seen them like that since I was a child. The spirits are happy. It is a good omen."

Taiwa walked out beside Shanoka, gnawing at the strip of meat in her greasy fingers. Her mother had pointed out the lights in the past, but she'd never been able to see more than a faint flickering. Tonight the entire northern horizon was a mass of undulating green light, pulsating into the heavens as it ebbed and flowed with a life of its own. Taiwa was held spellbound. The lights meant something; she could feel it—like the Power in the air before a thunderstorm.

Shanoka laughed as the meat Taiwa was chewing tumbled from her gaping mouth. "It is the essence of the spirits of the dead," Shanoka said, "traveling to the pathway in the stars. They're telling us that what they see on the earth tonight pleases them."

Taiwa watched, entranced by the rhythms of the shimmering shafts of light. Icy fingers slowly curled around her heart. Her breath caught in her throat, and she clutched at the choker around her neck. "No ... it isn't good. It's a warning." With a start, she swung her gaze over the ridge above them. She turned and ran out into the darkness on the other side of the fire, trying to see the top of the ridge to the south. Walking out a few more steps, Taiwa twisted slowly around as if drawn to something. She strained her eyes into the pitch-black veil that surrounded them, toward the first bend downriver. Ontarra ran to her side. In a moment Sannisen limped up to join them.

"What is it?" Ontarra whispered.

"I don't know ..." Taiwa answered mysteriously. "We must leave this place."

"Don't be silly," Shanoka's anxious voice came from behind. "The night lights are always a good sign."

At the first bend downriver from the camp, four dark forms huddled up against the riverbank. A frightened young man wilted under Taiwa's stare. "They're looking right at us!" he hissed under his breath.

"Don't be ridiculous," an angry voice shot back. "They can't see us out here on a night like this."

The family's time at the hunt camp had just run out.

"You're certain it's them?"

Adontayat answered with a quick dip of his chin. "We watched them; they're all there." Hiatsou glanced over at the new shaman who had traveled with Adontayat from Teotonguiaton. The young man was nervous, bobbing his head up and down every time Hiatsou looked at him. Hiatsou could barely contain himself. He started pacing, two steps in each direction.

"Ontarra too?" Poutassa asked.

"Yes. It appears they've been there all winter." Adontayat looked around the lodge for a stool. He didn't see one, so he settled himself down on a large sleep platform. He studied Hiatsou moving back and forth for a few heartbeats and then decided to continue. "After the big storm ended last moon cycle, we saw a tall column of dark smoke northwest of our town. Two of our warriors were sent out to investigate." Adontayat puffed himself up so his demeanor would match the importance of the role he'd played. "Our chief is a warrior, and I don't trust him. I insisted that Buzkit and I go along." Adontayat indicated the new shaman with a sweep of his arm. The young man still couldn't find his voice, so he agreed by jerking his head up and down again.

"Does he ever talk?" Hiatsou asked feeling a little annoyed.

"He's not accustomed to such exalted company," Adontayat apologized. "We have been through a terrible experience the past few days. The snow was too deep to make the trek overland. The warriors knew of a river that ran from the Lower Tranchi in the direction that the smoke was spotted, so we used the rivers. The melt had already begun, and the ice on the Lower Tranchi was covered with just enough water to let us use canoes. When there wasn't enough water, the warriors made us skid our own canoe over the ice.

We were soaked and frozen the whole time. They wouldn't even let us have a fire at night!"

Hiatsou was running out of patience. "So where are they?"

Adontayat wasn't finished telling about the ordeal, but the look on Hiatsou's face suggested he'd better get to the point. "There is a small river that runs north from the Lower Tranchi. It was covered in slush. We had to leave our canoes on the high ground at its mouth. For two days, we walked in slush." Adontayat glanced over at the young shaman, hoping he would expand on the great sacrifice they'd made, but the little slug just kept nodding.

"How long is this story?" Hiatsou fumed.

Adontayat sighed. "The river gradually loops around to the east. When we got up near the source, we found their camp. I would place it about halfway between the old Ounontisaston and Teotonguiaton."

Hiatsou nodded. "I remember. He used to go hunting down there somewhere. It must be them."

"It is them," Adontayat said, pursing his lips indignantly. "We watched them. Sannisen has a leg injury. He's walking around with a crutch."

"Why didn't you send the warriors in to get them?" Poutassa asked.

"We tried—they refused. They said if Shanoka is a truly witch, it is up to the shamans to get her."

"Where are the warriors now?" Hiatsou stared at the door, expecting them to appear.

"When we got back to the Lower Tranchi, the warriors told us to return to Teotonguiaton. They would come here to tell you what they'd found. I was suspicious," Adontayat added with a smug smile, "so we came along. The river was high, and the ice was breaking up. It was all we could do to keep the ice flows from smashing us to bits. The warriors got farther and farther ahead. When we reached the forks of the Tranchi, they sliced out into the current and disappeared downriver."

"They're going to Tontiaton," Poutassa said, thinking ahead. "They want to get Satwani and his warriors to go back and protect them."

"We can't allow that!" Hiatsou's voice was panicky.

"No, we can't," Poutassa agreed, running a hand over his face and letting it settle thoughtfully on his chin. "We will have to act promptly. Satwani will come upriver tomorrow or the next day. We will arrange a surprise greeting at the forks."

A depraved grin etched its way across Hiatsou's face as he unraveled the meaning of Poutassa's words. "Yes." He rubbed his hands together, picturing the scene in his mind. Hiatsou clapped his hands louder than usual in his excitement. Two of his young club-wielding fanatics rushed inside, anxious to wreak some sort of havoc. Poutassa calmed them with an upheld palm.

Poutassa waited for Hiatsou to say something, but he was pacing again, rubbing his hands together and grinning at the floor. "Tell the outsiders we wish to speak with them," Poutassa snarled, jerking his chin at the door to dismiss the two young men.

Hiatsou started mumbling to himself, bobbing his head as he paced. "We'll be rid of Sannisen and Satwani in one stroke," he gloated. Hiatsou hadn't felt this good in a long while, not since the night he dismembered Poutassa's mother and cast her into the Tranchi.

14

Taiwa couldn't shake the feeling that she'd been warned to leave. Her insistence that they go elsewhere put everyone on edge. "Ontarra and I will go to Tontiaton and come back with warriors," Sannisen suggested.

"No!" Shanoka was adamant. "It's too dangerous. If you don't return ... how would we ever know what happened?"

"We could go deep into the forest until we make a decision," Taiwa pressed.

Ontarra gave his head a negative shake. "If they find the camp, they'll track us. We'll have to stay here until the river breaks up."

With nothing to do but wait, tension in the hunt camp grew unbearable. Everyone found chores to keep them busy. Three days of sunshine had the melt well underway. Dead brown grasses of last cycle were poking up through fading mounds of snow. Knee-deep water flowed over the ice on the river. In one more day, the water would burst over the banks, and the ice would break into flows.

Taiwa and Sounia left early to gather firewood on the uplands. Deadfall in the walnut grove was long gone, forcing them to scavenge farther and farther afield. Ontarra climbed with them to the top of the ridge, pecked Sounia on the cheek, and headed for the deer trails south of camp.

He had three arrows now. The two with new shafts were still green. They wobbled in flight, but he would have to be content with them until the new shafts drying in the lodge were ready. There was no fresh sign on the trails closest to camp. Ontarra moved farther in, checking each trail, until he found himself in the old riverbed where he'd made his double kill just before the first snowfall. After a quick search, he found the remains of the buck's antlers.

They were badly chewed up by night creatures, but there were three points that could be fashioned into arrowheads.

He knelt down, tracing a finger across cloven hoof marks—fresh. They'd just passed through on their way to the river. If he was lucky, he could catch them drinking. Ontarra moved up out of the wash so they wouldn't spot him on their back trail. The forest fell away in a long, gradual slope until he was down in the river flat. Trees faded to scrub in the marshy soil. Ontarra caught glimpses of the river as he stepped silently through the tangled brush. He tested the wind on his face to be sure they wouldn't catch his scent. A stone's cast from the river, he came upon a stretch of wet mud that he couldn't get across without being heard. Ontarra studied the ground around him, taking note of the deep hoof prints pointed in several directions. Some of the bog willow branches were snapped. The deer had scattered here—something had scared them.

Ontarra moved to one side, skirting around the mud, nocking his best arrow as he went. He poked it through the last bush before the riverbank, forcing it aside to get a look. Nothing. He stepped out and crept along the shoreline. At a low point on the bank, deer sign was everywhere. Ontarra scrutinized the prints. No deer had watered today. He straightened up and scanned the river. It was wider here than at the camp. The current had already begun lifting out sections of ice midstream, leaving a submerged ledge protruding out from each bank.

As he watched, another section of ice cracked loose, rose to the surface, and was carried away by the rising floodwater. A strange mark caught his eye—a scuff on the submerged ice near shore. To one side, a pockmark gouged the slushy surface. Ontarra walked up the bank, stopping every few steps to gaze into the water. More scuff marks, more pock marks. Ontarra sat on his heels trying to decipher what had created them. The water erased the marks while he watched. His heart skipped a beat. A canoe had just been skidded through here by using paddles as poles to push it along.

Ontarra broke into a trot. He saw some marks in the crystalline snow up ahead. The current had pushed the canoe into shore. A paddle and a hand pushed it off again. A hand with three fingers missing! Ontarra's mind shot back to the battle on the Tranchi and a handprint in the mud. Hair bristled on the back of his neck. *One of the Agwa that escaped!*

Ontarra splashed out, mindless of the frigid water, to stare upstream.

The river hooked right and disappeared toward the camp. The shortest route back was across the uplands. Ontarra tried to hold back the panic, but the faster he ran the tighter it gripped him. He threw away caution for speed, crashing headlong through brush, jumping rocks and ravines that got in his way. He forgot to control his breathing; his lungs couldn't keep up. He fell gasping against a tree. A bone-chilling scream from the direction of the grove propelled him on again. He reached the crest of the south ridge and peered down through the trees. Two canoes were tied to the tree that blocked the river. The deadfall was down. Ontarra swung his gaze anxiously toward the camp. Two men where splashing headlong across a rapids, straight for the walnut grove. Ontarra ran along the ridge, nocking an arrow as he went. He tried to get a shot, but couldn't find a clear opening. He got a good look at one of the men—the dark-skinned outsider he'd fought at Tontiaton!

Sannisen hobbled out of the lodge and down the saddle, leaning on his rockwood club, a knife gripped firmly in his right hand. Ontarra thought his lungs would burst as he reached the ravine that ran down to the saddle. Shanoka charged over the top and onto the uplands to scream for Ontarra. When she saw him coming, she turned and skidded back down the hill. The two outsiders were running up the slush-covered creek. Ontarra noticed two more men trotting toward the camp from the direction of the downed tree where the canoes were tied.

Sannisen took a defiant stance on the highest section of the creek bank. Mox charged straight in as he always did. It threw fear into his enemies, causing them to falter at the critical moment. When Mox leaped for the bank, Sannisen slammed the butt of his club into Mox's forehead. Mox stopped cold, slowly sagged to his knees, and slid back down into the slush. Sannisen turned to face the second intruder.

Manak knew Sannisen had an injured leg. He moved down the creek just out of reach of the club and came up into the grove from a safe distance away. Pulling a black-headed ax from his waistband, he moved in. Sannisen swung the club. Manak ducked the blow, came up grinning, and swung the ax. Sannisen leaned away, and the ax cleaved air. A knife appeared in Manak's left hand, holding Sannisen at bay while he got the ax under control.

Ontarra sidestepped down the hill into camp, trying to get a shot. Sannisen was too close to the stranger for a safe release. Taiwa and Sounia charged down the east ridge and into the grove; they gripped thick tree limbs in their hands as clubs. They rushed up behind Manak, flailing at his head and shoulders with the hefty limbs. He forced them back with a swing of the ax. In the hairbreadth of time that Manak's attention was turned, Sannisen landed a stunning blow with the rockwood club and then opened a gash on Manak's cheek with his knife.

Manak leaped away. He hadn't anticipated so much opposition. From the corner of his eye he could see Mox climbing to his feet. Matoupa and Dekari were just now coming up the creek bed. The girls started pummeling him from behind again. Manak didn't dare take his eyes off Sannisen. He tried backing away so he could deal with the girls. Sannisen followed, slashing his blade across the tip of Manak's nose. The club ticked his chin a heartbeat later.

Sounia jumped on Manak's back, beating his head and face with her fists. "Get them off me!" Manak screamed in rage and frustration. Matoupa rushed up the bank and peeled Sounia off by her hair. Taiwa started clubbing Matoupa for all she was worth. Dekari tried to come up the creek bank, but slipped and slid back down into the slush. He tried again, using a tree trunk to steady himself. Reaching out when Taiwa got close, he yanked a leg from under her. She fell hard. Dekari slid back down into the slush.

Mox finally came to his senses. He climbed up into the grove a safe distance from the action. Matoupa threw Sounia down on top of Taiwa, pinning them both with his own weight. Ontarra was on the saddle in front of the lodge now. Everyone in the grove was mixed together, too close for a safe shot—except Mox. Ontarra lined up and let fly. The arrow wobbled through the grove, careened off a tree trunk, and veered hard left. Dekari was pulling himself up the bank for the third time when the arrow slammed into the walnut trunk he was holding, partially severing the tip of his longest finger. He screamed, falling backward as if the arrow had pierced his heart. The fingertip tore away, neatly pinned to the tree trunk.

Ontarra moved down the saddle, his arrow searching for another shot. Mox rushed up to hit Sannisen from behind; he raised a huge maul over his head for the fatal blow. Sannisen forced Manak back with a quick feint. Sidestepping, he rammed his club back, taking Mox square in the groin. Mox dropped the maul, swayed, and then settled into a fetal position and rolled on his side. He moaned once and choked up his morning meal. Sannisen jabbed the club in Manak's face and flashed a grin. "I think you're on your own now, skinhead."

Manak's rage boiled over. He batted the club aside, chopping at Sannisen's face and shoulders with a series of swings that forced Sannisen back. When Sannisen faltered on his bad foot, Manak lunged, pinning Sannisen's neck to a tree with his arm. "Now it's my turn!" Manak hissed in Tunican. Sannisen slammed his forehead into Manak's nose, staggering him back. Blood gushed from both of Manak's flattened nostrils. He raised his ax to hold Sannisen off. "Filthnee barbarian!" he gurgled.

Ontarra thought he had a shot. A flurry of movement to his right made him hold. Shanoka ran down the saddle and jumped on Manak's back, stabbing him in the neck and shoulders several times before realizing she had Ontarra's broken knife in her hand.

"Enough!" Manak screamed like a madman. He threw all his weight back, slamming into a tree. Before Sannisen could move in, Manak hammered his ax backward, catching Shanoka on the temple. Manak jumped forward and swung at Sannisen without missing a beat. Shanoka slid down the tree trunk into a heap.

Sounia and Taiwa started screaming, biting, kicking, and kneeing. Matoupa had no choice but to try dragging them down to the creek so that Dekari could hold one of them. Ontarra wanted to get to his mother. He had to move in close enough to take out Manak without hitting Sannisen. He sidled down onto the river flat. *Tree in the way ... Sannisen too close ... there!* Ontarra drew the arrow to his cheek.

"Ontarra! Look out!" Teota's voice screamed from the saddle.

Ontarra jumped to the side just as Mox's maul flashed by, taking his bow with it. Ounsasta's club came out. One of Mox's eyes was swollen shut. His face twisted into an imperious grin as he sized up his opponent's youth and inexperience. Ontarra feinted with a downward blow to the head and then spun into a crouch, coming around to try for Mox's knee instead. Mox jumped and swung the maul. Ontarra rolled backward—the maul blasted bark and splinters from a walnut trunk. Ontarra ducked under the big weapon and rushed behind Mox while he was still off balance. Ounsasta's club broke one of Mox's ribs on the way by.

Mox swung again; Ontarra parried. The huge maul had a long handle with a large black rock hafted into the business end. Mox needed both hands to control it. Each time Mox took a swing, Ontarra responded with two. Ontarra easily avoided the arcing swipes—if one connected, he knew he would be finished. Mox swung at Ontarra's legs. Ontarra jumped, and the club passed harmlessly beneath him. Ontarra got a piece of Mox's ear before his feet touched the ground again. His second swing went wild, glancing off a tree trunk.

Sannisen was satisfied that Ontarra could take the big one. He needed to finish this one and help Shanoka. He jabbed the butt of the club at the warrior's face, following it up with a sweep of his knife. The man was too fast. If only he could put some weight on his foot ... Sannisen backed up to a tree to steady himself.

Manak was insane with rage. This was taking too long. Dekari was down; Matoupa was fighting with women; he could see Mox flailing away from the corner of one eye. There were too many trees for the maul to be effective, and the young one was too fast for him. He saw bark fly as Mox wounded another tree, staggering back instantly from a blow to his thigh from the young one's club.

Teota ran down the saddle with his fishing spear. He almost got Mox's leg, but Mox kicked at the last instant, deflecting the spear without taking his eyes from Ontarra. "Teota, get out of here!" Ontarra lunged to pull him out of the way, jumping back again as the maul flashed by.

Mox saw the sudden look of terror cross Ontarra's face. He risked a glance at Teota, and Ontarra's club nearly took his head off. Mox recovered his balance, a malignant grin thinning his lips. The maul swooped down at Ontarra's hips. Ontarra faded back, letting the maul pass by. Teota didn't see it coming until the moment it struck his chest. Ontarra heard the bones crunch. Teota's body folded up around the stone head, the maul's momentum lifting him off his feet and tossing him into a fading snowbank like a discarded cornhusk doll.

"No-o-o-o!" Ontarra took one step toward Teota and realized his mistake. Mox followed the maul around, continuing the swing into a second blow that caught Ontarra above his left ear. A brilliant light exploded inside Ontarra's head, and the world blinked out.

Sounia screamed. Sannisen's eye's shifted to see what had happened. Manak threw his ax at Sannisen's injured foot. Debilitating pain locked Sannisen's muscles for an instant. His eyes screwed shut. Manak slammed the black knife into Sannisen's neck. Sannisen's eyes flew wide. He saw the horror on Taiwa's and Sounia's faces and felt a rush of grief through his pain, realizing he had failed to protect them. He toppled down the bank, landing face down in the slush on the creek. Sannisen's arms rose at his sides, fingers curling in the slush as he struggled to rise, but the effort was futile. He collapsed and didn't move again.

Sounia and Taiwa slumped against each other on the creek bank, sobbing hysterically. Tears ran down their faces as Matoupa bound their hands behind them. Manak jumped down, pulling his knife from Sannisen's neck. "Shut them up!" he shouted angrily, probing at his broken nose with a finger. Matoupa snapped two thumb-sized branches from a tree and forced them into the girls' mouths, tying them in place by fastening a cord around the back of their heads.

Manak pulled himself back up the bank. Kneeling down, he studied Shanoka's face, cursing under his breath. He poked at her right temple. The skull was broken.

Mox limped up beside him. "You killed her."

"I can see that, pissant! It might not have happened if I'd gotten a little help from you!"

"I never thought that one so young could handle a club like that." Mox pressed at his ribs, suddenly realizing that one was broken.

"You fight like an old woman!" Manak fumed, his anger beginning to subside. He reached down, yanking the mide bag from Shanoka's waistband. His fingers trembled as he untied the closure and shook out the contents, and he gasped when the crystal rolled onto his palm. He stared up at Mox with the closest thing to a smile that Mox had ever seen on that face. Manak's emotionless eyes took on an unnatural sparkle as he pictured what he could do with the Uktena Stone. He slid the crystal back into the mide bag and tied it to his waistband.

Manak got to his feet. He glanced over at Sounia and Taiwa leaning against each other, rocking back and forth, wracked by sobs. Matoupa looked like he was almost in tears as he watched them. Dekari was sitting on the bank like a blithering idiot, holding his new finger stub. Manak shook his head in disgust.

"We've got the little one," Mox said with a shrug. "She knows their rituals too." He poked at his rib again and winced.

"Yes." Manak rested his chin on a fist while he thought. "And look at the other one; she's a beauty." He lowered his hand and nodded. "We've done well. Check the two warriors—make sure they're dead," Manak instructed, his eyes still fixed on the girls. "Take them to the canoes!" he hollered at Matoupa. "Let's get out of here!"

Matoupa pulled the girls to their feet. There was no fight left in them. He could almost feel the grief and torment seeping through their skin. He pointed them at the canoes, shoving gently on their shoulders when they veered off course. As they slogged through the floodwater, he tried in vain not to think about what they were going through. He realized that his part in their misery would haunt him for the rest of his days.

Mox slid down onto the creek beside Sannisen. He rolled him over with his foot, studied his face, and then kicked him in the ribs. No sound—no movement. Mox crawled back up into the grove to retrieve his maul before approaching the young one. He held the maul high, ready to strike if necessary. Ontarra was face down. Dark red blood flecked with bits of gray oozed from a hole in the back of the head. Mox rolled him over with a foot. One eye was closed, the other half-open. Mox had seen that look before. He lowered the maul and stepped back. He swung his eyes around the camp to memorize the scene before turning and walking away.

"Well?" Manak demanded when Mox got back to the canoes.

"You got the big one through the spinal cord," Mox answered, taking his place in the rear of the canoe.

"And the boy?"

Mox grinned and stared at Sounia seated with her back to him. "I could see his brains." Sounia slumped forward, laying her head on her knees, shoulders shaking in silent sobs. Tears streamed down Taiwa's face and dripped from her chin as she watched helplessly from the other canoe.

"You can't just leave me here!" a voice called out in Attawondaronk. "I'll drown!"

Manak looked at Matoupa. "What did he say?" Manak chuckled as he listened to the translation. "Tell him we don't have room. I'll be happy to come over and finish him, though."

Matoupa called out in his broken Attawondaronk. There was no reply.

"I thought that would be his answer," Manak said. He shoved on the ice with his paddle, yawing the canoe out into the open current. Dekari sat in the front of Manak's canoe on the pack of treasures he was afraid to let out of his sight, whimpering while he wrapped his finger with a swath of rabbit skin. To Manak's annoyance, he made no effort to help guide the canoe. "Tell him to stop his whining!" Manak barked. "It's just another finger. It will probably improve his balance!" The rushing melt-waters tore at the canoes, lifted them off the ice, and carried them away.

A deathly pall descended over the walnut valley.

Ontarra looked down through the walnut branches at the carnage in the grove below. He wondered why he was lying down there. He saw Teota sprawled on a patch of dirty red snow; his mother slumped against a tree. A man was stooping over Sannisen at the creek. Ontarra was confused by his sense of detachment from the gruesome scene, devoid of any feeling. He knew he should help his father, but he was incapable of action—a witness only.

The man reached down. Ontarra wanted to scream. With two fingers, the big man gently closed Sannisen's eyes. When he stood, a tawny mound of fur became visible behind him. *The lynx!* Ounsasta craned his head back, staring up at Ontarra as if he'd heard his thoughts.

Ounsasta, why didn't you help us?

Ounsasta shook his head sadly. "I cannot change where you are going, young warrior. I can only show you the path. Your destination has been determined by a Power far greater than anything that I possess. That one out there"—Ounsasta gazed out across the river flat in the direction of the deadfall—"is one of many who have chosen wrong." Ounsasta looked back to Ontarra. "Your destiny is to save the innocents."

Why are you always telling me things that I don't understand?

The lynx made a mewing sound. Ounsasta looked down and nodded. "You must come with us, Ontarra."

Ontarra, Ounsasta, and Slammer stood on a dark hilltop above the junction of two rivers. The ghostly outline of a tumbledown farm lodge was profiled against the night sky. The sound of water charging relentlessly over and around everything in its path assaulted their ears. A shimmering ribbon of moonlight sparkled across an inundated floodplain below. The branches of half-submerged trees groped up at the sky as water swirled around them.

Ontarra knew this place. *This is where the hunt camp river empties into the Lower Tranchi.*

"Yes," Ounsasta said softly, jerking his chin up the hunt camp river. "Look."

Two canoes materialized out of the night into a ribbon of moonlight. The outsiders didn't need to paddle in the torrent carrying them along; they used their paddles only to keep the shore and ice flows at a safe distance. Sounia and Taiwa sat low in the center of each canoe. The gags were gone, and they were untied; they were emotionally spent. As the canoes approached the narrow river mouth, Ontarra yelled and waved.

"They can't hear you or see you," Ounsasta said in a low tone.

Taiwa could feel the canoes slowing as they entered the narrow defile at the river mouth. High hills on each side choked the floodwaters back. The canoes seemed to rise and hang suspended. The sudden weightless feeling sent an eerie flutter through Taiwa's belly. She sensed a presence. A familiar essence called out and touched her.

"Oh!" Taiwa's head whipped around. She stared wide-eyed up at the hilltop. Time froze for an instant as the canoes teetered on the edge of the cascade. Then the water regained its grip, and the canoes nosed over, accelerating down the torrent spilling out onto the floodplain of the Lower Tranchi.

She looked right at us, Ontarra said sadly, watching as the canoes yawed off to the left, slipping into a stand of submerged trees and brush to avoid the ice flows chasing them.

Ounsasta nodded, intrigued. "She has the Power of the ages, your sister. It grows inside her."

Ontarra could see Taiwa's face reflected in the moonlight, still staring up at the hilltop. *We must free them.*

Ounsasta folded his arms across his chest. "No ... it is all up to you now."

Then I will go after them, to Ounontisaston, and bring out whoever will come.

Ounsasta shook his head. "It's too late for Ounontisaston. They've made their choice. I know you, Ontarra. You will save your wife and sister first. Only then will you be wise enough to give the Attawondaronks another chance."

Ontarra gazed down at the canoes again, running Ounsasta's words through his mind.

The two canoes thumped and banged against each other on the turbulent water. The men yelled back and forth in their odd, guttural tongue. Taiwa cocked her head from side to side, closing one eye and then the other. She squinted up through the branches, trying to dispel the hazy fog left on her vision by all the tears she'd shed this day. Gripping the rail of the other canoe she subtly pulled Sounia next to her. "Ontarra is still alive," she whispered.

Sounia lifted her head, the effort almost too much. Her hair was filthy and matted. Puffy red eyes angled wearily over at Taiwa. "Don't say that."

"He is ... I can feel it," Taiwa whispered.

Sounia felt a glimmer of hope, but reality quickly invaded, shoving it from her mind. "You saw what happened."

"Sounia ... he's alive."

Sounia didn't have the energy to argue. She hung her chin on her chest, considering toppling from the canoe to let the river claim her, but it was obvious that these strange men would never allow it.

"Dekari!" Matoupa shouted. "Manak wants to know if there is a way out of this land without going back to that town!"

Dekari smiled to himself. He thought that would be the plan. "Head upriver!" he hollered over his shoulder. "Stay this side of the main current. We'll have to pick our way through the trees!" The men concentrated on swinging the canoes around to move off. Taiwa watched the men closely, waiting for just the right moment. She shifted her gaze to the branches above. In a flash, her hand shot up and she hung her choker on a stubby limb.

A light drizzle began to fall. Ontarra rotated his face up to feel it. It occurred to him that it was the first physical sensation he'd had since the walnut grove. As he stared up into the heavens, a brilliant star appeared in the east, rapidly growing as it approached and flashed overhead before trailing off to the west. In the twinkling of an eye, it was gone.

Ounsasta set a hand on Ontarra's shoulder. "Your father and Teota are coming with me. Your mother needs you."

Sounia didn't think she could feel more miserable—until the drizzle started. She lifted her head when the canoes started to move. Taiwa was clutching her chest, staring up into the sky with a look of anguish. Sounia glanced up in time to see a shooting star streak across the heavens and disappear behind the treetops to the west. She heard Taiwa moaning softly.

"What's wrong, Taiwa?"

Taiwa thought her tears had all dried up, but she felt the moisture spill out onto her cheeks. She lowered her head to palm it away. "It's Teota," she sniffed. "Mother said that when the spirit of a child is torn from this world, it doesn't have to follow the pathway through the stars. It goes directly to the Village of the Dead to begin the circle anew."

A pang shot through Sounia's chest. She buried her face in her hands.

Ontarra floated in an impenetrable void. Pain ebbed and flowed around him, probing into his head, searching for a way to drive his spirit from his damaged body. Slipping away offered release from the pain, but he fought to remain. In the distant darkness, a sound arose. *The whistles of the sentries?* It called out again, beckoning to him.

Ontarra tried to focus on the noise, searching his memory for its cause. It drew closer, forcing itself upon him and increasing his pain with its proximity. The noise and pain merged, growing in intensity until nothing else existed. It gnawed at his determination to fight on. He felt his lungs expanding and contracting; he became aware of a numbing cold in his extremities that added a new agony to be endured. Through the intolerable pain, his awareness grew. He was shivering, wet, and cold. He was injured. He had to see what had happened to him.

Ontarra concentrated all of his strength. Slowly, he cracked an eye open. Rain spattered in. He blinked and tried again. A web of branches swayed softly over a leaden sky. Ontarra lapped at the moisture on his lips. The ringing in his ears overPowered every other sound, imparting a surreal impression of silence. The incessant pounding centered itself in the back of his head, radiating in all directions with each beat of his heart. Ontarra let his jaw hang open so the rain could wash the rancid dryness from his mouth. He felt himself fading back to the void. He tried to resist, but it drew him in.

When he opened his eye again, the rain had ended. He lay for a long time, entranced by the pattern of branches floating on a drifting mat of mottled gray. The ringing in his ears dwindled. Another sound—rushing water—filtered through. Gradually, he remembered where he was. Slowly lifting an arm, he dangled the hand over his face to see if it still worked as he remembered. He rested the hand on the back of his head, exploring the crusted hair where the pounding pain was focused.

He found a hole and probed through the ooze with a fingertip. The finger fit neatly inside, to the depth of his first knuckle. The crimson blood on his finger was flecked with white—pieces of bone. Ontarra remembered the outsiders and forced himself up on his elbows. Teota was laying in a filthy snowbank to his right. He could see his mother's legs behind a tree trunk near the creek. Everyone else was gone. Ontarra rolled to his knees and crawled to Teota. Reaching out, he brushed the mats of hair from Teota's face. The little body was shattered, his skin pasty and cold. Ontarra sat back on his heels and lowered his chin to his chest.

He got one foot under him to try to stand but sank back down as the walnut grove spun round in a nauseating whirl. He flattened some snow on his palm and pressed it to the back of his head. The cold penetrated the pain, briefly numbing its intensity. He tried standing again. Staggering from tree to tree, he made it to the creek bank and propped himself against a big walnut trunk, waiting for the world to stop turning. He saw his father lying motionless in a slushy pool of blood.

Ontarra slid down the bank to his father's side, his heart sinking when he saw the oblong hole in Sannisen's neck. The image of Ounsasta closing Sannisen's eyes came back to him. Ontarra sank down into the bloody slush; tears blurred his vision. He set a hand softly on Sannisen's brow, working up his courage before slowly pushing to his feet to check on his mother.

Ontarra hobbled to the bank, wrapped his fingers around some exposed roots, and hauled himself up. He squeezed his eyes against the pain and sank to his knees to study her face. Red streaks tracked from her nostrils and ears. Biting his lip, he touched her cheek—still warm. Ontarra flattened some snow, nestling it gently against her broken temple. Shanoka groaned, and one eye fluttered open. "Are they ... gone?"

Ontarra pursed his lips, nodding slowly. "They took Taiwa and Sounia."

Shanoka's eye wandered the grove. "Teota? Your father?" Ontarra looked away, drew a choked breath, and shook his head from side to side. Tears glistened; Shanoka's eyes overflowed onto her cheeks. She looked over at the base of the east ridge. Groping for her mide bag, she realized that it was gone.

"Listen carefully, Ontarra ... you must do exactly as I say." Her voice grew steadily weaker as she gave him his instructions. Grief began to suffocate him. He had to put his ear to her mouth to hear through the relentless ringing in his head.

Shanoka saw the terrible wound behind his ear. She tugged his head down, running her fingers over the matted blood. It broke her heart to see him like this. Shanoka sobbed and then kissed Ontarra's temple. When he looked up ... she was gone. Ontarra wanted to scream, but every heartbeat hammered through his head. Instead, he folded her into his arms and did something unthinkable. He wept.

Ontarra caught a flash of movement from the corner of his eye. He brushed away his tears to focus on the top of the ridge. The wolves were staring down at the bloody grove below. Ontarra had to act fast. He peeled the broken knife from Shanoka's hand. An ironwood club lay a few feet away. He saw his bow through the trees—broken.

Propping himself on the club, he forced his way up the saddle to the lodge. A few embers still flickered in the hearth. Ontarra went out and lobbed some glowing sticks at the wolves to make them think twice about slinking any closer. He staggered to the back, tossing all the firewood from behind the lodge into a heap at the base of the east ridge. Loading the turtle-shell bowl with coals, he soon had smoke rolling up the hillside.

Ontarra carried Teota over and laid him by the fire. He tried lifting Shanoka, but the pain in his head was too much. He pulled her across the grove by her arms and laid her beside Teota. Sannisen was a struggle. Moving a few steps at a time, he managed to get him to the lowest section of bank. Ontarra saw the black ax lying on the ice and bent down. It was covered in his mother's blood. The ax was a filthy, evil-looking thing, and he didn't want to touch it, so he batted it aside with his club.

Ontarra tied enough rawhide together to use a tree trunk as a pulley, and he hauled Sannisen up into the grove. Dusk was creeping up the valley by the time he had all three bodies lying together at the fire.

He covered them in their sleep robes and sat, exhausted, draping the last robe over his shoulders. Smoke drifted through the grove, twining around trees and out across the flats. "Who is there?" someone cried from across the river. "Help me!" it came again, in clear Attawondaronk. Ontarra sat up, listening closely. The voice sounded familiar, but he had neither the energy nor the inclination to help a traitor.

He heard the wolves skulking around up on top of the ridge. From the safety of the darkness above, urine-colored eyes reflected the firelight. It started to drizzle again. As he stared up at the eyes on the ridge, a star shot over the brow, streaking for the western horizon. Were the things that Ounsasta showed him at the river mouth … just happening now?

Ontarra balled up some snow to try to wipe the crusted blood from his hair. He wondered if dark spirits might try to enter through the hole in his head. He struggled up onto the saddle to cut a swath from the doorskin. Returning to the fire, he tied the strip around his head to cover the hole and then promptly fell asleep.

When he woke, the wolves were in the river flat, just beyond the fringe of firelight. Ontarra threw a firebrand, and they moved farther back. Vaguely, he noted that the wretch across the river had either shouted himself hoarse or died. He added some deadfall to the fire. Using a paddle, he spread the coals out to cover the area he wanted to use.

Sleep came for him again and held him under its spell until the sky in the east began to lighten. The fire had burned down to a bed of shifting embers, and he raked them into a pile with the paddle. Then he scooped away the melted soil until he was knee-deep and hit frost again. Scraping the coals down into the pit, he piled on more wood and sat down. At midday, he repeated the process, using Teota's turtle shell as a shovel. The grave was waist-deep.

He laid Teota in first and then lowered Shanoka in on his left and Sannisen to his right. Their heads were inclined slightly up the hill, with their faces to the west, as his mother had instructed. Ontarra slumped down, head reeling from pain and hunger as he tried to recall everything she'd said. He wandered around the camp, collecting anything that might be useful on their journey.

Ontarra perched on his haunches over the grave. He set the broken bow, two arrows, and the good knife next to Sannisen. The firestones and a travel pack he gave to Shanoka; turtle-shell bowl and fishing spear to Teota. Ontarra pushed to his feet, wishing he had more to give them. He caught a flurry of movement as something scurried from sight over the top of the ridge. Ontarra crouched, grabbed Teota's spear, and made his way to the top of the hill.

He saw nothing at first. Then a mound of fresh soil and gravel caught his eye ... a marmot den. Ontarra slipped around to the back of the hole. Raising the spear to his shoulder, he waited. In a hand of time, a reddish-brown head popped up, staring intently down the hill for the intrusive human. It was an easy kill. Ontarra took the rodent down and set it in the crotch of a tree, returning the bloodied spear to Teota.

Stepping softly into the grave, he knelt to kiss his mother's forehead a last time. Ontarra ruffled Teota's hair. "Watch over me, Mosquito." He stepped over Teota to stare down at his father. He folded down beside him and placed his hand over his father's heart. Ontarra covered them with the sleep robes, crawled out, and began scraping the burned soil back. When the grave was level, he went up to the lodge, returning with Shanoka's prayer stone. He pressed it into the blackened loam and covered it over.

Now he had to keep a fire burning on the grave to light their way for the four days it would take their spirits to reach the Ojibwa Village of the Dead. The only firewood left in the grove was the lodge. Ontarra spent the afternoon tearing it apart, throwing the bark and wood down the saddle. He had enough coals left to get shreds of bark burning. When the fire caught, he dressed out the marmot, skewered it, and leaned it over the coals.

Wrapping the last sleep robe over his shoulders, Ontarra sat on a log to watch his meal cook, pondering whether the dream of Ounsasta had been real. If so, the strangers had taken the girls upriver, instead of to Ounontisaston, but why? Ontarra rotated the marmot so the stomach cavity was exposed to the flames. He shook his head sadly, thinking about how much had changed in the past cycle. His old life was gone. Like the ashes in a hearth ... nothing now but a memory.

The smoke carried the smell of frying marmot out across the river. "Help me! I need food!" the voice called from the deadfall. Ontarra cocked an ear. He knew that voice. He picked himself up and walked over to the creek. The voice called out again. Ontarra searched his memory. *Yadak! It's Yadak out there! He brought those men here to kill my family!* Ontarra felt a rage boiling up inside. *I'll go out there and cut his throat!* His jaw worked with tension and anger, but something held him back. He studied the deadfall. The rising river would reach it by morning. He didn't need to kill Yadak; the river would do it for him.

Ontarra walked back to the fire, his thoughts jumbled. He sat down and tore a leg from the marmot. *Why not kill him? Friendship? He betrayed us!* Ontarra's stomach was shrunken; he chewed and swallowed slowly. If only the pain in his head would go away so he could think straight. Ontarra gathered some snow and pressed it to his temples. The cold seemed to release a pressure inside his skull.

He ripped off a front leg and then took the marmot off the fire and set it to the side. Although his stomach couldn't hold much, the food was invigorating. He had to know for sure where they'd taken Sounia and Taiwa. If Sounia was dead, he wasn't certain he could carry on. The thought of Hiatsou and Poutassa having them was unnerving. He glanced over at the deadfall as he chewed. Not much daylight was left. The idea was fraught with danger, but he saw no other choice.

Ontarra tossed the naked leg bone on the coals, got up, and wandered out into the grove. Scanning the trees, he saw what he needed by the creek. The arrow was deep in the walnut trunk. A wry grin touched his lips when he saw a fingertip pinned on the point. He snapped the arrow's shaft close to the head and rocked the chert out of the wood.

Bending slowly, he slid it into the laces of a moccasin and pulled his legging over to hide it.

Ontarra walked back to the fire and picked up the broken knife. He studied the trees nearby. Deciding on the best one, he walked around to the backside. With a rock, he tapped the broken corner of the blade into the trunk, breaking off the handle so it wouldn't be so conspicuous. Ontarra scraped the guts, organs, and marmot skin onto a piece of lodge bark and buried it all under some snow.

Walking over to where the canoes lay inclined on the hill, he suddenly realized that his head wasn't pounding as hard. Ontarra dragged a canoe to the river and threw a paddle on the floor. Using the rockwood club, he poled himself out into the widening expanse of surging water. He had to time it just right before attempting to cross through the bobbing ice flows in the main current. Despite his caution, one nearly toppled him—it plowed the canoe around in a circle on its way by.

At the outside bends, the river was piling slabs of ice across the flats like firewood. Ontarra pulled the canoe up onto one and lodged it in a crevice. He picked his way through the maze of stacked ice, expecting to take a tumble with every step. A pair of legs protruded from beneath the big elm trunk. He laid the club on his shoulder and stepped around. Yadak stared up at him with panicked eyes. He'd been digging with his hands to get himself out, but the ground was a bit too frozen for fingers.

"Ontarra," he simpered in a raw voice. "It's you! Help me get out of here!"

"You brought those men here. Why?"

"I … I had to … I was ordered."

Random thoughts flashed through Ontarra's head. Taiwa said Yadak had sided with the shamans; he'd accused Ontarra of killing Tonayata. Ontarra raised the club over his head, aiming the blow at Yadak's face.

"No, Ontarra! Don't! Please!"

Ontarra's leg shook, and he swayed. He lowered the club to the ground to steady himself, buckling down onto one knee. "You're hurt," Yadak exhaled hopefully. "Get me out of here, and I'll help you." Ontarra opened his eyes and leaned on the club to push himself up. Walking around the upturned roots, he returned with the paddle and threw it down next to Yadak.

"You were my friend once, Yadak. I don't need the memory of killing you haunting my dreams. Get yourself out. I don't have the energy."

Ontarra made his way back across the river. The current carried him all the way down to the creek mouth before he could get in to shore. He climbed out onto the bank and gave the canoe a shove, watching the river carry it off. He hauled the last canoe down off the hillside and dragged it over to the fire, where he could keep an eye on it. Setting the marmot over the coals again, he pulled the sleep robe over him, sat down, and waited.

It was well after dark when Ontarra heard him coming. Yadak made no attempt to conceal his approach. He walked up into the circle of firelight. They stared across the fire at each other. "How did you get across the river?" Ontarra asked evenly.

"The fallen tree."

Ontarra gestured at the marmot. "Sit down … eat." Yadak sidled around the fire. Ontarra got up and crossed to the opposite side, keeping the flames between them. Yadak knelt, twisted a front leg off, devoured it, and went for the last leg. He pushed upright again, studying Ontarra as he chewed.

"It's overcooked," he grumbled. Yadak glanced over at the grave and back to Ontarra.

"My family." Ontarra felt a rush of anger but fought it down.

"How bad is your head?" Yadak talked through his food, trying to sound indifferent.

"Minor wound," Ontarra lied. Yadak nodded thoughtfully. He sat down and folded his legs in front of him. Reaching over the flames, he stripped a section out of the marmot's back.

"Why did you bring those men here?"

"I had to," Yadak answered casually. "My family is at Ounon', you know."

"Where did they take Sounia and Taiwa?"

Yadak stared into the fire, picking his words. "They'll make examples of them. We'll have to move fast."

"They took them to Ounontisaston?"

"Of course. Hiatsou and Poutassa can hardly contain themselves. They've probably got them right now." Yadak watched Ontarra's reaction.

Ontarra almost dove across the fire but held himself back. He studied Yadak, masking his emotions. They sat in silence a few moments. Ontarra calmed himself, timing his next question. "Why did you try to kill Taiwa at the deer trap?"

Yadak stopped chewing. Their eyes locked across the fire. Ontarra saw the hesitation he was looking for. Yadak realized he'd given himself away. Ontarra lunged, swinging the rockwood club as he came to his feet. Yadak rolled to the side and grabbed a log from the fire. Ontarra sprang across the flames. Yadak swung at Ontarra's legs the instant he landed. Ontarra lifted a foot, and the log passed harmlessly underneath. Ontarra jumped, landing with both knees on Yadak's chest. Ontarra let out a groan, and the club fell to the ground. He grabbed his head with both hands and made a strange gurgling sound. Ontarra toppled face first in the mud.

Yadak lay stunned, struggling to get air into his lungs again. He rolled over on top of Ontarra to pin him down, but Ontarra was limp. Yadak bent an ear and listened. He was still breathing. Yadak scanned the grove and saw rawhide bindings hanging in a tree.

Ontarra didn't stir until morning. His head slowly lifted to study his plight. He could feel warm blood on the back of his neck. He was seated, with his ankles and wrists tied. His knees were drawn up through his arms. The rockwood club was passed over his elbows and under his knees locking him into a fetal position. He looked across the fire. Yadak was sitting, wrapped in the sleep robe, eating the last of the marmot, a contemptuous grin on his face. The surprising clarity of Ontarra's eyes failed to register with Yadak. "I was afraid you weren't coming back."

"Where did you learn to do this?" Ontarra dipped his chin to the club that had him immobilized.

"Hah! I've learned many things," Yadak chuckled, flipping a section of backbone at Ontarra's face. "Did you really think that I would help you? I only fired on Taiwa because I couldn't get a clear shot at you. Look at you," Yadak snickered, rocking his head from side to side, "the great Ontarra, hero of Ounontisaston. Hiatsou and Poutassa have your women, and I have you. I've waited a full cycle for this."

"Why?"

The smug grin on Yadak's face, hardened into a scowl. "Don't play innocent with me. For what you did to Tonayata! You planted your seed in her—put your mark on her!"

"Tonayata hated me, you idiot!"

"Hmph." Yadak finished stripping the marmot and dropped the last ribs onto the coals. "You stole her from me!"

"Poutassa is the one who killed her, not me!"

Yadak shook his head and looked up at the sky with a bemused smirk. "Poutassa told me how the Midewiwin could put a mark on a person to control them—make her do things against her will. She denied it, just as you do." He looked at Ontarra with hatred in his eyes. "I tired of her lies and ended them!"

Ontarra's mouth fell open. "It was you? *You* killed Tonayata?" Ontarra squeezed his eyes shut and lowered his face to his knees.

"Did you think I was fool enough to marry her and raise your brat?" Yadak shouted. The grove was silent for a long moment. A deprecating grin wrinkled the corners of Yadak's eyes, watching Ontarra's anguish. "I killed her with your knife too. Your idiot brother let me take it when I helped him clean a fish last spring. I wasn't about to let you take advantage of me and get away with it."

"The shamans are behind all of this, Yadak." Ontarra raised his head wearily. "If Tonayata carried a child that wasn't yours, it was probably Poutassa's. He—wait … the mark on Tonayata. Was it a rake mark? Like a bear clawed her?"

Yadak jumped across the fire, snapping a kick into Ontarra's ribs. "You know it was!" he screamed, spraying spittle over Ontarra's face. "Poutassa told me you'd try this!" Yadak lashed out with the foot again. Ontarra couldn't even fall over with the club propping him on both sides. He gritted his teeth, leaning his head away from the vicious feet.

"Not so smart now, are you? Great hero of Ounon!" Drool ran from the corner of Yadak's mouth. "Look at what I've done to you: your family dead, Hiatsou and Poutassa having their way with your women." Yadak settled a bit, smiling as he congratulated himself. He chuckled and bent down, plucking a firebrand from the coals. He waved it in the air, delighting in the pattern of sparks that trailed off, and then blew, watching with fascination as it glowed brighter. "Yes," he gloated, "shamans back in control, Soutoten dead, Tsohahissen dead, and all because of me."

Ontarra's head snapped up, eyes wide. Sounia would be crushed when she found out. *Ounsasta was right. It's too late for Ounontisaston.* Ontarra glanced over at the tree with the knife blade in it. "I can't feel my feet. Why don't you tie me to a tree or something."

"Getting a little stiff?" Yadak jabbed the firebrand at Ontarra's face, waving it back and forth in front of his eyes. "What shall I do with you?" he contemplated dreamily. "I've been racking my brain, trying to decide. Maybe I'll let you starve and then feed your own flesh to you." He looked over at the grave and a crooked smile slanted his lips. "Or … perhaps I'll dig them up and feed them to you. How long before you'd be willing to eat your own brother, Ontarra?" Yadak laughed, pleased with the ghoulish workings of his mind. Yadak finished his ranting and sat down at the fire, rubbing his hands together with morbid anticipation.

"Hunger isn't so bad, Yadak." Ontarra fixed him with a cold look. "It doesn't even bother you after a few days. There are many worse ways to die." Yadak was wrapped in his thoughts and didn't see the deadly stare. Ontarra decided to try catching him off guard. "Who is the man with the missing fingers?"

Yadak looked up from his musings. "Dekari? He's an Erieehronon trader. He wanted your mother's medicine bag."

Ontarra ran it through his mind and shook his head. "Those men were warriors, not traders."

"Never mind them!" Yadak hissed. "You should be worrying about yourself. You know ... if you beg me, I might decide to let you go."

Ontarra's eyes narrowed to slits. He caught himself, and set his head between his knees, pretending to try to sleep. The evening grew cold. Yadak kept adding wood to the fire, but it didn't seem to help. He started pacing, mumbling to himself, and cursing Ontarra for the lack of food in the camp. It was late in the night before he finally sat down, pulled the robe tightly around him, and went to sleep. Ontarra bided his time, listening to the rhythms of Yadak's breathing before lifting his head. Yadak was slumped forward, arms wrapped around his knees.

Ontarra wriggled his face down between his legs so he could see what he was doing. With a thumb and forefinger, he got hold of the arrow shaft and tugged it free from the laces of his moccasin. He popped his head up and checked on Yadak. Then he started working on the rawhide at his ankles. The chert was dulled from long service. His fingers ached by the time the binding snapped.

He couldn't work the point around to a position to cut the cords on his wrists. Stiff fingers refused to hold the arrow shaft. He kept dropping it, getting nowhere. Frustrated, he stared over at the tree with the knife blade in it, judging it to be five steps away. Ontarra glanced at Yadak—he was still sleeping. Ontarra crossed his ankles, raised his knees, and slid the pole out. Slowly, he began pushing to his feet. He had to clamp his teeth to keep from groaning as his frozen joints unlocked. He worked the cramps out of his legs, before taking a cautious sidestep toward the tree. When he shifted his weight, a twig snapped.

Yadak's head jerked up. Ontarra ran behind the tree. He sawed frantically at the tethers. They snapped at the same instant that the rockwood club slammed into the trunk beside his face. Ontarra ran behind the next tree, working his hands to get the feeling back. Yadak followed with the club held high. He swung. Ontarra ducked the blow. He sidled around the trunk, smiling to himself. Yadak was slow. His life of leisure and bullying hadn't prepared him for this. Ontarra had a tingling sensation back in all of his limbs now. He stepped out into the open, baiting Yadak with a thin smile.

Yadak scowled and moved in. He raised the club, charging the last few steps with a wild swing. Ontarra spun and jumped off to one side, shoving a foot out as Yadak went by. Yadak took a hard tumble. Ontarra didn't follow up on his advantage; he waited while Yadak picked himself up. He saw the unfocused rage in Yadak's eyes and backed up against a tree. Yadak's swing was violent but poorly timed. It slammed into the walnut trunk where Ontarra's head had been only a heartbeat before. Ontarra leaned back and drove his foot up into Yadak's diaphragm. Yadak's eyes bulged in their sockets.

With a swipe of his hand, Ontarra threw the club away from the tree trunk. The sudden, unexpected force on the club turned Yadak sideways. Ontarra kicked again, downward, with the flat of his foot. Yadak's knee came apart with the sound of a snapping branch. Yadak howled and fell to the ground, both hands holding his dislocated knee. He flopped and rolled like a wounded doe, forgetting entirely about Ontarra. Ontarra circled cautiously, but Yadak was completely lost in his pain.

Ontarra kicked the club aside, picked it up, and trudged back to the fire. Wrapping the sleep robe around his shoulders, he sat down to watch Yadak's squirming. It was two hands of time before Yadak settled enough to remember where he was. He rolled his head over to Ontarra, watching from the fire. He rolled and tried to stand but fell flat with an agonized cry. Whimpering uncontrollably, Yadak pushed to his knees and started crawling, like a three-legged dog, dragging the useless limb behind him. Ontarra watched him disappear into the murk of the walnut grove.

"What are you going to do, Yadak?" Ontarra yelled. "Crawl back to Ounon?" He didn't expect an answer, and he didn't get one. "Why don't you try swimming? It would be a lot faster!" Ontarra stood up, peering out into the grove. Shaking his head, he turned to what was left of the woodpile and started gathering up what he needed to build a second fire a few strides away from the first. When he had it burning, he went over to the snow pile where the marmot guts where buried.

The heart and liver suddenly looked appealing. He pulled them off and set them near the fire. Cradling the bark under one arm, he walked partway up the ridge and lobbed the marmot's skin and head up to the crest. Ontarra made his way over to the saddle and pulled the kidneys off, tossing them up the hillside. He strung a length of intestines out on top of the saddle and then went down into the grove, dropping pieces of entrail as he went.

Yadak was easy to follow. The useless leg left a scuff that pointed right to him. Ontarra was surprised. Yadak had made it to the creek mouth already. Yadak heard him coming. "Ontarra ... don't kill me, please. I can still help you get Sounia and Taiwa back." Yadak kept crawling away as Ontarra approached. Ontarra stepped around in front of him, forcing him to look up.

Ontarra stared down pensively. "You know, Yadak, you strike me as someone who has never thought much about the next life." He looked at the star-spattered sky. "Tonayata, Soutoten, and my mother and father are all waiting for you on the other side. Do you think that Teota will still be a child that you can bully in the spirit world?"

Yadak hung his head. "Don't kill me, Ontarra. I'll do anything."

"I already told you ... I don't need the memory of killing an old friend haunting me."

Yadak's head rolled up. "Really? You'll let me go?"

"Certainly, crawl onward. I'm not going to stop you. Just one thing, though ... this is for Taiwa." Ontarra kicked Yadak's ribs. Yadak howled, curling himself up into a ball. Before Yadak could get his breath, Ontarra landed another one. "That was for my family over there." Ontarra repositioned himself, lining up on Yadak's face. "And this is for me!" Ontarra felt Yadak's nose turn to mush on the arch of his foot.

Yadak started caterwauling like an injured child. Blood gushed from both of his mashed nostrils, oozing out between the fingers clutched to his face. Ontarra bent down to study the bleeding. Satisfied, he walked back through the grove, seated himself between the fires, skewered the marmot heart and liver on a stick, and leaned them into the flames.

Yadak never made another sound. Ontarra gnawed on the organs, wondering how far he could have crawled by now. He heard the whisper of paws up on the ridge behind him. A wolf materialized on the saddle, staring over at Ontarra. Like kindred spirits, their eyes held, acknowledging each other with a grudging respect. Ontarra recognized the tinge of red in his scruff. "So you are their chief now? I hope you are not as brash as the last one." The wolf planted a paw and lowered his head, shredding a piece of intestine with a sharp tear.

The rest of the pack probed down the hill. The leader gobbled up the intestine before they could challenge him for it. "Only six of you survived?" The leader caught the scent of blood. He raised his nose to the night air and then lowered it and stared out toward the creek mouth. The yellow eyes swung back to Ontarra, gauging whether he was going to be a threat. "He went that way." Ontarra pointed his skewer stick out across the grove. The rusty gray turned and disappeared down the back side of the saddle. The pack bounded after him. Ontarra went back to chewing on the liver.

"Ontarra!" a voice cried in the distance. "There are wolves out here! Help me!" Ontarra placed Yadak somewhere up on the south ridge. He heard the throaty snarls start up, the smell of fresh blood creating a frenzy.

"Be careful, old friend," Ontarra muttered. "They haven't been eating well." Yadak's screams shattered the still night. Eons of predacious instinct demanded a cripple before the kill. When a blood-curdling shriek was cut short, Ontarra pictured the big gray shaking Yadak by the windpipe. "I told you there are worse ways to die, Yadak."

Ontarra couldn't have slept if he'd tried. The wolves fought over every scrap. It was dawn before their bloodlust was sated. Ontarra wandered over to the south ridge and found where Yadak had gone up. When he climbed over the crest, he screwed his face up and looked away. The wolves hadn't left much. Ontarra circled around the trample of mud and blood. He was intending to throw Yadak's bones in the river, to trap his spirit under the weight of the water, but the wolves had devoured all but a few shards.

He followed the tracks of the wolves along the ridge. At the junction of the two ridges, just above the camp, he found what he was looking for—Yadak's head. The wolves had chewed away everything but a patch of scalp and one eye. Ontarra kicked the grisly thing down into the camp.

The creek was breaking up now, shedding its ice in big slabs that wallowed out into the main river. Ontarra spent the rest of the day gathering stones from the creek bed and skidding them over to the grave in the canoe. Tomorrow morning, his family's souls would be finished with their journey. He could let the fires die and go after the girls. He arranged the rocks over the grave, hoping they would keep the wolves from digging.

At dusk, Ontarra laid down on his sleep robe. He slept the whole night. When he woke, the fires were nothing but cinder and ash. He scattered the ash around with the rockwood club to hide the signs of human presence. Then he picked up Yadak by the lonely lock of hair that was left and went up onto the saddle. Ontarra pounded the butt of the rockwood club into the ground with a flat rock. When he was satisfied that it was sturdy enough, he twisted Yadak's head down on top. No one would dare to disturb this grove with such an ominous warning staring down at them.

Ontarra sat down on the saddle, his eyes roving over the walnut valley as he thought about all the things that had happened—good and bad. He remembered the ax with the black stone head lying at the creek. He didn't want to touch it, but he didn't want to leave it so close to his mother either. Reluctantly, he plodded down to find it. He unwound the piece of doorskin around his head and wrapped it around his hand, using it to pick the ax up by its handle. Huffing up over the east ridge and then with a hand of strides into the woods, he lobbed it with all the strength he could muster.

Ontarra hauled the canoe down to the river, turning to take one last look, his eyes settling on the grave. "I promise that I will avenge you." He stepped in and shoved off. The water was receding from its peak two days ago, but the current was still fast and Powerful. Ontarra put all of his concentration into steering. Still, he pounded into the bank several times at sharp bends. Ice flows careening around him were impossible to avoid. He prayed that one wouldn't tear through the bark skin or roll him over.

The sun was settling down onto the treetops in the west, when he recognized the approaches to the river mouth. A fallen tree hove into view on Ontarra's side of the river. Using his paddle to steer, he angled the canoe across the main current to avoid the groping limbs. He didn't see the ice flow until it crunched into the side of the canoe. The big slab of ice started plowing water, trying to dive beneath the obstacle in its path. Ontarra dug his paddle into the ice to steady the canoe, barely keeping it from going over. Water appeared around his feet. Ontarra realized instantly that the bark was gashed.

With no other option available, he pushed himself upright on the paddle and vaulted from the canoe onto the ice. The canoe tumbled and went under. The slab of ice rocked from end to end as the canoe thumped and rolled beneath it. By leaning on the paddle, Ontarra managed to keep his balance, turning just in time to see the tree branches coming at him. He ducked, covering his head wound with both arms. The branches grabbed at his hair and clothing, clawing at him and snapping off when they caught. As suddenly as the crisis came upon him, it was over. The branches yielded to his weight, and the ice slab settled down. Ontarra floated down into the narrow cut that emptied out onto the floodplain of the Lower Tranchi. He shook his head, laughing for the first time in days.

If he stayed with the ice flow, it would carry him all the way to the forks, and Ounontisaston, or even Tontiaton if he desired. Despite what Yadak had said, Ontarra had a nagging doubt. When the ice slab got close enough to shore, he leaped but still landed in water up to his knees. Cursing his luck, he made his way up onto the hill. The swaybacked farm lodge looked exactly as he remembered when Ounsasta had brought him here. *Was it real?* He looked out across the floodplain, to the trees where the canoes had taken shelter in his dream. The retreating water had stacked slabs of ice over the entire flats. Everything seemed different. Ontarra swung his gaze to the right, studying each clump of trees and brush. The rays of the setting sun sparkled off something.

He skidded and slid back down to the river, walking along the bank until the spread of floodwaters barred his way. Shading his eyes to the glare, he scrutinized the object in the tree. He wasn't certain, but he felt a glimmer of excitement. Ontarra moved back upstream, eyeing the ice flows shooting past. As soon as one came close enough, he jumped on. By poling and paddling, he caught another, and another, until he was across.

His heart in his throat, he approached the tree. Taiwa's choker! On a branch … just beyond his reach. "They did go upriver!" Ontarra said aloud, smiling to himself. He poked the paddle up and knocked it loose. Picking up the choker, he held it to his cheek. "Good girl, Taiwa," he said softly. Caressing the thunderbird with his thumb, he stared up at the abandoned farm lodge. "I'm sorry I doubted you, Ounsasta."

Ontarra looked out across the wasteland of crudely piled ice. He would have to make his way across the uplands. He was glad he'd managed to keep the paddle. It made a useful walking stick. From the hilltop, he stared back at the western horizon, to where a town his father created ruled over a land of plenty … and sheltered a nest of vipers.

"I am coming for you. From this day forward, the family of Sannisen will be an unrelenting terror in your dreams. Some day you will turn, and I will be there. When that day comes, no shaman will be left alive in this land."

Ontarra rested his hand on Ounsasta's club. For the first time, he could feel its spirit. He turned and headed east … to Teotonguiaton.

15

"Why don't we just forget about the petun seed and get out of this land?"

Manak listened to Matoupa's translation and cast a scornful frown at Dekari. "If you wish to keep that travel pack full of goods you've become so fond of, I suggest you go down there and get the seed."

Dekari couldn't speak Tunican yet, but he understood the intent if he listened closely. He shifted his gaze downriver to the palisades of Kandoucho, knowing better than to hazard any eye contact with Manak at the moment. He'd seen enough of the man to last a lifetime anyway. Dekari took a deep breath, exhaling through his teeth. "You expect me to go in there alone?"

"Of course. You're a trader, aren't you? We can hardly go traipsing in there with these two." Manak tipped his head at Taiwa and Sounia, who sat, filthy and bedraggled, on a log behind him. "*We* have to stay here to guard them. You're going down there"—Manak pointed—"and get that seed."

Dekari turned a defeated look down the river gorge at the town two arrow-flights away. "What if they've already been told to watch for us, or they've missed the canoes we took at the landing this morning? We used up three days sneaking past Teotonguiaton on all those back trails."

"Those two idiots at Ounon' will just be realizing that something is amiss.

There hasn't been time for word to travel here." Manak pulled his knife, waving it under Dekari's nose. "This isn't open to discussion, trader. Go!" He shoved Dekari over the crest. Dekari continued skidding and sliding down the sheer riverbank without looking back. He uncovered one of the canoes and dragged it down through the trees to the water's edge.

Manak turned to Mox and Matoupa. "Tie their wrists to their knees. I don't want to have to chase them." Matoupa rubbed at his temples as if they pained him. Pulling a rawhide binding from his waist pouch, he turned to Sounia. Mox jarred him aside and grabbed Sounia's arms. He laid her wrists on her knees, letting his hand wander up her thigh, where it lingered a moment while Manak's attention was elsewhere. Mox's broken rib and swollen left testicle hadn't prevented him from paying special attention to Sounia whenever the opportunity presented itself. The look of loathing on her face would have wilted most men; it excited Mox.

Matoupa shot Mox a cold stare but said nothing. Instead, he turned to Taiwa, apologizing in a low voice as he wrapped her wrists. Taiwa looked at Matoupa's sad eyes. She had the feeling she understood him. He wasn't like the others; this man's soul held compassion. Matoupa plodded over to Manak, following his stare down the river valley. A hand of canoes surged out to challenge Dekari. His hand was held high in greeting.

"Do you think he'll get it?" Manak asked softly.

Matoupa ran a hand down his face. "We probably should have obtained it at Ounontisaston before we left."

Manak canted a sidelong glance. "Don't you think that the 'Feathered Sea Slug' would have been just a little suspicious if we'd asked for petun seed before we brought them the girls?"

Matoupa nodded lamely, shifting his eyes back to the river. "Dekari's sly; he'll get it."

Taiwa stared vindictively at her mother's mide bag, dangling like a profanity from Manak's waistband. "What is it you want from us?" Her voice was weary and strained. "Why don't you just let us go?"

Matoupa and Manak twisted their heads around. Mox yanked his hand away from Sounia's thigh. "From what I've seen, I think you'll be safer with us than your own people," Matoupa replied softly.

"Keep them quiet," Manak growled. "There may be sentries or hunters out here." Mox leered, wet his finger, and pressed it over Sounia's lips. Sounia yanked her head away.

Dekari strolled casually up the path into Kandoucho, escorted by several young warriors. He hadn't been here for many cycles; his eyes scanned around anxiously for some familiar face. "Is Takana still your chief?" he asked. "I need to see him about a trade." The young warriors remained silent as they herded him on through the plaza. Knots of people around the town studied the stranger as he went by. Dekari's darting eyes recognized no one. As they approached the chief's lodge, his nerves got the better of him.

He stopped outside the door. "Listen … I've been sent by Feathered Serpent and Windigo Killer to get petun seed. There wasn't enough to spare at Ounontisaston to complete our arrangement. I—" A warrior forced Dekari's head down and shoved him inside.

"I thought you might try something like this." The sound of that voice jammed Dekari's heart up into his throat. He sucked a breath. A shadowy figure rose from a sleep platform at the back. Dancing firelight shimmered across a shiny mica claw on his chest.

"Poutassa!" Dekari stepped back; rough hands shoved him forward again.

Adontayat and Buzkit stepped up behind Poutassa, grinning from ear to ear at the mortified look on Dekari's face. Poutassa crossed his arms. "Thought you'd sneak out of our lands through the back door, did you? You were supposed to bring me the females. Where are they?"

"Poutassa … I mean, Windigo Killer," Dekari stammered, trying to regain his wits. "They're … all dead. The fight got out of hand, and only the two girls survived. We had them, but our canoes toppled in the floodwaters. They were tied together. They … they drowned."

Poutassa curled a knuckle across his lips and gave his head a shake. "My people watched you stealing the canoes at the landing this morning." His voice rose to a threat. "Where are they?"

Dekari's heart sank from his throat to his gut.

Poutassa walked around the fire and stared into Dekari's eyes, a venomous smirk curling a corner of his mouth. "How do you suppose this looks to my people—you trying to worm out of our deal, making fools of us? Well … since I don't have the girls, I'll just have to make an example of you. Hold his hand out!" Four hands locked onto Dekari's arm, extending it out toward Poutassa.

Dekari struggled to pull away. An arm wrapped around his neck from behind and a chert blade pressed against his windpipe.

Poutassa studied Dekari's fresh stump with interest. "If you lose a couple more fingers, you're going to need help wiping away your own excrement." Poutassa grinned, and the warriors chuckled obediently. A dagger appeared in Poutassa's hand.

An appalling wail rent the night air.

Even walking on the uplands, Ontarra could feel the chill of the ice-clogged river flats. Only a breath of air disturbed the stillness. He was bone-tired and should have stopped to rest, but he felt compelled to make time. A three-quarter moon cast an eerie radiance over the landscape. Ontarra stopped. He could hear voices ahead. Cresting a rise, he came upon a handful of lodges. Hearth fires flickered behind doorskins; children's voices carried up the hillside.

Ontarra lay down behind the crest, pondering the situation. He hadn't expected to find an outcamp here. He poked his head up again. They weren't farmers, and they were too far from the river to be fishermen. He recognized the dark shapes lying around doorways as dogs, waiting for handouts. Ontarra licked a finger and held it up to the wind. The air was moving off the uplands, down into the river valley. He'd have to risk the river flats and the ice, or the dogs would give him away. He moved down a shallow ravine, keeping himself out of sight.

In the darkness, he didn't noticed how steep the ridge he was traveling along had become. He was forced to backtrack to find a way down the sheer face. Tossing the paddle over so his hands were free, he clung to the rocky outcrops and began a treacherous descent. Water seepage made the rocks slimy, but he managed to get down to the flats without mishap.

Ontarra could see his breath in the air. The valley felt like a winter storage pit. Glancing up at the cliff he'd just scaled, he saw instantly why those lodges were located here. These people were quarrying the gray slate from an exposed rock face. Ontarra moved out through the ice stacks to avoid detection in the glimmering moonlight. When he could no longer see the rock cliff through the trees, he turned and headed upriver again. Progress was slow. The paddle saved him from falls more than once. The effort was tiring him out; the cold was seeping into his joints.

He'd just decided to make his way back to the uplands when he saw a flicker of light through the trees ahead. Walking on his toes, he pushed ahead, crouched on his heels, and poked his head out from behind a fallen willow. A ramshackle lodge sat on a small rise directly ahead. He pulled his head back, cursing his luck. *Why would anyone put a lodge out here?* Ontarra peeked again. The door faced the river. He'd have to sneak around the back.

Quietly, he made his way from tree to tree until he was behind the lodge. A sound from the rear of the shack dropped him to his knees. Ontarra scanned in the direction of the noise. His heart skipped when he saw a dog tethered to a tree behind the lodge. *Could it possibly be Poutassa?* He had to know. Ontarra moved slowly back around front. The lodge had no doorskin. The dog was whimpering and whining in a familiar manner. Ontarra moved along the water's edge until he could see up the rocky rise into the lodge.

A cranky old female voice babbled from inside. He'd heard that voice before somewhere. She was complaining—grumbling and griping at someone. Ontarra leaned out to get a better look. A cackle of laughter jerked him back behind the tree. An ancient woman hobbled to the door and looked out. She stared sullenly at the swollen river for a moment. The laughter ended as abruptly as it had begun. The old girl turned grumbly again and disappeared inside. Ontarra leaned out. She appeared to be alone, but it certainly didn't sound like it. He planted the paddle on some ice, shifting his weight to get a better look. The paddle shot away, and Ontarra went down, his head smacking on a chunk of ice.

He wasn't sure how long he'd lain there. He was trembling with cold, and his head wound was bleeding again. Getting his knees under him, he tried to stand, but a wave of nausea settled him back down. He laid his face in his hands, but it didn't help. The hag came to the door, looked around suspiciously, and then retreated back into the depths of her hovel. Ontarra had to get out of the river valley or he was going to freeze.

He tried again to stand, holding himself upright against a tree, but a dizzying whirl slowly lowered him to his knees. He was shivering uncontrollably now. He squinted up at the lodge. Deciding he'd have to take the chance, he crawled over to the path. It was slippery; he kept sliding back. Rocky ledges and cracks gave him fingerholds, but they were covered in some kind of brown slime. His knees and fingers kept slipping as if the rocks were made of ice. A horrid smell overwhelmed him. He had to wait, holding back a heave. He held a hand up to his nose. It reeked. His stomach clenched again, and everything started to spin. Ontarra tried to call out, but all he managed was a choked groan before slumping forward on his arms.

Something was crawling on his face. Ontarra wanted to bring his hands up to wipe it away, but his arms seemed to be weighted down. His head was pounding again. The musty smell of sleep robes, left wet too long, assaulted his nostrils with every breath. The irritating sound of an old woman whining at someone forced Ontarra to open an eye. She had her back to him; she was fussing with something on the hearth fire and muttering under her breath. Ontarra opened his other eye to survey his surroundings. Whoever she was complaining to didn't seem to be in the lodge.

The top of the old girl's head was shiny and bald. A fringe of greasy gray hair hung in matted strands down her back. A worn and soiled buckskin dress hung from bony shoulders, with heavy buckskin leggings poking out below the hem. When she straightened up and turned around, Ontarra winced.

"'Bout time you woke up. Makin' an old woman like me drag around a youngster like you … bah! Typical man!" Her wrinkled brown lips puckered in and out as she talked, like a baby sucking on a teat. Ontarra had never seen so many cracks and crevices on one face in his life. Her lips and a large streak on her chin were stained a dark brown, and Ontarra realized she was chewing petun. His stunned expression struck her as funny. She rocked her head back and cackled. The sound was more like working up to a sneeze than any form of laughter. Only two teeth were visible in that mouth, both of them black from eons of petun juice. She stopped cackling to swish some flies from her face, and she studied her guest again. "Don't talk much, do you?"

Ontarra was deciding how to respond when she started the hacking and coughing again. She doubled over and horked three times, raising enough mucus to choke a bear, then she straightened up and twisted, blasting an end-for-ender that tumbled across the lodge and out the door, splattering down the rocky pathway. Ontarra sat up, pulled his arms out from under the musty sleep robes, and studied the brown slime stains on his hands. He closed his eyes and hung his head.

"You're not gonna pass out again, are you?"

Ontarra rolled his eyes up and let out a long sigh. "Maybe ... have you got any water around here so I can wash?"

"Water? This whole cursed place is water!"

Ontarra decided this might be an appropriate time to leave. When he swung a leg out, he suddenly realized he was naked. He lay back, pulling the robes up around his chin. "Where are my clothes?"

"Threw 'em out. They were filthy."

Ontarra looked at the rags she was wearing and then cast his eyes around the rubbish-strewn hole she was living in. He shook his head. "How am I supposed to travel without my clothes?"

"You can worry 'bout that later. Better eat—you've lost a lot of blood."

Ontarra felt the back of his head. The wound was cleaned, a skin patch stuck over the hole.

She watched him probing around with his fingers. "I checked it good. You're lucky. Looks worse than it is. Lost a nice clean chunk of skull, but nothing's shattered. Whatever hit you glanced off." She eyed him suspiciously and then sat on the side of the sleep platform, pulling his head forward to have another look. For no apparent reason, she started laughing again. Shoving herself forward, she pinned Ontarra to the platform. "You're a handsome young buck." Her eyes sparkled as she ran her hand up his leg beneath the robes. "I haven't had a man in my bed for ages."

Ontarra could see why. She was chewing again. Her lips puckered in and out like a sucker fish every time her gums ground down on the leaf. Those two black teeth were revolting. She rubbed her pelvis up and down his leg. He had to turn his face away from her rancid breath. He tried shimmying backward up the wall, but she had him firmly pinned. Ontarra had never been so terrified in his life.

"I ... uh ... uh ..." Ontarra stammered. "Since the blow to my head, nothing is working right ... or I would surely take you up on your generous offer."

The hag stared up at him, a skeptical look in her eye. Her face twisted into a frustrated look of acceptance. "All right," she said, rolling off, "but you don't know what you're givin' up." Ontarra didn't even want to imagine. He breathed a sigh of relief as he searched the entire lodge with his eyes for anything that might substitute for clothing.

She stepped over to the hearth, checking a charred pot as if nothing had happened. "I've had my fill of men anyway. Used up three husbands, you know. First one was a warrior, like you." Their eyes held each other a moment. She licked her lips. Ontarra shuddered as he imagined the taste. She returned to her pot and started stirring. "My name's Kratcha. You got a name?" Ontarra was uncertain what to say. "Okay, then, where you from?"

Ontarra searched his mind. "Sucker Fish Camp." Her head snapped up, eyes locking on him again. *Wrong answer.* Ontarra scolded himself.

"My second husband was a fisherman. Lake Iannaoa got him." She glanced over at Ontarra. "Sucker Fish Camp is gone." Ontarra stared out the door so he wouldn't have to meet her eyes. She handed him a wooden bowl with what appeared to be stew. Ontarra was thankful for the reprieve. He busied himself eating, trying to think of a way out of the lie. He noticed chunks of skin and hair in the stew, but said nothing.

"Why does your dog keep whimpering like that?"

"She hasn't eaten today ... and she's in heat. That's why I tied her up. Can't feed *her* proper, let alone a litter of pups."

The bowl was empty before Ontarra could think of a way out of his deceit. He set it aside. Kratcha was staring. "Thank you. What was it?"

"River rat."

Ontarra rolled his eyes up at the ceiling.

"I don't have anyone to hunt for me, you know," Kratcha chortled indignantly. "Food's kind of scarce this time of the cycle." She studied Ontarra a moment. "That's an interesting club you carry." She flashed a black-toothed smile. "It's Ounsasta's, isn't it?"

Ontarra stared at her warily, judging how many steps away the club was. "What clan are you, Kratcha?"

"Lynx, Ontarra. I'm Brata's sister. I saw you at the Festival of Dead. Had to bring my old man." Kratcha stared into the coals. "They've been looking for you all winter, you know. Phah! Young tyrants! Stomping in here unannounced, trying to boss me around. I sent them all over the countryside, and they soon left me alone." Kratcha tilted her head back, snickering with her tongue pressed against the roof of her mouth. Ontarra had to look the other way. The sound of an ice flow crunching into something interrupted her mirth. Kratcha jumped up and tromped over to the door. "That stupid old man of mine, building our lodge out here on the river flat," she railed. "Had to be away from people; hear the sound of the river." Kratcha's voice grew higher, shriller, as she worked herself up. "Lucky I wasn't drowned or crushed under all this ice!" She let fly out the door with a long stream of petun juice. Ontarra nodded his approval. Her distance and accuracy was amazing. Kratcha seemed to be two people living in one body. She stomped back, settling herself down at the fire. The lucid Kratcha returned. "How's your mother and father?"

Ontarra looked up, and their eyes held each other. "They've passed over," he answered softly.

"Oh, no-o-o!" Kratcha moaned. "Now there's no hope for any of us." She hung her head, rocking it in disbelief. Then she lifted her eyes again to look at Ontarra. "The shamans?" Ontarra nodded. Kratcha exhaled angrily. "I heard they killed Satwani and a lot of his men at the forks too." They sat in silence. Something occurred to Kratcha. "You're after those strangers, aren't you?"

"How did you know?"

"Brainless knotheads crashed right into my hump when the flood was at its peak. They were shoving off through the trees again when I got out there. Heard that weird language of theirs, though. Knew it was those strange men from Tontiaton."

Ontarra had to chuckle at the derogatory reference to their topknots. "Did you see the girls?"

"Girls? Didn't see nobody. Just heard their outsider babble. Probably went to stay with that fat slug Adontayat."

"Kratcha, I thank you for your help, but I need to keep moving. Do you have anything I can use for clothes?"

Kratcha crawled over to the sleep platform and rummaged around underneath. When she came up for air, she handed Ontarra a carefully folded buckskin bundle. He set it on the sleep robes and peeled it open, unable to believe his eyes—a finely crafted tunic, leggings, and matching moccasins. He glanced at the worn-out clothes Kratcha was wearing, folded the bundle, and handed it back. "Give me yours. You take these."

"Don't be ridiculous! They're way too big for me. The old man was about the same size as you last time he wore them, and *he* won't be needing them now."

Ontarra was in no position to argue. He considered climbing out from under the covers. A quick look at Kratcha convinced him to dress lying down.

"Kinda shy, are we?"

Ontarra pinched an embarrassed smile as he squirmed around, trying to pull the buckskins on. Finally, he had to roll out, stand up, and tug the leggings into place.

Kratcha grinned. "Everything looks functional to me. You know ... you look just like your father when he was your age."

The nausea swirled back. Ontarra sat down on the sleep platform, waiting for the room to stop spinning. "You knew him?"

"Of course. Everyone at the old town knew him. He was about your age when I had to move away. I was carrying a child. Unfortunately, it wasn't my husband's. He disowned me, so I came to live at Teotonguiaton. After Thozak was born, I married the fisherman."

Ontarra's mouth dropped open. "You're Thozak's mother?"

Kratcha gave her chin an affirmative dip, reached over, and lifted Ounsasta's club, cradling it as if it was a baby. Ontarra leaned forward, slowly tugging it from her grip before the other Kratcha could make an appearance.

Kratcha stood and went over to the door. She stared downriver a long time before returning to the hearth fire and folding herself down. "It's late in the day. You'd be wise to rest here until morning. The flats are treacherous with all this ice." Ontarra got up and stumbled over, propping himself against the doorframe to look at the sun. It was only a finger-width above the western horizon. He exhaled, a weary look of acceptance stiffening his face. He turned and made his way back to the sleep platform. Kratcha was right—he could barely make it across the lodge. He'd have to wait for morning.

Ontarra listened to the dog whining pathetically outside. "You should let her go, so she can find something to eat."

"Well ... if you've had enough, I'll give her the rest of the stew."

"Good idea." Ontarra bobbed his chin with relief. Kratcha disappeared outside with the pot. Ontarra swept his eyes around the shack, wondering how this was going to work out. There was no way he was going to share the platform with her. Kratcha slipped, falling heavily against the outside wall and setting her to cussing and griping again.

Her grating whine condemned every man she'd ever known. She cursed the river, the ice, and her third husband's lousy choice of location. Ontarra hobbled over to a corner and cleared a spot with his foot. He sat himself down with his back to the wall and rested the club across his legs. The pot flew through the door, tumbling across the floor.

It was going to be a long night.

Kratcha was just as loony asleep as she was awake. Several times during the night, she ranted at men who only existed now in her mind. Despite her obvious agitation, every time Ontarra checked on her, she was sound asleep. When she wasn't complaining, she snored. A puddle of mucus was rolling around in the back of her throat. The suspense of waiting for one of her snorts to move it kept Ontarra awake well into the night.

As dawn approached, she finally coughed it up and seemed to settle. She began talking tenderly to someone. Ontarra tiptoed over to the platform to listen. She was talking to her third husband. Kratcha's eyes cracked open. She smiled softly at Ontarra, studying him with a dreamy expression. "He was the best one, you know." Ontarra could see she was in another time and place.

"He was a trader. Wealthiest man in Teotonguiaton. We had a beautiful little girl together. Kiska."

Ontarra settled down on the platform beside her. "Where is Kiska now?"

Kratcha rolled her head to the side and stared at the wall. "When Kiska was in her eighth winter, she fell ill. Nothing we did helped. Adontayat convinced my old man that she had a sickness of the spirit, that only he could save her. The sickness lasted a long time. Her skin, even her eyes, gradually turned yellow." Kratcha palmed moisture from her eye. "I guess the manitos wanted Kiska more than we did. Adontayat took everything we had. He even lives in our lodge now—pompous fool!" Kratcha scowled. "He covered one of the walls with birch bark, but he couldn't find enough to finish it. Looks ridiculous," Kratcha chuckled. She shifted her eyes to the hearth fire with a bleak expression and lay back wearily. "The old man was never the same after Kiska left us. He came out here; threw up this shack. Said he wanted to be away from people, to listen to the river. He quarried a little slate, sold it in town, and faded away a bit every day ..." Kratcha's voice trailed off. "Now he's with her again." She closed her eyes and was instantly asleep. Ontarra brushed away a tear puddled on her cheek. It was the first period of relative calm all night. He sat back in his corner and drifted off.

"What are you doing in here? You sniveling little snake, coming around here, intimidating an old woman!"

Ontarra snapped his club up over his head, blocking the paddle before it could crush his skull. "Kratcha, wait! It's me—Ontarra!"

Kratcha hesitated, the paddle raised high for another blow. She bent and stared into Ontarra's face. He lowered his club cautiously, so she could get a good look. "Oh … Sannisen, it's you … I forgot."

Ontarra stood up slowly and twisted the paddle from her hands. He tossed it out the door, shaking his head in frustration. He sat Kratcha back down on her sleep platform and looked around the shack for something he could give her to eat. Seeing nothing, he went outside. He stripped some bark from a willow at the water's edge, filled the pot, and went back in.

Ontarra studied Kratcha sadly, thinking about Adontayat as they sipped the hot tea. A cold hatred settled over him. His jaw started working, and his hand unconsciously clenched and unclenched the handle of his club. He threw the rest of his tea on the coals and stood up. Ontarra went outside and brought the paddle back in. Leaning it against the doorframe, he went over and lifted Kratcha up by the shoulders, staring into her eyes. He wanted to catch her while she was lucid. He shook gently so she'd look at him.

"Kratcha, listen closely to what I tell you. I have to leave now. Tomorrow morning, some canoes are going to float by on the river. Go out and retrieve every one that you see." Kratcha nodded absently. "Every time you look at that paddle, you're going to remember the canoes, right?" Kratcha stared over at the paddle. Refocusing on Ontarra, she nodded again. "I want you to take one of the canoes, and go to Ounontisaston. You can live with Sakawa—Brata's husband. He's a good man."

Kratcha stared out the door into the distance. "I never talked to Brata after I left the old town. She stole a hair comb from me that summer. I never had much use for her after that."

Ontarra thought back to where he'd heard that story before and pursed his lips. "Kratcha," he said, shaking her to bring her back, "Sakawa will welcome you, but you must never tell anyone that you met me. It would be bad for both of us." Ontarra wasn't too worried. No one was likely to believe anything she said anyway.

Kratcha's eyes brightened. She pulled away from Ontarra, dropping down to dig beneath her sleep platform. She sat back with a large carry pouch on her palms and held it out to him. "Take this; you'll probably need it." Ontarra draped it over his head so it hung below his left arm. "Check inside," she said.

Ontarra flipped the closure and pulled out a large skinning knife with a double-edged blade. He smiled, admiring its symmetry and the solid chert. "Thank you, Kratcha. I'm sorry, but I have nothing for you."

"Sure you do! You just won't give it!"

Ontarra looked away. "Kratcha ... do you have any feathers here?"

Kratcha scratched her hooked nose, giggled, and broke into her insane cackling again. Ontarra pressed his tongue against the roof of his mouth, trying to decide how she made that gurgling sound. She reached under the sleep platform, dug around a moment, and produced a large turkey feather. "Just this one. I use it to scratch places that I can't reach. I really hate to give it up." Her head rocked from side to side as she thought about it. "Oh, well ... take it." Her lips peeled back into what must have once been a playful grin. A cavernous hole with a lonely black tooth hanging down made Ontarra wince. Gingerly, he reached out, took the feather between a thumb and forefinger, knelt, and laid it on the floor. He cut off the tip and then sliced three notches into one side.

"Attacked by three enemies, killed them all, and wasn't wounded," Kratcha mumbled over his shoulder. "The feather of Sannisen." Ontarra looked up with surprise written all over his face. Kratcha snorted a laugh and shot a brown stream out the door, making Ontarra's face screw up. "My first husband was a warrior, remember?"

Ontarra stood, tucking the feather into his carry pouch. Kratcha jumped up and smothered him with a hug. He held his arms out awkwardly, slowly closed his eyes, and forced himself to hug back. "Good-bye, Kratcha." Ontarra headed out. At the door he looked back. "Kratcha ... I'm going to take your dog with me. I'll let her go at the town. She can live off the rubbish heap if no one takes her in." Kratcha bobbed her head.

"The manitos be with you, Sannisen."

Ontarra didn't bother to correct her. He went out and untied the mangy dog, leaving the tether around her neck so she'd stay with him. He started upriver through the jumble of ice. When he was an arrow-flight upstream, Kratcha's enraged voice echoed up the river valley. "Now they've stolen my dog! Can't even shut your eyes at night without somebody sneaking round causin' trouble!" Ontarra looked back at the ramshackle lodge. Kratcha was wandering around, looking for her missing dog. He lowered his eyes to the dog that was rubbing her butt against his leg, and he shook his head sadly.

It was midday when Ontarra saw the curling smoke of Teotonguiaton. He'd soon be running into fishermen on the river. When he reached the bend where the river's course swung north–south, he decided to cross to the opposite shore so he could move along the uplands and avoid detection. He found rapids that appeared to be only waist-deep. A dark stone on the gravelly bottom caught his eye. He plunged his hand down and plucked it out. Dark ... rounded ... about the size of a husked walnut ... edges polished smooth by the water. Ontarra dropped it into his carry pouch, hoisted the dog up in his arms, and waded across. Hidden in the brush a stone's cast from shore, he came upon a drying rack with several weed fish hanging on it. Crouching down, he scanned the area and then trotted over, grabbed two fish, and slipped back into the brush.

Ontarra had to give some to the dog right off, to keep her quiet. The rest he stuffed into the carry pouch. They moved up onto the uplands, traveling through the woods until they reached the first fields. Ontarra dropped down over the crest of the ridge, working along the deer trails so he wouldn't be seen. The smell of food kept the dog close, so he removed the tether, rubbed her ears and belly, and tossed her a piece of fish occasionally to keep her interest as he stalked on.

When the sun was low in the west, he could see the town through the trees up ahead, just beyond a bend where the river's course turned east–west again. He settled himself down in some brush where he could watch the activity. Teotonguiaton was built on a gentle slope facing north. The Lower Tranchi's riverbed narrowed to only two canoe-widths in front of the town. The hillside swarmed with dogs. He tested the breeze to be sure he was downwind, afraid that all those dogs might catch the scent of a stranger and come looking. Ontarra chewed on raw fish and watched, waiting for darkness to quiet things down.

Teotonguiaton was a pretty place. As an interior town, it had no palisade surrounding it. Five hands of lodges lay scattered across the cleared area of hillside. The largest lodges housed only three or four families. Ontarra could see Adontayat's lodge in the middle, its single white wall a dead giveaway. People were milling around everywhere, enjoying the warm spring day. The first fish of the season were being brought in at the canoe area. Apparently, they felt the land was secure at present; Ontarra could see no sentries.

He scanned the faces but saw no sign of Adontayat or the outsiders. Settling back, he tossed another chunk of fish to the dog so she'd stop whimpering and rubbing herself against him. He could hear women working the fields above him. Slipping the tether back around the dog's neck, he dozed until he was awakened by the smell of evening meals. Some women were coming in late, moving along the crest above him. Ontarra straddled the dog, wrapped his arm around her neck, and held two fingers over her nostrils. She was so busy learning to breathe through her mouth, she never made a sound.

When the moon appeared over the eastern horizon, Ontarra stalked up into the fields. Moving in a crouch to the brow above the town, he peered down at the lodges. Everyone seemed to be inside. He untied the dog, pulled out the last side of fish and gave her a good whiff. Ontarra leaned back and lofted it down among the lodges. She watched it land and flew down the hillside.

She welcomed the first male that showed up. Even the second she was happy to see. When the third and fourth arrived, a fight started, and she'd had enough. In a few heartbeats, almost every dog in the town was chasing her down the riverbank. Doorskins peeled aside as people looked to see what all the commotion was. Heads shook, and the doorskins fell back in place. "You shouldn't be quite so frustrated tomorrow," Ontarra said softly, watching the pack disappear. He came to his feet and started down the hill for the back of the first lodge.

Quietly, he crept from lodge to lodge until he reached the back of the one with the white wall. Ontarra pressed an ear to the bark. There was no sound from inside. He slid along the wall to the front and sat on his heels beside the door. Pulling Kratcha's knife, he used it to push the doorskin back a crack. A bed of coals in the hearth cast ghostly shadows around the room. Three sleep platforms lined the walls. One had someone in it.

Ontarra poked his head inside. No one else was there. He stepped in, moving softly over to the slumbering hulk. The young shaman opened his eyes with a start. "Who are you? How dare you enter this lodge unannounced!" He glowered at Ontarra and started to sit up. "I am a sham—" Ontarra slapped a hand over his mouth and pushed him down, sticking the point of his knife up the man's nostril.

"Shut up!" Ontarra hissed. "Where's Adontayat?" The young shaman's eyes doubled in size. "Make a sound that I don't like, and it will be your last." Ontarra pulled the knife back and lifted his hand. The shaman lay there, quivering. Ontarra ripped the sleep robes off, tossing them to the floor "Roll onto your stomach!" The shaman looked at the knife and obeyed.

Ontarra pressed a knee into the man's back and twined his fingers into the man's ratty hair, pressing the knifepoint persuasively against the base of his skull. "I'm going to ask you one more time. Where is Adontayat?" Ontarra pulled the shaman's face up off the sleep platform so he could answer.

"He's gone to Kandoucho! Windigo Killer came—said they were going to meet a trader there!" Ontarra pressed the shaman's face back into the platform while he thought about this. *So, Poutassa is at Kandoucho.* Ontarra pulled the head up again. "Did some strangers come here with the witches?" The shaman's entire body started shaking. He rocked his head negatively. Ontarra pressed the face down and leaned into the knife.

The shaman's arms and legs flailed violently. The platform collapsed. It was all over in an instant. Ontarra sprang to the door and pulled the skin back. The town was silent. He wiped his knife on the doorskin and dropped it in the carry pouch. Gathering up everything he could see that would be useful, he wrapped it all up in a sleep robe. As he glanced around the lodge a last time, his eyes settled on a ceremonial bow and two medicine arrows in the corner. He set them on the bundle.

Ontarra emptied a bark pot, scooped it full of hot coals from the hearth, and balanced it on a sleep platform. Cradling the bundle on his arms, he ducked out—still no movement around the town. Deciding to take no chances, he moved in the shadows from lodge to lodge across the hillside and then slipped into the woods before making his way down to the river. When he reached the riverbank, all was still quiet in the town above. Ontarra crept along the shore into the canoe area.

He put the sleep robe, venison, and dried fish into the first canoe and pushed it out into the current. In the next he put a bag of cornmeal and two cakes of petun. The last got a bag of shell beads and a pot full of chert blanks. He pulled two hawk feathers from a tied bundle for future use, laying the rest on the seat of the canoe where they were sure to be seen. Ontarra watched as the canoe disappeared into darkness and then he settled himself down into one and headed upstream. When he reached the first bend he looked back.

Trees hid the town from view, but the night sky was a shimmering halo of orange. Teotonguiaton was going to be a lively place tonight.

It wasn't likely he would meet anyone upriver of Teotonguiaton. Only people traveling to the Kandia and Kandoucho would come this far up. The sky was a dazzling blanket of stars that reminded him of another night—on the bluff at Ounon with Sounia. A pang stabbed in his chest with the realization that it had been another lifetime.

He wondered why Poutassa would go to Kandoucho for the girls. It seemed the outsiders were intent on holding on to them until they got something in return. Ontarra thought about the man with missing fingers. Yadak said he was Erieehronon. *They're getting as close to Erieehronon territory as possible. They don't trust the shamans!*

It was the middle of the night when Ontarra saw the silhouettes of several grounded canoes ahead. He stuck his paddle down into the mucky bottom to hold himself in place while he scrutinized the small clearing that marked the overland route to the Kandia. There was no sign of people. He continued past silently until he was an arrow-flight upstream of the landing. Ontarra pulled the canoe up into a stand of last cycle's cattails and settled himself back in to try to sleep.

He listened to an early bullfrog croaking upstream, apparently wondering where everyone else was. An owl screeched somewhere deep in the forest. The sounds were reassuring. After Ontarra feasted on Adontayat's venison, he drifted into a slumber until dawn gathered in the eastern sky.

Slipping out of the canoe, he made his way silently through dead stalks until he struck the trail. He checked up it to its first bend, turned, and made his way back to the landing, certain that he was alone. Three of the canoes were badly scarred up. He ran a finger down a gouge in the bark. Ice flows. In one of the canoes he found a long strand of ebony hair. By the unusual length alone, he was sure it was Sounia's. He wrapped it around a finger, touched it to his lips, and stored it carefully in a corner of his carry pouch.

Checking the ground around the landing, he found a moccasin print with unfamiliar stitching. He looked up at the sound of black-head geese heading north but ducked down again when he heard another sound—footfalls. Someone was running. Ontarra slipped into a clump of bog willow and crouched low. A figure trotted around the bend in the path and then rested on his knees to catch his breath when he saw the landing. Ontarra studied him closely, searching his mind. He knew this person. He stepped out into the open and sauntered casually up the path.

The man glanced up with a start. "What? Who are you?" A concerned look lined his face. He took a few steps back.

"Ho, friend!" Ontarra held up a reassuring hand as he drew closer. "My name is Yadak. I've been sent to find Windigo Killer—a matter of grave importance." The man hesitated. His head slowly bobbed up and down as he recalled where he'd heard the name Yadak before.

"Windigo Killer is still at Kandoucho. He has the trader Dekari, but we haven't found the outsiders or the witches yet. I'm going to get more men so we can search the countryside." Ontarra's face rearranged into a puzzled look, the young man thought he was attempting to identify him. "I'm Buzkit, a shaman of Teotonguiaton. I helped to catch the witches," he said, preening.

Ontarra's eyes narrowed. He snorted a skeptical laugh. "Really? And just how did you do that?"

Buzkit frowned and pushed himself up a little taller, his face indignant. "I helped Adontayat find them. We watched them performing a witch ritual around a fire in the forest. They made lights dance in the sky."

Ontarra crossed his arms. "I remember that night well. Tell me—were there any men with them?"

"Of course! Sannisen and ..." Buzkit saw Adontayat's bow hanging around Ontarra's neck, and his face tightened. "How did you get that bow?" Ontarra pulled the bow over his head and started to string it. His malignant glare jarred Buzkit's memory.

"I stole it," Ontarra growled through his teeth. Buzkit leaned forward a bit, studying Ontarra's face. Recognition, then horror, flashed in his eyes. Ontarra's lips angled into a vindictive grin.

"No! It can't be you! Dekari said they killed you!" Buzkit started backing down the path, eyes frantically searching for some way to save himself. Ontarra slowly lifted the bow, nocking an arrow as it came up. Buzkit turned and ran. Ontarra let him get to the bend in the path. The gut string twanged. Ragged chert buried itself between Buzkit's shoulder blades. When he stopped rolling, he was already dead.

Ontarra walked over, staring down at the pompous little braggart. "Be sure to tell my family all about it," he said softly. The medicine arrow was broken but well spent. Ontarra dragged Buzkit down to the landing. Four strokes of the skinning knife removed Buzkit's head. He tied the cadaver upright on the floor of one of the canoes. With a quick twist of the chert blade, Buzkit's left eye popped out. Ontarra tossed it in the river.

Probing around in his carry pouch, he found the black pebble. It didn't quite want to fit, so he tapped it into the eye socket with the butt of his knife. Ontarra set Buzkit's head in his lap, laying his hands on each side to hold it in place. He pulled out one of the hawk feathers, smiling as he rotated it between his fingers. Pressing it against a sapling, he cut off the tip and notched the side. Ontarra squatted on his heels, studying the corpse with icy detachment. He shoved the point of the quill into Buzkit's mouth so that only the sliced tip protruded from his lips.

Ontarra placed several rocks around Buzkit on the floor of the canoe so it wouldn't roll over if it hung up at a bend or caught on a tree limb. He stood to admire his work for a few heartbeats and then shoved the canoe downriver. "In your next life, Bugshit, don't talk so much."

Ontarra thought about the other canoes in the landing a moment and then shoved all but one out into the current. He paddled the last one upstream, hiding it in the cattails beside his. If he was chasing anyone on the way back, they would have a sudden surprise. If he and the girls were being chased, they would have two canoes.

He set off down the trail for the Kandia, running a short distance and walking a short distance. If he conserved his energy, he could make the river by dusk. Ontarra gave up that idea when halfway there. The exertion was making his head pound. It felt like his brains were bouncing around inside his head. He stopped, seated himself on a fallen limb to let his heart slow, and ran his fingers over the scab at the back of his head. Kratcha's patch had fallen off somewhere. The wound was crusty and dry. If he probed at the soft spot in the center, a pain shot into the back of his left eye.

Ontarra forced himself to walk at a casual pace, despite the pressing urgency weighing on his mind. Swollen tree buds were threatening to burst in the warm sunshine. Flocks of ducks came in low over Ontarra's head, gliding down into some pool of water only visible from their vantage point. The land was coming back to life. As he approached a sharp bend in the path, flocks of startled birds lifted into the air ahead. Ontarra slipped into the forest. He found a boulder large enough to hide him and rested on his haunches behind it.

Keeping his eyes on the trail, he listened intently for a long time. He was just starting to think he'd been mistaken when a movement to his right caught his eye. He saw two warriors through the trees. They were moving cautiously, searching the forest. Ontarra pressed his back to the rock; his eyes darted around for a better hiding place. They were too close—he didn't dare move. Slowly, Ontarra lowered himself to the ground. He pulled wet leaves of last cycle up over him as best he could. Gripping his knife in one hand and his club in the other, he tried to control his breathing.

The warriors came on. Ontarra could hear the *shish* of their moccasins on the wet leaves. A hand holding a bow rested on the rock above him. Ontarra held his breath. The warriors spoke in low tones. Ontarra's legs and arms started to quiver with tension. He decided to jump to his feet and make the first blow count. The hand and bow disappeared. Ontarra allowed himself to breathe again.

Sliding forward a bit, he peeked around the rock. The warriors were on the trail, scanning it up and down. One held his bow up, signaling someone farther down. The two slipped into the forest on the other side of the path. Ontarra sat up, brushing away leaves and mud. Were they searching for him or for the outsiders? It had to be the strangers they were looking for, but it didn't really matter. If he'd continued running, he'd probably be dead now. He waited for dusk before moving. At times he heard men in the brush around him. No doubt many more passed nearby that he wasn't aware of.

As darkness settled, he moved off again, sticking to the cover of the forest this time. He found a wash that was lower than the surrounding terrain. The search had apparently moved elsewhere. Ontarra saw no one until the moon was high in the sky, and he hit the shoreline of the Kandia. A huge bluff rose from the water on the opposite shore. On the top, three times as high up as the crest at Ounontisaston, torch lights bobbed through the trees like giant fireflies. He saw occasional flickers down the ridge to the left and right, but the main concentration was directly across from him. An arrow-flight upstream, two torches illuminated the canoe landing that marked the end of the trail. They seemed to be counting the canoes. He would have to swim across.

The Kandia was wider than the Tranchi. Ontarra was numb when he pulled himself up into the brush on the east bank. He sat for a while, rubbing the feeling back into his limbs before starting the climb up. He angled left to make the crawl less tedious and placed himself off to one side of the big search party. Cautiously, he poked his head up over the crest. A clearing in a low trench, just back of the ridge, was ablaze with bouncing lights. Young warriors and shamans were circling in a search pattern.

He saw Poutassa, surrounded by a hand of his followers. His jaw tightened, and he felt the skin tingle on the back of his neck. Another shaman wandered over to Poutassa and pointed. Ontarra tugged his eyes away from Poutassa and scanned the clearing. In the shadowy light, he could make out four motionless forms. Men ... dead men. One's head was half-torn away. Ontarra realized that Mox had been here. He crept forward, crouching behind a big maple to get a closer look. There was no sign of the girls or the strangers.

The search was spreading out in his direction. Ontarra was about to slip back to the ridge, when a shout rang out from deeper in the forest. The men and torches all moved off into the brush. Ontarra followed. When the torches stopped, all gathering in one place, he made his way down from tree to tree. A hunter was talking to Poutassa, gesturing to sign on the ground and then pointing east into the forest. Ontarra took the chance, slinking down to a fallen elm spread out across the forest floor.

He stuck his head out beyond the roots, stopped his breathing, and caught a few words. "East ... run for it ..." Poutassa started giving orders in abrupt tones. The hunter and a handful of warriors headed off into the forest. Poutassa, Adontayat, and their bodyguards headed back to the clearing. As he thought about a multiple grave in a quiet walnut grove, Ontarra nocked his last arrow, sighting down its shaft on Poutassa. His hand shook as he considered Sounia and Taiwa. Ontarra lowered the bow. He had to think of the girls. He couldn't give himself away and risk capture.

He followed the shamans, moving up above the ravine until he was past the clearing and slipped down behind the big maple again. He heard Adontayat telling Poutassa to go on ahead; he would remain behind, he said, to ask the manitos to accept these unfortunate souls. Poutassa left with all the guards but one. Ontarra swung his eyes from Adontayat to Poutassa in frustration. Poutassa disappeared over the crest with his escort.

Adontayat instructed the warrior to hold the torch high as he started frisking the bodies. He tore open tunics, yanked fetishes from necks and war bundles from waistbands, picked out several knives, and stuffed everything into his waist pouch. Ontarra sucked in a corner of his lower lip and chewed on it. He nocked his arrow, stood, and let fly. The arrow plunged through the warrior's rib cage from side to side. It was hard to tell from their faces whether the young warrior or Adontayat was more shocked. Ontarra walked down out of the woods. Both stunned faces stared up at him. The warrior dropped.

"What is the meaning of this?" Adontayat tried to sound outraged, but his voice was shaking. Ontarra walked out into the clearing, threw down his bow, and pulled out the skinning knife. "Who ... who are you?" Adontayat started shuffling backward but stumbled over his own feet and fell flat onto his back.

Ontarra grinned and dropped on him, pinning the shaman's arms under his knees. The knife traced an arc under Adontayat's jaw. Ontarra never knew a face could express such terror. The shaman stared up, mouth opening and closing in silence, struck dumb as he recognized the wraith from the past that had come for him. "I've been sent back by a spirit that wishes to meet with you again, Adontayat. Do you remember a girl named Kiska?"

Adontayat tried to scream but barely managed a squeak before serrated chert plunged through his windpipe. Ontarra scanned the forest. They were still alone. He dragged Adontayat over to the crest of the ridge. The torches on the river were all headed for the protection of Kandoucho for the night. Adontayat had to have a canoe down there somewhere. Ontarra heaved the shaman up onto his shoulder and tossed him over the ridge. Heavy thumps and the crashing of brush seemed to go on forever. Ontarra heard a splash, and the forest fell silent again. He waited a hand of time to see if he'd drawn any attention, but the silence was complete. He skidded and slid down to the river.

Ontarra tethered Adontayat's canoe to a tree limb so he wouldn't float past the town in the dark. He seemed quite peaceful sitting there, with his head in his lap and a stone in one eye socket. He was badly battered up, but they'd know who it was. Ontarra pulled Kratcha's feather from his pouch. "This one's for you, Kratcha." He bent down, slid it into Adontayat's mouth, and straightened up with a wry grin. "Whewf! If you only knew where that's been."

He stared downriver to where he knew Kandoucho stood. He'd never get in there and back out alive. Buzkit said they hadn't found the outsiders or the witches. Those men seemed to want Sounia and Taiwa for themselves. The thought sent a shudder through Ontarra. He humped his way back up to the clearing to track the search party.

16

"Wait! I ... I can't run anymore. I have to rest." Sounia hauled back on the tether at her wrists. Mox almost pulled her shoulders from their sockets. Everyone came to an abrupt halt in the darkness. Manak stormed back, cursing under his breath.

"You will keep up or die right here," he hissed, hoping his voice wouldn't carry far through the forest. His Attawondaronk was stilted, but Sounia understood. Her eyes turned icy.

"Go ahead; kill me! I don't care anymore!"

"Sounia—no! Don't say that," Taiwa's voice quavered.

"Why?" Sounia shot back. "They've killed everyone we care about. We don't have any idea what they want with us or where they're taking us!"

"You still have your father." Taiwa was close to tears. "And I don't want to lose you."

Dekari was bent over, hands on his knees, catching his wind. He couldn't have gone much farther without collapsing himself. "Let her ... rest awhile," he panted. "She'll change her mind." Matoupa didn't bother to translate. He could see by Manak's expression that he understood.

Manak didn't know what else to say to Sounia, and he needed to vent his anger somewhere. He stomped back, grabbed Dekari's tunic, and stood him up on his toes, planting his nose a finger-width from Dekari's face. "Keep your thoughts to yourself, you imbecile! You brought those warriors right into our midst! How you ever managed to live so long is a great mystery to me!"

"They were going to torture me … cut off my fingers! What else could I do?"

"In the future"—Matoupa glanced at Manak from the corner of his eye—"if you should be lucky enough to have one, that is, go around the camp first, make some sounds, and give us some kind of warning! Don't walk right in on us!"

"I wasn't thinking clearly," Dekari muttered lamely. "If I lose any more of my fingers, I won't even be able to … well … dress myself."

Manak slammed Dekari against a tree, poking the black blade up against his throat. "Forget about your fingers. If you ever endanger us like that again, I'll cut your fool head off!"

"Calm yourself, Manak," Matoupa cautioned. "He's the only one who knows where we are and how to get us out of this land."

Manak relaxed. Dekari settled back onto his feet, trying to regain some composure. Manak spit in Dekari's face. Then he rammed the knife back into his waistband and twisted around to stare at Sounia. She glowered back with bitter defiance. "If you don't want to run, we'll carry you." Sounia didn't understand all the words. She looked over at Matoupa, the corners of her eyes wrinkling with confusion. "Mox, pick her up," Manak ordered.

Mox leered at Sounia, walked around behind her, and shoved his hands under her arms, fondling both breasts as he lifted.

"Get your paws off me!" Sounia caught the drift now and twisted away.

Manak cut the tethers from Taiwa's wrists and then walked over and snapped Sounia's. "Keep up. Don't try anything." Sounia pinched her lips together and nodded. Manak turned to Dekari. "What do we need to do to get out of this?"

Dekari hauled a deep breath. "We have only one hope. Keep heading east. The Kandia makes a big loop north. We'll run right into it again. If we can get there before morning, maybe get some canoes, we can keep ahead of them."

Manak put Mox at the back of the line, the girls in the middle, and Dekari out front where he could prod him to move faster. The effort was futile. As the night waned, Dekari slowed up as he stumbled and tripped over every exposed root. Finally, he went sprawling onto the forest floor, unable to pick himself up. Manak and Mox shook their heads at each other sourly. "The girls have more spirit," Mox said with a scowl.

Manak crouched down beside Dekari, waiting for the wheezing gasps to slow down. "How much farther?" Manak wanted to know. Dekari rolled his head up, mouth ajar and chest heaving. He lifted a limp arm and pointed but still couldn't talk. They waited anxiously, a full hand of time, before Dekari pulled his knees up and sat on his heels.

"Couple arrow-flights ... farther," he said, panting like an overworked dog. The eastern sky was already brightening. Manak paced back and forth, deciding whether they could afford to leave Dekari behind. He signaled Mox with a jerk of his chin. They each wrapped a hand under a shoulder and ran on, dragging Dekari between them.

Even Dekari couldn't endure such humiliation for long. He struggled to get his feet under him and shook himself free of their hands. His pace was pathetic, but it was still faster than dragging him. They crested a rise. The chasm of the river valley yawned ahead of them. Dekari stopped to rest on his knees a moment. Without warning, he straightened up and walked straight for the crest. Manak grabbed his hair and yanked him back before he could expose himself. He shot the trader a withering stare and slipped up behind a tree to study the river below. His chin fell to his chest, and he backed away. "Canoes—all up and down the river."

Dekari lifted a hand, memorizing the way his fingers looked. "We're doomed," he moaned.

Manak started stomping back and forth, thumping a fist against his leg. He turned to Matoupa. "Where do they expect us to go?" Matoupa translated to Dekari to be sure there was no misunderstanding.

Dekari pulled a defeated breath. "Down the Kandia to Lake Iannaoa or south through the forest to the lake."

"What is to the north?" Manak demanded.

"Nothing but empty wilderness until you hit the Great Lower Lake."

"Can we get to your land from there?"

Dekari gave his head a shake. "We have to cross Iannaoa to get to my land."

Manak tossed his knife down in front of Dekari. "Tell him to draw it."

Dekari understood. Picking up the knife, he drew a rectangle lengthwise in the dirt. "We're on a peninsula. Lake Iannaoa is at the bottom. The Great Lower Lake is on top."

Manak raised a brow and looked at Matoupa. "Did he just say the lower lake is on top?" Manak scowled and gave his head a frustrated shake.

"It's called the Lower Lake because it is the last lake in the chain," Dekari explained. "We came from the left side, over here. They'll be spread out all across here, looking for us." Dekari drew a line across the bottom of the rectangle.

"What is here?" Manak pointed to the eastern end.

"A massive gorge and the Great Cataract of Onghiara; beyond that is the land of the Sennikae. If you think we've got problems now"—Dekari looked up and snorted—"we wouldn't last a day in Sennikae territory without their permission." Dekari studied his map again. "My people are here, beneath Iannaoa." He poked the blade in the ground. "We have to get across the lake."

Manak and Matoupa crouched on their knees, talking in Tunican and pointing at the lines on the ground. Manak rubbed at his temples. "How far is this northern lake?"

Dekari sucked his cheeks between his teeth. "Day and a half."

Manak jerked his knife from Dekari's hand and stuck it into the ground at the eastern end of the peninsula. "Can we cross here?" Dekari considered this a moment and bobbed his head. "We go north to the lake, down the shore, then re-cross the peninsula at the eastern end," Manak said, tracing the route. "They won't expect that." Dekari thought about the distance involved and hung his head.

Taiwa leaned over to Sounia. "They want to go through the hinterlands, to the Lake of the Okis."

Manak put Mox out front this time, so *he* could set the pace. Then came Matoupa, Dekari, and the girls, while Manak brought up the rear. There wasn't time to worry about hiding their trail; they had to move fast. They kept up a steady gait, stopping only for brief rests until midday. The girls held up admirably, but Dekari had reached the limit of his endurance. They broke from the forest into a vast swamp. Ducks and geese exploded into the air. Water spread out in all directions, visible through openings in a maze of swamp grass and cattails.

Manak couldn't see any end to the water. "We'll rest here awhile," he said, to Dekari's immense relief. Dekari flopped to the ground. Manak glared down at him. "If you don't keep up, trader, I'm going to strip those waist pouches from you and toss them." The waist pouches Dekari had taken from the dead warriors at Kandoucho were bulging. Still, he'd been forced to abandon a fortune in that clearing above the Kandia. Manak offered tobacco to the girls. "Chew it. It will allay your hunger; give you energy."

Sounia turned her face away. "Give us something to eat."

Manak shook his head and stuffed the chit in his mouth. "Food would rob your legs of strength. We'll eat tonight." He looked up at Mox as he climbed to the top of a big willow and stared back in the direction they'd just come. "See anything?" Manak asked.

"No, the land is too flat. They couldn't have covered much ground at night. They're at least a half day back."

"Can you see any way around this swamp?"

Mox twisted, shading his eyes against the sun. "No, but I can see the other side."

Manak squinted out over the water. He couldn't see what Mox could see. Manak rubbed his chin, deciding to go straight across. It would save time and let everyone catch their wind.

Matoupa waded in, leading the girls, while Manak gave Mox final instructions. Mox hung back, catching up again when they were out in the middle, up to their necks in the water. Matoupa held a pouch with the last of their food over his head. The girls had to start swimming. In a stone's throw the bottom started coming up again. They sloshed out the other side. Manak immediately forced everyone back into a trot to fight off the chill.

When they hit forest, Manak stuck Mox out front to pick up the pace. Mox was good at this. He used deer trails, veered through openings in the underbrush, and always took the easiest path; he never lost track of his direction. Mox launched himself into the air to clear a fallen tree, cried out, and then disappeared from sight. Everyone skidded to a stop. Matoupa padded up to the blow-down, peering over apprehensively. Despite their current dilemma, he burst out laughing. Manak and the girls gathered around.

Mox was down in a shallow trench formed by a feeder creek. A tangle of low brush on top had hidden it from view. Mox picked himself up, cursing and holding his swollen testicle. He was covered from head to foot with mud. He growled angrily at Matoupa as he crawled out the other side. Sounia and

Taiwa smirked at each other. Even Manak's lips curled up for a moment before his stone face solidified again. He studied the layout of the terrain and its approaches and then ordered the girls across. They rested a short time while Manak and Mox snapped off brush and squished around in the creek bed. Then they were off again.

At dusk, the forest ended suddenly atop a sheer cliff. Mox crashed through a thicket on the brow and started sliding down a short, steep slope toward the precipice, almost skidding right off before saving himself on a tree limb. Lake of the Okis was spread out below them, melting into the sky in hazy hues of blue and gray at the horizon. Taiwa was awestruck as she tried to discern where the lake ended and the sky began. She felt as high as the clouds. The shoreline emerged from the horizon to the east, made a sharp turn directly in front of them, and faded back into the horizon in the north. Off to their left, in the corner of the lake, the two shorelines met in a huge bay. A sandbar at the mouth almost closed it off from the lake. A vast plain, bordered the bay, spread out in all directions and cut a swath of green up through the gray cliff face they were standing on. It was a magnificent sight.

"Look," Mox said, pointing to the sandbar. A wisp of smoke curled up into the sky. A small fire twinkled on the barren strip of sand. "I think I can see canoes."

Manak strained his eyes. All he could tell for sure was that there was a hearth fire burning. He turned to Matoupa. "Take the girls. Follow the cliff to that cut over there. Mox and I will catch up."

It was well into the night before they stopped halfway around the bay. Manak wouldn't allow a fire. Sounia scooped a depression into the sand, nestled the carry pouch of dried fish and corn meal into it, and added some water. They cupped the mush up in their hands, careful not to lose any. Taiwa fell asleep in the middle of a mouthful, slumping over on her side. Sounia crabbed over and sat her up. She wrapped her arms and legs around Taiwa to keep her warm, laid her head on Taiwa's shoulder, and passed out.

It was still dark when Matoupa rocked her awake. "We have to go. Manak and Mox will be waiting."

Sounia stared up at him as she tried to shake off the haze of sleep. "Why don't you just leave us here?" Sounia rasped wearily. Matoupa's lips pinched to a thin line. He shook his head in silence. Sounia gently rocked Taiwa awake.

When they reached the little camp on the sandbar, the two men were already dead. The girls preferred not to see the men beneath the robes, but Dekari went straight over and threw the hides back. Kneeling down, he tore at something and then straightened up again with a waist pouch in his hand. Dumping the contents on his palm, he started picking through it and did a double-take. "What? No … it can't be!" He knelt down to scrutinize the contorted face. Dekari gasped, lurched to his feet, and staggered over to a boulder. He sagged down with a low moan and buried his face in his hands. Manak and Mox traded bewildered stares. Manak glanced over at Matoupa.

"What's his problem?"

Matoupa rotated his palms up and gave his head a shake. "Seems he's suddenly developed a conscience."

Manak was fast reaching his limit with the trader. "Perhaps you might like to join them," he growled at Dekari with a nod toward the dead men. He twisted on a heel and headed for the two canoes overturned on the beach.

"You've killed my sister's mate," Dekari groaned, rolling his head back to stare up at the sky.

Matoupa looked over at the bodies and then back to Dekari. "You mean that these are your people? Why are they here?"

Manak and Mox rolled the two canoes upright. Manak paused to hear Dekari's explanation. Two large, willow wicker baskets with snug lids that had been hidden beneath one of the canoes started buzzing like a hornet nest. Manak and Mox instinctively backed away. They looked at each other, and Manak slid out his knife. He stepped cautiously forward and bent to pop the lid off one.

Dekari recognized the sound instantly. He watched Manak preparing to lift the lid, trying to decided whether he should let him. "No!" Dekari jumped up and pulled Manak back. Dekari swung his eyes around and scooped up a paddle. Standing well back from one of the baskets, he stretched the paddle out and pried the lid up. There was a blur of motion. Dekari jumped back, and the lid flopped back in place. A snake as thick as Dekari's wrist was clamped to the paddle, its fangs embedded in the blade. Dekari dropped the paddle to the ground and stepped on the snake's head, slicing it off with two strokes of his knife. The muscular body coiled and knotted across the sand. The head relaxed, teetered, and slid off the blade, with the tongue still forking in and out. Dekari picked up the paddle and flipped the head out into the surf. "Too mean to die," he muttered.

Manak was shocked. He'd seen many types of venomous snakes but never one so large. "Why do these men have bad snakes?"

"They've been hunting the rock cliff for them. The snakes sun themselves on the outcrops and ledges. The rattling snakes are hard to find in our land now." Dekari slumped down on his boulder again. "We've been warring with the Minqua for as long as I can remember. My people use the venom from these snakes on their arrows. Even if the poison doesn't kill you, you'll wish it had. You'll probably never remember who you are or where you came from, not ever again."

Manak nodded, settling his eyes on the baskets with sudden respect. "It seems I am in your debt, trader." He carefully slid the canoe away from the baskets, jabbing at one with his foot. It came alive, rocking from side to side and sounding like the rattles of an entire troop of shamans. He noticed Mox squinting up at the gray cliff; it was gilded in the first rays of morning sun. Manak followed his gaze. Three tiny figures were making their way down through the cut.

"Get the canoes ready!" Manak dropped to his knees and started digging.

Ontarra checked the dead warriors in the clearing above the Kandia, relieved that none was familiar to him. He stripped the waistband from one of the men and cinched it around his hips so he wouldn't have to keep carrying his club stuffed in his leggings. He located two good arrows and a small dagger that Adontayat had discarded, turned, and started after the search party.

The warriors left a path of tracks and broken brush that would have been easy to follow in daylight. In the dark, it was a different matter entirely. A silver moon cast ephemeral light through the naked branches overhead. Still, he had to walk slowly, stopping constantly to search for sign. It was soon obvious that they were headed due east. Ontarra lost the trail, found it, and lost it again. He shook his head in frustration. He was wasting valuable time. Climbing up into the branches of a big elm, he tried to get some sleep.

As dawn approached, Ontarra dropped down from his perch and set off toward the brightening sky. He could see the spoor well enough now to break into a jog. At mid-morning he came upon a small clearing. Moccasins had trampled the entire area. Stalking up a low rise, he peered over but then dropped back on his heels in despair. He was back on the bank of the Kandia. Canoes were patrolling up and down the river. He stared back in the direction he'd come, wondering if he'd traveled in a circle. Checking the position of the sun, he realized that the Kandia had looped around in front of him.

Ontarra cast around the clearing. The strangers had been here for some time. A party of six was after them. Other prints came up over the riverbank but turned back down again. The strangers and the search party went north into the hinterlands. Ontarra moved from print to print, picturing the size and age of each man. A lump formed in his throat. Dropping to one knee, he brushed back some skeletal leaves. He'd seen this print many times at the hunt camp—Sounia's winter moccasins.

He stared north into the hinterlands. No towns or people were in there. He nodded slowly. *And no one to stop them.* Ontarra heard a commotion down at the river. He crept over to the crest and poked his head up again. Dogs! Warriors were loading dogs into canoes to come across. Ontarra rolled his eyes and cursed under his breath. He was going to have warriors ahead; dogs and warriors behind. He slipped back from the ridge, turned, and sprinted north.

The wilderness north of the Kandia was flat, broken up only by occasional creeks and swamps that had to be circled. Swarms of geese, ducks, and grackles lifted off into the sky when he broke out of the woods into open marsh. Red-winged blackbirds scolded him from the cattails as he went by. In the shade of the forest, the white three-petal flowers that killed pain better than willow bark were already sprouting up. The trail of two hands of people moving through virgin brush was easy to follow. Ontarra kept up a steady pace until the sun was directly overhead.

He stopped, resting himself on his knees, and then sat on a boulder and pulled out some venison. He stopped chewing at intervals, cocking his ear to the south, listening for the dogs. He heard a low, throaty grunt off to his right and grabbed his bow. Rocking his head from side to side to see through the trees, he caught some motion. Ontarra stalked up behind a trunk for a better look. In a pile of boulders tumbled up against a low ridge, he saw the head of a black bear looking out at the world for the first time after a long winter's sleep. Another head appeared, and then another—a she-bear ... and two cubs.

Ontarra smirked and sat back, gnawing at his venison. He listened for the dogs again and then resumed chewing. A thought came to him. His scent was fresh and strong; the dogs were bound to follow him. He popped the last of the meat into his mouth and pulled out the skinning knife. Cutting away a hand-width of his left sleeve, he lifted his tunic and used the strip of buckskin to wipe sweat from his arms and torso. For good measure he jammed his hand down his leggings, rubbing around down there awhile. He grabbed his bow and stalked from tree to tree.

A stone's cast from the den, he dropped to one knee to study the situation. The bears had retreated back inside. Ontarra stood and dashed toward the boulders. Leaping up onto one, he threw the buckskin into the mouth of the den and kept on going over the top. A startled grunt kept him hauling until his lungs couldn't keep up. He allowed himself a smug grin and circled back to the trample of feet heading north.

The sun was halfway through its descent to the tunnel in the west when the forest opened up onto a huge swamp. He hunched down at the treeline, scrutinizing the vast area. In the depths of the forest behind him, he heard the faint sounds of dogs fighting. Barely audible shouts tried to call them off. Ontarra smirked. The dogs weren't likely to give up; the sow bear wasn't likely to lose.

He was ready to move out into the open when he saw something and ducked back down. A man was seated in the grass near the water's edge. Ontarra hadn't noticed him at first. His buckskins blended perfectly with the swamp grasses. No one else was around. Ontarra crouched, moving under cover as long as possible. A killdeer ran out ahead of him, dragging a wing to draw him away from its nest. Her shrill cries gave him away, so he stood and walked straight for the man, nocking an arrow as he went.

The warrior went for his bow. Ontarra shook his head. "Don't do that! Your bones will spend eternity in this swamp." The warrior's face stiffened. He stared at Ontarra for a heartbeat and then slowly lowered the bow to the ground. "Throw it over here," Ontarra instructed. The man picked it up again and tossed it halfway. "Now the club." He wriggled it out and cast it aside. "And your knife." The young warrior scowled, pulled the knife, and tossed it.

Ontarra laid his bow down, pulled his club, and circled around behind the man. The young warrior twisted his head, eyes glued to the big club, anticipating a deathblow at any instant. Ontarra ran a toe up and down the man's ribs and across the back of his waistband and then circled around front. He seemed about the same age as Ontarra. A chert dagger was skewered through his foot, moccasin and all. The point protruded a finger-length out the arch. Ontarra shook his head. "You've got big problems."

"Who are you?" the young man asked, his voice quavering slightly.

"I'm the guy that has the club." Ontarra crisscrossed the area, keeping one eye on the young warrior. He straightened up to stare out across the water. "They all went into the swamp?"

The warrior nodded. "I was about waist-deep when I stepped on this." He dipped his chin at the blade in his foot.

"When did you do that?"

"Midday."

Ontarra looked out across the swamp, calculating how far ahead they were. He stared down at the man's bloody moccasin, "You will have to cauterize that when you pull it out."

The warrior grimaced and looked at the sky. "Will you do it for me?"

"I don't have time." Ontarra stared back at the forest. "There'll be some warriors along after dark. They can do it." He looked down again. "Do you have any food?"

"No."

Ontarra dug in his pouch and tossed the man his last two pieces of venison. He picked up the club and knife, laying them a few feet away, so that he'd have to crawl to get them. Ontarra dipped his chin, turned, and sloshed into the morass, twisting the man's bow down into the mud at the water's edge before wading farther out.

Ontarra expected to feel the sear of sharp chert at every step. When he was waist-deep, he decided it was safer to swim. When it started getting shallow again, he drew himself along with his hands, feeling ahead as he went. The sun was only three finger-widths off the treetops when he crawled out the other side.

Ontarra loped along the trail of broken twigs and brush with a sense of urgency. The trackers seemed to be gaining on the outsiders. If they caught up, Sounia and Taiwa stood a good chance of being killed in the fight. Large gray humps of rock began taking over the forest floor around him. The stands of brush were getting patchy, and signs were harder to follow. He stopped, studying some moss that had been stepped in. Scanning ahead, he noticed a tangle of freshly broken branches woven into a thicket of brambles. An opening was smashed through the center. Someone had recently passed through them. Then he saw what appeared to be the top of a person's head, hiding from view in a depression just beyond the veil of brush.

Ontarra nocked an arrow and moved softly up behind a tree. He leaned his head around but quickly jerked it back, a baffled expression rearranging his features. He looked again and lowered his bow. Stepping down into the creek bed, he checked both ways to be certain he was alone. Four sharpened stakes were planted in the muck, slanting upward toward the tangle of brambles on the opposite bank. A young warrior was seated in the mud, hunched over as if he was relieving himself. Ontarra stepped around behind him, perching on his haunches to get better look.

He shifted his eyes from the warrior to the branches laced into the bramble patch above. The young man had charged through the brambles, seen the ditch too late to stop himself, and leaped to try to clear the stakes. Ontarra wasn't sure, but the stake appeared to have entered his rectum. It came out his left shoulder. The entire creek bed was a mass of tracks and blood. Ontarra stood up, marveling at how suddenly death could come for you. The lesson wasn't lost. These men were extremely dangerous when they knew they were being followed.

Ontarra kept on until he was afraid of losing the trail in the dark. He moved off into the forest, downwind of the track, in case any dogs were still following. Pulling himself up into a tree, he settled to wait out the night. An amazing number of bats flitted around the treetops. He watched them dip and whirl with interest. Then he realized that they weren't bats at all but cliff swallows.

The dogs never showed. As darkness crept away, Ontarra dropped down and made his way back to the trail. Most of the forest floor was rock now. Sign was hard to find, especially through sleep-crusted eyes. In a hand, the forest ahead seemed to open up into empty sky. Drawing closer, Ontarra realized he was on a huge cliff. Below him, spreading to the horizon, was Lake of the Okis.

Ontarra had heard of the giant escarpment that ran along the northern boundary of their territory, but he'd never imagined it being so awesome. A crescent of orange was rising from the lake to his right. A massive plain beneath him stretched outward to the sandy shores. He glanced down to see where to place his foot as he drew closer to the edge and did a double take. Recognizing the same weave of broken branches, he knelt down. They must have been in a hurry to be so obvious.

Ontarra moved around to the left to see what was hidden on the other side of the makeshift blind. He was about to step onto a steep slope that ran down to the precipice when he noticed skid marks. Moss and grass was all torn up and three elderberry stalks lay askew along the incline, one balanced precariously over the edge. Ontarra moved farther down to an overhanging ledge and crawled out. The height made his head swim. He lay flat on his belly and peered over. The broken body of another young warrior was sprawled on the rocks below; the elderberry stalks his life had slipped away on were scattered all around him.

Ontarra shimmied himself back from the brink and drew up onto his knees, shivering and shaking his head. He stared over at the weave of branches and exhaled a long breath. The blind was just a diversion to get the tracker to step on the stalks. Falling to one's death from such a height was frightening enough. Having so long to think about it was ... horrific. Ontarra stared out at the lake, trying to settle his breathing ... and he saw them. Two canoes were pulling out from a sandbar that stretched across the mouth of a deep bay.

He strained his eyes, trying to make out the occupants. Three figures were in each canoe. He was sure the ones in the center were women. Three men rushed out across the sandbar and into the surf. Ontarra could see by their stance that they were firing arrows. He prayed the canoes where out of range. Scanning the ridge to his left, he saw a valley that cut up through the cliff. He'd be half a day getting there and down. The canoes headed east along the shoreline. He grabbed a limb and leaned out. The cliff seemed to go on forever to the east. *There has to be a way down.*

Ontarra started running, staying a stone's cast back from the cliff to prevent surprises but still close enough to check their progress on the lake. He was keeping ahead. If he could find anything besides sheer cliff, he could get himself down. He ran on, jumping rocks, going around brush, and checking the lake whenever his nerves got to him. Suddenly, the forest disappeared, and a broad chasm opened in front of him. Ontarra's heart sank.

The cliff swung hard to the right, away from the lake. He dropped to his knees, crawling slowly to the edge. There was no way down. He had to go around. A rush of dread rolled over him like a wave. He couldn't lose them now! Ontarra crabbed back from the edge and jumped to his feet. He ran south, following the escarpment away from the lake, growing more desperate every time he checked for a way down. When he felt he could run no farther, he saw the cliff looping around ahead of him, making a swing back toward the lake. He looked to the sky and thanked the manitos.

Two warriors and a hunter struggled out of the surf and back up into the Erieehronon camp, cursing and blaming each other for the outsiders' escape. They fell silent as they studied the shambles of the campsite—two bodies lay face down in the sand. The youngest warrior approached a corpse, jabbing his foot under the rib cage to roll him over. A big snake uncoiled from a hole beneath the body, burying its fangs in the back of the young man's heel. Two more flashes of brown—a snake was on his calf, twining itself around his leg to rock its fangs in deeper. The second snake dangled from the buckskin of his tunic.

The young man screamed, hopping backward as he tried to tear the snake from his leg. On the second hop, there was a crunch. He dropped into the sand up to his knee. Gut-wrenching screams peeled across the sandbar. The warrior scrambled out and ran for water, snakes clamped all over him and squeezed their deadly juices into his bloodstream. Halfway to the water, he stopped. His head drew straight back and he stared up into the sky, as if he was praying for divine intervention. His entire body started to spasm. The young man collapsed and never moved again, even as sinuous bodies twined themselves around every appendage.

Snakes seemed to be leaping from the sand and slithering off in all directions. The hunter and warrior locked eyes. It had all happened so fast, they hadn't even budged.

"They're ... they're out on the water now," the hunter stammered, glancing furtively around the sandy strip for any other signs of tampering. "I can't track on water."

The warrior started backing out of the camp, one heart-pounding step at a time. "We'll tell them ... that they escaped."

When Ontarra reached the crest above the loop, he saw a waterfall. Over the ages it had cut a massive bowl down into the rock face. He dropped to his belly to see if there was a way down. Ontarra froze, his heart in his throat. Painted on a rock in front of his face was the figure of Glouscap, the trickster god, and beside it was the symbol of Orenda, magical Power. Ontarra held his breath as he stared all around. He saw a painting of Misshipeshu, the horned beast, and Pierce Head removing the brain from a corpse. Spiraling circles and red outlines of human hands were painted all around the bowl. Ancient symbols he'd never seen before were everywhere. Far down in the bottom, he saw a jumble of bones.

Ontarra climbed slowly to his feet and backed away. He didn't know if the bones were human or not, but this place oozed evil—he could feel it. He backed into the forest, hoping he hadn't awakened a force that he couldn't deal with. When he was well into the woods, he turned, running with renewed energy. He circled to give the bowl a wide berth and hit the escarpment again at a high promontory that jutted out beyond the ridge. He was much closer to the lake, but again there was no way down. The canoes were far off to his right now, hugging the shoreline and almost out of sight.

Ontarra sat on his heels, cradling his face in his hands. *No! Not when I was so close!* He forced himself up and made his way out onto the point. He could just make out Sounia's long black hair flying in the wind. Ontarra felt moisture brimming in his eyes. He fought back his urge to call out. He didn't want those men to know he was coming.

Mox stopped paddling to stare up at the gray cliff. Manak twisted around. "What do you see?"

"There." Mox pointed a meaty finger to a rocky outcrop on top of the ridge. "There's a man up there, watching us."

Manak squinted. All he could see was a vague outline against the sky. "That could be a tree or a boulder."

"No." Mox shook his head slowly, eyes shifting to Manak. "It's a warrior."

Kratcha turned her face up to the warm sunshine as she paddled into the canoe area of Teotonguiaton. She thumped the canoe into shore, balanced her way to the front, and hopped out. She'd cleaned herself up—pounded her buckskins with soaproot in the river, washed her hair and even combed it out, before tying two rows of hawk feathers down one side. Around her neck, a string of white and purple shell beads glittered in the sunlight.

Two slack-jawed fishermen helped her pull the canoe onto dry ground and then bent down, studying it suspiciously. Kratcha didn't really care; she felt great today. Besides, she had two more canoes hidden behind her shack. She just wanted to see Teotonguiaton a last time before leaving for Ounontisaston. If Sakawa agreed to take her in, they'd be quite wealthy.

Kratcha started up the hillside but stopped, her mouth sagging open. A crowd was gathered around a smoldering heap of ashes and charred poles—it had once been her home. She humped on up the hill, unable to take her eyes from the ruin. Pushing through the onlookers, she watched four men lifting a blackened corpse out of the cinders. An arm broke off the shriveled body, sending up a cloud of horrid-smelling ash. Everyone but Kratcha ran for air. A lopsided smile rearranged the lines of Kratcha's face, and her wet snicker started. People suddenly noticed who she was and moved away.

Someone shouted from the river, "Here comes another one!" Canoes had been floating by since dawn. The town's people shifted toward the river. Kratcha strolled back down to the landing, glancing back and chuckling and then forcing her face straighten again.

The canoe drifted lazily toward them. A woman screamed. Terrified voices cried out; wails and moans rolled along the river abreast of the canoe.

"What can it mean?"

"Who could have done such a thing?"

People stumbled back from the bank. Two hunters waded in and pulled the canoe to shore. Kratcha squinted from a distance. Buzkit was seated tranquilly on the bottom of the canoe, his head in his lap. A cloud of flies swarmed around the raw opening between his shoulders.

Men and women in the landing recoiled from the hideous sight—and then recoiled from Kratcha as she forced her way through. They didn't want to touch her accidentally—or worse, have her shadow touch them. Kratcha stared down at Buzkit. A black stone was jammed into one eye socket; the tip of a feather protruded from his mouth. A hunter bent and tugged the feather out—a trophy feather.

Kratcha rolled her head back, showing her two lonely teeth, black as ever, as her high-pitched cackle piercing the morning air. Kratcha threw her hands up over her head and reeled around in a circle, prancing on her toes and performing a little prayer dance she'd learned as a girl. Tears of laughter slithered down the creases of her weather-beaten face. She stopped for breath and palmed her eyes, glancing around at all the bewildered faces.

"Don't you understand?" Kratcha waved a bony hand at Buzkit. "The reckoning has begun! The last thing he saw was Shanoka! The last name on his lips was ... Sannisen!"

At Kandoucho, another canoe drifted past a landing. They'd found him yesterday, but no one dared go near him. Poutassa finally ordered one of his guards to go out and bring him in. The young man obediently paddled upstream and cut the tether holding Adontayat's canoe, but he didn't have the nerve to tow such a horror behind him.

Poutassa stared, mortified, at Adontayat's battered face as he floated by. Canoes coming in off the river veered away when they saw the cargo it carried. Poutassa gestured. Two guards waded out, hauled the canoe in to shore, and then removed themselves a good distance up the bank.

Poutassa studied the dark stone where Adontayat's eye should have been. A sense of foreboding crept over him. "Show me the feather." A guard bent down, gingerly tugging the feather from Adontayat's mouth. Poutassa's face drained. *Sannisen!* Afraid to hold the feather any longer, the guard let it flutter to the ground.

Poutassa felt as though his blood had suddenly turned to ice. Pulling his robe tighter around him, he swept his eyes up and down the river and then scanned the ridge on the opposite shore. Were they still alive? Or had their spirits remained to avenge them?

17

The only stops Manak allowed all day were quick jaunts to the beach to dump water from the canoes. These canoes didn't ride the swells as well as a dugout. Water slopped over the rails faster than Taiwa and Sounia could bail. The sun was sinking low when they saw a sheltered bay and headed in through a rocky inlet.

The men wearily hauled the canoes up behind the first high dune, where they'd be hidden from prying eyes. Manak had seen no signs of pursuit all day, so for the first time in a half-moon cycle, he agreed to light a fire. Sounia and Taiwa gathered driftwood while Matoupa sparked a fire using dead marsh grasses as tinder. Dekari wandered down to the water and started working on something with his knife. When he returned, he flopped down a gutted out snake carcass. Sounia cringed and pushed it away with her foot.

Dekari canted his head and frowned. "Cook it."

"I'm not eating a rattling snake! It's poison!"

"That's ridiculous," Dekari scowled. "The only thing that's poison is the head. My people have eaten them for years. It's better than turkey—no bones."

Taiwa could feel her bowels cramping just thinking about it. "Wait until tomorrow and tell us that."

Dekari stared at her, perplexed, and gave his head a shake. "Suit yourselves. I don't care if you starve." He picked up the big snake and laid it around the blazing pyre on the bed of coals that was already forming. Taiwa and Sounia shared a disgusted look.

"I'll starve anytime before I'll eat a predator again." Taiwa lifted her eyes from the snake to Manak. "Let me go check around the bay for cattail shoots." Manak glanced up from his thoughts. He nodded to Matoupa. Matoupa and Taiwa ambled up over the dune.

The bay was much larger than it appeared from the lake. Two arrow-flights wide, one arrow-flight across, Taiwa judged. Most of it was hidden by a tall dune that skirted the lake. Taiwa quickly gathered armloads of fresh shoots and loaded Matoupa down. When they were piled to his chin, she stopped, staring as if seeing him for the first time. It had been days since the Tunicans could shave the tops of their heads. Their fringe of hair seemed to stick out from beneath a fuzzy black mat surrounding their topknots. Taiwa giggled. Matoupa gave her a bewildered look, a grin curling the corners of his mouth.

"What?"

"If I put a dot here and here"—she poked his forehead with a finger—"it would look like you're wearing a river rat on your head." Matoupa chuckled. As they were about to leave, Taiwa stumbled onto a goose nest. It was a test, balancing the six big eggs on her arms, but she got them all back to the fire without an accident.

"Look," she said, beaming to Sounia as she revealed her find. Sounia grinned and scooped a hole in the sand. Taiwa laid the eggs in carefully, scraped some hot coals on top, and then shoved the sand back in place. Everyone started chewing on the sweet young shoots, too famished to take the time to cook them. Dekari tugged the snake from the fire, careful to keep the skin side to the sand. As it cooled, the skin curled off like stripped bark, leaving steaming pink meat. Taiwa was surprised. It looked a lot like the meat of a whisker fish. She was thankful she'd found the eggs—the snake meat suddenly looked very appealing.

Two eggs each, together with the shoots, was all either of the girls needed. Taiwa watched curiously as Matoupa slid each of the four logs farther into the sinuous flames. "Why do you always keep four logs sticking out?"

"They represent the four sacred directions. All fires are sacred, even temporary ones." Taiwa explained as she tossed the last of her egg to one of the gulls hovering overhead. She settled back on the warm sand, listening to the sound of waves breaking on the beach, and fell instantly into a deep sleep.

She dreamed she was flying. The vast country below her was parched and brown. The soil appeared sandy, unable to retain its moisture. The vegetation was dung-colored, as if it had been baked. She saw a fortified town on the banks of a muddy river. A sturdy palisade of thick logs started on the riverbank above the town, curved around three sides, and then butted into the river again, just below the town.

She swooped down. People with sad faces exited lodges with smooth walls of stone ... or perhaps it was dried mud. The steep roofs seemed to have grass growing from them. Four big red hills with flat sides towered over the lodges. A conspicuously large lodge sat on the flattened top of each hill.

The waves sound different. Taiwa opened an eye. It was still dark, but she sensed it was near morning. She sat up and raked the sand from her hair with her fingers. Sounia was curled up beside her. The men lay in shapeless heaps on the other side of the dying embers. Clouds had crept in during the night. She could tell by the crashes that the waves were bigger. Taiwa suddenly realized that Matoupa was gone.

She cast her eyes around in the predawn gloom for some sign of him and saw a faint silhouette against the lake. Pulling her feet under her, she unfolded upright and stepped softly around the fire. Manak rolled onto his side. Taiwa waited until his breathing fell back into a rhythm, and then she slipped silently past. She hesitated a moment, considering a dash for freedom, but she knew they'd catch her again. Besides, she couldn't leave Sounia all alone. Taiwa pursed her lips and continued down the slope toward the lake. She sat down in the sand, a stone's cast behind Matoupa. He was staring out at the lake, letting the surf roll up over his moccasins, with his arms crossed over his chest.

Taiwa was about to say something when a tiny thread of gold stretched out across the eastern horizon, separating the upper world from the lake. Two finger spans of sky lightened as she watched. The thread grew into a ribbon of pale blue, with a sliver of orange spreading out beneath it and pressing upward. Clouds captured the fiery rays, their bellies reflecting them back down at the lake. The blue rose higher, its shade deepening as the orange took on a crimson hue. The deep blue aura swelled upward, pushing away the night sky and fading the stars.

A blinding crescent blinked up over the horizon, shooting a trail of shimmering red across the water. It looked like Matoupa could step out and walk along the surface. The light of day took hold, and the vibrant colors melded into soft hues of white, gold, and lavender. Taiwa was overcome by a feeling of melancholy; she felt … homesick.

"Why are you with these men, Matoupa?" she asked softly. "You're not like them."

Matoupa spun around, embarrassed to be caught with his inner reflections. "Taiwa." He managed a tight smile. "You know, it has been a full cycle since I've heard my name spoken by a woman."

Taiwa climbed to her feet, moving up beside him to share the wonder of a new day. "So why are you with them?"

Matoupa folded his arms, stared out at the lake, and shook his head. "It's a very long story." He glanced down at her. "Why do you call it Lake of the Okis?"

"Okis are water demons. If your spirit is trapped beneath the waters of a river or lake in our land, it eventually ends up here. The okis gather here, tormenting those poor souls for all of time."

Matoupa arched his brows. "This is not a place where I would want to die in the water." Taiwa pursed her lips and nodded. Matoupa studied her. "Why is no one living in this part of your land?"

"It's said that in ancient times, evil men lived here. They worshipped the dark spirits, eating nothing but human flesh. Somewhere along that gray cliff is a passage to the underworld. If we could find it, we could burn it, cleanse it, and release the souls of their victims. Until then, they will haunt the cliff and the hinterlands of this peninsula."

Matoupa turned a sidelong glance. "You haven't seemed to be at all frightened."

"I don't believe those stories. Mother taught us that tales intended to frighten are generally untrue—made up for someone's ulterior motives. Besides, Sounia and I don't have much left to lose, do we? The next life has become appealing to me lately."

Matoupa drew a long breath and let it out slowly. "I'm sorry about all this, Taiwa." He stared out at the lake with a heavy heart.

"You're homesick, aren't you?" she asked. Matoupa bobbed his head. "The place you are homesick for … are there four square hills surrounded by lodges with smooth walls?" Matoupa locked eyes with her. Taiwa saw that she was right. "It's nestled up against a muddy river with a palisade of logs protecting it?"

"Taiwa, how could you know that?"

"I saw it in my dreams."

Matoupa shook his head. This girl had surprised him more than once. "You'll be amazed when you see it."

"What?" Taiwa stepped back, a dazed expression on her face. The urge to run crept over her again. It was the first time that Matoupa had actually seen fear in her eyes. He silently berated himself for being so stupid. "That's where you're taking us? How far is it? How will we ever get home again?" She backed away.

Matoupa gripped her shoulders. "Wait, Taiwa."

She twisted away. "You'll never get us there!" she shouted. "My brother is coming! And you'd be wise to not to be around when he finds us!" Taiwa spun around and stomped back to the camp. That she hadn't accepted that all her family was dead made Matoupa feel even worse. He hung his head and slogged up into the camp.

Everyone was starting to move around now. Taiwa sat silently at the hearth, drawing lines in the sand with a stick. Manak stepped up beside Matoupa and stared anxiously out at the wind-driven chop rising on the lake. "Can we travel on that?"

"Just barely. We'll have to hug the shore in case it gets any worse."

Taiwa headed off into the brush while the men were dragging the canoes down to the inlet. Manak signaled to Matoupa to follow her. Matoupa wandered over and stuck his head through the brambles. She yelled, and he backed away. When she finally came out, tears glistened in her eyes.

Sounia ran over. "Taiwa, what's wrong?"

Taiwa closed her eyes, rocking her head back and forth. "I've got the red gut worms." She dropped down on her knees next to the hearth, forlornly poking a stick in the sand and yanking it back out.

"We can't do anything about that now," Matoupa sighed. "Come on; we're leaving."

Taiwa glared at him. She scooped a last handful of sand and climbed to her feet. When they bobbed out into the lake, Manak poorly timed his turn. A wave swung him back toward the beach; the next broke over the side. They hauled the canoe in to shore, emptied it, and started off again.

An east wind swelled the waves to whitecaps. By midmorning, the girls couldn't keep up with the water crashing over the rails. Dekari pointed to a small river, and they headed in. "Do you know this place?" Manak yelled as they surged into the mouth.

Dekari gave his head a shake. "No, but we have to get across the peninsula anyway; we'd be at the gorge by nightfall, and they might be watching for us there." An arrow-flight up the stream, a beaver dam blocked their path. They struggled getting the canoes over it but got moving again, only to find that there was no way out of the pond above.

Manak wanted the canoes sunk, so they unloaded everything onto shore. While he was watching them slip beneath the surface, a beaver swam by, floating a huge limb toward his dam. When he saw the men, his tail smacked the water, and he dove from sight. "Did you see the size of that otter?" Manak whispered to Matoupa. "He grew so fat, the only place left to fill was his tail!"

They strolled through the forest at a more casual pace this time. Dekari assured Manak that they wouldn't be running into anyone out here. Taiwa's spirits brightened when she smelled lilacs, following the fragrance of a bush in full bloom. Manak reluctantly agreed to wait while she gathered sprigs to make the tea that kills worms. A bee decided it liked something about Dekari. He swatted at it twice and then screamed and ran, with the bee in hot pursuit.

The Tunicans roared at the sight of a man frightened by a bee. Dekari returned a hand later. "Their poison bloats me up until I can't breathe," he mumbled, flustered by their smirks.

The forest flowers were coming into bloom, sprouting up through the thick moss that carpeted the forest floor. Taiwa plucked some yellow coneflowers, weaving them into Sounia's hair as they walked. Mox trudged silently behind them, eyes glued to Sounia's supple form rippling beneath her tattered buckskin dress.

Late in the day, they hit a river that flowed south instead of north. They followed it until the sun was low in the sky. Three lodges in a clearing ahead marked a fish camp, the first sign that they were approaching Iannaoa. They skirted the clearing, seeing no other lodges until dusk.

A farm lodge sat alone in a burned-out clearing up ahead. Soaring seagulls in the distance indicated that the lake was close. A man and woman poked petun sprouts into mounds in their field. At the edge of the forest, an infant mewed from his cradleboard. Manak and Mox were gone a long time, circling around the little plot and investigating the immediate area.

When they returned, they stood just inside the treeline, watching the young couple and whispering, before slinking back into the brush. Manak held a finger up to his lips for silence. He gestured to move deeper into the forest. When Manak felt they were safe from detection, he sat the girls on a log, and stared over at Dekari.

"Where the river meets the lake, there are six canoes on the beach. Those two"—Manak jerked his chin toward the field—"are planting petun. They might still have some seed." Dekari rubbed his chin, nodding. Manak steepled his fingers, studying Matoupa and Dekari. "We'll pretend we're traders. You two just get me in close enough so I can use my club."

"No!" Sounia gasped. "You can't kill those people just for petun seed!"

"Keep them quiet!" Manak growled at Mox as they headed out. Mox pulled out his rawhide bindings, tied Taiwa's wrists to her knees, and wound a gag into her mouth. He turned to Sounia with a lewd grin, double-wrapping her gag as he watched Manak and the traders disappear into the brush. The look in Mox's eyes made Sounia's heart patter.

Without warning, Mox shoved his leggings down. His huge swollen member looked as if it should be poking out between the legs of a bear. He swung it back and forth in Sounia's face. She was appalled by the grotesque thing bobbing around in front of her and half-expected a forked tongue to flit out from the big slit in the end. Mox's bulging belly sagged down around it, completing the disgusting spectacle. Mox grabbed Sounia's shoulders, forcing her down on all fours like some forest creature. Before she could get over her shock and realize what was happening, he had her dress yanked up over her head.

Near the farm lodge, Dekari and Matoupa stepped out into the field and ambled casually toward the young couple. Manak stayed behind them. A scolding blue jay gave them away. The woman looked up, shouting a warning to her husband as she backed away. The man trotted over, scooped up the cradleboard, and then wrapped an arm defensively around his wife.

Dekari held up a hand. "Ho, friend! We have traveled far and seem to have lost our bearings!" The couple kept moving backward as they eyed the intruders suspiciously. "Can you tell me where Ouaroronon is?" The man hesitated. Manak slowly slid his club out.

A heart-stopping scream rang out from the forest. Then a second shriek—it could have been a woman in agony or some poor creature in its death throes. The young couple turned and ran. The men stared at each other. Matoupa spun around and ran flat out for the forest. "Go check the lodge for seed," Manak fumed at Dekari before turning and trotting after Matoupa.

Matoupa charged through the brush, pulling his knife as he went. This time he was going to kill Mox—if he could. Another high-pitched scream rang out. Matoupa crashed on, a sinking feeling in his gut. He charged into the clearing, prepared to die if he must. He glanced around. Taiwa was sitting where they'd left her. He followed her saucer-shaped eyes to his left.

Sounia was on her knees, pulling a gag from her mouth with her left hand, while her right hand squeezed Mox's swollen testicle. Mox was on his knees, mouth agape, tongue protruding between his teeth, with his leggings down around his ankles. His hands were up beside his head, fluttering as if he was surrendering to an enemy warrior. Sounia squeezed with all of her might. An ear-splitting scream died in choked gurgles. Saliva dripped from Mox's chin. His big snake had suddenly lost all of its muscle.

Sounia was surprised that the testicle expanded back to its original shape. She always thought that you could crush one like an egg. She tried again. "*Arrrrhh!*" Mox curled over backward, his legs bent at an impossible angle. Matoupa gritted his teeth and squeezed his legs together. Manak charged into the clearing and froze, staring in stunned silence at the ludicrous scene.

Sounia still had a firm grip on Mox. "Well, maybe I can rip it off then!" Sounia spat at him. "You filthy snake! You could kill a woman with that thing!"

Manak dropped down and poked his knife into Sounia's neck. "Let him go!" Manak ordered.

Sounia shot Manak a cold stare and squeezed Mox again. "*Ahhhg!*"

Manak moved the point of the knife to her cheek. "All right! You can spend the rest of your life blind!"

Sounia squeezed once more—"Ahhhhrr!" Mox's scream was weaker this time—she released her grip and stood up, brushing herself off indignantly. Mox moaned with every breath, his stomach spewing morning meal between whimpers. Manak rocked Mox with a foot, but he'd passed out, and judging by the fetal position, and low moans, he wouldn't be getting up for quite a while. Matoupa tried hard to keep the smirk off his face, while Manak stomped back and forth muttering oaths, trying to decide whether they could afford to leave Mox behind.

Finally, Matoupa and Manak each grabbed one of Mox's arms and headed for the lake, dragging Mox on his backside, with his leggings still trailing down around his ankles. Sounia and Taiwa followed along. "Look at that thing," Sounia said, dipping her chin at the source of her disgust as it dragged through the dirt in front of them. She screwed her face up. "I'd sooner couple with a rutting stag."

It was growing dark by the time they dragged Mox back to the farm lodge. Dekari met them out front. "It's all been germinated," he said. He glanced down at Mox. "What happened to him?"

"Never mind," Manak growled. "Let's just get to the lake."

"We'd best hurry," Dekari agreed. "Those two are going to come back with warriors."

When they reached the lake, they left Mox behind a dune and headed down to the beach. The six canoes at the river mouth were still pulled up on the sand, but four fishermen were loading nets into them for morning. Manak herded everyone in behind a stand of dune grass to wait for the men to leave. He whispered to Dekari, "How wide is the lake here?"

It's a half-day across," Dekari answered softly, "but no one ever crosses Iannaoa. You never leave sight of the shoreline, or the lake might rise up and swallow you."

"Don't start with the superstitious babble again."

"It's true," Taiwa piped in nervously. "Iannaoa was a man who lost his entire family to the lake. He never got over his grief, so he walked out into the lake and drowned himself to be with them. Since that day, when Iannaoa weeps, the lake boils up into huge waves. It happens in less time than it takes to tell the story. I've seen it many times. If you are out on the lake when that happens, it will swallow you."

Manak looked to Dekari. Dekari nodded. "No one ever tries to cross it." Manak shook his head and stared out at the lake. He started to ask Dekari something else but then followed Dekari's squint up the eastern shoreline. Two hands of canoes were coming around a point of land and heading their way.

"By the deities," Dekari's moaned, "this is never going to be over."

"Perfect," Manak muttered. "Well ... we can't go around the lake now.

Those people aren't going to let us." Manak jumped up and sprinted down the beach. He was among the fishermen before they could react. The first two fell, never knowing what hit them. The third had time for a single scream. The fourth turned and ran, plunging through the river mouth and disappearing into the twilight.

"Come on!" Manak yelled. Dekari and Matoupa hustled the girls down to the canoes. Matoupa splashed back through the surf, hauling a canoe along behind him. He raced up the dune and dragged Mox down, tumbling his bulk over the bow. He landed face down, with his head crammed in the front. Matoupa jumped in and pushed off. The war canoes had closed half of the distance. Matoupa winced at the sight of Mox spread-eagled over the brace in front of him, rocking with the waves. He wished Mox had taken the time to pull his leggings up.

"Push hard!" Manak hollered over the rumble of the swells. He checked on the war canoes again—they were bearing down fast. "Are you certain that they won't follow us out?"

Dekari's heart was in his throat. His voice wouldn't come, so he simply nodded his head. In the heartbeat that Manak's attention was diverted, his canoe rose up on a swell, yawing sideways down the backside, and taking on water when it pounded into the trough.

"I hate these flimsy toy canoes!"

Ontarra found a rockfall and managed to get himself down the escarpment. He crossed the plain that bordered the lake on a dead run. When he made the beach, the canoes were already out of sight. He rested on his heels to catch his breath and then set out on the hard-packed sand near the water's edge. Being cold and wet wasn't as much of a concern now as making time.

Whenever he rested, he scanned the horizon, hoping to see three specks against the skyline. About midmorning, he came to a river mouth that he had to swim to cross. Off to his right, the gray cliff jutted out toward the lake, forming two identical round-topped hills that looked like huge breasts. He studied the odd formation as he shook himself off. A fresh track up the sand dune caught his eye. Dropping to his knee, he ran a finger over the scuffs. *Snapping turtle.*

He tracked the turtle up into a patch of snakeweed. She was long gone, but Ontarra found two hands of eggs buried in the sand. He slid the leathery round eggs into his carry pouch and set off again, popping one into his mouth as he ran. Ontarra squashed out the contents, forcing it down his throat in one quick swallow and then spitting out the crushed shell. Snapping turtle eggs were horrid. They tasted like a combination of rotting fish and what Ontarra imagined skunk must taste like. If he ate while he was running, with his mind on other things, he could get them down and keep them there.

Twice he came across places where the outsiders had dragged their canoes up onto the beach to dump water out. There was no way that he could tell in sand how old the marks were. Day progressed into evening, and there was no indication that he was catching up. Ontarra sat down in the wet sand, letting the waves slosh up around him and slide away. He was reaching the limit of his endurance. He should rest and try to sleep ... but he just couldn't.

He climbed wearily to his feet and plodded on. He found a piece of driftwood that made a suitable walking stick. It seemed to help. The muscles in his legs ached. If he slept right now, he might not get up again for a while. Ontarra trudged on into the night. The stars were beginning to disappear behind clouds in the west, and he could feel the wind off the lake picking up. The weather was changing. He came to a marshy inlet and waded in. As he approached the opposite bank, he heard a familiar sound. Climbing out silently from the water, he walked on his toes to a stand of cattails. He could see the outline of a black-head goose on her nest.

Ontarra raised the walking stick over his head, but something that Toutsou once told him came back. *If you kill a black-head goose, make sure you also get its mate. They are devoted to each other for life and will pine away when separated.* Ontarra thought about Sounia and slowly lowered the driftwood.

He tried another turtle egg while he walked away, choked, and gagged it back up. For a hand of time, he sat washing his mouth out, but the taste remained. As night wore on, sleep tried to overtake him. Ontarra went out in the surf, dropping to his knees and letting the waves break over him. As long as he was wet, he could fight the need for sleep. He expected to see the twinkling of a hearth fire at any moment; he couldn't give in now.

The first glimmers of dawn ended any hope he had of catching them asleep. The sun rose in a spectacular display of colors that were totally wasted on Ontarra. His feet had grown so heavy, every step was an ordeal. His mood turned dismal. They'd be moving again by now. When the sun was a finger span over the horizon, he came to a channel running inland to a large bay. The water was deep. He'd have to swim it, and he didn't have the energy left. Ontarra flopped down, hanging his head in frustration.

Elbows on his knees, he rested his face in his hands, listening to the raucous sounds of gulls bickering on the far side. Ontarra popped his head back up. They were at the base of a tall dune, hovering on the breeze and then swooping down with quick snatches and gliding away to the safety of the lake to gulp down whatever was dangling from their beaks. Ontarra pushed himself up. Leaning on the driftwood, he walked down the inlet toward the dune. He saw the furrows left by the canoes first. Ontarra broke into a trot, scanning the base of the dune as he went—the charred remains of a hearth fire!

Ontarra waded in and swam across. Gulls scattered to the air at his approach, screeching indignantly. He poked his walking stick under the tattered remains of a snakeskin, tossing it down the beach to get rid of the gulls. He stirred the ashes. A few faint embers glowed to life as fresh air hit them.

Ontarra ran down to the lake, staring east along the shoreline. There was no sign of them. The waves were high—canoes wouldn't be visible for far. Ontarra slogged back up to the hearth fire. Two white spots beside a hearthstone caught his eye. Dropping down, he brushed the sand away and plucked out two fat goose eggs. He shook one next to his ear. Already cooked. Ontarra looked east, a faint smile touching his lips. *They know I'm coming.*

Ontarra tore the shells from the eggs and wolfed them down. They tasted wonderful. He sat and scooped a hole in the sand. He laid the turtle eggs in the hole and then smoothed it over with sand. His eyelids grew heavy as the chore of digestion sapped his strength. He rested his head on his knees a moment.

When he woke, it was late afternoon. He cursed his stupidity. He'd wasted valuable time, and if the sun had been out instead of this solid gray overcast, he'd be burned and blistered.

Ontarra lurched upright but flopped back down, rubbing the muscles of his legs before trying again. While he was working the stiffness out, he noticed a set of tracks heading up into some brush. He hobbled over and poked his head in but yanked it back when the stench of human excrement struck him. He didn't have the stomach for that right now. The corners of his eyes wrinkled quizzically. Had he seen what he thought he'd seen? Sucking a breath he stuck his head back in. An arrow was scratched in the sand, pointing east.

Ontarra alternated between running and walking to save his strength. Several times, he had to swim the mouths of rivers and inlets. The outsiders would have to cross the peninsula soon. They wouldn't want to risk being seen at the towns along the Onghiara River, and the Erieehronon would know better than to try and cross into Sennikae lands.

As the sun settled toward the treetops, Ontarra saw the smoke of hearth fires in the distance. He moved up into the trees, padding ahead cautiously until he could get a better look.

The widest river he'd ever seen blocked his path. Across the enormous river mouth, was a fortified town. People moved in and out through guarded entries. At the shoreline, a canoe landing was a hive of activity. Ontarra slumped back on his heels, twisting his head around to stare bleakly in the direction he'd just come. This had to be the Onghiara. Somehow, he'd missed where the outsiders came in off the lake.

He sat for a long time in a black depression. There was no way he could prevent their escape now. A day—perhaps two—and they would be in Erieehronon lands. Ontarra heard his mother's voice inside his head. *It isn't the problems that you have but how you handle them that matters.* Ontarra stood up and sucked a weary breath, a grim look of acceptance settling on his face. Turning on a heel, he headed up into the forest. He had to get across Iannaoa.

The terrain climbed slowly as he made his way inland from the lake. Moving along inside the treeline, he kept the Onghiara in sight to keep his bearings. The river appeared to be quite deep, yet the current flowed incredibly fast. The surface of the river was a maelstrom of swirls and eddies—impossible to swim or even get a canoe across. He struck a hill, trudged to the top, and stared down through the trees. The river was hidden from sight now, in the depths of a deep gorge. He could see sheer rock walls on the far side, and he thought he could see the outlines of people standing along the top.

He made his way down the backside of the hill to keep out of sight. An arrow-flight farther on, he veered back toward the river. This time the far side appeared deserted. Stalking down out of the trees, he crept to the edge of the gorge, crawled out to the brink, and peered over. The height took his breath away. The river was tightly packed between two canyon walls, higher than the escarpment along the lake. Water surged and swelled in white-capped breakers, crashing in foamy sprays over boulders the size of lodges that had tumbled down from the cliffs. Fish jumped, trying to make headway against the torrent. The little white specks bobbing on the surface seemed to be gulls.

Beneath him, the river made a sharp turn, pounding into the cliff face and swirling, eating away at the rock. The water churned and whorled as it looked for a way out of the cauldron. A gaping black hole opened up, twining its way across the pool before disappearing. Another formed as the first died away. It snared a tree limb, upended it in the swirling vortex, and sucked it into the depths of the river. Another hole surfaced; flotsam and debris whirled around the edges and then disappeared down its maw. Ontarra shuddered. He had the unnerving feeling the okis were staring up at him through those holes, drawing him to them and trying to entice him over the edge.

Ontarra backed away from the brink. He stood on quivering legs and then ran. In the safety of the woods, he stopped to get his breath. He wasn't sure why he felt so shaken, but one look at that place was enough for a lifetime. The farther up the river he went, the deeper the gorge looked. Before long, he detected a sound. Or was it a feeling? The ground seemed to be trembling under his feet. Ahead, above the treetops, he could see white mist billowing high into the air. *The cataract.*

Ontarra moved up onto a ridge an arrow-flight back from the gorge. He could hear a steady rumbling now, like distant thunder. As he drew closer, he could see water tumbling over the edge of an abyss. Ontarra's heart was in his throat. He felt as if he was approaching an enemy camp. He saw faces floating in the mist, swirling and melding together, and then fading away again. He settled himself down on a rocky bank well back from the deafening roar. Through the shrouding mist he could see a white wall of water bending around in a crescent. A shaft of sunlight broke through the blanket of cloud and a rainbow arced up over the gorge. It disappeared instantly when the sunlight faded out again. So much Power focused in one place was wondrous and frightening. The noise alone was enough to chill a man's soul.

The entire area was drenched from the mist settling down like a heavy spring fog. An overhanging table rock protruded out over the cataract, creating a large open area that was covered in offerings to the divinities. Corn, petun, shells, and spring flowers were set in cracks and depressions. Ontarra knew his mother would have wanted him to see it, but he wasn't going any closer.

He noticed an unusual rock lying next to his leg and picked it up. A perfect leaf that looked like maple was frozen in the stone. His mother had kept several of these in the basket under her platform. Power objects, she called them. The manitos were unhappy with the first world they created, so they turned everything to stone and started again. Ontarra heard a sound above the perpetual din and glanced up.

A big man worked his way out onto the rocky shelf overhanging the gorge, dragging a girl by the arm. They were screaming at each other, but their words were drowned out by the thunder of the cataract. The girl appeared to be no older than Taiwa; the man, perhaps a hand older than Ontarra. He wore only leggings and moccasins. The club hanging from his waistband marked him as a warrior. The girl leaned away, throwing her legs out ahead of her. She sank her teeth into the man's hand. The warrior slapped her and then used both hands to haul her toward the chasm.

Ontarra instinctively pulled his club but hesitated. He dropped the club to the ground and stripped off all his clothing. Scooping up some black mud on his fingers, he smeared three lines on each cheek and circles around his nipples and navel, and then he smacked handprints over his belly and legs. He grabbed the stone with the leaf in it and dashed down through the trees. Ontarra stepped out onto the table rock. Ignoring the warrior and his victim, he began dancing and swirling across the ledge. As he got closer, he was shocked. The man was a monster—even bigger than Mox—but there was no turning back now.

Ontarra spun to a sudden halt, as if he'd just noticed the man and woman for the first time. The brute released his grip on the girl and started pulling his club. Ontarra molded an insane grin to his face and danced up within a few paces of the murderous eyes glowering down at him. "Your mother must have wintered with a bear to spawn a fat slug like you!" he shouted. He threw his head back with a maniacal laugh, watching the man through slitted eyes. Nothing could be heard above the crashing roar of falling water.

The corners of the man's eyes wrinkled with confusion. The club lowered a bit as he studied the shaman lines on Ontarra's naked body. Ontarra laughed again, mouthed a few words, and then pointed at the leaf in his Power rock. The brute lowered his club some more, tilting his head to one side.

Puzzled wrinkles tracked across his forehead. Ontarra tossed him the rock. The monster caught it against his chest with his free hand, glancing down to take a better look at it.

Ontarra prayed—and leaped. Springing off his left foot, he kicked out hard with his right, slamming the hand and the rock into the man's chest. The monstrosity staggered back three steps but stopped himself, teetering right on the brink, arms flailing wildly and eyes bulging with terror. He seemed to regain his balance. Ontarra stepped closer for another kick. The warrior lashed out with his club. Ontarra leaned away, and the momentum of the club carried the man over the edge. Time seemed to slow as Ontarra watched the horror alter the man's face. Mouth wide open in a silent scream, he toppled backward into eternity. His feet were the last thing to leave.

Ontarra dropped to his knees and crawled apprehensively toward the edge. The cloud of mist shrouding the falling water seemed alive. Vaporous shapes surged in and out. Ghostly features formed wispy arms that beckoned to him and then melted together, sliding into oblivion. Ontarra summoned his courage, sucked a deep breath, and peered over. A boulder-strewn river lay far below. The height was staggering … hypnotic. Power seemed to emanate from everything: the thundering roar, the white wall of water, the rocks, the mist.

The big warrior was smashed across a boulder directly below, head and arms still intact but his torso a gory red splash. His shredded leggings were floating in the foaming current. Ontarra felt a tingling sensation in his hands and feet. It shot him back to his adolescence at old Ounon, when he'd slid down the roof of a longhouse, trying in vain to get a grip with his hands or feet before the inevitable fall. He dropped to his belly and squirmed back from the edge, heart pattering. The forces of more than one world were centered here. It was mind-boggling why such a place as this should even exist.

Ontarra climbed to his feet, scrutinized the frightened girl sitting with her mouth agape, and offered her his hand. She crabbed backward. Ontarra dropped his arm, shrugged, and trotted off across the ledge and up into the brush. He tried wiping himself clean with wet leaves, but only managed to smear the mud. As he was pulling his leggings on, he saw the girl coming up the hill. She stopped a stone's cast away.

"Who *are* you?" she shouted.

Ontarra didn't answer. He finished dressing and slid his weapons back in place. Then he jerked his head toward the forest. He studied her with from the corner of his eye as they walked, the head numbing sound of the cataract fading behind them. She was a little older than Taiwa; very pretty. A knee-length buckskin dress and three hawk feathers hanging from a tiny braid over her ear indicated she was of some stature. "Why was that freak trying to throw you over?" Ontarra asked.

The girl raised a brow and smiled. "You talk. I'm glad; I was beginning to wonder."

"That place doesn't exactly accommodate good conversation." Ontarra grinned back. "So what was that all about? You yank out a handful of his pubic hair or something?"

She didn't laugh; she looked off into the distance, pursing her lips and letting her breath out in a long sigh, "He is ... *was* ... Brak. He was our greatest warrior. All he's been doing for the past cycle, though, is guarding the shamans. More wealth and prestige, he said. He's been forcing gifts on me since my moon flows began. I tried to tell him that I wasn't interested. He wouldn't listen ... until last night, that is. Said if he couldn't have me, no one could. I think he was hoping I'd change my mind before we got here."

"That bite you laid on him probably didn't improve his mood any." Ontarra tipped his head to one side. "He defected to the shamans?" He stared off through the trees toward the cataract. "Can I have one of your feathers?" The girl shrugged. Unraveling one from her hair, she handed it over. Ontarra held it against a tree, notched it with his dagger and sliced the tip off. "Wait here."

He trotted back down the ridge and out onto the table rock, searching until he found a suitable stone. Then he crawled out to the overhang. He balanced the stone on top of the feather near the edge of the drop, smiling as he climbed to his feet and turned to head back. She was at the edge of the forest, watching. They moved in silence back up onto the ridge.

"So, who are you?" she shouted.

Ontarra thought a moment as they continued into the forest. "I'm from a faraway place. My name really doesn't matter."

"I need to call you something." She frowned, gazing up at him. "I think I'll call you ... Mud-Face." She giggled.

"That's a good enough name." Ontarra nodded. "What is yours?"

"My name is Kiska."

Ontarra stopped in his tracks and turned to her with a slack-jawed expression. "Have you ever been to Teotonguiaton?" Kiska gave her head a negative shake, wondering what she'd said to put that look on his face. "Ever heard of a woman named Kratcha?" Kiska rocked her head. Ontarra turned and started walking again.

"What is it?" Kiska asked with concern, trotting to keep up.

"Nothing ... just an odd coincidence. Who are your parents?"

"I hardly knew them," Kiska said. "They died on the river when I was young. Their canoe got caught in the current, and they jumped off onto rocks just above the cataract. They were there for days. People floated food down to them, but there was no way to get out and rescue them. One morning ... they were gone."

"What clan are you, Kiska?"

"Myeengun—Wolf."

Ontarra nodded. "Is there a town ahead?"

"Not on this side. There are three towns on the far shore, but no one lives on this side. The men hunt and fish over here. Everyone comes back at night, though. They fear the eaters of human flesh that live out in the hinterlands. Just last cycle, a girl was found half-eaten near the cataract." Kiska was taken aback by the malignant look that crossed Ontarra's face. She didn't say anything more until the silence grew uncomfortable. "I'm from Gaousge, where Iannaoa empties into the Onghiara."

Ontarra stopped, gripping Kiska by the shoulders. "So you have a canoe? You can get me across the river?" Kiska bobbed her head. "Can you show me how to get to the land of the Erieehronons?"

Kiska's eyes flew wide, and she stepped back. "It would be your last journey, Mud-Face. An Attawondaronk warrior cannot travel into their lands and expect to live."

"I can't explain, Kiska, but I have to go there."

Kiska shook her head reluctantly. She looked around for a bare patch of soil to draw on and then looked at her left hand. She made a fist over her breast, pointing her thumb straight up at the sky. "The eastern end of Iannaoa looks like my hand; my thumb is the river. Gaousge is here," she said, pointing to her largest knuckle. "All across here is Sennikae lands." Kiska traced a finger across her knuckles, stopping on the outside edge of her smallest knuckle. "You don't reach Erieehronon territory until you get to here."

Ontarra studied his fist, trying to visualize the distance. He shook his head and started walking again. They came out of the forest at the edge of a small river.

Kiska pointed. "If we go downstream, there's a rope bridge." The bridge was at the river mouth where it joined the Onghiara. The Onghiara above the cataract was a torrent of surging swells and whitecaps. Ice flows still coming off the lake piled up against boulders, careening around their sides, and rushing madly toward destruction.

"It's the biggest river I've ever seen," Ontarra mumbled, awestruck by the wide expanse.

"That's not even the other shore you're looking at," Kiska said, grinning as she tried to keep her balance on the swaying bridge. "That's an island."

A well-worn path wended through the trees along the Onghiara's bank. "Are we likely to meet anyone?" Ontarra asked.

Kiska stared up at the gray clouds, judging how low the sun might be. "No, it's too late in the day. Everyone with their wits about them is already back across." Kiska studied her feet as she walked. "Do you think you could take me with you?" Ontarra turned, a curious look on his face. "Everyone saw Brak drag me out of the town," she explained. "The shamans are going to persecute me."

"Who is your chief shaman?"

"Chinnotai."

Ontarra shook his head. "I've never heard of him. I'd pay him a visit if I had the time."

"You could leave me with the Sennikae. I think they would accept me. I could try to make a home with them. There's nothing left for me at Gaousge."

"Kiska?" Ontarra said softly. "Have you ever heard of Sannisen?"

"Of course, he—haven't you heard? Word came that he is dead."

"Then you know that the shamans have gained control throughout the land?"

Kiska nodded sadly. "Yes, here too. Our chief grew ill and died during the winter storms."

Ontarra cursed under his breath, staring out across the river as he walked. Kiska saw he was troubled and left him to his thoughts. It was dusk when they reached the lake. The Onghiara's mouth was jammed with ice. "Ice keeps coming off the lake for a full moon cycle each spring," Kiska cautioned. She slid down into some brush and uncovered a canoe. "We have to go wide, out into the lake, to get around it." She made her way up into the bow. Ontarra shoved off and hopped into the back.

The top of an orange moon appeared over the horizon, splashing the bellies of some low clouds in a pale magenta. When the moon pushed up through the cloud layer, the lake was utter darkness. Chunks of ice scraping along the elm bark was disconcerting, but Ontarra couldn't see to avoid them. Kiska pointed to some twinkling lights along the far shore. "That's the town," she said softly. Ontarra headed in. He thumped the canoe into the sand just below a group of lodges.

"Kiska," he whispered, "can I have another of your feathers?" She unwound one and gave it to him. "I can't take you with me," he said, avoiding her eyes as he notched the feather and removed the tip. He could feel her sense of betrayal cutting like a knife. "There is only one place you can go. Have you heard of Khioetoa?"

"Yes," she whispered hesitantly, "near the west end of the lake."

Ontarra nodded. "You will be welcome there. Go and take whatever you need from Brak's lodge. Leave this"—he handed the feather back—"on his sleep platform. Then take a canoe and leave tonight. It will take you about four days to get there. When you come to a river almost as big as this one, turn up it, and then turn into the mouth of the first river on your right. The town is a half day up. You'll see canoes on the south shore, but don't stop or talk with anyone until you get there." Ontarra started to push away.

"Wait," Kiska said in a low tone. She trotted off into the darkness. After a hand of time, Ontarra started growing nervous. He was about to leave, when he saw her silhouette, hunched over and tiptoeing along the shoreline. "Here," she said breathlessly, dropping two dried fish on the floor of the canoe.

"Thank you, Kiska." Ontarra shoved off with his paddle, swinging the bow out toward the lake. Kiska bobbed her head, rotating the feather curiously between her fingers. Her voice floated out to him through the pitch. "The story of these feathers has preceded you. The manitos be with you, Sannisen."

Ontarra made a wide arc out into the lake to avoid any curious eyes at Gaousge. Then he swung back in close to follow the shore. He laid a fish over his knees, tearing off chunks between strokes and devouring them both as he worked his way east. The shoreline began a wide swing to the south. A light rain started to fall. Heat lightning flickered in the western sky, and the rain grew heavier. Ontarra had to put in.

He dragged the canoe up the beach and over the first hill of sand. Exhausted, he rolled it over and crawled underneath. He was already drenched, but it felt good to be out of the weather. The warm rain awakened the mating desires of the frogs. A chaotic medley of chirps, rattles, grunts, and croaks calmed his nerves, lulling Ontarra to sleep.

An eerie presence jolted him awake. It was still pitch black, but the rain had ended. He held his breath, eyes searching warily out beneath the rail of the canoe. He saw a movement in the dune grasses. Frilled leggings and low-cut moccasins padded across the sand toward him. The moccasins stopped a handspan from his nose.

Ontarra grabbed the ankles and threw himself upright, the canoe flying off to the side as the warrior took the full impact of the fall on his shoulder blades. Ontarra dropped with both knees on the warrior's diaphragm, twisted a club from his hand, and raised it high in one fluid motion. Someone behind snatched it away. Ontarra rolled across the sand, coming to his feet a canoe-length away.

Young warriors, with bows and clubs at the ready, surrounded him. Two older men stood farther back, arms folded across their chests, waiting to see what his next move would be. Ontarra glanced around him at grim faces. *Kiska was right. Not even one night, and the Erieehronons have got me.*

The warrior on the ground got his wind back. He crawled to his knees, cursing and demanding his club back. Ontarra searched his mind for some means of saving himself. "I have come with an important message ... for the trader Dekari," he said slowly. The young warrior was coming at him now. Ontarra laid his hand on his club. He'd take as many with him as he could. One of the older warriors barked a command. The young warrior froze in his tracks, eyes blazing.

The older warriors talked to each other in low tones. "Why would he tell us something so stupid?" The other rubbed his chin without answering.

Ontarra heard the word "stupid," surprised that he understood it so clearly. He studied the angry young warrior in front of him and realized his mistake. His head was shaved on both sides, leaving a thick swath of hair down the center that ended in a long tail hanging down his back—symbol of the Sennikae warrior elite. Ontarra looked over at the older men. He pulled his club between a thumb and forefinger and dropped it to the sand. Reaching behind his back, he tossed his dagger down beside it.

"I am the grandson of Togo, False Face of the Sennikae, at the town of Joneadih."

"Bah!" the angry young warrior hissed. "He is Dwakanah! I will remove his lying head from his body!" He took a step toward Ontarra. One of the older warriors stopped him with a sharp rebuke.

Ontarra understood the word "head," and he bristled at the insulting sound of the word "Dwakanah," although he had no idea what it meant. The older warriors talked to each other again, all their heads bobbing in agreement. "Tie him and gather his weapons. We'll take him with us to Cattaragus."

"What do you mean, all the shamans of Teotonguiaton are dead?" Hiatsou demanded. "How can that be?"

Poutassa stared vacantly at Hiatsou—his eyes were sunken and dark—as he decided how to answer. He snuggled his robe tighter around his shoulders. He seemed to always be cold lately. Poutassa shuffled over to the door. Pulling the skin back, he scanned the faces of Ounontisaston, making sure his guards were still nearby before wandering back to sit on a platform. Hiatsou's face was anxious and impatient.

"Their heads were cut from their bodies," Poutassa said, rubbing at his eyes. "Their left eye was popped out; a round black stone was driven into the socket."

"What?" Hiatsou slumped down. "Who would dare to do such a thing?"

Poutassa got up and started to pace, wringing his hands together nervously. The two guards inside the lodge tried moving with him but soon gave up and stood near the door. "They had a feather stuck down each of their throats; a trophy feather ... unlike any other." Poutassa's eye started to twitch. The nightmares were so vivid lately, he hated sleep. He rubbed a palm into a bloodshot eye.

Hiatsou chewed on his lip, annoyed at being left hanging. "Well?"

Poutassa lowered the hand, clearing some mucus from his throat before continuing. He fixed Hiatsou with a morose stare. "It was the feather of

Sannisen. And the stone in their eyes was identical to Shanoka's prayer stone, only smaller."

Hiatsou's brows arched. His head rocked back as if he'd been slapped in the face. "That's impossible!" he croaked. "The strangers must have killed them to get the girls."

"Perhaps they did," Poutassa answered in a brooding voice.

Hiatsou twined his fingers, staring into the dancing flames as the full impact of what Poutassa was suggesting sank in. "We have to find out what happened at that hunt camp." Hiatsou glanced over at the guards on the door. "Take a party of warriors. Go find that camp and see what happened there!" The two young warriors were shocked at being offered such a responsibility. Their indecision lasted only a breath, and they were out the door.

Poutassa glared at Hiatsou. He trudged to the door again, scanning the town. "You could have sent someone other than my guards."

"You've got eight more," Hiatsou said, scowling. "Are you continuing on to Tontiaton?"

Poutassa dropped the doorskin back. "No. It would be dark before we got there. I don't like traveling at night. Who has Soutoten's lodge?"

"Winona."

Poutassa rolled his eyes. "Ounsasta's?"

"Some of the young shamans."

Poutassa nodded. "I'll use it. They can sleep outside tonight." He ducked out the door. The doorskin tumbled into place. It flew up again, and Poutassa stumbled back inside. He shuffled backward across the lodge until the sleep platform hit his legs and dropped him on his backside. An old woman stuck her head in. She started to say something when she was suddenly grabbed under each arm and dragged inside by two of Poutassa's guards. More guards poured in behind.

"Why did you let her get so close to me?" Poutassa raged at the guards, his voice shaking as he picked himself up to turn his bile on the woman. "If you ever approach me like that again, you old bag of bones, I'll have you skinned alive!"

"She … she says that she has an important message for Feathered Serpent," the oldest guard tried to explain.

"I'm sorry," the old woman rattled meekly, lowering her head. "My name is Kratcha. My lodge is on the Lower Tranchi, near the slate quarry."

Poutassa was in no mood for small talk. "Say what you have to say, and get out!"

Kratcha nodded obediently. "A half moon cycle after the river broke up, Sannisen and Shanoka came to my lodge." Poutassa's mouth fell open. "Sannisen wanted petun," Kratcha continued. "I offered them some food too, but they said they didn't need it. They told me they were traveling the land, bringing peace back to our people by visiting all the shamans, and they would never rest until they met with each one."

Poutassa sagged back down onto the sleep platform. Hiatsou laced his fingers together again, staring off into a frightening future. "Are they traveling on the river?" he asked in a hollow voice.

"Don't rightly know," Kratcha answered mysteriously. "It was all very strange. Sannisen dropped something when he left. I followed them out to give it back, but they were nowhere to be seen. When they come to see you, would you return it for me?" Kratcha thrust an arm out and dropped a trophy feather. She watched it flutter down onto Hiatsou's lap.

"Aah!" Hiatsou recoiled backward.

Kratcha hobbled across Ounontisaston for the south entry. It was all she could do to choke back the manic laughter trying to burst from her throat. Halfway down the bluff, she allowed herself some wet giggles. She could see Sakawa already seated in the front of their canoe for the journey, talking idly with two fishermen.

Sakawa's lodge essentials were neatly stacked on the floor of the canoe; sleep robes were draped over the pile. Hidden at the bottom was a fortune in chert blanks, shell beads, and feathers. Kratcha had no intention of living among all these shamans. Khioetoa was the only place left.

The fishermen glanced up at Kratcha shuffling down the bluff. "How can you share a lodge with that crazy old hag?" one asked, his disgust obvious.

Sakawa looked up, confused at first, and then slowly nodding as he grasped the man's meaning. "I suppose all you see is an eccentric old woman, but I knew Kratcha when she was a young maiden at old Ounon." Sakawa looked up at the bluff. As he watched Kratcha for a heartbeat, the corners of his mouth curled up with the memory. "She was the most attractive girl I'd ever known. All the young men wanted her, but I was a hunter; she desired a warrior. I had to settle for her sister. When I look at her now, I still see that beautiful young girl."

Kratcha lurched up, studying the two fishermen suspiciously. They stepped back, giving her lots of room. She settled herself into the rear of the canoe and picked up her paddle. "Well, don't just stand there," she barked. "Give us a shove!" The two men jumped down in the river, pushing the canoe out into the current. The river would carry them all the way to Khioetoa; all Kratcha had to do was steer. She took a final glance at the fortress up on the bluff, relishing that look on Hiatsou's pudgy face when the feather landed in his lap.

The two fishermen watched the canoe disappear around the first bend. Kratcha's cackling laughter echoed up the valley. The men winced at the sound of it. "Whewf! By the manitos," one said, shaking his head. "Brave man."

It had been a long time since Sakawa was out on the Tranchi. The landscape shining in bright sunlight seemed even more spectacular than he remembered. He lifted his face to the warm rays, feeling drowsy. Sakawa drifted off. Kratcha pulled out a bone hair comb—Brata's. Sakawa had given it to Kratcha as a memento of the old days. She brushed it against her cheek, remembering those enchanted times at old Ounon.

Kratcha smiled, sliding the comb back into her waistpouch for lack of anywhere else to put it. She leaned forward with her paddle and jabbed it into Sakawa's back. He jumped awake with a start. "This is our last great adventure, old man. Don't sleep through it."

18

"Togo never took a wife! He has no children, so how could he have a grandson?" Wasakah, the sachem of Cattaragus, tended to be irritable when he was summoned from his sleep robes in the dark. Ontarra listened from the doorpost he was tied to as the two older warriors who had brought him in explained.

"We saw him come in off the lake. It was our intent to dispose of him and be on our way, but he claims to be Togo's grandson." The warrior pursed his lips. "I, for one, do not want Togo holding me responsible for the death of one of his relatives."

"Nor I," the second warrior added, shaking his head as he considered the possible consequences of such a mistake. "Besides, why would anyone claim to be related to Togo if he wasn't?"

Ontarra found that if he listened closely, he could pick out about half of what was being said. Their language used many of the same words, but they were clipped short, like grunts, the end of the word left hanging or dropped altogether. It sounded like they were in a hurry to spit everything out before they forgot what was on their minds.

"I can think of only one possibility," Wasakah said. He rubbed his chin, staring over at Ontarra. He walked around the hearth fire to study Ontarra's eyes. Ontarra returned the stare and then realized the chief wasn't looking into his eyes but scrutinizing their shape and color. "Tell me how it is that you can be Togo's grandson."

Ontarra was astounded. Not only did Wasakah speak in clear, concise Attawondaronk, but he sounded exactly like Sannisen. "I ... he ..." Ontarra couldn't get over the shock. "He adopted my mother. She grew up with him at Joneadih."

Wasakah's cold eyes warmed slightly. "And this woman's name?"

"My mother's name is Shanoka."

Wasakah nodded, a faint smile curling one corner of his mouth. "You have her eyes. How is Shanoka?"

"Gone ... to the Village of the Dead."

Wasakah's face became impregnable again. He turned, walking back to his stool beyond the hearth fire and seating himself. "Tell Chakadda to come in here," he commanded. Chakadda must have been listening; he ducked inside instantly. Ontarra recognized the young warrior who had wanted to remove his head at the beach. "Chakadda, you will take this man to Joneadih. Leave now; take the young warriors with you."

Anger colored Chakadda's face, making the lines of tattooed dots running down his cheeks even more vivid. "I am to lead the escort for the dignitaries going to the canyon," he protested in a disrespectfully loud voice. Wasakah glared across the fire. Chakadda shifted his eyes to the floor. "As you wish." Chakadda backed to the door and barked some orders. Several young warriors came in to remove Ontarra.

"Chakadda," Wasakah said, waiting for Chakadda to turn so they had eye contact, "if he doesn't get there alive, I will hold you responsible. If he is lying to me, don't bother to bring him back."

Outside the lodge, Chakadda tied Ontarra's hands in front of him. He straightened himself up so he was nose to nose with Ontarra and glowered into Ontarra's eyes as he removed the tether around Ontarra's neck. Ontarra remained expressionless. Chakadda looped each end of the tether around an ankle, making sure the knots were tight enough to be uncomfortable.

Chakadda hollered some more instructions, gave Ontarra a rough shove, and the young warriors fell into line ahead and behind, setting off for the forest at a brisk trot. The best Ontarra could do with his feet hobbled was a stiff-legged lope. He managed well enough at first, while the land was still relatively flat, but as the hills and ravines grew more frequent, the unnatural gait began to tell in his thighs and buttocks.

By midday Ontarra began to stumble, falling occasionally. The line of warriors had to keep stopping to help him back to his feet. It was suggested to Chakadda that he untie the Dwakanah's ankles. Chakadda yanked his club out, threatening the presumptuous young warrior with a barrage of obscenities. Nothing more was said on Ontarra's behalf that day. By dusk, Ontarra was totally worn. His legs finally gave out, and he tumbled down a steep bank, sprawling into a jumble of roots and debris in the bottom of a wash.

Chakadda was over him in a heartbeat, waving his club, and yelling so fast, Ontarra couldn't understand a word. He'd caught enough of Wasakah's warning to know that Chakadda was forbidden to kill him, so he refused to get up. When Chakadda realized there was nothing he could do, he stormed off down the wash, slamming trees with his club, ranting at all the young warriors as if this was somehow their fault. Two of the young men came down and helped Ontarra out of the tangle of flotsam. They sat down on a nearby boulder while they watched Chakadda's childish display.

Ontarra heard them talking in muted tones to each other. They seemed to think Chakadda was a tyrant, not suited to lead the women planters, let alone warriors. They held little respect for him but were wary of his violent and unpredictable temper.

Chakadda finally wore himself out. He glared at the young men standing around in the wash and watching from the bank above as they waited for something sensible to happen. "Make a fire!" Chakadda growled, turning on a heel and walking farther down the ravine to sit on a downed tree.

Ontarra scanned around the gathering gloom of twilight. For the first time today, he realized that the forest was different from what he was familiar with. The budding trees were taller and thicker. There were several types he hadn't seen before. A young warrior offered him some dried venison. Ontarra smiled and nodded his thanks. He studied Chakadda's angry face as he chewed and then stared into the flames. If he was going to survive tomorrow, he had to ignore Chakadda; he'd pretend he was somewhere else.

He searched his mind. Tomorrow he would track deer on the uplands above the hunt camp.

Ontarra fell asleep sitting upright. He toppled over on his side sometime during the night, but it didn't wake him. He dreamed he was in a canoe, traveling the lower Tranchi, a gray fisherbird flying toward him. He wanted to get out of the way, but he couldn't move. Suddenly, the bird changed into a swarm of wasps, stinging his face and his neck. Ontarra screamed, lurched up, and jumped to his feet. Chakadda was there, laughing, enjoying the effects of the hot coals he'd kicked on Ontarra to wake him.

Ontarra brushed hot embers from his tunic, the acrid smell of burned hair filling his nostrils. It was all he could do to keep from going at Chakadda, despite the bindings on his wrists and ankles. Ontarra slowly sat back down. "Get up, Dwakanah!" Chakadda shot a well-aimed kick into Ontarra's ribs. "We go now!" Ontarra tilted his head up, shaking it slowly from side to side. Chakadda pulled his club and raised it for a blow.

"Untie my legs, or I'll never make it."

Chakadda's eyes wrinkled in confusion. He stared back at one of the warriors. The young man translated Ontarra's words. Chakadda turned back to Ontarra, grabbing the shoulder of his tunic to pull him to his feet. Ontarra refused to budge. "Get up, Dwakanah! Or you will taste my club!" He swung, brushing the top of Ontarra's head.

Ontarra understood a few of the words, and all of the threatening actions. "Kill me then. I may as well die here as on the trail somewhere." Chakadda listened to the translation. Fuming, he walked a few paces away, thought for a few moments, and then nodded reluctantly to one of the young warriors. The warrior sliced off the hobble.

Ontarra climbed stiffly to his feet, groaning as his muscles and joints screamed. Chakadda gave him a violent shove. Everything seemed to be working, so Ontarra trotted off down the ravine. The young warriors fell in behind, and Chakadda was left standing by himself. The warriors started chuckling among themselves at Ontarra's audacity. Two got out in front, so that Ontarra wouldn't be accused of trying to escape. Chakadda didn't catch up until they stopped at the top of a high ridge to rest.

The young warrior who spoke Attawondaronk sat down beside Ontarra, keeping his eyes fixed on some distant place out in the valley. In a low voice, he told Ontarra to stay two back from the front for the rest of the journey. If he could keep up the pace, the young men could keep some distance between him and Chakadda on the narrow paths.

They never stopped again until mid-afternoon. Chakadda started wearing out before anyone else. The young warriors knew he was too arrogant to call for a rest, so none of them intended to stop. Chakadda lagged back, stumbled, and fell. Everyone pulled up, gasping as they rested on their knees. Chakadda instructed the warriors to go on ahead; he'd turned an ankle.

An arrow-flight further on, the young men started laughing, ridiculing Chakadda's stamina and his ancestry, from what Ontarra could glean from their amused chatter. He was thankful for the more relaxed pace. The hills had grown into mountains over the course of the day. Ontarra had never realized before that parts of the world reached to such heights. The warriors tried to stay on the ridges, only twice having to descend to the lowlands and back up again.

The sun was sinking low behind them when they loped down into a vast valley, where a large river looped around through its center. They jogged along a path at the base of the ridge, rounded a point, and then the crop fields of Joneadih opened up before them. Off in the distance, Ontarra could see the palisades of the chief town of the Sennikae. An inexplicable sensation rushed over him. He felt like he'd just come home from a long journey.

The young warriors slowed to a walk as the procession made its way through the fields. Women planters and young maidens stopped hoeing and poking seeds in the mounds to watch the captive being brought in. The young warriors held their heads high at the honor it bestowed to them. A group of older warriors came out of a gap in the palisade to meet them. There was a quick discussion. Ontarra was escorted inside, taken directly into the plaza. His arms were wrapped around the war post and his wrists tied.

"Tawanda, our sachem, and Togo are both at the canyon," the youth who spoke Attawondaronk explained. "Wasakah sent runners for them when we left Cattaragus."

A large crowd started to gather. Many women and young maidens had followed them in from the fields. A group of boys started throwing rocks and shouting insults. The older warriors stopped them, explaining that the prisoner claimed to be a relative of Togo's. Skeptical murmurs passed through the onlookers. An old woman hobbled up, leaning on her hoe while she scrutinized Ontarra's features. Her eyes narrowed dubiously. She twisted around on a heel shaking her head. "Dwakanah!"

People moved closer, scrutinizing his clothes, hair, and nose. A pudgy girl who seemed to have no neck—as if her head grew directly from her shoulders—walked around Ontarra slowly with a curious fascination that Ontarra found humiliating. She ran her hand up his legs, testing the muscles, and pulled off one of his moccasins to smell his feet. She curled his lip back and squinted into his mouth. The huddle of young maidens started to giggle. Ontarra yanked his head away.

The tubby girl was unfazed. She wandered off through the crowd, with the ugliest dog that Ontarra had ever seen lapping at her heels. As he watched them disappear, he wondered if it actually was a dog. It wasn't anything like the dogs he knew. Its ears dangled flat against its head; its hair was so short it didn't seem worth having; and as it padded along behind her, its back legs kept trying to run out and pass the front ones. Ontarra gave his head a bewildered shake. *Somehow, a marmot got into that creature's lineage.*

As time for evening meal approached, the townspeople grew tired of ogling the prisoner and drifted off to their hearths. Ontarra studied the height of the war post. He could easily shimmy up and free himself. He knew they'd track him down before he got far, though. He had to wait for Togo. Ontarra slid his arms down, wrapped his legs around the post, and tried to get comfortable. He saw some figures approaching through the gathering gloom.

The pudgy girl knelt down in front of him; a dumpy, overweight boy—her brother, no doubt—squatted down beside her. She set a bowl of stew in front of the post and laid a stomach bag full of water beside it. Her dog-thing went straight for the stew, letting out an indignant yelp when she cuffed him. The boy straightened and wrapped a sleep robe over Ontarra's shoulders. The two wandered off without a word. The dog tarried for a heartbeat, slavering over the stew. Ontarra tossed a handful of dirt in his face, and he dashed off.

It was a cold night. Ontarra probably wouldn't have slept without the robe. He found it was easiest to crouch on his hands and knees, resting his head on his forearm. At dawn, he awoke to the shrill sound of an angry voice shouting oaths and epithets. A chirpy, frightened voice was pleading for mercy. Ontarra lifted his head. Chakadda had the fat boy by the arm, shaking him violently. He swatted at his face and shoulders with an open palm. A bowl of stew was scattered across the ground. Chakadda shoved the boy away, landing a kick to his backside as he ran off. Ontarra stood up, letting the robe slide to the ground. Chakadda looked over, their eyes meeting like daggers across the plaza. Chakadda kicked the bowl, turned, and disappeared inside a longhouse.

The town was just coming to life. Wisps of smoke began to twine up out of the smoke holes of nine longhouses, rising in straight columns on the still morning air. Mist from the river was burning off under a bright blue sky. The tree-covered mountains on each side of the valley faded into the horizons to the north and south. Big, black birds, with bald pink heads soared along the ridges, never flapping a wing. Ontarra could see lodges sitting in clearings on the sides of the mountains. *A beautiful place*, he thought, *if you had the freedom to enjoy it*.

As he stared up at the incredible height of the mountaintops, something grappled with his leg. Instinctively, he jerked it away, but something was locked on tight. The dog-thing had its front paws wrapped around his right thigh and was blissfully humping his knee. Ontarra tried to shake him off. All it did was increase his amorous desires. Ontarra worked his other foot around and got it up against the dog creature's throat. He landed on his back, jumped up, and ran between the longhouses. "Filthy mutt!" Ontarra shouted at him.

Ontarra saw some chiefs and dignitaries coming through the entry. They split off left and right, heading for their lodges and morning meal. Two carried on through the plaza. To Ontarra's relief, one of them was Togo. Togo didn't seem to recognize him at first, but as he drew closer, he saw through the welts and burns.

"Ontarra! It is you!" Togo spread his arms wide, hugging Ontarra, war post and all. Embarrassed, Ontarra tried to wriggle free before any of the warriors saw the embrace. Togo leaned back. "You're a mess." He pulled a knife and cut the cords at Ontarra's wrists. "Come on, we'll go up to my lodge." Togo wrapped an arm around Ontarra, nodded to the chief standing a few paces away, and then headed across the plaza.

Outside the palisade, they took a path toward the western ridge. It hit the mountain at an angle, sloping up the face of a steep incline. "What are you doing here? Why didn't you send word that you were coming? It would have been safer." Togo turned to hear Ontarra's answer. Ontarra was probing absently at the wound on the back of his head. Togo turned him around. "Who battered you up like this?"

"One of your warriors, named Chakadda, except for the one on my head here." Ontarra touched it. "Some warriors from a land in the west did that."

Togo pressed around the scab behind Ontarra's ear. Ontarra jerked his head away. "Where do you feel that?" Togo asked.

"Behind my left eye … and in my teeth." Ontarra sighed wearily.

Togo turned, continuing up the slope in silence. "Something's wrong, isn't it? That's why you're here without warning." Togo stopped, twisting his head around to see Ontarra's face. "Is it Shanoka? Has something happened to her?"

Ontarra looked up into the forest, pulling a long breath. "She's dead." He felt the moisture well in his eyes. "Father and Teota too."

Togo took a step backward, easing himself down on a boulder by the path. He stared out over the valley in abject silence. Ontarra sat down quietly to wait. "She was such a beautiful child, so full of promise." Togo's voice sounded as if it were coming from the far end of a longhouse. He palmed the tears from his eyes and looked over at Ontarra. "Hiatsou and Poutassa?"

Ontarra nodded. "And the men from the west … and a trader named Dekari."

Togo's head snapped up. "I know him!" He sucked on his lip, shaking his head. "Never did like him."

Ontarra explained how the tragedy had come to pass; how everyone barely escaped Ounontisaston with their lives; surviving winter and starvation at the hunt camp, only to be attacked unexpectedly by some strange men brought into their lands by an Erieehronon; the chase cross-country to try to save the girls; and his foolish capture by Sennikae warriors.

"How did you bury her?" Togo asked softly.

Their eyes held each other a moment. "As an Ojibwa. Father and Teota too. We all agreed in the winter that we would meet again in the Ojibwa Village of the Dead."

Togo stood up, nodding his head. "She always wanted that. I'm glad she admitted it to herself in time." They continued on up the path, with Togo reminiscing about Shanoka in her childhood and Ontarra only half-listening, until they came out onto a rocky ledge. A tidy lodge was set back against the mountain. The view of the town and valley below was breathtaking. Ontarra could make out the chubby girl and her brother in the plaza.

"Who is that strange-looking girl with no neck?"

Togo stared down Ontarra's finger. "That's Scajaweda, daughter of our sachem, Tawanda."

"The boy is her brother?"

Togo glanced again to be sure and gave his head a shake. "They call him Stoolmaker, for obvious reasons. He's been an orphan since he was a child. Nobody wanted to adopt such a voracious appetite, so he moves from longhouse to longhouse, until people tire of feeding him. He and Scajaweda seem to have become close friends. Come inside now. I want to check your wounds."

Togo's lodge was crammed full with interesting treasures and trinkets from his travels. Ontarra pulled a beautiful hide bag from the wall and studied it. It was covered in intricate beadwork—designs and patterns he was unfamiliar with.

"Menominee," Togo mumbled absently. Ontarra looked up, confused wrinkles around his eyes. "The people who made that," Togo said, jerking his head, "are called Menominee. Now put it back and take your tunic off." Ontarra hung the bag back, settled down on a platform, and peeled his tunic up over his head. Togo started applying a salve to the burns.

"Togo, I don't have time for this. I have to go after the girls."

Togo settled back with a sigh. "I don't know any easy way to tell you this, but you can't risk another blow to your head. You have bad blood in there. It has to be drained away, before dark spirits can take advantage."

Ontarra pushed Togo back to make him see that he was serious. "I was right behind them until a few days ago. There was no place left for them to go, except across Iannaoa. They're in Erieehronon territory right now—I'm sure of it." Ontarra studied Togo tentatively. "You can get some warriors to help us."

Togo rocked his head and walked to the other side of the hearth fire. Prying open some space in the heap of exotic trade goods, he sat himself down on the opposite platform. "We are constantly warring with the Erieehronon. I certainly have no love for them, especially that weasel Dekari. We've had an uneasy peace with them now, for two cycles. If we go into their lands with

Sennikae warriors, there will surely be a fight and then reprisals. How many deaths do you suppose we would be responsible for?"

The bleak look on Ontarra's face sent a pang through Togo's soul. "Ontarra," he said softly, "you can't go any farther right now. Too much exertion could kill you. You need to build your strength." Togo stared into the flames, pinching at his lip. "I think your chances of finding them now are very slim."

Ontarra stood up and ran his hands over his face. He folded his arms with determined resolve. "Sounia is my wife. Taiwa is my blood. I would rather die now, trying, than die in fifty cycles, wondering if they still live or if I might have saved them. If you won't help me, just tell me how to find the Erieehronon."

Togo twined his fingers together, a reproachful look masking his true feelings. "You're a foolish young man. I'm not going to be responsible for sending you to your death. It appears you may be the last family that I have. You can stay here; have a good life."

Ontarra's eyes narrowed with a look of betrayal that cut through Togo like cold chert. "While there is still breath in my body, blood in my veins, I will never give up. Sounia and I had something that no one else could ever know or understand."

Togo watched Ontarra's reaction closely. The controlled anger was impressive. He decided to goad him a little further. Togo canted his head cynically. "And just what might that be?"

"Each other!" Ontarra's voice was vehement, his eyes ablaze.

Togo shook his head. "You have much to learn. It is the great lesson of this life, to lose all that you hold dear a little at a time, until finally there is nothing left."

Ontarra's mouth opened and then closed. He spun around and headed for the door.

"Ontarra, wait!" Togo jumped up, following him outside. Ontarra was already walking down the path. Togo sauntered to catch up, grabbing him by the arm. Ontarra twisted around, his face flushed and bitter. Togo pursed a humbled smile. "I knew that would be your answer. You have your father's spirit." He let go of Ontarra's arm. "Of course I'll help you, but I fear we will not come back from this alive. If we all must die, I had to be convinced it was the only way."

Ontarra took a deep breath, the anger melting from his face. Togo rubbed his chin thoughtfully. "We are going to need a safe place to bring the girls ... if we manage to get them. I have to talk to Tawanda. Wait in the lodge, and don't wander off anywhere." Ontarra smiled, gripping Togo's arm before going back up to the lodge.

Togo didn't return until the sun was directly overhead. Ontarra was sitting on the ledge, feet dangling over, watching the activities in the town below. "What river is that?" he asked as Togo settled down beside him.

"The Alhegalena. Looks a lot like the Tranchi here; much bigger downstream, though."

Ontarra studied the river where it looped just below the town, turned southwest, and disappeared behind the ridges in the distance. He bobbed his head in agreement. "I never realized that the world contained so many wondrous things," he said in a soft voice.

Togo nodded. "You have no idea. Every land and its people are different." He cocked his eyes at Ontarra. "Did you see the cataract?"

"Yes. It was magnificent—and frightening."

Togo was surprised at the forlorn look on Ontarra's face. "What's wrong?"

Ontarra looked out across the valley, lips pinching together with disgust. "I've got the gut worms."

Togo rolled his head back, staring up at the sky. "Wonderful. Well ... I'll start making some lye and lilac paste. It's still going to be a half moon cycle before you're rid of them." Ontarra's face screwed up at the thought of the horrid mixture. "Tawanda says that I can adopt you, but ..." Ontarra looked over quizzically. Togo thought he had better get right to the point. "He sees an advantage in this. It seems that you've made a favorable impression on Scajaweda. I'm not sure why, considering the way you look right now. He's going to gift her to you."

"Gift her to me? What in this world am I supposed to do with her?" Togo leaned back and raised his eyebrows. "No, Togo! Tell me you're not serious! I already have a wife!"

"Our warriors take many wives."

"I have no desire for another! Especially one that needs two sleep platforms and whose food goes right from her mouth to her stomach when she swallows!"

Togo let out a long breath. "The way I see it, you have two choices. You can wait until nightfall and run, and our warriors will bring you back hanging on a pole, or you can accept Scajaweda and adoption into the Sennikae."

Ontarra's chin fell to his chest. His head snapped back up with a hopeful thought. "Can I give her to someone else?"

"You could ... but she is the sachem's daughter. She knows her standing. I agree that Scajaweda is no prize—Tawanda has been trying to marry her off for two cycles now. Still, it will be expected that you share a hearth with her. Any other arrangement would be bad for both of us. It will give you and Sounia a safe home to come to," Togo reasoned.

Ontarra climbed to his feet and started pacing while he ran it through his mind. Togo waited patiently, watching Ontarra's fingers lace and unlace. He stopped and stared at Togo, throwing his arms out in surrender. "Agree to whatever you must. Let's get this over with."

Togo climbed to his feet with a sly grin. "She's waiting down the path a ways. She wanted to come up and meet you." Ontarra closed his eyes and rubbed his temples. Then he turned and went inside to work up his nerve. He could hear Scajaweda's husky voice chattering to Togo as they came up the hill. She ducked inside. Treating Ontarra to a coy smile, she started to walk over to him but paused suddenly, as if something had just occurred to her. She unabashedly hiked up her skirt and scratched herself before dropping down beside him on the platform. A Powerful odor struck him instantly.

When she finally got out of his way, Togo seated himself amid the trade goods on the platform across the lodge. Ontarra was staring at the ceiling but managed to force a smile to his face and look at her. Her hair was parted down the center of her skull, pulled tightly together at the sides, and braided into two long tails that stuck out at odd angles, reminding him of the hind legs of a frog. Scajaweda grinned and babbled something. Ontarra didn't understand a word. He shook his head, turning a withering look to Togo.

"She hopes that you are well." Togo pinched his lips together and looked out the door so he wouldn't laugh. "And she wants to know if she can pull out that hair that's growing on your chin. She thinks it's ... disgusting." Scajaweda reached up to Ontarra's chin. He cringed, yanking his head away and jumping to his feet. The thought of her touching him was too much. He ducked outside, walking over to the ledge to stare out at the valley.

"Aah!" Ontarra's reflexes jarred him back from the precipice as something struck his leg. Scajaweda's dog was showing his affection again. Ontarra clamped both hands into the scruff of the thing's neck and peeled it off. He briefly considered heaving it over the edge but tossed it to the ground a canoe-length away instead. Scajaweda came out of the lodge, prattling away to Togo. She flashed a toothy smile at Ontarra and waddled off down the path. Togo waited until she was out of sight before turning with an amused smirk.

"She thinks you will be quite suitable, once she cleans you up, gives you some manners"—Togo put a hand to his mouth to hide his grin—"and gets that hair off your chin."

Ontarra didn't see the humor.

"We don't have time for all this! We need to make plans!"

Togo's face turned serious. He strolled over, lowering himself down to dangle his legs over the edge of the cliff. "I've already been making some arrangements. Council has been called for tonight, to adopt you."

Ontarra sat down beside him. "I was talking about Sounia and Taiwa."

Togo bobbed his head. "The trader Dekari lives at the northern end of a lake called Cha-ta-kwa. It is only a day's journey from here."

"Only one day away?" Ontarra was elated. "We can go tomorrow!"

"The only hope we have of getting in and out of their land alive is to pretend we are traders." Togo could see in Ontarra's face that he didn't like that plan.

"Can we travel with weapons and profess to be traders?"

"A bow, three arrows, and a skinning knife is considered to be a trader's essentials."

Ontarra thought about this, looked over at Togo, and shook his head. "I have no intention of dickering with any of those men. I want them dead."

Togo expected that. "Or," he continued, "we strike suddenly—without warning—with only a few men, and get our hides out of there before they know what happened." Togo locked eyes with Ontarra. "If we're caught, we die game. We don't want to be prisoners of the Gahkwas."

"Gahkwas?"

"That's what we call them." Togo stared down at the town. "If we are to go with only a handful of men, I know who it is that we need. Our people are meeting in the canyon right now, with some of our neighbors to the east. They're trying to arrange a peace." Togo sighed, rocking his head from side to side. "It never lasts. We are friends for a while, and then someone raids for revenge or women, and we become sworn enemies again. We seem doomed to always repeat that cycle."

"Togo …" Ontarra canted his head impatiently.

"Yes … anyway, the Onondaga are one of the nations meeting at the canyon. There's a young man with them who has never been bested at personal combat. Tadodaroh has become their most feared warrior."

Ontarra's pride was bruised. "No one is unbeatable, Togo."

"He is; I've seen it. With or without weapons, it makes no difference." Togo eyed Ontarra. "Don't you let your conceit make an enemy of him." Ontarra snorted and shrugged it off. Togo squinted suspiciously. "I know him well, and he owes me a debt. I've sent word that I wish to see him." Togo got up and brushed himself off. "For now, we better head down and get you cleaned up for the ceremony."

Togo took Ontarra to the lodge of a woman who was conspicuously happy to see Togo and to meet his grandson. She sat Ontarra on a platform, gave him a bowl of water and some hide strips to wash with, and then filled bowls with roasted venison and succotash stew. Yalonda talked incessantly, bubbling away as she wandered around the lodge, tidying things up, only stopping long enough to share an intimate smile with Togo before chattering on again.

Togo appeared engrossed in what she was saying, but he winked at Ontarra when he knew Yalonda wasn't looking. He answered her queries with occasional grunts and nods. When Togo set his bowl down, Yalonda settled herself on his lap and wrapped her arms around his neck. They spoke in muted tones for a hand of time. She pecked his cheek and went to the door to check the plaza. Yalonda dropped the doorskin back and dipped her chin to Togo.

"Come, Ontarra, the council is ready," Togo said, strolling over to Yalonda. She flashed a smile, offering Ontarra some words of encouragement as he followed Togo out.

"She really likes you," Ontarra said to Togo with a sly grin.

Togo reflected on that before answering. "Yalonda is a friend to many of the men. In return, she is well taken care of. We are well suited to each other."

The plaza was filled with chiefs and dignitaries, all sitting together on a long bench attached to the south palisade. The wives sat cross-legged on the ground in front of each man. Across one side of the plaza, the clan mothers were seated; the maidens gathered in groups along the opposite side.

Scajaweda beamed at Ontarra from a knot of girls off to one side. The rest of the townspeople milled around in the background. Seeing a relative of Togo's was an event worth witnessing. Togo ushered Ontarra across the plaza, instructing him to kneel, facing the oldest chief.

Tawanda dipped his head to Togo, and Togo stepped back a few paces. Tawanda gestured to some warriors off to the side. One brought a rolled hide and set it on Tawanda's lap. Tawanda started talking to Ontarra as he unwrapped it. He swept his arm around the plaza and then handed Ontarra his weapons back, one at a time. Ontarra glanced over at Togo.

"As with all people, you are the progeny of the Creator," Togo explained. "You have come far to join us, and we are honored to welcome you."

Tawanda waited for Togo to finish before continuing. "I return to you the necessities of a warrior, with the understanding that they may never be used in anger against us." Ontarra dipped his head in esteem for Tawanda's generosity.

Picking up Adontayat's ceremonial bow, Ontarra handed it to Tawanda. "For your generosity, it is my wish that you accept this bow. Hang it in your lodge. It has magical Powers that will protect your home from all of your enemies."

Tawanda held the bow up to the fading sunlight, admiring the multicolored sinews wrapped around the shaft, and the stringer of dappled feathers dangling from the grip. A delighted smile etched its way across Tawanda's creviced face. He leaned the bow against the palisade. "Your gift pleases me." Tawanda clapped his hands. To Ontarra's dismay, Scajaweda knelt down at his side. "In return, I give you my only daughter." Tawanda smiled again as Togo finished translating. This was truly a happy day for Tawanda.

Tawanda shouted out to the onlookers in a perfunctory manner, ending the ceremony. "And if anyone among you objects to the grandson of Togo being welcomed among us, you must speak now."

To everyone's surprise, an angry voice started shouting from the back of the plaza. Ontarra twisted around and looked back but couldn't see who it was. Then he heard the word *Dwakanah* and saw Chakadda pushing his way through the onlookers. He strutted out across the plaza, waving a war club, and hollering oaths to people in the crowd; then he spat insults at Ontarra. Ontarra straightened up, turning to face him as he drew closer. Chakadda stopped a stone's cast away, cursing and pointing his club at Scajaweda. Ontarra glanced at Scajaweda and then looked to Togo.

"He wants her?" Ontarra asked.

Togo stepped closer, turning his back to the chiefs and Scajaweda before answering. "Of course not," he whispered. "He wants the prestige that holding your head up in front of all these people will bring him. He can't object to your adoption, so he is challenging your right to be counted among our warriors." Togo turned to the chiefs. Tawanda's arms were folded across his chest, eyes glowering at Chakadda, but he remained silent.

"My grandson has a head wound," Togo said. "He is in no condition to fight."

Tawanda nodded. Chakadda rolled his head to one side, grinning to some of the warriors watching from the crowd.

"What did you just say?" Ontarra asked Togo, bristling at the obnoxious grin on Chakadda's face.

"I told them that you are ill and not able to fight." Ontarra shot Togo an icy stare. He bent down and picked up his club. Taking three steps to the left, Ontarra slashed it through the air twice to get its feel. Chakadda jumped back, spinning away defensively at the sound. The grin fell from his face when he saw the big, ornately carved rockwood club, stained from use and covered in battle scars—a wooden ball the size of a fist firmly clamped in the jaws of a lynx.

Ontarra smiled to himself at Chakadda's shocked expression. "I see your ankle has healed up," Ontarra chided. Ontarra noticed the young warrior with whom he'd traveled from Cattaragus, grinning as he translated Ontarra's words to the warriors standing around him. Laughter rippled through the group. Chakadda got his wits about him. Strutting back and forth, he flashed cocky grins to faces in the crowd, moving subtly closer to Ontarra with each stride. Ontarra held his club in both hands, swinging it slowly back and forth—eyes following Chakadda's every move. Chakadda stopped suddenly and bowed his head to Ontarra. Ontarra dipped his chin.

"Don't!" Togo yelled.

Chakadda swung at Ontarra's head, but Ontarra was watching. He leaned back, wind from Chakadda's club fluttering his hair as it went by. Ontarra used the backward momentum to heave his arms straight up. His club tore the lobe from Chakadda's right ear. Chakadda reeled away, clutching the side of his head with one hand. Ontarra felt the club warming up in his fingers, and its spirit spoke to him.

Feel him out. Take your time and wear him down.

Ontarra pranced in with practiced moves, swinging at Chakadda's head and then at his body and his legs. Chakadda flailed back but was still off balance. Ontarra ducked, spun, and twisted gracefully around the plaza, his club slicing through the air with the sound of arrows passing too close. He moved constantly, with purpose, intentionally glancing blows off Chakadda's legs and arms and tearing gashes in his buckskins. A part of him saw what Chakadda was going to do before Chakadda even knew. It was clear to everyone watching that Chakadda was never going to land a blow. He was getting winded just trying to keep Ontarra in front of him. Ontarra pranced and weaved, drawing Chakadda in close, spinning away from his angry swings, toying with him—and humiliating him in front of the entire town.

Ontarra ducked a blow aimed at his head, smacking Chakadda's ankle with the rockwood ball as it slid past. Chakadda tumbled, rolling to his knees again to protect himself from another blow. He howled and grabbed the injured ankle, but Ontarra saw what was coming as Chakadda's arm snapped up again. Ontarra dove, rolling back to his feet in one fluid motion. A knife thudded into a palisade post only a handspan from Tawanda's head.

Chakadda tried to stand, but groaned and dropped back to his knees. Ontarra raised his club, circling around Chakadda once, before coming to a stop in front of him. Chakadda rolled his eyes up, hatred burning in their depths. A smug grin slowly thinned his lips and eyes. He spread his arms out at his sides, dropping his club in the dust. Ontarra cast a puzzled glance to Togo.

"He concedes defeat," Togo said, grinning with pride.

A shadow settled over Ontarra's face; his eyes narrowing to venomous slits. Togo saw a tendon bulge as Ontarra's jaw clenched. His fingers rippled up the handle of his club, rotating it slightly as he perfected his grip. The eerie sensation that another person had crept into Ontarra's body made Togo's skin crawl. The town was utterly silent.

Togo's head rocked from side to side. "Don't."

Ontarra's club flashed. The rockwood ball in the lynx's jaws obliterated Chakadda's forehead from temple to temple. Red and gray mush splattered across the wives of the chiefs. Four streams of blood spurted out around the plaza with the final beats of Chakadda's heart. A baby started wailing in its mother's arms. Chakadda seemed to turn to stone. Arms still spread wide in submission, his eyelids didn't even flutter. The crimson spray petered out. Ontarra was actually considering hitting him again, but Chakadda finally tottered over on his side, that smug grin frozen on his face—where it eventually would rot off.

The council was struck dumb. Warriors surrounded Ontarra, a wall of arrows penning him in. The club was wrenched from his hand, and his arms were yanked back and tied behind him. They dragged him across the plaza and forced him to his knees in front of Tawanda. The blade of the chert ax that was about to cleave his head from his body was rotated in front of his eyes and raised high for the fatal blow.

Taiwa studied the group of men huddled around a fire halfway down the hillside. Then she shifted her gaze to take in the lake. Cha-ta-kwa was long and narrow, stretching away to the south before looping east to disappear behind a point of land. She turned her attention back to the midday meal, adding handfuls of cracked corn to round-bellied ceramic pots simmering on the hearth in front of Dekari's lodge. Sounia reached across, dropping in chunked fish, venison, and turkey. She sat back to sip at her lilac tea. At least they'd eaten well since coming here.

"I think they're getting ready to take us somewhere." Taiwa said softly. Sounia looked up but didn't answer. Since the journey across Iannaoa and the discovery she had the gut worms, Sounia seemed distant, as if her spirit had left her. Taiwa stirred the coals with a twig, staring out across the lake at three longhouses and a smattering of lodges on the west shore. Dekari acted like he owned that village.

His lodge sat majestically on the northern shore, on a hilltop that dominated the entire area. The hillside down to the lake was burned clear to improve the view. Dekari's lodge displayed all the trappings of wealth, accumulated over a lifetime of barter and conspiracy.

Taiwa studied Sounia's desolate expression. "How long do you think it would take someone to come around the lake?" Sounia set her tea on a hearthstone, shrugging absently. Taiwa twisted around with a fleeting glance at the men talking on the hillside. Manak and Matoupa shared a pipe with

Dekari and three others he'd brought up from the town. "I think they're making another attempt to get petun seed," Taiwa mumbled, turning back.

Mox glared vindictively at the girls from a bench a stone's cast away. He was moving around now, slowly; he still couldn't stand straight. Manak had threatened his life if he harmed either of the girls. Since then, he'd hardly spoken. Glowering eyes and occasional grunts were the only interactions he'd had with them for days. He was scarier than ever.

"Maybe we should try to escape before they move us again," Taiwa whispered, pretending to be occupied peeling cattail shoots.

"And go where?" Sounia asked, her voice bleak. Mox tossed a length of firewood at the girls—his way of telling them to be quiet. Sounia snatched it up and drilled it back at him. He got his hand up just in time to keep it from mashing his face. Mox slit Sounia's throat with his eyes.

"We better try to get a knife or something, before they leave us alone with him again," Sounia muttered. She noticed an enormous brown spring beetle lurching across the ground and plucked it up. Glancing over at Mox to see if he was watching, she dropped it into a pot and stirred it under. "Don't eat the fish stew," she said softly.

Taiwa giggled. She noticed Matoupa and Manak coming back up the hill. Dekari barked at Sounia to bring down more petun. Sounia frowned, but she stood and walked listlessly to the lodge. It certainly was an interesting place—a trove of treasures, trinkets, and junk from his wanderings. It reminded Sounia of what her father said a pack rat midden looked like.

Dream-catchers dangled from the walls and rafters. Two hands of strange arrows and darts were mounted horizontally along the back wall. Masks made of wood, corn husks, reeds, mud, and clay ran in a long row around the roof line. Mats covered in beadwork hung on the walls. Fresh food brought up from the town lined all the rafters. A black, withered human arm, severed at the shoulder, hung from the smoke hole.

Sounia winced, grabbed a brick of petun from the pile in the corner, and headed out. Manak and Matoupa were talking quietly with Mox. Sounia ambled down the path, trying to ignore the ogling eyes and ugly tattoos of Dekari's associates. She dropped the brick on the ground at Dekari's feet, spun around, and left without a word.

"Not very friendly, is she?" one of the men said with a smirk.

The man beside him leaned over with a twisted grin. "I can soon break her of her arrogance."

"Just make sure you bring enough men," Dekari said in a low tone. "I've seen them fight—it won't be easy. When we're rid of the Tunicans, she's all yours." Dekari rubbed his chin, squinting up the hill. "I'm going to keep the little one—for a while, at least." Dekari popped some greenstones out of his waistpouch, handing three to each of the men. As an afterthought, he handed three more to the oldest man. "Give these to my sister; I have heard that her husband is missing." The man nodded, cramming them into the tobacco pouch hanging around his neck.

Dekari handed the brick of petun to the men as an added bonus. "We'll set it up for midmorning, three days from now."

"What about the seed?" the older man asked.

"Just bring ordinary tobacco seed. If they realize it's not petun, it'll still be too late."

The men rose together and made their way up to the lodge. Dekari insisted that among his people, men always ate first, so Taiwa and Sounia handed out bowls of fish stew, waiting patiently while the men devoured the entire pot, before helping themselves to venison. Mox hit something crunchy. He spat it onto his palm to examine it, shook his head, and tossed it away.

"Is there no shorter route we can take?" Manak wondered, culling out chunks of fish and ignoring the rabbit food.

"The Minquas are killing everyone who ventures into their land," Dekari mumbled through a mouthful of gruel. "Iannaoa is the only route. Besides, you already know the way."

The Tunicans started discussing the journey. The men from the town decided it was a good opportunity to leave. Taiwa had trouble looking at the menacing blue and green swirls on their faces. She'd grown to hate tattoos. Dekari walked down the hill with the men before coming back.

"We've decided on a site for the trade," Matoupa advised. Dekari cocked his head to one side, squinting to focus. "We'll meet here, of course."

Manak and Matoupa rocked their heads in unison. "We will meet out in the open, in the dunes, where we can see who is coming. We want to be on the lake as soon as the trade is completed." Matoupa studied Dekari's reaction. "We'll tell you where, when it becomes necessary."

Dekari frowned, but caught himself and made a show of shrugging the whole thing off. "Certainly, whatever you wish. Just let me know, when you feel like it." Dekari strolled over to his lodge, trying to appear unperturbed. He disappeared inside. Manak and Matoupa looked at each other suspiciously. The girls started picking up the bowls.

"Let Sounia clean up." Matoupa lifted a travel pack to his shoulder, handing a smaller one to Taiwa. "We're going to start taking some of our things down to the lake." Taiwa propped her hands on her hips, refusing the pack with an icy stare. "Mox can't do it." He thrust the pack out at her again. Taiwa rolled her eyes at Sounia; then she reached out and took it.

The trail to Iannaoa was heavily traveled. Two people could walk abreast. Brush encroaching on the path was slashed back. Benches had even been built for rest stops. Taiwa was amazed at the size of the trees that grew here. Huge trunks shot up into the sky, to the height of fully matured trees at Ounontisaston, before the first branches even poked out. Then the tree grew on upward to double the height that she was accustomed to. The trunks were as thick through at their centers as she was tall. It felt like she was in a completely different world, with her body reduced to the size of a field mouse.

Manak and Matoupa walked ahead, talking in whispers and looking back occasionally to be sure she was keeping up. The trail gradually changed from packed loam to sand. Taiwa could feel cool air off the lake on her face. The immense trees faded downward into thick stands of brush and white poplar. She was thankful to be out in sunlight again.

They came out on a dune, two drifts back from the lake. Manak and Matoupa left the trail, bearing east through the snake grass and reeds. An arrow-flight further on, they went up over a hill of sand and down into the trough. At the far end of the depression, they moved a heap of brush hiding three elm-bark canoes. "I wish we could get some real canoes," Manak complained. Taiwa stared up at the wall of sand between her and the lake, sloughed off her pack, and humped her way to the top.

The white caps of Iannaoa glinted back at her in the sunlight. The most frightening experience of her life was being out there with no land in sight. Riding up the swells in the darkness and then accelerating down the backsides, plunging into the next wall of water with a crashing spray. She'd bailed water with her hands all night long—certain the whole time that they were all doomed. Glimpses of the boiling lake in the flashes of heat lightning made the memory seem like a terrible nightmare. Dekari said that the rainstorm had actually saved them, keeping the wind and waves down while hiding their trespass on the Lake from the Okis.

Taiwa swept her eyes up the shoreline to the east. Iannaoa was angry today. Only the gulls were venturing out, bobbing on the surf as if they had nothing better to do. She knew Ontarra would never try to cross the lake, and she had no idea how far it was around the end. She didn't even know why she kept expecting to see him—it was just a feeling. She hung her head, thinking back to the hunt camp, wondering if she was wrong. *Even if he is alive, he can't get here in time now. He can't track us on the lake.*

"Get down from there before someone sees you!" Matoupa yelled. Her hopes melted away. Taiwa turned, dejectedly making her way back down to her captors and an uncertain fate. The trip back to Dekari's lodge seemed to last forever. Twilight was falling when they walked in off the trail. Mox and Sounia sat on opposite sides of the fire, ignoring each other. Taiwa watched sadly as Sounia drew lines in the dirt with a stick, a bleak look on her face. She knew how Sounia felt now. The future seemed empty and hopeless.

"Aaaah!" A shrill scream erupted from inside the lodge. Manak and Mox had their clubs out instantly. Matoupa pulled a knife. Crashes were followed by more screams, and Dekari flew out the door, flailing his arms around his head.

Matoupa stepped closer but couldn't see anything. "What is it?" he asked, bewildered.

"Something stung me! Ooh!" He shook his hand up and down, his face a mask of fear and agony.

"Let me see." Matoupa grabbed the hand flying around in front of him.

"Argh!" Dekari yanked it back and held it up, quivering. The palm was already swollen to twice its normal size. Dekari stared, moaning, as if the palm might burst. His mouth dropped open. The pain was centered in his little finger—the one that was no longer there!

Ontarra heard the distant singsong voice of an old man, chanting. He tried to concentrate on the ethereal words floating around him. They were peculiar, meaningless ... mystical. A pungent odor filled his nostrils. He tried to open an eye, but it was crusted shut. Ontarra slowly rolled his head and tried the other.

The lodge was a haze of gray smoke. A thin man with long strands of wispy white hair sat cross-legged at the hearth fire. He finished his noisy spell, leaned forward, and sprinkled a fine powder over a perfect bed of glowing coals. Togo sat across the hearth, chin on his chest, eyes closed. He raised his left hand, holding it out to the old man. The man grasped Togo's fingers and pulled them close. The man's body hid his actions. Togo flinched and turned his head away, gritting his teeth. He drew the hand back, resting it on his leg, fingers flexing as if he was working a stiffness out. The old man returned several items to a medicine pouch, stood silently, and left. Togo opened his eyes and saw Ontarra staring at him from the sleep platform.

"You're finally awake." Togo plucked something off his little finger, crunched it, and tossed it on the embers. Ontarra caught a glimpse of a copper-colored mud wasp, writhing in agony, before disappearing in a puff of flame.

"Who was that?" Ontarra rolled upright, knocking a hand of trade goods onto the floor. He ignored the mess and tried to scrape the sleep crust from his eyelid.

"No one knows his real name. We just call him No Name. He feels it protects him from other … well … people of his calling … who might want to bring him harm." Ontarra pried the eye open, only half-listening to Togo's explanation. He stretched, wishing immediately that he hadn't.

"Oooh! Glouscap … everything hurts."

"I'm not surprised." Togo poked a stick at a bead bracelet burning on the embers to be sure the heat had devoured it all. "That was quite a nice speech Scajaweda made, don't you think? She almost had me believing you were a gift to us from the manitos."

Ontarra let out a long sigh. "Are you sure I can't give her away?"

Togo gave his head a shake. "She intends to be your wife. After she civilizes you, that is." Togo looked over with a faint grin. "And gets that hair off your chin."

Ontarra pursed his lips, the corners of his eyes wrinkling. Searching his chin with a finger, he found one lonely little strand. "Hm-m-m, I think I like it."

Togo's expression turned serious. "You know ... just for future reference, the man surrendered! You didn't have to spread him all over the plaza!"

"Never leave an enemy behind you, Togo."

"Sometimes an enemy can become a friend."

Ontarra's lips pinched together as he stared out past the doorskin. "I've yet to see it. He would have shown me no mercy. Why should anyone expect me to let him surrender?"

"They didn't, really." Togo rolled the bracelet over again, watching it fall to pieces on the coals. "The warriors were obliged to disarm you. You weren't even adopted yet. The decision to punish you was Tawanda's to make. He just needed some excuse to let you go, and Scajaweda provided that." Togo looked pointedly at Ontarra. "It seems you are in her debt."

Ontarra gave his head a frustrated shake. "Well, the world is a better place today without Chakadda."

"Apparently, most of the town agrees with you. He wasn't very well liked. I offered his clan two cakes of petun as restitution. They snapped it up. Pretty cheap." Togo looked at his hand, flexing the fingers again. Ontarra saw that they were swollen.

"What happened?"

"Mud wasp sting—very nasty. No Name and I are making sure that our friend Dekari stays in one place for a while." Togo picked up a bark container and dumped black rocks over the embers, spreading them out evenly with a stick. Before Ontarra could ask him why, blue flames started to lick up around them. Togo laughed at his shocked expression. "You've never seen fire rocks before?" He tossed one over.

Ontarra rolled the black stone on his palm. When light hit it the right way, the surface mirrored like water. "How does it work?"

Togo shrugged. "It's a rock that burns, that's all. No Name wanted a perfect bed of coals to burn the bracelet. Fire rock lasts much longer than wood."

Ontarra studied the charred bracelet, Togo's swollen fingers, and the blue flames dancing from the rocks. He tossed the stone back. He didn't want to know any more about No Name.

A girl's voice called a greeting from outside. Togo answered, flashing a grin at Ontarra. Scajaweda ducked in, with Stoolmaker right behind her. He plodded around the hearth and presented Ontarra with a beautifully crafted bow. Stoolmaker mumbled a few words and stepped back. Ontarra strung it, tested its tension, and glanced over at Togo for an explanation. Togo asked Stoolmaker a few questions before answering.

"You know the young warrior named Kadai?" Ontarra shrugged and shook his head. "He's one of the ones that brought you in," Togo explained. "When you ... disposed of Chakadda last night, he went to Chakadda's lodge and took that bow." Togo inclined his head to the weapon in Ontarra's hand. "He asked Stoolmaker to present it to you."

Ontarra stared at the bow, a smile spreading across his face. He set it on the platform and walked over to grip Stoolmaker's shoulders. A rank smell at that end of the lodge almost floored him. Ontarra stepped back, and then remembered where he'd smelled it before. His eyes shifted to Scajaweda. She was scratching again. "Thank you, Stoolmaker," he said, still eyeing Scajaweda, "and you also, Scajaweda, for your help last night." Togo translated. The two of them beamed from ear to ear as they listened to Ontarra's words. They ducked out again, bubbling with excitement as they headed down the path. Ontarra turned to Togo, asking, "What is that horrid smell?"

Togo fought back a grin. "It's a love potion." Ontarra's eyes widened. Togo chuckled. "Sumac and tobacco boiled down to a paste. The women make it and spread it over their bodies. Makes them ... irresistible."

Ontarra groaned. "That's an awful habit she's got, scratching herself all the time."

"That's not a habit. She got into blister bush last autumn. Must be driving her mad by now. I gave her a jewelweed salve for it, but she refuses to use it." Togo smirked. "Says it stinks."

Ontarra rolled his eyes to the rafters and stepped outside. He pulled out a hollow wooden vial as he walked to the ledge to look out at the valley. Swiping some of the paste out with his finger, he shoved it to the back of his tongue and choked it down. Togo came up beside him. Ontarra screwed up his face. "This stuff is awful."

"Lye and lilac paste is the fastest way to kill the worms. It's still going to be a while, though." They watched the activity in the town below. Togo shielded his eyes, staring out across the fields toward the river. Ontarra followed his gaze. Two warriors were drawing a lot of attention from the women planters. Ontarra looked at Togo, waiting for him to say something. Togo lowered his hand. "Tadodaroh and his brother are coming."

Ontarra studied the two as they strolled with self-assured strides along the north palisade, clubs and bows in plain sight but stowed in respect to Tawanda and his town. They moved with the haughty confidence of men whose reputations had preceded them. Black-maned heads held high, proud of who they were, and certain of their freedom to move unchallenged wherever they pleased. They headed across the fields for the path up the mountain. Ontarra went inside the lodge. He came back out wearing his waistband, with the club and dagger prominently displayed.

Togo looked over, annoyed. "We're just going to talk. You don't need those."

"I have no intention of talking to armed men without my weapons," Ontarra said flatly.

The two warriors walked up into the clearing. One was about Ontarra's age but a hand taller. Heavy skins covered a muscular frame. He stopped at the head of the path, coming no closer. The other, a cycle or two older, walked directly to Togo. They gripped each other's forearm and exchanged a few words. Togo smiled and dipped his head to the younger man. He returned the greeting.

"This is Tadodaroh," Togo said, releasing the warrior's arm to gesture at the man guarding the path, "and his brother Shonennkari." Ontarra dipped his head to each of them in the Sennikae manner. Togo and Tadodaroh started talking rapidly; Ontarra picked up pieces of the conversation. Tadodaroh was apparently not pleased at being called upon. The conversation shifted, centering on Ontarra. Togo pointed to him; Tadodaroh shot an unamused glare. Ontarra was growing irritated at being left out.

Tadodaroh made a fist, jabbing it toward the west. He used the word *Gahkwa* several times. The discussion was getting heated. Tadodaroh looked over at Ontarra and then back to Togo. The next word out of his mouth was *Dwakanah!* Ontarra's hand dropped to his club, and he took a step forward. Tadodaroh spun to face him, his club already half out.

"Ontarra, no!" Togo yelled.

"What does the word Dwakanah mean?" Ontarra kept his eyes fixed on Tadodaroh as he spoke.

"It's the name we use for your people."

"It sounds like an insult."

Togo rubbed his chin. "Well ..."

"That's what I thought! Any man not my friend is my enemy!" Ontarra shot a quick look at Shonennkari, surprised that he hadn't budged.

Togo looked apprehensively at the two warriors in front of him as they sized each other up—two stone wills, fearful of no man, ready to fight to the death at the slightest provocation. They were kindred spirits. Togo sensed that this was a momentous meeting, if only he could keep them from killing each other. "Ontarra, remember what I said about Chakadda. Enemies can become friends." Togo shifted his eyes to Tadodaroh. "Tado ... you owe me."

"This is the one who killed Chakadda?" Tadodaroh asked.

"Yes."

Tadodaroh saw Ontarra in a new light. He nodded slowly, sliding his club back in place, his ebony eyes never leaving Ontarra's.

"If we talk slowly," Togo suggested, "Ontarra will understand most of what we say."

Tadodaroh canted his head to one side, scrutinizing Ontarra. "I will help the ... Petun?" Tadodaroh waited to see if that word was acceptable. Ontarra gave his chin a dip. "I will help the Petun go into the land of the Gahkwas to get his woman back." Ontarra took his hand off his club and stepped back a few paces, calming himself. "I feel that I should warn him," Tadodaroh said, speaking haltingly to be certain he was understood, "that when she and I meet, she will probably want me."

Ontarra seemed baffled for a moment and then his hands came up, and he charged across the ledge. Tadodaroh turned his body slightly sideways to Ontarra, waiting for him to get close. The unusual move flustered Ontarra at the wrong moment. Tadodaroh's left hand shot out, slapping Ontarra's face as if he was an unruly woman being shown her place. Ontarra stopped cold, stunned by the stinging insult. Sannisen had spent a lot of time teaching Ontarra to control his anger in a fight. Ontarra was proud to have mastered the skill.

But not this time. Ontarra's eyes flared. Uncontrollable rage shot through him. He lunged with both hands for Tadodaroh's neck.

"Tado! Don't—" Togo never finished.

Tadodaroh's right arm uncoiled with the blinding speed of a rattling snake strike. Ontarra took the full impact on his chin. It snapped his head back, rocking him up onto his heels. His eyelids spasmed and fluttered shut, a swarm of fireflies swirling in behind them. Ontarra never felt the ground come up to meet him.

"... hit him in the head," Togo sighed, running a hand down his face as he finished his sentence.

19

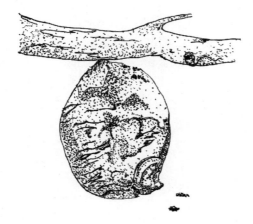

CLAN COUNCIL AT OUNONTISASTON WAS a sham. Hiatsou had appointed Winona to settle disputes between the moieties. Now she had the Power that had obsessed her for so long, and she was determined to use it. It was soon apparent in her prejudiced rulings that she intended to abuse the Land clans.

The daily workings of the community held little interest for Hiatsou. With the tribal chiefs all dead or missing, everything was so easy. He simply dictated his whims and desires to Winona. Occasionally, he made a formal appearance at council, regally folding himself down, honoring everyone with his presence. When he felt he'd spent enough time for them to admire his feather robe and headdress, he'd pretend to share an insight with Winona, and he was gone.

When anyone complained to Hiatsou about the new council, he sent them to Winona. If a person criticized the shamans, Winona made sure Hiatsou heard of it—the miscreant was soon performing menial tasks for the good of the community.

Unwilling to continue with the charade, the Land clans stopped attending council. Then Land clan families started to disappear. Men went out to hunt and never came back. Their women and children weren't missed until evening meal, when the planters came in and hearth fires were found empty. Overnight, the Power and authority Winona lusted for trickled away. She was nothing more than a glorified grandmother of the Bird clans again.

Winona marched the procession through the plaza, muttering to herself, her walking stick punctuating the air at the end of each string of epithets. They'd caught the Land clan maiden at the river, trying to steal a canoe. Her betrothed was already at Khioetoa. Winona intended to put an end to this once and for all. As they approached Hiatsou's lodge, the girl tried to squirm free of the shamans holding her. Winona got in front, cracking the girl's shin with the walking stick and raising a howl that reverberated around the town.

"Wait here! Don't let her get away!" Winona ordered. The doorskin of the lodge peeled back. Poutassa's face appeared for an instant, scowling when he saw Winona. The doorskin dropped back in place. Winona stormed up to the door, and the guards moved out of range of her stick. Winona didn't bother with formalities. She leaned onto her walking stick and barged inside. Hiatsou and Poutassa were seated on tripods across the hearth from each other, in the middle of a discussion.

"Finally caught one of 'em." Winona's voice was high-pitched and aggravating. "We have to make an example of her. We've already lost the older warriors and the experienced hunters." Hiatsou and Poutassa waited to be sure she was finished.

"We had the same problem at Tontiaton," Poutassa said. "Block all of your entries except one. Put four guards on it constantly." Poutassa smiled at the simplicity of the plan. "Keep all the Land clan women inside to perform the daily chores in the town—only the Bird clan women can go out into the fields. The men won't leave without their families." Poutassa turned back to Hiatsou to finalize their scheme.

"What about this girl that tried to run?" Winona pressed.

Poutassa's first impulse was to give Winona a swat, but he pursed his lips. "Cut the big toe off of each foot—she won't do any running after that." A grin spread across Winona's face as she turned to leave. The girl heard. She started putting up a fight as they dragged her toward the plaza. Winona cracked her across the temple this time.

Poutassa turned his attention back to Hiatsou. "We have to get some shamans to Teotonguiaton if we are to retain control there. The problem is, none want to go to a town without palisades now."

"I'll order them to go," Hiatsou huffed indignantly. "They'll have no choice." He locked his arms over his chest as he fumed. "We'll send some warriors along to protect the cowards if we must. They can keep the townspeople busy building a palisade."

"Feathered Serpent," one of the guards called from outside, "the party you sent out to find the witches' camp has returned. The warrior Kwonda asks to speak with you." Hiatsou and Poutassa settled their eyes on each other.

"Send him in."

The doorskin shoved back, and Kwonda ducked inside. He canted his head around, squinting while his eyes adjusted to the dim light. Hiatsou shoved a stool under him and sat him down. "Well?"

Kwonda nodded a greeting to Hiatsou and then to Windigo Killer. "We found it," he began, "way up the river that you told us about. It was in a strange valley of walnut trees. There's a ridge that wraps around a grove, with a creek running through it. We studied it from the river and then made our way up onto the ridge and followed the crest around until we were above the camp. A small rise extends out into the flats from the juncture of the two ridges. The remains of two lodges sat there—one burned, the other torn to shreds. At the base of the north–south ridge there appears to be a large grave."

"Appears?" Poutassa was aghast. "You didn't check?"

The color seemed to drain from Kwonda's face. "We spent two days circling around that grove. There are bones everywhere—deer, wolf, raccoon, marmot, turkey, fish ... and human. We found burned bones, bones chewed to pieces, bones with chert cuts in them, even the jaw of a wolf with the end of a chert blade in it. On the hillock down in that grove is a human skull mounted on a pole, with some hair still fluttering in the wind."

Poutassa's eyes snapped up to meet Kwonda's. "Was there a stone in the eye socket?"

Kwonda shrugged. "None of us dared to go down in there. Everything that goes into that grove dies. There are no birds, no animals, no fish in the river. It is a frightening place. We felt it would be best to report back. Maybe one of you could come, sanctify the place, and drive out the spirits that are lurking there."

Hiatsou's heart crawled up into his throat just thinking about it. "This is ludicrous!" He jumped to his feet and started stomping back and forth. "Are you telling me you're afraid of dead people? We need to know what is in that grave! You take your so-called warriors back there and finish the job I entrusted to you!"

Kwonda felt a surge of anger and came to his feet. "You have no right to imply that I am a coward until you have seen this place for yourself. You're the ones who are frightened. Feathered Serpent hasn't even gone outside the palisades in the past half cycle!"

"How dare you speak to me like that!" Saliva shot from the corner of Hiatsou's mouth. He clapped his hands. Two guards flew through the door. Kwonda stopped them short with a cold stare and a hand on his club. "You will carry out my orders!" Hiatsou's voice quaked.

Kwonda's mouth narrowed to a thin slit. He spun on a heel, elbowed the guards aside, and ducked out. Kwonda fumed all the way to the south entry. His men were waiting down in the canoe area where he'd left them. He'd suspected something like this would happen. Anxious eyes followed him as he drew closer. No one wanted to go back to that valley of bad spirits. Kwonda read the apprehension on their faces and made his decision.

"You can all go up and see your families." He smiled as the tension drained from their faces. "I have another trip I need to make." Kwonda watched somberly as they slogged up the bluff with their weapons and travel packs. He dragged a canoe down and pushed off. At the Tranchi, he swung downstream.

A woman's horrified scream echoed down out of the valley of the Entry River. Kwonda hung his head. Setting the paddle across the rails, he groped at his neck. With a yank he snapped off the raptor claw fetish that Poutassa had given to all the young warriors and tossed it in the river.

Kwonda looked over to where Ounontisaston was hidden by the forest, cursing under his breath. He picked up the paddle and headed for Khioetoa.

Ontarra sat up, swinging a puzzled gaze through the empty forest around him. Towering trees with ragged limbs groped at billowy clouds scudding past. He didn't know this place. His head hurt, his jaw hurt, and he had a pressing need to relieve himself of a healthy portion of Yalonda's stew.

Glancing around, he noticed some burdock leaves and tore several from the stalk. He tugged his leggings down, folding his arms behind his knees for a perch. The strain made his head throb. When he stood, he staggered sideways, tangling his feet in his leggings, and took a tumble.

"That was foolish, Ontarra."

The voice was familiar. Ontarra rolled onto his back to get a look. *Ounsasta.* He tugged his leggings up, lacing them before climbing to his feet again. *I ... I tripped over my leggings.*

Ounsasta folded his arms across his chest. "I didn't mean that. I was talking about losing your wits—letting the Onondaga bait you like that." Ounsasta shook his head slowly, staring off into the forest. "The deities have claimed you for a purpose. Many will suffer if you sacrifice yourself needlessly."

Slammer padded up to sit beside Ounsasta. He noticed something and stalked off again. Ounsasta followed the cat with his eyes. Ontarra turned. Slammer cautiously circled Ontarra's stool. Squirming gut worms made it seem alive. Slammer stared over at Ontarra and then buried the disgusting heap with a few Powerful sweeps of his rear paws. He padded back to take up his place beside Ounsasta, clearing the memory from his nostrils with two head-snapping snorts. Ontarra felt like crawling under a rock.

"He finds some of your habits ... distasteful," Ounsasta said bluntly. He shifted his eyes back up to Ontarra. "The girls are at the trader's lodge."

Are they all right?

"So far, but you must hurry. They leave in three days."

Ontarra nodded vacantly. He pressed at his temples, trying to gather his thoughts. It felt like someone was twisting a blade inside his head. Ounsasta turned to leave. *Ounsasta,* Ontarra said slowly, *did you ever know a woman named Kratcha?*

Ounsasta stopped, looking back at Ontarra with guilt-ridden eyes and holding the stare for several heartbeats. He ignored the question. "The Onondaga is chosen too. Don't destroy each other." Ounsasta turned and disappeared into the forest without another word. Ontarra sat himself down, squeezing his temples between both palms to keep them from bursting.

Six heavily armed men, in clothing designed for travel, appeared on the ridge above Teotonguiaton. They scrutinized the town and the faces in it and then continued on down with a boldness born of resolve. A young girl noticed the ominous group first and ran to her mother.

"He's back!" Anxious faces around the town glanced up at the men who suddenly appeared in their midst. Children ran up the hill to the first man in the party, clinging to his heavy leggings. He had a kind word and a smile for each of them. He hopped up onto a hollowed-out boulder that served as the community mortar. People came from all directions, gathering around in a circle. Two of the man's companions continued on down to watch the river. Two split off left and right toward each of the tree lines. The last took up a position on the hill behind the leader.

The man on the boulder studied the faces turned up to him. "Some of you have known me since I was a child," he began, "most of you have known me only this past half cycle. Still, I hope that all of you will believe the words that I speak today." He paused a heartbeat for effect. "I have been successful in the duty you entrusted to me. Shadaki and I discussed many things. People are arriving at Khioetoa from all of our territories, people who have abandoned all that they have in order to gain freedom. In Khioetoa we can start over, rebuilding our lives in the harmony we once knew, without being dictated to or preyed upon." The man swung his eyes over the Land clan faces in the crowd.

"Shadaki welcomes his brothers, the Land clans of Teotonguiaton. Already the Fire People have heard of the turmoil in our lands and plan to take advantage. He needs your help to feed the town and to protect it from the Agwa raiders." Bird clan people started forming into groups, muttering apprehensively among themselves. The man on the mortar stone understood their concerns.

"Shadaki sends this message to the Bird clans of Teotonguiaton." The mumbling stopped as all eyes focused on the speaker. "Shadaki appeals to you for your assistance in helping him to feed all the newcomers. There are not enough fishermen or planters to provide for everyone's needs. All of the Bird clans are already represented at his council. Shadaki welcomes you all with open arms." Excited voices started chattering all across the hillside.

"Is there room for everyone?" a man called out.

"The town is full. Three new longhouses are being erected outside the walls. The palisade will soon be expanded to accommodate everyone. There is much that needs to be done." The man rested his hands on his hips as he studied the crowd. "Any among you who wishes to run to Hiatsou and Poutassa, you are free to go now." He pointed to the canoe area. No one moved.

"Very well." He nodded. "We have warriors waiting at Iannaoa to escort you—" A bird-bone whistle shrilled from the river, interrupting him. His two companions trotted up from the canoe area. They whispered in his ear, pointing to the river. Three canoes sliced out from behind the veil of trees and turned in toward shore. The man on the boulder gestured to his men on the hill. They moved down into the crowd, where they'd be less conspicuous.

Four Bird clan warriors, followed by two shamans, jumped out of the canoes and strolled up toward the gathering with suspicious eyes. The leader stopped a stone's throw away, studying the man standing on the mortar. "Who are you?" he demanded.

The man on the mortar ignored the warrior as he turned back to the crowd. "Everyone who is coming with us, go get your things, and gather on top of the ridge." The people began to disperse.

The Bird clan warrior looked at all the people heading back to their lodges; his face turned dark. "Going where? We've been sent here by Feathered Serpent and Windigo Killer to be sure the people of Teotonguiaton are safe and secure."

The man on the boulder folded his arms. Penetrating eyes swung from the warrior to the two young shamans. "Are your shamans not concerned about the wrath of Sannisen and Shanoka?" He could see from their startled expressions that they were.

People were already gathering on the ridge above. The angry Bird clan warrior glanced up at them. "You people get down here! We've brought shamans to tend to your spiritual needs!"

The man on the boulder shook his head, "They're going with us"—his arms unfolded, dropping subtly to his sides—"to Khioetoa."

The warrior's jaw dropped; his hand fell to his club. The men behind him rushed to string their bows. "You dare to defy Feathered Serpent! Do you know what he will do to you when we bring you in?"

The dauntless man on the mortar stone canted his head to one side. "Hmm ... Poutassa will probably turn me into a she-bitch and tie me to a tree. Hiatsou will want to watch."

The club was out now. The Bird clan warriors started fanning sideways. "You think that we'll let you take all of these people to Khioetoa? Hah! The warriors of Ounontisaston and Tontiaton will be on you before you got halfway to Iannaoa."

"Yes, I suppose they would ... if they knew." The man stepped down off the boulder, leveling a withering stare at the arrogant traitor. *Fwoosh!* The people gathered on the ridge saw a blur streak across the gap that separated the two men; it stopped abruptly at the Bird clan warrior's face with the sound of a stone bouncing off a hollow tree trunk. The impact lifted the warrior off his feet; his club tumbled through the air. He landed with all his weight on the back of his head. Even the people up on top of the ridge heard the unmistakable sound of vertebrae crunching.

The shamans hit the dirt, trying to become invisible. Arrows shrieked across the hillside from the lodges and the western treeline. Two more Bird clan warriors went down. The last warrior dropped his bow and ran for the river. A man stepped out of the trees below, blocking his path. The Bird clan warrior judged instantly that the man was smaller than he was and that his only visible weapon ... was a walking staff. The warrior charged on.

Unfazed, the smaller man held his ground. Leaning carelessly on his staff, he bent his left leg up at an odd angle, resting the foot on his right knee while he casually watched the man bearing down upon him. Not until the last instant did the warrior have any misgivings, but it was too late. Taskinao dropped flat on his back, planting the butt of his staff firmly in the ground, and angling the point up at the warrior's chest. It drove through his rib cage, hit something solid, and vaulted the man over Taskinao into one of the canoes in the river. The canoe burst into shattered pieces of sapling and elm bark. The warrior sat waist-deep in water and mud, staring in shock at the shaft he was impaled upon.

Taskinao walked up. To the warrior's horror, he grabbed the staff and tried to tug it out, but it was lodged between two ribs. The terrified warrior grabbed hold and pulled back. Taskinao walked his hands down the shaft, pulling the warrior closer, and kicked him off with his left foot. The warrior rolled face down and floated off with the hulk of the canoe.

Taskinao plunged the point of his staff into the muddy river bottom to clean it and then strolled up the hill. He cast a wicked grin at the two mortified shamans quaking on the ground and studied the mashed face of the warrior lying next to them. He slapped Toutsou on the back as he bent to pick up his throw-stick, "Great shot, Toutsou!"

Toutsou slid the weapon into a special pocket laced into the right thigh of his leggings, sharing a quick smirk with Taskinao. He glanced over at the shamans and pulled his skinning knife.

Ontarra smelled smoke and forced his eyes to open. He didn't recognize the lodge at first, until Togo came through the door. Then it all came back to him. He pushed himself up on the platform. The pain in his head was gone, but his jaw made up for it. Wrapping his fingers around his chin, he rocked the joint back and forth, expecting to hear the crunch of bone fragments.

"I warned you about Tadodaroh."

Ontarra shot a perturbed glare at Togo, working his mouth a few more times to be certain everything was functioning properly. "How did he do that?"

Togo threw his hands up, giving his head a bewildered shake. "I've watched it many times, and I'm still not sure." Togo settled down beside Ontarra to check the dressing on his head wound. "All I can tell you is that he plants himself in one place, and lets his adversary come to him. He never allows him to get close enough to touch him, and he strikes with his hands."

Ontarra studied his hand skeptically, shook his head, and rubbed his jaw again. "It feels like a war club cracked me." He jerked his head away as Togo hit a tender spot.

"Sorry. There was a lot of bad blood in there. I had to cut the wound open and let it out." Togo picked up a rabbit hide stained with Ontarra's blood. "You should be okay now. The bleeding seems to be stopped."

"How long have I …"

"Been resting?" Togo grinned. "All day."

Ontarra looked out the door at the fading daylight. "Good, there's still time. Ounsasta said that the girls will be at the trader's lodge for three days."

Togo sat back so he could see Ontarra's face. "Ounsasta speaks to you in your dreams?"

Ontarra nodded and then paused. "Actually, he seems to come to me when I'm sick or injured."

Togo rested his chin on his fingers thoughtfully. "Three days. That's exactly what No Name told me. You know," Togo said, studying Ontarra, "you aren't in very good shape for this. You should at least rest another day."

Ontarra stood up, teetered a bit, took two wobbly steps and turned. "I'll be fine by morning. If you don't want to take me, just tell me how to find him."

Togo sighed and steepled his fingers. "Tadodaroh and I have already discussed it. I will leave tomorrow, traveling as a trader."

"He's still here? After what happened?"

Togo answered with a dip of his chin. "He and Shonennkari are down at the town. He said that if you live, they'll go with you."

Ontarra couldn't fathom it. He would never have been so noble. He sat himself down again. "Why?"

Togo moistened his lips. "He owes me a debt, which I'd rather not talk about, but he feels he owes you one too." Togo smiled at Ontarra's puzzled look. "For killing Chakadda. He's been waiting for an opportunity for two cycles. Now you've saved him the trouble."

Ontarra shook his head in wonder. "Mother always said that every life touches another." Ontarra stared outside. Twilight was settling over the land, but the hillside across the valley was still ablaze in brilliant sunlight. He wondered if Sounia and Taiwa were watching this sunset. He knew Teota wasn't. "Togo," Ontarra said, swinging his eyes, "we have a real chance at getting the girls back now."

Togo got up and walked around the hearth fire, perching on his haunches to add some sticks. "I will leave during the night. That will put me in Gahkwa territory at sunup. They won't bother a harmless old trader traveling in daylight." Togo stirred at the coals as he pictured the journey in his mind. "Tado has been to Cha-ta-kwa, but I am going to leave a single slash on trees along the way so you can follow the same trails. If I meet anyone, or there is any danger in the area, the tree will have three slashes in its bark." Ontarra stared into the fire, bobbing his head almost imperceptibly.

"When will we leave?"

"I will send word down that you'll be ready to move at midday. They'll come up here to prepare. You'll be able to get through the mountains before dark. With luck you can make the lake by sunup." Togo stirred the coals again and tossed his stir-stick on the embers. Resting his hands on his thighs, he fixed Ontarra with a somber stare. "Promise me you will do whatever Tadodaroh asks, Ontarra. He knows the Gahkwas and their ways."

Ontarra's fingers laced and unlaced as he returned Togo's stare. "I would follow anyone to anywhere right now, Togo, if they could help me get Sounia and Taiwa back."

A voice called out from beyond the doorskin. "Togo, it's me, may I enter?"

Togo straightened up and went over to hold the doorskin back. "Come in, Yalonda."

Yalonda breezed through carrying two reed baskets. She set them down near the hearth and then spun to peck Togo's cheek before nestling two bark pots and what appeared to be three bricks of mud on the coals. Yalonda took a seat on the platform across from Ontarra, flashing a dazzling smile. Ontarra had to smile back. "Your ... head." She patted the back of her head. "It is ... gooder?" Ontarra arched a brow and glanced at Togo.

He smirked. "She wants to know if you're feeling better." Ontarra grinned and nodded.

Yalonda's smile melted away, her face turning solemn. "I am ... with Shanoka ... much sorrowed. We share ... happy times ... us."

Ontarra's eyes swung back to Togo. "She knew Mother?"

Togo pulled a tripod stool over and sat at the hearth. "She was like a mother to Shanoka. When Shanoka first came to live here, Yalonda took her for long walks on the mountains. She'd never seen such large mountains before. Shanoka loved being so high up, watching the turkey vultures soar along the ridges. Yalonda spent many hours sitting with her, watching the birds, while she taught her our language and our customs."

Yalonda laughed suddenly and started talking to Togo in the fast, clipped Sennikae tongue. Ontarra caught a few of the words but couldn't keep up. Yalonda finished by smacking her palms together and rotating her hands around each other as she dropped them to her knees. Togo and Yalonda shared a long laugh. Ontarra canted his head, scowling at Togo for being left out.

Togo felt Ontarra's stare. "Oh ..." He wiped at the corner of his eye, still giggling. "Your mother and Yalonda were out on the ledge in front of my lodge one day, watching two hands of the vultures flying wingtip to wingtip."

They were showing off, dipping and diving at each other like they always do. Shanoka started telling Yalonda how amazed she was at the vultures' flying skills, always being able to avoid calamity at the last possible instant." Togo started chuckling again. "And as the words came out of her mouth, two collided head-on and tumbled down into the trees." Togo rocked with laughter. Yalonda started up, and Ontarra couldn't help himself.

They talked on into the night. Ontarra wasn't tired, and Togo didn't dare to sleep. Yalonda served fish stew. When they finished, she cracked the tops off the mud cakes to reveal quails roasted in their own juices. Ontarra heard stories of his mother's life at Joneadih. He related the last days that they had all been together at the hunt camp. Togo finished his quail and set the mud bowl aside.

"The walnut valley sounds like a beautiful place," he said, unfolding himself upright. "She'll be happy there."

Ontarra set his bowl beside him on the platform, staring wistfully back into time in the pulsing embers. "I didn't realize it then, but it is one of the happiest times I've ever known," he said softly. The lodge was silent for a while as Togo started loading a travel pack. Yalonda cleaned up her things and then dug into the other basket and pulled out four buckskin-wrapped bundles that she laid on the platform.

"Travel food," she held both of Togo's hands a moment, staring up at him. He gave her a hug. She picked up her baskets and ducked out.

"I like her very much." Ontarra smiled. "In many ways, she reminds me of Mother."

"She was a big influence on your mother." Togo threw his pack up on his shoulder and moved to the door but turned back to Ontarra. Their eyes held each other, both realizing it could be their last moments together. "Ontarra, if I don't get back and you do, promise me you will take care of Yalonda." Ontarra pursed his lips, looked away, and nodded.

"Togo," Ontarra said, reaching out to squeeze his arm, "the manitos be with you."

Togo flashed a smile and disappeared into the night.

Ontarra knew he should try to sleep, but he couldn't. He laid his weapons out on the platform, checked them, and cleaned them. He packed his carry pouch with Yalonda's travel food. He paced for a while and checked everything again.

He went out and sat on the ledge to watch the sunrise, wondering how many more he would see. A river of fog flowed down the valley below him, hiding everything from sight. He listened to the harsh, abrupt noise the Sennikae dogs made. Togo called it barking. Ethereal voices and the spectral sounds of children told him the town was coming to life. Ontarra ambled back in, shoved his weapons aside, and lay down. He sifted through his memories, staring up into the rafters a long while before finally drifting off.

He dreamed he was flying over sand dunes bordering a vast lake. He saw three canoes on the beach and swooped down low. In a hollow, one dune back from the shore, men sat in a circle. No fire was lit to give them away. He saw the bare heads and topknots of the outsiders. His eyes searched around for Sounia and Taiwa, but he couldn't see them. Movements caught his eye. He saw men stalking in from three sides behind the surrounding dunes. He scanned desperately for the girls, so he could warn them.

Ontarra jerked upright, drenched in sweat. The air in Togo's lodge was stifling hot under a midday sun. Swinging his feet to the floor, he wiped away perspiration with his hands. Out on the ledge, the breeze felt almost icy as it played across his skin. He saw Tadodaroh and Shonennkari leaving the town and heading out across the fields. Ontarra went back inside, tied his waistband on, sheathed his dagger, and hung his club in place. He had Chakadda's bow but only three arrows. Footsteps approached on the path. The doorskin drew back. Shonennkari's face appeared. Ontarra motioned him inside.

Shonennkari laid a burden pack on the free platform and rolled it open. Tadodaroh ducked and stepped inside. He locked eyes with Ontarra for a heartbeat and then dipped his head. Ontarra returned the gesture. Both were dressed in heavy skins. Ontarra felt a little embarrassed at his own worn-out clothing.

Their bows and arrows were tied tightly together with a carrying strap. Shonennkari unrolled several buckskin bundles. Tadodaroh slid chert daggers into sheaths sewn in his clothing, behind his neck, and at the small of his back. Shonennkari set two long, pointed bones off to one side. Ontarra picked one up curiously—the shinbone of a deer, split in half, smoothed into a small flat handle with a carefully honed, handspan-length point, half the thickness of an arrow shaft. It would reach any organ in the body with a light jab.

Ontarra handed it back. Shonennkari slid it into a sheath in the top of his high moccasin. Ontarra sat down to watch. They hung a carry pouch under each arm, filling one with what appeared to be round stones with white dots painted on one side. Shonennkari looked over at Ontarra. "Food?" He put his fingers to his mouth.

Ontarra jumped up and grabbed Yalonda's packs, handing one to each of them. They stuffed them in the other carry pouch. Shonennkari pulled out a handful of porcupine quills. Splitting them with Tadodaroh, he set the rest on top of the food in his carry pouch. Then he stepped over and checked Ontarra's clothes and weapons, shaking his head.

He went back to the pack and came up with some extra arrows and a carry strap. He bundled Ontarra's bow and arrows together and tossed him a pair of heavy, lace-up moccasins. Ontarra accepted gratefully. He watched as they smeared their faces and hair with bear grease and tied headbands on. Tadodaroh threw the grease to Ontarra. Clubs and skinning knives were hung in place, and they were ready to go.

Ontarra struggled with the bow-and-arrow bundle. Tadodaroh slung it over his back properly. Ontarra swallowed his pride. "I thank you both for staying to help me."

Tadodaroh settled his eyes on Ontarra with a blank expression. "I just pay ... debt."

They went up the mountain from Togo's, over the top, and down into the next valley. The climb up the next ridge was slow and tedious. At the top, Ontarra was surprised to see only a few rolling hills and then flatlands stretching off to the west in the setting sun. "No more mountains?"

"No." Shonennkari shook his head. "At bottom, in Gahkwa lands, no more ... talk."

At the base of the ridge they picked up a well-worn trail heading west. The going was easier as they left the hills behind. Tadodaroh picked up the pace. They kept a steady gait, even after darkness had blanketed the landscape. The moon rose behind them, bathing the forest in a ghostly light. As the night wore on, Ontarra found his vision was becoming as keen as in daylight.

Tadodaroh pulled to a stop, whispering softly to Shonennkari. Then he looked to Ontarra and pointed to a tree. A slash cut in the bark showed clearly in the moonlight. They continued on without stops until the moon was high in the sky. Ontarra was amazed at the trails they were using. Worn deep and smooth through the forest, two men could easily walk abreast on them. He wondered if the Gahkwas had cut them out. Tadodaroh stopped again. Ahead of them in the moonlight was a wide swath of burned-out forest, smoke still rising from the charred stumps and timbers.

The fire swept through a stretch of lowland where only pines and cedars had grown. Jumping from tree to tree and roaring along the carpet of dried needles, the inferno had spent itself without spreading into the hardwood forest around it. "We can't expose ourselves crossing this. We'll have to go around," Shonennkari whispered. They wasted valuable time before finding their way back onto the trail again.

The sky in the east was hinting at dawn when they came to a sharp bend in the path. Tadodaroh pulled to a halt. He held a finger to his lips as Shonennkari and Ontarra came up. He tapped his finger on a tree. It had three slashes in the bark. Tadodaroh gestured for them to remain as he prowled off around the bend. Returning in a hand of time, he held nine fingers up. Shonennkari shook his head.

Tadodaroh nodded agreement. He held up one finger and indicated they should follow in complete silence. They skulked along in a crouch. Off through the trees on their left, Ontarra could see the twinkling of hearth fires in a low gully. To their right, a rushing stream bordered the path, preventing them from circling silently around the camp. Tadodaroh held up a hand, pointing to a tree ahead.

The Gahkwas had placed a sentry to watch the trail. He was reclining with his back to a tree, sound asleep. Tadodaroh stalked up silently and wrapped his left arm around the tree, covering the man's mouth. His right hand swept around the other side. After a moment, he waved to Ontarra and Shonennkari. Ontarra was amazed; he hadn't heard a sound. Creeping up, he glanced over Shonennkari's shoulder, grimaced, and looked away.

A porcupine quill was rammed into the man's ear canal. Tadodaroh plucked a leaf from a bush, tugged the quill from the man's ear, and used it to stuff the leaf in and stop the blood. He wiped away the telltale specks on the man's ear lobe and padded off down the trail again. Ontarra studied the Gahkwa, sleeping just as tranquilly as when they had arrived. It was going to be a long sleep.

The sun was coming up. Tadodaroh picked up the pace again. They were late, possibly jeopardizing Togo. As they loped along, daylight began to reveal the depths of the forest. Ontarra was stunned by its beauty. It was unlike any place he'd ever seen. The trees grew to stupendous heights, trunks stretching upward a full stone's throw before even sprouting branches. The trunks were as thick as the length of a longbow, huge knobby roots snaking out in all directions.

The forest was dim, cool, and open. Hardly any underbrush grew. Instead, a green moss carpeted everything, even growing up the tree trunks and dripping from boulders. The trees were widely spaced, their first leaves now beginning to sprout high overhead. Some kind of vine draped down from the branches, giving the canopy a feathery look.

With daylight came the melodious sounds of cicadas, spring peepers, and wood frogs. The trio trotted down through some boulders into a low swampy area that was teeming with mosquitoes. Shonennkari scooped up some of the thick black muck beside the path as they dashed through the swarm. When they reached high ground again, they stopped and smeared the muck over their exposed skin to deter the insects.

"How did these trails get here?" Ontarra whispered between breaths. Shonennkari gave him a look that made him wish he hadn't asked.

"Buffalo," Shonennkari grunted and started off again. Ontarra shook his head and followed. He'd have to find out what that meant another time.

The forest gradually started to change. The enormous pillars of oak, hickory, and beech diminished. Stands of silver maple, white elm, and birch began to appear. Ontarra could see clumps of rockwood in the distance, shimmering in morning heat. The sun was two fingers above the eastern horizon when he saw glittering flashes of sunlight on water up ahead.

They came out onto a hillside covered with cedar and tamarack. The hill sloped down to the shore of a long, thin lake. Wildflowers were blooming in a wild display of color. Ontarra was astonished to see a bright orange bird fly by him. Tadodaroh pointed across the lake. Three longhouses and a smattering of lodges sat on the far shore. They moved down the hillside to a vantage point where they could see the north end of the lake. The slope on the north shore was burned clear. On the top sat a single lodge.

They crept back up into the forest and followed a buffalo trail running north along the lake. As they neared the northern end, they came to a tree with three slashes in the bark. Tadodaroh and Shonennkari whispered. Tadodaroh pointed to some marks on a rock, scratched there with the black burning stones. Shonennkari looked over at Ontarra and pointed up the path, mouthing, *Togo*.

Togo's position might have been compromised because of their late arrival, so Tadodaroh slipped off the trail and into the brush. They crept forward as if they were entering an enemy camp. Togo was hunched down in the branches of a tall cedar, eyeing the lodge up on the hill. Tadodaroh stole up behind him in perfect silence. Ontarra wished he could warn Togo, but there was nothing he could do.

Tadodaroh clamped a hand over Togo's mouth, hauling him backward out of the cedar. Ontarra felt a wave of guilt when he saw the terror in Togo's eyes. Tadodaroh lowered Togo down, holding a tight embrace until he was sure he'd settled from his fright, and then he slowly released him. Togo propped himself up on one arm, laying a hand over his heart while he caught his breath.

"Tado, if you ever do that to me again ... I'll have No Name infest your nether-regions with the red lice!" Togo snarled between gasps. Tadodaroh's features cracked open into the first smile Ontarra had ever seen on that rigid face. Togo sat up and stared over at the lodge. "The three strangers and the girls left at dawn."

"You saw Sounia and Taiwa!" Ontarra whispered, his voice trembling with excitement.

Togo nodded. "They were all carrying packs. I think they're going somewhere. Two women from the town just brought Dekari his morning meal and left again. He's still inside. I think he's alone, but I'm not sure."

Tadodaroh checked the sun. "We can waste no more time."

In a hand, they were crouched in the woods behind the lodge. No sounds came from inside. "I'll go in first," Togo whispered. "It'll throw them off. If he's not alone, you'll know by the voices." Tadodaroh pulled a headband down over his forehead to keep any stray strands of hair from marring his vision; he nodded. Togo stood up, straightened his pack, and walked into the clearing and down the side of the lodge.

"Who's that?" a voice called from inside. "Who's out there?" Togo disappeared around the front. "Who are you? What do you think you're doing, traipsing into a man's lodge with no warning?"

"Hello, Dekari. It's been a long time. Whewf! That arm looks awful! Those mud wasps pack a lot of venom, don't they?" The warriors in the brush listened intently to the conversation only a few feet ahead of them. Dekari's angry voice turned quavery and uncertain. "Togo? Is it you? What … what are you doing here?"

"I've come for my daughters." Togo's voice changed instantly. "Where are they?"

"Are you addled? How would I know? I've been lying here sick for two moon cycles now … arrhh!"

Ontarra sprang to his feet, dashed to the front of the lodge, and burst through the door. The trader writhed on his sleep platform in obvious pain. Togo was wringing his swollen arm. Ontarra lunged, landing with one leg on each side of Dekari's chest, his skinning knife pressed to the windpipe. "Try telling me you've been in here sick for two moon cycles!"

Dekari forgot all about the pain in his arm as he stared in horror at the mud-encrusted apparition ready to cut his throat. "You … it can't be you … I saw them kill you!"

"You made a big mistake, trader." Ontarra pressed on the knife. "You didn't finish me."

"All right! All right!" Dekari choked. "But it wasn't me who killed your family and took the girls. It was those crazy Tunicans!" Ontarra relaxed the knife a bit. Dekari looked past Ontarra at the two mud-caked warriors who followed him in and realized there was only one way he was going to survive this. "Look—they're all down in the dunes making a trade. I'll take you there."

Ontarra tilted his head to one side. "Is that what this has all been about? They just wanted the girls for barter!" Ontarra almost pressed the knife home.

Togo stopped him. "We need him to show us where they are."

Ontarra stepped to the floor, pulling Dekari up by his hair. "If you're lying, trader, I'll cut you apart, piece by piece." Shonennkari wanted to tie Dekari's hands, but his left arm was so swollen he didn't dare. "Tie a tether around his neck," Ontarra growled. "I'll take care of him." Tadodaroh stepped outside and checked to be sure that the area was still secure. He stuck his head back in with a quick dip of his chin.

Dekari led them down the trail to the lake. Ontarra kept him on a short leash, yanking his head backward occasionally just for spite. The trail was wide and well used. When they came upon a bench designed for rest stops, Tadodaroh insisted that they leave the trail before running into someone.

Twice they had to stop and put a knife to Dekari's throat as people passed by on the path.

The sun was at its highest point when the trees began to diminish in size. White-barked saplings began to encroach on the hardwoods. The soil turned sandy under their feet. Dune grasses and clumps of poplar were springing up. Dekari pointed off to the right. They followed the trough of a low sand drift until Dekari stopped, looking around at his surroundings. He jabbed a finger toward the sound of the waves. "Show us!" Ontarra growled in his ear.

They went up over the drift and then climbed to the top of a higher dune. Clumps of scrubby bush and cattails were scattered everywhere through the hollows and partway up the slopes. The warriors didn't like the amount of cover that adversaries could be hiding in.

"They're over the next dune," Dekari choked out—a little too loud.

Ontarra yanked the leash, wrapping it up in his left hand until his knuckles were right behind the trader's neck. He stuck his knife to Dekari's ear and whispered, "You first." Ontarra stood him up, and they all splashed down through the sand into the hollow, using Dekari as a shield. At the bottom, Dekari came to an abrupt stop. He tried shuffling backward, but Ontarra wouldn't let him. Ontarra shook the trader's head until his teeth rattled. "What's wrong with you, maggot?" Dekari croaked something incoherent, the words bunching up in his throat. He pointed a trembling hand to the top of a poplar ahead. Ontarra glanced up and saw a paper wasp nest waving gently in the breeze off the lake.

"He's terrified of bees and hornets," Togo said softly.

Ontarra tried pushing Dekari, but he planted his feet and refused to budge. "All right, if that's the way you want it." Ontarra pulled the buckskin swath from his head wound, forcing it into Dekari's mouth. He reefed the knot up so tight that Dekari looked like an old woman with no teeth. Ontarra started hauling him forward by the tether. Dekari shook his head, balking and dropping to his knees to resist. Ontarra leaned into the tether, dragging Dekari by the neck across the sand, almost pinching his head from his body.

Ontarra stopped under the poplar with the wasp nest in the top, sat Dekari upright, and pried the noose open so he could breathe again. Mucus blew out of Dekari's nostrils and mouth as his lungs started working. Ontarra slapped him. Winding the tether around the tree and Dekari's neck, he knotted it, and used the remainder to bind his wrists behind the trunk. When Ontarra sat back on his heels again, Dekari was staring straight up at the wasps, a glassy look of abject fear fixed in his eyes. *He really is terrified of the wasps.*

They clawed their way to the top of the dune and poked their heads up over. Ontarra recognized the scene instantly from his dream. The outsiders were seated cross-legged, facing three men across a trade blanket spread out between them. A pipe was passing around. Behind them, partway up the next dune, Sounia and Taiwa were sitting in the sand. Ontarra yanked his head back down.

Tadodaroh grabbed his arm. "Is it them?" Ontarra nodded, his mind elsewhere ... thinking back to his dream. He must have seen himself and the Onondagas stealing up on this trade meeting.

Tadodaroh drew a circle in the sand with his finger, poked a hole in the center, and pointed toward the men in the hollow. "On-ta-ra, Togo, remain here." Tadodaroh poked a hole at the bottom of the circle and then another at the top. "Shonennkari—other side." Tadodaroh poked one final hole on the right side of the circle and pointed to himself. "We must wait for Shonennkari. When he attacks, we all go. Use your arrows first and then clubs."

Ontarra gave his chin an affirmative jerk. "Don't risk hitting the girls."

Tadodaroh and Shonennkari gripped each other's shoulders and cascaded down the dune in opposite directions. Ontarra lay on his side and untied his bow-and-arrow bundle. Togo kept bobbing his head up over the top, watching the bartering progress. Ontarra finished stringing his bow, set his arrows just behind the crest, and popped his head up.

Shonennkari hadn't had enough time to get into position on the far dune yet. Ontarra slid back down, sucking deep breaths to calm his nerves. He noticed that Dekari was unconsciously gnawing on his gag out of raw fear, his eyes still glued to the wasp nest.

"There's Shonennkari," Togo whispered, pointing across the hollow toward the next dune. Ontarra rolled to his stomach and wormed his way up. Shonennkari was nestled in some brush on top of the far dune; he looked across. Ontarra pointed to the men in the hollow. Shonennkari shook his head, pointing east down the dune, and then made a petting motion with his hand.

"What does that mean?" Ontarra muttered, slipping back down.

"Tadodaroh isn't in position yet." Togo answered. Ontarra's heart was racing. He couldn't take much more waiting. Togo was still peering over the top.

"What are they doing now?"

"One of the strangers is angry. He threw a bag at the Gahkwas. He's getting up ... Ontarra! Look!" Togo pointed at Shonennkari again. Ontarra poked his head up.

"What?"

Off to Shonennkari's left, something moved in the brush. Ontarra squinted, scrutinizing every branch and leaf that waved in the breeze. Then he saw an elbow ... and a moccasin. Ontarra locked eyes with Togo. "The dream was a warning that this is a trap!" Ontarra muttered aloud.

Togo's eyes wrinkled. "What are you talking about?"

Ontarra's mind was racing. He tried to think of some way to warn the others before it was too late—and then another thought sent a chill through him. Ontarra grabbed his bow and whirled around. A Gahkwa warrior was standing beside Dekari, his bow already coming up. Ontarra put a foot against Togo and pushed off. Togo flew sideways, and Ontarra landed on his back—the Gahkwa's arrow burrowed into the sand at his feet.

Ontarra nocked and fired from his waist. The Gahkwa warrior was already drawing his second shot. Ontarra's arrow disappeared into his mouth and kept on going. The warrior froze up in wide-eyed astonishment. His hand started to spasm. The arrow released, flying off into the brush. As the tremors traveled up his arm, the man dropped to his knees—and fell flat on his face. Ontarra sat up, looking over to see if Togo was all right. Then he glared at Dekari.

"You filthy little worm!" Ontarra snarled through his teeth. He raised his bow, lining up on Dekari's heart ... but he hesitated. The trader was still fixated on the wasp nest. Ontarra raised his bow and let fly. The arrow blew an opening through the center of the nest, swinging it wildly back and forth. An angry cloud billowed out through the breach. Dekari made a high-pitched squealing sound.

Ontarra didn't have any more time to waste on him. He grabbed his arrows and went over the top, screaming, "Shonennkari! Behind you! Look behind you!" Ontarra ran halfway down the slope, slammed his arrows into the sand, nocked, and aimed at the intruder. He raised his bow to the sky for the longest possible trajectory. Twenty pairs of eyes locked on the arrow-flight. It plunged into the dune a canoe-length short, but Shonennkari saw his adversary and was on him.

Ontarra swung to his right, scanning the crest for Tadodaroh. He saw him standing at the far end, firing down the backside at someone. Ontarra turned his attention to the group at the trade blanket. Weapons weren't allowed during barter; all they had were knives. Ontarra launched four arrows in rapid succession. The stunned men scattered, and two Erieehronons fell to their sides on the blanket.

Ontarra glanced over to see how Shonennkari was faring. He had the first man down, but he was fighting two more, swinging his club in one hand and a knife in the other. Ontarra nocked and fired. One of Shonennkari's opponents took it in the thigh. Ontarra saw Mox, who'd been sitting near the girls, pick up his maul and start slogging his way across the face of the dune toward Shonennkari. Ontarra drew down, but suddenly Tadodaroh was screaming at him.

Ontarra swung right. Tadodaroh charged down into the hollow with three warriors hot on his heels. Ontarra bowled the first one over with an arrow to the chest. Tadodaroh turned on the remaining two and started drilling round stones with white dots at them. Manak and Matoupa grabbed the girls on their way up the dune, pulling them toward the top. Ontarra couldn't risk a shot at them now. Mox was closing on Shonennkari from behind. Ontarra drew a lead and fired. The arrow plowed into the dune just below the lumbering brute. A second arrow splashed in, spraying sand up just behind Mox's head.

Ontarra whirled around to see who was behind him. Togo was firing from the top of the dune with the Gahkwa's bow. Ontarra spun back for another shot. A horrendous scream echoed through the dunes, shooting icy tendrils through every soul who heard it. It was followed by another … and another. Even the war clubs stopped in midair, as everyone tried to determine the source of the blood-curdling sound. Only Togo was in a position to see the cause.

The wasp nest had rocked loose from the tree, crashing apart like a shattered egg at Dekari's feet. Dekari bit through his gag to make the last sounds of his life. The angry cloud transformed into a whirlwind of yellow fury. It ebbed left, swirled right, then honed in on the smell of fear emanating from Dekari's pores, and it engulfed him. The screams choked out as Dekari disappeared beneath a hideous, crawling shroud. Togo had to look away.

Tadodaroh dropped his last adversary with a flurry of blows. He turned to stare over at Shonennkari in dismay. Mox was almost upon him. Shonennkari caught his last man off balance and drove a knife up under the rib cage. The warrior slumped forward. Shonennkari threw him off. Ontarra fired at Mox again—and missed. He threw down his bow, cupped his hands to his mouth, and screamed. Tadodaroh hollered. Shonennkari had started to turn when the maul slammed into the back of his head. Ontarra closed his eyes.

Shonennkari went down hard, but Mox wasn't finished. Any man whose testicle had been clubbed and squashed had a right to take it out on someone. Mox swung the big maul again and again. Ontarra knew Shonennkari was done, so he grabbed his bow, leveled, and fired. The chert point cut a slice across the back of Mox's neck. Mox lowered the maul, felt his neck, and staring over at Ontarra like a man just coming out of a trance. He plodded up over the dune and disappeared.

Ontarra heard a scream. Tadodaroh dropped to his knees, a chert blade protruding from his thigh. The Gahkwa warrior Tadodaroh had pummeled with his fists started to sit up but fell back with a deer-bone stiletto in one eye. Ontarra turned slowly in a circle. No one was left. Togo ran down the dune for Tadodaroh. Ontarra ran over, his last arrow still nocked. The blade in Tadodaroh's leg was deep.

Togo grabbed Ontarra's arm, "Ontarra, we have to get out of here before more show up." Ontarra looked up at the dune standing between them and the lake.

"We will, Togo, I promise, but I have to see if I can catch them on the beach."

"Don't you abandon us here, Dwakanah!" Tadodaroh snarled, hiding his pain behind clenched teeth.

Ontarra ignored the insult. He laid a hand on Tadodaroh's chest. "I'll be back." Ontarra handed the bow and the last arrow to Togo, turned, and sprinted for the dune. He scrambled to the top, standing breathless as he scanned the beach. The three canoes were already an arrow-flight out into the lake. Ontarra sank to his knees, grabbing a fistful of sand in each hand, trying to squeeze it into stone. He could plainly see the girls seated in the front of two of the canoes. They'd never even know he was alive now. He wanted to scream, but he couldn't risk attracting more warriors.

He saw Taiwa's face turn toward him. Her arm rose up, slowly at first and then with a sudden joy, palm forward, fingers spread wide. Ontarra choked as moisture filled his eyes. He got to his feet, scrubbing the sand from his hands. He raised his arm, spread his fingers, and greeted her back.

Tears streaked down Taiwa's face. The little sobbing sounds she was making made Sounia look over. She stared at Taiwa, crying, and waving to one of those mud people standing up on the dune. The figure looked familiar. Sounia felt a jolt of recognition.

Ontarra saw Sounia staring. A warrior doesn't cry, but sand was falling from his fingers, blowing back into his face, forcing tears from his eyes and down his cheeks. Ontarra lowered his hand to his chest, made a fist, and threw his heart across the lake to Sounia.

"Ohh!" Sounia put both hands over her mouth. Tears overflowed in streams, slithered down her cheeks, and dripped from her chin. "Oh, Taiwa … it's Ontarra! It's really him!" she choked out. Manak gave Mox a look that could spell death. Sounia lowered her hand to her chest, nestled it between her breasts, and flung her heart across the waves to Ontarra with all of her might.

In that fleeting instant, above the waters of Iannaoa, they touched once more. The world was whole again. Five enchanted heartbeats pulsed through every filament of Ontarra's soul. The canoes turned wavery in his glistening eyes and then faded into blemishes on the water … and speckled out.

Historical Note

The Attawondarons were also known as Petun, after their strain of tobacco, or Neutrals, because they managed to remain neutral from the ongoing warfare and raiding between the Huron and the Iroquois Confederation of upstate New York This story starts in 1538, approximately seventy-five years prior to the first European contact with the Attawondarons.

If our knowledge of the Attawondarons relied on the few European incursions into their territory, it would be seriously incomplete. Etienne Brules account of his 1615–1616 expedition was written secondhand by Samuel de Champlain. The Jesuits Brebeuf and Chaumonot visited at a time of disruption caused by climate and disease. Nicholas Sanson's map of 1656 creates further problems by placing towns and settlements in the wrong locations.

Hence, it is the archeological record that provides the most important and accurate understanding of these people. I have placed many of the towns, such as Ounontisaston (Lawson) and Tontiaton (Southwold) in their known locations. I also mention an abandoned town on Ontarra's trek down the Lower Tranchi. This is the Calvert site near Dorchester, Ontario, abandoned about 1250 but still existing as an eerie "ghost town" in the Attawondaron oral tradition when Ontarra slips silently past almost three hundred years after the town was abandoned.

Sites given mention and approximate locations in the historical record but never actually found or excavated, I have placed in locations that seemed to me to best control the rivers and territory of the nation, while still offering good defensive capabilities for the settlement itself. Town and river names, as well as most of my characters, are purely fictitious, but in all cases I have tried to stay true to what is known of the Attawondaron dialect.

One name, recorded by the Jesuits, is "Tsohahissen," the Attawondaron "chief of chiefs" at the time of the Jesuit visit. This name and title implies some form of political structure to control all of the Attawondaron territories, rather than a simple scattering of tribal settlements—in effect, a nation.

People familiar with Southern Ontario will recognize the Upper Tranchi and Lower Tranchi as today's upper and lower branches of the Thames River. The Kandia is the present-day Grand River. I have tried to write in an informative and revealing manner that will allow the reader to understand this unusual and fascinating culture. I have also attempted to include enough detail for you to follow Ontarra's chase for the girls—or perhaps to visit some of the sites described.

For those who wish to learn more, *The Archaeology of Southern Ontario to AD 1650*, a publication of the Ontario Archeological Society, is a wealth of information. Also, *The Jesuit Relations* are a sketchy but interesting firsthand account of the Attawondarons and their land.

In book two, *The Reckoning*, Ontarra and Tadodaroh will take us on a journey to strange new lands and cultures in their quest for the girls—and retribution.